HOW OPERAS ARE CREATED BY COMPOSERS AND LIBRETTISTS

The Life of Jack Beeson, American Opera Composer

HOW OPERAS ARE CREATED BY COMPOSERS AND LIBRETTISTS

The Life of Jack Beeson, American Opera Composer

Jack Beeson

The Edwin Mellen Press
Lewiston•Queenston•Lampeter

Library of Congress Cataloging-in-Publication Data

Beeson, Jack, 1921-
  How operas are created by composers and librettists : the life of Jack Beeson, American opera composer / Jack Beeson.
    p. cm.
  Includes index.
  ISBN-13: 978-0-7734-4947-3
  ISBN-10: 0-7734-4947-7
  1. Beeson, Jack, 1921- 2. Composers--United States--Biography. 3. Opera--United States--20th century. I. Title.
  ML410.B399A3 2008
  782.1092--dc22
  [B]
                                    2008041799
hors série.

A CIP catalog record for this book is available from the British Library.

Front cover: Jack Beeson, composer-librettist of *My Heart's in the Highlands*, in the role of the Young Husband in his opera's televised premier by NET Opera, March 1970.
Photo by Conrad White
Back cover: Jack Beeson, May 2007
Photo by Richard Marshall

The Edwin Mellen Press   The Edwin Mellen Press
        Box 450   Box 67
  Lewiston, New York   Queenston, Ontario
  USA 14092-0450   CANADA L0S 1L0

The Edwin Mellen Press, Ltd.
Lampeter, Ceredigion, Wales
UNITED KINGDOM SA48 8LT

Printed in the United States of America

For Nora and Miranda

Table of Contents

Acknowledgments

I acknowledge gratefully publishers and others who have permitted the reprinting of articles and other material first published by them and those who control the copyrights of two deceased composers and one deceased poet for permission to publish their letters to me. I am also grateful to two fellow composers, Michael Dellaira and Phillip Ramey, for their careful readings of my manuscript and helpful comments.

- The American Academy of Arts and Letters: "Tribute to Otto Luening." (*Proceedings*, No. 47, 1966.)
- Albany Records: Liner Note (Troy 382, 2000).
- Peter Bartók: a letter from his father to Beeson.
- Boosey and Hawkes: "Ruminations of a Dowager Villa" and a passage from, *Dr. Heidegger's Fountain of Youth.*
- *Columbia,* the Magazine of Columbia University: "Magic, Music, and Money," "McMillin Theatre Remembered," and "Three Biographical Essays."
- *Current Musicology*: "Opera at Columbia."
- Faber and Faber: four letters to Beeson.
- Sheldon Harnick: a letter to the Hagen Theater.
- Opera America: "Way Back, Later, and Now."
- *Oxford University Press*, for *The Opera Quarterly*: "The Autobiography of *Lizzie Borden*"; "Marriages of Convenience"; "The Making of Peter Grimes."
- *Parnassus*: "Virgil Thomson's Aeneid."
- The San Francisco Opera: "The Birth of *The Mother of Us All.*"
- The *SCI Newsletter* (and the University of Iowa): "Bartók's Last Year" and "Teaching Composition."
- *SONY BMG Music Entertainment*: three essays by Jack Beeson, Sheldon Harnick, and William Saroyan.

- The Stanford University Libraries: seven letters from William Saroyan to Beeson.
- The Virgil Thomson Foundation Ltd.: two Thomson letters to Beeson.
- Stephanie Anne Viereck Gibbs Karnath: a letter from Peter Viereck to Beeson.

Chapter 1

Growing Up Untypical in *Middletown*
(1921-1939)

When we read or hear "As Holmes said . . ." we expect wise words from Oliver Wendell Holmes, an important Supreme Court Justice from the early twentieth century. Once we disentangle his father, also named Oliver Wendell Holmes, from the other New England poets with three names, we may remember reading his "Old Ironsides" in high school. That he was also a well-known wit, physician, and professor in the Harvard Medical School is forgotten. Dr. Holmes is supposed to have said to those of his patients who suffered from chronic incurable diseases and who also followed strictly his advice, "You are the healthiest of my patients." I've never known a physician who has heard these words until I've quoted them, but once past grinning at the paradox, they tend to agree with Dr. Holmes. So do I, and with reason: I've been an adult-onset diabetic since 1980; I was inaccurately diagnosed as a juvenile diabetic at the age of six and given six months to live—eighty-one ago. Diabetes is a chronic incurable disease. For all these years I have followed strictly the advice of my three successive physicians: my father, Mack Lipkin, and Murray Berenson. I am generally thought to be healthy, if one discounts a 1988 triple bypass and a demand pacemaker installed in 2003.

When Mack Lipkin, a remarkable physician much interested in psychosomatic matters, retired from practice, he moved to North Carolina. In the spring of 1983 he happened to attend a lecture at Chapel Hill by Dr. Arthur Rubenstein on his research in Chicago concerning the differing molecular structures of human insulin. After the lecture Lipkin told Rubenstein that he had, for years, cared for a highly atypical diabetic about whom he'd often thought of writing a paper. Rubenstein said that he was interested only in the atypical. I was asked to provide him with a comprehensive medical autobiography and with copies of all relevant medical records from my three physicians. Dr. Rubenstein must have been astonished to receive a thick packet of prose and records from a person who had been a patient, if only on consultation, in 1927, of his University of Chicago predecessor in insulin research, Dr. Rollin Woodyatt. The Canadians, Best and Banning, had isolated insulin only six years earlier, in 1921. For several years thereafter, the treatment of juvenile diabetics remained difficult or impossible. From the foregoing and the medical autobiography (to 1983) which follows, those who might well imagine that this is yet another of those books telling, at length, how the writer/sufferer has survived this or that awful disease will be heartened or disappointed to learn that it is not. After this page and the letter to Dr. Rubenstein—which gets the required subject of my birth out of the way—the subject of diabetes is diluted with opera gossip at a dinner party, and thereafter will hardly ever be mentioned. My disease is my familiar and we have been together for a lifetime. It is my intention to introduce the reader to my familiar, who, as Webster says, "is a spirit that attends and serves or guards a person" and who may do so quietly and invisibly.

May 26, 1983

Arthur H. Rubenstein, M.D.
Professor and Chairman
Department of Medicine
The University of Chicago

Dear Dr. Rubenstein,

In accordance with Dr. Mack Lipkin's request and my telephone conversation with you I'm sending an informal medical autobiography, the more informal because I usually write in longhand and have never—until this evening—used my wife's *electric* typewriter. I shall be somewhat impressionistic, writing what I can remember—or what I *think* I am remembering, in the full knowledge that memory sometimes seems to have a personality of its own. Much of what I write now I told Dr. Lipkin at what appears to have been his first examination of me in 1947. Where there is variance between what I write now and what he noted then and the letters from the later doctors I visited on consultation, it is the latter who misconstrued what I suppose I told them. Dr. Murray Berenson has been in charge of me since Mack retired from practice here some years ago. Berenson has extracted from the Beeson/Lipkin/Berenson files what he thinks would be of use to you, and would, of course, be pleased to provide whatever else you might want to have.

I was born with difficulty on July 15, 1921, at the Home Hospital in Muncie, Indiana. My mother needed considerable "repair" thereafter. As Mack dutifully recounts in what is apparently my first visit with him (my memory tells me that my wife and I had pre-marital visits with him in the spring of '47). I was told later that I was born paralyzed on the left side, with a broken left arm. I remained a mess for some years. I remember excruciating pains in the legs, abscessed teeth, and more than two lanced ear-drums. For these, and obviously other reasons that I knew nothing of at the time, my father took me and his mother to the Presbyterian Hospital in Chicago for consultation with Dr. Rollin Woodyatt. W. confirmed my father's diagnosis of his mother, Diabetes Mellitus, and made much the same diagnosis (or the same) of my condition, saying that I was unlikely to live more than 6 months. Naturally I knew nothing of these matters at the time, and experienced only the oddity of having to urinate and eat very strange meals on those several days in the hospital, and of having blood taken.

It was some time in my teen years that my father told me of W.'s diagnosis, began to give me simplified lectures of biochemistry, and helped me to set up a home chemistry lab, outfitted with an alcohol burner and Benedict's solution, with which I tested my own urine—and anyone else's who would cooperate. He told me that he was as proud of proving W. wrong as he was in having once proved Harvey Cushing wrong about some patient of his with a suspected brain tumor. He told me at that time that I was not a diabetic and had not been at the age of 6, but that I had "renal glycosuresis." I spell it that way because my father was very proud of his Greek and that's what I remember his saying. His way of explaining the matter to the boy was, "It's as tho the sieve that's supposed to keep the sugar from the urine has too-large a mesh and lets your sugar pass through."

My father had practiced internal medicine and diagnosis, but with a mother and son with metabolic problems he began specializing in diabetes, a disease he developed in the Thirties, *his* forties. He was ostensibly on the weighted diet common to those times (amplified with such items as cherry pie, which I sometimes saw him eat on the way to the office, to my horror and the despair of my mother), took insulin, and drank very heavily. Though he was his very worst patient, I assume that he was an excellent physician for everyone else, including me, for he was the first FACP [Fellow of the American College of Physicians] in that part of the state and on the basis of some papers on diabetes he delivered at FACP and other meetings was invited to join the Mayo Clinic to do research on the subject. I think he knew by that time that he was too far gone as an alcoholic to accept the position. He died at 53 of an intentionally untreated left-arm wound that led to blood-poisoning and heart failure, a kind of suicide, I suppose. Fifty-three is the average life-time of the last half-dozen male Beesons in our line. (By the way, he is supposed to have had coronary disease too.) I'm 61.

As for me, some information is provided by the one medical report I have in my father's hand, written on my seventh birthday. I suspect that the comment "Feels good. Much pep" held for much of the time. I do remember vividly, however, having to sit down on a wall halfway back home on the 3-block walk from elementary school from lack of energy-hypoglycemia I'd now think. The bouts with "acidosis" continued intermittently, with much vomiting, liquids, orange juice, and a day or two in bed. I also spent time intermittently soaking an infected toe or finger in hot salt water. At 13 or 14 I began wearing glasses for astigmatism, my father insisting—against the wisdom of his eye-specialist colleagues—that my bouts of nausea could be caused by an uncorrected astigmatism. The earlobe and finger stickings continued; my father told me later that the blood sugars in those earlier years (and in the teen-age years when the "biochemistry lectures" were taking place) rarely exceeded the high normal range.

In those teen-age years the bouts with "acidosis" and infected toes and fingers decreased; there was less trouble with teeth and I don't remember hypoglycemic incidents. I avoided, as I'd been trained to do since at least 6 years old, sugars and much starch. At seven I'd begun piano lessons (and read a lot and consistently got A's in everything). I was a typical "over-achiever": small stature, childhood illnesses. Perhaps inconsistently, I was a Boy Scout and had no trouble with the 7-mile and 14-mile hikes. In Junior High School the track coach tagged me as a dasher, but I gave up the 100 yard dash when each race led to vomiting on the sidelines. Similarly, when swimming I had a tendency to set too-high goals and often ended up vomiting on the beach. I assume that my reactions to over-exertion were related to whatever my disease was. Throughout these years I, or my father, did urine tests; I consistently, though not constantly, showed sugar in small amounts; the blood sugars I referred to in the preceding paragraph.

At eighteen my parents divorced and I went away to school. There were no blood-sugars taken except on annual visits to my father; they followed the same pattern. So did urinalyses, when I remembered to do one. The diet remained the same. There were rare instances of infected extremities and no hypoglycemic incidents, unless an occasional beach-vomiting counts. (I was, by the way, by then less inclined to over-do.) There may have been an "acidosis" incident or two between the ages of 18 and 30, but if so I don't remember them as such; by that time I'd discovered that I couldn't tolerate a large intake of fats (particularly with alcohol) without getting sick. On such occasions, for no intelligent reason, but out of childhood memories, I drank orange juice in quantity. In short, between the death of my father in 1944, when I was 23, and when I went to Mack Lipkin for the first time in '47, when I was 26—after which I saw him regularly—I had no occasion to take my "disease" seriously or to see a doctor. (The exception was my physical examination for induction into the WWII army in 1942. The Army would have nothing to do with a conscript with sugar in his urine.)

*   *   *   *   *   *   *

All that prose brings us up to about the time the Dr. Lipkin records take over, and I need add little more, except, perhaps to enlarge upon two events that took place on Shelter Island, out of the reach of Lipkin/Berenson.

The first was to do with 1963 and the Wantz surgery report on page 11. In August of that year I told the local GP on Shelter Island that I had appendicitis, but he refused to accept my diagnosis because the white count was "too low" and filled me with tetracycline or whatever. Five weeks later he had me on the table, shaved, to take a biopsy from the mass when his conversation with an intern about various lethal matters that reminded me of my father's text books that I'd read as a youth led me to get off the table, flee to NY, and to NY Hospital. By that time I was on low dosage Orinase, which had begun, I think, shortly before. As a precaution I was put on insulin (how much?) during surgery. For 1 or 3 months thereafter I was sugar free.

By June, '80, some continuing weight loss and elevated blood sugars led to Berenson's suggestion that I go on insulin. I countered by suggesting that we wait until I'd returned from summer vacation. In that August I was conned, or conned myself, into doing some unaccustomed squats and popped an interior right calf vein. After 4 days of increasing difficulty in getting around I came to NY and Berenson threw me forthwith into the hospital. We took advantage of the hospitalization to put me on insulin, which I've continued. At present I'm on 37 units of NPH 100.

I am coming to Chicago on University business on June 23rd and returning on the 24th. I have to be at lunch at the Palmer House to give a CU award at 12:30 on the 24th. I could see you earlier that day, should you wish me to and let me know—or perhaps late on the 23rd.

Cordially,

Jack Beeson
MacDowell Professor of Music

* * * * * *

The university business referred to above was to represent the President of Columbia in granting the Ditson Conductor's Award to Julius Hegyi of the Chicago Symphony by speaking briefly and then reading the citation—ostensibly written by the President. Telephone messages from Dr. Rubenstein were not delivered to me by the Palmer House and so I checked out at noon on the 24th. When I then discovered that blood was to be taken at 3 o'clock, I told the hotel assistant manager that I was a participant in a University of Chicago experiment and that a doctor would be drawing blood at 3, that I had checked out at noon, and that I wouldn't mind in the least being bled on one of the comfortable couches in the lobby. He was horrified by my sensible solution.

As I reported by letter to Dr. Lipkin, "So Dr. Cohen [Rubenstein's associate] showed up with an ice-packed picnic basket and filled 11-13 tubes with blood—in the newly made-up room, the new occupants of which were made to wait in the lobby. Actually, I still cherish the idea that we'd used the elegant lobby—itinerant business men clustered around the white-coated medic and the victim of some awful disease, maybe AIDS."

I conclude this discussion of the now common disease of diabetes with a tale of operatic hors d'oeuvres and a half-eaten dinner. But first a few words on physiology. The isles of Langerhans are not in the Dutch East Indies, but in our pancreas. In normal people they produce insulin that makes possible the metabolism of sugars and starches. If too little or none is produced, the insulin (or the new Humulin, DNA human insulin) must be injected either before meals or once a day. In the latter case the insulin must be "fed" specified amounts of food at specified times, in my case at 8, 12, and 6, with specified snacks at 3 and 10. In this unvarying regimen my wife, Nora, cooperates uncomplainingly and is as strict with me as I am with myself. Accordingly, fashionably late dinners are avoided or coped with by having a half-dinner at 6, the other half whenever.

Two or three years ago I found myself unavoidably at the National Arts Club attending a benefit of the Center for Contemporary Opera, seated to the left of a former chairman of the board of the Metropolitan Opera. He introduced me to his guest, Dr. So-and-So from Mt. Sinai Hospital, seated to his right. The Met-Man and I enjoyed an uninterrupted exchange of operatic gossip. In return for his contributions I offered two stories not very complimentary to the Met:

Back in the mid-sixties my friend John Gutman, Assistant Director to Rudolf Bing, was annoyed to hear that my opera *Lizzie Borden* was to be premiered at the New York City Opera. Why had I not first offered it to the Met? I replied that the Met had commissioned an opera by Marvin David Levy on O'Neill's *Mourning Becomes Electra*. Surely the Met wouldn't produce yet another New England up-dated Electra opera. He was insistent that I submit the score. Months later when I asked for its return, he said that the Met really couldn't produce yet another New England up-dated Electra opera in addition to the Strauss in their repertory, and asked me to speak to his assistant for my score. I did so and was told to ask *his* assistant who took care of such matters. Much later, the assistant of the assistant to the Assistant Manager of the Met did so.

In the early seventies my wife, Nora, and I received an elegant invitation from Rudolf Bing to attend a performance. Because it was addressed to Prof. and Mrs. Jacques Besson, we suspected that it was intended for my famous colleague, Jacques Barzun, and postponed replying. A while later, a secretary asked curtly if we would attend. We did so and other invitations arrived intermittently for a few years. The company in Bing's box consisted of various contributors, plenipotentiaries, and some repeaters, including a Viennese masseuse. The routine was unvaried: first intermission with Bing at his table, with pre-ordered whiskey and soda and very small talk on non-controversial subjects. If one excepts the personal representatives who were also the husbands of singers, there were no musicians when we were present. Bing did once confide to me at a *Die Walküre* performance that he would not remain for the second act because he couldn't stand family quarrels. This private remark was the closest he ever came to recognizing me as a composer. Perhaps he thought, indeed, that we were the Barzuns? I asked John Gutman if Bing knew that I wrote operas on occasion. "Why yes, of course!" Perhaps it was, similarly, his successor's unfamiliarity with living composers that led someone in his office to call a friend of mine at ASCAP to ask if it would be proper to invite John Corigliano to his box to attend the premiere of his *Ghosts of Versailles*.

While the Met-Man and I exchanged stories,—Dr. So-and-So, left out of the conversation, watched me nibbling on one course after another and interrupted in a professional tone: I had no appetite? Did I feel ill? Could he help in any way? I explained that I had had to eat at least half my dinner at 6 o'clock, unfortunately, "Why?" "I'm a diabetic," I said, hoping that would satisfy the doctor and end the subject. Then, as often happens when I meet a doctor, "Are you related to the famous Dr. Paul Beeson, Sir Paul?" I admitted to being a distant cousin and to having met him. Not wanting to leave out the Met-Man in the middle of our conversation, I added that Paul's son, John, was the head coach at the City Opera and worked also at the Met. He shrugged. As though I were a patient in his office, Dr. So-and-So persisted: "I assume you inject insulin once a day at breakfast. How many units?" "37." "From what you said about the two half-dinners, I assume you eat at regular times and are fussy about it?" "Yes, very." "And are you annoyed at misspellings and those who are late at appointments . . ." "I suppose so." ". . . and are you upset by your own and others' mistakes?" "Perhaps." "Well, we don't see many diabetics who follow our advice strictly.

When those few do, they're likely to remain healthy, as you appear to be. But they tend to be pains in the necks to their friends and relatives."

While they enjoyed their elaborate sweet desserts and I was served a small amount of fresh fruit, I pondered the cause-and-effect mystery hidden in his words. Were pain-in-the-neck qualities the result of a strict regime or had they always been there, making the strict regime just another way of being on time, accurate, and avoiding error? In any case, it was a pleasure to hear a latter-day version of Dr. Oliver Wendell Holmes's words.

* * * * * * *

Sometime during my last two years at the Eastman School I quite serendipitously found a copy of Laurence Sterne's eighteenth century novel *Tristram Shandy* and became enchanted by it; my copy is now quite worn and marked up from our long and intimate relationship. Perhaps because at that time I was writing instrumental works of some length, I admired Sterne's easy control of chronological time over the whole of nine volumes published over eight years and the shaping of the volumes themselves, in spite of their long and short chapters dealing with the most diverse characters—unborn and living—events from here and there, and time present, time past, and time future, all threaded together. And all managed with wit and humor as in a friendly conversation with the reader. Probably I aspired at the age of 20 or 21 to being able to control in my music such movement-to-moment and minute-to-minute sections within a satisfying whole; I know that in the years since, particularly in my ten operas, such has been my aspiration.

There is another, but purely verbal, cause-and-effect mystery lurking here: long before my early twenties I was much given to telling stories that were both discursive and allusive. These are the adjectives that describe *Tristram Shandy* and may, therefore, have attracted me to that odd novel. On the other hand, once granted the Shandean license to be discursive and allusive, I have exercised the right in a growing repertory of stories and prose—as here.

I did not meet another committed Shandean until I became friends with my Columbia colleague, Robert Merton. He was, indeed, one of the leading sociologists of the 20th century, but he was surely the greatest Shandean since Sterne himself, as the subtitle of his most widely known book suggests: *On the Shoulders of Giants, a Shandean Postscript.* His is one of the few scholarly books known by its acronym, *OTSOG*.

Occasional meetings with Bob Merton and savoring *OTSOG* reminded me of my Shandean debt in composing, story-telling, and prose-writing. In 1990 I was seeking appropriate texts for what was to become *Magicke Pieces*, a large, difficult work for mixed chorus, three winds, and bells. What better as its central movement than parts of the excommunication written by Ernulf, bishop of Rochester from 1114 to 1124, transcribed and translated by Sterne and to be found (also in Latin) in Volume III of *Tristram Shandy*? Among the series of horrifying curses is surely the first published musical setting of "May he be cursed in eating and drinking and fasting . . . in pissing and shitting and blood-letting!"

One of Tristram's father's dislikes was a small, short nose. He insisted in chapter after chapter that a long nose is a sign of strength and character. During the decade of 1980-'90 when Sheldon Harnick and I were writing our opera *Cyrano* I would recall such lines as "My nose has been the making of me" and "How the deuce should such a nose fail?"

But it is the father's other hobbyhorse, often ridden, that is likely to intrigue even a disbelieving reader: "There is a strange kind of magic bias which good or bad names . . . irresistibly impresses upon our conduct." He abhorred his son's name, Tristram: "Who ever heard tell of a man call'd Tristram performing anything great or worth remembering?" In a highly comic scene not to be retailed here, the child had been christened Tristram, instead of Trismegistus "which would have shed luster on a life of great and heroic action." These two names are clearly Shandean exaggeration, but Mr. Shandy *could* be reasonable. He lists four names, Jack, Dick, Tom and Bob, and adds that as many knaves and fools as wise and good men had borne them, so that "they mutually destroyed each others effects." Doubters should notice that when we speak today of the generality of men we still say "every Tom, Dick, and Harry."

But, even if readers resist Mr. Shandy's conviction that the name given a child will influence its future and think it no more than whimsy, they must agree that they regularly recognize the congruities between adults and their names— sometimes commenting on incongruities. Why else would fiction writers, playwrights, librettists, and scriptwriters in other media take such trouble to find names they think their audiences will believe fit their characters' actions, bodies, and souls?

On page 2 of *The Life and Opinions of Tristram Shandy, Gentleman*, Tristram describes his own conception. Four pages later he discloses the *date* of his birth, November 5, 1718. There follow close to two hundred pages of life and opinions until his actual, difficult birth. Poor, misnamed Tristram was delivered by a mid-wife and Dr. Slop, whose forceps flattened his nose irretrievably.

Now, in a Shandean reversal, let us return to July 15, 1921, when I was born "with difficulty"—still with forceps, probably—and given two names to go with Beeson on my birth certificate. It was surely a fine day, for it was St. Swithin's Day, the anniversary of the translation of the saint's body from outside to the inside of his church; if it rains on St. Swithin's, it will continue for forty days, it is said, and no second Flood is recorded in the ten centuries since his translation.

Deciding on my middle name turned out to be troublesome. My father's middle name was Hamilton because his father, a lawyer, was strongly Hamiltonian. My mother's family was Pennsylvania Dutch, her great-grandfather having emigrated from Germany in the early nineteenth century. He named his son Thomas Jefferson Siegfried in 1825, when Jefferson still had a year to live. Those three names continued into the next generation, to my grandfather, whom I remember vividly. I speculate 87 years later that there must have been a renewed Hamilton-Jefferson contention in 1921, not on political, but on family loyalty grounds: my middle name became Hamilton, not Jefferson. Perhaps my parents compromised at first; my mother often told me with some pride that my first name was to have been—and should have been—her maiden name, Siegfried. How and why Jack was chosen I have no idea.

If some readers have thought that I actually believe the Shandean theory of the influence of names on lives, they may not have noticed that Mr. Shandy is not predestinating but invoking only "a strange kind of magic bias…"

Because I was not named Siegfried I can only speculate what its effect might have been: a large, muscular man, probably blond and slow-witted? Instead, I was given a nickname as a name, one listed by Sterne as a "neutral name borne by as many knaves and fools as wise and good men"—by Jack the Ripper on the one hand and on the other Little Jack Horner, Jack Sprat, and a dozen other fine fellows in Mother Goose. Nicknames often suggest intimacy, sometimes are belittling. Whether because of "magic bias" or genetic endowment I was belittled, achieving only 5'6". Scrawny as a youth, I've been pleased since to have considered myself slender. In my middle-age, Virgil Thomson—not one to restrict his criticism to music reviews—chastised me for having no paunch and recommended that I develop one. I neither would nor could.

The name Jack was briefly advantageous when I reported to my draft board at age 21. When I gave my name to the official, he told me that Selective Service did not accept nicknames and wrote John on the form. I suggested that I might not receive their misnamed mail and that they might lose track of me. He considered that possibility, made out a new form and muttered that it was very much against the rules to write in Jack.

The name Hamilton has been without effect except for some weeks in 1976, when it surfaced unpleasantly in connection with Sheldon Harnick's and my plan to write a chamber opera to be entitled BURR vs. BURR.

The real given names are those that are inherited. When one is changed for ethnic or whatever reason, the new name is chosen by its dissatisfied bearer or his or her agent or movie studio—let it be noted—to be consonant with the person and personality of the "re-made" bearer or newly-made star. I don't recall as a youth in Muncie, Indiana, ever knowing anyone with a changed last name. But I do remember that my father was the physician of a family named Gullet. When the Gullets came into money they insisted that their name be pronounced "in the French way!"—a sixty or seventy year anticipation of Hyacinth Bucket's Bouquet.

Beeson is an uncommon surname in this country. In England there are eleven towns and hamlets named Beeson or Beeston. Genealogists differ in their explanations of the origin of the name. Those with a penchant for finding a 1066-and-all-that origin cite Godfrey de Buizon (Bezon), a knight who accompanied William is credible because within decades of the Conquest two impressive Beeston Castles were built, in Cheshire and Nottingham. It is likely that the name Beeston, later also Beeson, was already used by the Anglo-Saxons long before the Conquest to name a person or place east of the town, just as Weston derives from west of the town. Whatever the origin of the names, a coat of arms was used by both Beesons and Beestons, with six bees emblazoned.

Although two Beesons are known to have immigrated from England in 1657 and 1676 and others may have done so in later centuries, most of us American Beesons trace our lineage back to Edward Beeson, who arrived with his relative by marriage, William Penn, in 1682. The exact familial relationship is not yet certain, but the two men, both in their thirties, were united also by their membership in the Society of Friends and, as Quakers, much abused. Penn had been "sent down" from Oxford and several times imprisoned for his beliefs and writings, then disowned by his father, Sir William Penn, Commander of the Fleet. A decade after Sir William's death, William, Jr. approached Charles II, who agreed that Sir William's services to the Crown had not been properly recognized. Charles gave what he, himself, named Pennsylvania and three counties of Delaware to Penn, in 1681. A year later Penn came to his colony, accompanied by Edward Beeson and his brother, Richard, who returned soon to England. Penn was generous to his relatives and friends: Edward eventually possessed some three thousand acres.

I am omitting comment about the nine generations from Edward to me, including those several early Quakers who were "disowned for marrying out of Meeting."

There are, though some rural particulars on my mother's side of the family. Her father was the last of the Thomas Jefferson Siegfrieds already mentioned. He married Hattie Sutliff, an English name derived from the Anglo-Saxon south of the cliff. They were locals from in and around the village of Benton in the northeastern corner of Pennsylvania. Hattie was, it seems, the granddaughter of what used to be called an Indian, a matter to be discussed later when I discovered her existence. My grandfather was at first the owner of a hilly farm known as Butter Bowl, then moved into the village and became a mason. I know nothing of my grandparents' schooling, though the naming of their children suggests that there was very little of it or a great deal of imagination. My mother was named Autum A Siegfried. There was no n on the first name, a misspelling, I suppose. There was never a period after the A. When I asked her why that was, I was told it was because she had two aunts whose names began with A. That made no sense to me as a schoolboy and still doesn't. There was one son named Schuyler, but the name was never used, even professionally. He was always called Skie, not Sky. It was said that as a very young man he had come to Muncie and babysat for me as a very young child. He then became a baker, later ran his father-in-law's department store most efficiently—in spite of having left school after a few grades. The other daughter was my Aunt Flossie. Some of her words I didn't understand, for they were Pennsylvania Dutch. Once I began to study German I realized that, "Isn't that shone-pretty?" meant "schön-pretty."

I saw my grandparents with some irregularity until I was about twelve. By train, Mother would take me and my brother Tom, younger by two years, to visit her family, who were all in or nearby Benton. I particularly enjoyed my grandfather's stories:

There was a young woman whose parents tried unsuccessfully to prevent her from going to New York City. She was suffocated when her Murphy bed suddenly closed while she was asleep.

There was the relative, a farmer, who one autumn fell on a cut corn stalk and died of blood poisoning because it pierced his anus.

And then there was the elderly couple, also related, who engaged a young couple hardly known to them to look after them during their last years. They promised the farm and the house to the young couple for payment of their services and made the mistake of telling them when the will had been drawn up and signed. Not long after, the farmer died mysteriously; shortly after, the widow hanged herself in bed, the rope tied to the bedpost. I was appalled to learn that the police had found nothing mysterious.

Whether all boys of twelve relish such stories and remember them, I've no idea, but I know that at 6 or 7 I had not yet developed a taste for them. My parents unwisely took me to a traveling production of the play, *The Cat and the Canary*, an event rarely to be seen in Muncie. In the scene I remember a woman lay asleep on her bed. On the wall above, a picture was pushed somewhat aslant from behind and a hairy arm—was it an ape's? —reached out for the woman. I was carried out of the theatre screaming.

*　　*　　*　　*　　*　　*　　*

From the vantage point of 87 I see clearly that at the ages of 6 and 7 I enjoyed a mid-childhood crisis. At 6 I entered first grade at the nearby Washington Elementary School, was ill and absent for a while, was given six months to live, then rarely absent.

When I was six we had moved from a bungalow near the Home Hospital to a large, to me enchanted, house; and at seven I began piano lessons.

Of the bungalow I have but two memories. The first was being told to climb up on the dining room table and to lie down on my back—a preposterous request to a 6-year-old. Then someone in a mask put something smelly over my nose and I seemed to lose track of what was going on: the extraction of one or more teeth under ether.

Perhaps as a reward for such frequent indignities, my father came home one evening with a black English bulldog. I didn't know at the time that black bulldog pups are rare because breeders eliminate them at birth. Jim was but the first in a long succession of bulldogs to be enjoyed by Tom and me, and then by our own two children.

That we could move to 803 East Washington Street was the result of good times in the late twenties and my father's flourishing medical practice. Eight blocks east of the center, it was in the old and proper part of town; the new and more elegant expansion was toward the west, as was common at the time in the Midwest. A large, brick, 3-storied structure with a slate roof, it was close to the cross-street. On the other side a large lawn met the large lawn of the larger building near the next cross-street, called by us "the Elk's Club" —The Benevolent and Protective Order of Elks. In Muncie there were also the Moose and the Masons: my father was a 32nd degree Mason, with a large decorative sword to show for it and aspired to 33rd degree status.

No doubt the house was smaller than I thought it was, but the enchantment of the front downstairs rooms and the staircase remained until I left Muncie at eighteen. The large dark entrance hall was oak-panelled and when nobody was around I drummed on it, convinced that somewhere there was a secret compartment. All the doors were sliding, disappearing into their wall-slots. The dining and breakfast rooms were paneled in red-brown mahogany; the living room walls were covered in fabric with sculpted fleur-de-lis, with three pairs of window-hangings of wine-red silk velvet. The three pairs of hangings are in my Lloyd Neck studio today, much worn and split, resembling those seen in English country houses badly in need of restoration.

The main staircase handrail seemed designed for sliding down. Near the top was a large landing with an offset in which stood an oak Roman-style chair, throne-like, in which one could curl up and gaze at the beautiful young lady in windblown draperies plucking fruit from a tree. This improbable scene—she was certainly life-size—was a stained glass window quite different from the ones I'd seen in church. I assume now that it was a Tiffany knock-off and could have dated the design of the house.

To match these elegancies my father splurged on several oriental rugs. One of these, a 5' by 7', was placed under the Gulbransen baby grand piano purchased for me at about the same time. It is under the Baldwin grand in our New York apartment now, none the worse for wear.

Why I wanted a piano at age seven I've no idea; no one in my family played or sang. I said that if I could have an instrument, I would practice and one was provided. My parents then and thereafter were always supportive.

Nor do I know how Luella Weimer became my first piano teacher. She lived in the neighborhood, taught music in a public school, was proud to have attended Teachers College at Columbia and to have studied piano with Perceval Owen, to whom she sent me some years later. When I was assigned my first piece by Beethoven, *Für Elise*, she told me that I could trace my lessons back to Beethoven: she had studied with Owen, who had studied (together with his classmate, Artur Schnabel) with Leschetizky, then through his teacher, Czerny, to Beethoven. She was indeed in the tradition that dated from Leschetizky: a strong, arched hand, with an imagined ball within and independence of the fingers, insofar as the linked fourth and fifth would permit.

The music lessons—for they were more than just piano lessons—were much more interesting than the six years of grade school. In fact, my only vivid memory of school is of an Assembly theatrical performance of *Bubbles Concerto*. Quite by chance I found in a copy of GEO in 1984 an illustrated profile of its creator, a Hoosier who had given 1,400 performances of it since 1932, when I was in 5th or 6th grade. I had long since forgotten the title of the event—if I'd ever known it—but even his earliest version consisted of a series of numerous bubbles blown in all sizes, shapes, and colors, some of them with children inside. The article included photographs of the more recent and elaborate creations, but omitted his middle initial, G., which I could supply, having thought its creator-producer's name one of the most preposterous I'd ever heard, Eiffel G. Plasterer.

I suppose it is shameful that we do not remember those epiphanies in elementary school when one mystery after another is solved in reading, writing, and arithmetic. Instead, I see only routine on my twelve semesters of grade sheets—each divided and reported on in segments of six weeks—mostly grades of A, and the tiresome "very commendable" for Attitude Toward Work and Conduct. To whom did I whisper what, in the first segment of Grade 2A, where there's the blight of "Whispers"?

My impression of the conduct in Washington Elementary is that it, too, was commendable. Those who were then known as "colored people" were migrating north, many of them to Muncie. Our school was "integrated" if the word would have meant anything at the time. I think we mixed in class, corridors, and in recess without problems. The only prejudice I recall was directed at the students of the nearby Catholic school, who were called Catlickers. I remember no fistfights from the taunts.

Two of the recent migrants from the South were a "colored" couple, Elmer and Emma Cloyd, who moved into the back part of our house and were quickly integrated into our lives. Elmer was a lean Jack Sprat and Emma, with a passion for "southern fried," was often in need of my father's aid. She took care of the house and the cooking; Elmer took care of the yard, window-washing, and a regular supply of self-caught catfish. From him I learned that one dips catfish in very hot water, then skins them with pliers. Modest and quiet-spoken, he told Southern tall stories with a straight face: his walk to school had led through a section of poisonous hoop-snakes. On the way down a steep hill a snake coiled into a hoop and rolled toward him. Terrified, he turned quickly behind a large oak tree; the snake uncoiled and impaled itself into the trunk. When he returned late in the afternoon the leaves of the tree were already shriveled.

Elmer and Emma lived comfortably in the back part of the house, a large living room on the first floor, a bath and porch on the second, and a bedroom on the third, all off the three-story back staircase.

On the third floor was also what I disbelieved had been intended as a ballroom: in the movies ballrooms always had high ceilings. Two dark, mysterious attics flanked the large room; Elmer hinted that my father was using his knowledge of chemistry to brew beer there during Prohibition.

Aside from the bulldog, which during the winter sometimes pulled us to school on a sled, Tom and I cared for other miscellaneous animals. Two foot-long alligators lived under Emma's kitchen sink, but they were given away when it became impossible to find enough flies during the winter. Chameleons adorned one curtain after the other, their colors changing accordingly. Some bantam roosters lived in the garage. When one was eviscerated by the bulldog, the others went back to Uncle Otis's farm. And when the piglet that lived in the back hall developed bruised hips from climbing and falling down stairs, he had to go back too.

My paternal grandmother was a Johnson and one of 13 children, most of them living on farms in the neighborhood. Not far away was Johnson County, full of them. Unfortunately, they all insisted on meeting once a year. My annual nightmare was the Johnson Reunion, held in a Muncie park next to the dark brown White River. The tables were full of food I couldn't eat, uncles and aunts and cousins by the dozen, flies, bees and softball games, which I avoided because of my hands and fingers.

We did often visit the farms of two of my grandmother's siblings, especially that of Aunt Mandy and Uncle Otis Cranmer. There we marvelled—in the days before Roosevelt's REA (the Rural Electrification Authority)—at the windmill attached to a generator that produced electricity stored in huge batteries in a separate fireproof outbuilding. (The recent interest in wind as a source of energy is hardly new to us elderly Midwesterners). We could watch the new mechanical milkers at work on a dozen cows. We carried water sometimes to the harvesters. Once I was mystified by the castration of pigs and horrified by their squeals.

In short, this child, from 6 to 12 led a varied, protected, and happy life.

*   *   *   *   *   *   *

The one team sport in the Indiana of my day that brought out the crowds was basketball. Honored above all else was a city that had a championship basketball team. Muncie Central High School's team, the Bearcats, were almost as famous as the Ball canning jars, all of which were then made in Muncie. For a city of some 40,000, the Field House seemed too large, but all four of the inclined rows of seats above the basketball court and its running track were often filled. Ingeniously, beneath all these seats was the McKinley Junior High School for all of us 7th, 8th, and 9th graders—mostly 12, 13, and 14 year olds. The classrooms and workshops were spacious and the Bearcats' athletic facilities were for our use.

I suppose the curriculum was typical of its time and place: besides the usual courses there were Typing and Home Ec(onomics) for the girls and Industrial Arts for the boys. The latter were one-semester courses in Printing (type-setting), Electricity (general, and making our own radio crystal-sets), Wood-working, and Metal-working. I elected the first three and have never regretted it. Physical Education was required, but the choice of sports for me was slim. As already mentioned, I soon gave up competitive running and was too short for basketball. I turned out to be a not-bad wrestler when I could substitute wiliness for brawn. My grades for Phys. Ed. were consistently Bs, for trying hard, surely. Otherwise I continued making mostly As. When I received my first-ever B—in Algebra—the principal called me in for an explanation. I told him that the answers to the problems were all in the back of the textbook and that I didn't want to waste my time on the routine of finding what was already known. He seemed puzzled but satisfied.

What I told him was the truth, but it masked a larger truth: my entrance into Junior High School in 1933 at the age of 12 coincided with my realization that music was a larger and more interesting subject than just playing the piano two or so hours a day—or Algebra. Somehow I found the time—or took it—to add lessons on the clarinet with Mr. Garrett. Once reasonably proficient I joined the McKinley Band, while filling in at the piano the missing instruments in the McKinley Orchestra. Mr. Garrett offered to give me lessons on the xylophone too, if my parents would give me an instrument. They did, a good one, a Leedy. I learned to play, I was told, "a mean *Nola.*" To prove to others—and to myself— that I had a "xylophone period" there still exists the purple cloth banner that hung between the Leedy's front legs emblazoned with "Jack Beeson, Soloist with Garrett's Boys Band." For a short time I was lent a piano accordion. The left hand keyboard wasn't interesting, but the right-hand chord buttons could be played two at a time, resulting in fascinating poly-triads and bitonalities.

These other instrumental studies did not seriously interfere with my piano studies with Miss Weimer. There were occasional piano recitals, sometimes held in our living room, which served also for meetings of Mother's bridge club. I always contributed a couple of solos, joined Phoebe Yeo for a four-hand piece, and once played a xylophone solo, *Yuki.* When I was asked occasionally to play something for my parents' guests I did so; if I had a memory lapse, I discovered that I could improvise the rest of the piece without anybody's noticing.

Miss Weimer had been encouraging me to improvise and my pleasure in doing so led me to compose my first piece, at 12, a *March in F$^\sharp$ Major* that exists in her fluent hand. It is original only in its odd choice of key for a march. She had a number of students whose parents were well-off and she thought would benefit from supervised practicing. She asked me if I would give them these paid "practice lessons." I agreed, of course, it was the modest beginning of a teaching career.

It was also in the autumn of 1933 that the Metropolitan Opera began its Saturday afternoon broadcasts, some years before Texaco began its long-lived sponsorship. As my initial interest grew into a teenage passion I began to buy and study Schirmer vocal scores with my newly-earned practice lessons money. When a score matched a broadcast I tuned in the console on the far end of the living room and a small radio on the piano and attempted to accompany the Met. Given my enthusiasm for some films and the few theatrical events I'd attended, my first appearance as an actor in a 3-character play, and the sound of the Met voices and orchestra—not to speak of my fledgling composing—I thought when I grew up I would write operas, too.

I suspect that I kept this intention very much to myself; to my school chums it would have seemed grotesque and sissified. Doubtless my ambition to write operas was encouraged by the first public performances of music I'd written—a music-theatre piece. The occasion was a festivity celebrating the McKinley Junior High School graduation in 1936. Fifteen hundred guests filled the basketball court and track of the Field House. We in the orchestra began the evening; then a prayer and a speech; special honors were presented. I received the Citizenship Award—for continuing good deportment, I suppose. As I read in the morning *Star* the next morning, "Following dinner a 'fun festival' was presented by 9A pupils." I had helped to devise a skit with three characters, Popeye, Olive Oyl, and Whimpy, and a cartoonist. The music I wrote was a set of variations on "Popeye, the Sailor Man" for two pianos played by Phoebe Yeo and me. Neither I nor the faculty knew anything about copyright infringement.

I'm certain that my father hoped that I would become a doctor, though he never told me so. I probably misled him unintentionally by showing a real interest in those parts of his practice he made a point of sharing with me. Why were those enormous bottles of same-shaped pills of different colors in his office? Answer: otherwise perfectly healthy patients with neurasthenia (a new word!) could be helped by giving them the three colors of harmless aspirin tablets in as complicated a sequence as possible. I was astonished by how he could diagnose diseases as we walked together along the street. "That man has locomotor ataxia and syphilis." Then a discussion of syphilis and other venereal diseases until another victim appeared: "That's poliomyelitis," and how common polio was in boys of my age. I enjoyed accompanying him on hospital rounds occasionally.

Once I attended, as a special favor, a post-mortem. It was interesting to see in real life what was pictured and written about in his medical library shelved in my parents' room.

In those days doctors were as often on house-calls as in the office. Occasionally I went along and on one occasion I went in with him. As he opened the door he sniffed and, though the patient was upstairs, gave me his diagnosis: "diabetic coma—the odor of new-mown day." It was not a New York City physician's simile.

One other house-call I remember well, in part because I've sometimes recounted it—for its punch line. As we drove out to the "colored" part of town— the south side—he explained that he would be delivering twins. I wondered how he could know; he explained that he had heard two heartbeats. The bulldog and I remained in the car until he returned, all smiles. He explained that he'd told the couple to have names ready for the birth certificate; for two boys, two girls, or one of each. Two girls were born, to be named Syphila and Gonora.

There's no doubt that my interest in medicine during those three years was related to those matters referred to in my *Medical Autobiography*. It was then, at 12 or 13, that I was told of Dr. Woodyatt's diagnosis and prognosis in 1927, that my father gave me simple lectures on biochemistry and helped me set up my modest laboratory in a walk-in closet, the light provided by an oval window of stained glass, no less. Aside from the urinalysis paraphernalia and a chemical set, he lent me a disused microscope through which was the fascinating world of fly-legs, my own spermatozoa, and creatures scraped off catfish skins. If I occasionally toyed with following medicine as a profession, I gave no thought to a general practice, interesting and varied as my father's was. Perhaps research in diabetes? Unless a doctor's specialty comes about by chance events, it is often a reflection of his own body or psyche. During my half-century at Columbia I met many pre-meds and developed a sense of who would likely specialize in psychiatry. I've never figured out, though, what leads one into proctology.

A few classes in ancient history sparked a passing interest in becoming an archaeologist, but my fascination with ancient Egypt led to frustration in keeping the dynasties in order. Besides, I thought that my duty would require specializing in the New World. Central and South American archaeology, though fascinating, was hardly local. A visit to a mound Builders site in western Ohio was dismal and cured me of this passing fancy.

*   *   *   *   *   *   *

My entering high school in 1936 marked a change in my life much greater than the longer walk to and from Central High School. I had been taking seven courses a term in Junior High in addition to piano, clarinet, and xylophone lessons, the latter two of which I dropped. During my first, transitional, semester I continued by fill-in duties as orchestra pianist, quit the band, and signed up for five courses only.

Just before the second term, I paid an extended visit to the principal, Roscoe D. Shaffer, and told him of my newly-made plans: I had begun practicing the piano and sight-reading for four hours a day and planned to become a composer specializing in opera. Because I planned to attend a music conservatory, I would not need to take college preparatory course. I added that "study halls" were a waste of time; I'd do my assignments at home. I probably mentioned something of my stringent diet and concluded with the request that I attend all my necessary course-work in the morning, go home for lunch, and stay there to do my music and my assignments. Surely he must have been astonished at this 15-year old's comprehensive plan and request. After a few questions about my academic record—which he'd had no chance to check—he agreed to everything. During the next five terms I took only four courses a term. My grades remained as usual except for my first-ever C in advanced Algebra, which led to no comment from on high. What homework I did was done in a snug alcove of the panelled hall downstairs while Tom did his at our bedroom desk.

One generation later our daughter Miranda was in the 9th grade at the Brearley School, one of the finest girls' schools in Manhattan, noted for its high academic standards. She had for some years been studying dance seriously, had the right build for it, and was enrolled in the Martha Graham School. A visit to the doctor disclosed that she was losing weight and that she would have to give up either the compulsory gym classes or the Graham School. It seemed to us an obvious choice, but I suspected that it would be difficult to convince the headmistress, a redoubtable Scotswoman, to agree. For that reason I asked the Music Department secretary to call Miss Jean Fair Mitchell and ask her to make a personal or phone appointment with Professor Beeson of Columbia University concerning an important curricular matter. She phoned at the appointed time urging me not to leave my duties for the East Side and asked about the curricular problem. When I explained, she expressed some dismay about relaxing their strict rules and the danger of running afoul the N.Y. State athletic requirements. She did agree to call a meeting of her Athletics Committee to consider making a very special exception. Eventually the problem was solved in favor of Miranda and Martha Graham. Had I been so foolish as to tell her of my principal's measured and easy acceptance of my plan for almost three years of high school, she would have been convinced that in 1936 anarchy had reigned in the public schools of Muncie, Indiana.

It is unlikely that Miss Mitchell would have heard of Muncie, but she might well have heard of Middletown. *MIDDLETOWN: A Study in American Culture*, by Robert and Mary Lynd, published in 1929, was the first major study by sociologists to examine every aspect of an American city: how it was organized to provide health, wealth, education, welfare, and entertainment for its citizens. Lynd, a Hoosier himself, was insistent that Middletown was not a typical city, that there could not be one in the varied USA. And he went out of his way to hide evidence that Muncie was the subject. The several Ball brothers, very rich from the world-wide sales of their Ball canning jars, and memorialized in Ball Memorial Hospital, Ball State Teachers College, became the X family. Muncieites' names were evaded. Sometime in the 1950s my fellow Shandean, Bob Merton, arranged an impromptu luncheon at what was still known as the

Columbia Men's Faculty Club, with his fellow-sociologist and my fellow-Hoosier, Robert Lynd. Naturally, he and I discussed Muncie and Middletown; he remembered well that Dr. Beeson had been helpful to him in researching medical services and public health for his two books, regretting that he could not name names. He also regretted that his secrecy had been unsuccessful: Muncie and Middletown had become inextricable.

Indeed, Muncie soon after 1929 became known in the press as "Middletown, USA, the typical American city." The effects on the Muncieites of the time I was unaware of, for I was only 8, but they reverberated for years. The book's subjects were said to have been flattered by all the attention, but embarrassed and angered by having their civic, business, and social lives dissected and read about. They must have been shocked by the headline of H. L. Mencken's review of the book, *A City in Moronia*.

Middletown had appeared during good times, a renewed "era of good feelings." Its successor, *Middletown in Transition*, was published in 1937, during the sourer times of the Depression. As a teenage Muncieite I had just entered high school, where there was talk of "that Columbia professor who's been snooping around here for years." Getting a haircut was entertaining because of the talk and violent cursing of the new book and its authors.

In the years since, these two volumes have become classics in the sociological canon. Among journalists Middletown was always associated with the word the Lynds had avoided: typical. For years the *N.Y. Times* ran articles headlined "What is Muncie Reading?", as a quickie substitute for the best-seller list. Thirty-five years later, Alden Whitman of the *Times* wrote a long article with many photos—one of Edmund F. Ball of the no-longer-secret X family.— *Middletown Revisited: Still in Transition.* By that time, among laymen, Muncie and Middletown had become synonymous, either one designating a usually idealized typical American city.

While shuffling through these decades, I recount my first hearing of the last phase in the development of the Lynds' forbidden "typical": any Muncieite is necessarily a typical American. Just before I left Rochester for New York City in 1944, my mentor at the Eastman School, Bernard Rogers, telephoned me to give me the telephone numbers of his friends Aaron Copland and Samuel Barber and to say that I was to phone them because he was asking them to introduce me into New York new-music circles. Copland I met for most of an afternoon at his loft-studio, where the north side of Lincoln Center now is. He was informal, friendly, and helpful. He wondered how I had managed to overcome Béla Bartók's refusal to teach composition when I told him that I was just then beginning to meet with him. Copland wanted to hear some music and so I played a couple of piano sonatas. His compliments were welcome, but I wondered—as I still do—whether his comment, "It sounds Egyptian" was a quip or a reflection of his then purely diatonic-major style. To be sure, I was a "chromatic composer," but there were few if any augmented seconds.

When he asked where I'd been born and raised and I replied, he broke into a great smile—as if he were an agent who had unexpectedly signed on a star-singer. "Well, so you are now our typically American composer! You can make a great deal of that distinction if you handle it right! People all think I reflect the American heartland in my music, but I'm just a Jew from Brooklyn. What I know of the midwest and southwest is what I can see from an airplane on my way to Mexico City to visit my friend Carlos Chavez." We spent the rest of our time together listening to Chavez on 78s.

There was less time to chat with Samuel Barber when he invited me to accompany him to a concert in Carnegie Hall. At intermission he, also, was amused and surprised to meet a composer from Middletown/Muncie. As we left the concert he remarked that he'd seen some reviews of a concert with a Beeson piano sonata included. As it happened, it was my first New York City performance. "Had I seen them?" "Yes, of course," I answered. "Did you read them?" "Why yes. Don't you?" "No." he answered. "I just measure them." I supposed that I'd get used to such Big City sophisticated and cynical remarks, and I did. But as I began to receive more reviews of my music—there were half a dozen newspapers regularly reviewing music in those days—I noticed that passing friends on upper-Broadway complimented me more warmly on long, mediocre reviews than they did on short, excellent ones. It occurred to me that Aaron's evaluation of a *Middletown* background and Sam's measuring the print devoted to his music were both attitudes more realistic than cynical.

*   *   *   *   *   *   *

Entering high school in 1936 at the age of 15, the idea of my ever meeting Copland and Barber would have seemed preposterous, not to speak of remaining their friend for their lifetimes. Considering the plans I had for music studies and high school for the next three years—plans carried out—the popular notion that anyone born and bred in *Middletown* had to be a typical American should have allowed for an exception here and there.

Although I continued to give practice lessons to some of the pupils of Miss Weimer, she suggested that I now study with Perceval Owen, reminding me jokingly that I would then be one teacher closer to Beethoven. (Years later, when I had my first publications, I remembered the joke, for I noticed that I was snuggled up next to Beethoven alphabetically: it was easy to find him in catalogs and library cards; my few titles always preceded his.) Mr. Owen came to Muncie one day a week to teach at Ball State Teachers College and to teach privately a couple of advanced students. He proved an excellent teacher, strict and forgiving, and enlightened. He would not accept private students unless they agreed to study music history, theory, and strict counterpoint with his assistant, Lorin Woodward. The lesson with Owen and the instruction with Woodward consumed an afternoon a week. I was told to practice piano and sight read four hours a day, so what I had told R. D. Shaffer in my plan for high school was honest. When I was assigned the first in a series of Beethoven sonatas, in Owens's friend Artur Schnabel's edition, I was given the four volumes by Owen, inscribed, "From his Helper and Friend." The music history assignments filled in the gaps in my already wide knowledge of opera and its environs. The harmony lessons confirmed what my ear had been teaching me. But the species counterpoint appealed to some atavistic pleasure in working within limits and rules. The combining of independencies into a larger, coherent whole—counterpoint in the largest sense—has been a characteristic of my music ever since, whether clearly projected as such or not.

These studies showed me that there was much more to composing than improvising piano pieces and improvising vocal lines with their accompaniment to the words on the music rack, then writing them down and polishing their surfaces. I did not need a goad at that time; I needed a guide, but there was not one in the neighborhood.

*   *   *   *   *   *   *

The regular Saturday afternoon Met broadcasts were a constant spur to me to write my own opera. Surely by the time I'd written my libretto I'd be able to set it to music? It did not occur to me that I might find a play that I could adapt for a libretto. Instead, as an admirer of Shelley's lyrics I found his tragedy in five acts, *The Cenci.* It contained all and more of the strenuous emotions I thought were the stuff of opera: requited and unrequited love, incest, guilt, murder, and executions. Nevertheless the verse seemed too ornate and diffuse to set to music and the dramaturgy . . . well, too un-Verdian. Borrowing the play's characters and their entanglements, I put my Shelley volume away—so that I would not be tempted to crib from it—and wrote my own libretto, mostly in verse. I completed the music of the first scene. I remember but one other scene and its last line. In a dark chapel of the Cenci palace in Rome there stands a catafalque on which lies the body of Beatrice's murdered younger brother. The only light is provided by two very tall candles in floor-stands on either side of the catafalque. Count Cenci pursues his daughter Beatrice around and around the body of Rocco until he topples a candle, falls, and sings "The dead burns me."

When at a loss for rhymes or telling phrases, I tried setting passages to music, but I was always disappointed. I had far greater reason than did Shelley to believe the words in his Dedication to *The Cenci,* "I can also perceive defects incidental to youth and impatience; they are dreams of what ought to be, or may be." What happened to my musical settings, such as they were, I do not know. They have long since disappeared; I'd be interested in seeing them today.

I was clearly more satisfied with my libretto's words than with my music. I put the completed libretto in one of my father's aromatic cigar boxes and included a note to myself: "To await the completion of my musical education." I kept it with me, unopened, until the early forties when I showed it to Albert Rivett, a composer-classmate and opera buff at the Eastman School. What his reaction to reading it was, and mine to re-reading it, I don't remember—but we destroyed it.

In the late forties, my wife and I first saw what is thought to be the portrait of Beatrice Cenci, attributed to Guido Reni, in the Barberini Palace in Rome. It may be that it was then that I first told her of my teenage affair with Beatrice. She did not forget my confession, for some years later, while working at the Metropolitan Museum, she frequented the Parke Bernet 84 Gallery auctions and acquired a quite decent pastel copy of the original portrait, or the copy of a copy. She presented it to me and it was treasured until it was unaccountably left in our Shelter Island house. Retrieved by our daughter Miranda, it was re-presented to us on our fiftieth wedding anniversary. From across my studio here on Lloyd Neck, Long Island, Beatrice is gazing at me pensively as I write of our unconsummated relationship.

During the year I was at work on *Beatrice Cenci*—the first of my three years of high school—I was doing a great deal of highly extra-curricular reading. Somehow I found and became absorbed and troubled by Oswald Spengler's *Decline of the West*. I was impressed by his theory of historical cycles, but wondered if it was not a mistake to plan a life as a composer in a period of general decline in music and the theatre. My history teacher was appalled that I was reading Spengler and tried to be reassuring.

Our Carnegie Public Library provided me with a number of handbooks intended for beginning writers, but not one had anything to say about the writing of librettos. All, though, suggested that a writer should choose subjects of his own time, place, and station. Perhaps I had made a mistake in choosing Beatrice Cenci as a subject? She had been executed in Rome in 1599; that was far away and long ago. Perhaps Red Wing, supposedly an Indian princess, would be more suitable for me as an operatic heroine? She had died not too long ago and was said to be buried under the only building of our Boy Scout Camp just outside Muncie. Sometimes, after singing the national anthem, with our right hands over our hearts and merit badges, we'd sing the still well-known popular song of 1907, *Red Wing*. With the tune stolen from a Robert Schumann piano piece, the first line was, "There once lived an Indian maid."

The lyrics were full of love-sick sentiment and sorrow for her fallen "warrior bold," but shy of facts and plot. Somehow I pieced together from legend and my imagination a story-line, then began the libretto for an opera to be called *Red Wing*. For *Beatrice Cenci* I had had at least a model for the over-all structure in Shelley's play. Now, on my own, how long should an act be? Was it proper in 1937 or 1938 to follow the Italian pattern of recitative-aria? Or should I through-compose as had my favored Wagner? Somehow, I persevered, completed the first act libretto and 2 or 3 musical numbers, one of them modeled on Wagner's Senta's Ballad.

On some Saturday afternoon broadcast I must have heard Lawrence Tibbett singing Amonasro, for when he came to sing a recital at Muncie's local teacher's college I took along my piano-vocal score of *Aida* with the hope that I might have the courage to acquire his autograph. That I did is proven by his name signed in now fading ink next to Amonasro on the cast list of my Verdi score. (His accompanist's name, Stewart Wille, is scrawled crosswise on the page.) Tibbett was so cordial that I hazarded a technical question: "Mr. Tibbett, could you please tell me how long an opera act should be?" He seemed surprised by the question and answered something like, "As long as it has to be." A teenager pondering this Delphic answer from someone he thought an expert on the matter naturally thought that a composer-librettist could do what his inspiration dictated. But I soon noticed that the inspiration of Verdi and his librettists operated within bounds: Verdi acts are rarely more than forty minutes—most of them are less than that or in the forties; in *Don Carlo* there's a rarity of fifty-two minutes.

For some reason, long since forgotten, I dropped my Indian project and turned to Byron's *Manfred*. My intention this time was to use the words of an admired poet rather than my own, but to cut and rearrange them in order to capitalize on the several rhymed speeches of the Spirits, actual song lyrics, and ensemble possibilities. Byron called *Manfred* a dramatic poem, though he shaped it into three acts of several scenes each. I was naturally undeterred by reading that Robert Schumann's very elaborate incidental music for spoken performances of the play was thought to be undramatic in the extreme; I thought that my operatic setting of the Cataract Scene, Act II, scene 2, was my best effort so far. Reading the play seventy years later, I remember a line here and there and what were my intentions. Unfortunately, my manuscripts of both *Red Wing* and *Manfred* are long since lost. There was no formal destruction of them as there was to be in the early forties when *Beatrice Cenci*, the opera, was condemned and executed by Al Rivett and me.

Looking back over those three aborted attempts to write an opera, spread over the three high school years, I am interested to note that the only overt influence of Wagner seems to have been the shaping of a *Red Wing* aria after the Ballad of Senta, a conventional model from his early *Flying Dutchman*. My enthusiasm quickly led me to his later music dramas, broadcast often by the Met, with Flagstad and Melchior. I devoured Wagner's *Mein Leben* (in English, of course) and Ernest Newman's biography. I accompanied my mother on her shopping expeditions to Indianapolis for the purpose of borrowing or renewing Henry T. Finck's 2-volume *Wagner and His Works*, large chunks of which I copied out by hand, and orchestral scores of Wagner scheduled to be broadcast. My most vivid aural memory of Wagner's music from that period is turning on the car radio toward the end of the long drive from Muncie to our Michigan log cabin, turning up the volume as I opened the car door and Siegfried's horn call rang out into the small grove of trees and over the nearby lake. Then, as Siegfried continued on his Rhine Journey and the crescendo built in F major to a climax, the sudden shift to A major brought to me a kind of epiphany. A red circle and two exclamation marks in my vocal score remind me of that moment still.

*   *   *   *   *   *   *

A series of seemingly unrelated events at the beginning of my junior year made it possible eventually to understand better Wagner's music-drama texts and brought about a small change in the curriculum of Central High. I was supposed to take third year Latin that year. Because I was so obsessed with spoken and sung language, before the first class I asked the teacher if we would be taught to speak Latin. She replied that Latin was a dead language and could not be spoken. (Later, four years in Rome disproved that assertion.) I suppose I told her that in that case I'd take French, the only other language offered, though I didn't want to do so; I was not yet an admirer of *Carmen* and *Manon*, my only French acquaintances.

Someone had the information that Miss Hutzel had once taught German, perhaps before WWI. She was well-known to all of us as a teacher of mathematics—had she given me my C in advanced algebra? She was tall, intimidating, of a certain age, with white hair, cut—completely out of character—in a Clara Bow bob. I asked her if she would like to teach German again and she said she would, enthusiastically. As I had a few months earlier, I went to see Mr. Shaffer, the principal, explained my problem—such as it was—and told him that Miss Hutzel would be pleased to exchange a math class for a German class. He didn't fuss at all and offered a deal: if I could find another five students willing to take beginning German, it could be offered. I did so and we began immediately. Fräulein Hutzel, as she directed us to call her, had been brought up bilingually and so the classes were carried on in German. Because all six of us were good students, in two years of high school we did the equivalent of two college years: all the grammar and some short stories of Storm and Heyse in the first year and *Wilhelm Tell* and *Faust*, Part I, in the second—each, to my delight, the basis of an opera.

As we began our second year of German, another group of motivated students began their first year. When they began their second, I had already left for the Eastman School. A former classmate wrote me that an ugly rumor had led the press to report that the students hailed Miss Hutzel at the beginning of each class with a Heil Hitler salute. it was true that the classroom's large windows were matched by windows across the small court, but that argued against the truth of the rumor even more than in its favor. World War II had begun in September. Fear and fervour were abroad in the land, as were American Firsters and waving flags. German classes were dropped at Central High, not to return for 44 years. *Middletown*, if perhaps not full of typical Americans, surely was not populated by ideal Americans. After all, on one of my last trips to the barbershop in Muncie, I'd had to hear yet again that our president was Jewish and his name Rosenfeld.

*   *   *   *   *   *   *

During my junior year I coped with the four courses in the morning—enlivened with the new language course—and spent the rest of the time on *Red Wing*, studying scores, practicing, reading, and biking. I was serious about the piano and needed to be, for Mr. Owen was planning recitals of his students; George Cook (my senior, so to speak) and I were to perform Beethoven sonatas. More taxing was that Mr. Owen, still loyal to his Canadian birth, insisted that in June I take the examinations in piano, music history, theory, and counterpoint at the university of Toronto Conservatory of Music. Mother and I drove to Toronto where there were two days of lengthy exams. Mr. Owen was pleased by the piano examiner that "this candidate has been well taught."

Perhaps as a reward he invited me to accompany him to Cincinnati to hear and to meet his old friend Artur Schnabel from their Leschetizky days. It was the first recital by a stellar pianist I'd ever heard and I've seldom since heard its like: two Schubert sonatas and two Beethoven sonatas, with another, shorter, Beethoven sonata as the encore.

*   *   *   *   *   *   *

Not just for convenience have I divided my adolescence, my years from 12 to 18, into two segments: the first three years, those of junior high school, paralleled by the early Met broadcasts and my idea of becoming a composer, and the various instrumental studies and early compositions; the second three years, those of high school, paralleled by the writing of three librettos and attempting to set them to music, and serious piano and music study. If a declaration of independence is required for entering adolescence, mine, at 12, was my refusal any longer to attend Sunday School and church. Mother took Tom and me regularly to the Methodist Church and then—for social reasons, I suspect—to a "high church" Episcopal church. I liked its incense and costumes, but was bored with the sermons and developed a dislike for hypocrisy that has continued lifelong. Our father never accompanied us, with the ready excuse of having to care for patients. Tom, two years my junior, continued to attend for the rest of his life. Jack and Tom—our names as like as were our genes—as youngsters had constantly quarreled and tussled until Emma yelled at us, "You boys quit fighting or I'll call the PO-lice!" Tom took a few piano lessons, then took up the cornet, as our father had once upon a time. When I began to accompany Tom at the piano it was a sign that a truce had been arrived at. he went on playing ball, going fishing with Elmer, and being an undersized all-American boy and I went on with my projects.

By this time, 1933 or so, our father's hay fever and asthma had worsened and so it was decided we should spend the hay fever season in northern Michigan, the usual haven for Hoosiers. As preparation for the next season the garage was turned into a workshop and he turned his handyman talents and excess energy into building an elaborate trailer-housecar, with his sons as assistant carpenters. The next August we drove north to a few miles northeast of Petoskey and got stuck in the sand. A few steps away was a small grove of trees on the edge of Pickerel Lake. The car and trailer rescued, the isolated grove for sale and purchased, we returned every summer through 1939. During our first season, in the housecar, it was arranged to have the major part of a log cabin built before the next summer, when we would roof it and do the interior. That we three did, with Elmer's help. Tom and I were responsible for putting in the walls and floors of our bedrooms. Because I had never found a hidden space behind the panelling in the Washington Street house, I built one into my flooring using cut-off nailheads to hide the entrance. Unfortunately, I never found anything important to hide in it.

During that summer an upright piano was provided for my use—and a clinker-built rowboat appeared. I built a small mast fort it, jury-rigged it, and taught myself to sail. I was to relish sailing for long periods—if intermittently—until 1980. Both my experience in carpentry and sailing I passed on to my son Christopher, who surpassed me in both and turned them to professional use.

A similar routine was followed by two more years. During the first winter and spring my father built a metal motorboat; I wasn't allowed to help much because of possible injury to my hands. It was trailered up to Pickerel Lake for much of the summer. In the second year an eighteen foot sloop was built—with my enthusiastic cooperation—trailered north and sailed almost daily.

On one occasion, with my father as crew and a mild breeze, we had sailed across the lake when my diabetic father broke out in a sweat, became incoherent, and lay down in the cuddy cabin. I knew that it was the result of low blood sugar, hypoglycemia, and could soon lead to unconsciousness. The wind having failed, I tried again and again to start the occasionally undependable outboard engine, but without success. Meanwhile a following breeze arose and we scudded home, where orange juice and sugar soon revived him. The experience so terrified me that rarely thereafter did I sail without a companion and a supply of orange juice; and I have since then seldom been able to trust any engine in an emergency.

It used to be said that the best sailors come from the land-locked Midwest and I hoped it was true. I took to sailing as I had to swimming. It seemed to me then, as it did later, that combining one's knowledge and careful use of wind, tide, and currents to bring about a seemingly easy and satisfactory forward movement was a perfect analogue to writing music.

When I became overly familiar with Pickerel Lake, I negotiated the narrow passage to a larger lake and began frequenting the docks at nearby Harbor Springs, filling a scrapbook with photos of Great Lakes yachts. Fresh water led in the imagination to salt water, to the Pacific and its western islands. In fantasy I imagined owning a 35-foot ketch—the best rig and maximum length for single-handed sailing—and going to the South Seas. (In fantasy one doesn't need to remember that one is an incipient diabetic subject to hypoglycemia!) I read widely, from Cook's *Voyages* to *White Shadows in the South Seas*, and everything about Pitcairn Island from the mutiny to the present inhabitants. In saner moments it occurred to me that I knew of two painters and the writer, Stevenson, but no composers who had gone there. I was too uninformed to know that it was just in those years of 1934 and '35 that Colin McPhee was in Bali writing the music that would make him famous—but Bali was not in my South Seas. These dreams ended with my adolescence, the end of summers at Pickerel Lake in 1939, and the sale of my sloop.

During the two years in the early thirties when our garage became a boat-builder's shop there occasionally appeared a nervous, scruffy fellow named Fred Bohlinger. He avoided the bulldog and the house because Mother disliked and distrusted him. He and my father did not so much speak to one another as mumble together. Once or twice he handed my father a wad of bills and I heard the magic name of George Ball (of the X family) and the famous name of George Dale, a mayor of Muncie. Sometimes, when Bohlinger appeared suddenly, I'd be sent to some fool's errand or it would be suggested that I go practice. I was fascinated because I thought I was on the edge of some mystery, perhaps some conspiracy. Some years later, in going through my father's papers after his death, I discovered that I had been correct.

To make sense of some of these cryptic sheets I looked up George Dale in *Middletown Revisited*, which I had only skimmed through when it was published in 1937. Dale was there by name, for he had put Muncie, rather than *Middletown*, in the national press in the late twenties. He had long run a local Democratic newspaper that attacked the enormously powerful Indiana Ku Klux Klan so consistently that he was jostled, spat on, and beat up on the street—twice nearly shot. Elected mayor in 1930, he tried to bring an end to some of the corruption in the city. On trumped-up charges, an indictment was brought by his local enemies in Federal Court, ended by a presidential pardon in 1932. Other indictments were brought against him and thrown out in 1933. These matters were also covered by the national press in 1932 and 1933. Those are exactly the first two of the several years listed in the cryptic sheets, one of them signed by Fred Bohlinger, the go-between who was keeping track of the payments of a few thousand each from George Ball to my father. On which side of this extended battle had the three men been? I decided that my statute of limitations had run out and forgot about the matter until now. I find it troubling anew.

*   *   *   *   *   *   *

In Michigan the summers passed unchanged and idyllically, often enlivened by long visits from my father's sister, Iva, and her two children, our favorite cousins. Both were good Floridean sailors and instrumentalists: Claire, my age, was an accomplished cornettist; Joe Julian, a little older, hoped to become a concert violinist. Accompanying him at my upright piano, I had the opportunity to savor a new repertory.

In Muncie, though, changes were apparent from year to year. The effects of the 1929 stock market crash had been delayed and first affected the well-do-do. One day a truck delivered a handsome antique grandfather's clock; a wealthy patient had fallen far behind on his medical bills and was paying "in kind"—a new term to me. Then Mother received a large amethyst ring, another payment in kind. Doctors in those days had always taken care of "charity patients." By the middle thirties, with medical insurance unheard of, charity patients became all too numerous and my father's income diminished. On occasion the lights went out or the telephone wouldn't function. I learned from Emma, usually discreet, that the electric or telephone bills had not been paid.

Some of my father's financial troubles in the middle thirties were of his own making, and as the decade wore on, the major cause. To his diabetes, asthma, and coronary disease he added heavy drinking, which developed into alcoholism. When hung over he could not make hospital rounds or go to the office. Mother cared for him as only a nurse could. When she remarked that "Doctors are their worst patients" she spoke from experience. They had met in Philadelphia when she was in nurses training, with a perky, pleated cap to show that she had been at Old Blockley. My father was then doing his residency at Philadelphia General. As soon as she was graduated they married and moved to Muncie, where he began his practice, which flourished for years. But, although Mother was the most selfless, caring, and generous person I've ever known, there was nothing she could do in the middle thirties to prevent deterioration or his alcoholism. I tried a couple of son-to-father talks. He responded with embarrassment and promises, but I was too inexperienced to know that heavy drinking can have deeper causes than just a taste for liquor. I had always enjoyed his profanity and Hoosierisms: "That shade of brown is piss-muckle brown"; a particularly nervous patient reminded him "of a fart in a hot skillet." But by my senior year in high school, his casual profanity was becoming cursing and the quick temper turning into fits of anger. On a few occasions, when he came home drunk, Mother, Tom and I took refuge behind locked doors upstairs. Once, when Emma served him a too-hot cup of coffee he threw it at Mother, missing her but scarring the polished mahogany of the wall, yelling that the trouble was that she was part Indian.

Tom had school, games with his chums, and fishing with Elmer. I had school and my music, but we were both all too often aware that the grown-ups were having troubles. Once Mother confided in me that my father was sleeping around with colored women. That she said it to me seemed as preposterous as what she claimed. Later my father confided that Mother was having an affair with the manager of the A&P grocery store. My reaction was exactly the same. I thought to myself, "If even one's parents can say such things—even it they are not true—what's the point in growing up?"

When I overheard Mother say something to a friend about "getting a divorce after Jack graduates," I thought, "that's just the sort of thing grown-ups say they disapprove of and then go do anyhow," tried to put it out of mind, and began to look forward even more eagerly to leaving home for a conservatory somewhere and living in a dormitory with people of my own age who shared my interests.

I had long since decided that I would go to the Curtis Institute of Music in Philadelphia, the Juilliard School in New York City, or the Eastman School of Music of the University of Rochester in upstate New York. I favored the first two because they were on salt water, which I had not yet experienced; Eastman was on just another of the Great Lakes, Ontario. Sensibly, though, I found the names of the composers on their faculties and ordered music written by them. There was nothing to be had from the Curtis composer, I wasn't interested in the scores of the Juilliard composers, but I was impressed by the music of Hanson and Rogers at Eastman, where I applied. Naturally, samples of my compositions were required. The opera scenes were too out of context to be submitted and both Mr. Owen and Mr. Woodward advised submitting something more conventional. Accordingly, I swiftly wrote a pseudo-Mozart piano sonata movement and made a fair copy to send. Then, without thinking at the time how bizarre it was, I *re*-wrote, in my own fashion, a favored passage from Act III of Wagner's *Die Meistersinger*, the "Wach' auf" chorus. In my application I would have listed my musical activities to spring, 1939: 11 years of piano study, some ability on clarinet and xylophone, membership in orchestra and band, some chorus accompanying, and the University of Toronto Conservatory examinations in piano, music history, theory, and strict counterpoint, a couple of modest compositions that had been performed, and three libretti, only partially set to music. That, indeed, is a lot of musical activity, but I was applying in composition and their jury must have been taken aback by the two submissions. They may have thought that this off-beat applicant from Muncie—from *Middletown*—from Moronia—was desperately in need of being shown the straight and narrow path to becoming a composer. For whatever reason I was admitted and awarded a full-tuition George Eastman Scholarship, renewed for three years.

While our parents remained in Muncie tending to their divorce and the house and its contents, the pain of the break-up of our family for Tom and me was diluted by a truncated summer at the Michigan cabin with Aunt Iva, our cousins, and Elmer. We knew very little about the divorce proceedings and its provisions. When I learned that my father was to provide for his sons during their minority, it occurred to me that if we and Mother were to remain together, she could benefit from our allowances. When everybody thought that a good idea, I was pleased to forget about the pleasures, if any, of living in a dormitory and we left for Rochester in the late summer.

*   *   *   *   *   *   *

Chapter 2

At the Eastman School of Music During World War II
(1939-1944)

It was not long before we three found the sunny end-house of row-houses where Mother and I lived for my five years at the Eastman School, a healthy walk to and fro; Tom, of course, was with us for his last two years of high school, which was only a couple of hundred yards away. On the third floor was an extra bedroom, which we rented out to an Eastman student. Mother soon found employment at the Strong Memorial Hospital of the University Medical School as assistant to the director of the "solutions room," an ambiguous term, to be sure. In those years, saline, glucose, and other medical solutions were prepared in hospitals rather than bought in quantity from suppliers, as they have been in more recent years. She and the director, who had been a Swiss nurse, became friends and shared a house after I left Rochester for New York City. Together with our furnishings trucked from Muncie was my baby-grand piano and a large bookcase that had been built into the Washington Street house for Tom and me in 1928. This I had extracted and have built into every apartment since, the only trace of its origin hidden: the cut-out that had originally been made to fit the first highly-curved baseboard.

From this comfort and domesticity every walk to school—even in Rochester winters when yard-high snow banks into April formed a narrow path—

was to me an exciting journey to the neo-Renaissance place of the Eastman School of Music, inhabited only by musicians, many from Europe and Asia.

On Gibbs Street one entered a high and wide corridor that stretched the block to Swan Street across which were the outbuildings, so to speak, the very tall one with stacked practice rooms and a gym and handball court on top, and the low jewel of the Sibley Music Library, where every conceivable piece of music, in manuscript, print, and recording, was available on open shelves.

Off the main corridor to the left was access to the palatial Eastman Theatre; to the right the entrance to Kilbourn Hall, with its daily noon solo and chamber music recitals and space for the Eastman-Rochester Orchestra at the readings of new works, a unique service to the young composers of the time.

On the second floor was a duplicate of the main-floor corridor, even less encumbered, with corridors leading to the private offices of the faculty, from which one heard dimly the familiar sounds of singers, instrumentalists, and from the composers' studios sounds never before heard. The buildings, their fittings and decorations, were so different from my earlier "typical American" experience that my first impressions remained enduring ones, elaborate stage settings in which we were to play our varied roles.

But first all was technical: a battery of Seashore tests, designed especially for musicians to test various aspects of hearing, and motor tests for quickness of reactions. And then there were, for me, not one, but two or three Stanford-Binet intelligence-quotient tests with results both middling and high, none conforming with those sent from Muncie Central High. I explained to the puzzled technician that my I.Q. tests always were better indications of my varying blood-sugar levels than of my presumably unvarying I.Q.

There was a concerted attempt by the registrar and others to talk me into double-majoring in composition and piano, but I resisted successfully. I knew that if I were assigned a major piano teacher I would be required to practice more than I might wish and to learn the standard repertory for public performance, which I had no intention of doing in the future. I wanted the piano as a composition tool and to study contemporary piano works toward the same end. It was my good luck to be assigned to Lyndon Croxford who was broadminded enough to permit me to choose Bartók, Bloch, Griffes, and Prokofieff sonatas. There were to be his choices of representative works of the past, as well as the Schumann as a token concerto. It was Croxford, a nut for "double-notes," who led me through all scales in 3rds and 6ths and all Chopin and Debussy etudes in "double notes," with a startling result during my first meeting with Bartók, to be described later. (Since the Croxford years I have substituted a warmer-upper, a homemade finger-breaker of chromatic augmented fourths a minor tenth part.)

Those of us who had already studied theory and had done well on the ear-tests were assigned to the "fast class" of Irvine McHose, the autocratic head of theory. We soon learned that the rules of part-writing and harmonization in whatever conventional book of theory we had studied were to take second place to the actual practice of Bach in his 371 chorale settings. In the first counterpoint course, the species system we might have studied (as I had) was ruled out in favor of the actual practice of Palestrina and Lassus. Both of these points of view had the advantage of being based on first-class composer models; both were limited in scope, though after our first years of the subjects, the models were more varied.

A couple of us composer-wags in the "fast class" learned that McHose's early training had been as an entomologist specializing in the classification of insects and promptly named the theory class "taxonomic harmony." McHose had for some years set graduate students in theory the task of converting Bach's 371 chorale settings into a series of percentages listing how often each of the seven triads and the seventh-chords in Bach's vocabulary was used in the total corpus and how often certain pairings of them occurred. One of the pairings was of "first-class chords" (those leading to the tonic chords at cadences) and "second-class chords" (those preceding the "first-class chords"). It may be understood from this over-simplification that the student, when given a chorale melody to harmonize, was to do so by choosing his chords largely by relying on the tabulated percentages. Woe betide the inventive student who crammed into his harmonization of a melody in a minor key to a grieving text more of the expressive events used by Bach than the list of percentages permitted.

Warren Fox was the one musicologist on staff. Witty, erudite, and unpublished, he was very friendly to us composers and an obliquely-spoken and perceptive critic of our emerging works. Typical of his sly ways was a prank he played on the whole "taxonomic theory" enterprise. He returned one fall from Germany with the 18th century manuscript of a chorale setting which he successfully passed off as a Bach manuscript. McHose was appalled, for to add one more to the canonic 371 would necessitate refiguring the contents of 372 into new percentages, and his findings were nearing publication. After Fox had savored the effect of his joke he took pity on the graduate theory students who had begun the tiresome manual recomputation and confessed, hoping that he might have had the effect of showing a weakness of "taxonomic theory"—which he had not.

Because only composition and theory majors were required to take two years of counterpoint, our classes had but a half-dozen students, all taught by Gustave Soderlund, the only foreign-born teacher I had at Eastman. As I had enjoyed species counterpoint with Lorin Woodward, so I enjoyed in the first year the rigor of Soderlund in seeing to it that we wrote our exercises in accordance with the practice of late 16th century composers. In the second year, mostly given over to 18th century canon and fugue, the bonds were changed and retightened. As a final exercise we were assigned to compose a longish piece written to a model of our own choosing and I turned in *A Fragment of the Passion of St. Matthew*, in the style of K. H. Graun, perhaps out of mischief.

It was always a pleasure to witness the tall Swede react so passionately to a small musical mistake, a pair of parallel fifths or octaves, for instance. Once, though, someone made a more flagrant error and Soderlund flew into a rage. Intending to leave the room, he chose the wrong door and shut himself into his closet. Naturally, we decided to do the correct thing and sat in our places until the end of the hour. We didn't see him again until the next class.

Though the three years of theory and two of counterpoint were taught in a remarkably well-organized fashion and were instructive and interesting, it often seemed to me that there was something illogical about requiring such a regimen of composers who had already been through the same material, albeit from different points of view with differing terminologies.

It finally occurred to me that our much enlarged *second* dose of these two subjects had the merit of assuring the Eastman School (there having been no entrance examinations in the subjects and therefore no possibility of advanced placement) that each of its student composers could indeed crawl and walk, although some of us were up-and-running composers while taking third-year theory. As a freshman from the Midwest I did not know that teaching in universities and conservatories was the usual employment for composers and almost always included teaching theory—thus the required Eastman Pedagogy of Theory, taught also by McHose. Inasmuch as the Midwest colleges were filled with Eastman graduates, it was in the interests of both the School and McHose that the Eastman Way be thoroughly inculcated in all students and then widely exported.

And it came to pass that when I began my first classroom teaching, at Columbia University, I was assigned an elementary theory class—but only for a year. It was necessary, first, to be indoctrinated, for I was fresh from enemy territory. The head of theory at Columbia was William J. Mitchell, who had studied in Vienna with Heinrich Schenker, a theorist with a highly original and for a long time influential analytic method. Mitchell's textbook was not to be deviated from or quarreled with by us juniors. The "Columbia Way" was known as "common practice;" Mitchell's *Elementary Harmony* resembled my conventional Muncie harmony textbooks more closely than the "Eastman Way." There's no doubt that the coherent and comprehensive courses in harmony and counterpoint during my first year at Eastman and later were of great value to a ripening greenhorn from Muncie, particularly as they introduced me to other ways of looking at and listening to the subjects in the fast company of fine teachers and committed students. The same could be said of the Historical Survey course of Warren Fox, with whom I later took a musicology course and became friends.

Such was much of the first and some of the other of my five years at Eastman. Accustomed as I had been in the past to filling my time with what I enjoyed doing, I took courses also in three of the summer sessions and thereby earned both the Bachelor and Master of Music in four years. My fifth year was a residence year for the PhD, during which two large works were composed, either of which would have served as a dissertation, had I wished to complete that degree.

Naturally, during the whole of that time I was in the care of the staff composers: in the first year, Edward Royce; in the second, Burrill Phillips; for two years with Bernard Rogers, and in the fifth, Howard Hanson. I would gladly have spent that final year also with Rogers, but I sensed that Hanson expected PhD candidates to attend his seminar and I had no wish to offend him. As it turned out, he was such a fine and experienced musician, conductor, and composer—and sight-reader at the podium and piano—that much was to be learned from him, though as composers he and I were very different in age and style.

Not having had even one word of advice about my composing in Muncie, I entered Royce's class with a naïve and romantic notion of the teacher's role in the development of a young composer. It was probably gleaned by having read of such pairings as Bach and his sons and Leopold and Wolfgang Mozart. My adolescent idea of the composer as free artist was jolted by being asked by Royce to model new pieces on standard works.

Of Royce and Phillips I wrote briefly and of Rogers at length in 1980. Kenneth Gaburo, an excellent composer who had studied with Rogers a few years after I did, asked a few of us who had known Bernard well to write of him. Rogers had died in 1968 and the collection of tributes was intended to be published by Gaburo under his own imprint as a kind of memorial. The following *Job and J. B. at Eastman* was to be my contribution. The publication was several times postponed and then, with Gaburo's death, cancelled, causing great distress to Bernard's widow, who was not able to retrieve the material that had been submitted for publication.

Job and J. B. at Eastman

In late summer, 1939, the guns of August seemed very distant to four teenagers who were entering Eastman as the freshman composition majors. With Europe closed to study Eastman appeared to be the finest school anywhere for composers, but there was one striking anomaly even in our disorientation period: our composition teacher, Edward Royce. Had he been hired to amuse us, to confuse us, before some later-to-be-revealed Eastman system would set us aright? Had we been chosen, not as composers, but to serve as an audience for his reminiscences of Josiah Royce and William James and his renditions of Schumann and Brahms; or, once we had begun to carry out his assignments (to write a, b, or c in the style of x, y, or z) to play little Wagners to his Hanslick? With all the cultural disadvantages and the pragmatic advantages of 18 years in Middletown, USA, I decided to make the best of the investment, to value his teaching method as I had valued my strict counterpoint studies, as bonds within which to develop suppleness and strength. In retrospect it seems to me that there was some sense in his teaching, but very little sensibility.

To a Hoosier, Burrill Phillips, assigned in the second year, was familiar. He was reticent, but salty; down-to-earth, but not earth-bound; picturesque, but not "poetic." A wrong note was simply a wrong note; an unjustified rhythmic dislocation was "off-base;" factitious passages were "not heard" and unacceptable. He sight-read well; if the student played, bumbling was not tolerated. When he composed at the blackboard standards were set; when we did so, we aspired to a standard. To me this way of building a craft was familiar. When I had accompanied my father on house-calls and hospital rounds I had learned that a quick, seemingly intuitive, diagnosis was possible only because practice had made perfect the ability to select the right few decision-making necessities from the mind's storehouse. . . .

The above abbreviated comment on the valuable year with Burrill Phillips leads me to postpone the entrance of the title character of *Job* and to recount a singular event that took place early in the Phillips year. A discussion by the five of us about Schönberg's practice in the early twenties—only 20 years before!—of sometimes using 19th century formal structures to shape his new 12-tone materials, led Phillips to assign us a similar task: using a two-part form, write a short piece in whatever idiom, including what we took to be our own. In preparation for doing so, I read through a number of Scarlatti sonatas and then quickly wrote out the short piece he asked for. When we next met, I played what I had written. The consternation and giggles of the others led me to realize that I'd written out almost note for note one of the sight-read Scarlatti sonatas.

I had always feared memory lapses—and with reason—even in pieces I'd prepared for weeks for recitals or piano exams. I could never have accomplished the feat—as Mozart could—of reproducing by memory a piece I'd but once or twice read through. Later, in teaching composition, when a student brought in music that was too redolent of, or too literally dependent on, music already written, telling the student of my early experience tended to take the sting out of whatever criticism I might make.

To my knowledge I have never again committed such an unconscious plagiarism as I did in 1940. However, to a greater extent than most composers, I have *consciously* chosen to quote from—and to give credit to—a wide variety of composers of many styles and periods, usually in operas, and always with a reason for doing so.

. . . Though we Juniors had acquired a thin patina of sophistication and toughness, the thought of studying with Mr. Rogers was unnerving. One could not be certain that the stories about him were true. To a student with a voluminous first symphony: "Brahms was over forty when he finished his 1st, but I suppose you may as well get your early ones out of everybody's way, so that you can get on to the later ones." Or, to a student with a large gnarled work: "Are you having trouble in your life?" But credence was lent by overheard quips at concerts. At the first performance of new work by Roy Harris: "If at first you don't succeed, tri-ad again." At the performance of a symphony by a composer, now well-known: "It sounds as though he's afraid the wrong people might like it."

What we discovered in class was that if such stories were true, they had paled in the re-telling, but that such pungent, even acid, comments were made in such a manner that the sting was somehow delivered together with the restorative. Always the intention was to prick the conscience of the student, to quicken his ability to ask the right questions of himself and to find his own right answers … and to avoid compromise. Bernard's use of that word, compromise, resonates down through the years, for he used it often and pronounced it—softly—as though the word itself were evil. Only over the years did I come to suspect what had led him to warn his students against it: he considered it to be the sin just short of the worst sin against self, suicide. Indeed, he may have equated the two.

A teacher who insisted that his students find their own musical truths, resist irrelevant influences and compromise, and work unremittingly—as he did himself—reminded one of some Christian saint, Protestant to be sure. But other aspects of Bernard resembled an Old Testament prophet. Was it Jonah, the bearer of bad tidings? Or was it, rather the suffering Job, for Bernard suffered from all kinds of ills, real and imagined, psychic and physical. But how enjoyable he made seem much of that suffering! The wailing wall was also a place for puns, jokes, and clowning.

This aspect of Bernard's personality, surely a part of his Jewish heritage, was mysterious and exotic to the young man from Indiana and I was to understand it later, only after years in New York. At first I saw no connection, for example, between his use of the shofar in the orchestra and his insistence that a tuba was a tuber: later the connection seemed certain, or at least logical. Back in Muncie I had wondered why the parents of my friend Bert Roth were not building their house in Westwood, the elegant new suburb, but on farmland across the road. I was told it was because the family was Jewish. I supposed that was something like being Amish.

Bernard as Job from New York seemed exotic in yet other ways. His house had been designed by a leading modern architect, Lescaze. He was a painter as well as a composer, and his familiars, Degas and Hokusai, accompanied him to class. In fact, his conversation, his music, and his book *The Art of Orchestration* were hued and highlighted with visual imagery.

If a student needed some understanding of the varieties of human experience to become a friend of Bernard, and an eye to savor the sauce of his teaching,* he required an acute ear and a fast hand to live up to the standards Bernard set for a developing composer. He resembled Phillips in the rigor with which he examined and criticized stylistic problems, pitch and melodic contours, rhythm, and texture. But Rogers' ways with rigor were very much his own: his non-pianist's hand's ability to find only the trenchant chord (as simultaneities were called in those days) whether to demonstrate that it was maybe the right one or maybe the wrong one; his cracked voice (accompanied by a dangling cigarette) following a line to its fulfilled or (unfulfilled) conclusion. His suggestions for instrumental and orchestral usage remain unparalleled in my experience.

Most of us do not remember when and with whose help we first learned to parse a sentence, do subtraction, or resolve a dominant seventh. We do not remember as often as we should—or perhaps we do not choose to remember—those to whom we owe our debts. Though I owe much to two with whom I later studied formally, Hanson and Bartók, and much to many others, my largest debt is owed to Bernard Rogers, for he first taught me the largest truth: one must sing his own song, no matter how few—or how many—may be listening.

---

* He infected several students with his love of mixed metaphors and his chronic synesthesia.

The teacher of orchestration was also Rogers. In the required first year he covered all the instruments, singly and in combination. Memorable were the weekly meetings when he went painstakingly phrase by phrase through a series of late 19th century through early-Stravinsky scores, each of us with his/her own copy in which the salient passages were marked—and still remain.

In the advanced orchestration class, with a few students each, we were treated to the equivalent of another composition class, for Rogers considered the orchestration of a passage as important structurally as the pitches and rhythm, just as he considered the colors and hues in an art work as no less important than, and inseparable from, its "line."

It is not surprising that Eastman graduates in those days were all known to have a command of the orchestra, though they were thought to be somewhat conservative in style, if not Hansonian. Not only did we have expert teaching, we were expected—if we did not play instruments in the orchestra—also to attend all orchestra rehearsals for four years, armed with miniature scores. In addition, each of our own new works was accorded a reading by the expert sight reading of the Eastman-Rochester orchestra under Hanson's direction. In my fourth year I heard my *Concerto Grosso* for piano and orchestra, the slow movement of which was specially rehearsed and broadcast on the CBS network. In my fifth year my *Concerto* for piano and orchestra was read and rehearsed.

All this musical activity was making me into the composer it had been my ambition at age twelve to become when I grew up. To be sure, there was more to be learned and more growing up to be done. It is strange that the other part of my ambition, "to write operas," to become "an opera composer," seemed to have become lost as soon as I entered Eastman. It is true that my Saturday afternoons were no longer as free as they had been to listen to the Met broadcasts. On the other hand, the first live performances I'd ever seen took place in the Eastman Theatre occasionally. They were all repertory pieces, often with decent young singers, but their staging did not live up to the standards I'd set in my imagination during the numberless broadcasts I had heard.

I became friendly with a few singers, Zelda Goodman (later Manacher) a musicianly mezzo among them, and accompanied them in whatever, whenever I was asked; but it seemed that composers and singers—especially opera singers— were segregated in fact, if not by edict. It is perhaps fortunate that it never occurred to me to volunteer to accompany in the opera department in order to learn about singers, singing, and repertory, for I would have been reported to the office as deranged. I knew only one other composer who had considered writing for the stage and heard little or no vocal music on the spring symposiums.

Not unrelated, in those days when the press was eagerly awaiting the Great American Symphony and composers were vying to become its composer, songs and choral pieces were written mostly by specialists. When such pieces were brought to composition classes they were examined and discussed as usual, but there was never any discussion of vocal style as such or the problems of setting English to music, even by Phillips, Rogers, or Hanson, all of whom had composed vocal and choral music. In fairness I should add that when I was in Hanson's seminar working on a large chorus and orchestra work, he was supportive and helpful. He would not have known that it was his *Lament for Beowulf*, for the same medium, that had brought me to his school.

It was said that the opera department had been vibrant and nationally well-known in the late twenties and early thirties, but had been on short rations since 1933. It was in that year that Hanson's *Merry Mount*, commissioned by the Met, had been premiered there with Laurence Tibbett in the leading role. Apparently Hanson had been terribly upset by its cool reception and thereafter had turned against the medium in his school, which he ran efficiently but autocratically. Such wits as there still were in the opera department dubbed Hanson's opera 'Merrily Mounted.'

Had the subject of composing operas ever come up—Rogers never mentioned his "grand opera" of 1931—my interest might have been rekindled. I suspect, though, that I was subconsciously remembering the note I had included with the libretto of *Beatrice Cenci* in the destroyed cigar box: "To await the completion of my musical education." If so, I must have thought the moment had arrived toward the end of my last year. I somehow discovered a copy of *Hello Out There*, a one-act play by William Saroyan, whose short stories I had been struck by as a teenager. Requiring only three singers and a couple of speaking parts and with a straightforward, touching story, it seemed to be exactly the sort of play I could adapt as a libretto myself and set to music. I learned somehow that he was in the western Pacific and imagined his storming some beach heroically. I had enough sense to know that I shouldn't begin work on the opera without asking permission to do so and wrote his publisher for Saroyan's address, without having the sense to inquire of Harcourt Brace concerning the rights. I was given an Army Post Office address and wrote him at length of my plans and for his permission. There was no answer.

I learned later that he was, indeed, in the Army, posted to Astoria on Long Island, to New York harbor's Governor's Island, and to London, writing a novel on Army time. Later I was to write operas on my libretto versions of two of his plays: *Hello Out There* (1953), and *My Heart's in the Highlands* (1969). We became Bill and Jack and I was to learn that his life was as much fiction as his fiction was autobiography.

It is not the case that until that moment arrived when I thought I could write an opera, all my time and energy had been spent with music. Eastman offered a small number of English courses and an Art History course, all taught by the versatile and always interesting Charles Riker. I took the few that satisfied the liberal arts requirement and then everything else he taught. When I ran out of non-music courses and needed more to keep the non-musical part of my mind in working order, I searched the catalog of our parent institution, the University of Rochester, for others. The Prince Street campus of the U. of R. was but a short walk away, but on each of my successive trips to the Eastman registrar to sign up for a U. of R. course, there was a hurdle to be jumped: convincing him that electing non-music courses was not wasting my time.

I took courses with two stellar members of the English Department (a term on T. S. Eliot with an expert on the subject) and a summer course, Ethics, with a well-known Kantian philosopher recently arrived from Europe, Julius Kraft. The last-named was my first experience with traditional German scholarship. The class consisted mainly of divinity students. Though some time was allowed for discussion, for the most part Kraft lectured, without notes. We were expected to convert each lecture into a précis-paper; some unlucky student would then be asked to read his at the beginning of the next class. Kraft was so deeply in thought on his way across campus before class that he would not-could not-respond to a "good morning," even a "guten Morgen." He was a trained musician, a piano student of Egon Petrie, who occasionally invited me to his home to play chamber music, with him as cellist. We maintained our acquaintance for some years. He would call me in New York to accompany him to F.A.O. Schwarz to help him shop for his grandchildren's Christmas presents. He was one of those unfortunate refugee professors who found it difficult to adapt to our ways.

In our musical cocoon, World War II was at first a presence only to those who read newspapers. December 7, 1941 was audible, though, and there may have been enlistments after our declaration of war the next day. It was not long before the draft began calling up students. After one term of cello lessons, my teacher was inducted. (I had decided that though I had some hands-on experience with winds and percussion, I needed some with strings.) Other friends began disappearing, some to the Army Band in Washington. A close friend, the composer Seth Chapin, left for the Navy and was killed shortly thereafter. A newspaper article was quickly passed from one to the other: his ship, the USS Eagle, off the Maine coast, had been lost after a boiler exploded. To this amateur boatman it seemed possible but improbable. Only in the past few years has the Navy admitted that it had lied, not wishing to let it be known that submarines were marauding off the East Coast and that the USS Eagle had been torpedoed. Even more recently the U-Boat, and its number, has been identified. Seth and Doriot Anthony were close friends, as she and I were, and still are. Writing for her a small piece for flute and piano, *Song*, dedicated to his memory, was a small solace to me and perhaps to her in her many performances of it.

I am certain that my choice of taking Kraft's Ethics course was determined by my growing quandary at the time related to the war and its implications for me. Kraft, though, had been explicit in his lectures that what he and Kant had to say could not advise an individual on every moral choice. My quandary, complicated by the temporary and permanent loss of friends, was that although I knew well enough that almost every citizen in a country at war is to some small or large extent a part of its war effort, a member of its armed forces is directly involved in killing. That I would not have a part in. To cite Kant, "to say that I should act as though my act could become a universal law would be persuasive to nobody but myself." I was to become 21 on July 15, 1942 and some time after that, when my number came up, I decided I would apply for "exemption by reason of alleged conscientious objection to participation in war."

My father and I had been regular correspondents since we left Muncie. His letters—sometimes enclosing a little spending money—were as interesting as he had been in person, describing patients with offbeat diseases and lectures and papers he was preparing. I tried to visit him at least once a year. One of these visits took place during my quandary-period and I told him of my plan to become a C.O. He was his old self, exclaiming in some such words as "Nobody but a God-damned fool would go to the trouble of trying for C.O. status if he often carries sugar in his urine. Have some sugar for breakfast before the medical exam! You know as well as I and the Army medic that there's such a disease as stress diabetes, either on its own or as part of what you may have or would develop under any army stress. The Army doesn't want a diabetic on its hands." I said I wouldn't cheat by eating sugar. He hit the roof and suggested that if I were that stiff-necked I should make a tea from the bark of a tree, the name of which I promptly forget—was it maple?—and I would show sugar. In a subdued voice he asked whether I realized that if by some chance I passed the physical and could not convince a judge of the validity of my beliefs I could be sent to prison. I said, "Yes."

Because I wanted my beliefs to be validated on their own and wanted no church involvement, least of all one that Mother might have been responsible for, while I was in Muncie I paid a visit to the office of the Methodist Church I had attended as a small boy. I asked the attendant whether a person with my name had once been made a member. He examined the records and my name was missing. He was about to enlighten me as to how I could join when I told him that I had come to withdraw it if it has been listed. He was not pleased.

Back in Rochester, this "stiff-necked damned fool," whether from high moral principle, priggishness, stubbornness, or a combination of them, proceeded exactly as though he expected to pass the inevitable physical exam and then have to defend his strongly-held ethical beliefs for C.O. exemption. I had long since made the choice to join no church, and to believe in no God, Heaven or Hell, or afterlife—as though by way of another categorical imperative, as I would today. That was that; come what might.

I first wrote to Rosemary Morrow, a Quaker classmate for 12 years in Muncie, now in Earlham College, a Quaker institution in Richmond, not far from Muncie, in which my father had earned his B.A.

Rosemary put me in touch with Craig Rosenbaum of the American Friends Service Committee, who wrote me at length about the ever looser Selective Service definition of its phrase "religious training and belief" as the courts determined that "religious" could include the humanitarian beliefs even of atheists. Rosenbaum sent me much relevant material on the subject, which I studied, as I did treatises on the doctrine of the just war and the relevant writings of Aldous Huxley.

In November 1942 came the long-expected notice of classification, provisionally 1A, with 10 days to appeal. This I did. In January 1943 I was told to plead my case before a federal judge. I went to him well prepared to plead my case and to answer what were said to be the usual questions: "What would you do to a man who threatened your wife or sister with rape? What would you do if someone attacked you?" Instead, after questioning me briefly about my physical disability, whether my objections were to serving in any war or just this one, and other such matters, having sized me up, the judge insisted on talking about music for the rest of the session.

Shortly thereafter, partly in reaction to the press and public constantly equating cowardice and conscientious objectors and partly in the knowledge that one can never know all the reasons for one's actions, I wrote the judge a well-meant letter. I said that I was now prepared to accept alternative service if assigned as a medical aide on a submarine, where I would be subject to the same dangers as the crew. He did not respond. Neither he nor Selective Service could have made such a singular exception and he probably thought that I suffered not only from an underpowered pancreas, but also from an over-active conscience.

In April '43 I received a new classification. C.O., subject to the result of the physical examination which took place in May. Sugar was found in my urine. I was found unfit for service and classified 4F. I rationalized that the whole effort had been a good mental and moral exercise. There was to be no more worry about Selective Service until the anxiety of waiting for the draft number to be drawn for our son Christopher in one of our later wars, the one with Vietnam.

*　　*　　*　　*　　*　　*　　*

My resumé for five years at Eastman has been seriously unpopulated. In fact, in addition to the few friends so far mentioned, there were very many others, some of whom I continued to see in New York and who became well-known to the musical public at large. David Oppenheim, a year or two younger, was a clarinetist whom I sometimes accompanied. One day he dropped by my practice room with a clarinet sonata by his often-mentioned composer-friend, Lennie. On the manuscript that we ran through and then rehearsed a bit, Lennie was Leonard Bernstein. He was in his twenties and relatively unknown. I thought it lively, well-made, and a bit Coplandish. Dave asked for a manuscript by me and I lent him my second piano sonata, which he took back to his friend, together with my comments about his clarinet sonata. Mine was returned with Lennie's comment that it was "very talented"—an early New York "review" of a piece I've long since renounced.

Dave and I met unexpectedly and exotically when both of us were later firmly fixed in New York. I went late one Wednesday or Saturday afternoon to see the interior of the Schwab mansion at the foot of Riverside Drive. It was shortly to be wrecked, but was open to those who wished to make bids on the many mantel pieces and other embellishments still in place. Wandering through the empty spaces I ran into Dave and his wife Judy Holliday, whiling away her time between matinee and evening performances. We strolled together enjoyably. Dave had been one of the few Eastman students with a social commitment and so I was not surprised when he later told me that he was giving up his flourishing performing career because he thought that being just a clarinetist was not useful enough to the world to justify a life. He went on to help build Columbia Records into a home for Stravinsky, Copland, Bernstein, and others and to become Dean of Arts at NYU. I met Judy but that once, but there was more to the pair than being only a handsome couple: When she was called before the McCarthy Committee for God knows what, its members were so struck by having a real star before them and by believing her to *be* the dumb blond she was famous for portraying on stage that she was let off easy.

William Warfield was one of the singers I sometimes accompanied and my regular handball partner. I suppose there may have been witnesses to the comic pair of a very large Black and a small White banging a small ball against the wall of the handball court. It was a stupid choice of exercise for a pianist, for in spite of a glove, my right hand was always swollen thereafter. Later, when I read Virgil Thomson's lyric review of Bill's debut recital in Town Hall, with special mention of his excellent foreign languages, I remembered his habit of loudly practicing Lieder and chansons in the Eastman locker room and showers. I had the opportunity of meeting Leontyne Price occasionally at the apartment of a friend who was one of her supporters. Just out of Juilliard, she was very nervous at having been cast as Bess to Bill's Porgy in an important revival of Gershwin's opera. They married thereafter.

At the start of our third year, we composition majors, were joined by a very exotic transfer from Reed College. Jacob Avshalomoff, known as Jascha and later, with a respelling, as Avshalomov, had been born in Tsingtao of a Russian father and an American mother and educated in American and British schools in Tientsin. Trilingual in Russian, Chinese, and English, he could get along later in other European languages. He had studied music off and on with his composer-conductor father, but while we here had been learning to play instruments, he had been making a living in China by exercising his talent for distinguishing sheep from goat intestines under cold running water for the Oppenheimer Casing Company—and becoming the champion high-diver of North China. These snippets are but tastes of the very full meal of his and his father's peripatetic lives served up in *Avshalomov's Winding Way*, published in 2001. We at Eastman had the opportunity to savor orchestral pieces by Jascha and his father Arosha— differing versions of West meets East—conducted by Hanson. Because Jascha lacked instrumental facility he took up conducting and formed a madrigal group, asking his fellow students to write for it. I provided four madrigals and a canon. He was then drafted and was within a day of being landed in the Normandy Invasion when the Army finally decided that a translator of Russian and Chinese might be more useful elsewhere. We met again after the war when he came to Columbia, led the chorus and sometimes the orchestra, and had a work performed by the Opera Workshop. Our friendship has continued, lamed only by the width of the continent during the forty years of his conducting the Portland Junior Symphony and the years since. His father, Arosha, was for a time my copyist in New York, where Jascha's son, Daniel, the violist, is an ornament on the chamber music scene.

Among one's friends were those who played his music on the noon or evening concerts in Kilbourn Hall. Eugene Altschuler offered to play my new violin and piano sonata there in 1941. Just as I was beginning to write it, Henry

Cowell treated an interested few to an informal performance of his music played with fists and forearms on the keyboard and plucked and strummed on the strings. I was captivated and then carefully integrated some plucked piano bass strings into the sonata's slow movement. At its first performance I was accompanying Gene and when the plucking began, we heard the whispers and buzz of comment that almost drowned out our playing. The applause at the end was generous, with bravos from a couple of "modernists," but I found the earlier audience reaction upsetting. Why should such a modest foray into such an obvious and convenient sound-source cause such a stir?

During the next season Doriot Anthony asked me to write a piece for her and I complied with a *Sonata for Flute and Piano*. During our rehearsals she remarked that the piece was well-written for the flute, but that I was asking the flutist for technical and expressive effects not often met with. That seemed to be the impression also of the audience, some of whom quizzed me for days.

The reception of these two pieces, sharing the centuries-old conventional name of sonata, seemed to suggest that if I had not yet written and been performed enough to have developed a recognizable style, I might be on my way to doing so. That's what Doriot thought, but she was prejudiced in my favor, for we had been fast friends since we entered as freshmen in 1939. She remained partial to my sonata, though, and played it in Los Angeles when she joined that orchestra, in Washington when she was in the National Symphony, and when she joined the Boston Symphony as the first woman in the US to hold a first-desk position. Like her ancestor, Susan B. Anthony, she was—is—persistent, and remained in that position for decades, after which she was proven irreplaceable.

My vagrant thoughts concerning developing a recognizable style returned a few months later with the performance and reception of *Music for Two Earnest Instruments* for trombone and organ. Bernard Rogers was as delighted with the title and the combining of two wind instruments not usually associated, as was I. It was the second of my descriptive but jocular titles. Ever since, I have sought titles, whether jocular or serious, long or short, that catch the attention of the performer and audience, and that invite the listener into the piece while succinctly describing it. Titles have come to me as sudden inspirations or, more often, after much thought. When the right one is found, it is known to be right.

This earnest piece was written also because a performer-friend asked for something. Dorothy Ziegler was a double major of a unique kind: piano and trombone, and built like a brass player. The organist for the performance was one of the few women composers at Eastman in those years. The mixture of the two wind instruments was as mellifluous as I expected and the earnestness as ironic. After graduation, Dotty, as she was known, became the first woman member of the St. Louis Symphony. When the next conductor, Dutch, took over, he was appalled to find a woman as first trombonist and demoted her to second chair. The next music director, Brazilian, solved the female brass-player problem by firing her. She then organized her own local orchestra, conducted it herself, and commissioned me to write a fanfare for it. She also conducted my opera, *Hello Out There*, several times in the fifties and early sixties.

The last to be mentioned of those friendships made in school that endured thereafter was with Nora Sigerist, whom I met in my last year. She was a Swiss citizen, born in Zürich, a year younger than I. From the age of 4 to 10 she had lived in Leipzig, Germany, and then immigrated to Baltimore—with not a word of English—where her father became the Director of the Institute of Medical History at Johns Hopkins. After two years of living at home while pursuing a BA at Goucher College and studying music and violin at the Peabody Institute, she hankered for a freer atmosphere and transferred to the University of Rochester because she could easily continue violin study at Eastman. On her visits for harmony classes and violin lessons she became acquainted with Dave Oppenheim and Seth Chapin, one of whom introduced her to me. Because, as she said, she found us composers more interesting than the generality of performers, she was often in the company of our small composer circle. We did meet alone occasionally, especially when she was helping me with my German while preparing a paper on the concerto grosso for Warren Fox.

When I left for New York she remained in Rochester for her final year, then went to Cornell for a graduate year and then transferred to Columbia University for further graduate studies in Russian. There we met again. Our friendship was renewed, ripened, warmed, and we married in August 1947. We have remained in that blessed state for 61 years.

*   *   *   *   *   *   *

During my last two years at Eastman there were occasional meetings of what we jokingly referred to as our soiree. Although it was open to anybody, there was a nucleus of six or eight, including a couple I have already mentioned. Two of the regulars were faculty members, Charles Riker the English and Fine Arts man, and the musicologist Warren Fox. Two musicology students, Lee Fairley and Frank Campbell, I would not have met had it not been for these meetings.

Frank later became the Music Librarian at the Library of Congress. While there he invited me to the premiere of *Appalachian Spring* at the Library. He had acquired three tickets, 2nd-row center, for himself, Doriot Anthony (then flutist in the National Symphony), and me, just behind Elizabeth Sprague Coolidge, who had commissioned the ballet. One of us suggested that we fiddle with the hearing aid built into the arm of her regular seat, but we did not, so impressed were we by the Copland chamber ensemble score and the Graham choreography.

Mostly the soirees existed just for talk, though there was also beer. Fox led some amateur experiments in hypnotism, accompanied with much talk about his ideas about the friendship between Mesmer and Mozart. A few proved susceptible to his dangling pocket watch, or pretended to be. I proved to be immune. It was at one of the sorirees that I tried marijuana for the first and last time. Perhaps the puffs were too few, for I proved to be immune to it as well.

For the most part, all deferred to Fox, but there was deference shown also to William Bergsma out of fear of his sharp mind and even sharper tongue. Most of the time he could answer any question on any subject; when he could not, he invented. If I knew the answer I'd remain silent, waiting for him to answer or invent.

Bill had been born in California and bred in comfortable circumstances in a house built directly over the San Andreas Fault. He learned to play the piano and viola passably and composed from early on, but nevertheless enrolled at Stanford University where he made an enviable reputation during his two years there. He was fond of reminding me that his mentor, Witter Bynner, had told him that he "was too clever by half."

At that point Howard Hanson heard his ballet *Gold and the Señor Commandante*, sought him out, and talked him into transferring to Eastman. If my remarks suggest that I knew him well, I did; when be came to Rochester, for two years, he rented our extra bedroom. Aside from seeing him in school, Mother often invited him for dinner. When we were not otherwise engaged we helped one another copy out instrumental parts and during a couple of mock air-raids we improvised Hidemith four-hand pieces by candle light.

Hanson took him immediately into his composition seminar, during his second year in which we were seminar-mates. All of us other composers recognized him as "the white-haired boy." That others elsewhere also thought so was demonstrated by the composer-prizes he won while yet a student. When he won the Columbia University Bearns Prize, the check for $900 was on the Corn Exchange Bank, the University's bank at the time. "Corn in exchange for corny music!" he remarked.

His special status was made obvious by Hanson, who often introduced only him to visiting celebrities. Bill came home one evening and told me of such an event. Hanson arranged for Bill to use his office-studio so that he could play a tape of his *First String Quartet* for Roy Harris. All too soon, Harris nodded and then went to sleep. Bill seized the opportunity to open Hanson's files to Beeson and Bergsma. He reported to me with some pleasure that the average of my two or three I.Q. tests was lower than his and then shame-facedly admitted that my Seashore music scores were higher than his. He was sorry that he hadn't risked the time to copy out the numbers, he said.

His singularity was demonstrated by Selective Service. At his medical examination he was asked by the doctor about his tall, thin nude body, oddly at variance from the normal. Bill confessed that he had been a tubercular child. The doctor opined that it might be useful to him as a composer to serve in the army and to learn to know ordinary listeners. Bill's answer sent him on down the line to the psychiatrist. During that interview, Bill happened to remark that his musical talent was God-given; he probably had other Bergsmaish things to say that he didn't confide in me—I've forgotten nothing that he _did_ tell me—for when his classification card arrived he had been place in the category reserved for men over 40! He was 22 at the time, as was I, for we had both been born in 1921, he on All Fool's Day. To Hanson's dismay, Bill chose not to apply for the Eastman B.M., but for the university B.A., so that he could qualify for—and then earn—Phi Beta Kappa.

After the Eastman years, he taught at Juilliard. When he became its dean, he asked me to take over his graduate seminar called "From Wag to Imp" (from Wagner to Impressionism) with strict instructions as to what I was to do. For two years I moonlighted from Columbia at 116th and Broadway to 122nd Street, doing as _I_ thought best. The Juilliard moved to Lincoln Center in the middle sixties. A little later, when William Shuman resigned as president of the School, it was his wish that Bergsma succeed him—and Bill coveted the position—but Peter Mennin was the Board's choice. Peter, two years younger than we, was well-known to both of us from Eastman, where he had become the new "white-haired boy" and was usually to be found scrunched over in a basement practice room writing some new prize-winning symphonic work. After running the Peabody Institute and having married an Eastman-trained violinist, this charming and uncomplicated pair of tall, dark, and handsome people no doubt predisposed the Juilliard Board in Peter's favor. Bill was severely disappointed and told me he was damned if he would serve as dean under Peter. On the rebound he became director of the School of Music of the University of Washington, a continent away. We saw one another on the annual weekends of a New York music jury and at a last long dinner of the four of us before the premier of his second opera at Queens College attended by not even one music critic. Toward the end of his life he was suffering from a mysterious disease he was too proud to admit or to name. It was that disease, I choose to believe, that led him gravely to betray our friendship, rather than another reason I can imagine. Nevertheless, as the length of this memoir suggests, he and his music do not deserve the neglect they are receiving after his death.

At our soirees Bill was as voluble as Al Rivett—already twice mentioned herein—was withdrawn, or suddenly prickly present. Al was cursed with too many talents, mathematical, linguistic, and musical, the latter of which he had been exercising for years. His was the most acute and well-trained hearing of any in my acquaintance except that of Jacques Monod. He also possessed perfect pitch-memory (sometimes known as absolute pitch). Without trying to emulate his ability, and knowing that Richard Wagner had unsuccessfully tried, I left home each day with an F in voice and mind. On the walk to school I would sing it intermittently and then test the F when I arrived at a piano. Because I retain the successful results of that practice only intermittently. I don't claim to have "perfect pitch." There was some comfort in knowing that if Jascha pitched a piece lower than that written in the score when leading his madrigal group, Rivett, singing in his resonant bass, would have to transpose accordingly at sight.

Upon graduation he joined the Navy and accomplished the feat of navigating his ship in stormy weather from the Canal Zone to Cape Hatteras by dead reckoning. After service, he showed up at Columbia and, pursuing his early interest in opera, became a coach in the Opera Workshop, which performed his *Poor Eddy* with no less a pair than Humphrey/Weidman involved. In those years he was often a dinner guest of Nora and mine. He ceased composing, seemingly turned against music, tapering off via Gilbert and Sullivan. By the time our son was born in 1950, he had come out of the closet, moved in with a man from our theatre, and come to terms with the problem that, I suppose, had long troubled him. We lost touch with him little by little and then saw him not at all because, I learned later, he had died of a heart attack.

*　　*　　*　　*　　*　　*　　*

To return from two lives, one with a troubled death, the other with an early death, to the musical cocoon of our soirees in the war years of 1943 and 1944: at the ends of these two academic years, Fox and Bergsma prepared very long letter-reports to be sent to ex-students in service or elsewhere. Both were breezy accounts, in small part quasi-gossip about faculty and composition and musicology students, prizes and positions won, and in large part an account of new music performed on the American Festival and the Symposium. Only some of the works were reviewed, usually unattributed, by Fox or Bergsma, or by the pair. These capsule reviews were smartly written, knowledgeable, sometimes cutting to well-known composers represented on the Festivals, friendly but frankly outspoken on the locals' music. In 1944 I was asked to contribute an account of a Rogers premier in Cincinnati. For Bill and me these were our first attempts at organizing our thoughts about new works for a readership larger than a correspondent.

Though the whole of the two letter-reports might merit publication as a time-capsule of a time and place, I include only the Fox/Bergsma comments about my two piano-and-orchestra works because they are relevant to my wondering at the time whether I had already, or could, or would, develop a recognizable style of my own. My contribution concerning the Rogers *Passion* follows:

Jack Beeson's *Piano Concerto*, played by Helen De Jager, is the very puzzling and very annoying work of a very talented young man. On the credit side: an individual, crabbed, linear treatment of rough thematic ideas which stick like burrs. He treats his instruments with a virtuosity curiously at variance with the somber and half-angry effect. On the debit side: the music remains puzzling despite familiarity, perhaps because of its individuality, perhaps because of too many trees and not enough forest. The second movement, where the tempo and time-scale do not admit of much cluttering, presents a stern but moving impression with point and power. The first proved as difficult to play as perhaps to understand; no adequate reading of it was obtained. The last movement, a brilliant scherzo, has an interrupted final statement, a rowdy second theme, and cyclic thematic implications. Some, but not all, found the ending anti-climatic; Beeson, perhaps, to be filed for reference.

There was a small pilgrimage [by Bernard and Betty Rogers and Jack Beeson] last week to Cincinnati, to hear the first complete performance of Bernard Rogers's *Passion*, Goossens conducting. For a review of this, and a few side-swipes at Bergsma's quartet, we bring in Jack Beeson:

Bergsma's beautifully-made *Second Quartet* received an excellent performance by the Gordon's. This new work, together with the *Music on a Quiet Theme*, written and performed last year, may well be Bergsma's first mature work. Particularly in the third and fourth movements, which together form the slow section, the quartet has a fine emotional depth not to be found in the early music. This feeling is got across in an idiom which, though personal and consistent, is not strikingly new. But within its limits perhaps the only flaw is one of texture, in the first two movements a lack of clarity and dramatics resulting from too much four-part writing arranged in SATB order within a somewhat limited high-low range. Bergsma can handle this later; let there be no complacency.

The Rogers setting of the *Passion* may well be the first great piece of music in a large form to have been written by an American composer. In it all forces are made to contribute to one end, a dramatic presentation, a reliving, of the Holy Week. Arias, set choral pieces, treatment of the orchestra now as an accompaniment, now as a symphonic group, none of these parts combine to form a whole; thematic material, of which there is little in the conventional sense of the term, is not developed into a formal-musical whole. Instead, *all* of the medium used—the large orchestra, the chorus, and the solo voices of Christ, Pilate, and numerous nameless characters; the purely musical structure—that is, the notes themselves arranged within their own whole of color, harmony, counterpoint, rhythm, and melody inextricably mixed; and the text itself—all of these make one vast living canvas of the scene.

Rogers has said that the work is influenced mostly by two painters, Rembrandt and El Greco. There is, in addition, a strong, influence of the East, not only in his use of the percussion and free, often barbarous rhythms; but also in his music's intensely emotional appeal, which is a far cry from the detached, almost contemplative spirit of the Bach settings. It is this emotional quality which will either enkindle or repel a hearer; he will not be cold to the work.

There is no space for details, the fine text adaptation, or an account of the performance, which was very good, though not flawless. It is enough to know that great music is being written.

This, my first review, is surely that of an acolyte as yet unacquainted with many other large works by American composers. The event was memorable, and also for another reason. There were drinks after the performance with Goossens (the conductor) and his first hornist, the 18-year old Gunther Schuller, Gunther was also first horn in the premiere performance of Rogers's one act opera, *The Warrior*, at the Met in 1947. Thereafter Gunther became the one conductor to perform the *Prelude* to that opera and other works of Bernard.

Some time in the late winter of my last year, Casey Lutton appeared at Eastman. He ran a college teacher's agency in Chicago and was intent on signing up everybody who would not return to school for next year, or who might not. I was in the latter category and filled out his quasi curriculum vitae form, including my teaching experience, which now included two years of theory and keyboard harmony. Although I was serving the first year of the two required of residence for the PhD and was composing a large work for chorus and orchestra, *Three Settings from the Gaelic*, which could serve as a dissertation (as could the just-completed piano concerto), I needed a second language, French. I had taken all the required courses and all the others that interested me and saw no point in remaining to fill out a required year in residence with French and a continuation of Hanson's Seminar. Perhaps as a convenient rationalization I conceived the notion that there was something illogical about a Doctorate in Philosophy in musical composition. What I really wanted to do was to get away to New York City.

At about this time my brother Tom arrived to pay Mother and me a brief on-leave visit from his North Carolina training camp. After completing his last two high school years in Rochester, he had enrolled in the University of Michigan. Because he was interested only in joining the Air Force as a pilot, he was often on probation. A successful operation on a carcinoma of the perotid gland prevented his flying, but permitted enlistment in the Air Force as a weather specialist, for which he was then in training. His questions about my future I could not answer.

Shortly after he left, the Lutton Agency informed me that I could have a teaching position in Enid, Oklahoma if I wished. My consideration of a paying job in Enid versus an unaffordable life in New York City was interrupted by a telephone call that my father had just died on March 31. Tom, on special leave, Aunt Iva from Florida, and I converged on Muncie. Because my father had told his ever-faithful office nurse, Naomi Crane, that there was to be neither a church service nor a memorial service, she and the three of us met at the grave-side for the burial. There was something sadly congruent between the simple casket and the small hotel rooms he had lived in for five years. Our few figures, lost in the vast deserted cemetery, seemed a visual image of the loneliness he often confessed to me in letters and in person. It was largely my knowledge of those private feelings and that what was left of his health was deteriorating, and then learning that he had for several days refused to be hospitalized, that led me to think that his death had been a kind of suicide.

There was little for us to do, for there were no possessions. We soon learned that there were unpaid taxes and money owed to the patiently long-suffering Naomi Crane, not quite covered by the meager assets. Tom and I covered the difference. We knew that he had long since cashed in the large policy that would have been paid to Mother; we were touched that he had somehow managed to retain a small policy intended to provide for our college education, though he had borrowed against it. One half of it would be payable to me in June, the other half payable to Tom in August when he came of age. After a day or two Tom returned to camp, then shipped out to do Air Force weather prediction in Foggia on the Italian boot and I returned to Rochester.

Sixty-four years ago $5,700 was a sum that would permit me to leave what remained of my family and to venture out on my own. I had toyed with the idea of studying with Ernest Bloch. Two years earlier I had become so enamored with his music—especially the piano quintet—that I had ceased writing a string quartet that was becoming too derivative. A few months before my father's death an exploratory letter to Bloch brought a strange reply that I showed to Rogers, who had studied with him. Bernard was encouraging, but said that I would have to put up with someone now even more neurotic than himself. That was ambiguously off-putting.

In any case, I was now engaged in listening to the few recordings there were of Béla Bartók's music and studying his scores. Now that it was financially possible to do so, I was determined to move to New York and to study with him.

I had a long conversation with Hanson at the end of the school year about by future plans. He tried to talk me into finishing the PhD, now that there was so little left to do. He was indignant that I would go to New York, as he was with Bill Bergsma, who planned to do the same. To Hanson, New York City was enemy territory; Eastman graduates were supposed to live and work between the Appalachians and the Rockies. In many ways, some unpleasant, he had maintained the conservative ideas one might attribute to his having been born and brought up in Wahoo, Nebraska.

When I told him that I hoped to overcome Bartók's aversion to teaching composition, he was dismissive and asked "So you want to find out all about folk music?"

During the summer I did what was becoming a habit: write a sonata for piano. I had written an un-numbered one in 1941, #1 in the summer of '42, #2 in '43, and now #3 in '44. To follow were #4 in '45, and, the last in the series, #4 in '46. When #3 was completed I set about breaking and loosening ties with the past: I sold the piano and traveled to Michigan to arrange the long-term rental of the log cabin, which Tom and I had inherited. During these varied activities I pondered what to say in a letter to Bartók that might induce him to do what everybody kept telling me he had not done and would not do—teach composition. Finally, on September 4, I sent him my brief attempt at doing so.

352 Mount Vernon Avenue
Rochester 7, New York
September 4, 1944

Dear Mr. Bartók,

I have been told that you do not accept students in composition, that you do not believe that it is possible for one man to teach another to compose. Nevertheless I write to you asking if I may not study with you this winter; for even if it be true that one cannot teach another, is it not possible for one to learn from another?

I plan to come to New York in October and remain at least throughout the winter. May I look forward to meeting you and showing you something of what I have done? Perhaps then, if you find me worthy, we can meet again.

Yours very truly,

Jack Beeson

I had phoned Bartók's publisher, Boosey and Hawkes, to ask for his address and was referred to his editor, Hans Heinsheimer, who gave it to me after asking why I wanted it. He and Bartók had long known one another at Bartók's Viennese publisher. It was said that Ralph Hawkes had flown one of his own Spitfires from London to Vienna just before World War II in order to acquire all the Bartók publishing rights for Boosey and Hawkes, his music no longer being performed in German-speaking countries.

Bartók's reply to my letter arrived, dated September 20, from Saranac Lake where he had spent the summer. I don't know what the doctors thought his illness was, but Saranac was famous in those days, as it had been for many decades, for the treatment of tuberculosis. He actually was suffering from leukemia, from which he died just a year later.

32 Park Ave.   September 20, 1944
Saranac Lake, N.Y.

        Dear Mr. Beeson,

You are quite right in supposing that I do not "teach" composition (I have my several reasons for that). However, something could perhaps be done, if I will know that you wish me to do.

        As you plan to go to New York for the winter, the best would be, if you would come to see me there, and show me some of your compositions. I will be there from Oct. 3 on. I can not yet give you any address. The best will be to ring up Mr. Hans Heinsheimer, the manager of my publisher Boosey & Hawkes, 43-47 West 23 (phone: Gramercy 5-(1146 or 1147), he will give you my address.

        Yours, sincerely

        Béla Bartók

*   *   *   *   *   *

Chapter 3

To New York City, Béla Bartók, and Opera at Columbia
(1944-1945)

With at least one meeting with Bartók assured and a comfortable sum in my checking account, I looked forward to New York. By coincidence, two friends were planning a trip there and offered to show me around as my guides and to help with my luggage. Also by coincidence, the names by which they are now known were not then their names. Peter Mennini was becoming Mennin out of deference to his younger composer-brother, Louis; José Velez, a Peruvian and recently arrived at Eastman to study composition, was to change Velez to Malsio when he discovered his biological father, the provider of horses to the Peruvian cavalry. On the train south they asked if I knew where I wanted to live in the city and I replied on the upper West Side in the Columbia University neighborhood, which they seemed to know well. When I was asked why, I replied: they remembered that Hanson had conducted the premiere of Douglas Moore's *In Memoriam* on the most recent American Festival. I continued: well, after the concert Warren Fox had invited a few friends to his apartment to meet the visiting composer. Moore and I had a long conversation over drinks. He was most affable and asked me about my plans for the coming year. When I told him my reasons for not completing the Ph.D. he smiled mysteriously. When I mentioned my hope to study with Bartók he counseled me not to get my hopes up, for he taught only piano. He knew Bartók well, he added, or as well as it was possible to know such a shy man. He told me that shortly after he had become Chairman of the Music Department in 1940, he and Paul Henry Lang had talked Columbia into granting Bartók an honorary degree. In that same year Moore had become the person in charge of the Alice M. Ditson Fund, which had made its first grant to Bartók and then followed it up with three more grants. He then said that, Bartók–lessons or not, if I did come to New York, I should live near Columbia and he'd see to it that I was given a library card. I was much impressed that such an eminence would make such an offer to a new out-of-town acquaintance.

Peter, José, and I spent the night in a YMCA and then took a double-decker bus up Riverside Drive. José wanted us to get off at 116th Street, but Peter insisted that we stay on it till 119th Street. As we got off there and arrived at the second apartment house south of the corner, it was clear he'd been doing his homework: the Douglas Moore family lived in 464 Riverside Drive; there was an unmarried daughter, said to be very attractive and intelligent, and about his age. He wanted to meet her. José and I accompanied him to apartment 52 where Peter rang the bell and we hung back. The door was opened by a colored man in a white working jacket, a more elegant version of Elmer Cloyd: "No, Miss Sarah is not at home. She recently returned to Bennington College."

In short order we found me a furnished room with kitchen privileges in the Arizona, on 114th Street just off Amsterdam Avenue. Peter and José left to go on the town and I settled in. My first two acts were to rent a small upright piano and to arrange for my first meeting with Béla Bartók.

As Bartók had suggested in his friendly letter to me, I called Heinsheimer at Boosey and Hawkes for his New York address. Heinsheimer was at first suspicious and asked why I wanted it. When I explained he was incredulous and asked me to read both letters over the phone. He thought that my first two sentences had been well-judged and that Bartók had been curious about their writer-composer. He gave me the address and asked me to let him know if I were to be invited to return for a second visit.

BARTÓK'S LAST YEAR
(a radio interview)

. . . Whereupon, in early October I went to 309 West 57th Street, where his apartment was and is now, as well as a bust and a plaque.

There's also a disco on the ground floor a little bit west in the same building. I took the elevator up to the apartment and somebody was playing the piano inside—playing *Mikrokosmos* with one hand—very distinctly and very loudly—so I thought, "Well, he can't be practicing his own *Mikrokosmos*," (which is a series of six volumes of teaching pieces—some of them quite complicated). So I waited until the sound stopped, knocked on the door, and there came to the door a short, youngish woman with long pigtails. I thought at the time, that she looked as though she were a refugee from a chorus of a performance of the opera *Freischütz*. She'd been playing. So she disappeared into the back of what was a small apartment (probably a one bed-room apartment—there was a big grand there) and out came Bartók.

I'd seen pictures of him, though you must remember that at that time, in the fall of 1944, Bartók's music was little played here or abroad; therefore his picture was not well-known either. He was about my height, as a matter of fact he was about an inch shorter—about five-five. He was deeply tanned, from Saranac, and was very strongly made, so to speak. But what I remember was the tan and the fact that the skin seemed almost translucent. He was very courteous, and a little formal, and said very little. We sat down on the couch and he looked at a piano sonata which I had written that summer, the Third Sonata, and he said very little except that this stem ought to go down and that one should go up and that I shouldn't use double bars when the meter changed because double bars really have to do with ends of sections, and comments of the sort that many people would find pedantic. As a matter of fact, I learned from my sessions with him that year not to be afraid of seeming to be pedantic because anyone who listens to Bartók's music would never think of the word pedantic in any sense whatsoever. It's astonishing that the kind of vigorous music that he wrote came out of such a—not frail but—small, well-made body. It occurred to me that if he could spend the time worrying about double bars and stems when someone else might have expected great artistic statements and questions and answers of some sort, then I could afford later when I was teaching—so called teaching—composition to graduate students over 30 – 40 years, I could afford also to talk about stems, double bars, and things of that sort, no matter what the students thought.

Anyhow, he came across a passage in the Second Sonata that I showed him; he tried the right hand out on the side of the couch, had trouble with it, went to the piano and had trouble with it and then he said, "Well, you can't play that either, can you?" You must remember, as you probably know, that he was an excellent pianist, that he had taught as a professor of piano in Budapest for many, many years–never composition–and that he played widely, very often Mozart concerti with orchestras in this country and elsewhere. He couldn't play the passage and I did and he asked why. I told him why–because I'd had a nut of a piano teacher who liked me to work on double notes–and then he launched into a discussion–a very interesting one–about how the hand of a pianist-composer always determines the kind of music he writes for the piano. He played some Liszt and said, "Of course you can tell from the way Liszt wrote for the piano what his hand was like, as you can with Brahms." I've never heard anybody else talk about that. It's one of those sophomoric ideas which is true and which grownups don't like to discuss, even with graduate students–especially with graduate students. In any case, this went along very well, except that I was astonished after half an hour sitting on the couch looking at the music when he asked me, "Well, let's see how you play the piano," so I had to go play it. At the end of the session, which was two hours long, we stood up, and I wanted to pay him, but I had somehow the sense that he wouldn't like to talk about money. He was, as you know, not "well-off," and as I discovered from talking to my colleague at Columbia, Paul Henry Lang (who was also Hungarian and who had known Bartók and Kodály in Hungary as a student), that middle-class Hungarians don't discuss money. It's a dirty subject. He had, in fact, told me this before I went, so I stayed away from the subject. On the other hand, sitting for two hours with a person, I thought I should do something, so I brought a wad of bills of various denominations in my pockets and somewhat surreptitiously put $20 (which was quite a lot of money in 1944) on a table without his having to smirch his hands with it. The he said–because I said something about payment–that I was welcome to come back again if I wished to. And then if I wished to come back and if I wished to pay him I could perhaps pay what I would were I his piano student, which is rather roundabout. So I thanked him and left. And then, this was October '44, from then into March I went back with some irregularity, at the shortest interval a week, sometimes longer that that, taking him up on his offer that if I had anything to discuss with him or if I had some music I'd like to show him for comment, I was welcome to come back. This continued, as I said, into March. At that point he developed pneumonia was ill off and on, and then back up at Saranac for the summer, and then died in September–September 26th was it?–in 1934.

The other sessions I could tell you about if you like, but that was the substance of it . . .

WKCR: I'm curious about whether you and Bartók discussed his music . . .

JB: Yes, at least twice that I remember. I brought in a set of songs, a cycle for contralto and piano, the Crazy Jane songs of William Butler Yeates, and thought I'd like to have his comments about them. He looked them over and said, "Oh, they're songs in English," and I said, "Yes," and he said, well he couldn't make any comment about songs because the essence of a song is the text which one is setting and that his English was not good enough to make comment about that which was the basis for the songs. Then he went on to say what I thought was very curious and shall not forget: that he didn't believe any composer could set to music words that were not in his native tongue. He said that because I asked him why he hadn't written more songs and his answer was Hungarian does not have a large amount of lyric verse suitable to musical setting. And then I asked him why, since his German was at least as good as his English, he didn't write Lieder. He said, "Because German is not my native language." Although it must have been close to a step-mother-tongue. That was his comment about it.

So, we went on discussing texts. He liked those I had set—perhaps we had similar tastes—and I left and he kept the songs—although he'd said he wouldn't look at them. But he said, "I'll look at them while you're gone, at my leisure," and "why don't you come back next week."

During that week I looked up a song cycle–one of the few sets of songs by Bartók—in Hungarian which is not very well known, even today, and examined them. When I went back to 57th Street the next week, he had my songs and his set—the same . . . that I had looked at in the Columbia library–and we discussed them. He said, "Well, the texts were very erotic," and they were seldom done. In Hungary, people looked on the texts as being too erotic. It was difficult to translate them into English–as all Hungarian is difficult to translate into English because it really has no roots in our Western languages–and even if they were translated, the people here would object to the texts,

When we discussed my cycle—there were two or three songs that he liked very much (oddly enough, the more erotic texts—if you look up the Crazy Jane poems, you'll see why). And that was, to me, very instructive.

Another time we discussed his music–it was in January 1945–because the Boston Symphony had come to town having, in Boston, just given the first three or four performances of the Concerto. I went, naturally, to the first New York performance of the Concerto (it's odd to think of going to the first performance because it's now such a standard work—in the twentieth century repertory at any rate) and I happened to have a meeting (I'd hate to say lesson) with him the next day. So we discussed the Concerto and he wanted to know what I thought about the form of the first movement. I doubt that I was sitting there listening to the form of the first movement section by section, but I said it seemed to me that it was a modified sonata-allegro structure with the recapitulation somewhat awry and he said, "That's just exactly what it is."

We also discussed two other things. One had to do with the fact that Koussevitsky had some small limitations as a conductor sometimes—though he was a wonderful conductor. He got lost in the last movement, which scurries around at a great rate, very difficult to play—or it was then, the first time. There happens to be a grand pause toward the end of the movement and he went on conducting through the grand pause—while the orchestra stopped—and they then started up—together—and finished the piece. That he found rather amusing.

He also, at that session, said he had heard his first Sibelius symphony. Now it's not correct to say that the British invented Sibelius' music—obviously—but it was the English orchestras that first played it, largely, and the Americans who played it at the time of the Russian-Finnish war for political, if not musical reasons. Sibelius was not often played in central Europe, so he had never heard one! Which is rather astonishing because he was not a homebody—he was traveling around constantly. It was the Second Symphony of Sibelius and I asked him how he had reacted to his experience with Sibelius and he gave me a very wry look. (I might add, parenthetically, that as we met during the year his shyness somewhat disappeared and he turned out to have quite a sharp tongue, particularly about other composers of his generation). Though Sibelius was, of course, older, he said that he had not liked the Second Symphony at all. I asked him whether he'd heard it in Boston and he said, "Yes, one of the ladies on the Board told [me] that Sibelius wrote wonderful music . . . [you] must hear it, particularly since [you have] never heard one."

He asked me what I thought of the Sibelius Second Symphony and I told him that I never like the First or Second, but that if he wanted to find something that I thought he might like, he should listen to the Fourth or the Seventh . . .

WKCR: . . . on Bartók at Columbia . . .

JB: Bartók had a position at Columbia that was not a faculty position. It was paid for by the Alice M. Ditson Fund which is in the university and which is not and cannot be used for regular teaching purposes. The first grant ever made by the Ditson Fund was made to Bartók. The second one was given to Britten and Auden for their *Paul Bunyan* production on campus in 1941. The third grant was given to Bartók, for aid. Now, since he was very persnickety about money, as I said, he would not accept what he thought of as charity, (we might not think of it as charity, but he did), the Ditson advisory committee gave him $2,500 a term for what turned out to be four terms—which doesn't sound like much money—but it was then—to do more or less what he liked. What he did was to have an office on campus and to transcribe some Yugoslav materials which were then later published. The manuscript is, as a matter of fact, at the Columbia libraries.

He gave lectures, I think, once in a while. I heard, I think, one of them. But most of those took place before I ever got there. Since he remained in New York, or outside New York, he came back to Columbia often and I have the impression that there would be those who heard him speak under what would have been visiting lecture circumstances—which he didn't have to give but which would have been interesting.

I know that he came back to the library once in a while because I dropped in on a Saturday once and there he was, fussing around with the card catalog. This was during the period when I was working with him. We greeted one another and I asked him what he was doing. This is another one of those persnickety aspects, almost pedantic aspects: he was very concerned about the transliteration of Slavic languages in English and was worrying about how we did and how we should spell Tchaikovsky in English. His researches, so to speak, on the subject were later published in *Music and Letters*. It's difficult to imagine a composer—*we* know toward the end of his life (he didn't know that necessarily)—worrying how to spell Tchaikovsky . . .

The foregoing reprint of *Bartók's Last Year* had its origin in a radio interview that was part of a 26-hour broadcast devoted to Bartók and his music by WKCR-FM, the Columbia University station, on March 25, 1998, Bartók's birthday. Ji Seuk, the Classical Director of WKCR, was the originator of the idea of this marathon and my interviewer. I was asked for a recording of the interview by the editor of the SCI Newsletter (The Society of Composers, Inc.) who had a transcription made and published its slightly abbreviated version in April 1999 with the title *Bartók's Last Year*. Because the first part of the article outlined the correspondence and events leading up to my first meeting with Bartók, already described in detail in this memoir, I have deleted it.

Given the fact that Bartók's connection with Columbia University, by way of his honorary doctorate and the Ditson Fund grants, had been his one institutional relationship in the U.S. (aside from ASCAP and his publisher) and that my half-century at Columbia began in September 1945 at the time of his death, it is not surprising that I became a participant in an ongoing series of on- and off-campus events. The thread tying most of these together was my Columbia colleague, Paul Henry Lang. Some of these event—by no means all of them— were the following: Bartók's burial in Hartsdale, N.Y. in September 1945 and the exhumation of June 1988 (for re-burial in Hungary); a splendid all—Bartók concert at Columbia on the tenth anniversary of his death; a continuing effort in the Sixties by Lang and me to acquire the Bartók Archive for the Columbia Library, which failed; two television documentaries, NET, (now PBS) Bartók: A *Portrait*, November 1963 and BBC, *Bartók*, 1988; lecture and benefit recital of songs by me, and other aid toward the restoration of the cottage in Saranac Lake in which he spent his last summer 1945, at 89 Riverside Drive. It is now open to visitors. In 1984 the Hungarian Government presented the University with a handsome bronze bust of the composer, which is now in the Music and Arts Library.

At some of these events, whenever I was introduced as "the only composition student of Bartók," or a television script made the claim, I insisted on the qualification "one of the few." It is a fact that the Canadian composer, Violet Archer, studied with him in the early 1940s at two-week intervals for a while. I do not know of another American, nor have I ever met any of those composer-pianists who were said to have smuggled their own piano music into piano lessons.

Nevertheless, whether "the only," "the only American." Or "one of the few," over the more than sixty years since '44 – '45 there has been an ever-growing correspondence with European and American musicologists and Bartók specialists and enthusiasts, especially those interested in his American years. At first, I answered their questions if I could, without undue elaboration. I was asked to contribute a *Conversation Piece: First Lesson with Bartók* for the New York Philharmonic concert program of early March 1960—a Fritz Reiner, Bartók, Kodaly concert. With copies of it I could satisfy casual correspondents. Since 1999 I have been able to provide the curious with copies of *Bartók's Last Year*, although there are those who expect me to be more knowledgeable about his life and works than I am. I do admit, though, that I heard stories from Bartók's intimate Hungarian friends shortly after his death that I do not repeat.

*   *   *   *   *   *

Shortly before my first meeting with Bartók I had made an appointment with Douglas Moore to speak with him in his office. In those days the Music Department was in the Journalism Building, much to the irritation of the Dean of Journalism. Moore was too much of a power in the university and the City to be evicted against his will. Accordingly, some time after he retired in 1962, the Music Department found itself deposited in Dodge, across the street in a twin McKim, Mead and White building, on similar partial floors—plus the attic—and somewhat expanded. It is still there today.

Moore (hereafter, often Douglas) had invited Paul Henry Lang to our meeting. Lang (hereafter, often Paul) was tall, dark, and impressive, with a cigar and a mixed-European accent. Douglas had told Paul of my wish to study with Bartók and both were surprised and pleased that he had written and invited me to meet with him. Both asked me to report on our coming first meeting and thought that the first would be also the last meeting. Douglas told Paul that he might see me in the Music Library, for which he'd already arranged for me to acquire a card, that I might be working there toward the completion of my PhD at Eastman. I thanked Douglas for the favor and added that my presence in New York was proof that I would not be completing the degree, about which—as I'd told him in the spring—I had some misgivings. My comment let to a short tirade from Paul. I learned that he had been carrying on for years a feud with Hanson about "his" PhD in composition, both in print and at musicological national meetings. It was a disgrace that Eastman and some of the Big Ten in the Midwest were granting such a degree, as though English and French departments should be permitted to grant PhDs with novels as dissertations! Not one of the Ivy League universities was granting it; and they all regularly hired composers with only the MA and the equivalent of the doctorate—i.e., a body of work and a reputation—just as did departments of physical education! Douglas did not enter the discussion, for he had heard it all before—often. Nor did I, for my ideas on the subject had added up rather more to a rationalization than a conviction, as I indicated earlier. Paul and I were to continue the discussion some twenty years later.

It was useful to have access to the Music Library, but after the upstate Sibley Music Library at Eastman, it was the Columbia collection that seemed provincial. The standard reference books and the works and biographies of all the celebrated composers were there, but not many of 20th century composers. It was a fine place to browse in, but not a place to find an off-beat modern score.

I was on my own and on the town and in no mood for browsing. I soon learned that New York City is a place for walking, the buses and subways convenient for finding new places to walk in. One long hike was down the West Side along the river almost to South Ferry, stopping off half-way to marvel at the transatlantic liners then lined up in one pier after the other. I savored whiffs of salt air from the sea.

I soon discovered that near the Music Department, in Dodge, was the McMillin Theatre in which first-class concerts and recitals regularly took place. A ticket for a seat in the rear balcony of Carnegie Hall cost 90 cents; score desks at the Metropolitan Opera were available to me through the Music Department for almost nothing; the subway and the buses were a nickel a ride. Quite apart from the permanent and changing exhibitions in the many museums were the originals, always on view, of some 18th and 19th century, and many 20th century buildings I had seen illustrated in art and architectural volumes. The more intimate art galleries on 57th Street and Madison Avenue were a far cry from the frame-shops I'd seen in Rochester. To one of them I returned several times, for I wanted to buy a small Paul Klee painting and a townscape by Lyonel Feininger, each only a few hundred dollars. I could have afforded one or both, but it did not occur to me that they were good investments and I was thrifty, as were—and as are—those of us who were teenagers during the Depression years.

The McMillin Theatre, referred to above as my unexpected neighborhood source of concerts, was renovated in 1988 and re-named the Miller Theatre, in honor of its benefactress, Kathryn Bache Miller. With its acoustics improved and an orchestra pit added—though the stage remains where it was, not where it belongs—the Miller Theatre has become an important part of the new-music scene. At the time McMillin became Miller I was asked to the university publication *Columbia* to write *McMillin Theatre Remembered*, which was published in October 1988.

McMILLIN THEATRE REMEMBERED

One of the minor pleasures of attending the theatre in London is reading the article in each program that gives a history of the building and rebuilding of the theatre and a resumé of memorable productions that have taken place in it. Now that Broadway theatres are adopting this British custom, perhaps we should consider the past of *our* Broadway house, even as it begins its new life as the Kathryn Bache Miller Theatre.

McMillin Academic Theatre was dedicated in 1924, as was the building as a whole, our first School of Business (now Dodge Hall). The theatre memorialized Emerson McMillin, a mid-western industrialist and the chief donor.

The theatre was built to house the Institute of Arts and Sciences, a part of the University's adult-education program. In its heyday the institute sponsored 200 events annually, from October through April. On Monday evenings there were lectures on "Our World-Today and Tomorrow," sometimes organized as short non-credit courses; lectures and short courses on Tuesday considered "Men and Ideas in America"; books, the fine arts, and music (including folk music and jazz) were the subjects on Wednesday; on Thursday and Friday motion pictures and travelogues were offered; on Saturday mornings there was entertainment for children, and in the evenings instrumental or vocal recitals and occasional concerts by the Columbia University Orchestra or Chorus. The lectures were often given by well-known figures and were widely advertised and reported in the press. Churchill, General Marshall and members of FDR's cabinet and Brain Trust made news, even at Broadway and 116th.

On the 25th anniversary, in 1949, the institute could boast of having presented over 8,000 events to 2,500,000 persons. I became one of those persons in the autumn of 1944 when I moved to New York City to study with Béla Bartók.

To my surprise an excellent series of recitals was taking place three blocks away in a smallish hall for half the price charged for hearing the same artists in too-large halls downtown. During that year there were recitals by Casedesus, Huberman, Grace Moore, and Singher, and a string quartet series to boot.

Students, faculty, and the neighborhood-at-large continued to enjoy the concert series until 1957. In that year the Institute was discontinued. Audiences for the lectures and travelogues had dwindled, for in the fifties adults were seeking more demanding fare and academic credit for their efforts. It was rumored that some in the University had long been embarrassed by the entertainments in McMillin *Academic* Theatre. But it had been the "profit" from the most popular events that had made possible the inexpensive tickets to the Saturday concerts. For the past 30 years there have been very few downtown recitals uptown.

It was toward the end of my first year in the Columbia neighborhood, in May 1945, that the first week-long American Music Festival took place. The orchestral, chamber music, and choral concerts were held in McMillin; at the same time, performances of chamber operas took place in Brander Matthews Hall, another University theatre built in the late thirties for the production of plays. Supported by the Alice M. Ditson Fund, the festival presented over the next decade numerous premieres of works by Hindemith, Barber, Ives, Porter, Sessions, Talma, and Wolpe, among others. The festival chamber operas commissioned for performance in Brander Matthews included Menotti's *Medium* and Stein and Thompson's *The Mother of Us All.*

McMillin's long-standing reputation as a center for new music and as *the* center for electronic music dates from the American Music Festivals. There was nationwide coverage and standing-room-only at the concerts and operas, all free to the public. I remember relinquishing my seat to Leopold Stokowski; a colleague became a standee so that Koussevitsky could be seated. After many complaints, a guard was dismissed for intermission *frottage.*

But the presence of the CBS, Juilliard, and other orchestras, and the dance companies of Martha Graham and (later) Alwin Nikolais-not to speak of the long-suffering local orchestras and chorus—drew attention to the inadequacies of McMillin as a *theatre.* Of the 1,500 seats, not more than half had good sightlines and decent sound. The Institute's purposes would have been served as well, or better, had the stage been placed at the short east end of the hall. It was not, and flies, wings, and a pit were omitted because of strong opposition in the early twenties to dramatic and music theatre performances at Columbia. Undergraduate romps such as the Varsity Show were encouraged but the burgeoning Little Theatre movement could not easily invade the campus if there was no proper theatre. Upstart playwrights such as Eugene O'Neill were to remain where they belonged, at the Provincetown Playhouse in Greenwich Village.

In the late forties the Columbia University Opera Workshop summered in stifling McMillin and in the early fifties wintered there. Participating were several singers later to have major careers: Teresa Stich-Randall, Gladys Kuchta, Leopold Simoneau, James McCraken and Josh Wheeler. Among my coaching and assistant conductor colleagues were John Kander, who was promoted to other Broadway theatres downtown and John Crosby, who left the workshop one spring to found his own opera company the next year in Santa Fe. The loudest sound ever achieved by our singers—if not the most artistic—was a rendition (with piano) of the first part of Act II, *Die Walküre,* with 16 Valkyries instead of the usual eight.

In the mid-fifties the razing of Brander Matthews and the elimination of its annual subscription series of plays, operas, and operettas, coinciding with the demise of the Institute and the festivals, deprived Columbia of strong links between town and gown. In 1968, the Students for a Democratic Society decided that the revolution required revolutionary music: an excellent student performance of the Boulez *Sonatine* in McMillin was almost obliterated by cat-calls and whistles. A year later, a grenade was thrown onto the stage during a Cuban rally.

During the last 20 years McMillin played host to innumerable miscellaneous events, including some important conferences. There were full-houses for semi-staged revivals of Sousa's *El Capitan* and *Fly with Me* by Rodgers, Hammerstein, and Hart. But after the palmy days of the institute and the festivals, McMillin's role in the University became unclear. Unsuitable as a theatre, too unattractive for University ceremonies, it was too large for most of the events taking place within it. Unmanaged and untended, the butt of the *Herald Tribune* (which regularly denounced it as the worst concert hall in the city), deserted by critics and the other gentry, little by little it took on some of the pleasantly Bohemian qualities of a public garret. Accordingly, as a seedy shelter for the new and the untried, it welcomed new-music enthusiasts from all over the city, attending the births of new-music chamber ensembles and nurturing innumerable composers, young and old.

After only a few days of enjoying what New York City had to offer, both uptown and downtown, I fancied myself becoming a New Yorker: a person born and bred elsewhere who would not and cannot go home again. There were no close relatives left in Muncie and whatever was left of Hoosierdom in me would remain ineradicable, but on Columbus Day two reminders of my nurturing foster-home, Rochester, arrived by mail. A somewhat squishy package turned out to be one of Mother's well-known fruitcakes, prepared without sugar and wrapped in brandy-soaked cloth, delicious and long-lived at a slice a day. The other was an application for a Guggenheim Fellowship, sent, an appended note said, "at the suggestion of Bernard Rogers." I was touched by his thoughtfulness and dutifully filled out the form, bothering him, Phillips and Hanson for recommendations, but realizing that the application was very premature, as it turned out to have been; I had never heard of a 23-year old being granted Guggie, as they were nicknamed.

Shortly after mailing the hopeless application, as if by some benign coincidence, I received a letter that I had been awarded the 1944 Lillian Fairchild Award for my *Concerto for Piano and Orchestra*, for which I had not applied. Enclosed was a handsome certificate and a check for $100. I learned that the Award had been made annually for 20 years "for the most meritorious and praiseworthy creation" in arts and letters by a citizen of Rochester. I was the third composer to have been honored. The letter was signed by the chairman of the jury, Richard Greene, Chairman of the English Department of the University which administered the Award for the City. Though I suspected my name and the *Concerto* were likely to have been nominated by someone at Eastman, Greene may have remembered the name of that Eastman student who had recently been in one of his courses. If so, it was possible that there was yet another reason that the Eastman Registrar had been wrong in thinking I was wasting my time electing non-Eastman courses. Furthermore, it was in Greene's course, I think, that I heard of Laurence Sterne and became infatuated with *Tristram Shandy*.

Encouraged, and as a change of pace, I decided to write a song cycle for contralto and piano. I was drawn to the inviting title *Words for Music Perhaps*, by William Butler Yeats. While making a selection of eight from the twenty-five "Crazy Jane Songs," I oiled my old rusty and unused—to-writing— songs hand with a single setting, that of Rupert Brooke's *Clouds*, also for alto and piano. I had so far written only three songs, Carl Sandburg settings in 1940-41. The writing of the Yeats cycle took some time and, as they were composed, served as the subject-matter of several of my sessions with Bartók, not just the two that I described in *Bartók's Last Year*.

Some of these songs and the recently completed third piano sonata served as my audition pieces for membership in the Forum Group of the ISCM. That audition afforded me an insider's view of what I'd already been hearing about the intricacies and simplicities of the politics of musical style. In the Twenties two groups, chiefly of composers, had been organized in New York to perform and to promote new music: the American section if the ISCM (the International Society for Contemporary Music) and the League of Composers. The ISCM dates back to Vienna, 1922, when its concerts provided a hearing of new works by Schönberg, Webern, and Bartók, and a host of other, mainly, avantguardists, including French and English composers. A year later, in 1923, the other New York group, the League of Composers, was organized, primarily to perform new music primarily by Americans and to report on the new-music scene in its excellent quarterly, *Modern Music*, which endured for 24 years. The League was initiated by a cross-section of the composers of the time, though with a preponderance of those who had, or soon would, study with Nadia Boulanger and were partial to French music and Stravinsky's works.

A score of years after their beginnings, the American section of the ISCM and the League of Composers had become polar powers on the New York new-music scene. Each had become more strongly and clearly representative of the musical attitudes already manifest in their beginnings. In the early autumn of 1944 I was hearing the ISCM and the League referred to simplistically as the "twelve-toners" and the "Boulangerie" or, in impolite conversation, as "the Germans" and "the French." As a non-joiner by temperament and a disliker of either-or formulations, I found the scene distressing.

This over-simplified division of the two differing styles of composing, hearing, and discussing new music was to continue into the fifties and sixties, given more credence as the "Second Viennese School" and its 12-tone procedures grew in importance and remained identified with the ISCM; that style's detractors, holding fast to tonality of one sort or another, centered in the League. There were examples of apostasy, nevertheless. In 1954, because both groups were experiencing financial troubles, in a fit of ecumenicity the combined League/ISCM came into being. Nevertheless, the earlier division was thought to be continuing unchanged, accounting for the *whole* of the new-music scene mid-century and became a dogma chewed over in the *New York Times* and elsewhere for all too long.

It is probable that the request of Bernard Rogers that his friends Copland and Barber show me the ropes in NYC (described earlier in detail, and unchronologically) led them to put my name in the mailing lists of both ISCM and the League, and soon after meeting them I began receiving notices of their concerts. Copland had been among the organizers of both groups; Barber, more consistently conservative, would have been a member of the League.

It is also probable that Copland arranged that I should be phoned by Miriam Gideon, who invited me to attend a meeting of the ISCM Forum Group in her upper Central Park West apartment. She explained that the Forum Group was a quasi-independent organization of the youngest composers of the ISCM who would like to make the acquaintance of me and my music, some of which I should bring with me.

There were perhaps 10 to 12 composers at the meeting, informally led by Miriam, who introduced me to them one by one, none of whom I knew except by reputation. There was merriment at having someone from Middletown in their midst and someone inquired if I considered myself a typical American. Someone else remarked that he had heard of no Hoosier composers except for Hoagie Carmichael and Cole Porter. (The Quaker Ned Rorem, born two years after me in Richmond, 40 miles from Muncie, was not yet a part of the NY scene). There was some surprise and disbelief that someone from such a conservative place as Eastman could have been accepted by Bartók, and some questions asked about our sessions together. I was asked to play a sonata or two and to pass around multiple copies of those of the *Crazy Jane Songs* that had been completed.

By the time I had finished playing and the scores had been examined, a couple of latecomers had arrived; I found myself seated on the floor, surrounded by commentators and questioners. Kurt List, with a pronounced German accent, and Ben Weber—both 12-tone serialists—commented that some of my more chromatic passages suggested that I might be on the verge of composing in the new idiom. Had I considered doing so? I replied that I had no a priori objection to any style, but that I sought a greater variety of sound could be found by using only the "total chromatic", i.e., the constant reiteration of the 12 pitches found in the chromatic scale. That exchange let to an animated discussion of the music they had heard and the scores they had examined, their tonal, quasi-atonal, and pre-12-tone aspects, and in what directions my future pieces might lead. As the discussion turned argumentative, I became extremely uncomfortable, as though I were a patient surrounded by doctors and medical students trying to make a diagnosis and prognosis of some disease. I told them that I thought they should continue their discussion without me, got up, said "Thank you and good night," and left abruptly.

From someone present I learned that Bill Bergsma had "auditioned" earlier in the evening. From someone else I learned that his music had been found "inappropriate for the Forum Group." Bill was uncharacteristically mum on the subject of his "audition." Shortly thereafter he began writing occasionally for the League's quarterly, *Modern Music*.

Miriam phoned to thank me for attending, invited me to attend meetings and said that the Forum Group would try to program some of the *Crazy Jane Songs* later in the season. It was gratifying to have been accepted, after however much discussion and argument had continued after I left. It was also instructive to have heard what I *did* hear, for it aided me in placing my music in the stylistic continuum of the time: hard to pin down because variable, but on the average, so to speak, somewhat left of center. At that time political terminology was often applied to musical stylistics, ISCM being left, League right. I might add that I was voting for the socialist Norman Thomas for President for as long as he ran, in 1944 and '48.

A little later, as she promised, I was asked to prepare four of the eight songs in the cycle for a Forum concert. I was fortunate in finding Jean Handzlick, a contralto, as the singer. She was young, tall and handsome, and a fine musician with clear diction, and quickly learned and memorized the four songs selected. I add—somewhat parenthetically—that low voices are usually found in both men and women in tall bodies, in accordance with the fact that it is their longer and thicker vocal cords that make the low notes possible. Those with the lower voices also tend to have longer necks than do those who have the high voices, who are usually shorter in stature, in accordance with their shorter and thinner cords. Though there are exceptions—Joan Sutherland, for example—it is usually possible to identify high and low voices by sight when a vocal quartet enters a stage. Not surprisingly, the strong, dramatic high voices are usually packaged in burly—not necessarily fat—packages and need not be "no-neck monsters." The incomparable Birgit Nilsson was built like a fire hydrant.

Handzlick and I agreed that it would make sense to perform the first four, which were designed to follow one another – as were the eight, needless to say. But there was a problem in the lyric of the first song, *Crazy Jane and the Bishop*, which involved my first name. I, little me, was to be the accompanist and my tall regal, and handsome contralto was to sing "Jack had my virginity." We feared that the audience would react to Yeats's unintended humor with laughs and giggles. We discarded the idea of cutting the line or changing to some other one-syllable name, and decided that nobody would notice, especially if she muffled her diction and the text was not reprinted in the program.

While we were wrestling with this amusing problem, I had a session with Bartók, with whom by this time it had become possible to discuss just about anything. Because he had become familiar with most or all of the cycle, I told him of our unexpected predicament. He thought my story very funny and wished he'd had a similar experience with Béla. He then recounted his experience with his ballet, *The Miraculous Mandarin*. He had completed the score in 1919, but had waited until 1931 for a performance in Budapest, which was cancelled after the dress rehearsal: too much lewdness and nudity.

Shortly before the performance, it occurred to me that I had neglected to clear the rights of the copyrighted Yeats poems for setting them to music and for having them publicly performed, the texts perhaps to be reprinted in the program. I went to Douglas Moore for advice. He was sympathetic but stern and suggested that I *not* approach the publisher at this late date. He added that he had set the Yeats lyric *Brown Penny* to music after requesting from the publisher the right to do so, and receiving no reply. Yeats had died in 1939. Both the publisher and Douglas had to wait until the widow arranged a séance during which she asked if her husband would grant permission. He had said yes. Better, Douglas said, to plead youth and inexperience if I got caught, than to alert the publisher of my intentions and lose the performance while waiting for Mrs. Yeats to get in touch with William Butler again.

The performance did take place, successfully, and was followed by a later ISCM broadcast performance. From the premiere I learned at least two important lessons: first, an audience can be inattentive to the words and lack a sense of humor: second, not to set copyrighted words to my music without having the permission of the publisher and/or the writer to do so.

In 1959 I thoroughly revised numbers 2, 3, 5 and 6 of the cycle of eight and relegated the others to the closet. Before the four were published by Boosey and Hawkes in 1999 they were again thoroughly revised. I finally obtained the right to set them—55 years later:—and to perform and publish them, Mrs. Yeats long since having joined her husband in some Irish heaven.

I have spent much of my adult life in setting words to music for solo voice, chorus, and the stage; consequently, I have had all too much experience in acquiring permissions for all copyrighted words, except for my own—for those, too, on occasion! In general, if a composer approaches living authors—unless they are on principle averse to being musicalized—they are flattered, and may easily be persuaded to permit the omission or repetition of a phrase or line, or even a change of word, if there is good musical reason for doing so. After all, a musical setting of a lyric is not unlike a translation of it into another language. On the other hand, a surviving spouse or an agent representing an estate may be extremely protective of the deceased author's words and may require the composer to set the words verbatim. T.S. Eliot presented a special problem to composers: he would occasionally permit musical settings, but he denied permission for those of his poems that *he* thought inappropriate for music. After his death, his widow tried to preserve this distinction. It is fun to consider whether Eliot would have approved his *Old Possum's Book of Practical Cats* as the libretto of *Cats*. Probably. Whether yes or no, that musical's world-wide success has been a gold mine for his estate and his publisher, Faber and Faber.

I have learned that young composers do not learn the facts of copyright life from anybody but their untutored friends. Consequently, every year I impressed upon the 6 new members of a composition seminar the importance of protecting their music by running a "copyright line" on the bottom of the first page of their new score. When a student composer intended to use a copyrighted text, I insisted that he write for permission to do so immediately, to avoid the disappointment of its being denied or proving to be too expensive.

When it became known to ASCAP that I had long been interested in bringing this information to young, and older, inattentive composers, I was asked to write *Suggestions to Composers Who Wish to Set Words to Music*, which ASCAP published and also put on the Internet.

Relevant to the subject of T.S. Eliot and his relationship with composers is the following correspondence, initiated by his publisher. In my letter I refer to "enclosures": I sent copies of correspondence initiated by me in 1955, and reprint them here, except for my long, routine, initial letter, the contents of which are rehearsed in the letters that follow. Inasmuch as the performance by a dramatic soprano coloratura of concert arias about the mating and other habits of hippos and elephants was such an attractive prospect, I was intent on winning my case. Though the two arias are certainly not lyrical in style, they are far from being declamatory, as musicians would define the term. I was counting on Eliot's defining the word in his own, poetic fashion, as I suppose he did.

And to conclude this discussion on rights, copyrights, and permissions, I include a poet's letter of permission that, if not unique, is of a kind seldom received by a composer.

8th July 1983

ff

Mr. Jack Beeson
404 Riverside Drive
New York
NY 10025
U.S.A.

Dear Mr Beeson

I am writing to you because we are the London publishers of the work of T.S. Eliot and we have been informed recently that you have included a section of 'The Waste Land' in a musical composition called 'The Shakespearean Rag'.

Faber and Faber deal with all requests to set the words of T.S. Eliot to music and we have not been asked about this use. We do, as a matter of principle, have to deny permission to include Eliot's words in musical settings. Eliot, during his lifetime, was insistent that his words must be allowed to stand on their own without the super-imposition of any other imagery, be it musical, dramatic or visual, and we continue to respect his wishes today. The fact that Andrew Lloyd Webber's musical 'Cats' has used the poems from the book *Old Possum's Book of Practical Cats* has in no way affected this decision. These latter poems written in the first instance for his God-children, are not of the same calibre as his longer work and Mrs. Eliot, herself, has co-operated personally with the composer in the presentation of this material

We look forward to hearing from you and to having your assurance that no further use will be made of T.S. Eliot's words.

Yours sincerely

Mavis Pindard
Permissions Manager, Faber and Faber Publishers

July 27, 1983

Dear Mr. Pindard

Upon my return from London last night I discovered your letter on the 8th of this month; had I received it some weeks ago I could easily have disposed of the matter in person—in fact, I several times walked past the Faber & Faber offices, noting each time its presence.

I should be most interested to know who is spreading false information about me in London—flattering though it may be to be spoken of in London. I have never written a work called "The Shakespearean Rag" and I have never succumbed to the temptation of setting sections of "The Waste Land". There is a composition "Shakespearean (sic) Rag", recorded on CRI (Composers Recordings Inc.), but because I don't at the moment have access to the record, I can't tell you if there's an Eliot passage in it. He teaches at the University of Illinois, in Urbana, Ill. I have a sneaking suspicion that there's another piece with such a title, but I can't place it.

In any case, I am not the guilty one, if there is one. In fact, I am very conscious of the necessity for clearing access to another's property and am something of a bear on the subject to my students here.

I wonder if Faber & Faber may not risk being thought to be, so to speak, "holier than the Pope" in rejecting out of hand all musical settings of Eliot's poetry—except Webber's. Indeed, Eliot was himself not altogether restrictive as you will see from the enclosures. I send them to you for what interest they may have to you, though to be sure they concern a matter of the mid-Fifties.

It is likely that no reply is necessary to this letter, but should you write, it would be best to address me in the country (a rather unfortunate, unintended pun).

Seaforth Lane
Lloyd Neck
New York, 11743

Cordially

Jack Beeson

17 August 1983

ff

Mr Jack Beeson
Department of Music
Columbia University
New York
NY 10027
USA

Dear Mr Beeson

Thank you for your letter of 27 July. I am sorry that I had to trouble you about something with which you are obviously not concerned. We do get these flurries of interest in T S Eliot's work from time to time and up and coming young composers are always quite sure that we have already given permission for other people to set T S Eliot's work to music and it is only with them that we are being difficult.

I am grateful to you for your understanding in this matter. I should, I think, point out that there have of course been notable exceptions when permission has been given for some of the short lyrical pieces to be set to music and obviously this is what happened when you made your application in 1955. I did work closely with Mr. du Sautoy when he was the chairman of Faber and Faber in dealing with requests to use T.S Eliot's work and as I explained to you, today we act on behalf of Mrs. Valerie Eliot who likes to be involved in requests to use her husband's work.

Yours sincerely

Mavis Pindard
Permissions Manager

FABER AND FABER LTD PUBLISHERS
24 Russell Square London WC$_I$

FABBAF, WESTCENT, LONDON
MUSeum 9543 (4 lines)

5th April 1955

FFdus/JGC

Mr. Jack Beeson
Dept. of Music
Columbia University,
New York 27

Dear Mr. Beeson,

Thank you for your letter of 27th March. Mr. Eliot prefers to give permission only for lyrical or passages of his work to be set to music. "The Hippopotamus" hardly seems suitable for this purpose, although it might be used for recitation. In the circumstances, we should be reluctant to agree to your proposal, though we should be glad to consider a request to set some other poems.

Yours very truly,

P.F. du Sautoy

FABER AND FABER LTD PUBLISHERS
24 Russell Square London WC$_I$

FABBAF, WESTCENT, LONDON
MUSeum 9543 (4 lines)

April 18, 1955

Mr. Peter F. du Sautoy
Faber and Faber, Ltd.
24 Russell Square
London W.C.1, England

Dear Mr. Sautoy:

Thank you for your prompt reply to my request for permission to set to music "the Hippopotamus" by Mr. Eliot. In truth I was asking permission somewhat after the fact inasmuch as I had already completed the setting of the words in both version—for voice and piano and for voice and orchestra—and had in fact copied out the orchestra score and parts. Though, frankly, it had occurred to me that my having committed a considerable amount of time and effort to the work would put me in a most disadvantageous position should any bargaining be necessary in connection with the terms upon which permission might be granted, my experience with authors in the past had been such that it had not occurred to me that the permission itself might not be granted.

Upon reading a copy of my letter to you I realize that you quite naturally would have assumed that I had not yet set the poem to music. Had I not done so, Mr. Eliot's preference in giving "permission only for lyrical poems or passages of hi work to be set to music"—should he have remained adamant in such a preference—would certainly have dissuaded me from continuing. Under the circumstances, however (circumstances which include the fact that Curtis Brown, Ltd. assures me that Mrs. Lawrence will surely give me permission to use the text of "The Elephant" by D.H. Lawrence as the other of the *Two Arias*) I trust that Mr. Eliot will make an exception on this occasion in favor of a composer who was so enthusiastic about the possibilities of the poem as a concert aria that he proceeded with the composition without first cautiously—and correctly—asking for permission to do so. I would assure him that I, too, would find a lyrical setting of "The Hippopotamus" incongruous and that I have therefore set it in a declamatory style.

I very much hope that you—or Mr. Eliot—will find it possible to reconsider. I should be delighted of course, to send a score of the music to you, or perhaps Mr. Eliot would care to see the music when he is in New York next month.

Very truly yours,
Jack Beeson

JB.ri

FABER AND FABER LTD
PUBLISHERS
24 Russell Square London WC$_1$
FABBAF WESTCENT LONDON   **Museum 9543**

27th April, 1955

FFduS/JGC

Mr. Jack Beeson
Department of Music
Columbia University
New York 27,
N.Y., U.S.A.

Dear Mr. Beeson,

Thank you for your letter of 18th April. In the circumstances, Mr. Eliot agrees to the performance of your musical setting of "The Hippopotamus" and I am therefore returning two copies, duly signed, of the agreement that you have sent. Please would you note that no permission for publication may be given.

Yours very truly,

P.F. du Sautoy.

- - - - - - - - - -

Department of History
MOUNT HOLYOKE COLLEGE
South Hadley, Massachusetts 01075
Telephone 413 538-2377

From Prof. Peter Viereck, 12 Silver St., Nov. 10 1974

To whom it may concern:

I own the copyright to my various poems and books and herewith give carte blanche to Prof. Jack Beeson to set to music and publish whatever he chooses of mine; I have complete faith in his good judgment and fairness so far as setting any fees or rental for me goes and leave that to him.

signed – Peter Viereck

Nora and I first met Viereck in Rome at about the time he was awarded the Pulitzer Prize for Poetry in 1949. He was eager for me to set some of his lyrics to music, but I was then busily writing *Jonah*. Since 1951 I have set a dozen of them, most recently *Three Viereck Songs* for bass voice and piano, premiered in October 2004. (I overcame the temptation to use the title *Three Four-cornered Songs*, a bilingual pun, as too arch and professorial.) I have been attracted to Peter's off-beat subject matter and humor and to his easy control of scansion and rhyme. He is much given to rewriting and republishing his work, the earlier, simpler, versions of which I find suitable for music. As implied in his letter, written thirty years ago, he has proven to be a genuine collaborator, permitting me to retitle, mix lines from early and late versions of a poem, and to make minor changes when the musical settings suggest them.

*   *   *   *   *   *

From these Shandean forays into the future we return to autumn 1948.

Though there were a few friends who knew my address and phone number, there were no visitors to my miserable room but one. José Velez, Peter Mennin and I had found the Arizona apartment house, and José occasionally returned there to pay me a visit, always without warning. A knock on the door and there he was, as casually as he might have left a bar stool or a table in a restaurant to appear at my table to say hello. If he was talkative—as he usually was—I listened to the news from Eastman and postponed practicing and collaborating with Yeats on *Crazy Jane*. If not, we'd arrange a time to meet again, usually in the company of the South American friends he'd come to see, most of them Chileans. Some years older than the others, Rafael de Silva, a pianist and teacher who prepared advanced students to study with Claudio Aarau, soon became my friend also, as did Claudio Spies and Juan Orrego-Salas. Aarau was the paterfamilias of this circle of friends, but because at that time he was committed to as many as 140 recital and concerto performances a year, he was seldom in evidence. When he was to be at home in Forest Hills for a short time, Rafael arranged for me to accompany him to see Aarau, suggesting that bring along my latest piano sonata, the Third. When we arrived, the small-talk in Spanish became, for my benefit, more serious talk in English. The short, muscular virtuoso was also a highly articulate, widely knowledgeable, sophisticated conversationalist. He asked what the score was and I answered that it was some of my music that Rafael had insisted that I bring. He took the music and was about to sight-read it when I said I'd play it for him. When I finished he commented to Rafael, "He plays very well for a composer." He then added, to me, that I should use more arm weight and that Rafael would be happy to show me how. I hazarded the comment "That would be difficult, for I don't have any." I left the two to consider further the problem of thin pianists and arm weight while I examined the large collection of pre-Columbian and other rare objects in two of the rooms. Rafael explained: "Aarau is the most widely know Chilean in the world and, as is the case with other such worthies in Latin America, has been appointed an ambassador, with a diplomatic pouch that is never examined by customs; he can buy whatever interests him and take it home with no trouble at all."

As we took our leave from Claudio—he insisted on the first name—he was unnecessarily and defensively embarrassed, I thought. As though I'd come with the intention of trying to "sell" him my *Third Piano Sonata*, he told me that he was sorry he no longer performed new music and that his personal representative, Frieda Rothe, was averse to his programming the Bartók, Schönberg, and other such works he had performed as a young man.

Claudio was also the father of a family. In 1944 two of the children were about 4 and 6; a third was born much later. As sometime baby-sitter for them and as company for his wife Ruth, once a promising mezzo soprano in Berlin who had given up a career for Claudio, there was often a young woman in attendance. At this time it was Felicia Montealegre, a former piano student who had turned to acting. She was soon to make what was said to be her New York acting debut in Synge's *Riders to the Sea*. The Chileans trooped off to the performance of the Chilean-American debutante and took me, the one all-American, along. The performance as memorable, as was the festive supper-party afterwards, mostly in Spanish. It occurred to me that this one-acter was suitable material for a chamber opera. But the music of the piece was in the Irish lilt of its spoken language and I had no idea of how to set that lilt without smudging it.

Shortly thereafter, Aarau invited me to spend an afternoon with him. When I arrived he was practicing and then continued playing Chopin *Etudes* as I listened, quite overcome with his ease. He ended with the one in thirds, which led to a discussion of double-notes. When he asked if I'd ever studied the piece, I went on about my "specialty" in thirds and sixths and played a double-trill on a perfect fourth and perfect fifth that had troubled Bartók. Aarau played it easily. It turned out that he had invited me, in part, to hear about sessions with Bartók, whose music he had always admired. He was fascinated to learn that at the end of my first meeting with him I'd been told all I needed to study were all the Mozart piano concertos, to learn how I could find the freedom to do this and that while following a rigid formal structure. And Aarau agreed with Bartók's observation that a composer-pianist's piano music is an accurate record of the composer's hand—and, he added—his wrist, arm, and body-weight. "Absolutely! For instance, Brahms . . ." He rattled off a loud, tumultuous passage in sixths from the Brahms-Handel variations . . . "He must have been build like a bear—with huge paws!"

Because he had noticed my interest in his collection, he showed me around, object by object, encouraging me to heft and stroke whatever I wished.

Over coffee he said he was sorry to have been on tour when Felicia had performed. Had I been as impressed as had the others? "Yes," I said and added that I'd thought about and discarded the Synge play as a one-act opera project. I was delighted to hear that he admired some operas; very often instrumentalists abhor them all. He then confided that he was responsible for Felicia's welfare and was upset that she was determined to talk Lennie into marrying her and it was all his fault because he had introduced the pair to one another: "It's even crazier to marry a bi-sexual than a homosexual!" He added—not entirely logically—that he'd been very annoyed in a performance with the City Symphony to have been cued in at every entrance by that 26-year old Lennie in the Brahms D minor, which he'd been playing for decades—and on this occasion, as a favor to Bernstein, for free!

The on-again, off-again marriage of Felicia and Lennie, the genius of ambivalence, took place seven years later, in 1951.

Whenever I was in the company of two or more of the Chileans, Peruvians, and an occasional Mexican, there was Spanish spoken. Sometimes there was a discussion as to whose Spanish was the purest. I found their prejudice amusing, as I did their agreement that the Puerto Rican Spanish, heard more and more often on the streets and subways, was the worst on earth. Intrigued, I decided to learn the language, bought a Hugo's grammar, and began attending the neighborhood Spanish-language movie-house. My intention always was to see the film twice, during the second showing to concentrate on the spoken dialogue. The trouble was that there were more tearful death scenes than in any 19th century Italian opera—in which they are usually packaged neatly at the end—throughout. I rarely managed even one showing. After a few months I took a train to Rochester to visit Mother and carelessly left the grammar in the Albany station. This, I thought, was an omen and decided to get along with what I could pick up by ear.

If these somewhat exotic events seem to form "an Hispanic period" it is only because they have been recounted in sequence; in reality, they were isolated adventures in the continuum of the other activities already described. In any case, I continued to enjoy the company and varied talents of José Veléz, Rafael de Silva, and Claudio Aarau for as long as they remained in this country.

I divined from the highly personalized English of José's letters that Eastman had become too boring and that he would transfer to Yale to study with Paul Hindemith. Shortly after he had done so, he appeared at the door—as usual, with no warning—with a description of these composition seminars that described his own combustible nature, as well as Hindemith's all-too-personalized teaching of composition. Examining a short piece by a student, Hindemith quickly found a passage in the middle of the piece that pleased him. He copied that passage out on the large blackboard, explained its excellence—José said that it was purely Hindemithian—and then completed the piece on the blackboard, backwards to its beginning and forward to its end: a virtuoso performance but of doubtful value to the student. I don't remember what it was that José said in class on this, or on other occasions, to cause Hindemith to throw chalk-laden erasers across the room at him.

When José Veléz returned to Lima he became José Malsio and was installed as Director of the National Conservatory of Music. Once a week an army general made a visit to check up on things. A little later he was appointed also to be Conductor of the Orchestra against his will. What José didn't tell me of these matters I learned second-hand from Rafael de Silva. Unforewarned as usual, a phone call from José in Lima seemed at first for the purpose of greetings and gossip. He then casually informed me that he had arranged for me to teach music in the University of Cuzco. Would I accept? While pretending to be considering the matter, I was estimating how much was left of my once-upon-a-time interest in the Incas and their impressive ruins: none—and replied lamely that my Spanish wasn't good enough for such an important position.

Not long after, I noticed the last name of Alba accompanying the somewhat Indian face and the Spanish accent of a Columbia Collage student attending my class for the first time and asked him to see me after class. I learned that he was a Peruvian and had heard of, but not met, José Malsio. I was curious about his grand Spanish name: He somewhat embarrassedly admitted to being a descendent of the Dukes of Alba and the Inca Emperors. He was amused by my having turned down a job in Cuzco, and even though it had been his ancestors' capitol, he thought I'd been wise not to have taken a job in such a touristy place.

I last heard from José years ago when he wrote asking me to recommend him for a US Government grant. I assume his application was unsuccessful, for he has not since rung any doorbells. I do, though, skim through articles datelined Lima, in the hope that he has been forced into some even higher Peruvian post.

Rafael de Silva remained a friend for years after my "Hispanic period" came to a close. His fear of performing had led him to teach piano to advanced students, or, rather, to teach music to pianists. He was a discriminating listener and critic of new music. When I happened to mention that I was revising my *Third Sonata for Piano*, he remembered my playing it for him and Claudio ten years earlier, in 1944, and made some useful suggestions. He agreed with Bartók's comment to me at our second session on the piece that the first, movement had too much literal repetition and not enough development. Rather than trying to re-write myself at age 33 as I had been at 23, I—we, Rafael and I— discarded it. Bartók had liked the slow movement, variations on a sea chantey, a tune that intrigued him. (He had added that too many modern composers choose as their subject matter folk material too imbued with eighteenth century idioms.) So the second and third movements, both revised, were published as *Two Diversions: Sea Chantey* and *Fast Dance*.

Rafael played the first performance of the *Fourth Sonata* on a WNYC radio festival shortly after "our" revisions of the *Third Sonata*.

My "collaboration" with Rafael was followed a few years later by a joint project carried out with Claudio Aarau. After attending a recital played by him in Rome, I went backstage to speak with him. Somewhat shyly he asked me for a favor: would I please accompany him on a shopping expedition the next morning? When I met him at the Excelsior Hotel early the next day he asked if I knew of a shop specializing in Roman antiquities. I replied that I'd window-shopped one on the Via Margutta, a short interesting walk down the Spanish steps and to the right of them. As we ambled down he explained that he wanted to purchase a votive object for his collection, in particular, *un fallo*, a phallus, and he wanted me to do the talking, in English or Italian, as I wished. Trying hard not to giggle, I was tempted to ask "Why me?" He explained "I speak Italian quite fluently, but it embarrasses me to do so because of my terrible Spanish accent."

At the small *antiquitá* there was but one salesman. Beginning with the obligatory "Buon giorno" and trying to keep a straight face with my Italian singulars and plurals in order, I told him that my friend wanted to buy a phallus; did he have any? "Yes, many," he answered, as he let us into the back room and pulled out a drawer full of *falli*, in all shapes and sizes. Claudio went through them and chose one—I'd no idea on what basis—paid the man a fistful of lire and we left. He tucked the tightly-wrapped, oddly-shaped, package under his arm; we had *espressi* in the nearby Café Greco and said our goodbyes.

Not so much in return for that small favor as because I knew that his favorite nephew was enrolled in Columbia University, I was able to talk Claudio into playing a recital, gratis, on campus the next season for students and the neighborhood. The only loser was his agent, Frieda Rothe, who received her percentage of nothing for yet another of Claudio's benefit recitals.

*　　*　　*　　*　　*　　*

Surely, the placing of a Chock Full O' Nuts restaurant on Broadway and 116th Street and Broadway, directly across from the main entrance to Columbia University, was no accident, but very likely a symbolic act. William Black, with generous financial aid, was graduated from the College of Engineering in 1926. Thereafter, he noted the large number of shops selling nuts, which got rid of their broken nuts very cheaply. These he bought and, mixing them with cream cheese, invented the sandwiches that made his chain Chock Full O' Nuts famous and him rich. In the early sixties, in return for his college financial aid, he donated six million dollars to the Columbia Medical School toward the building which bears his name.

Shortly before Christmas 1944, I went to the crowded Chock Full for a store-bought breakfast and took a seat to the left of an early-middle-age man having a coffee and reading a newspaper. While ordering, I noticed that he was reading a review of a concert I had attended the night before and leaned over to read it. Saying nothing, he moved the paper toward me so that I could read it more easily. He could have repeated the W.C. Fields line, "Here, have half of my doughnut, too!" but he didn't. I muttered my thanks. Interested, he asked if I'd heard the concert and I answered, "Yes, and there was an excellent soprano!" "That was my wife, Ethel."

Such an exchange naturally led to our exchanging our names and what we were doing in New York and in the neighborhood. He was Otto Luening (1900-1996), who had been teaching at Bennington College during its early and most interesting years. He had taken a leave from there to prepare and to conduct the premiere of the first Ditson Fund commissioned opera the past spring, Bernard Wagenaar's *Pieces of Eight*. Since September he had been on the Barnard College (and, by extension, the Columbia) faculty and would be musical director of the 18th century and newly commissioned American operas in the local Brander Matthews Theatre. When I told him that I'd been at the Eastman School until recently, over a second cup of coffee, he launched into a detailed description of the glory days of opera at Eastman in the middle and late twenties, about which I'd heard only out-of-date gossip. The many productions had been under the musical direction of Eugene Goossens, stage direction by Rouben Mamoulian and Vladimir Rosing, and with dance and movement by Martha Graham—all famous names by the time of our conversation. Yes, all that activity had gone to pieces for the reason I'd heard, some remnants of it becoming the American Opera Company, which specialized in new American works and the standard repertory translated in English. Then . . .

(Luening's detailed account of the above, his teenage years in Zürich with James Joyce, Strauss, and Ferrucio Busoni, and his highly personalized composer-conductor-teacher's view of the American musical scene from 1925 to 1980 are included in the 600 pages of his *The Odyssey of an American Composer*, Charles Scribner's Sons, New York, 1980.)

When I told him that I wanted to write operas, he wished me an ironic "good luck" and added that he had completed his so-far-unperformed *Evangeline* twelve years before. By this time we had long since left the Chock Full and were ambling along snow-covered Riverside Drive. As we parted, he invited me to attend the evening performance of Pergolesi's *The Jealous Husband*, which he was conducting in Brander Matthews.

Otto's brief account of our first meeting is included in his autobiography. If my account is much longer and more detailed, it is because it could be titled, "How I got my first job at Columbia."

*　　*　　*　　*　　*　　*

The performance of the Pergolesi that evening was enjoyable, in particular because the well-translated libretto was clearly projected by the young actor-singers in the theatre seating not quite 300. Even more enjoyable was my first visit to the innards of a theatre. I poked around the orchestra pit and the backstage area at length before finding Otto and thanking him for the invitation and the experience. He introduced me to Willard Rhodes, who cheerily invited me to pay a visit in his Music Department office.

Before I did so I asked Otto about the man I was to visit. Rhodes had come to the attention of the Chairman, Douglas Moore, when he produced and conducted one of Moore's early theatre works in a Westchester high school. He had been put in charge of the Opera Workshop in September, only a few months before we met. He had been a coach and conductor of the American Opera Company in the early thirties; as a young man in Paris he had been an accompanist to Josephine Baker. Before we met he had presumably checked me out with Otto. After pleasantries, he said that I would be welcome to join the Workshop as a volunteer coach. I would not be paid, but the usual tuition would be waived. I learned that many of the singers in the Pergolesi opera were Workshop singers, including the wonderful French-Canadian tenor, Leopold Simoneau, and the opportunity to work with such singers led me to accept his offer on the spot. So it was that in mid-January—the middle of the second year of the Workshop—I began enjoying myself hugely, coaching singers and ensembles and playing for the staging rehearsals, immersed, finally, in my first love, opera.

Soon after, Otto Luening, whom I was seeing almost daily, mentioned that the President of Barnard had called him in, told him that he was being overworked, and offered him $500 to hire somebody to help him. Would I be agreeable to being his coach and assistant conductor on the spring premier production of *The Scarecrow*, the second in the annual series of Ditson Fund opera commissions? That offer, too, I accepted on the spot.

In the spring, in addition to my duties in the Workshop, I had the opportunity as an insider to see and hear a new opera come into being. Its composer, Nornand Lockwood, was a dryly humorous delight—and claimed to like the way I played his piano score; his wife and librettist, Dolly, was quite dotty—Otto remarked that he always expected her to fly up on a chandelier and start swinging on it: and Percy MacKaye, on whose play, *The Scarecrow*, the libretto was based, was silently present. Though only 70 at the time, to us youngsters he seemed a ghost from another age, as indeed he was.

For the next three years (including two summer sessions) I served as coach for the Workshop and for the productions of forgotten and newly written operas, with the exalted title of assistant conductor of the productions. Then, after two years in Rome, I returned to both responsibilities only intermittently, sharing the coaching with the two Johns, Crosby and Kander.

The following reprint is self-explanatory. The list of operas (and plays with incidental music) is not incidental material, but the essence of the undertaking; it is reprinted in appendix A, page 511.

columbia report
Opera at Columbia University, 1941-1958

By Jack Beeson

Introduction

The following essay was written, and the accompanying material compiled, in 1961. With the exception of the addition of some singers' names, the essay has been only slightly revised: at this late date it would be difficult to find and to correct any errors in the production data.

My purpose forty years ago was simply to record a short but vibrant period in the history of American opera through my experience as coach and conductor in the Columbia Opera Workshop and the closely related series of

American opera premieres. For some years thereafter, I offered copies to anyone who showed an interest and to those on campus who—naively, I thought—were eager to revive the Workshop and/or produce new operas at Columbia with some regularity. Over the years, as opera workshops, small companies, and the writing and producing of chamber operas burgeoned, copies of the essay were requested more frequently—even by such organizations as Opera America. In celebration of the Music Department centenary in 1996, both a Low Library exhibition and a publication highlighted the Workshop and its related productions. It was at the same time that the Glimmerglass Opera and the New York City Opera revived *Paul Bunyan*, drawing attention to the premiere of Britten and Auden's opera at Columbia in 1941. Shortly thereafter, the two companies revived Virgil Thomson and Gertrude Stein's *The Mother of Us All* and invited me to speak to their audiences about her birth, largely from Workshop singers, in 1947.

Long before this period of interest in events of the past, I had given a copy of the material to a former graduate composition student, Jim Stepleton—by coincidence the son of my Junior High School music teacher in Muncie, Indiana. His interest led to his producing, in collaboration with the Friends and Enemies of Modern Music, a concert of excerpts from operas first performed at Columbia from 1941-1958. This retrospective in Miller Theatre in 1997 received extensive press comment. Finally, an inquiry from a graduate student at another university, addressed to Elizabeth Davis, Columbia's Music and Arts Librarian, requested a copy of a specified "unpublished document." Ms. Davis then insisted to me that this long drawn-out nonsense should cease, and that the material should be published. I complied, insisting only, in light of my many years at Columbia, that the publisher be *Current Musicology*.*

I add, more as a coda than a preamble to what follows, that through the energy of Jim Stepleton there has recently been incorporated the Douglas Moore Fund for American Opera, which will become active some months hence. Its purpose is to provide young composers of opera—Moore Fellows—with residence in opera companies that produce new works; to learn the ways of singers, conductors, and stage directors; to experience the pleasures and perils of collaborations and perhaps to play rehearsals, coach singers, and conduct a bit. In short, to serve apprenticeships similar to those some of us enjoyed during our years with the Workshop and its productions half a century ago.

* * *

In 1940, four years after its organization, the Columbia Theater Association (CTA), a small repertory company specializing in new and neglected old plays, moved into the newly built Brander Mathews Hall on the Columbia University campus. The Facilities of the new theatre were most inadequate for the production of even modest opera, but there *was* an orchestra pit—or the

* *Current Musicology*, no. 70 (Fall 2000)

semblance of one—and a production of two one-act chamber operas was undertaken immediately, in collaboration with the Juilliard School Collaboration with musical forces more readily at hand seemed preferable, however and during the next two seasons Columbia's Music Department augmented the musical forces from both inside and outside the Columbia community that were assembled by Milton Smith, who ran the school's Theatre Department, and the CTA. In order to serve better the musical needs of the Brander Mathews productions and to provide an outlet for the Music Department's interest in lyric theatre, the Opera Workshop was organized in the 1943-44 season. In addition, Otto Luening was brought to the University in the spring of that season to rehearse and conduct the first performances of *Pieces of Eight* by Bernard Waganaar. *Pieces of Eight* was the first opera commissioned by the Alice M Ditson Fund, a grantor committed to advancing the cause of American music, and which after 1942 was administered by its Advisory Committee, with Music Department representation.

In the autumn of 1944, Professor Willard Rhodes was selected as executive and musical director of the Workshop, and Otto Luening was appointed to the Barnard and Columbia teaching staff and named musical director of the CTA. Through these changes in leadership, and with the Ditson Fund made available to commission and underwrite the production of a new opera each spring, a *modus operandi* was established which was to continue for about thirteen years with several changes of stage director.

The Opera Workshop existed as a General Studies course for four points, meeting twice a week (Tuesday and Friday) for a total of eight hours. Membership in the Workshop was open to aspiring conductors, stage directors, composers, and librettists, as well as to singers. Singers were admitted to the course only after an audition, and an attempt was made to achieve a distribution of voices in accordance with the repertory under study. Ditson tuition scholarships were available to the most promising singers. A program of study combining courses from the Music Department and the School of Dramatic Arts was available to those preparing for careers in the lyric theatre.

During its most flourishing years, the Workshop resembled a small opera repertory company in the amount and scope of activity. Friday classes were given over to staging arias and ensemble scenes that had been rehearsed musically in the Tuesday class sessions. In addition, numerous solo and ensemble coaching sessions were held, usually in the Music Department, under the guidance of the music director, his musical assistants, or the student-coaches. Occasionally student stage-directors were entrusted with special rehearsals; for a period, sessions in Italian and English diction were provided. Limited space in the Department and the busy schedule and play production in Brander Mathews drove us frequently to Earl Hall, McMillin (now Miller) Theatre, and Casa Italiana; it was not rare for classes and rehearsals to be occurring in two or three places simultaneously. Several times a season the arias, scenes, and acts from the standard repertory studied in class were presented to invited audiences. Piano accompaniment sufficed.

Of greater importance to the opera project as a whole were the full productions, usually mounted twice a season and typically produced in collaboration with the Theatre Associates. The productions were about equally divided between neglected eighteenth-century comic operas, always translated into English (performed in mid-winter), and new works by American composers, commissioned by the Ditson Fund. Usually both productions were included in the regular subscription series of the CTA. In addition, the new works were given prominent place in the annual spring festivals of American music presented by the Music Department and the Ditson Fund for six successive years to distinguished invited audiences.

These large scale productions of premieres—usually of chamber operas, it should by added—were well attended and given full attention by the metropolitan and national weekly press. As often as not they were directed (both musically and dramatically) and sung by persons not necessarily regularly connected with the Workshop. Several of the premieres, for instance, were conducted by Otto Luening and staged by directors or chorographers from off-campus. But even productions not given under the aegis of the Workshop were made possible by the existence of that organization, for the Workshop provided continuity—that is, it could be depended on to supply the singers for small parts, a chorus, and, frequently, talented singing-actors for the important roles. Other roles were cast from "downtown" from the ranks of those who were delighted to perform without pay for free coaching, stage experience, and critical notice in the press. Orchestras for the productions were made up partly by Columbia students and partly by outsiders. An arrangement with the Musicians Union made possible the payment of instrumentalists out-of-pocket expenses, a very much smaller amount than union scale. The size of the orchestra varied, from thirteen instrumentalists, required by several of the chamber operas to about thirty. The inadequate pit, the small size of the house, the orchestral budget, and (by no means the least important factor) the interest of everybody concerned in a production of musical and dramatic intimacy—all these elements determined the size of the orchestra as well as the style of the production.

Particularly during the forties and the early fifties, the Opera Workshop and the opera productions were a vital part of the city's musical and dramatic life. Of more widespread importance was the commissioning and performing of new works. The astonishing interest in the lyric theatre shown by American composers since the Second World Was and the new directions their works have frequently taken have certainly not been altogether the result of the Columbia project. But its influence can be imagined, if not measured, when one realizes that during its existence Brander Mathews was prominent among all theatres in the United States in the number of new operas it brought into being and that the recent interest in dramatically viable operatic productions was from the beginning the aim of the Brander Mathews productions. The current practice of casting choreographers as stage directors was anticipated at Columbia in a number of productions: Gian

Carlo Menotti's *The Medium*, Virgil Thomson's *The Mother of Us All*, Otto Luening's *Evangeline*, and Albert Rivett's *Poor Eddy*, among others. The emergence of Menotti as a successful and well-known composer and his debut as a stage director occurred on campus in 1946—and one might in passing draw attention to the fact (glossed over by their biographers) that the first operatic efforts of those two stalwarts, Benjamin Britten and W.H. Auden, took place in May 1941 on West 117th Street.

But though the quality of individual productions during the late fifties did not decline, there was a notable diminishing in the number of productions and in Workshop activity. The reasons were various: other workshops sprouted inside and outside parent institutions: the G.I. Bill came to an end and men and women who might previously have been able to nurture their talents in the Workshop were forced to rely in Lady Luck; professional and semi-professional opera companies and even Broadway producers began to show an interest in new works and in the revival of eighteenth-century repertory. More significant, however, was the fact that the academic and administrative community at large had not exhibited sufficient interest and support to organize this branch of theatre at Columbia on a secure academic, artistic, and financial basis. An Arts Center with three theatres had long been planned, but was not built; it was said that a large gift was proffered by William Paley and rejected. Those who had led the opera project were not interested in continuing what was now being done elsewhere—frequently in imitation of Columbia's efforts—and development along new lines seemed impossible under the conditions that prevailed. Their patience exhausted, their energies no longer buoyant, and their efforts recognized in the main outside the University, they turned their attention to other matters. The assistants, having served their apprenticeships, were not tempted to continue the struggle with the old unsolved problems and the new unsolvable problems posed by the scarcity of rehearsal space in the Music Department, the disappearance of Milton Smith and the School of Dramatic Arts, and the disappearance altogether of Brander Mathews Hall.

In spite of difficulties, much was accomplished during Columbia's operatic years. It is not necessary to emphasize further the encouragement given to new works and ideas and to the revival of neglected operas of interest to the University community and the New York public at large. (One notes with some smugness that Paisiello's charming *Barber of Seville* was first rediscovered, not in Berlin in 1960, but in New York in 1946.) Equally important ends were served in training conductors, stage-directors, and singing-actors. One may single out from the names on the following pages four coaches and assistant conductors who have turned their apprentice years to professional use: Jacob Avshalomov, composer-conductor of the Portland Junior Symphony; John Crosby, founder and artistic director of the Santa Fe Opera; John Kander, composer and conductor on and off Broadway; and the present author, a composer.

* * *

In 1961, it seemed to me invidious to list any singers who had once been members of both the Opera Workshop *and* the casts of related productions. Now that forty years have passed, there are but few still performing and some have died. Of those singers whose names or recorded voices may be familiar today a partial listing may suggest the quality and variety of the young artists who enlivened opera at Columbia from 1941-1958.

Everett Anderson	Leopold Simoneau
Ellen Faull	Teresa Stitch-Randall
Alice Howland	David Thaw
Gladys Kuchta	Josh Wheeler
James McCracken	

As indicated earlier, the new American operas were cast in part from "downtown." By prior arrangement, the title role of Menotti''s *Medium* served ClaraMae Turner, successfully, as her audition for the Metropolitan Opera. The first *The Mother of Us All* led Dorothy Dow to Zürich, La Scala, and the New York Philharmonic. Two sopranos who appeared in the series of new American operas were also involved in two Douglas Moore premieres at the time: Shirlee Emmons and Leyna Gabriele.

In the Introduction to the preceding listing, Milton Smith is named as the Director of both The Theatre Department and the Columbia Theatre Associates (CTA), the latter the producer and host of almost all the opera productions in Brander Matthews Hall. He is also credited as stage director in eleven of the old and new operas produced in the forties.

It was his proselytizing in the early twenties that led to there being live theatre on campus for the benefit of town and gown from 1927 on for thirty years. He had been responsible for all the Columbia instruction in acting, stage direction, playwriting, and stagecraft, as well as directing most, if not all, plays presented by CTA. It was he who planned and oversaw the building of Brander Matthews in 1940 and may have witnessed its razing in 1958, after having been forcibly retired at age 65. From then until the organization of the School of the Arts in 1965 there was no instruction in theatre and few theatre productions on campus.

After his retirement I often visited him and his wife, Helen Claire, who had been a Broadway star. I learned that he was writing a memoir of his Columbia theatre years. Because I offered to try to find a publisher for it, I was in possession of a manuscript copy at the time of his death and deposited it in the Columbiana collection.

Perhaps because Milton knew that important members of the administration and faculty found theatre instruction and productions inappropriate to the university, he often felt put upon and was irascible. He knew much more about music than he let on, for his brother, Melville, was a composer and one of the very first students of Nadia Boulanger. He could barely tolerate the presence of orchestra players in his theatre on our opera productions, all of which he insisted on calling operettas. He was surprised and delighted when I occasionally volunteered to join the stage crew in building stage sets. Once, when tacking canvas to a frame over my head, I hammered a finger. He felt as proudly responsible for the accident as solicitous, but not at all concerned that I was hampered for days in playing rehearsals. On another occasion I heard him fire a stagehand on the spot, saying that he was never again to enter the theatre. But he rushed to tell his secretary, Gretchen, "Make sure we have his address and number in case we need him again!" In short, Milton and I enjoyed one another.

He solved large and small problems as would the editor of a small New England newspaper, in a tiny office, seated on an uncomfortable chair in front of a rolltop desk. He once came into the pit where I was playing a piano dress rehearsal to summon me to see him during the next break. When I appeared he asked what I knew about a woman named Friedelind Wagner. I told him that she was one of the four grandchildren of Richard Wagner; that she had been appalled by her mother's affection for Hitler and her brothers Wieland and Wolfgang toadying to him and to her; that she had angrily left her family, Bayreuth, and Germany, in 1938. He then told me that she, speaking English well and saying little about her past, had dropped into his office seeking theatre experience. He, thinking she was a refugee and wanting to be helpful, had hired her to work in the box office and to usher! After our opera opened I was standing in the back watching and listening when I looked to my left and saw her profile in the dim light, my knees almost giving way: it was the young Richard Wagner, the high sloping forehead, the long hooked nose, and the same lank hair. During the run of whichever opera it was we had several brief, guarded conversations when she wasn't selling tickets or ushering. Soon after she disappeared as mysteriously as she had arrived.

Years later Nora and I attended a *Wozzeck* performance in Munich, seated by chance in the royal box, I suppose once upon a time the box of Ludwig II. During an intermission, while wandering around, I thought I spied Friedelind Wagner sitting alone on a bench. Circling about to make sure it was she, I put my memories in order: she had published a justifiably nasty book about her family; when an uneasy truce with her brothers had been arrived at, Wieland had put her in charge of the Bayreuth master classes; Wolfgang had fired her. I greeted her and initiated a brief conversation in which she let me know that she had indeed been in New York, but that she had never been on the Columbia campus, had never been in Brander Matthews, and that we had never met before.

*   *   *   *   *   *

The staging rehearsals of an opera are presided over by a stage director. The conductor is present to set tempi, cue singers, and keep things tidy. A pianist plays a piano reduction of the orchestral score. The Friday staging sessions of the Workshop followed this pattern, During the 15 years of the Workshop the stage directors were all Central Europeans, their training and experience in the many German theatres the most thorough in the world at the time. Herbert Graf had to schedule his Metropolitan Opera rehearsals so as to be available to us for three hours on Friday.

When Willard Rhodes was late or absent, someone subbed for me at the piano while I conducted, having learned the rudiments of conducting at Eastman in a too-large class of 25 or so. Those simple arm movements were hardly sufficient for what I was now sometimes called upon to do. Fortunately, Rudolf Thomas, who taught orchestration in the Department and sometimes conducted the University Orchestra—and who was to take over the Workshop in the fifties— occasionally taught conducting on a one-to-one basis. He was the opposite of the phlegmatic Paul White at Eastman, known for his diffident, monotonic appeals to his orchestra, "Please, more expression, more passion." Rudolf was a man of many large enthusiasms, another superbly trained German opera-man, who had studied with Nikisch. Shortly after immigrating to New York, he conducted, in 1933, *Champagne Sec*, a version of *Die Fledermaus*. The "Adele" was Kitty Carlisle (Hart). In my several meetings with her over the years I avoided mentioning that subject, not wishing to embarrass her. Last year, in her nineties, finding ourselves apart from the crowd, I asked her if she remembered the conductor of *Champagne Sec*. She said, "Oh, yes, Rudolf Thomas. He had a clear beat, was very strict, and very charming." Then, confirming what Rudolf had told me half a century ago, she added, "And, you know, the pianist in the pit was Frederick Loewe, who went on to write the score of *My Fair Lady!*"

Rudolf's training of a conductor was simple and effective. I would play a piano score, following his beat, or he would play, following mine. In either role he commented constantly on what I was or was not doing. We began with the *Carmen* accompanied recitatives—as John Crosby and Jacques Monod were to begin their lessons with him a year or two later. Next on the agenda was the whole of *De Fledermaus*. We also worked on those scenes that were being staged, some of which I was to conduct in the public recitals.

I thought then—and have continued to think—that some experience in conducting is useful to composers. A composer-conductor's physical feeling for how his music will be conducted and played can lead him to find the best and simplest notation for even very complicated music and lead to better performances.

A similar attitude toward learning to do the things that I was involved with in the Workshop and productions led me to study voice. A fine singer, Everett Anderson, asked me to coach him privately on some roles in the bass repertory. I agreed, in return for voice lessons. I had been intrigued by hearing singers say that they couldn't really *hear* themselves in the studio, but that they knew they were singing well by way of feelings in their throat and head, chest, and diaphragm—

feelings that they were not very good at explaining. Though I didn't vocalize as much as I should have, I soon experienced what they were talking about. When Anderson, after some months, told me that my light baritone, with more study, would become a tenor, I quit, fearing a possible personality change too.

My conducting and voice lessons ended as the casting and rehearsals for the 5 premiere performances of Gian Carlo Menotti's *The Medium* began. In addition to all his other talents, Gian Carlo Menotti had a genius for casting. He had in his mind's eye and ear the perfect embodiments of the characters he had created. All we had to do was to find them, and he, Otto, and I heard everybody available. The Metropolitan suggested that we hear ClaraMae Turner, who had auditioned for them recently. She was tall and of commanding presence. We cast her; the Met saw one or more of her performances, as Baba, the medium, and hired her immediately. Otto and I were eager to have Gian Carlo hear and see a fine lyric soprano from the Workshop; he found her too normal and healthy-looking for the part of Monica; he agreed to let her cover the role and perhaps sing one performance. He was enthusiastic about another, with an attractive but oddly timbred voice. After a second audition we cast her, though Otto confided to me that there was something unhealthy about the voice and that we were lucky to have a cover for the role. Not long after the performances, nodes were surgically removed from her vocal cords. All the rest of the parts were cast to Menotti's great satisfaction.

I was drafted to play the piano in the small orchestra or, rather, the *piano primo*, for Gian Carlo's score requires piano, four hands, and Avshalomov was to cope with *piano secondo*. The Brander Matthews pit accommodated only a chamber orchestra and the commissioned composers had to orchestrate accordingly. Menotti chose an instrumentation that became, with variations, the model for chamber operas: 5 solo strings, 4 woodwinds (with alternations, flute and piccolo, oboe and English horn, etc.), horn and trumpet, 1 percussionist, and a piano or harp. (Britten was to follow this model in his chamber operas of the late forties.) I asked Gian Carlo why he was requiring two pianists—a question probably posed by producers and conductors of *The Medium* ever since. "Well, Jack, I'm Italian and I'm superstitious. The instrumentalists I need add up to thirteen, which would mean bad luck, so I added another pianist."

Because the composer was also directing the staging rehearsals at which I was accompanying and occasionally conducting in the absence of Otto Luening, Menotti had a chance to observe me and asked if I'd like to conduct one of the performances. He'd already asked Otto, who'd thought it a good idea and would be agreeable to practicing and playing the *piano primo* in my stead. I was flabbergasted and said I'd think it over. Actually, I dreamt it over for several nights: I was in an orchestral pit with a score I had never seen before—hardly the case with the score of *The Medium*! Ready to give the down beat, I could not raise my arms. During the day I remembered my father's discussion of stress diabetes with me and wondered if it was a good idea to commit myself even to this modest "debut," that could, if I wished to let it, lead to more serious opera conducting commitments. I thanked Gian Carlo and Otto for their well-intentioned offer and was content to go on playing *piano primo*.

At that time Otto was living alone on Claremont Avenue and refusing to have a telephone. One of my duties as assistant conductor was to ring his doorbell in very late afternoon and accompany him to the theatre. Well into the run, when he came to the door he was unusually disheveled and drunk. While he dressed with difficulty I made strong coffee; on my arm he stumbled to the theatre. Fortunately Avshalomov had arrived early to practice his part and I let him in on the all-too-open secret. While he and I plied Otto with more coffee, knowing that he would insist on conducting, we decided that should he fall sideways from the tiny podium—we hoped not onto the piano strings just in front of him—after he was carried out, I would, willy-nilly, conduct the rest of the performance. Jascha would then try to cope with the four-hand piano part.

Though there was much swaying there was no fall. Afterwards Gian Carlo asked Otto why the tempi had been slower and more varied than usual. The imperturbable ClaraMae Turner asked me if Otto was ill, his cues having been often missing or erratic. Otto and I never spoke of the performance, though he did thank me rather gravely when I saw him home that evening.

The Columbia performances were so successful that plans were made for a Broadway production. Gian Carlo quickly tossed off a "curtain raiser," *The Telephone*, to fill out the evening. With his genius for casting he found another superb singing actress for *The Medium*, Marie Powers, who had been singing repertory in the French provinces. He asked me to prepare her for the previews at the Heckscher Theatre and the Broadway run. I accepted, of course, and found Powers both very musical and an extraordinary woman. She insisted that we meet daily at 9 am at Columbia, after her breakfast and attendance at mass. She arrived always from far downtown on a bicycle.

At her insistence I attended the tryouts at the Heckscher in which she was perfection itself. I was invited to the opening at the Ethel Barrymore Theatre. After *The Telephone* two women, to my left and right, asked me the same questions. "What kind of a show is this? Do you know if they're going to go on singing all evening?" An operatic double-bill was something entirely new for Broadway theatergoers. After the performance I visited Powers in her dressing room, which—except for the bicycle—looked like an elaborately decorated chapel in Lourdes.

The "show" was well received and ran for six months. One music critic wrote that it had been improved by revisions and cutting. In fact, the meter of *one* measure had been changed and a prayer-scene *added* for Baba.

Exactly a year later, during the premiere production of the Virgil Thomson/Gertrude Stein *The Mother of Us All*, Otto was confronted with a run of nine performances. This time, he suggested that I conduct a couple of the shows and Virgil was more than agreeable. My same dreams reoccurred at night and my same stress-diabetes doubts by day. This time, though, it occurred to me that any 24-year old with the unquenchable ambition, ego, and drive necessary to be a conductor would accept anxiety dreams and health hazards as pebbles to be kicked aside on the road to a career. That I had twice turned down opportunities to conduct new operas before audiences that included critics and VIPs was not so much that I was a fool as that I lacked the makings of a conductor.

In this rondo of my non-conducting career there was one more long-delayed final repetition of the tune. I was coaching the principals and sharing with David Effron the playing of the staging rehearsals for the premiere of my *Lizzie Borden* by the New York City Opera in its old house on 55th Street. Only occasionally did I conduct the singers and Effron at the piano. The General Director, Julius Rudel, dropped by occasionally to watch and listen. He and I were by chance in an elevator one day when he complimented me on my playing and conducting. He went on to say that the company was planning a series of performances in Los Angeles. If I cared to come along, I could conduct a *La Traviata* or two. (He did not need to add "with no orchestra rehearsal, of course.") I was astonished, flattered, and said, "Thanks, but no. I can't." I could have, probably, but wouldn't.

*   *   *   *   *   *

Chapter 4

Britten's *Grimes* and Virgil Thomson's *Mother* and *Aeneid*

At about the time we were premiering *The Medium* in May 1946, it was announced that the American premiere of Benjamin Britten's *Peter Grimes* would take place at Tanglewood that summer. Its premiere was to have taken place there, for Koussevitzky had commissioned it, but problems related to the end of World War II led to its having been first performed in London in 1945; it had turned out to be a turning point in the history of English opera.

Avshalomov was in Tanglewood studying with Copland. He invited me to join him and his wife Doris in their rented cabin at the time of the *Grimes* dress rehearsal, if, he quipped, I could stand hearing another opera in English by a non-American. I noted the allusion to Gian Carlo's slightly Italian-accented English settings and accepted.

Fifty-one years after the *Grimes* premiere, *The Making of Peter Grimes* was published in two volumes, priced at $531. Fifty-one years after my visit to Tanglewood I was invited by the *Opera Quarterly* to write about this new publication. Casting aside my long aversion to writing reviews, if only to receive such volumes free, I agreed to do so. I reprint the review here, in part because it describes my reactions to a few of the events that took place at the dress rehearsal of the first American *Grimes*; it also alludes to the first production of Britten's first opera, *Paul Bunyan*, which has only recently been rediscovered. *Bunyan* is the third entry in the list of Brander Matthews musical productions, on page 510.

The Making of "Peter Grimes"
Volume I, *Facsimile of Benjamin Britten's Composition Draft*
Volume 2, *Notes and Commentaries*

Edited by Paul Banks

Rochester, New York: Boydell and Brewer, 1996
122 folios, 251 pages, $531.00

Beleaguered as "serious music" publishers are, it has been common in recent years to find that the publications of contemporary operas have been reproductions of the composers' fair copies of vocal scores. Instructive though such a score may be—if indeed, the hand is that of the composer and not that of a copyist—the publication may be as idiosyncratic as it is unclear. Given the expense of publishing vocal scores even today when composers may have provided print-ready, computer-generated scores, it is astonishing that in recent months two far more expensive and surely less salable opera manuscripts have been published in facsimile: the orchestra score of Kurt Weill's *Die Dreigroschenoper* by European American Music and Britten's composition draft of *Peter Grimes*, in honor of the work's fiftieth anniversary. To my knowledge, there are no other such publications of twentieth-century operas.

Although the title of the first volume uses the phrase "composition draft," Britten himself used the word "sketch," boldly written on *his* title page in red crayon. Then follow the complete sketch and three related pages, all produced in four-color offset litho at 92 percent original size, but clearly legible. Information usually found on a title page is included with the colophon.

The second volume is handsomely printed in large, widely spaced type, with color plates of Kenneth Green's costumes and set designs of the original Sadler's Wells production, and reproductions of typescripts, handwritten libretto drafts, and discarded pages of the orchestra score. There are eight chapters related to the creation and early productions of *Grimes*, most of the contents either written years ago and now first published or prepared for this celebratory publication by authors who have written extensively on Britten and his music. Bibliographic material covers every conceivable aspect of manuscript scores and libretto states, publications, sound recordings and film, even the first box-office receipts, print runs, and sales acquired from the Boosey and Hawkes files. Particularly fascinating is the information that Britten's own copy of the Passacaglia (interlude 4) includes a highly specific program, the action cued to bars.

Both Philip Brett's chapter, "The Growth of the Libretto," and Philip Reed's chapter, "Finding the Right Notes," are, respectively, detailed studies of the words and the music and refer to the comprehensive holdings of the Britten-Pears Library at Aldeburgh. (The music sketch, long considered lost, was restored and bound by the British Library and is also at Aldeburgh, having been donated by Reginald Goodall, the conductor of the premiere.) Helpful in following the details of these two chapters is the preceding "A Peter Grimes Chronology, 1941-1945," which quotes extensively from letters, program notes, radio interviews, and other sources in detailing the progress of the work from the first scenario ideas of Britten and Pears in Escondido, California, through the rehearsal revisions in London.

The composer's work habits were often described by him and his collaborators. They are confirmed by this facsimile manuscript. We cannot know his thoughts during his long, fast, afternoon walks, during which formal ideas and notes were decided. But we can all now see what he set down on these pages in the three-hour stints later in the afternoons and the following mornings. The general impression is that of fluency and assurance. Britten always wrote in pencil, a gum eraser close at hand; for the most part in the *Grimes* years he did not use sketchbooks and odd sheets, though there are occasionally fragmentary jottings in the sketch itself. Apparently the manuscript shows many erasures, the original notes sometimes legible: these *pentimenti* are sometimes legible in the facsimile. Obvious are the rejected bars and short passages decisively crossed out. Except in the orchestral passages, a pair of staves usually suffices to limn the orchestration; except where a favored woodwind is to be remembered or strings are to be disposed unconventionally, instrumental notations are rarer than in other such scores I have seen. Almost throughout Britten indicates triplets in duple meters and duplets in compound meters with brackets, without the usual *3s* and *2s*. The engraver of the piano-vocal score followed the composer's notation except when he slipped into the old-fashioned manner and was not caught by the proofreaders. It is not usual for a composer to "edit" an opera sketch so thoroughly, to include most of the dynamic indications that are to be found in the engraved vocal score. (Some of the latter may well have been added by Britten in the copyists' intervening ink fair copy, as well as metronome indications, which are not in the manuscript.)

Philip Brett's chapter does not seek to provide commentary on every subtle aspect of the score and indeed could not be expected to do so, even in his thirty-six-page discussion. This composer-reviewer can add only that on every page there is more than a little to catch the ear and the eye: a plain vocal line, later to be chromatically inflected; a word setting bettered in blue pencil; a vocal line completely foreign to the words beneath, Britten realizing that the *words* must be altered to fit his music.

In fact, one has the impression from the sketch and the extensive commentaries that Britten's well-known tendency to avoid confrontation served him ill in his collaboration with his librettist, Montagu Slater. At least three other persons contributed to the *Grimes* libretto. To be sure, Slater did rewrite when pressed to do so, but he was soon to publish the libretto, claiming that it was (without the composer's repetition of phrases) the text that had been sung at the premiere. The more inclusive credit "Libretto by Montagu Slater" would have been more accurate than the printed credit "Words by Montagu Slater," for not all the words were his. I wish—as I suspect that Britten wished—that more of the words had been Britten's, or Pears's, or Crozier's, or Duncan's. Reading other of Slater's stage works discloses a poet often unable to adapt his voice to those of his characters.[1] Slater is not a character in *Peter Grimes*, but he remains too often onstage.

Since the early nineteenth-century, composers have been free more often than not to choose their libretto subject matter. In the last century the amounts of time, energy, and money invested in writing an opera have greatly increased; it is not surprising, therefore, that composers have chosen—or rejected—subjects with care, often unaware of their psychological reasons for doing so. If we know comparatively little about the subjects Britten considered and then rejected, we do know that his chosen subject matter provided protagonists as outsiders of one kind or another. There are many inhabitants of outsiderdom, and their citizenship derives from various sources, composing operas the most obvious. I believe that writers in these Gay Nineties err in ascribing the choice of *Grimes* by Britten and Pears so exclusively to their homosexuality. Britten was a pacifist already in his school years; returning to England in 1942, he and Pears registered as conscientious objectors and were each heard twice by tribunals. Britten rejected alternative service but accepted a simulacrum. Their friend Michael Tippett followed a similar but more rigorous course and spent three months in prison. These events took place while the scenario was in work and deserve to be given their full weight in considering the choice and treatment of their *Grimes*. Britten's continuing belief in pacifism surely animated his choice of *Owen Wingrave* twenty-five years later. Those of us Americans who registered as conscientious objectors during World War II were well aware of the terms *adolescent, immature,* and *failure to adjust,* implied by Philip Brett as having been code words solely for British homosexuals in the closeted forties. Might they not have referred also to Britten's noncombatant status, at least in part?

There was reason for some Englishmen to believe that *Grimes* was Britten's first opera, for *Paul Bunyan's* only performances had taken place at Columbia University four years earlier, in 1941, and had been little noted abroad. Until after its premiere Britten and Auden vacillated between calling their work an opera and an operetta. It *was* an opera quite unlike any other, and no more an operetta than it was the musical comedy they thought for a time it might become. Nevertheless, all commentators have agreed in calling it an operetta, and it was so designated on the Faber Music vocal score of 1978. (Boosey and Hawkes held the 1941 copyright and then, in 1974, generously—and perhaps ingenuously—assigned it first to Britten in order that he might revise the work, and later to Faber.) More important than its appellation were Britten's comment in 1941 that

"I feel that I have learned lots about what not to write for the theatre" and Humphrey Carpenter's comment that "the most obvious lesson he learnt from it was not to be dominated by his librettist."[2]

Concerning the less important matter, Milton Smith was the stage director of the first *Bunyan* as well as being in charge of the Brander Matthews Theatre. His unpublished autobiography includes a fascinating account of the audition of the work that took place in the New York City apartment of Douglas Moore, 464 Riverside Drive.[3] (In an apartment eight buildings to the south Busoni had been at work on *Arlecchino* in 1915.) As Moore, Smith, and Auden listened, Pears sang all the roles to Britten's accompaniment. Milton Smith, much to the annoyance of all his theater colleagues, always insisted on calling *all* theater pieces with music "operettas." It was he who wrote the program note beginning *"Paul Bunyan* is the first operatic collaboration . . ." and then reverting to his habitual ". . . this operetta."[4] Perhaps the holdings of the Britten-Pears Library can answer the question: Was the birth of *Paul Bunyan* as an operetta pre-Milton or post-Milton?

In early August 1946 I was seated on the aisle, down front, at a dress rehearsal for the first American performance of *Peter Grimes* at Tanglewood. Leonard Bernstein was conducting an opera for the first time in his burgeoning career. In addition to my pleasure in knowing that I was present at the second coming of a great work, I remember vividly three details of the event: at the first break, as Lenny was bounding over the orchestra barrier, the sight of Britten popping out of his seat and asking, in an anxious, demanding tone, "Do you think we have time for a cup of tea together?"; the close of act 2, scene I, the D-flat sung by Phyllis Smith (later Phyllis Curtin) still spinning in my ear; and the passage for two flutes, several times repeated in that beautiful trio-quartet. At each subsequent performance of *Grimes* I've wondered if the part writing of that passage had come about during its orchestration. Now, with this remarkable publication at hand, I see that the optional D-flat was parenthesized from the outset and that the evocative intertwined falling thirds were provided with "Fl." The last repetition is crossed out (together with "Fl ob") and the whole close transposed up a perfect fifth. Every other admirer of *Grimes* can now seek the answer to his favorite mysteries.

Jack Beeson

NOTES
1. Montagu Slater, *Peter Grimes and Other Poems* (London: John Lane, The Bodley Head, 1946).
2. Humphrey Carpenter, *Benjamin Britten: A Biography* (London: Faber and Faber, 1992), p. 150.
3. The typescript of Smith's memoirs has been deposited in the Columbiana Collection of the Columbia University Libraries. The relevant pages are 465-82. Copies of these and a relevant letter from Smith to Beeson have been deposited in the Britten-Pears Library.

4. The publisher's note in *Paul Bunyan* (London: Faber Music, 1978) reprints much of the program note but is not clear concerning its authorship.

The cadre of those involved with new American operas—composers and librettists, funders, producers, and performers—is much larger today than it was in the forties. Now, as then, its members tend often to combine or exchange categories. As in most minority groups the members help one another. Sheri Greenawald was a splendid evil stepmother in the Glimmerglass revival of my *Lizzie Borden* in 1996. Six years later she became director of the San Francisco Opera Center (an arm of the larger company) and soon brought about a production of Sheldon Harnick's and my *Dr. Heidegger's Fountain of Youth* on a triple bill of one-act chamber operas. As a specialist in American repertory she knew that I had served as one of the midwives of the second Stein/Thomson opera and I was invited to write of its birth, for the program of *The Mother of Us All*, which was to open the 2003-04 season of the San Francisco Opera.

Immediately following the reprint of that article is another concerning Virgil Thomson. It was Virgil's suggestion to the editor of *Parnassus* that I be asked to write about his operas for the Spring/Summer issue 1977, largely devoted to a tribute to Thomson on his 81st birthday. I reprint only the first and last parts of that tribute, eliminating the detailed discussion of his three operas, described more briefly elsewhere.

The Birth of *The Mother of Us All*

"Out! Out! Out!" This unscripted line, the diphthong "ou" exaggerated, the "t" exploded, was sung out in a high-pitched voice by Virgil Thomson as he strode down the center aisle. The 27 singers became silent. The small orchestra straggled to a stop and the conductor, Otto Luening, waited patiently for yet another lecture on the importance of projecting out to the audience every word, including every final consonant.

The Place: Brander Matthews Hall, a theatre seating about 200 on the campus of the Columbia University in the city of New York.

The Time: The "Sitzprobe" of *The Mother of Us All* by Virgil Thomson with libretto by Gertrude Stein in early May 1947; that is, the first meeting of the cast and orchestra in the theatre, in preparation for four performances for invited audiences and five for the general public.

Until a few days before this rehearsal, Otto Luening and I, the assistant conductor, coach, and rehearsal pianist, had kept Thomson away from the singers until they were prepared to be heard by the composer, who was also the highly feared, but respected chief critic of the *Herald Tribune*. Now, in a large classroom, he listened attentively and approvingly. "Then," as Otto reminisced in his autobiography, "he began barking at the singers. . . . One of the singers said, 'If you keep carrying on like this, we won't be able to sing at all.' I took Virgil out of the room and told him he should control himself . . . the young singers are doing their best . . . we returned and he apologized. . . . Have I been naughty? I'm sorry. I'll control myself."

A few minutes later Virgil called a halt when he thought Otto's tempo needed adjustment. When Otto couldn't suit him, he handed the baton to Virgil, who took over decisively—but twice too fast. I, at twenty-five but already a veteran of opera composers being present at rehearsals of their Columbia Premieres, said mildly from the piano, "Virgil, we're still learning your piece. Please try half-tempo." He did. "That was just fine. Thanks, Puss."

The assembled singers had been cast after some 200 auditions. The majority were young professionals from downtown, but ten of the twenty-seven were members of the Columbia University Opera Workshop. Operas as elaborate as *The Mother of Us All* could not have been produced at Columbia without the Workshop, its musical staff, and its 25-some singers, who could compete for major and minor roles, understudy, and serve as a chorus when needed. Unique when it was organized in 1943, it was widely imitated at its demise in 1958. Its stage directors were highly experienced Central European refugees, among them Herbert Graf, moonlighting from Wagner and Strauss at the Met. Taken together, the Workshop, the premieres (of which *The Mother of Us All* was the ninth) and the annual revivals of neglected older operas, resembled a small German opera house. A number of the Workshop singers went on to major careers: Ellen Faull, Gladys Kuchta, James McCracken, Leopold Simoneau, and Teresa Stich-Randall. Open to budding conductors and composers, the coaching staff included this writer, who has composed ten operas; the composer-conductor Jacob Avshalomov; John Crosby, who left the Workshop to found, conduct, and lead the Santa Fe opera for decades; and John Kander, the composer of *Cabaret, Chicago,* and other musicals, two new ones opening in New York City this season.

Thomson was familiar with the occasional productions offered by the Workshop itself and often reviewed the better-known series of opera premieres presented in Brander-Matthews each May. The first of that series was also the first opera by Benjamin Britten, *Paul Bunyan* in 1941. Thomson was not enchanted with its music or with its libretto by W. H. Auden. Beginning in 1943,

The Alice M. Ditson Fund of the University began commissioning each year an opera by an American composer and underwriting its production.

Douglas Moore, whose *Carrie Nation* and *The Ballad of Baby Doe* have been performed by San Francisco Opera (the former presented by Spring Opera Theater), was the prime mover behind the Workshop, the Ditson Fund, and its commissions. He approached Aaron Copland for the 1947 opera, but Copland was otherwise engaged and wary of what he called *la forme fatale*. And so it was that Thomson and Gertrude Stein were invited to collaborate for a second time. Given the success of their *Four Saints in Three Acts* at its premiere in 1934 and on Broadway immediately thereafter, it's odd that nobody had done so earlier. The commission was $1,000 to Thomson (and $500 for orchestral parts-copying) and $500 to Stein.

After the pair accepted their commissions, barely eighteen months passed between their agreement and the selection of their opera's subject matter, characters, and style, and the Sitzprobe described above. Stein had completed the libretto in March 1946 and died in July. Virgil and his friend Maurice Grosser, who had provided a detailed scenarios for *Four Saints*, then set about making minor verbal and dramatic adjustments in the text. Virgil, often playing hooky from the *"Trib"* [*Tribune*], was able to compose the music in three months and to score 500 pages for an orchestra designed to fit the peculiarities of the Brander Matthews pit. He was reveling in being permitted to choose his favored designer and costumer and a choreographer, John Taras as director. In fact, the Columbia premieres very often used choreographers rather than directors, a practice then thought strange and still uncommon. Otto Luening, Taras and I lent eyes and ears to those singers whom Virgil had long admired and wanted to cast in roles Stein had devised from among her friends.

Most of the auditions took place in Virgil's apartment in the Chelsea Hotel. Otto and I had pre-selected those Workshop singers we wanted Virgil to hear; the very numerous others from downtown were eager to be seen and heard by music professionals in the world premiere of an opera by a well-known composer and critic—without pay! (The orchestra players, by arrangement with the Local 802, received only expenses.)

Virgil's drawing room—as he called it—and adjoining library were full of trophies: to the right of my piano bench were the serial LOVE paintings by Robert Indiana; to my left was a larger Florine Stettheimer, the artist who had designed the cellophane sets and costumes for the first *Four Saints*. He would listen to nothing but Handel in English, and American and British art songs or arias. He sat bolt upright or slouched on the couch, betraying his reactions. I remember little else but day after day of sight-reading and miles of left-hand, fast-moving, Handelian sixteenth notes.

Finding a Susan B. Anthony proved difficult until at the last moment Dorothy Dow appeared. A broad-shouldered, no-nonsense Texan, she was then being auditioned by the Met for a revival of *Fidelio* for which Flagstad was not available. She was called time after time just to sing the "Abscheulicher" aria to find out whether she ever cracked on one of the high B's. In one of our later coaching sessions she remarked that she found the role of Susan B. to lie a little low for her. Nevertheless, nine performance in eight days would prove taxing; she told Otto and Virgil that if she had to sing two Saturday performances, she could not sing the final Sunday performance.

That problem was solved by my spending many hours at the piano with Teresa Stich, helping her to prepare the role of Susan B. for the last performance. Stich, a wondrously gifted and very young Workshop singer, had been chagrined to be cast as Henrietta M., whose role consisted of four scattered lines: "Daniel Webster needs an artichoke," "Be where?", "In winter" (sung twice), and "I have never been mentioned again." To sweeten this pill, she was to understudy Gertrude S., and sang that role when Hazel Gravell became indisposed. Finally, with Gravell recovered and Stich prepared to undertake Susan B., Dow became disposed to sing the final performance.

Teresa Stich-Randall—the Randall was added to honor her benefactress—shortly thereafter sang in two operas under Toscanini, at the Met, and became the first American Kammersängerin at the Vienna State Opera. Dorothy Dow was also to have a European career, often in contemporary operas, and to realize her Texan ambition to sing *La Fanciulla del West* at La Scala.

How did this long-draw-out but intense experience affect me as a twenty-five-year-old composer? My composer friends, mostly writing "advanced" instrumental music, knew I was lucky to have a job, but thought playing triads for opera singers was wasting my time, and enjoying it, some new kind of madness. It was true that there were only well-chosen triads in the Act 1 exchange between John Adams and Constance Fletcher—as most everywhere else. But the characters' alternation between G-Flat Major and G Minor was delicious to the ear and lent the scene exactly the low-temperature passion of the words. The score was filled with other striking key relationships, strong musical characterizations, and the exact rendering in the vocal line of vowel quantities and inflections. Nowhere did the orchestra unintentionally cover the voices, as was the case in operas by the "more advanced" composers of the time—and since. Virgil's music went in neither for sentimentality nor the emotional high temperatures usual in opera. In common with all successful opera composers, he chose a librettist who could provide him with words that invited him to compose the music he wanted to write and knew how to write. A year after *The Mother of Us All*, I asked Virgil why he didn't set Stein's libretto, *Dr. Faustus Lights the Lights*. He answered, "Because it requires dissonant music and I don't want to write that way."

At that time—and often later—I listened to Virgil's instrumental works. They were always deftly made, often charming or witty, and usually hard to remember. I also read Stein's plays, which seemed un-theatrical. They were in need of Grosser's clarification and Virgil's music to put flesh on the bare bones of her characters. A parallel comes to mind: Gilbert and Sullivan. Thomson or Stein, alone, resembles Sullivan's music without Gilbert's lyrics, Gilbert's words without Sullivan's music.

By then I had begun what was to become my first completed opera. I had resolved to find libretti (if I had to write them myself) that permitted—that required—the full range of musical and dramatic temperatures: triads in all their seven-tone families, twelve-tones, whatever was required to bring to life their words, characters, and conflicts. It was then and remained for some decades a fairly heretical idea, but Virgil approved of my early efforts in that direction.

- - - - - - - - -

Virgil Thomson's *Aeneid*

Mozart once remarked that a whiff of stale air from an opera theatre made him immediately envious of all the other composers who were writing operas. That he was not then writing one meant simply that he had no commission at the moment. It would not have occurred to him or his contemporaries, as it would not have occurred to his predecessors, to compose an opera for a possible performance sometime, somewhere.

A commission usually included among other things a prescribed, or at least suggested, libretto. When it did not, the composer was at no loss for a libretto; he could re-use or re-fashion one already long since proven stage-worthy or he could turn to a professional librettist, for in those days there was such a profession. And in those days there was a general agreement in the first place as to what an opera was and what particular type of opera would be appropriate for a particular occasion, theatre, or public.

This happy state of affairs was to continue in Italy for some generations, but soured elsewhere as the nineteenth century wore on. The opera composer's language—his musical vocabulary and syntax—became ever more idiosyncratic, his choice of libretto subjects ever more impervious to outside suggestion and criticism. Sometimes his new composer stance intrigued the public; more often it confused the critics and repelled the new patron, the box-office. It certainly did not encourage commissions from the usual sources. As composers sought subjects of ever broader significance—at least to themselves—they fought longer and harder with their librettists (when they did not write their libretti themselves) and they spent ever larger amounts of time, effort, and money on composing and orchestrating, and frequently re-writing ever smaller numbers of operas. Naturally, given the ever-growing investment in writing ever fewer operas, the choice of a libretto subject became correspondingly more difficult, excruciating for some (and, one might add, the opportunity to learn from experience ever diminished). Beethoven found his first libretto subject, *Leonore* (later re-titled *Fidelio*) when he was 33, after some search. He revised it twice and failed in almost a quarter of a century to find another subject equally high-minded. Given his all-or-nothing approach to *Fidelio's* subject matter, Freedom and Conjugal Love, it is not surprising. At the other end of the century Debussy spent nearly a decade writing *Pélleas et Mélisande* after dallying with other subjects; during his remaining seventeen years he completed neither of his two operas based on Poe.

By then, the end of World War I, it was clear—or by now it surely is— that for more than a century practical considerations have played the smallest role in composers' libretto choices; rather, composers' acknowledged and unacknowledged psychological drives have determined their choices. A list of libretto subjects rejected and accepted by a composer is as clear an index to his personality as would be a list of his rejected and accepted lovers and mates.

If one cites such one-opera composers as Beethoven and Debussy—R. Schumann, Wolf, Fauré, Bartók, Copland, and W. Schuman come quickly to mind—it is only because in part they personify the gradual remove of opera from its once central position on the crossroads of music and theatre to an expensive suburb.

Virgil Thomson has written not one, but indubitably, three operas. Though these three works are as nothing in a numerical listing of his works, they are substantial and I am neither the first nor the last to remark that they are the works by which he is likely to be remembered, cherished, and influential. The reputations of Beethoven and Debussy are hardly dependent on their operas, secure though these are in the repertoire and the canons of taste.

However, to insist upon these differences between Thomson and the one-opera composers cited is hardly to put him in the camp of the specialist "opera composers" of whom the 20th century has produced more than a few. His *Four Saints in Three Acts, The Mother of Us All* (both to libretti by Gertrude Stein), *Lord Byron* (libretto by Jack Larson) inhabit one of the more exclusive suburbs of contemporary opera, the first two in seemingly simple but sophisticatedly similar houses in an enclave of their own. In fact, it is happy accident or the genetic inheritance of longevity that masks his relationship to one-opera composers and obscures his similarly long journey through writers and writing to find a successor to his first librettist, Dido-Gertrude . . .

. . . By the time Thomson had set his first Stein poem, "Susie Asado," he knew that he had found "his poet" and, shortly afterward, "his librettist." She responded to his gift of the manuscript, "It is very nice to have words and music and to see them at the same time when by accident it is where they need it best." The sentence succinctly and presciently sums up two operas. It is idle to quote critical approbation of his text-setting thereafter, for examples are as numerous as the reviews. Perhaps the first dates from 1931, when no less a *savant* than Henri Prunières wrote in *La Revue Musicale* and *The New York Times* concerning settings in *French* of his "remarkable feeling for musical declamation" and of his being "destined for the opera."

In his autobiography of 1966 Thomson had this to say about his "Susie Asado" setting:

> My hope in putting Gertrude Stein to music had been to break, crack open, and solve for all time anything still waiting to be solved,

which was almost everything, about English musical declamation. My theory was that if a text is set correctly for the sound of it, the meaning will take care of itself. And the Stein texts, for prosodizing in this way, were manna. With meanings already abstracted, or absent, or so multiplied that choice among them was impossible, there was no temptation toward tonal illustration, say of birdie babbling by the brook or heavy heavy hangs my heart. You could make a setting for sound and syntax only, then add, if needed, an accompaniment equally functional. I had no sooner put to music after this recipe one short Stein text than I knew I had opened a door. I had never had any doubts about Stein's poetry; from then on I had none about my ability to handle it in music.

In 1976 he rather overstated his case by remarking on the occasion of a delayed and taped broadcast of *Byron's* premiere, "Nobody else was doing anything about [setting English properly], so I did." There have been some other composers who have set English extremely well in our time, but nobody else has so frequently thought, spoken, and written about it. And no other composer similarly interested and consciously so well-versed in the subject has been also so powerful a critic, able to do something about the improvement of singers' diction, without which the best word-setting will remain garbled.

In fact, his numerous written comments on declamation have to be searched for in his *Herald Tribune* reviews and Sunday articles and in his two other books. Some of his thoughts on the subject were organized into the lecture "Words and Music," which he has given widely. Though he has been offered publication, he has declined on the grounds that the royalties would never add up to the lecture fees and that, anyway, he hasn't wanted to fix the content. At least twice he was offered publication contracts for a book on the subject. One regrets that he did not accept, for we might now have at least *one* book on the subject of English declamation and prosody from the musician's rare point of view.

But his widely dispersed written comments and his own practice (and my long-treasured notes on his lecture) provide the gist of the book, for which he has spent a lifetime providing the musical examples. Were he to write it, somewhere near the beginning one would surely find the proposition that although European languages do not make use of quantitative verse (16th century *vers mesurés* and 17th-century Campion are late examples), all poetry (and prose) is quantified when set to music—at least when composers do more than add pitches to words conversationally paced. The composer must therefore know which vowels may and may not be extended without losing comprehensibility and which should not be too much diminished in length. He must realize that sung vowels are often modified, where and why; that diphthongs are tricky to handle, neutralized vowels trickier still, that the kinds of consonants surrounding the vowel determine in part its extensibility, its color, and its feasibility in the upper range.

At least a chapter would be given over to matters of handling stressed syllables. An early paragraph would state that of all European languages English is the most dependent on tonic accent for its meaning, that correct musical accentuation is correspondingly crucial to comprehensibility. The implications of this characteristic of the English language would be pursued at length, with examples of musical formations deriving from the differing personalities of French (especially), Italian, and German, and maybe others. The varied meanings attached to "How do you do?" as different words are stressed would be adduced, with an invitation to the reader to reproduce the effect of the question in translation to other languages. What are taken to be Purcell's idiosyncracies and the growth of jazz in this country (and speculation of why not elsewhere) would be shown to derive from the fact (largely un-noticed by others) that only in English do we find the coincidence of two-syllable words with initially stressed "short" vowels followed by unstressed "long" vowels, resulting, naturally and necessarily, in verbal and therefore musical syncopation. Two examples are: "Tit willow, tit willow" and "Coming Through the Rye."

Once the local quantitative and stress problems have been covered, they would have to be set in their larger verbal and musical contexts. The composer would be advised to hang on to the few extendable vowels he can find (when the context permits) and to put his articles, conjunctions, and prepositions, together with their piddling vowels, tidily to one side. The tempo of English, compared to other languages; the vowels proper to high notes (male and female) and to low; questions of *tessitura*, particularily as related to the *cantilena* and *parlando* styles; syllabic and melismatic settings, the vexed problems of *Sprechstimme* in German and in its imported varieties, and if and when and how to change to and from speech to song; ah, what a myriad of matters to be discussed, some for the first time—not even to mention those deriving from voice and orchestra in combination!

This adumbration is but an educated guess at the partial contents of *Words and Music*, the book not yet, but perhaps yet to be written by Thomson. It would be more authentic and better written than anybody else's without much question. That it would be less idiosyncratic than have been his opinions and compositions would derive from the nature of the subject matter.

In his libretto-choices and operatic music Thomson has avoided those emotional entanglements—verbal, dramatic, musical—that have enticed other composers (and audiences) to the genre. Not for him the extremes of religious or carnal passion, the energies of adultery, envy, or hate, the quiet of shared confidences, introspection or nostalgia—and never the pleasures of the forbidden: sticky sentiment or crude gesture. One does not mention these matters to accuse him of a narrowness of expression in his operas. His means are perfectly adapted to his ends. It is, rather, to suggest that the more intensely composers indulge their passions operatically, the greater and more varied will be their demands on voices. It is precisely the most indulgent who have the most need to study declamation and who would be the least likely to seek it in the music or a book by Thomson, unfortunately.

Because it had been Virgil's idea that I write about his three operas, I was nonplussed concerning *Lord Byron*: how to express my disappointment with it as a whole without giving offense—not that he and his other composer-friends did not often anger one another with what they said in print. Because I was interested in his new work, I attended several of the late rehearsals at the Juilliard School in April 1972. Virgil no longer behaved as he had in Brander Mattheas 25 years earlier. Now, embittered and ill-tempered by his ambiguous exit from the Met, deprived of his chosen designer and choreographer, he took advantage of his position as Artistic Director to upstage and argue with his old friend John Houseman, the stage director, and, in the presence of the orchestra, to belittle its conductor, Gerhard Samuel—who had overlapped with me at Eastman.

As a stage piece, *Lord Byron* seemed to have been buried in the Juilliard School in 1972. There were concert performances of it in 1985 and 1991. A review in the *Boston Review* by Anthony Tommasini of the latter performance, in New Hampshire, I read hastily and then, reflexively, thought I'd seen my name. Rereading, I was astounded to learn that Virgil had decided that *Lord Byron* was too long and ". . . got composer Jack Beeson to make drastic cuts, thinking the job needed a distanced perspective."

This misinformation led me to the telephone, to Information, and to Tommasini himself. In answer to my puzzlement he said that he was guiltless, that he had long wanted to "pick my brains about Virgil" and the rehearsals and premiere of *The Mother*, and that he would come to New York to tape my memories and to explain the *Byron* matter. He soon appeared at our apartment and said that he had been taping innumerable interviews with Virgil in preparation for a biography. (His *Virgil Thomson, Composer on the Aisle*, New Haven, Norton, was published in 1997). On one of the tapes was the longer version of what Virgil had said about my cutting his opera. I replied that it was nice to be so misremembered, that I had never been asked by him to do any such thing, and added—with some heat—that I wouldn't have done it for him or any other composer. Virgil was by this time in his nineties and we decided that his memory must already have been failing when he spoke about *Byron.*

Tommasini taped my lengthy account of the premiere of *The Mother of Us All* and then we chatted amiably about new operas and their critics. He went on a bit about my *Lizzie Borden* and I mentioned that a well-known music critic in two publications had mentioned my serial procedures in *Borden,* in which there's not a shred of serialism. As though personally offended, he asked to see my *Lizzie* scrapbooks. "Oh, him!" he exclaimed when he saw the critic's name.

In Virgil's *Aeneid* I mentioned that Thomson had twice been invited by publishers to write a book about the setting of English to music. The first offer had been initiated by me; the second led to the following exchange of letters.

VIRGIL THOMSON   222 WEST 23rd STREET
                                  NEW YORK 11, N.Y.

February 13, 1978

Dear Jack,

Nice piece in *Parnassus,* for which I thank you.

About the text or handbook for words and music, why don't we write it together? And to prepare for that, we might even give a course together. That would enable us to organize the material, simplify the problems, and find examples for everything. We might even use a modified version of the "case" method for deriving principles.

Anyway, you might phone and meet with me for discussing all this if you find it feasible.

Everbest,

Virgil

Jack Beeson, Esquire
445 Riverside Drive
New York, New York 10027

tal

Columbia University in the City of New York / *New York, N.Y. 10027*

DEPARTMENT OF MUSIC   Dodge

February 25, 1978

Dear Virgil,

I enjoyed your letter and your offer. In face, it's a second offer, this time made directly. You may remember that quite some years ago a lady with a thin German accent called you, suggesting a book on words and music for her publishing house. Which one it was I don't remember, but I'd said no, and then suggested a few possibilities, first and foremost you. You said no—for reasons outlined in my article—but suggested to her that you might do one in collaboration with me if I were willing. I was, but couldn't at the time.

Well, it's still an intriguing idea, mine, I mean, that you should write it. Why don't you? I can think of a number of reasons I think it would make sense for you to do so these days, quite apart from the reasons that were always in force.

As for the collaboration, that would be engaging, but I'm in the middle of making a vocal score of a new one-act chamber opera (not at all a big job, one would think, but more troublesome than any other I've made) and can't even think of it now. And I'm supposed to be writing next a long-promised flute concerto for my old girl-friend flutist in the BSO. I don't know if I shall; only flutists think there is *that* much variety in their instrument.

Anyhow, we might talk about it after I've delivered the 90-100 pages of piano score.

The course idea is intriguing. Have you thought about drawing together all your *written* ideas on the subject? As I think I wrote, they're hard to find and put together. You have those first-rate indexes now. Has anyone a tape of your lecture? If not, why don't you invite someone in and deliver the lecture to an audience of the tape recorder operator, at least?

Cherrily,
yrs,
in waiting,
Jack

Jack Beeson
404 Riverside Drive
NY, NY 10025

VIRGIL THOMSON   222 WEST 23rd STREET
                     NEW YORK 11, N.Y.

                                    March 6, 1978

Dear Jack,

Thanks for detailed answer.

The reason for giving a course would be to find more examples (in both old & new English-language music) and to give answers to all sorts of questions that bright students might raise.

A half-course would be enough, and I think it should be a composition seminar limited to, say, 10 students. 2 hours once a week.

I wonder if, being busy yourself, you might know somebody prepared to take it on with me. Alone I fear the library work and my lack of teaching routines.

The main lecture is already typed out, but I think of a book as containing lots more material—how to project the meaningful syllables for instance, how to distort for passionate statement, to go into and out of patter, to syncopate the line for verbal clarity, all sorts of devices that we know and they don't. Also, constant references to methods that fit German or French or Italian but not English.

It's not really a job to take on casually.

                              Everbest,

                              Virgil

Jack Beeson, Esquire
404 Riverside Drive
New York, New York 10025

tal

At the time of this correspondence I had long since been devoting several sessions of my graduate seminars in composition to a discussion of all types of voices and to what they can and cannot do. We then considered those prosodical and other matters I listed toward the close of *Virgil's Aeneid* that I expected a words-and-music book by Thomson to include. When I retired from Columbia in 1988 I became a charter member of The Society of Senior Scholars, the Society of Elderly Professors, as Nora and I call it. As a member I was enabled for quite some years to offer biennially exactly the kind of "course" that Virgil outlined in his second letter to me. In that seminar for graduate composition students there was now time to consider all those problems in detail, with examples culled from the past and from the vocal works they were writing. By this time, the late eighties, Virgil was finally writing, without me, his words-and-music book, a compilation, with additions, of his earlier writings on the subject, while I was giving the "course," as he called it, without him.

During the summer of 1989 Nora and I heard that Virgil was failing rapidly and we paid him a brief visit. He was slouched on his favored couch, his paunch resembling an advanced state of pregnancy. His attendant, Jay, hovered helpfully. Virgil was his old self, or, rather, himself, but very old, still acerbic and funny. He constantly fiddled with the hearing-aid control perched on his belly; when he was silent it occurred to me that he was tuning in and out some program on what was really a small radio. He was alert enough to tell me that he had finished his words-and-music book and that he would send me a copy. Virgil died on September 30, 1989, a month before his 93rd birthday. The book arrived a few days after his death. I noted that he had very sensibly changed the order of the words of the earlier title to *Music and Words, a Composer's View*. (New Haven, Yale University Press, 1989). Written perhaps a little too late in his life, it is nevertheless by far the best book on the subject of setting English to music, only in part because it's the only book on the subject.

*   *   *   *   *   *

Chapter 5

Living Miscellaneously
(1945-1948)

New Year's Eve remains the time of celebration it always has been, but the beginning of the new year has lost much of its earlier meaning. For those in business the beginnings of their fiscal years are more meaningful. For students, teachers and professors the holidays are the pause between semesters; the academic year begins in September and ends in May or June and goes by the double name of 1939-40, 2004-5, or whatever. Ex-students soon grow out of this bifurcation, but teachers and professors measure out their lives in academic years, the only use of the word academic these days that is nor completely pejorative.

To apply the above observations to the welter of musical and operatic activities that took place from the time of my arrival in New York, early October 1944, through the Stein/Thomson performances in May 1947 were three academic years that had flown by. In this newly-written prose and in the reprinted articles there have been occasional references to the past and numerous forays into the future. These are present, not so much because of my Shandean tendencies—for which I make no apologies—as because I have wished to follow a topic such as my conducting from its beginning to its end, or a person such as Virgil Thomson from out meeting until his death.

The reader may remember the breakfast of Otto Luening and me at the Chock Full of Nuts in the middle of my first year and my comment that it led to "my job at Columbia." So it did, at first by way of the Opera Workshop and the productions, the rehearsals for which led me constantly to the Music Department. There I often ran into Moore, Lang, and made the acquaintance of the other faculty members. But the offer that I join them was made under more exotic circumstances than the Chock Full.

To recover from the exhausting rehearsals and five performances of Normand Lockwood's *The Scarecrow* in May 1945, Douglas invited its composer, Otto, and me to the Moore country house on Peconic Bay, way out east on Long Island. Douglas added, to me, "If I can get permission. Emily strenuously disapproves." His wife, Emily, was not invited to this stag event; Sylvester, their servant, had to remain in town to look after her needs; she could not imagine four men managing a weekend on their own. I had come to know Emily and Sylvester well during the first year, for I was several times in the Moore apartment, twice on musical evenings. During one of them Otto accompanied his wife, Ethel, in his and others' songs; on another I played some of my piano music. The once beautiful Emily, elfin and alert and always ailing, had strong opinions and usually had her way with the devoted Douglas. Sylvester I had seen but not met on my first day in New York when Peter Mennin had called at the Moore apartment seeking the younger daughter Sarah. On these musical evenings Sylvester served drinks and both looked and acted like a more elegant version of Elmer Cloyd, who had lived with his wife Emma with us in Muncie. Sylvester was chief cook and bottle washer and clearly indispensable to Emily during the frequent absences of Douglas.

Having finally received permission to absent myself for the weekend, Douglas drove the three of us to Salt Meadow, near Cutchogue. I reveled in the comfortable, capacious house, the oak grove around it, and my first swim over in buoyant salt water. The weekend was also the first time I'd ever spent in the company of grown-up composers. Otto and Douglas, separately or together, seemed to be members of every American composers' organization, and board and/or jury members of every organization aiding composers. They spoke openly of the musical politics and personalities involved. I learned that Henry Cowell, whom I'd met at Eastman, had been imprisoned on Alcatraz for a sexual offence; both had played small parts in his release from prison.

There was a good deal of drinking before and after meals. I resolved never again to permit any member of the Moore clan—today sadly diminished in number—to pour my one drink a day. Otto and Normand collaborated in telling one drinking story:

> O.L. You remember that concert at Yaddo?
> N.L. Yes, I certainly do!
> O.L. At intermission we went to the bar and then down the hill. Then I asked what had happened to your drink.
> N.L. Well, yes . . . at first I was puzzled, for I'd not yet even sipped it. Then I remembered that I'd put it in my jacket pocket, as I often do. But I tipped it over getting it out. I was so smelly and wet I had to leave.

In some quieter time Douglas took me aside and said that he and his colleagues had decided that I should be invited to join them as Assistant in Music. It could be arranged that my operatic duties—so far, for the one semester, mostly unpaid—would be the bulk of my assignment, but there might be a course or two in addition. The salary was very small, but he would see to it that I be granted the Seidl Fellowship in addition. He than added, with some embarrassment, that few of the faculty had had a conservatory education and that nobody had been trained at Eastman. Because Bill Mitchell, the theory-man, and the musicologist Paul Lang had been feuding for years with their Eastman counterparts, it was thought I should be . . . well . . . indoctrinated in Columbia ways. Would I mind auditing for a year Lang's Proseminar, taken by first-year graduate musicologists? I agreed to attend, thinking it would be interesting to be in the company of the author of *Music in Western Civilization*. I may or may not have added that I thought their idea of what a composition student at Eastman had available there was based on both prejudices and ignorance. Bergsma, Rivett, and I had elected Warren Fox's equivalent of Lang's Proseminar, in which we were assigned Lang's tome; furthermore, Fox had the quirky idea of assigning each student quite a number of pages of the proofs of Apel's *Harvard Dictionary of Music*, in which he or she was to find and report on wrong dates and errors of fact, to be checked against Warren Fox's astonishing long list. It was a research project far beyond anybody else's idea of proseminar, surely.

So it was that in the fall of the 1945-46 academic year, the *Medium* year so to speak, I took the first step up the long academic ladder. In my second year, the *Mother* year, I ascended to the second rung, Associate of Music. In the third, which turned out to be the Luening *Evangeline* year, I was promoted to Instructor, the rank at which these days most juniors begin. By the time I reached the top rung, the MacDowell Professor of Music Emeritus, in 1988, and had gone on for a while with the voice-and-prosody seminars, I could look down, and back, on half a century of teaching and administration at Columbia. There was to be one more, very much off-the-ladder, promotion at the 2002 Commencement, Doctor of Music, *honoris causa*.

In 1996 the Department of Music celebrated its centennial. By that time, though no longer teaching, I was still involved in University matters: the Ditson Fund, the related University Press publication of new American Music, the Pulitzer Prize of Music, and doing odd jobs for the Department when asked. Accordingly, enmeshed as I had been for a little more than half of the Department's past, I was asked to help plan its centennial events and to speak at the celebration luncheon. I refused, though, to write a departmental history because I didn't want to and was busily writing my ninth opera. I remembered Douglas Moore complaining bitterly about losing a composing summer, having been coerced into writing the one earlier history, in 1954, the year of the Columbia Bicentennial. In any case, the comprehensively annotated catalog of a celebratory exhibit in the Low Library rotunda by Mary Monroe was in itself an excellent illustrated centennial history, published in 2000.

As of now, Twelfth Night, 2005, the University had finally completed its year-long celebration of the 250th anniversary, 1754-2004. Such celebrations, including the Music Department's Centennial, are, of course nothing new, but have become ever more elaborate in this Advertising Age. They are always an excuse for looking back. Accordingly, the University began its celebration five years early with a long series of "Living Legacies" in the quarterly *Columbia*, each reviewing the life of a deceased important former faculty member or two or more of them contributing to some scientific or scholarly end. I was invited to contribute biographical essays on Lorenzo da Ponte, the first Professor of Italian at Columbia, and three musical figures, Edward MacDowell, Douglas Moore, and Paul Henry Lang.

The da Ponte essay, the earliest figure included in *Living Legacies*, is omitted here because its subject matter is included in *Marriages of Convenience*, see page 454, in connection with his collaboration with Mozart, The MacDowell essay is included because when I entered the Opera Workshop and then the faculty I became a part of a continuum that began with him in 1896. Though he died in 1906, he had envisaged for music at Columbia three goals that were achieved only much later: a required music course for all undergraduates, part of the core curriculum that is unique to Columbia College and which matured during my first years in the Department; a School of the Arts, which I played a part in organizing; and collaboration with a school of music, which I spent a great deal of time and effort in helping to bring about. The Moore and Lang essays offer information about the lives of two colleagues already often mentioned and who were to remain my friends until their deaths.

The third major musical figure during my Columbia years was the already often-mentioned Otto Luening. He had shepherded me into the Workshop and the Department and became my mentor thereafter in matters musical and professional. Shortly after his death in 1996, the American Academy of Arts and Letters invited me to read a commemorative tribute, which was then published in the Academy *Proceedings*. It is reprinted here because, as do the Moore and Lang essays, it attempts briefly to describe his life before we met, to limn his individuality, and his contribution to the Music Department and its students.

A thousand years ago, more *and* less, music, together with its then-related subjects astronomy, arithmetic, and geometry, formed the *quadrivium*, the part of the medieval curriculum that led to the Master of Arts. Music has had long since had no such honorable place in universities, and in the American university had no place at all until well into the nineteenth-century. When it reappeared it had lost its connections with both astronomy and mathematics. In these interplanetary days the "music of the spheres" is but a poetic image; professors of music are more likely to visit departments of anthropology, computer science, history, and language than mathematics. In fact, music departments lead somewhat sequestered lives, puzzles to administrators who try in vain to fit them into conventional patterns. Nevertheless, they are valuable public relations assets, for they train musicians who sometimes become successful performers and harbor composers who also become known to the larger public.

Edward MacDowell

In the year of Da Ponte's death, 1838, Lowell Mason, noted hymnodist and publisher of hymns, introduced music into American public schools in Boston. Almost immediately music worked itself up the academic ladder, appearing in the curricula of Midwestern and women's colleges, then in graduate schools. Joining in the trend, Yale appointed a German, Gustave Stoeckel, instructor of vocal music in 1855 and promoted him to professor in 1890. Harvard named John Knowles Paine instructor in 1862 and professor in 1875, but not without opposition: it was said that the establishment of music led the eminent historian Francis Parkman to cry out, parodying Cato the Elder, at each meeting of the Harvard Corporation, *musica delenda est* (music must be destroyed), and to vote against funding it. Both Stoeckel and Paine were composers, but it is probable that their fame as performers was more persuasive to their appointers than their compositions.

Columbia President, Seth Low, was not to be outdone by Yale and Harvard. Spurred on by a promised gift of $150,000 (nearly three million in today's dollars) for instruction in music, he sought advice from the Episcopal bishop and John Burgess, professor of political science and law. They quickly agreed that composition and the philosophy and history of music should be the subject of the new department, not the technical training more suitable to conservatories: that choice would not preclude a glee club, perhaps a student orchestra, and token instrumental study. (The dichotomy between what was thought to be proper to a university on the one hand and professional study—applied music—the other has bedeviled the study of music ever since, except in those universities that have added schools of music or have formed alliances with conservatories.)

Having seemingly so simply settled the matter of what should be taught, the committee incongruously asked two pianists, William Mason (son of Lowell) and Ignace Jan Paderewski, who should lead the department. They recommended

MacDowell, who had been composing and concretizing in Boston for eight years, making a living chiefly as a piano teacher. Their recommendation was strengthened by there having been a recent New York concert by the Boston Symphony Orchestra, during which MacDowell played his *First Concerto* and his *Indian Suite* was premiered. The concert had been rapturously received by the press and public. Two days after the Morningside campus site was dedicated on May 2, 1896, MacDowell was appointed professor of music and the Department of Music was created, shortly thereafter empowered to offer undergraduate and graduate instruction. The news was received by the musical public and the University with enthusiasm, for MacDowell was thought to be the preeminent American composer and pianist.

A brief curriculum vitae outlines how MacDowell arrived at his preeminence. Born in New York to prosperous Scotch-Irish parents, he studied the piano from the age of eight. He progressed so rapidly that at the age of sixteen his mother removed him from school and took him to Paris for advanced study. Perhaps because of a misunderstanding about the age limit for entrance to the conservatory, at about this time his birth date was changed from 1860 to 1861. A memorial plaque at Columbia has the later date case in bronze; the correct date was established 110 years later. (Draft-age men have discovered since how difficult it can be to reestablish a birth date.)

In Paris he began to compose and studied piano and theory assiduously. He had sketched for years, and a surreptitious caricature of one of his teachers so impressed the subject that he was offered three years of instruction in painting by an eminent École des Beaus-Arts faculty member. (MacDowell was later often to design the covers of his published books.) After a period of teenage indecision, inhibited by his weak spoken French and dissatisfaction with some of the instruction (shared by his classmate Debussy), mother and son left for Germany, the goal of almost every young composer of the time.

Settled down alone in Frankfort, MacDowell quickly made a strong impression as pianist and composer on the much sought-after Joachim Raff, who arranged for him to play his music for Franz Liszt. Liszt was so impressed by the young man's first piano concerto that he accepted its dedication and arranged for MacDowell's first publications. With such support, his music soon became widely known in Europe and was often performed in the U.S. by the virtuosa Teresa Carreño. Edward Grieg, with whom and with whose music MacDowell had much in common, was later pleased to become the dedicatee of two piano sonatas. After this European sojourn, MacDowell and his wife—at 24 he had married one of his American students—left for Boston in 1888, where they were to remain for the eight years before he left for Columbia.

The correspondence between President Low and the new professor, before as well as after his appointment, is fascinating. MacDowell, in his middle thirties, was both ignorant of and unencumbered by university ways. He outlined courses for undergraduate and graduate study intended for music specialists. He also designed courses for the general liberal arts student and argued for similar courses in the fine arts: "Our doctors, lawyers, literary and scientific men know but little of the arts except what comes to them through . . . social intercourse: (Courses in music and find arts became part of the Core Curriculum half a century later.) He and Low agreed that Columbia should establish a School of the Arts, to include music, painting, and sculpture—and Low added architecture. (A building to house these, and theatre arts, was promised in 1954 and not built. Columbia's School of the Arts, with theatre arts but not architecture, came into existence in 1965.) They agreed that Columbia should also establish a school of music or affiliate with one. (The college formed an attachment to the Juilliard School in 1989.)

Had MacDowell been better acquainted with the universities of his time, he would not so wholly have committed his boundless energy, imagination, and teaching abilities to such ambitious plans. He had, indeed, accepted the appointment with qualms: he suspected—correctly—that his performing and composing career would be relegated to summer, spent on the large farm his wife had just purchased in Peterboro, New Hampshire. He could willingly give up the concert career: though he enjoyed performing his own works, he suffered from stage fright and disliked playing conventional recitals and concerti. He had earlier given up concertizing for composing, which he considered his reason for existing.

During the eight years at Columbia, he wrote (mostly in the first four years) two excellent piano sonatas and short piano pieces, some songs to his own texts, as well as numerous choruses for the glee club and commencement fanfares. Clearly there was not the time necessary to conceive and carry out any more substantial orchestra works.

It must be conceded that MacDowell, the good citizen, took the time peripherally to "center the arts" elsewhere, in Jacques Barzun's phase of 1954. As befitted his reputation, he was the first composer nominated for membership in the National Institute of Arts and Letters (1898) and then was instrumental in organizing the interrelated American Academy of Arts and Letters. He justified his efforts on behalf of the fledgling American Academy in Rome: "For years it has been my dream that the arts of painting, sculpture, and music should come into such contact that each and all should gain from their mutual companionship. . . ."

With the advantage of hindsight we know that he had but four post-Columbia years to live, some of them clouded with mental illness. We cannot know what other important mature works he might have written at the height of his powers between the ages of 36 and 44 had he not accepted the professorship. Was it a "total mistake" as one of his early biographers wrote?

Having devised the curriculum. MacDowell proceeded for more that two years to teach all the classes. He was then given an assistant, and the faculty was later modestly increased as the curriculum enlarged and students flocked to his classes. Among them were Upton Sinclair and John Erskine, who wrote at length in reminiscences about the enduring impression their teacher had made as a person and musician.

It is painful to recount even briefly, the dramatic falling out that took place in MacDowell's eighth and final year (1903-4). After President Low resigned to run for mayor of New York City, Nicholas Murray Butler was appointed. He had his own ideas about education in the arts, and when MacDowell returned from a sabbatical he found his music offerings—and those of fine arts—intermingled with the courses listed in the bulletin of Teachers College. Butler was unresponsive to his strong objections to this and other matters. MacDowell agreed to a frank "off-the-record" interview with *Spectator* reporters: within a few days six newspapers entered the fray. Both MacDowell and Butler published letters in *The New York Times* and elsewhere. MacDowell resigned. The Trustees, appalled, accepted his letter of resignation (as of June 30, 1904) with a rebuke for his offenses against propriety.

During this unpleasantness, MacDowell sometimes seemed to lack his usual vivacity and resilience. Then, over the next two years, he lost his robust health, and finally his mind. The death certificate state "Paresis (Dementia Paralytica)." Had his physician dared to write what was very likely tertiary syphilis, Columbia would have been spared the often-repeated accusation that it had been largely responsible for MacDowell's "depression," "nervous exhaustion," "brain fever," and death.

To aid the two MacDowells financially during his illness and to promote his music, at least three organizations were formed. The MacDowell Fund in New York included among its 400 members all the financial and artistic leaders of the city, among them Seth Low. MacDowell Clubs were established in 66 cities, and contributions were received from England and the continent.

Even in his late moments of lucidity MacDowell often spoke of centering the arts on the New Hampshire farm. With the aid of the accumulating funds, the Edward MacDowell Association was formed to administer the property as the MacDowell Colony, a haven for the undisturbed work of composers, writers, painters, and sculptors. Months before his death there were two colonists in residence. Since then residencies have been enjoyed by more that 4,500 individuals—an enduring legacy of a farsighted man.

Douglas Moore

The North Fork of Long Island resembles the upper tail fin of a fish whose head is Brooklyn and Queens. Flat, fertile, and embayed, to the north are Long Island Sound and Connecticut—to the south, Peconic Bay. For 250 years immigrants from New England and their descendants sailed across the Sound rather than trekking overland to distant New York City. Even Walt Whitman's central Long Island was far "up-island" (that is, upwind), though he taught school for a while on the North Fork, living at a crossroads known thereafter as Sodom's Corner

In the first 1640 boatload of settlers from New Haven was Thomas Moore, a teacher. His descendants were farmers and tradesmen. Douglas Moore (1893-1969) '63HON, C.U., relished repeating the comment of a local historian who claimed that the Moores never had amounted to much because they had been too addicted to music and sex. But Douglas's father amounted to a great deal: the first to leave North Fork for the city, he founded the *Ladies' World* magazine, lived in a Stanford White house in Brooklyn, and built a shingle-style villa on Peconic Bay.

The father went along with his son's early passion for music because there were two much older brothers whom he expected to take over the magazine (later sold to Hearst). Given these comfortable circumstances, Douglas went off to prep school, Hotchkiss, where he made many friends, among them Archibald MacLeish ("Archie") '54HON, C.U., with whom he was later to collaborate, and who—much later—was to officiate at the Columbia memorial for his old friend in 1969.

Yale was proper after Hotchkiss in those days and there Moore earned two degrees, the second in music. Going to New Haven was also symbolic, for it was from there that Thomas Moore had left nearly three centuries earlier.

Douglas Stuart Moore is remembered today not only for his 36 years at Columbia—he shaped the music department as chairman from 1940 to 1962 into what it largely still is today—but also as the founder and tireless supporter of several organizations that aid composers. The wider musical public knows him as a composer of operas, particularly *The Ballad of Baby Doe* and *The Devil and Daniel Webster*. It is always written of Moore that his seven operas are based on American subjects. And so they are, as are his several other theater pieces, two films, and even much instrumental music. But they are more specifically engendered: the subject matter is intimately related to his birthplace, Cutchogue, and its surrounding farmland, and to a long life of summers spent in his father's villa, Quawk's Nest, then next door in his own smaller shingled house, Salt Meadow. Almost all of his music was composed in a secluded studio overlooking a tidal inlet.

It is true that since Beethoven composers usually have chosen subjects for their operas, whether consciously or unconsciously, that are close to their preoccupations, Moore is a prime example. Most of his opera libretti deal with strong, protective husbands, often close to the earth—in *The Ballad of Baby Doe*, the powerful Horace Tabor literally digs for silver—and loving, often ailing, wives. In the above-mentioned operas there are two strong wives: one is ailing in her last scene; the other, Baby Doe, is indomitable, even as she freezes to death. In *Devil and Daniel Webster*, the husband, a farmer, tries to better his family's lot by making a pact with the devil; he is supported loyally by his wife. The farmer-lawyer, Daniel Webster, wins his client's case against the devil by converting a jury of the worst blackguards in American history. *Giants in the Earth* (Pulitzer Prize, 1951), and *Carry Nation* carry on this Moore-ish tradition, although in the latter the traits switch genders: Carry chops up bars with a hatchet and her husband succumbs to alcoholism. Moore's one transatlantic foray, based on James's *The Wings of the Dove*, differs from the above in its English setting, but the heroine is mortally ill; and Moore knew about Americans abroad, for he lived among them for three years in France during the twenties.

Given the above relationships of life-as-opera and opera-as-life, it may be unnecessary to mention that Moore enjoyed a large vegetable garden near his studio and that his wife was beset with lingering, overlapping illnesses during their long marriage. But many singers who have impersonated the four gossips in *Baby Doe* would be surprised that the models for their roles—Sarah, Mary, Emily, and Effie—were Douglas's two daughters, wife, and sister-in-law. Moore's intimate collaborations with his librettists permitted these and other such semi-private references.

From his earliest years he had the ability to write catchy, humorous songs. At Yale-Harvard games his "Goodnight, Harvard" is still bellowed. John Kander, who once introduced himself as Moore's illegitimate son—and this writer as Moore's legitimate son—can be talked into performing "Naomi, My Restaurant Queen" and others of Moore's Yale and World War II navy songs.

His ability to write pop songs and later a dozen "art songs" had something, but not much, to do with composing operas and hardly anything to do with his writing a number of orchestral works and a decent amount of chamber music. That necessary craft, developed in a personal way, he was slow in developing.

He revered his main composition teacher at Yale, but later had to unlearn much else learned there. Mustered out of the Navy in 1919 in Paris, he stayed on to join those of his contemporaries who were arriving to study with the already fabled Nadia Boulanger. She and Moore did not get on: she was becoming accustomed to Americans with limited craft, but she was not sympathetic to what he wanted to write and he was not enamored of the composers she favored. He decamped to the Schola Cantorum to study composition with Vincent D'Indy and organ with Tournemire. D'Indy was a profound influence in part because he was a composer of operas and sometimes based instrumental works on popular and folk melodies. One sometimes catches whiffs of his harmonic progressions even in Moore's later works.

Leaving Paris for home, Moore accepted the position of curator of music and organist at the Cleveland Museum. He took advantage of the presence at the Cleveland Institute of the Swiss composer Ernest Bloch for further study. On the side he took several acting roles in the Cleveland Playhouse, then it its heyday. His passion for the theater had been thwarted at Yale, where that Hoosier upperclassman, Cole Porter, was favored as lyricist and show-composer. (Later Moore was to provide incidental music for two Shakespearean plays on Broadway; later still he added a stage to the huge living room at Salt Meadow, suitable for charades and family theatricals, the first of which he had written and composed at about the age of seven.)

In 1926 he was offered a teaching post at Columbia, but through the back door at Barnard College, so to speak, a subterfuge used occasionally by Columbia to acquire composers. He became one of the five faculty members of the Barnard-Columbia music department. There were but two classrooms, a number of books, scores, and pianola rolls, and no librarian. It was said that the shorter professors used Bach Gesellschaft volumes as chair-heighteners. Moore climbed the academic ladder rapidly and succeeded Daniel Gregory Mason as chairman in 1940. (Mason, by the way, was the grandson and nephew respectively of the two Masons earlier mentioned.) In that year Yale attempted its by-then well-known alumnus with a deanship. President Butler countered by alerting Moore to an expected large legacy "for the aid and encouragement of musicians," composers particularly, not to be used for educational purposes. Moore turned down the Yale offer and then, after the will was probated, engineered the resignations of the self-interested members of the advisory committee of the Alice M. Ditson Fund and their replacement by others more likely to carry out the implications of the will.

In this maneuver, he showed two qualities that served him well both at Columbia and in the numerous other organizations he served and often led—and sometimes had helped to establish: great charm and velvet-gloved toughness. He sweet-talked Butler into dismissing a professor he thought poised to set up a rival music department. When John D. Rockefeller, Jr. invited Butler and Moore to move the music department to Lincoln Center, then in the planning stage, Moore refused on the grounds that Music Humanities and other liberal arts students couldn't be expected to attend classes by subway. It was an action MacDowell would have approved. When I told William Schuman, president of the Juilliard School, that his school had been second choice, he was aghast. So was Rockefeller.

In addition to being charming and tough, Moore was also thoroughly knowledgeable about and in love with music. Accordingly he was a Great Teacher (the award of 1960), a fair-minded critic and music juror, and the author of two books intended for Music Humanities students and other laymen. In his day, chairmen were appointed "at the pleasure of the Trustees," and he pleased them for 22 years until his retirement in 1962. By that time he had accomplished much of what MacDowell had envisaged in 1896.

Moore was a more fervent spokesman for the music of others than he was for his own because, I think, of a certain musical modesty that bordered on insecurity. His early interest in Americana was bolstered by the strong encouragement of Vachel Lindsay. Later he was to move amiably among sophisticated composers of all kinds, some of whom, as usual, looked askance at one who insisted on writing operas and may not have recognized in his conservative music the "modesty, grace, and sound construction" noted by Virgil Thomson '78HON, C.U.

He was also a better protector of other composers' rights than of his own. He neglected to ask formally for the operatic rights to his friend Philip Barry's play *White Wings*; heirs and lawyers held up its premiere for fifteen years. When his friend Stephen Vincent Benét suggested his short story *The Devil and Daniel Webster* as an opera subject, the two worked out the libretto together. The dramaturgy was chiefly the composer's. Foolishly, there was no written agreement. Benét published the almost unchanged libretto as a play that was to be performed hundreds of times and then filmed—starring Walter Huston and with a score by another composer—all without credit and royalties to Moore.

When such unpleasantness occurred or an unkind review was let into the house, Moore was never outwardly angry. He simply adopted, as his allusively literary family called it, his Eeyore manner.

Paul Henry Lang

Sometime in 1932 an acquaintance of Moore insisted that he meet Paul Henry Lang, a tall, dark and handsome Hungarian in his early thirties then teaching at Wells College. Moore invited him to lunch at the Faculty Club. According to Moore's account it was a long, animated lunch hour. One can assume that these two good, digressive talkers covered their separate and common interests and that Moore was piecing together in his head the outlines of Lang's curriculum vitae: born in 1901; studied music at the Budapest Academy with Zoltán Kodály—and Béla Bartók '40HON as his adviser; orchestral bassoonist and vocal coach at the Opera (Moore would have perked up at the mention of coachee, Marie Jeritza, one of his favorite sopranos at the Metropolitan Opera); to Germany to study musicology, history, and literature; to Paris for more of the same; wrote a dissertation there, but could not meet the requirement of its publication because his father had lost money under the Horthy regime; emigrated to the U.S.; another dissertation at Cornell on the literary history of French opera (Moore would have enjoyed pointing out that Otto Kinkeldey, the musicologist at Cornell, had been a MacDowell student at Columbia); taught at Vassar and Wellesley; and—oh, yes!—while in Paris had been on an Olympic rowing team.

Then, according to Moore's recollection, the two walked toward Broadway until they arrived outside Journalism (which then housed Music) and they went their separate ways. On a sudden impulse he turned, shouted to Lang to wait, ran after him, and asked, "Would you like to teach at Columbia?" When he said, "Yes, of course," Moore went immediately to Mr. Mason (under his chairmanship, first names were not commonly used) and shared with him his plan to add a musicologist to the staff. Mason demurred: there was no need, for there was already a year of music history and music literature courses, symphony and chamber music; besides, there was no money for another salary. (The department had been somewhat somnolent since MacDowell had left; his successor had added little and subtracted some; his successor, Mason, occasionally requested no increase in the annual budget and refused to answer correspondence concerning summer session.)

Although Moore was too much the gentleman to tell me so, it may be that Mason was also put off by Lang's name (then spelled Láng, with an accent). His writings include encoded anti-Semitism. When I asked Lang toward the end of his life if he were Jewish, he answered, "Well, no, I'm a Catholic, though I don't often go to mass. In the thirties there was an influx of Central European refugee musicologists and I was naturally thought to be one of them, though I'd been here for a decade." That he was telling the truth—if anyone still cares—was already proved at his christening. Paul Maria Henry Ferdinand László Láng. Whatever the objections of Mason, Moore went to the Carnegie Foundation and arranged for a grant to cover the first two years of Lang's salary.

Lang's mentor at Cornell, Kinkeldey, was the first professor of musicology in the U.S. Lang immediately began to teach the subject at Columbia—he was among the first in the U.S. to do so—though he was not recognized with the same title until 1941.

Laymen see the word *musicology* most often in CD booklets. The discipline was a mid-nineteenth century German and Australian conflation of all studies in music except composition and performance. It made its way here by way of returning Americans who had done their graduate study abroad (as had Kinkeldey) or by way of immigrants (such as Lang). For a while, there were turf battles with the reigning composers. Once it was established, there were other turf battles as the all-too-encompassing discipline divided into specialties: historical musicology, ethnomusicology, the speculative aspects of theory and aesthetics, and (as of today) of whatnot. By the time these later battles were joined, Lang's position had become so impregnable that he rarely seemed embattled. In any case, he was tolerant, and when he had to give ground, he could take pleasure in his decided streak of masochism.

That high ground he achieved in part (with the eventual collaboration of at least three colleagues at the time) by training innumerable graduate students who were then to find important far-flung teaching positions.

In addition, the restless, energetic, and ambitious Lang became the editor of *The Musical Quarterly* in 1945 and remained so until 1973. He could not accomplish the impossible: make a profit from a learned journal for its publisher, G. Schirmer. But he was proud never to have a budget deficit.

When Virgil Thomson unexpectedly gave up his post as chief music critic on the high-minded *Herald Tribune*, its owners realized that no second Virgil Thomson existed and turned to a professor who wrote fluently and interestingly and who was happily married with four children. For almost ten years (1954-63), Lang enjoyed covering concerts and opera and writing Sunday articles (both later the substance of published books). In those days, review copy had to be submitted for the next day's morning edition—and for Lang there was a long commute home.

These non-university activities—not to speak of service on behalf of musicologists and learned societies and assembling a groundbreaking series of books on music for the publisher W.W. Norton—exacted a price that his students and colleagues were paying. He might have disregarded that debt with his usual insouciance, but he was deeply offended when the University's president at important functions introduced him as the chief critic of the *Trib*. When he decided to quit his post, the *Trib's* owners offered to add the whole of his Columbia salary to his critic's salary if he would remain. He resigned. He was not the only one of my seniors to say, ruefully, that universities are insecure in judging qualities of their professors: therefore, reputations within the university are made on the basis of outside accomplishments.

Lang once confided that he preferred cabinetmaking to practicing music history, "particularly now that steam-shovel musicology has become the thing." True, he was not always to be believed, but his favorite phrase, *se non è vero, è ben trovato* (if it's not true, it's nicely invented) was disarming. The Langs changed houses often and in each there was something to be improved. One of the more impressive was a converted early poured concrete structure built by Horace Greeley. In it was a study that could be compared only to the library of an English country house. It was full of his handiwork, including double-height bookcases. In the basement of each house were innumerable bottles of identified hardware, like three-by-five cards awaiting some new scholarly undertaking.

My first acquaintance with Lang was by way of reading his *Music in Western Civilization* as a student at the Eastman School of Music shortly after its 1941 publication. I had never read anything like it, nor have I since. It read like a 1,000-page essay, placing music in the context of the other arts, philosophy, and history; it was at once magisterial and intimate. I was disturbed, though, by the regretful tone that suffused his decision of the twentieth-century musical scene— which I was preparing t o enter.

When I met Lang himself in the fall of 1944, he was delighted that I had come to New York City to study with his friend Bartók. In friendly fashion he cautioned, "Don't put any currency in Bartók's hand at the end of a lesson: some Hungarians are uncomfortable with money and he has no talent at all for making it." . . .

. . . [A year later I attended] Lang's Proseminar in Musicology. It was exhilarating to experience his book brought to life: he improved brilliantly on themes from an overflowing mind. There was inventive speculations that could be followed by alert students. That he loved the sound of music was obvious when he played recordings, even when he fumbled at the keyboard. He had a habit of suddenly asking difficult questions. When nobody could answer, he would call on me (or on William Bergsma, an Eastman composer friend who occasionally audited for the fun of it). I remember one such exchange: "What are the dates of Giovanni Pergolesi?" When nobody knew, he called on me. "1710-36," I answered. (What 24 year-old composer would not remember the dates of a composer who had written so well and so much in 26 years?) There was then yet another opportunity to castigate his students for not spending enough time reading and listening and for not living up, even, to schools-of-music standards.

Late in life he was to write the impressive *George Frederic Handel* and to look forward to preparing a new edition of *Music in Western Civilization*. Much later, deteriorating eyesight permitted him only to add an occasional essay and many record reviews to the several hundred he had already amassed.

In 1997, six years after his death, his 1941 magnum opus was reprinted unaltered. The perspicacious foreword by Leon Botstein includes the following tribute: "The passage of time has not diminished its virtuosity and stature as a tour de force . . . [It] would be a good place to begin the debate that increasingly occupies scholars and listeners alike concerning the future of the classical and serious music tradition in the United States and Europe."

- - - - - - - - - -

From *Proceedings*: 2nd Series – number forty-seven, 1996[*]
OTTO LUENING
1900-1996

I am not certain whether Otto Luening ever followed my suggestion that he read Laurence Sterne's *Tristram Shandy*. If he did, he must have enjoyed the numerous English-Latin puns, for Otto was a discriminating and outrageous punster, often straddling English and German. Sterne and Luening were also both digressionists; but mostly he would have approved Tristram's father's conviction that the name given to a child determines its future.

Luening's middle name, Clarence, is to be found only in biographical dictionaries. *He* rarely used it, perhaps because he found it not worth living down to and because he was reacting to the habit of composers of his father's generation of flaunting three names: John Alden Carpenter, David Stanley Smith, and Daniel Gregory Mason, to name but three of them. Whether he believed that his first name symbolized his life—as Sterne would have insisted it must—I don't know, but I do know that he enjoyed the implications of his palindromic name OTTO. The name backwards evoked the musical traditions of the past that he revered; frontwards it promised new and better tines; his view of the future was rosy, he liked to insist, because Midwesterners such as he were not only more down-to-earth-sensible, but also more optimistic than others, particularly New Yorkers. Small wonder that he enjoyed reciting the lines of Dadaist artist Kurt Schwitters: *"Die schöne Anna, die ist von hinten wie von vorne"* (The beautiful Anna, who's the same from the rear and the front")

It was characteristically accommodating for Otto to arrange for his birth in 1900: we need no arithmetic to place him in his own century's past 96 years. When he was 12—need I remind you, in 1912—he completed the 7th grade *and* his formal education, though he was later tutored at home and studied at the conservatories in Munich and Zürich. Sixty-nine years later he was awarded an honorary degree from Columbia University, just a few months after receiving an honorary diploma from his Madison, Wisconsin high school.

Otto's exit from the 7th grade was the result of his composer-conductor father's decision to continue his career in Germany, in Munich, after a confrontation with his superior, the President of the University of Wisconsin. As a young man, he, like many his generation, had studied music in Germany. During my half-century friendship with Otto I was often chronologically disoriented when remembering that Otto's father had known Richard and Cosima Wagner

---

[*] Read at the American Academy of Arts and Letters Dinner Meeting on November 7, 1996.

well, and that he had sung in the Beethoven Choral Symphony under Wagner's direction at the laying of the Bayreuth cornerstone in 1872.

There was no schooling for Otto in the Munich years, only the study of music and visits to libraries and museums. He barely escaped becoming an enemy alien in 1917, when the United States broke off relations with Germany. He left for Zürich, where he remained for the 3 years that strongly colored the remaining 76.

During world wars, Zürich becomes a haven for the young and disaffected and the older famous. Luening, almost starving until rescued by a patroness, Edith Rockefeller McCormick, soon became acquainted with some of the former, in particular the first Dadaists. Among the latter was James Joyce, still in his thirties and not yet famous. They became fast friends: Joyce was interested in what the young man had to tell him about contrapuntal manipulations and the music of Schönberg, incorporating some of his findings in the "Sirens" chapter of *Ulysses*, parts of which he would try out over lunch with Luening. Their friendship resulted in an invitation to join Joyce's English Players, in which Otto played juvenile leads in several English and Irish comedies.

But these were diversions. Luening had become such a proficient flutist that he joined both the Opera and Tonhalle orchestras. His studies at the Conservatory and his compositions brought him to the attention of the composer-teacher Philipp Jarnach and then to Ferruccio Busoni who became his mentor. Otto's nascent, perhaps predestined, notion of using older styles, renewed in the present as a bridge to the future, had long ago been written about by Busoni and composed into his music. Encouraged by Busoni, Otto composed his first string quartet and a sextet, juxtaposing old and new styles the simple and the polytonal, the lyric and the contrapuntal, all as form-building means. Busoni actively promoted the works in prestigious concerts in Berlin and elsewhere, where audiences found them futuristic. Though Luening was later to subtilize his methods—incorporating his study of the overtone series into what he called "acoustic harmony"—his more than 400 compositions in all their bewildering variety were of one piece. His last, a work for cello and orchestra, was completed shortly before his final brief hospitalization.

With typical OTTO-ish contrariness, he left his German-speaking world for America in 1920 when he was just 20, just as his contemporaries were leaving the US for Paris. At the bidding of Mrs. McCormick he was briefly in Chicago. But until he settled into teaching responsibilities in Bennington in 1934, and at Columbia ten years later, he was everywhere doing everything: arranging gospel hymns for export to Japan, composing anonymously parts of the film score "Of Human Bondage" in Hollywood, improvising to silent movies, conducting for J.J. Shubert on Broadway, managing and conducting three opera companies specializing in American operas—leading to the later impressive chamber opera achievements at Columbia—and concertizing as flutist and accompanist for his first wife, a singer, both here and abroad.

At Columbia, he invigorated the composition program and, with his colleague Vladimir Ussachevsky, initiated and developed the composition of music by electronic means, receiving international attention. At Columbia and elsewhere, he welcomed the talented, whatever their style, insisting as had Busoni, that they find their own ways under guidance, not direction.

Besides aiding the young, he labored on behalf of established composers, not least in urging them to cooperate rather than to compete for the spoils—"the peanuts," as he called them. He was instrumental in founding half a dozen still-flourishing organizations that promote American music, including two record companies. Both guru and fundraiser, he was, as Virgil Thomson wrote, "a handy man around the foundations." Few American composers have not benefited directly or indirectly from his largesse. Fortunately for Otto, into this ceaseless activity of composing music and promoting the music of others, his second wife, Catherine, was able to bring a large measure of order and serenity.

Anybody, student or not, was free to ask him advice about anything at all. But no one ever received a yes or no, for Otto always rephrased the question in a broader context in which only "maybe" was applicable. Those not satisfied with ambiguity were dismissed with a Busoni quotation: "Well, one knows what one means, doesn't one?"

*   *   *   *   *   *

At about the time I entered the Opera Workshop, in January 1945, I completed the *Crazy Jane Songs* and was still seeing Bartók, on no fixed schedule. During that term and the following two academic years, so much time and energy were spent in the works of opera composers of the past and such living composers as Lockwood, Menotti, and Thomson that it might be thought that I had unselfishly given up composing my own music. Such was not the case. Constantly in the company of singers, it is not surprising that I wrote two cycles of songs for soprano and piano, one of them to three poems of William Blake, the other to five poems by the almost forgotten Francis Quarles. Both sets were performed here and there, complete or in part. After they were revised in 1951, and the Quarles *Five Songs* published soon thereafter, they were performed more often, here and abroad. When the Blake Songs were finally published, I re-set them for tenor, as I should have in the first place.

It was mentioned earlier that I had acquired the habit of composing a sonata for piano every summer. So it was that the fourth and the fifth were composed during this period, in the summers of 1945 and '46, after which I quit the series. Each of the last two was performed first in New York by a different woman. Other performances were related to the efforts of Olga Samaroff—a former Mrs. Leopold Stokowski—to present new American piano music played by her most advanced students. Both in Town Hall and in the Washington National Gallery she sponsored performances of the second and fifth sonatas.

The two most recent in the series, the fourth and fifth, were revised in 1951 and eventually published by Theodore Presser. Music publication, then and now, has always been eagerly sought after by composers and is usually fraught with difficulties. On rare occasions circumstances may require going swiftly into print; more often publication is a lengthy process. The publication of the *Fifth Sonata for Piano* was drawn out over two decades for reasons, fortunately unique, worth recounting.

Presumably one of the well-reviewed performances of the *Fifth* came to the attention of John Fitzpatrick, who heard that I was revising it and asked if he could premiere the new version. I was dumbfounded, for Kirkpatrick—whom I'd not yet met—had for decades been cajoling his much older friend, Charles Ives, into revising his *Second Sonata for Piano, The Concord Sonata*, into its final state. Kirkpatrick had then performed it, in his edition, in Town Hall in 1939 to great acclaim from both critics and the public. In one of the more exuberant reviews Kirkpatrick was referred to an "an unobtrusive minister of genius."

He first performed by revised *Fifth* on a Composers Forum concert in November 1951, in McMillin Theatre. This long-lived series presented in each concert several works by each of only two composers, after which there was a three-way discussion led by some older eminence. On this occasion Virgil Thomson was the moderator. After the music and the talk, Virgil approached and complimented me on the new violin piece, the Blake songs, and especially on the large concert aria for large soprano, *The Hippopotamus*, to the Eliot text. He then added that he thought the sonata was a fine piece, but he could be sure that it was better than that "Because John never plays anything but the best."

Kirkpatrick performed it several times in New York and then a dozen times on tour and in Washington and elsewhere thereafter. From a couple of far-flung places he dropped me short notes suggesting that I might consider making this or that small change in the voicing of a chord or a dynamic indication. I often made changes that he suggested, with the realization that I was experiencing a little of what Ives and he had experienced together over the years.

During this time there was interest in some of my music by Music Press/Mercury Music, which had published the first two operas of Thomson. Curiously, Kirkpatrick had been in touch with that publisher about the unrevised *Fifth* two years before his performance of the revision. It was not long before a copy of my revised manuscript, tweaked a bit by him, was sent to Vienna to be engraved. In those days, still, copies of a printed work were made from a master copy pressed from copper plates into which—in reverse—all the notes, staves, and the rest had been incised. Eventually I received the "green proofs," pages printed on green paper. Then, the first calamity: the plates had been somehow irretrievably lost. Time passed until it was decided to invest in re-engraving with another, more dependable, company. By the time I had read and corrected the first and second proofs, we learned that the engraving establishment had become bankrupt and its plates melted down and sold on the copper market.

My fellow sufferer in these long drawn-out bouts of bad luck was Milton Feist, the Director of Publication of Mercury Music. Whether he had been or was still a rabbi, as was rumored, I did not know. By now, wheelchair bound, he had the patience of Job and was a friendly, wise and witty conversationalist. Naturally, the expense of a *third* engraving was out of the question, but there remained a possibility: he and I had seen copies of Kirkpatrick's own too tightly spaced, but painstakingly edited—with fingerings added!—beautifully copied out version of the sonata in his own hand. He had made just such a version of the Ives *Concord Sonata*. If I could acquire his original transparencies, it might be possible to print from them as masters. (Until the advent of Xeroxing, composers—or their copyists—made ink fair-copies on high quality vellum transparencies, from which copies could be made by the blueprint process.) A phone call to Kirkpatrick at Cornell disclosed that he might still have the sheets. He brought them to New York and I delivered them to Feist, taking no chances. Before too long both Kirkpatrick and I were reading proofs.

By then Mercury Music was to be sold to Theodore Presser, Inc. Feist called me in to tell me that all Mercury's publishing commitments would be honored by Presser. Because I had been so uncharacteristically patient a composer—sixteen years having passed—if I would tell him which of my works would be most difficult to get published, he would happily give me a contract that would be honored by Presser. I quickly chose the *Sonata for Viola and Piano* (1953, rev. 1967). Inevitably, with the change in publishers, four more years passed before the *Fifth Sonata* appeared in print in 1973, with a special credit on the cover: "Facsimile Edition of the Manuscript of the Editor, John Fitzpatrick." Twenty-two years had passed since his first performance of the piece. In the same year *Viola Sonata* was printed. The *Fourth Sonata for Piano*, subject to the same Mercury/Presser arrangement, was published in 1984, thirty-three years after its 1951 revision!

Though there were the special circumstances detailed above concerning publication of *The Fifth Sonata*,[1] the time from publication contract to print in the case of each of these works was extraordinarily long, even by the standards of the time—or of any time—and has not, fortunately, been duplicated in my life since then. Composers tend to blame publishers for their laxity and bad taste, but surely standard business practices and complex sociological truths are responsible. The publication of music that is not likely for many years to sell sufficient copies to reimburse the publisher for his expenses in printing is not likely to be hurried, if undertaken at all. Such an observation holds true today, even though many changes have taken place in the printing and dissemination of new works.

---

[1] The *Fifth Sonata* was recorded by Yvar Mikhashoff in 1981 on a disc entitled American Historic: The Piano Sonata, released by CRI Records. It is available on CD from New World Records/CRI.

Ars longa, vita brevis, as the Romans had it; or, as is often the case, vice versa.

*   *   *   *   *   *

Having followed the progress of the *Fifth Sonata for Piano*, its early performances, its revision and emendations by John Kirkpatrick, to its publication, let us return to the time of its birth in the summer of 1946, twenty-seven years earlier, and the drawn-out compositional stumble that followed. That academic year, 1946-47, was so filled with teaching and opera rehearsals and productions—playing and conducting in a Workshop evening of excerpts, eight performances of the American premiere of two one-act Etienne Méhul operas on a double bill, and the Stein/Thomson opera in May—that was little time for me to compose.

In the fall, after I had played my new sonata around a bit, mostly for friends and colleagues, Otto Luening asked me one of his typically oblique, but loaded, questions. "Do you mind that the word around town is that you are a composer of sonatas?"

"No, I don't, really," I answered, knowing that, decoded, his question was: "Jack, why aren't you writing an opera?" In fact, I was already searching for a suitable subject. Accustomed as I had become to new operas designed to fit Brander Matthews, chamber operas, I wanted a subject that would benefit musically and verbally from the intimacy of a small theatre. I sought suggestions from Sarah Moore, now living with her parents since graduating from Bennington. She was widely read, of a writerly disposition, and had since childhood heard her father discussing with friends and librettists the pros and cons of this or that play, person, or story as the stuff for an opera. She suggested that I look into the Wakefield cycle of medieval mystery plays for a subject. I did so and while settling on *Noah* ran across Andre Obey's recent play, *Noah*. Sarah proved to be a fascinating conversationalist, but an undependable collaborator. Mostly on my own, I concocted a conflation of the two Noah plays, wrote the first small part of the libretto, and began setting it to music.

I believed then, as I still do, that singing actors on the stage are the essence of opera. Nevertheless, the orchestra—of whatever size—besides accompanying actors and occasionally coming to the fore, provides its various colors to create and to enhance voices, words, and actions. If, as I thought at the time, instrumental color is so essential in the mix that is opera, shouldn't a composer choose his colors directly on the canvas of his orchestral score, rather than sketching in the black and white of the traditional short score? Composers of operas have almost always sketched out what the instruments are to play in a "short score" that resembles an unplayable piano score, often with several staves and with some notes indicating what instruments are to play what. Because writing in short score need not inhibit the composer's having in his mind's ear the final instrumental sound, my idea of composing and orchestrating at the same time was uncalled for and unwise. The composer has enough to do in planning short-term and long-term shapings, discovering his notes and rhythms, setting the text, and timing actions and reactions, without bothering at the same time with details such as harp tunings, changing from oboe to English horn and back, and mutes in and out and on and off.

I could have continued the opera in the time-honored short score, but I tired of "the just and perfect" but tippling Noah and his nine hundred and fifty year life-span, his well-meaning large family, and I "repenteth me that I have made them." In short, Noah and His Sons became a seven-minute torso. *Noah* became the fourth of my aborted operas, the timing of its end coincided with the preparations for the birth of *The Mother of Us All*. Nevertheless, my brief immersion in *Genesis* may have predisposed me to choose a Prophet as the subject of my first completed opera, *Jonah*, to be begun a few months later, in the early autumn of 1947.

*   *   *   *   *   *

Tempting though it might have been to have lived all the past year in the never-never land of writing an opera, taking part in the preparation and performances of scenes from golden oldies and the whole of a premiere, there had been the real world to contend with: teaching classes in Columbia College, with a number of students on the GI Bill older and more experienced than I, and with relatives and with relationships. As to relatives: Mother had remarried, adding to my small family a large collection of pseudo-relatives; as to relationships: the birth, in May, of the second child of that odd pair, Thomson and Stein, was to be followed, in August, by a more conventional couple, Beeson and Sigerist.

My occasional trips to Rochester to visit mother—and to see Bernard Rogers and others at Eastman—had become trips to Shamokin, in northeast Pennsylvania to visit her and my new step-father. The groom, so to speak, was Will Haupt, whom I'd occasionally seen when we were visiting Mother's family in my young days, for they all lived in the area. Will was a widower, older than Mother, large, overweight, and often ailing, fortunate to have a trained nurse as company and wife. He moved so slowly that his new-fangled watch that was powered by the movement of his wrist frequently ran down and stopped. He was amusing as the epitome of Pennsylvania Dutch conservatism, well enough informed to tell me that he regretted that I was teaching in "a pinko university." He was fond of such old saws as "A penny saved . . ." When Mother moved in, she found old tea-bags on the clothes line, hung out to dry and to be reused. I was very pleased by the unexpected marriage, for it assured Mother comfortable circumstances for life. Will owned a furniture store and was a director in two banks.

There was also some pleasure to be found in trying to untangle the familial imbroglio that had resulted from Mother's having married the father-in-law of her brother Skie. He was now also her stepson-in-law; her sister-in-law, Mary, was now also her stepdaughter; the two daughters of Skie and Mary were both her nieces and her step grandchildren. My Aunt Mary had become my stepsister, and Uncle Skie also my stepbrother-in-law. This litany, which could be extended, nobody else found interesting, but I found useful to repeat as a sleep-inducer.

I, too, had changed my living arrangements, but far more modestly. Farther to the west of 114th Street, almost to Riverside Drive, the owner of a brownstone was converting it to apartments; if I would pay the rent a year in advance, he would convert ground-floor space into a studio apartment. I acquired what became known as The Mousehole. There was room for my upright piano; when the sofa-bed was extended there was space only to sidle through. Except for four years in Rome and summers occasionally in Europe, often on Shelter Island or on Lloyd Neck, all addresses since have been in the neighborhood, on Riverside Drive: 3 Claremont Ave. (the backside of 440 RSD), 445, and 404.

A few weeks after the 1946 fall term began, my Eastman acquaintance, Nora Sigerist, suddenly appeared on campus. Though we had not seen one another for three years, we had corresponded occasionally. After completing her liberal arts degree at the University of Rochester, she had just spent a year of graduate study in Russian at Cornell. During that year, Columbia, where Slavic studies had deteriorated, had been arranging a coup: to bring from Cornell to Columbia the well-known Slavic scholar, Ernest Simmons, together with some of his teaching colleagues and graduate students.

Nora had arrived late for classes. She and her family had spent their first post-war summer in Switzerland. The only transportation back for her and her mother had been a freighter with no radio or doctor; with a port of call at Oran and an engine breakdown in mid-Atlantic, the voyage from Genoa had taken a harrowing five weeks!

We soon discovered that we hade more in common than having been former Eastman friends and began attending the theatre and concerts together. Otto, still separated from his wife, had a good deal of discontented time on his hands, was lonely, and sought my company for dinner at the Gold Rail and/or evenings to talk. After Nora appeared on the scene, he often found me otherwise engaged. He was relieved to hear that I was seeing a girlfriend and astonished that I had picked a Swiss from Zürich. He invited us to the Gold Rail for one if its pseudo-German dinners so that he could meet her. They spoke some High German together, he with his Bavarian accent; he remembered and faked some Swiss German in the Zürich dialect, Züri Dütsch. He had left that city just two years before she was born there in 1922. I re-heard yet again his tales of Joyce, Strauss, and the early Dadaists. For the benefit of Nora, studying Russian literature and history, he went on in detail about having gone to the station in 1917 to watch Lenin and his followers board the train for the Finland Station.

There were three other composers around whom Nora had known at Eastman: Rivett and Avshalomov, now at Columbia, and Bergsma, only a few blocks away at the Juilliard School. They formed a continuity with our past, as though we had not been apart for the intervening three years. Because she and I were in different directions so busy, it was a while before she became acquainted with other musical colleagues, with Rhodes of the Workshop, Rudolf Thomas, then still my conducting teacher, who enjoyed having someone to speak German with, Lang, and Douglas Moore, of whose household we were over the years to become almost informal members. Because for a short time I was often discussing my *Noah* Libretto with Sarah Moore, Otto one day said he's heard Douglas say that he hoped I would marry Sarah. I suspected that Otto was simply prying for information about Nora and me and offered no information about anything.

As the year rolled on, Mother came to New York to see the Mousehole and to meet Nora; she and I then visited Shanokin in return, for Nora to meet Will and my aunts and uncles at a holiday dimmer with the requisite amount of far too much food.

Sometime in the spring, Nora and I decided that we would marry, but would simplify matters by waiting until her parents left Baltimore to move back to Switzerland, to its southernmost canton, the Ticino. What I had heard from Nora about her father leaving Johns Hopkins I read in a long and laudatory article in *Time*. During his fifteen years there he had taught and headed the Institute of History of Medicine, founded and edited its Journal, and written over a hundred articles and half a dozen books. Upon his resignation from Hopkins he would become a Research Professor *in absentia* at Yale, enabled, finally, to write his long-postponed multi-volume History of Medicine.

A few days after the last of the *Mother of Us All* performances Nora ad I heard Dr. Sigerist give a rousing fund-raising lecture in a private eastside home for the American-Soviet Medical Society, now fallen on difficult times in the opening cold-war battles. After the lecture, Nora had introduced me to her father, I thought to myself: if my father had lived to learn that I was to marry a daughter of Henry Sigerist, he would be astonished and find me disloyal in the extreme. My father had delivered a lecture, *State Medicine*, to the Indiana State Medical Society, which published it in 1933. Well written, it decried any great intervention into medical insurance and treatment by government of the sort being carried out in other countries. My father must have become aware in the thirties that one of the strongest voices in favor of what was called "socialized medicine" was that of Henry Sigerist. He could have, might have, read the long article about Sigerist and seen his face on the cover of *Time*, June 30, 1939, not long after I'd left Muncie.

This irony I kept to myself— even when Nora and I spent a few days in Baltimore helping with the preparations for her parents' trans-Atlantic move. Most of my time was spent in packing Henry's vast private library. Much of it and most of the house furnishings had traveled from Leipzig to Baltimore in 1932. Because Henry read thirteen languages, including the classical languages of Greek, Latin, Hebrew, and Arabic, language and subject-matter determined hat went in which carton, rather than my being able to pack as usual, by size and shape. There were also musical scores and volumes of cello music and *Lieder*; Henry had played cello and Emmy had a trained voice, still singing until recently for small audiences. I had met Nora's mother briefly in New York. She spoke English fluently, but preferred German, her mother having been born in the Rhineland. On her father's side she was an Escher, an ancient Swiss family traced back to the early 1300's and as close to aristocracy as Swiss dare claim.

Because Henry was still attending testimonials in his honor and giving lectures widely, it had been wise of us not to plan out marriage for this time, but to wait for their departure. By the time they went—leaving their Chevrolet as a wedding present—I was involved in my commitment to the Summer Opera

Workshop. At the end of those six weeks we went downtown to the County Clerk, were married—in a room with a stained-glass window—and set off in the Chevy on a leisurely trip to Nova Scotia, with side trips to abandoned lighthouses along the way.

*　　*　　*　　*　　*　　*

The summer Opera Workshop had served as a long, joyous, and appropriate wedding prelude. With me coaching and accompanying, Otto, conducting, and Ernst Lert staging, we prepared most of the vocal ensembles from four of Mozart's major operas, enough to fill two public recitals. All four operas are about, or include, marriage: *Flute, Figaro, Don G.*, and *Così*: purification for the rite, the enjoyment and protection of it, marriage won against odds, and the subversion of it.

If, in my opinion, the quality of composers of operas is to be judged by their ability to create characters by way of *composing* them, Mozart remains unsurpassed. In his vocal ensembles there are numerous passages in which the several characters with their several musics are combined seemingly as simply as a conversation may take place, any hesitations or disagreement composed into the musical flow. (A splendid example, considered in detail, is to be found in *Marriages of Convenience*, see page 454.) Constantly studying and hearing these marvels of imagination and construction over six weeks had been a spur to my beginning work on *Jonah* upon our return from our wedding trip. In my opera there would be naturally occurring ensembles of various sizes and in the comic Court Scene a quintet, sextet, and septet.

*　　*　　*　　*　　*　　*

Chapter 6

Jonah
(1947-1952)

Rome and the Ticino
(1948-1950)

It was Al Bauman who suggested, months before the autumn of 1947, that I consider Paul Goodman's recently performed and published play *Jonah* as the basis of an opera. Al was on the junior teaching staff, an excellent pianist specializing in new music, a great believer in the merits of the Orgone box, and well acquainted with varied young talents on the fringes of things—those outside the ken of our older colleagues. Before he arranged for me to meet Goodman I made sure of my commitment to the play and how I would adapt it if its author would permit me to do it myself. I learned that Goodman had studied and taught widely and I read around in his published poetry, short stories, and non-fiction, ranging from criminology and academic freedom to urban planning and gestalt therapy. (A few years later he was to become widely known and a hero to many from his book *Growing Up Absurd*.)

Somewhat daunted by meeting such a polymath, I feared our first meeting, but needlessly, as it turned out. He was pleased that I was enchanted with his play and gave me permission to do whatever necessary to musicalize it: to cut it as needed, to repeat or transpose lines or sections, anything but writing new lines unless he approved them. He added that he had neither the time nor the expertise to carry on a composer-librettist collaboration.

On our first and subsequent long meetings—mostly filled with animated discussions and arguments about matters non-operatic—I confessed that those of the Jewish jokes I didn't find funny I was planning to cut. He was regretful but understanding, remarking ironically that after all there were some others in the opera-world who weren't Jewish. I asked him to explain the inflections and implications of "Nu" and "Nebich" to me. He did, saying that he was flattered that someone who had not grown up with those words could be attracted to his play. I responded that they were but part of the local color necessary to the characters and to a very serious subject being dramatized by comic means—my favorite way of telling a story. I added that his subtitle "A Biblical Comedy with Jewish Jokes Culled Far and Wide" I was changing to "An Opera to be Played, Sung, and Danced," the _played_ having several meanings.

Some fragments from Goodman's _Preface to Jonah_, 1942, describe his intentions for his play and apply also to the opera and its libretto.

> This play follows the incidents in the _Book of Jonah_.
> Among the books of the Bible, _Jonah_ seems to be unique, as the only comedy, although a kind of sarcastic irony is almost omnipresent elsewhere. The essential situation, the Prophet whose prophecy proves false and who then says to God, "I told you so!" is perfectly comic and the conclusion is a little fable. . . . Even the style has a genre realism not altogether serious, as "He found a ship going to Tarshish and he paid his fare.". . . The idea of the Empire City, such as it is, and its perils, such as they are, are taken perhaps a little too closely from the current national emergency; but those who are offended can believe that the poet, too, is one of the playful Ninevites, as indeed he is.

I include a brief scene-by-scene synopsis of the libretto as finally completed, because it is not available elsewhere.

Jonah and his wife are asleep in their poor room in Gath-Hepher. Awakened by three thunderous knocks on the door, Jonah rises and is met by his Angel (a male). He is commanded "to go to Nineveh, that great city, and cry out against it." He objects. He is disliked and feared as the bearer of bad tidings; sometimes the Lord changes His mind and he is made a fool. They argue. Jonah packs and they leave.

Jonah boards the *Glory of Tammuz* at Joppa for Tarshish, fleeing from his duty. A storm arises. Jonah wants to be thrown overboard because "Whatever I turn my hands to is an evil . . ." Others hold him responsible as a foreigner and a Hebrew. The crew see him swallowed by Leviathan.

Inside the Great Fish Jonah is asleep. He wakes, rambles in his thoughts, prays. The Angel arrives with a lamp and repeats the Lord's command. To the sound of rushing water they disappear.

In the Nineveh public square are acrobats, a peasant and sight-seeing guides, sirens, and two spies. Jonah appears, crying out "Yet forty days and Nineveh shall be destroyed!" His warning is enjoyed by all as some new traveller's act and made into a popular song.

He visits the Court with his warning, now of thirty-nine days. The foolish king is but thirty years old; three court ladies and a duke are also young. The king forms a committee and issues a proclamation: repentance, new costumes of sackcloth and ashes, and fasting.

Outside the wall Jonah has set up a tent to await the city's end. On the wall the days are marked off one by one by gloomy dancers. Bets are laid on the outcome; the spies are alarmed. On the final day the Angel appears and draws a luxuriant plant from the earth. Jonah reclines in its shade; from the plant hangs a watermelon with a spigot from which he and the onlookers drink. A storm suddenly arises as the melon explodes and the crowd runs off. The Angel speaks to Jonah. ". . . Should I not spare Nineveh, that great city, wherein are seven million people who know not their right hand from their left?"

I was in Rome in 1949 at work on *Jonah* when the Soviet Union acquired the atomic bomb. I could not but marvel at the timely irony of some news from the Music Department: Al Bauman, who had led me to Goodman and his play, had become terrified by the warnings of several latter-day Jonahs that New York would be destroyed; he had left our Empire City to join a California commune as a baker. As we know, our city has so far been spared. Nineveh, though, in Iraq, is not what it once was.

When I began composing the music of *Jonah* at the outset of the 1947-48 academic year, there wee already some random sketches, one of them of the first few bars of the opera, dating back to when I first read the play. Except for minor changes to be made while setting the text, the libretto had emerged from the play during the period when Paul and I had been conversing. Had we not become such good friends, it might have occurred to me to draw up a letter of agreement—as I should have—granting me permission to use and to adapt his play as an opera. The youngish Douglas Moore, as related earlier, had twice neglected to have such a written agreement and twice suffered. In my case no problem ensued: when, years later, Boosey and Hawkes took *Jonah* under its wing, Paul's widow, Sally, was graciously cooperative about the rights and copyright in my name.

The more pleasurable it was to be working on my opera, the more frustrating were the interruptions. In this, my third full Columbia year, as the routine of class meetings and Workshop coaching hours and rehearsals asserted themselves, it became difficult to find the time-spans necessary for conceiving and carrying out the long musico-dramatic passages that contributed to the time-scale of a large-scale work. *Jonah* was planned to be in six scenes, in two or three acts, lasting two hours, an unconventional re-telling of an old story by somewhat larger means than those of a chamber opera; a large cast with doublings; a small chorus and dancers; an orchestra of 36-40 players.

If Henry Sigerist could resign his professorship and commitments and move to Europe to carry out his enormous life-fulfilling *History of Medicine*, surely I could ask for a year's leave of absence to write my modest opera? To make such a thing possible I met the early deadlines for applications for the Rome Prize and the Guggenheim Fellowships, the results of which would not be known for several months.

In the meantime I could become more time-efficient and keep in mind that my writing deadlines were of my own making. I was compromising with my failed *Noah* scheme of composing on the full-score page by orchestrating scenes shortly after completing them in short score. I managed to compose and score the first scene while juggling with teaching and the Workshop. When the auditions and rehearsals for the eight premiere performances of Otto Luening's *Evangeline* began in the spring, I had to set my opera aside in favor of his.

During that year the Opera Workshop had a number of stars-in-the-making on its roster. I had the experience of preparing and conducting long scenes from *The Magic Flute*. My Tamino was James MacCracken, surely the most stentorian Tamino then alive. He was soon to be discovered, in Zürich by Herbert Graf, and was to become the preeminent Otello. My Papageno was David Thaw, soon to become the leading character tenor in Berlin. Gossip had it that it had been Thaw's grandfather who had shot and killed the architect Stanford White, whose mistress had been Thaw's grandmother. In our close of Act I, *Boheme*, those three evenings, was Teresa Stich (Randall) as Mimi. Because of the high quality of the singers at hand, we had to do very little casting of *Evangeline* from downtown. I was relieved of some coaching of principals, for Otto was pleased to do much of it himself. Also on hand were trained voices for the chorus, important in the work. Otto invited Nora to join his pick-up orchestra as a violinist. It was her first experience in playing in an opera-pit orchestra—from manuscript—as it was for many of our advanced students and semi-professionals in our spring premiere productions; conducting and following the beat are very different in opera from the concert stage.

In his autobiography Otto wrote in detail about his shaping of the story (from Longfellow) and the libretto and the music; he also described his trips to Grande Pré, Nova Scotia, and to the Cajun villages in Louisiana, the beginning and ends of the journey forced on the French Acadians by the British in mid-18th century, a nearly forgotten example of the relocation of an ethnic minority. *Evangeline* had been commissioned for a production that did not take place; nor did any other promised production until ours in 1948. It was written during an extended Guggenheim Fellowship, 1930-32.

*   *   *   *   *   *

Some time during the spring Douglas Moore waved me into his office with what he said was very good news for me, but would cause him great inconvenience: I had been awarded the Rome Prize *and* a Guggenheim Fellowship. Only one could be accepted. Because the Rome Academy preferred relatively young Fellows, he suggested that I choose the Rome Prize; I could then re-apply to the Guggenheim in some later year; that Foundation rarely granted a fellowship to a composer as young as I, then 27, preferring the older and more experienced. I thanked him for the unexpected news and the advice and asked for a leave of absence, which he granted readily, saying they'd get along somehow without me.

Before returning to the Mousehole and telling Nora that we, too, would be going to Europe—to Rome in September—I went to Otto's and my studio to think over the implications of what Douglas had said. He was much too large and wingless to be Mercury, bringing two gifts and instructions from the gods, but how else could he be so knowledgeable? If he knew before I did about the two awards, he must have been on one of the juries and there have heard about the action of the other that had met earlier, or had he been on both? How large were the juries and who else had been on them? Could one juror, friendly with an applicant, swing one, or two, in favor of a favorite? Surely not. Such thoughts were chastening.

There was, though, no need for me to mention my winning double-header: declining the Guggenheim would avert any public mention of my name. Most of my composer-friends and acquaintances of my age were regular applicants for the few prizes and fellowships available in the post-war forties. The gossip among them—especially the non-winners—was that because music juries had to compromise, the winners were always those without strong musical personalities. It was thought that luck was all-important: one could never predict whether one would have close personal friends, former teachers, or musically like-minded composers on a jury. Composers belonging to a minority—women, blacks, Jews, homosexuals—thought themselves out of the running unless at least one of their number was judging. I thought it curious that Juries—anonymous or not—were rarely considered able to come to fair-minded, purely musical, decisions; it was too often thought that some one juror was responsible for the jury coming to a "right" or "wrong" decision.

Now, sixty years later, human nature not having changed—not even that of composers—the above list of half-truths is still current. There are now far more and plumper plums to be picked from the serious-music tree, but there are far more pickers. Between now and then the National Endowment for the Arts grants to very many composers over many years have come and gone. Today the awards and fellowships to composers (and one librettist) of the American Academy of Arts and Letters are greater in number and value than then, amounting annually to over $250,000. About nine Guggenheim Fellowships are award to composers each year.

The music juries of these and other contests have in common with other arts juries that their members are professional practitioners of what they are judging. To avoid ties in consensus decisions three or five jurors are common; the American Academy's seven is large. By now most music juries use the Australian ballot, particularly useful if there are many candidates and a rank-list is desired. For example, if there are 90 applicants, the number is winnowed to, say, 15. When the final vote is arrived at, each juror lists his choices from #1 (high) to #15 (low). When the ballots are counted the lowest number is winner and a rank-list results. The only disadvantage of the Australian ballot is that a juror intent upon preventing a seemingly favored applicant from winning or doing well, can assign him/her the highest available number. One or two well-known composer-jurors were dropped from the Guggenheim jury by Henry Allen Moe, that paragon of frank speech and honesty, who led the Foundation from its beginning in 1925 until 1963. Henry strongly believed that his jurors should remain anonymous;

others thought such an idea undemocratic. He thought his little group of five, who worked very well together, should change its membership as little as possible; others warned of the dangers of stylistic inbreeding. I confess that I served on that demanding jury for twenty-five years, with the greatest pleasure and instruction. Several days, annually, of looking at scores (sometimes playing them at the piano for the others, in the days when recordings were rare), hearing sections of works by innumerable composers, sharpened the eye, ear, and critical ability, and charted the shoals and depths of the always changing new-music scene. All the other New York and NEA juries that I've served on have been similarly beneficial to me, but without affording such a long-term, synoptic view.

As has already been discussed in some detail, American new music in the forties tended toward one or the other of two very different stylistic attitudes. Except for a very few juries, most were known to veer in one direction or the other. Their membership was chosen accordingly. More recently, musical styles have become so numerous and diverse (and overlapping) that it would be impossible to represent them all on a jury, as some recommend. Rather, composer-jurors should be sought of whatever style, who by temperament, catholic taste, and perhaps with teaching experience, can recognize talent and promise when they hear it. Those so qualified are few in number and may hold— and argue strenuously—in favor of unacceptable prejudices. For example, the first jury of consequence on which I served was that of the Rome Prize, only shortly after I had returned from Rome. My distinguished elders were Howard Hanson and Randall Thompson (both of whom had been very early Rome Prize winners) and Edgard Varèse. I was shocked to find that Howard expected me to second his enthusiasm for those applicants who had studied with him and annoyed when in the discussions I was often partial with Varèse's point of view. Douglas told me that Hanson had been dropped as a juror thereafter for undue partisanship.

Service on numerous juries while closely observing one's colleagues is a prerequisite for one who is responsible for nominating or naming jury members and their chairmen. Such a person requires a combination of common sense, political acumen, a wide knowledge of the contemporary scene and its composers, and a thick skin, to the possession of all of which one can only aspire.

I admit for the first time to having been chiefly responsible for the membership of the Pulitzer Prize in Music juries for 36 years, from 1968 through 2004. In a sense I inherited this difficult and unpaid responsibility from Douglas Moore, who had originated that prize. I tried, short of lying, by verbal sleight-of-hand, always to remain anonymous, as had he. Though the monetary value of the Prize is not large, a Pulitzer Prize is the most prestigious available to a composer. It is the only one ever to be found in the first sentence of an obituary. As a creature of the press, it is highly publicized; as such, it is highly coveted. Consequently, those who don't win in the annual competition—and their partisans—often belittle the winner, criticize the jury and "whoever it was that picked such a bunch." Even the winner may accept ungraciously, feeling that he/she has for too long been passed over.

If the Pulitzer Board, some 25 well-meaning and intelligent, mainly newspaper-people, choose to exercise their right to overturn the decisions of their appointed professional jury, the jury is angry, the two or three composers known to have had their places exchanged are hurt, each in a different way. There is then a scandal for the critical fraternity to explore, to the detriment of everybody concerned. The political judgments in Washington that led to the demise of individual art and music grants were not unlike the substitutions occasionally by the Pulitzer Board of its "I don't know anything about music but I know what I like" decisions for those of its music jury. On such occasions—and there have been others over the years—there was talk on the Board that the Music Prize should be dropped. Determined to do what I could to prevent the loss of the Prize to our "profession," I countered with seemingly good-humored obstinacy and mollification. In a fit of frustration I drafted a long letter of resignation to the Board in 1998, filed it away, and went on doing my duty for six more years. That letter and its covering pro forma letter of resignation were delivered at the close of the 2004 competition.

It need hardly be remarked that the Pulitzer Board acting as a supra-jury, its Music Jury, and all other juries are necessarily, if unfortunately, restricted to memberships of human beings. It is tempting to allude again to the gods who could decide between the fortunate and unfortunate and then send Mercury down from Olympus to bring the glad tidings. But in a contest of playwrights, could the gods have been fair-minded toward Euripides, who reviled them? From all accounts the Olympians often differed among themselves, as how could they not, conceived as they were in man's image?

*   *   *   *   *   *

In response to my brief letter to Henry Allen Moe declining the Fellowship and saying that we would be going to Rome in September, Moe phoned, cherrily inviting me to come speak with him in his office. On my way there I lingered a bit in the lobby of 551 Fifth Avenue, admiring the elaborate and well-known brass castings. Almost his first question was "Who's the other part of 'we'?" he perked up at the mention of Nora Sigerist, saying that he knew Dr. Henry Sigerist well. "He's one of the few whose letters of recommendation of Fellowship applicants I can believe!" We spoke of Moore, Luening, and other friends in common, but he gave away no secrets. He added that I was welcome to reapply whenever I chose.

*   *   *   *   *   *

Yes, once upon a time it was said that all roads lead to Rome. By 1948 New Yorkers wee flattered to read that they lived in the latter-day Rome, even though the writers insisted that it was the vices that were the same and would lead to a similar decline and fall. By this time all roads, rails, and planes led to and from New York. Our way from New Rome to the old one, via Naples, was to be by way of the Italian liner Vulcania, third class, in early September, the passage arranged early on. In the meantime I re-wrote what I'd written of the first scene of *Jonah*, Nora picked up her Master of Arts Diploma—having skipped Commencement—and we both studied Italian grammar. Fortunately, a year of marriage had added little to our meager possessions, which went into storage; we turned our wedding-present Chevrolet into cash.

For me, my first ocean passage on a liner would likely be more humdrum than my teenage imagining of a single-handed voyage to the South Seas in my own ketch, but it would be, nevertheless, crossing the Atlantic, passing Gibraltar in sight of Africa, and seeing much of the Mediterranean. For Nora, not quite a year after her west-bound 5-week passage, it would be only a new variation on an old experience. Every summer during the thirties there had been a family round trip from New York to Le Havre, a stop-over in Paris, en route to an 18th century chalet on the shore of Lake Luzern at Kastanienbaum, sharing with the Wagners, so to speak, the same view of the lake and mountains as theirs from Triebschen, a couple of kilometers to the east. Records of the Sigerists' 5-day crossings exist in a packet of postcards picturing the liners, on the backs of which Henry Sigerist, ever the historian, recorded the dates of departures, arrivals, even the cabin numbers.

By coincidence, also on the Vulcania and in third class were Sarah Moore and her former Bennington classmate, Judith Bailey—who was to become Judith Jones, senior editor at Knopf. The latter part of the voyage was enlivened by the presence in first class of Judith's cousin, Jane Gunther, and her husband John , the author of *Inside Europe, Inside Asia*, and other such insider books. Whenever our two friends were invited to dinner in first class, John introduced them to the waiters as his two mistresses. Sarah could have become one, for also in first class was the husband of Beatrice Lillie, who invited her to accompany him to his villa on Capri. She declined to go, but she told me she'd been flattered to have been asked. Nora and I were invited once by the Gunthers to tea and while surveying the upper class I caught sight of two operatic worthies, the tenor Lauri-Volpe, and the composer Castelnuovo-Tedesco.

But these amusements took place in the Eastern Atlantic under picture-postcard-blue skies. On our second day out the radio in the lounge carried the news that the violent storm leaded for New York had turned eastward and was "passing harmlessly out to sea." Already the clouds were scudding and the sea gray. Soon there was pitching and rolling such as I'd never experienced in my sailboat in an unexpected storm, perhaps because I was in control of the tiller and sheets and could anticipate heeling and other motions. When, for the first time ever, I began to feel queasy, the highly experienced Nora suggested that I go on deck for the fresh air and the immovable horizon—never mind the wind and rain. That I did, trying to find a set of stairs not covered with vomit. Finding none and more affected by the messes than the ship's motion, I slithered my way to the deck and recovered—waiting there until the stewards had cleared the stairs before going below.

The cleft cone of Vesuvius, still steaming after its 1944 eruption, announced that we were entering the Bay of Naples. Unexpected were the superstructures of sunken ships in the shallow parts of the bay, the wreckage still not removed four years after the war's end. As we disembarked, two long rows of beggars entreated us for alms. Many were women carrying babies. I learned later that many of the babes-in-arms were rented out to the beggars in return for a percentage of the take. The four of us may have had twinges of guilt: Sarah and Judith were to be picked up by car, invited for a stay at the villa of an American in Positano; we found the chauffeur of the Rome Academy station wagon, Nicola, who was to drive us to Rome, where we were to remain for a year—as it turned out, for two years.

As we drove out of Naples, first west a bit and then north along the coast, paralleling the ancient Roman road, we passed the Phlegrean Fields with their many spumes of sulfurous steam, Greek and Roman ruins, the Grotto of the Cumaean Sibyl, and Lake Averno, the fabled entrance to Hades. I wonder now whether it occurred to me then, as we passed these exotic and ancient sites, how much my life had changed in the nine years since this "typical American" had been graduated from Central High School in Muncie, Indiana.

In a few hours we were at the gates of the American Academy on the Janiculum, the highest hill of Rome. As we made our way up the steps, passed the cortile, quiet except for its fountain, and into the impressive building, I felt quite at home, for both the Academy and the Columbia campus had been designed by McKim, Mead, and White in their expansively Classical style and in the same years.

Those architects favored impressive staircases leading to the entrances of their buildings; inside, their high ceilings demanded even more. With help from the staff we were shown up to our spacious room on the second floor; one looked out on a small and a large villa, both belonging to the Academy on its eleven acres. Baths and showers were down the hall, shared with a few others.

During the years when we were at war with Italy, the Academy was closed. It had reopened the year before we arrived, in 1957, and was now operating much as it had before the war, except that married couples without children could now be in residence. There was a happy combination of a coeducational dormitory with a comfortable hotel: the rooms and beds were cared for by staff: downstairs there was a large lounge, a billiard room, and the dining room, with an enormously long table at which the varied and delicious breakfasts, lunches and dinners were served to all residents. One could choose one's seatmates from among fellows and their spouses, painters, sculptors, architects, classicists, and archaeologists. There were also a few residents, older and well-known in their field, and occasional short-term visitors. The company embodied a version of MacDowell's vision for Columbia, a centering of the arts, and his legacy, the MacDowell Colony. I was the only composer for the new year, but Alexei Haieff and Andrew Imbrie had been the first postwar fellows in composition and were remaining for a second year, both good company in their very different ways.

During the early years of the Academy, three years in residence were usual. By our time the Rome Prize was for one year, extended for a second year if requested and circumstances warranted it. At the time I requested it—the following spring—and was granted it, the Fulbright Fellowships had just come into existence, without the usual long process of applications and jury determinations having been put in place. The Academy Board arranged that those of its continuing fellows who qualified be granted Fulbrights, and then discontinued paying their stipends, which were considerably smaller as it happened. On her own, Nora applied for a Fulbright for study of Russian literature at the University of Rome, and Polish, and was granted it immediately. We found ourselves in the second year awash in lire, our board and room, my studio and her library carrel taken care of by the Academy.

Every Fellow was provided with a studio. The four sculptors' studios near the Academy entrance are buildings in themselves. I was shown to mine, across the street from the main building and in handsome, park-like, surroundings. The street, Via Angelo Masina, is split in two parts by a small informal garden. On the far side is the gated entrance to the grounds of the Villa Aurelia, umbrella pines and formal gardens. The Villa Aurelia itself is a renaissance villa remodeled. It contains the director's apartment, large rooms for entertainment, and, on the top floor, a handsome space perfect for chamber music. Off to the south side of the villa's façade is an elevated small extension, part of which was my studio, separated by two stairways from the gatekeeper's house. The music studio is isolated, perfect; two large arched windows provided light and the sun's heat on cool days, a wood stove for cooler days, a grand piano and a worktable. Shortly after I'd begun work I asked one of the other composers if he knew why there were bird-droppings on the piano strings and sounding board. I learned that a young composer-friend of Menotti had used the studio for a brief time helping Menotti complete an orchestration. Apparently the orchestrator had a parrot. It seemed that Menotti was late with a deadline, as usual. (Some of the orchestra parts for *The Medium* were delivered to us just before the dress rehearsal of its premiere.)

For Nora and me—and surely for many of the Fellows—for the first time since early childhood there were no classes to attend, and for me none to teach and no rehearsals to superintend. Our time was our own to do with what we wished: composing, reading (what better place to read Gibbon's *Decline and*

Fall?), studying the Italian language and observing the Italians, conversing with the Americans at the Academy and seeing their work in their studios—whatever, whenever.

Even day-trippers in a tourist bus who see only the Forum and St. Peter's Basilica must be struck by the more than 1500 years that separate these two sights. No one would be so foolish as to claim to know all of Rome, but many long-term visitors can name places not distant from one another that can add almost a thousand years to the 1500.

It is said that there are as many churches in Rome as there are days in the year; my excellent Roman guide lists *only* 258, many often closed. It is also said that there is actually a Santa Maria Sempre Chiusa (Santa Maria Always Closed).

One of my favorite churches, often revisited, was San Clemente, typical of many in its layering of time. One enters from street-level the eleventh-century church, much altered in the Baroque eighteenth-century. Interior steps lead down to the earlier church of San Clemente (discovered in the nineteenth-century) built in the fourth century and altered in the eighth and ninth, with some frescoes remaining from its earliest years. *Under* the lower church are the remains of Clemente's villa and, descending more steps, one enters the several rooms of a temple to Mithra, a Persian god as popular among religious dissidents at the end of the second century as was Jesus Christ. The addition of a modern altar in the lower church and the reuse of decorations and parts of the older buildings in building the new ones do violence to any American's sense of passage of just decades in our meager two or three centuries.

Other such layered churches have on their lowest levels access to extensive catacombs with the remains of early Christians often visible. Even more gruesome than the catacombs are the five subterranean chapels below Santa Maria della Concezione, the Capucini church. The walls, ceilings, and altars are decorated in geometric designs with the skeletons, skulls, and bones of 4000 Capuchin monks. These baroque conceits easily surpass in luridity the twenty-fist century works of Damien Hirst.

If I seem to dilate on these relatively unknown and bizarre churches, it is in part because they are time-layered—the essence of Rome—and in part because, unfortunately, they resonate with our own time. Other Roman monuments, the Coliseum, for instance, have lost their original grisly meaning and have become but advertising symbols.

The friendly name of the church of San Giuseppe dei Falegnami (Saint Joseph of the Carpenters) in the Forum belies what lies beneath: one of the most important prisons of ancient Rome, with several rooms in which prisoners were starved, tortured, and strangled, their bodies thrown down a hole leading to the main sewer and then into the river Tiber. The prison has been sanctified and is now a chapel, San Pietro in Carcere, for Peter may have been imprisoned in it. I doubt that there is a lesson to be learned there by the architects of memorials to our modern versions of places of such atrocities.

In addition to Christian churches built directly into the walls of temples to the older gods, the center of Rome consists of buildings of whatever century adapted to modern uses. The Romans live and work, as they always have, in a temporal minestrone, a rich thick soup, full of everything. To be sure, all Mediterranean peoples have a relaxed attitude toward time, but living among the Romans, one becomes aware that their sense of it is based on an elasticized version of our finite minutes, hours, and days. Appointments for whatever are kept, but whenever. One often hears *"dolce far niente"* (sweet idleness, or sweetness makes nothing); it is rarely a call to action. I was already too time-bound and work-prone to enjoy more than a light case of *dolce far niente*. More destructive to my time sense was the absence of recurring academic years and their pairs of semesters, which tend to fix in the memory the sequence of events, travels, and conversations that take place. Without such markers I remember what took place, but not when.

Accordingly, the following vignettes date from Rome, 1948-50 or possibly—such are the effects of *dolce far niente*—from our two later years at the

Academy, 1958-59 on a Guggenheim Fellowship, or 1965-66, when I was composer in residence.

Laurence Roberts was the perfect Academy Director, He and his wife, Isabel, were able, it seemed, to supplement the Director's entertainment budget, for there were numerous social events at the Villa Aurelia, often coinciding with the visits to Rome of celebrities, some of them guests of Laurence and Isabel. Often, all the Fellows and residents were invited. It was generally thought that we three composers (and sometimes Nora) received special treatment, for only we were invited when composers were honored guests.

One of these visitors was Igor Stravinsky, whom I'd met a few times before in New York at the Russo-American parties of Kyriena Siloti after his annual appearances with the Philharmonic to conduct a new work. Stravinsky was in Rome to hear his rarely performed *Les Noces.* I attended rehearsals and the concert, armed with a miniature score, which included translations of the original Russian text, failing often to match the verbal accents of the original text settings.

Present at the Roberts dinner party for the affable Stravinsky were only Andy Imbrie, Russian-born Alexei Haieff, and I. Alexei had been an intimate in the Los Angeles Stravinsky home in the p.C. (pre-Robert Craft) days. After dinner I was invited to join their Russian tête-a tête, which then turned into English. I remarked to Stravinsky that the Italian translation we'd just heard was awkwardly set to the vocal lines and at odds with the chugging rhythms of the instruments. Had he minded? He answered that he had conducted *Les Noces* in several languages: all the translations shared the same problem; he paid no attention and conducted as though everybody were singing in Russian. That was that.

Alexei remained mainly in Rome for many years. On one of our later year-long stays he and I continued our discussion of Stravinsky's attitude toward word-setting. By that time, Stravinsky's *The Rake's Progress* had been premiered in Venice in 1951, which Alexei had attended and about which he had an amusing story. Stravinsky, dressed comfortably to conduct the performance and surrounded by camera crews and well-wishers, was denied entrance to the opera house because he was not properly attired! By the time of our later conversation I had heard several of the Met performances of the opera and studied the published vocal and orchestra scores. By then and thereafter Robert Craft had written knowledgeably and intelligently about *The Rake's* libretto, dramaturgy, and music, but without explaining why it was so difficult to understand its sung text, even when well sung by those with excellent diction and projection. I told Alexei that I loved everything in the work except for the obscuring of the amusing and sometimes moving text, too often unidiomatically, even awkwardly, set to music.

Alexei agreed and offered a simple explanation: Igor's Russian settings were exemplary; his settings of French, English, Latin, and Hebrew, were of two languages he spoke fluently, but with a very strong Russian accent, and two that he spoke not at all. Native speakers of the four languages always had trouble making out the words. Alexei and I agreed that Stravinsky's writings and those of his spokesmen about his wish to use words simply as generators of pitches and colors were half-true, high-flown rationalizations.

I repeated to him Bartók's comment to me that composers successfully set to music only those languages that are native to them; we agreed that he may well have had Stravinsky in mind, among others, at the time.

Alexei had known the *Rake* librettists, W. H. Auden and Chester Kallman, in Los Angeles. He could have collaborated with them on their next opera libretto, *On the Way*, as composer, but didn't; his description of its detailed scenario seemed unpromising to me and, apparently to him, for he declined. He told me the following story dating from the years when the *Rake* was being composed. The librettists heard the composer sing and play through the new work. Impressed, naturally, they took notes of words and phrases that were awkwardly set to the vocal lines. After they left, Auden rewrote his words to fit the music and returned to Igor passing them off as improvements on his first version. According to Alexei, Stravinsky had seen through the subterfuge and refused to make any changes in the words or the music.

I showed Alexei what I'd found that must have been one of these bones of contention. In the Boosey and Hawkes vocal score in Anne's Aria at the end of the first act, page 63, straddling rehearsal number 88, are two rhymed lines separated by a comma,

> And warmly be the same,
>
> He watches without grief or shame;

In the separately printed libretto there is a period between the lines, as one would expect. I'd guess that the comma is not a publisher's error, but is in the Stravinsky manuscript for some reason—perhaps his mis-reading. Any English speaking-composer—any composer—would provide a break here—at a comma or a period—for a breath. Stravinsky forbids a break here by indicating with a comma over the vocal line that the breath is to be taken after "watches," difficult to do after managing "tches" on a sixteenth-note. The awkwardness results from the composer's trying to force the well-set high-lying phrase on the page before to fit different words that require two phrases. I know of no better example of what can result when a composer permits his "purely musical" intentions to disregard the meaning, sound, rhythm, and singability of the words. The ideal, of course, is that words and their musical setting should be so inextricable that they seem to have been born together, identically twinned.

In about 1965, in New York, I was invited to cocktails by Ellen Faull, who had been the first wicked stepmother in *Lizzie Borden*. She introduced me to her former student, Judith Raskin, whom I had admired at the New York City Opera and at the Met for her voice, musicianship, and clear diction. She had recently completed the second recording of the *Rake*, as Stravinsky's choice for the role of Anne Truelove. We spoke admiringly of the Nick Shadow at the sessions, the similarly gifted John Reardon, who had sung the Young Gambler on my *Hello Out There* recording. I then asked her if she had been troubled by "that odd passage toward the end of the b-minor part of Anne's Aria." She knew immediately what I meant and replied that she'd tried hard to make sense of the passage, but failed to do so. At the recording session she had dared ask Stravinsky if he could give her time to take a breath between the two phrases—she'd been afraid to say "two sentences" —and he'd said absolutely not; she had to sing and to breathe as he'd written it. She thought that *The Rake* had been for him a kind of "in-job training," that the word-setting had improved as he progressed through the two and one-half hour long opera.

Though Auden was not permitted to edit this or other such passages, the German translator, Fritz Schröder, was, so to speak. In the passage discussed, there is one sentence in German, separated by a comma. It fits the music perfectly, and is easily singable and understandable. The same can be said of many of the other awkward English settings in their German version.

*　*　*　*　*　*

Is it only coincidence that at least five of the major composers of the 20th century were so short? Ravel was only five feet tall; Stravinsky was but 5'3"; Schönberg was also diminutive; Bartók was barely my height, 5'6"; and the guest at another of the Roberts's dinner parties, Paul Hindemith, was shorter than that. On the Hindemith evening at the Villa Aurelia the guests were the same as those for the Stravinsky except that Nora was there and also Hindemith's wife, a *Hausfrau* type, who hardly spoke. All evening I was bothered that she reminded me of some opera, the title of which I finally remembered: *Die Schweigsame Frau,*[*] a late Strauss opera. Her husband was talkative and—ever the teacher of young composers—asked to hear some music by one of us. Andy Imbrie volunteered to play a piano work.

While Andy went to his studio to get the score, Hindemith said that he'd heard that I had worked with Bartók and quizzed me at length about the experience. They had known one another well, of course. He said that when he had been on tour as the violist of the Amar Quartet, even in the most out of the way places, when the four went to a pub or bar after a concert, they were likely to see Bartók—also on tour—sitting in a corner drinking alone. I asked him how he

---

[*] (*The Silent Woman*)

reacted to Bartók music and he responded, "I can't hear it." I suspect that was his answer to any such question about the music of any composer very different from his own, for by that time Hindemith had fixed his own late style and codified it in two volumes.

Andy returned with his music and sat down at the piano. Hindemith offered to turn pages and found a nearby comfortable chair. He turned pages a couple of times, then dozed off and slept through the rest of the piece. Andy's music at that time tended to be strongly influenced by his teacher Roger Sessions in its length and chromatic expressionism. Doubtless Hindemith "couldn't" — wouldn't—hear it.

*   *   *   *   *   *

Not a guest at the Villa Aurelia or at the Academy, Leonard Bernstein was in Rome for a few days at some point; always looking for company, he hung out with us three composers. Still searching to become the musical director of a major symphony orchestra, he was guest conducting everywhere and had just arrived from Israel. Though posters announced that he would conduct and play the Ravel G Major *Piano Concerto* with the Orchestra of Santa Cecilia, I was astonished to find him at my studio door one afternoon. He greeted me as though we were close old friends, rather than the casual acquaintances we were at the time. He came in as though I'd been expecting him and referred to our "first meeting," the exchange of our sonatas via David Oppenheim, maybe five years earlier. Because Lennie's musical memory was so phenomenal, it's possible that he was not just being polite when he spoke a bit about my *Second Piano Sonata*. I could certainly not have remembered his *Clarinet Sonata* half so well and didn't try. Was I still writing sonatas, he asked. I said that they had been detours off my main road, the Via Opera, and told him a bit of what I was doing; he seemed to enjoy the idea of Nineveh-New York. He hoped to continue on the parallel ballet-musicals road, he said.

I asked if the rehearsals had begun. "Yes, just," he answered, "and, Jack, I think we're on to something new, because all these foreign orchestras have the same trouble in the Copland with getting the hang of equal eighths." ("Equal eighths" probably had their origin with Stravinsky. A number of American tonal-modal composers in the forties, notably Copland, began the use of predominant and subordinate lines of eighth notes in changing meters, for example, exaggeratedly: 4/4 7/8 3/4 5/8 2/4.) Though simple enough in themselves, it was for a time difficult to train the unaccustomed to make such passages sound so and not bizarrely accented.

After a stream of talk, Lennie paused and then went on to murmur that he envied the three of us being able to compose unencumbered. Why couldn't *he*? I'm afraid I said he could, if he really wanted to. Just for the asking he could surely become the Resident Composer for a year—an apartment next to the Villa, a piano, board, and a small stipend—everything necessary for composing. But the conversation was turning serious; his endless battle between composing and conducting, conducting vs composing, would be in for another bout. He suddenly remembered that he'd not yet looked at the Vivaldi Concerto he was to rehearse the next morning and he took a hurried leave.

I made a point the next morning of taking the pleasant short bus trip to the Piazza Argentina on which is the eighteenth-century Teatro Argentina, home of the Orchestra of Santa Cecilia. The center of the piazza one cannot enter, for it consists of the excavations of four Roman temples dating from four centuries before, to the birth of Christ—a typical mixture. The ruins are inhabited by scores of very untamed cats, a couple of which followed me around to the stage entrance, begging for a handout.

I never entered the theatre without remembering that it was here that took place the noisy fiasco of the premiere of Rossini's *Il Barbiere di Siviglia* in 1816. (Mention of that later very successful opera inevitably leads to the mention of Act I, *Tosca*, in San Andrea, a block or two away; the Palazzo Farnese another two blocks away, the scene of Act 2; and hardly a mile down the Corso and across the river, the Castel San Angelo, scene of Act 3.)

Inside the theatre I was about the only one attending the rehearsal. Lennie got along fine with just Italian musical terms and rehearsed the Vivaldi as though it had been in his repertory for years, not less than a day. And he teased the orchestra into smoothing out the Copland "equal eighths."

At the concert the audience was enthusiastic about the musical, lively young man on a podium and the piano stool. The Ravel *Concerto for piano* was clearly a favorite of his, with its jazz-flavored last movement. At the end of the slow movement he laid his head on his hands for much more than a moment. Was he fatigued, having spent much of the night with Vivaldi? Was he overcome by the music? Was he play-acting? Impossible to tell.

After the concert Lennie, Nora, and we three composers went to one of the music studios. After a good deal of wine, Lennie sat down at the piano and began playing and singing passages from *Boris Godunov*. Nora joined him in singing and at a pause asked him when and where he'd learned Russian. "Oh, I don't speak it. I just memorized the sounds of the words along with the music."

The kind of musical memory exemplified by that casual remark is not unique, but very rare. There may very well have been a price paid for the sponge that absorbed and retained all that Lennie heard, for throughout his serious-music career the accusation "derivative" dogged him. Turns of phrase, passages from the music he most admired—by Copland, Milhaud, Stravinsky, Mahler, and others— seeped back into his orchestral and choral works. Because he did not conduct and fall in love with ballet and musical comedies, his works in those media are free from unintended influences, and in *Candide*, for instance, there is intentional parody.

One of those present in the green room after Lennie had just conducted the premiere of a new piece, reported that Copland ambled over to the new score and said, as he leafed through it, "I wrote this in so-and-so . . . and that in so-and-so . . ." Lennie seemed unoffended.

Another composer-conductor-pianist, Stravinsky was not blessed—or cursed—with such a musical memory. In his early forties he wrote, especially for his own performance, the *Concerto for Piano and Wind Instruments* and played it frequently. Often he suffered memory lapses, once not remembering even how the slow movement began. Whenever I was present when Stravinsky conducted his own music, he had his nose in the score. He was frank about his problem, saying that because he had such a poor musical memory he had no choice but to be original.

*   *   *   *   *   *

In the first Academy post-war year, 1947-48, Sam Barber had been the Resident Composer. Fortunately for me, he returned as a long-term guest in the spring of '49, housed in one of the apartments of the Villa's wing. He had no Academy duties, and, essentially a shy man, was seldom if ever seen in the Academy. He and I—and the gardeners—had the Villa grounds to ourselves. He, as had Lennie, showed up unexpectedly at my studio door one morning. Apologizing profusely for disturbing—as Lennie certainly had not—he explained that he had asked Roberts to return in order to complete, undisturbed, his large piano sonata, commissioned by Rodgers and Hammerstein and to be premiered by Horowitz. (Barger's premieres were famously stellar events.)

We spoke of having seen one another last at *The Medium* rehearsals and performances, and he added that the New York City Opera had added it to its repertory; Gian Carlo would stage it, of course. He and Menotti were still sharing the house in Mount Kisco; Gian Carlo sent his greetings and wished me well in writing my opera. He was thinking about writing another, perhaps to be titled *The Consul*. After some more news about his hyperactive friend, he invited me to drop by his apartment any day before lunch for an aperitif and left, apologizing again.

I was chary of accepting his open invitation and so he frequently came by to walk me across the lawn for a Campari. He spoke little of his progress on the sonata, but I gathered he was having trouble. One tid-bit of conversation remains in the memory: Leon Kirchner had arrived from California and his piano sonata had been a sensation in some composer circles. Kirchner had played it especially for Sam—conservative in taste and in his own music—and Sam had told him that it reminded him of the Bartók Piano Sonata. He had intended the comment as a put-down, but it had been accepted as a great compliment.

On another Campari occasion we spoke of setting English to music. He saw no problem: one just did it. I replied that before I had to teach others who had never done it, or did it poorly or badly, I had to find out for myself what the basic problems of setting English are and what the solutions had been from Purcell to the present. "Oh, you and Virgil!" he exclaimed. I added that for years I'd accompanied auditioning singers and that most chose his songs as their American offering. He set English perfectly, but what other composer of songs had studied voice and concertized, accompanying himself? (Sam had recorded his own *Dover Beach* with string quartet for RCA when he was only 25.) And what other composer had grown up with an Aunt Louise (Homer) singing around the house, after she'd retired from the Met as the reigning contralto. He didn't argue further.

Later in the spring he showed up much too early for drinking and said that he needed help with his sonata. Puzzled, I traipsed along. It turned out that he'd finally completed it and needed help in determining the metronome markings. While he played very well from the manuscript, and up to tempo, with most of the right notes, even in the final fugue, I noted down the metronome numbers, quite a few, which we then toyed with and finally determined.

Sam was interested in my story about Bartók and metronomes. Bartók would not use one because he found the ticking intrusive and dictatorial. Instead, he used a weighted pendulum, the string marked off with gradated speeds; if he was playing the piano to set the tempi, an assistant or his wife Ditta operated the pendulum. A curious combination, setting twentieth-century tempi with eighteenth-century technology.

*   *   *   *   *   *

During warm weather a long luncheon table was set up under the arcade in the cortile, the several conversations accompanied by the splash and spatter of the Paul Manship fountain in the middle. Lunch was well under way one day when the breathless Japanese-American sculptor, Isamu Noguchi, took the adjoining seat. He had recently arrived and we had not yet met. To my innocent question, "Have you been sightseeing?" he answered that he had just been to St. Peter's and that he was appalled. He railed at the size of the basilica and its chapels, everything ridiculously out of scale with human beings. I was puzzled by his angry comments because I didn't know if he was speaking as a sculptor who often collaborated with architects in suiting his work to buildings and plazas, or whether we was personally affronted because he was so short. I probably refrained from saying that even the very tall and brawny Swiss Guards—some of them half a yard taller than he—could make the same objection. He went on to upbraid Bernini for the size of his *baldacchino*, but I got him to admit that at least it was in scale with the crossing and the dome. He disliked, too, the too-large statues.

I pointed out that he would surely find all the baroque churches, government buildings, and palaces designed to bully their beholders with the power of the church, government and nobility and therefore out of human scale. "Then isn't there anything worth seeing in Rome?" I recommended several of my favorite medieval churches and chapels. He thanked me and we went on talking about the stage pieces he'd been designing for Martha Graham, and how careful he had to be in scaling them to the size of her dancers. He was so upset that he may have left Rome soon after.

*　　*　　*　　*　　*　　*

Several times each year Fellows were invited to volunteer to fill the station wagon on three-or four-day excursions to Tuscany, to Florence, the Abruzzi, Etruscan-tomb country, wherever. I always volunteered. Shortly after we arrived, there was space for both Nora and me to return to Naples, this time to visit its museums, Pompeii and Herculaneum, the palace of the Kings of Naples at Caserta, and to visit the sites on the inland road to Naples and the coast road back to Rome.

All these trips were memorable, of course, but hardly need recounting. In any case, as has surely become apparent, I am given to remembering most vividly conversations that were incipient dramatic scenelets, sometimes with props.

I was waiting in the back of the empty station wagon to take off on a Tuscan jaunt when Philip Guston joined me. Nora and I had made friends with him—as many of the other Fellows had not—in spite of his prevailing glumness and irritability. He had made a considerable reputation with a series of imaginative but realistic scenes, easel-size and deftly painted, which no doubt had led to his Rome Prize. Now, in Rome, he was making a violent change in style, large works tending into the abstract. Nora and I had been invited to visit his studio and were impressed by what he was doing, but though he complained of being alone and lonely, we suspected that he was made edgy and unsettled by, as he said, "I am searching for my own painting."

In our station wagon conversation, somehow Virgil Thomson made an entrance and I mentioned his friend, the painter Maurice Grosser, who had supplied the dramatic scenario for the two Stein librettos. Philip snorted. (Grosser did portraits of southern children for a living, and specialized in still-lifes with eggs.) I unwisely went on to say that I had just read Maurice's little book for laymen, *Painting in Public* and that I'd found it very sensible. I am sure that Philip would have left my side in irritation had there been an empty seat.

His mood changed as we approached Arezzo and what he'd been talking about, on and off, since we left Rome: the large and elaborate fresco series by Piero della Francesca, which he knew only from reproductions. We parked in the piazza in front of the church of San Francesco and I tagged along with him into the church and straight to the Pieros in the main chapel. After a curse of pleasure, he lapsed into silence and stood transfixed. The striking, almost geometric shaping of the scenes that he'd been talking about, was plain to see, and much else. After a while, watching him studying the fourteen scenes, I walked away without his noticing. I must have thought then, as I had earlier in that first year in Rome when visiting a museum with a painter, how alike painters and composers are in at least one respect: laymen look, painters see; laymen hear, composers listen. A painter only glances at and passes by what doesn't interest him; he sees and studies what does. A composer tunes out, literally or figuratively, what is not of interest; he listens intently to what intrigues him.

All of us but Philip showed up on time at the excellent *trattoria* to the left of the church. When lunch was about finished, he appeared. Our next stop—perhaps at his suggestion—was Borgo San Sepolcro, birthplace of Piero and the resting place of his wonderful Resurrection. I have never been able to see the connections between Philips's painting and Piero's, often noted by others, but I suppose a painter would not hear my indebtedness to Bach either.

*   *   *   *   *   *

Some time later I returned to Arezzo and went through piles of prints and drawings in the shop next to the trattoria and the church of the Pieros, already described. Foolishly, I bought only one of the two large unsigned ink drawings of an ancient in chains; it turned out to be a Kurt Seligmann, drawn when the young Kurt was visiting in Italy and somehow left it behind. I also found there a watercolor, "Castel San Pietro, above Palestrina, Oct. 1836," by a young American, I am told, and later a member of the Hudson River School; which one is not yet determined. These are but two in our eclectic collection of oils, watercolors, drawings and prints, the nucleus of which are gifts or purchases from American and Swiss artists we met during our four years in Rome. There are also five Piranesi etchings (including two of the Prison Series, found on the cart of a street vendor) and a very large, more than two by six foot engraving of St. Peter's and Vatican City dating from the time of Pope Paul V, before the Bernini colonnade was added. Purchased in the Vatican, it is an early twentieth-century impression from two huge early seventeenth-century copper plates.

*   *   *   *   *   *

I was once asked by an interviewer, "How does one go about writing an opera?" Flippant and evasive, I answered, "Well, one sits down, as does a novelist, and writes. After a couple of years or more one gets up for the last time and there it is." Trying again, he asked, "How do you write an opera?" "Well, if the libretto is more or less ready to be set, or if the libretto is being written and pages of it are arriving ahead of need, I sit down at the piano (as most but not all composers do), conceive the music and write it down in pencil, in sketch—called a short score. Then I sit at the table and expand the short score on to the large pages that form the orchestral score, notating everything that the instrumentalists are to play. Still at the table, with short trips to the piano to test playability, a piano-vocal score is devised, an amalgam of the short score and the orchestral score—a necessity for those who want to examine the piece and for the singers and others to learn and rehearse from. I do my own—as some composers don't—because I've had a lot of experience in playing from others' scores and they are tricky to get right. If the opera ha been orchestrated in pencil, a fair copy in ink must be made at some point for duplication, almost never these days on transparencies (hard to find!) for blueprint duplication, but on opaque staff-paper for Xeroxing. Then one gets up for the last time from the several hundred pages of short score, one or two orchestral scores, and the piano-vocal score—that is, if it's an evening-filling opera, two or so hours of playing time. In the course of writing these three or four scores the composer has copied out the words of the libretto three or four times—not to speak of providing the repeated words for the choral sections. This is the sequence I've followed, more or less, in writing ten operas. Other composers, using hired orchestrators, copyists, or computers, can avoid some or all of the handwriting. But they must end up with the three scores and a separately typed libretto.

To apply the above comments to *Jonah*: in addition to the six months in New York writing and re-writing the first scene, the whole of the Roman two years, September 1948 to August 1950 were required. Writing an opera, just the music, or libretto and music, is a solitary activity; the only company is that of those imagined characters one is trying to bring to life in words and sounds.

To imply that I was spending my time with the *Jonah* characters during "the two Roman years" is less accurate than "during our two years abroad," for though we were mostly in Rome, we spent some weeks both years at Christmas and many weeks both summers with Nora's parents at their villa in the Italian-speaking Swiss canton, the Ticino. By the time we arrived at Christmas, 1948, they had had more than a year to settle in. Besides Emmy and Henry Sigerist, Nora's elder sister, Erica, had been serving as her father's secretary, typing manuscripts and extensive correspondence; she was followed by a series of live-in secretaries. By the time we arrived an upright piano had been rented from someone in the nearby village of Pura and placed in a solitary garden house known as the Cathouse, because Babyface, the house-cat, lived there. Cathouse was Henry's punning allusion to one of the workplaces of the painter Toulouse-Lautrec, a brothel. During our eight sojourns in our four "Roman years" to Casa Serena, as the Sigerist home was called, the piano was always rented, tuned, and ready for my use, as it was later, on our occasional summer trips to the Ticino from New York.

Casa Serena was wondrously sited on the flat top of a foothill of the Alps. From a glassed-in room one looked east down over vineyards and across a farmed spit of land to an arm of the Lake of Lugano. I often hiked down for a swim and sunbathed while improving my German by reading a set of translated *Dr. Doolittle* books.

On the other side of the main arm of the lake was the village of Bissone where the architect Borromini was born. Curiously, several of the architects and builders of seventeenth-century Baroque Rome hailed from the local villages. When Italians had trouble understanding my name, I found it convenient to pass as Gianni da Bissone.

To the left, north, were the Swiss Alps and Lugano itself, quickly accessible by a narrow-gauge Toonerville Trolley look-alike. To the right, south, was Italy, only a scant mile away across the Tresa River, which split the small town of Ponte Tresa into Swiss and Italian halves. From the third floor of Casa Serena, looking across the river one could see the hill town of Cadegliano, a name that stuck in my memory. Jogging it constantly, I remembered: the birthplace of

Gian Carlo Menotti. We made a pilgrimage, naturally, and were shown through part of the Menotti villa by a housekeeper. I sent Gian Carlo a postcard from Ponte Tresa memorializing the event and learned, later, that he rarely returned to where he'd been brought up.

There was a constant stream of visitors, sometimes from the Sigerist side, more often from the Escher side, three of whom later lived and worked in the U.S. Most spoke at least some English and made a point of speaking it or High German with me, the first American to be married into the family. Swiss German was occasionally to be heard, always spoken to the cat.

Henry's eminence as a medical historian and medievalist, and his service as a public health consultant to the governments of India, South Africa, Saskatchewan—and others—had led to a wide acquaintance and to varied guests eager to see him in his isolated retreat. Each, on his first visit, was presented with a *boccalino*, a regional specialty in the form of a very small pitcher used as a wine glass. Made in quantity by a local ceramicist, each bore the name of Casa Serena and they are now widely dispersed.

On special occasions the village cook-maid was demoted to helping Henry, who took over the kitchen, for he was an accomplished chef in the French style. He not only cooked, but also provided a hand-drawn menu with listed wines. On only our first visit were Nora and I treated to such a special dinner, for I could not tolerate the rich and buttery fare.

The psychiatrist Gregory Zilboorg, a long-time friend of Henry, was a visitor more than once when we were in residence. He was also an accomplished chef and the two would prepare a dinner together, sipping wine the while. On one occasion Henry was puzzled by Gregory's dropping by overnight on his way from Paris to Rome and the Vatican. What business did a Jew with both Russian and American medical degrees have with the Vatican? The explanation was that Gregory was upset that French priests, nuns, and monks with psychiatric, alcoholic, and sexual disorders were being treated in French public hospitals. He had convinced the French prelates that the Church should set up its own, more private, facilities and he was on his way to convince the Curia to agree. Apparently he did, although there was little or no public mention of it, naturally.

Back in New York, The Zilboorgs occasionally invited us to a Sunday brunch, together with a number of psychiatrists. (May one say a disputation of psychiatrists?) It was then that I realized that Zilboorg was something of a controversial figure. Among his celebrated patients, some of whom he accompanied on their travels, was George Gershwin. Because he had not diagnosed Gershwin's fatal brain tumor he was criticized by some; others maintained that even if it had been found, it would not have been operable in 1937.

Not to speak of the charms of Lugano and the magnificent Thyssen art collection nearby, there were many attractive rural wayside chapels and village churches in the neighborhood of Casa Serena. All were photographed, captioned, and put by Henry in his numerous scrapbooks, now at Yale. The hilly Collina d'Or (the hill of gold) appeared from Casa Serena to be the other side of the lake and turned out to be of special interest to me. When Henry happened to mention that Hermann Hesse had lived and died in Montagnola near the hill, my curiosity was aroused. Otto Luening had spoken of Hesse often and warmly and of how strongly he had been influenced by Hesse's writings. They had met in Zürich when Otto was but seventeen and he had then set one of his poems to music. A year earlier the Dada group had organized itself—or, rather, disorganized itself—and Otto both attended and performed at some of their meetings. The Dadaists, war resisters and dissidents of all kinds, Germans, Swiss and Rumanians, they met and performed usually in the Café Voltaire, at #1, Spiegelgasse, in the old town. Among the early members were Tristan Tsara and Hans Arp, later well-known artists; two Germans, Hugo Ball, a writer, and Emmy Hennings, a singer who turned to writing, later married, lived later on the Collina d'Oro and died there. I was determined to trace their ends, and finally succeeded. On the crest of the Collina is the church of Madonna d'Ongero. We searched through the adjoining cemetery and found a gravestone: Hugo Ball, died 1927, and Emmy

Hennings-Ball, died 1948. According to the locals, she, as a widow, had toiled in a small tobacco workshop, which I often passed on my way to a swim and another chapter of *Dr. Doolittle*.

Sometime later, in New York, we were visiting a German-American painter-friend, Adolph Fleischmann. He introduced us to another guest, Dr. Richard Hulbeck, a psychiatrist. In the course of an animated conversation with Hulbeck, we mentioned that we had been often in the Tessin—as the Germans call it—and that Nora was from Zürich; I learned that his name had originally been Hülsenbeck, a name that was somehow familiar to me. "Why?" I asked. I then learned that he had been one of the half-dozen or so original Dadaists and therefore had known Ball and Hennings intimately. To his growing astonishment I told him of my mentor, Otto Luening, whom he would have met many decades ago, my interest in the Dada movement, and my success in finding the graves of Ball and Hennings. I sent a copy of my photo of their headstone to Dr. Hulbeck's office on Central Park West, with a note inside to Richard Hülsenbeck as a memento of our chance meeting.

During our many summers from 1949 through 1957, when Henry had just died and Emmy was planning to move to Zürich, Casa Serena's location made possible short trips by Nora and me in the family Volkswagen to the main cities in Lombardy: Milano and the Scala, Verona, Vicenza, Bergamo, and Brescia; Como was but a daytrip. Trains from Lugano led us in one year or another to Zürich and Basel and farther-away places—all nearby to an American. A belated wedding present from Nora's grandmother Sigerist made a three-week visit to Paris possible; there followed, one year or another, *Die Meistersinger* and *Tristan und Isolde* in Bayreuth, Venice, Vienna and its opera, and Salzburg. In the last-named there were two memorable opera performances and two unexpected events. Loitering in the Mozarteum, I was approached by a man I took to be a CIA agent from his manner and his questions. I was quizzed at length about Herbert von Karajan, who, I had heard, was still undergoing de-Nazification. I had to confess that I knew nothing about him but gossip. It was said that he had been forbidden to have anything to do with the Festival, but that unofficially he was running it. More pleasant, also in the Mozarteum, was dropping in on a rehearsal of *Dido and Aeneas* and finding that the two singers on stage were erstwhile Opera Workshop singers, mezzo Shirley Sudock and soprano Judith Liegner.

All these summer trips were to places new to me, though mostly not to Nora. They exercised the mind and the eyes, the palate in Italy and France, and the ears in the opera houses and the Roman amphitheater—the Arena—in Verona. Each excursion led to a stimulated me back to my cathouse and a continuation of my very long imaginary stay with Jonah and his friends in Nineveh.

Thoughtful Swiss and Italians agree that the Ticino enjoys the best of Switzerland and Italy, without the stiffness and formality of the former and the disorder, even lawlessness, of the latter. Though snow-capped mountains can be seen in the north, the weather is mild: tobacco, grapes, and camellias thrive. No wonder that Mussolini called the Ticino "Italia Irredenta" and proselytized among the Ticinese for its return to Italy.

The camellia buds would have been forming when we left Casa Serena for our 1950 "spring semester" in Rome. Shortly thereafter I completed the short score of my opera and began its orchestration. As I did so, it occurred to me that with our abundant lire and the excellency and inexpensiveness of Italian copyists I might save myself the trouble of making my own fair copy of it in ink by having it done professionally.

Aldo Carnevali was famous in Rome for his accuracy and beautiful music calligraphy. He lived in a walk-up apartment in an ancient building about equidistant from the Palazzo Cenci and the Teatro Argentino. As I completed, checked and re-checked a number of pages of the orchestration, I took them to Carnevali. Some time passed before I noticed that he was blind in one eye. It took even longer for me to notice that his wife—his copying associate whose calligraphy was indistinguishable from his—was blind in the other eye. Between them they possessed one pair of eyes—and seemingly one hand.

I completed my penciled full score, appropriately, on All Fools Day (1950). By that time the Carnevalis were at work on its first pages. My 578 pages were to become their 588 pages on twenty-four-staff, high quality, almost vellum-like transparencies. As they carried out their transformation, I was copying my 212 pages of penciled piano-vocal score in ink on similarly high-quality Roman transparencies. I interrupted occasionally to proofread Carnevali pages; their only errors were beautified versions of the errors I'd overlooked in checking my own penciled score. Their score and my piano-vocal score—the 212 pages expanded into 241 pages—were completed at about the same time, well into the summer.

While I was under the pressure of these two tasks I had little time for sightseeing.

A pleasant and unexpected interruption was a visit to my studio by Ned Rorem. Though he was born two years later than I and only forty miles away in Richmond, Indiana, and we shared Quaker backgrounds—his parents, mine several generations in the past—we had known one another only casually in New York. Ned was very interested in my opera project, for he was a close friend of Paul and Sally Goodman. A few years earlier he had, as a student, composed part of an opera based on Paul's play, *Cain and Abel*. His 1947 setting of Paul's lyric, *The Lordly Hudson*, had aroused comment and he was to set many other of his poems.

Years later I was startled and amused to find our brief meeting memorialized in a paragraph or two in one of Ned's fifteen volumes of diaries and reminiscences. He wrote that he had been impressed by the beauty of Carnevali's score-copying. He also wrote that he thought my opera would not be performed—an opinion I surely would have remembered had he shared it with me that day in Rome.

Upon our return to New York a few months later, Douglas and Otto briefly considered producing *Jonah* in the spring, but it was clear that my orchestra, chorus, and a few dancers would not fit into Brander Matthews. Nor would they fit into two other chamber opera theaters, whose producers specialized on operas with Jewish subjects and were eager to premiere what they called my "Jewish opera." These reactions and the fact that orchestral parts had not yet been extracted, led me briefly to consider making a chamber orchestra version of the score, but the storm scene and the several choral scenes argued for leaving the score as it was—and as it remains. So far Ned's prediction has proven correct, but I'm not certain that he ruled out a posthumous production.

In any case, these three aborted productions of *Jonah* did not relegate the 1,619 pages in pencil and in ink to the closet. That act was postponed by the intervention of another opera composer, Giuseppe Verdi, who died in 1901.

I had no occasion to relate the story of this comic intercession until 2001, when a committee was formed by New York University to memorialize the centenary of Verdi's death, primarily with a short series of lectures by composers.

I was chosen to initiate the series with a lecture at the Morgan Library. Unfortunately, a storm of *Otello* proportios was raging that evening and the audience was hardly the size of an *Otello* chorus. It did, however, include Lady Bing, the widow of Sir Rudolf Bing, who was madly talkative at the reception thereafter.

Presumably we lecturers had been chosen because we were thought to have had some connection with Verdi and his works. Accordingly, I began with myself when young, frequently accompanying Verdi opera broadcasts from the Met at the piano from my own vocal scores. I mentioned the influence they may have had on my writing three librettos and of my music to them; the five years at Eastman School and the consideration there of Verdi's music only in the history courses, never in theory, orchestration, or composition classes; the coaching, accompanying, and occasional conducting of Verdi arias, ensembles, and scenes in the Columbia Opera Workshop over some four years. This first part of the lecture is omitted here, its contents having been already described in detail.

The second part of the lecture had to do with my opera *Jonah*. What follows is an edited version of a transcript of the recording made of the lecture, which was not read; it continues seamlessly from the time when the Carnevalis were copying and I was devising my piano-vocal score.

The third part of the lecture was concerned with my sixth opera, *Captain Jinks of the Horse Marines*, the subject matter of which is directly related to Verdi's *La Traviata*, from which there are many almost literal quotations. That *Jinks* part of the lecture will appear later in its proper chronological setting, the early and mid-seventies.

*   *   *   *   *   *

. . . During the summer of 1950 we were again in Pura, where I was completing my piano-vocal score. When it was completed in August and the full score was received from Carnevali in Rome, there remained the task of reproducing both in multiple copies. Because there was nobody in Lugano who could do the job, I delivered the manuscripts by hand to an establishment in Milano that could. A few days later I drove down to pick up the copies and the original manuscript, all unbound, which made several piles of paper in the back seat of the Volkswagen.

I drove up to the barrier at Chiasso, the Italian-Swiss border, was asked the usual questions, and was then queried about my importation of unbound musical manuscripts. The customs official was about to unload the piles for weighing and figuring the import duty when he thought to ask, "Who wrote it?" I replied, "I did." "What kind of music is it?" "It's all one opera." "It's all your opera?" "It's all mine!" With a broad smile and a friendly gesture, he waved me through, saying, "We don't charge composers for their operas. Ciao!" Fortunately this exchange was carried on in "proper" Italian; the local dialect is impenetrable:

Ticinese: Piöcc fa piöcc e danee fa danee.
Italian: Pulci fanno pulci e denaro fa denaro.
English: Fleas make fleas and money makes money.

Otmar Nussio, a composer and the conductor at Monte Ceneri, the Swiss-Italian radio station, was a cousin of my wife and was later occasionally to program my music on the Monte Ceneri station. Because he had not composed an opera and knew that I had, he gave me a newly published La Scala brochure. It announced that in honor of the 50th anniversary of Verdi's death in 1951 a contest was underway for a full-length opera. It was open to composers of any age and nationality; the winner would receive 5,000,000 lira and the premiere of his work at La Scala during the 1951-52 season; the judges would include Stravinsky (as chairman), Honegger, Ghedini, Cantelli, and two others. As Nussio remarked, I now had available the numerous required scores and libretti and nothing to lose in applying. I did so, as instructed, enclosing in an envelope my name, date of birth, and nationality. On the envelope and on the submitted material was my chosen pseudonym—I hope not Joseph Green, but I'm not sure.

Shortly thereafter we returned to New York and to my teaching at Columbia, where my Opera Workshop duties had been taken over largely by John Kander and John Crosby. During that whole academic year of '51-'52 I heard not a word from La Scala about my Verdi-contest submission, though I read somewhere that the winner, the Argentine Juan José Castro's *Proserpina e lo Straniero*, had been a fiasco at its Scala premiere.

During the summer of '52 we were again at Pura in the Ticino. After settling in I set out by train to Milano to find out what had happened to *Jonah*, if anything. After my short train trip I found myself at the La Scala stage door explaining my mission to a friendly attendant who rattled off very elaborate directions to the office of the librarian in charge of the scores submitted to *Il Concorso Internazionale per L'Opera Lirica*. I took the elevator to the 4th floor, turned, turned, and turned again (as instructed, I thought), knocked on a door, and stepped in—to find myself standing on the gridiron, that set of steel bars at the very top of an operatic or other stage from which sets, or other things—such as Rhine maidens—are hung—or flown, as they say. Floating up the 80 or 90 feet from the stage was a soprano voice, identifiable even at that early part of her career as the voice of Maria Callas, singing *La Gioconda*! I walked out a few steps on the gridiron and then stood transfixed—as who wouldn't—partly because you don't want to fall through and partly because you don't want to fall on Callas.

Though tempted to stay longer, I left my exotic perch, found the door I had been seeking, and entered a very small dark room. I saw immediately my pile of *Jonah* material in a large locked case, otherwise almost empty. In the gloom was the librarian, with a stylish black patch over one eye. Could it be an augury? Jonah had blamed God himself for his bad luck. The half-blind keeper of my two-volume score copied out by a half-blind couple of autographers: all three had overcome their bad luck. Had I? I gave him my name and he became distinctly uneasy, I thought. "Those are my scores over there," I said, pointing to them. "And who, exactly, are you?" I repeated: "My name is Jack Beeson and I'm the composer and librettist of *Jonah*. I've come to collect my music. I've been wondering why I've heard nothing about my application." He answered my question at length, handing me a copy of the handsome illustrated brochure that recounted in detail the course of the competition, which I still have. There had been 138 entrants, one by one 133 had been eliminated. He pointed to the page listing the remaining five, and to *Jonah*, #4. He explained that when the envelope was opened and the composer-librettist of #4 was discovered to have been only in his twenties when he wrote it, the jury and the administrative committee decided that perhaps some fraud had been committed. It had been decided to await more information about #4, or his arrival in person.

"Well, here I am," I said. He asked to see my passport. I gave it to him, but he was unsatisfied. "How do we know that you are that person?" and I answered, "Look at the picture! Look at the picture!" My annoyance was quickly erasing my euphoria at discovering how well I'd one in the competition.

He remained friendly, but insisted that I go around the corner to the American Consulate for a letter stating that I was indeed Jack Beeson. We had lived in Italy long enough to have learned not to become upset at Italian bureaucratic habits. The official at the Consulate was equally suspicious and gave me a letter stating that I claimed to be the owner of the passport. Irritated, I returned to the librarian, who could not read the letter written in English. I was pleased to mis-translate it in a way that satisfied him.

"Very well," he said pleasantly. "The Director, Mr. Ghiringhelli, told me that should you ever show up I was to bring you to his office so that he could meet you." With this unexpected invitation, I filled my arms with the two large volumes of the orchestral score, two piano-vocal scores, and five synopses in Italian and we set out through the back-stage maze. There was time for me to recollect some of the gossip about Ghiringhelli that Otmar Nussio had shared with me when he had given me the application form two years before. La Scala had been damaged during the Allied bombings of 1943. After it had been put back together in '46, someone of the right political party and wealth was needed to head it. Signor Ghiringhelli knew very little about music and opera, but a great deal about making money, raising money, and the manufacture of shoes. Shortly after he became director, the musical director came into his office and asked if he would care to come into the theatre and hear singer auditions. "What kind of singers?" "Mezzo sopranos." "No! I'll have no half-sopranos in my theatre!"

I was ushered into his regal newly-restored eighteenth-century office. He seemed not in the least suspicious, but very friendly and ordered two double *espressi.* He was unable or unwilling to speak English. Naturally I told him of our two years in Rome and our frequent stays in the nearby Ticino. He claimed never to have heard that during the war sausages had been smuggled by one-man submarines from the Italian end of the Lake of Lugano to the Swiss end. We spoke at length about the opera competition and he presented me with a handsome very large volume of essays and Verdi stage sets, published by La Scala in commemoration of the semi-centennial. He was reticent about the premiere of the winning opera, polite about an American having come in fourth, and obviously delighted that Italian composers had come in second and third. As I left he invited me to attend La Scala as his guest whenever I should be in Milano.

I am delighted to have had small parts to play in the commemorations of the semi-centennial and the centennial of Verdi's death, for he and his works have been a great influence on mine. Wagner's music dramas have also been a strong influence. The two were contemporaries and the celebrations of the bicentennials of their births in 1813 are now but years away. The two composers never met. During their lives and thereafter the values of their works have risen and ebbed, often one up and one down, and influenced not only by changing taste but also by nationalistic politics. I wonder which one will get top billing in 2013.

*   *   *   *   *   *

To return briefly to Casa Serena and to August 1950, when I first heard about the La Scala/Verdi opera contest; we were about to return to New York, both of us to Columbia and the real world. We booked passage on a Holland-American liner as an excuse to travel north and visit Amsterdam. This we did, as well as Enschede on the northeast border with Germany, where Nora's cousin Margerite Lely and her engineer-husband made it possible to visit out-of-the-way museums and World War II sites accessible only by car. There was something touchingly personal in the way Lely explained the construction of the protecting dikes, for some of them had been designed and built by earlier Lelys.

On an extended boat trip through the Amsterdam harbor and canals we were astonished to find Lennie Bernstein in front of us with a younger man who turned out to be his brother Burtie. When we disembarked occasionally to be shown this or that, Lennie paid so little attention to Burtie that Nora took him in tow. The two brothers and their sister were spending the summer sightseeing around Europe, Lennie guest conducting the while.

When our watery tour finally came to an end, Lennie asked us if we would show him around the red-light district after dinner. Startled to be asked, we did know where it was to be found: just across a canal from the back of our fine hotel, with its well-known high, glass-ceilinged dining room. After dinner, the three of us—Burtie was thought by Lennie to be too young to come along? —traipsed slowly along the one-sided street, gawking at the windows of each house. In each was a red light bulb or a candle and a flimsily dressed siren looking bored.

This sadly comic jaunt was the end of European sightseeing. We embarked on the Veendam in Rotterdam and left for the Empire City. On board, by chance, was Jim Lamantia, a Fellow in Architecture whom we'd known well at the Academy. He seduced us time after time into endlessly playing cards all the way across the North Atlantic.

*   *   *   *   *   *

Jack Beeson at age seven. Muncie, Indiana, 1928

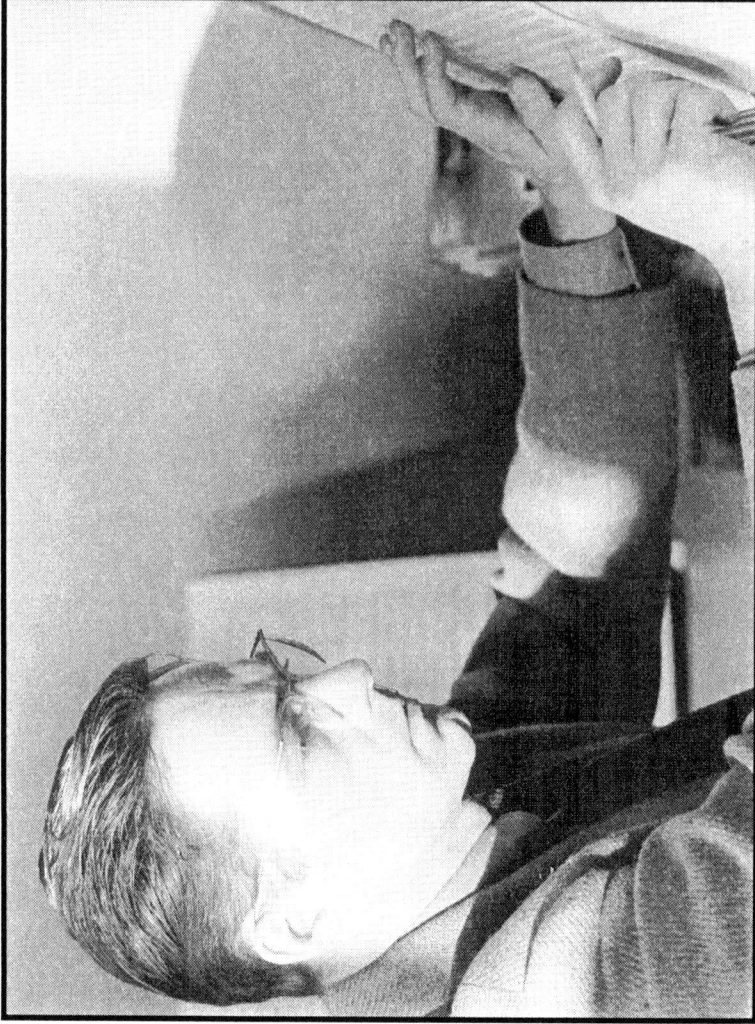

Jack Beeson at work on the *Lizzie* score, Shelter Island, NY, in the early 1960s
Photo by William Barksdale

Ralph Farnworth (the Young Gambler) and Leyna Gabriele (the Girl)
in the premiere of *Hello Out There*, the Columbia University Opera Workshop,
May 1954.
Photo by Fred Fehl

The opening scene of *The Sweet Bye and Bye*: Bathers versus the Lifeshine Flock, led by Mother Rainey (Ruth Kobart). Premiere, the Juilliard School, November 1957.

The composer (Jack Beeson) and Lizzie (Brenda Lewis)
during a rehearsal for the premiere of *Lizzie Borden*,
the New York City Opera, March 1965.

The "bitch scene" of *Lizzie Borden*: Lizzie (Brenda Lewis) and her stepmother, Abbie (Ellen Faull), in the New York City Opera revival of 1967.
Photo: © Beth Bergmen, 1967, NYC

Lizzie (Phyllis Pancella) in *Lizzie Borden,* Glimmerglass Opera, July 1996.
Photo by George Mott

Principals in the original cast of *My Heart's in the Highlands*, NET opera, March 1970.
Left to right, sitting: Kenneth Smith as Jasper MacGregor, Allen Crofoot as Ben Alexander, Gerard Harrington as young Johnny.
Left to right, standing: Lili Cookasian as Grandmother, and Spiro Malas as Mr. Kosak.

Jack Beeson, the composer of *My Heart's in the Highlands*, as the
Young Husband in its premiere, NET Opera, March 1970.
Photo by Morris Warman

In the cast of Shakespeare's *Midsummer Night's Dream*, Shelter Island, NY,
Summer 1966,
Hermia (Edith Lechmanski) and Lysander (Jack Beeson).
Photo by William Barksdale.

In the first scene of *Captain Jinks of the Horse Marines*, Col. Mapleson
(Eugene Green) descends from the liner The Flying Dutchman.
Premiere, the Kansas City Lyric Theater, September 1975.

In the premiere of *Captain Jinks of the Horse Marines* the two principals meet: Aurelia (Carol Wilcox) and Jinks (Robert Owen Jones). Kansas City Lyric Theater, September 1975.

Dr. Heidegger's Maid (Miranda Beeson) is spooked by a dangling skeleton and a dusty tome at the outset of *Dr. Heidegger's Fountain of Youth*, premiered by the National Arts Club in November 1978.
Photo by Marbeth

Three of the four ancients briefly enjoy rejuvenation in *Dr. Heidegger's Fountain of Youth* during its premiere by the National Arts Club.

Left to right: Colonel Killigrew (Robert Shiesley), Rachel Lockhart (Carol Wilcox) and Reuben Waterford (Grayson Hirst).

The composer (Jack Beeson) and the librettist (Sheldon Harnick) collaborate on taking a bow at the end of the first performance of their chamber opera, *Dr. Heidegger*, at the National Arts Club in November 1978. Photo by Marbeth.

Cyrano (Werner Hahn) casts an uncharacteristically baleful glance during one of the twelve premiere performances of *Cyrano* by the Hagen Theater, Germany, in the autumn of 1994.
Photo by Dietrich Dettmann

In the premiere performance of *Sorry, Wrong Number*, Patricia Dell enacted and sang the wheelchair-bound, and telephone-bound heroine. The Center for Contemporary Opera at the Kaye Playhouse, May 25/26, 1999.
Photo by Susan Lerner

The operina, *Practice in the Art of Elocution*, was performed May 12, 2007 by Wendy Hill, soprano/actress, and Gerald Sheichen, pianist/actor, in the Skirball Performing Arts Center, sponsored by the Center for Contemporary Opera and the New York City Opera.
Photo by Richard Marshall.

Chapter 7

New Yorkers and Ticinesi, Miscellanea
(1950-1952)

It is said that the two apartment houses on Riverside Drive at 116th Street, #335 and #440, were once conventionally shaped, but that a corner of each has been eroded over the years into its elegant curve by the violent winds coming down the Hudson River from the north. The larger of the two, #440, sports in its east side a second entrance and address, 3 Claremont Avenue. On Claremont, which runs north and south parallel to the Drive, unbroken by side streets for three blocks, almost all of the buildings are owned by Columbia and are inhabited by its faculty, known locally as the Claremont Avenue Gang. They resemble a professorial enclave in a small college town, with the usual enlivening scandal and gossip. On the other side of the street is the back side of Barnard College. We joined the Gang shortly after disembarking from the Veendam, by finding an apartment in 3 Claremont with two bedrooms, the small one intended for the baby expected to be born in late November 1950.

Hardly were we housed, when I was teaching full-time in Columbia College, in those days three courses a term. One was permitted to take on a fourth course each term in the School of General Studies for an additional pittance, and that I did for a while.

No longer committed to the Workshop, I nevertheless—for fun—helped out on the spring '51 premiere production of Douglas Moore's *Giants in the Earth* (which was awarded the Pulitzer Prize in Music) and served as coach and assistant conductor a year later on the premiere production of *Acres of Sky* by Arthur Kreutz.

While we had been abroad, Al Rivett had taken my place in the flourishing Opera Workshop and its more frequent public performances (aided by coaches Everett Lee and Anley Loran) and on the two Ditson Fund sponsored spring premieres. He wrote me such frequent very long letters, mostly about operatic activities—repertory, singers, and stage directors—that I hardly missed being present. He also complained bitterly about being overworked and underpaid, having kept accurate account of his coaching hours and computed his pay per hour. Because he had taken over exactly my schedule in the classroom and the theatre, I wondered if I had been too busy and pleased with my work not to notice the hours and the pay, or, for three years had been too passive and complaisant.

In any case, now that I had returned, he continued exactly as before, at what pay I had no idea, and I was teaching my four courses. Two of these were Music Humanities, known as MB1. The General Studios Music I course was designed as an analogue of MB1. In those years the College was not yet coeducational; General Studies students were men and women of all ages over 21. So, except for taking into consideration the two differing kinds of students, I was teaching one course three times each term—time-consuming and time-saving—but, so to speak, instructive.

More than once during the couple of years when I was teaching these three section and later when teaching but one (finally having arrived at a total of forty of them) I had occasion to remember and re-read the ten pages Virgil Thomson devoted to the subject of the "appreciation racket" in his 1940 book, *The State of Music*. His phrases "Appreciation Racket" and "the Fifty Pieces," soon became useful to polemicists and sociologists to music. Virgil, in a fine fury, argued that those teaching (or, as he also said, "preaching") the subject using as examples the fifty masterpieces—usually orchestral works composed between 1775 and 1875—were but cogs in the publicity machines of record and radio corporations and symphony orchestras. Because Virgil wrote of teaching music appreciation on its lowest, most popular, level he gave the term a bad name in musical circles. We who were teaching MB1 and GS Music 1 avoided the term altogether, though we were teaching a form of it. We began with a nod to the Greeks, continued with medieval monody and on through the centuries to include the up-to-the-minute present. Musical example in all media, including opera and chamber music were included. That we succeeded in introducing at least some students to what they had so far missed, had come to enjoy, and thereafter taken much pleasure in, is certainly the case: time after time, in New York and more often elsewhere a seeming stranger approaches, introduces himself as one of my former Humanities students, and says so fervently.

My fourth course that year required a change of role: teacher, rather than student of composition, in this case teacher of those who were just curious how one writes music mixed in with those who already had written or improvised a bit, were floundering and eager to learn how to give shape to their errant musical ideas, in short, Composition I. Otto Luening preferred, he said, to help the beginners rather than the more advanced, who were often already certain of their genius and resistant to anybody's suggestions. Because by 1950 more composers than before were applying and being accepted for our terminal MA in composition, Otto had to relinquish his teaching of undergraduates in favor of the graduate students. After a year I had to do the same for the same reason, more graduate students. As I did so, Henry Cowell took over the undergraduates for a while; I subbed for him on occasion when he was unwell.

In 1966 a doctorate in composition was established and the number of graduate student composers burgeoned. By that time, and slightly later, other tenured composers had joined the department: Vladimir Ussachevsky, Chou Wen-Chung (who attracted a large number of Mainland Chinese and Taiwanese students), and Mario Davidovsky (who attracted South Americans our way). At the height of this efflorescence, 1976 to 1990, we registered annually some sixty graduate composers, so large a number that it was widely disbelieved by our

214

colleagues in other American universities and conservatories. Columbia-trained composers for a while seemed to win more than their share of Guggenheims, Rome Prizes, Academy of Arts and Letters grants, and other such awards. There were reasons accounting for the very large number of applicants: the attraction of New York City's music life for talented and ambitious young composers; the Ditson Fund's partial funding of several new music performance groups at Columbia, in New York, and elsewhere; the reputation of some of the students and faculty; and the reputation of Douglas Moore. (He never taught composition to composers, but to musicologists, during the period when there was also an elective seminar in musicology for composers.)

Shortly after I had retired and was no longer offering my seminar for composers concerning the voice and setting English, I was interviewed by David Gompper of the Society of Composers concerning teaching composition. Transcribed, edited, and published, it is reprinted here as a short retrospective account of some experiences daring from the years hurried through above. Much of the comment about Bartók is deleted, he having been extensively discussed earlier herein.

*　　*　　*　　*　　*　　*

"Teaching" Composition—
An Interview with Jack Beeson

DKG: How do you prepare for a career in composition? I see many students who start off in composition but become confused in their search for a career and drop out.

JB: Then they aren't destined to become composers. No harm done! Composers compose; if they cease composing, they cease being composers. If they drop out and then feel guilty enough, they'll return to the habit and join the profession, if that's what it is. The drop-out who feels relieved of a burden has learned things about music that can't be learned by those who have not composed.

[I think what Virgil Thomson once wrote about painting is equally true of composing: "Painting is still learned rather than taught."] One can teach only aspects of composing, not composition itself: notation, some aspects of instrumental and vocal usage, and orchestration (when, if ever, it's separable from creation): clarity and projection, texture, coherence, and shaping time over short and long spans—not to speak of the line-writing, pitches and rhythms. I guess that covers it. Which of these elements dominate and to what expressive end are what forms a style. And *that* is none of the teacher's business. Oh, one can say, as I did back in the 60's and 70's, "If you write that way, you pay a price for it. Do you know the price and are you willing to pay it? If you want to write extremely difficult music, are you willing to put up with performances that don't come about, or with performers who don't like it, or with poor performances or none? It is a free country and you can do it if you want. But don't come to me later complaining that no one is performing your music." Or you can say to a student who churns out quickly one piece after another, stylistically all over the map and with no trace of self-criticism: "Write a piece for solo oboe. Never mind the two pianos and the rest of it. You don't have to write an orchestral piece to have somebody tell you that you can't write a musical line."

DKG: It isn't easy to do—or to teach composition, for that matter.

JB: Yes, I know, and the trouble is that there's no way of objectively testing success either. Let's be modest: after all, what do <u>we</u> remember learning from <u>our</u> teachers? It is possible to aid the talented by helping to clear the brush along the paths to their goals, or sometimes by helping them to discover a path that they had neglected or avoided, perhaps one that someone else had forbidden. Talented students, I think, pick up quickly on the things we say in passing. Hints usually work better than pronouncements. With the less talented and hopeless, one tries to be encouraging—up to a point-and at least to let them get full value for their tuition. We should not say, "You're untalented. Drop it." Let them discourage themselves.

DKG: The same with pianists, who are always trained to become the next concert artist. I think this is wrong. You are trained to be a pianist not only to produce those warm tones, but more importantly to sight-read, to be a useful musician.

JB: Not counting composers I've tried to help elsewhere. I had about 300 composition students at Columbia, over a span of forty-some years, mostly graduate students. They ran the gamut from Wuorinen and Sollberger to John Kander. I certainly had nothing to do with the latter's ability to write memorable tunes for his musicals, but he admits to my having introduced him to *Wozzeck* and still calls me by his nickname for me, "Teach".

"Teach" has the duty to share his longer and wider musical experience with the young, sometimes in unconventional ways. Though I never studied with Otto Luening, he said to me as I was just beginning to teach, "You know, Jack, you won't have to worry about their pitches and rhythms. They will be no problem to you." And he added, "that is not the problem teaching composition.

The problem is being a lay psychiatrist. You will find that the blocks that people have are not about musical problems; they are something else, and it is up to you to get them unblocked or send them off to the clinic for professional help." He was right: as in any large group of persons immersed in an art, many did seek counseling. On my own, though, I made two diagnoses of manic-depression, one of diabetes, and one thyroid disorder. Thereafter, we could more easily get down to the problems of their musical choices.

I remember well a too tightly-wired student with a special kind of talent. He was writing something with words and wasn't getting very far with it—everything was oblique. I looked at him, I asked "Are you gay?" And he looked at me as though I was absolutely crazy, didn't answer, then thought for a while and said "Yes, why do you ask?" Well, because I think you ought to come to terms with that aspect of your being, because nothing that you are writing projects. You are keeping *everything* in the closet. When you write music, you are presumably writing it for somebody, one or two, or lots of people. There are words here that you don't exploit and I don't see why you should hurt yourself by keeping your music so inexpressive." We had a long conversation that I think was beneficial to both of us.

DKG: How did he turn out?

JB: He died of AIDS. I don't think he wrote much music after he finished the master's program.

It was also from Otto Luening that I learned the importance of a teacher's accompanying students on their search for their means toward their ends. He once told me of a 3-day-long convivial visit with that great musician-composer, Paul Hindemith. The latter spoke of his forthcoming *Craft of Musical Composition.* "You'll like it. It tells you what's right and what's wrong." When Otto read it upon publication he was not charmed. Hindemith's students acquired great craft, but only the most self-directed could avoid becoming lesser Hindemiths
. . . And it was also from Otto that I learned the danger of <u>too</u> successfully identifying with a student's ends and means. As a young man, Frank Wiggleworth studied with Luening and then continued showing him his music for many decades. Late in the game, Frank told me that he had just shown him a very small opera. After Luening had spent hours on the piece, he had so wholly become Frank's alter ego that he could tell Frank nothing that he did not already know. After hearing that story, and the death if my remarkably frankly-speaking son in 1976, I became more forthright in sharing my reactions to student's pieces—but not less careful in my choice of words. One has to remember that students are as affectionate toward their music as we are to ours: theirs may be puppy love and ours a more mature affection, but nevertheless.

DKG: What was your experience with Bartók?

JB: That's much too long a story. . . . Although many of Bartók's comments over several months were substantive, he fussed about such matters as notation, double bars, phrasing, etc., that might have seemed oddly pedantic to those knowing his idiosyncratic and vigorous music. Thereafter I had the courage to run the same risk and to limit my teaching to what was teachable.

And there are those subjects, too often neglected, that should be part of a composer's education, some of them easily discussed in seminars or meetings: music copyright and text rights-clearing, finding a publisher or self-publishing, Internet usage, membership or not in composers' organizations and in a collection society (ASCAP, BMI, SESAC). In private with a student: if, when, in what order, and how to apply for grants, fellowships, and prizes, his or her suitability for teaching career and its relevance to pursuing graduate degrees; the pleasures and perils of collaboration in the theater, film, TV, and other matters of a delicate nature, such as are already included above. All these, and more, are packaged in what's called "teaching" composition, though few are in the job description

There is nothing like teaching to force one to define one's views on the subject and how it can be taught to whom. If the subject is painting or composition and perhaps cannot be taught—to borrow from Virgil Thomson and from the crucial sentence in my letter to Bartók written when I was 23—then one can at least let students know what it is they need to learn. In any case, teachers will have to exercise their critical abilities when seeing and hearing new pieces put before them, distinguishing carefully between their personal—perhaps quirky—tastes and what may pretend to some general truths, if there be any.

Perhaps because my pre-*Jonah* pieces were at least three years old and I had not the time to plan another large work or to write even little ones, or because I was for the first time responsible for examining and reacting to music by composers only a few years younger than I, I set about reviewing the music by myself when younger. In doing so, I set about ordering and numbering all the titles and manuscripts of what I had written before *Jonah*. (The manuscripts of 5, including the 3 teen-age operas, had been lost or destroyed.) The little *Song* for flute and piano had been published and, still in print, has remained safe from tinkering. Of the 53 pre-*Jonah* works, 5 were revised during that 1950-'51 year of retrospection—the 4ᵗʰ and 5ᵗʰ piano sonatas, the 5 Quarles songs and the three Blake songs, and the choral *A Round for Christmas*; a little later the 3ʳᵈ piano sonata was revised. There remained then, and remain still, 45 works, large and small, in the limbo of the closet, a few unfinished and to remain so.

To combine this foray into bibliography, a few years later Nora and I were invited to one of the annual Twelfth Night parties hosted by John Latouche. Whether John was flush with money, or without any, he had presents for the guests. Ours was a handsome blank-page volume bound in red leather with a hand-drawn caricature on the flyleaf of his chubby self waving a banner "to Jack and Nora, Noel, John Latouche." Such a volume called for some special use. It has served over half a century as the registry of my compositions from the first, *March in F ♯ Major* from 1933, through #134 *Four Gallows Songs* (for chorus) of 2007. If one includes those songs and individual pieces of larger works that can be, and are, performed separately, there are more than 134: 240.

When I put the book to use, in 1956, because *Jonah* still seemed to me to have been a watershed, it was the *first* entry, number 54. The earlier 53 works, with dates of composition and performances—if any—were entered into the last pages of the book. Beginning with *Jonah* each new piece has been entered on its own page, or pages, with all relevant information and comment, including performance data when known. And, in what may seem to be a note to a music executor, each of the operas (except *Jonah*) has at least one scrapbook to itself, containing reviews, publicity, photos, etc. There are now seven volumes concerning *Lizzie Borden*. Similar material relevant to the non-operatic works and their programs, photos, etc. fill another seven scrapbooks.

*   *   *   *   *   *

In that "year of retrospection," 1950-51, while I was engaged in bringing older works acceptably into the present and writing new pieces—not to be enumerated here—there was an event that looked only to the future, the birth of our son Christopher Sigerist Beeson, November 27, 1950, a birthday that was often to coincide happily with Thanksgiving. His name was chosen as one with well-known European cognates, as befitted a half-Swiss with a Swiss middle name. He was healthy, rambunctious, and demanding. Because of my teaching commitments I was often unable to be with the new mother and child, but our neighbor, Celia Hecht, was often with them. Celia and her husband Selig were the parents of Maressa, who had been a classmate of Nora at the University of Rochester; they had become, and remained, friends who introduced us to many of the interesting members of our Claremont Avenue Gang, the Trillings, Rabis, and Lorches, among others.

Mention of a birth and a modest cocktail and dinner-party life may permit the recounting of a later curious post-death adventure. Selig Hecht was widely known for his work on vision and the eye. It was said that he had been several times nominated for a Nobel Prize; though it eluded him, he was very proud of one of his students who became a laureate. Before his too-early death he directed that he be cremated and his ashes be strewn on campus near the physics building, Pupin. When the melancholy time came to carry out his wish, his son-in-law (Maressa's husband) and I volunteered. We thought it best to do so in the dark, fearing that if seen, gardeners or guards might misunderstand or object to our mission.

At that time there was on the campus at Broadway and 120th Street a small unkept garden, hardly a hundred feet square, protected on the street sides by a high iron fence, on another side by the physics building itself. We therefore entered the deserted campus, with the urn, at 116th Street and walked north to the wall above the fourth side of the garden and descended the long steel staircase that was its only access. Lou and I shared the service of scattering the ashes on the bare ground next to the Pupin building until we noticed the figure of someone at the top of the staircase peering down suspiciously. Although we had intentionally dressed in dark clothing, we took refuge in the shadows until the figure disappeared and we could finish our task.

A few days later the secretary of President McGill phoned to ask if I would drop by the president's office for a short chat. I assumed that he wished to discuss some matter concerning the Ditson Fund, about which we sometimes spoke. Not al all. He had heard a rumor about the scattering of Professor Hecht's ashes on campus and that I was somehow involved. Was it true? Far from being reprimanded when I explained our deed done under cover of darkness, he was quite overcome by the underlying loyalty of a professor to his university and his laboratory home. He and I suspected that there had been no burials or ashes strewn on the campus of Columbia since its land was purchased from the Bloomingdale (Insane) Asylum in 1892.

Imagine our adventure taking place today and the continuation and follow-ups of a newspaper article beginning. "Two youngish men dressed in dark clothing were apprehended last night by a university guard who immediately summoned the NYPD and the FBI. The two men were spreading a considerable amount of a powdery, grainy, substance next to the wall of the physics labs of Columbia University. The men denied any criminal terrorist intent and claimed . . ."

*　　*　　*　　*　　*　　*

When the time came that Christopher's father could be substituted for his mother for short periods, Nora began, tentatively, to continue her studies toward the PhD in the Department of Russian and Slavic Languages. These were interrupted again, three years later, with the birth of our daughter, Miranda, on October 30, 1953. The name Miranda, like Christopher's, was chosen to be familiar to Swiss relatives and other Europeans; I—still with my Shandean beliefs—thought that the name would insure beauty and a talent for the theatre—as it has.

The Russian Department had been thriving ever since the arrival of Ernest Simmons from Cornell in 1946, together with some of his colleagues and graduate students, including Nora. With the end of World War II and the onset of the Cold War Russian studies were flourishing.

Simmons, though a fine scholar, writer, and administrator, was also an example of a kind of professor now thought to have become extinct: he believed that it was wasteful of time and energy to train women graduate students because they too often married, bore children, and left the field. Nevertheless, because he knew, admired, and had engaged Henry Sigerist to participate in the Cornell Russian Summer Sessions, he took a special interest in Nora, in addition to her own promise. He put up with her marriage, her absence abroad for two years after earning the M.A., welcomed her return, and then, undoubtedly, was disappointed at the birth of her first, then second, child. His opinions on the subject were more often implied than stated and did not interfere with our frequent visits to the Simmons apartment just around the corner from ours. He must have been surprised and gratified when Nora earned her doctorate in his department in 1960, the first woman to do so.

* * * * * *

The three years between the births of our two children, November 1950 and October 1953, were by coincidence also those that separated the completion of *Jonah* from the completion of my second opera, *Hello Out There*. In retrospect, the months seem to have passed pleasantly enough, as do the anonymous faces of persons one passes on a crowded sidewalk; there was routine shared with family and old and new friends, routine broken by small excitements.

The day-to-day routines in the music department were presided over by Ruth Ihrig. Ruth was already present before we left for Rome and remained until her retirement, after which she was often in the department trying to be helpful until her mind failed. She was known as the "Mother Hen" of her sometimes raucous flock of faculty and students. There was room under her large wings for everybody's problems. Accordingly, she scheduled my classes so that they did not conflict with Nora's attending seminars. On occasion Nora and I had to take advantage of the campus-wide ten-minute interval between classes and would sometimes cross paths on the short fast walk between the intellectual life and baby-sitting—and its reverse.

A year after my return, Betsy Low became secretary to Douglas Moore, the chairman. Recently graduated from Oberlin College with a degree in music, she was prepared to assist Douglas in matters concerned with the Ditson Fund and the Pulitzer Prize in Music. Douglas was responsible for nominating the members of the Pulitzer Music Jury; for Betsy there was much correspondence with publishers, performers, and applicants, not to speak of caring for their scores and recordings and attending the jury meetings. After marrying an architect she became Betsy Mahaffey widely known today in the new-music world. When I took over the Ditson Fund and Pulitzer responsibilities from Douglas in the early sixties she continued as my ever-responsible partner. She is now only the second woman to have served as a member of the Advisory Committee of the Ditson Fund and also the officer in charge of it, only the fourth Secretary since the inception of the fund in 1940.

Some months after Betsy arrived, she was responsible for recruiting John Kander into the department for a few years and into the Moore and Beeson families for life. She and John had known one another in Oberlin, where he had begun writing musicals in collaboration with the Goldman brothers, William and James. (That troika was to have a musical produced on Broadway in 1961, *A Family Affair*.) While John was on his way from home, Kansas City, to New Haven, where he was applying for entrance to Yale for graduate study in composition, he stopped over in New York and phoned Betsy. She urged him to come uptown and meet Moore, for they had many interests in common. A short appointment was made for the early afternoon of what must have been a Thursday, for on that day in the spring, Douglas always left his office for a long week-end at Salt Meadow. The two met and were soon absorbed at length in discussing music, theatre, and musical theatre—and probably popular songs of the time and back into the twenties. Emily called the office, alarmed. "What has happened to Doug?" Douglas, reluctant to put duty before pleasure, broke off the talk and—though a Yalie himself—told John not to bother going to New Haven, for he was welcome to enter the MA program at Columbia. That he did.

So it was that I found John Kander in my small Proseminar in Musical Composition in September 1952. Interested in all aspects of music in the theatre, he soon became a valued coach in the Opera Workshop, where he remained for three years. In his second year, in Luening's Composition Seminar, he completed a one-act opera in collaboration with Jim Goldman. Though *Da Capo* remained unorchestrated, some years later I was phoned by someone trying to trace *Da Capo* and its composer for a possible production. I called John about the matter: "Absolutely not!" He went on to tell me that the thick bound score of his little opera was just where it would remain: under his backside as a heightener of his piano bench. Though uninterested in his own opera—he later began one he didn't finish—he was a knowledgeable critic of others'. As coach preparing my *Hello Out There* for its premiere, he made excellent suggestions about vocal and dramaturgical matters that I took seriously.

In my teaching years it sometimes occurred to me that similarities could be found between team sports and teaching classes. Fall and spring semesters resemble fall and spring seasons. Class sizes, though more flexible in size than teams, were no more than 6 in composition seminars and no more than 20 (later 25) in a Music Humanities section (with the real team members often in the back row.) The "Rules," set by a committee of all those teaching the numerous sections, consisted mainly in deciding on the musical works to be studied, and in what order. Conformity was necessary because in addition to the three classes a week, there were several listening sessions during which the longer works were played complete and any student could choose a convenient one. Though each teacher had to make the contents of his (her) section fit the sessions, the staff as a whole hardly amounted to a Sports Federation. The teacher of one of these multi-section courses was acting as his team's coach and trainer. If he allowed class discussion to get out of hand, he'd act as umpire.

In the composition of seminars it was wise to settle for being an older more experienced member of a team of seven. As years passed and I took on courses not taught by others at the same time, analogies with sports tended to disappear. In the Senior Seminar there were only Columbia and Barnard music majors, a dozen or so, with whom one tried to cover subject matter and repertoire that seemed to have been passed over or slighted. In Score Reading, Orchestration, and Conducting (one course) the subject matter was technical, but on occasion it was possible to keep everybody busy at once, singing, or playing, or waving his arms.

In the Opera Survey course the large classroom was over-flowing; the only problem was in preventing the opera buffs from intimidating the others, without giving offense.

In the late sixties, when students' ideas and ideals became public—even strident—there was an official outlet for their opinions about their professors. These were solicited, converted into grades, their comments quoted anonymously, and published. I was delighted to discover that my high grades in the public schools of Muncie had not deteriorated. I also read that what had been only hinted was what I'd thought: the Grout *Short History of Opera*, though the best book of its kind, was unsuitable for an opera survey, too long and detailed and, for me, too prim. When I dropped it in favor of three paperbacks, one of them the then inflammatory Kerman *Opera As Drama*, I read in my reviews that my audience was pleased.

Several students had been telling me that I was being too modest in not including one of my operas in a course of this kind. Indeed, I had been. I reformed and thereafter treated these young people to a large dose of how a frustrated daughter, Lizzie Borden, went about murdering her parents with impunity. I expected at least one student to be publicly quoted accusing me of incitement to murder, but nobody did.

Naturally, as in sports, coach-trainers of classes remember their stars. I have not been permitted to forget some of them, for several of the composers continue to send me scores and recordings, their ideas for librettos, even operas. I always respond—even to composers I've hardly know—sometimes at length, as I do when I go out of my way to hear performances of their music. It is difficult to break the habit of playing teacher.

I shall have nothing mote to say about classes, as such, though some students may re-appear in other contexts. Nine years before I retired, in 1988, the Society of Older Graduates of Columbia presented me with its Great Teachers Award for 1979. The long citation ended with a short encomium about my teaching. The first part consisted of a lengthy recital of good works, of how I had participated in University affairs outside the classroom. I include an edited list of what could have been known to the citation's author, with a warning to young composers seeking a teaching position that all that might be expected of them is not included in their job description: Chairman of the Music Department and often Acting Chairman of it and the School of the Arts Music Division; the first Chairman of the first University Committee on the Arts; member of the first University Senate (and of its Rules Committee, which set forth the rules of behavior for students *and* faculty, the aftermath of the '68 Time of Troubles); the Committee of Instruction of the School of the Arts and Columbia College; and the President's Committee on Academic Priorities in the Arts and Sciences. None of the above will be mentioned again except in passing. It is possible that I enjoyed meetings more than did most of my colleagues. At their best they could be fodder for the mill, grinding out more finely made libretto dialogues and ensembles. At their worst, they were wastes of time; one came to realize that in universities and elsewhere, if one wants to evade or to postpone the solution to a problem, appoint a committee. I found that going straight to the evader or the postponer saved time and therefore often used "the backstairs approach", in Low Library and elsewhere.

I offer another comment to young composers seeking teaching positions because they want to or they must: those polar opposites, Stravinsky and Virgil thought that composers should not do so. The above list of University commitments would be shorter or non-existent if I had simply said, "No, I can't. I'm too busy composing music." But, for everybody, departmental meetings and other parochial duties cannot be evaded. One makes one's choices and mine, apparently, ware made and determined early on, as suggested by my excellent marks in Deportment (now an obsolete word?) in grade school.

*   *   *   *   *   *

During the teaching months of the first two of the those post-Rome years there was also the routine of hunting for time to write a number of little pieces for one voice and for two, for chorus, and a violin and piano *Interlude*—in addition to the already mentioned revisions of some pre-*Jonah* works. Fortunately, the promise of a long break in these routines came in the form of an invitation from Emmy and Henry Sigerist—eager to see their first grandchild—to spend the summer of 1952 with them in the Ticino. To simplify the trip, we splurged on our first trip by air, by Swissair, naturally, to Zürich, and then the ever splendidly scenic trip to Lugano by train.

Life in Casa Serena was as serene as it had been during the earlier summers there. With Christopher being looked after by his mother, grandmother, and the maid, Henry could often retreat to his study, writing and doing his research, and I could be in my Cathouse, where I had the time to plan and compose longer works. In a short time there was a cycle for soprano and piano on English and American poems called, simply, *Six Lyrics*, and a *Sonata for Viola and Piano* under way. The sonata was to include both some 12-tone passages and, in the last movement, a set of variations of *La Folia, The Follies of Spain*, the famous 17th century tune often played by violinists, rarely by violists.

That I was again writing a sonata, was the idea of the violist Jascha Veissi. He was for years a member of the Kolisch Quartet, known for its premieres of new music. He and his wife were friends of the Sigerists, who introduced him to me. He had married the heiress to the Maxfield House Coffee fortune and after the Kolisch Quartet disbanded in 1939, he and Harriet traveled in high style as he gave occasional sole recitals on his rare and beautiful instruments. We had heard in a recital in Rome: the 17th century music was played on an instrument of the period, the 20th century music on a smaller instrument in which the very high pitches were more easily manageable. When my sonata was completed, we played it through together and he seemed pleased, especially with my giving him a rare chance at *La Folia* and its variations. He took a copy of the score with him back to California, where he and Harriet divorced, he began teaching and married a student. Whether he ever played our sonata or not I do not know.

As always, there were many visitors from far and wide to Casa Serena. Among the locals were Nora's cousin and her husband, Otmar Nussio, the musical director if the Swiss Italian-language radio station in Lugano who had alerted me two years before to the La Scala opera competition in honor of Verdi. Nussio, a composer himself, broadcast many contemporary chamber and orchestral works. He had programmed my *Fifth Sonata* just a year earlier. In 1947 he commissioned Richard Strauss, then living near Zürich, to compose for the Lugano radio *Duet-Concertino* for orchestra and solo clarinet and bassoon, which turned out to be his last instrumental work.

Otmar was high-spirited, had studied in Milano, and was just the person to enjoy hearing the details of my recent trip to La Scala, overhearing Callas, the silly bureaucracy insisted on by the half-blind librarian, and coffee with Ghiringhelli. He was delighted with how well I'd done in the competition and asked what I was writing at the moment. We went out to the Cathouse and I showed him the score in progress, an arrangement for small orchestra of a concert aria composed earlier for soprano and piano, *The Hippopotamus*. He was tickled by the text—though his English was faulty and we mostly spoke German and Italian together—and said he would program it on his station once he'd received the completed score and the extracted orchestral parts.

I am informed by my registry of compositions in the Latouche volume that the *Hippo* orchestration was completed on August 31, 1952, so the three Beesons must have said—and waved—farewells to the Sigerists soon after in order to be present at Columbia registration. Nussio was forced to wait for my promised new piece for some months and then found it doubled in length, for I decided to pair *The Hippopotamus* with a setting of *The Elephant* by D.H. Lawrence. Fortunately, the poet's widow answered my request for the rights to do so promptly and pleasantly, as T.S. Eliot and his publisher had not, as explained earlier. *The Elephant* was composed directly into the orchestral score, from which the version for voice and piano was derived. This odd coupling of *Two Concert Arias*, preferably to be sung by a dramatic-coloratura voice in a body of some girth (accompanied by either a small orchestra or piano), was then performed for the first time on the Italian-language Swiss radio in Lugano, with a Swiss-German soprano, and an American guest conductor, Theodore Bloomfield.

*   *   *   *   *   *

Chapter 8

Hello Out There. The Sweet Bye and Bye
Librettoless in Europe.
(1953-1959)

Back in harness in New York City, I spent what composing time I could snatch, not only in the enjoyment of bringing my odd couple of arias to life, but also in reading numerous one-act plays and some short stories. After the pleasure of finding three producers eager to premiere *Jonah* and the disappointment of their not having access to theatres equipped to take it on, I decided to be sensible and to write a one-act chamber opera. A successful play with operatic possibilities—or occasionally a play that has failed because it needed music to begin with—gives a composer-librettist a skeleton on which to shape his music, fleshing out the characters and their interactions. A short story—or a novel—may not be adaptable to the theatre and presents the problem of adapting dialogue from the page to the actor-singers on the stage.

Nevertheless, a short story by John Collier, *Evening Primrose*, was tempting. A fantasy, its few characters were refugees from city life who were living in a large department store, sleeping hidden in odd places when the store was open for business, wakening to a complicated life when the store was closed, their enemies the night watchmen. I went so far as to inquire of Collier's agent, Harold Matson, if I could acquire the rights to adapt it. I could not, for *all* rights had been optioned by Laurence Olivier, who planned to combine *Evening*

Primrose and two other Collier stories into the script for a movie. As it turned out, he eventually dropped the plan and the option. My conviction that the story had musical possibilities was confirmed when Steve Sondheim and Jim Goldman collaborated on an hour-long musical for television.

It may be remembered that during World War II, I had tried in vain to find William Saroyan to ask if I might be permitted to make an opera of his play, *Hello Out There*. Now, reading the play again, I knew immediately that it was exactly what I was looking for. Either I had rationalized my disappointment back in 1944, thinking that it was not really possible to adapt it and set it to music, or I was then too inexperienced to know how to go about it.

As I had done the first time, I approached its publisher, Samuel French, and its rights editor, a Mr. O'Leary. Highly protective of his writer, in my presence he phoned Saroyan's agent, Harold Matson—also Collier's agent. Even at our first encounter, both men seemed suspicious of my plans. Samuel French published innumerable plays in soft-cover acting editions and some high-school operettas—and the word opera to both men required translation into English. They decided that I should write a letter to Saroyan of my plans and send it to O'Leary for forwarding, refusing to give me their client's address.

That letter and the year-long exchange of letters that followed form a detailed account of how I made the libretto from the play and a succinct account of its composition, the premiere of the opera, and its reception. As implied by the frequent mentions of O'Leary and Matson, there were many inconclusive letters between them and me—all omitted here—until Saroyan gave up on the pair and referred me to his lawyer, about whom I shall have more to say.

3 Claremont Avenue
NY, NY 10027

June 3, 1953

Dear Mr. Saroyan,

This afternoon I was in the Samuel French office to speak with Mr. O'Leary about the possibility of my acquiring the rights to turn your *Hello Out There* into an opera. While I was there he phoned Harold Matson and the two decided that I should write to you in detail about my plans. If you have no objection to the project, then—presumably on this end—we can go into the matters of rights and percentages.

It is no new idea of mine that the play will serve as an excellent libretto for a chamber opera. Eight years ago I took the initial step of inquiring whether the rights were free. But it seemed that you were in the Pacific and that correspondence from me to French to you was difficult. Anyhow, other projects intervened, including my writing a full-length opera and so it is only now that I am again in a fever to try my hand at my first choice for a one-acter.

As you may know, in the last 3 to 10 years there has been a mushrooming of college and civic opera workshops and repertory opera companies which amounts almost to a second Little Theatre movement. Most of these groups have limited resources from a Metropolitan or San Francisco Opera point of view. But these resources have in fact made for the creation of a new kind of opera—one calling for few singers, no chorus, few sets, and a very small orchestra, for just the sort of opera *Hello Out There* could be. This is to say nothing of the fact that there is a touching story and appealing characters who have words which will go well with music. A good many of subtle changes in mood in the first part could be pointed up well with music and the end could be made really upsetting. The fact that the story is serious is an advantage. There are so many comic operas around that many groups have trouble in finding a work for the heavy end of a double bill. Mr. O'Leary asked whether there are many outfits capable of putting on chamber opera. Since we gave the 1st performance of the *Medium* here in '46 there have been more than 200 different productions of the piece. A much lighter one-acter, Weill's folk opera, *Down in the Valley* has had 2 or 3 times that many.

It is my feeling that *Hello Out There* would need little revision to be suitable for music. Words take longer when sung and so some cuts would probably be necessary. In order to be able to develop longer melodic lines, various speeches could be telescoped. This would really be necessary in order to give Emily a chance to sing longer by herself. (The baritone—I am sure the Young Man is a baritone—has to have a chance to rest, too.) With your permission, I should like to be able to do this kind of reworking myself, since the changes are slight and since they would be in the direction of making *musical* forms. Many times the changes suggest themselves only when the music is being written. Naturally any suggestions you cared to make would be most welcome.

I have spoken of the possibility of my being permitted to do the work to two music publishers. Both of them are experienced in handling operas of this sort and both expressed interest in seeing the work in progress and when completed. In addition I should mention that Peter Herman Adler, in charge of the NBC TV opera project has asked to know if I should find a text which might be suitable for his series. The length of your play and the number of characters should make it easily adapted to the television opera set-up. . . .

. . . To come to the rights themselves, I am not too concerned about having the *exclusive* rights to musical adaptation. Naturally, one feels a little more secure if they have been granted, but I would not count them very heavily against the possibility of not being permitted to do the work at all. I think precedent shows that one-third of the performance fees to the author, two-thirds to the composer is fair for this kind of work in which the composer must invest a great amount of time and actual cash. The 50-50 is fair, too, but only when it applies to the Broadway-type musical comedy in which the music is relatively less important. Should *Hello Out There* ever have a chance at a Broadway run I would agree, if you wished, to the equal split for those performance. We could talk about publication percentages later, but there again I would suggest one-third and two-thirds on score sales, recording rights, etc.

I should like to invest the free summer and as much of the winter as will be necessary in writing the opera. Naturally I should like to begin as soon as possible, but I hesitate even to look at the play again before hearing from you.

Sincerely yours,

Jack Beeson

cc: to O'Leary at Samuel French

24848 Malibu Road
Malibu, California
July 7 1953

Mr. Jack Beeson
Columbia University
Department of Music
New York 27 New York

Dear Mr. Beeson:

Thanks very much for your letter of June 3rd which began its way to me by means of Mr. O'Leary at Samuel French on June 29th, and having been sent to an old address, I received it only yesterday: I hasten to reply.

I am of course very much interested in your plan to put *Hello Out There* into operatic form. Business terms I can't discuss, I'm afraid, because I don't have any experience in this particular kind of arrangement, but I would expect a fair arrangement, on both sides.

Will you let me know more about this, and inasmuch as there is a good chance I shall be associated with CBS TV I wonder if we oughtn't to agree now that if there is to be a televising of the opera when completed that it will go to CBS. Also, I would like to call attention to this fact—the Sam. French edition has been superseded, (if that's the word) by a revised edition, published [in *Razzle Dazzle*] by Faber & Faber, London, and if and when the time is at hand to get to work I will get a copy of that edition to you, along with further ideas for revisions and changes. Also, would you let me know your ideas for changes—and for solo songs. With thanks.

Yours truly:

(signed William Saroyan)

234

24848 Malibu Road
Malibu California

Mr. Jack Beeson
Mrs. Sam Darby (in care of)
Cutchogue, L.I., New York

Dear Mr. Beeson: Here's the English (Faber & Faber edition of *Razzle-Dazzle*, containing the revised and proper version of *Hello Out There*, along with other plays and prefaces etc. I think the wisest procedure will be to move along with the work and to take up matters as the work proceeds. I shall presume as you do that business details will be in order in due course—borrowed typewriter, in San Francisco, sorry—

　　　do you have any recordings of your music; if so I'd very much like to listen: in the meantime I hope the going is good and that the opera turns out nicely.

Yrs

(signed: W. Saroyan)

in care of Mrs. Sam Darby
Cutchogue Long Island, New York
July 15, 1953
[my 32nd birthday]

Dear Mr. Saroyan:

Needless to say, I am delighted that you like the idea of my turning *Hello Out There* into an opera. I have already phoned O'Leary and have done as he suggested—sent a copy of your letter to him. He and Harold Matson are to get together to decide upon percentages and other gory details. I have so little doubt that these matters can be worked out satisfactorily that I should like to start work on the opera in the next few days. I am a slow worker and my free summer is fast slipping away. . . .

. . . I was very careful not even to re-read the play after writing you, for fear of having still more inflated hopes punctured. Now I am reading it every 6 hours. As yet I haven't many specific revisions or requests to submit. But I don't want to wait longer to write you.

There is no problem in the beginning, that is, up to what would be the "lonesome music" on page 362 of *Razzle Dazzle*. From there on to the middle of 380 I want to figure out ways of combining speeches and cutting others so as to provide sometimes longer speeches, the content of which would move consistently from one subject and emotional plane to another—the tension and the warmth of the feelings between the two always increasing. In this way places of rest would be created and the music would have a chance to blossom—music needs more time than words to make its full emotional effect. For example: the Young Man's words about San Francisco are beautiful but there should be two or three times as many—would you care to write some more? —so that a real lyric feeling results musically. This should be a kind of plateau emotionally.

The content of "people are the same ev'rywhere" could be transposed into the body of the text. The girl has her line "Nobody anywhere . . ." and goes. Then a very powerful effect could be had by cutting the Young Man's shouting speech and letting the music make the transition to the tense stage business and the Man's entrance. (Naturally, the transition could be made with the speech not cut.)

Similarly, it's very touching on 377 when the girl runs back afraid. Musically the "Hello out there" is an interruption of what should be singing lyricism on her part. It would help to have 2 or 3 times the number of words about the lonely town. Her little song then is a kind of parallel to the San Francisco one a little later and serves as a resting point in the activity and conversation.

When real lyricism doesn't develop—that is to say when the music isn't more important than the words and there isn't formalized expression ("songs")—then the short simple lines exchanged between the two are good and provide contrast in what is really a very long duet.

The various speeches of the Young Man about himself beginning on the bottom of 366 naturally form one long song if combined. (Naturally there is no objection to an occasional interruption.) The lines about the seasons are fine, especially the little extension about swimming which will be good musically. But the "working like a dog" lines won't work in this context, partly because the idea is complicated and the sentence long. The season sentence is long too, but is good for music because there is a series of ideas and nothing doubling back on itself.

The parallel of his song about himself should be her song about herself. The situation is similar to one in Act I of *Bohéme*, but set in a Texas jail: "Nobody ever talked to me that way. All the fellows in town—well—they laugh at me." Then she continues, perhaps with a selection of lines from 372-373 about the father and those beginning with the musical "I'm nobody here." But in any case new lines are really necessary, letting her give information about herself not now in the play, or expanding poetically on the ideas already there. I think it's very important here and perhaps elsewhere (certainly in the "lonely town" section) to give her a chance to make herself *musically* sympathetic. Besides, the man's voice ought not to dominate too much. Other revisions would inevitably take place around these four "reflective" sections but they'd require no new lines, only words changed or repeated here and there. Though cuts might be necessary, the last eight pages would set almost as they are now.

I should explain that I don't require *lyrics* for the songs. They aren't to be songs in the musical comedy sense. Prose with simple, direct words, clear images, short sentences, and singing rhythms is what is needed and the play is full of it.

The one thing I want to avoid is a Puccini-like one-act thriller. Your play could very easily have been a grim, realistic problem play, but it is ever so much more than that, thanks to its people and what they say. Taking its cue from the words, the music ought to make the personal framework even larger, and so, make the tragedy the more poignant.

It is a pity that by my having to send my other letter through French things were held up. I am grateful that you answered promptly and hope that you'll find time again soon to put your ideas on paper.

You will have noticed that I have a different address for the time being. Until Sep. 15.

I look forward to seeing you in New York this winter and to being able to talk things over without the typewriter in the way.

Sincerely,

(signed: Jack Beeson)

*   *   *   *   *   *

Our "different address for the time being" was an apartment over the garage of an estatelet, Anchor Ridge, on Nassau Point, jutting out from the North Fork into Peconic Bay and only a few miles from the Moores' Salt Meadow. Anchor Ridge looked out from its perch onto the Bay; our apartment had a view of the small inlet in which the Darby sport fisherman was docked when not out joy-riding or tuna fishing. Because the daughter, Connie, had married a cousin of Sarah and Mary Moore, there was much visiting between Anchor Ridge and Salt Meadow. The not-yet three-year-old Christopher dared the long steps to the beach and the sea water; Nora, pregnant with the Miranda-to-be, managed nicely. I, as reported to Saroyan, was at the table and the rented upright piano working on *Hello*—when not otherwise engaged.

in care of Darby
Cutchogue, Long Island
August 3, 1953

Dear Mr. Saroyan:

I have waited too long to thank you for sending me the book and for sending it so promptly. I shall keep the copy unmarked and return it to you one day. I have transferred all the variants into the French acting edition, which itself differs from the other two, and if I have neglected writing you it is because I have been busy working out the libretto—my fourth version of the play.

And as a matter of fact I have been writing the music too, scoring it as I go along. So far, I am terribly pleased with the ease with which it moves—but Emily has only just entered, and there will be more complications as I go along. It is being scored for string quintet (that is, with double bass), woodwind quintet, trumpet, percussion, and harmonium. The harmonium begins the opera all by itself and it seems to me that it is just the right sound to set the opening. It should be loud enough for the small halls in which the work would most likely be done, and would be fine for TV.

A most surprisingly pleasant letter came the other day about the opera, but until next week when I know more about the matter myself, I should not tempt luck by talking about it.

Inasmuch as I have not heard from O'Leary (who, after all, may be on vacation) I have written Harold Matson to ask that *someone* clear up for me the situation in regard to rights and royalties. I shall hope to hear from them soon.

I am sorry that I have no records here and that the ones in town are unavailable for the summer. Do you happen to know John Collier in Hollywood? For some time I was trying to get a story of his for a work and at one point sent him a pile of things which you might get hold of . . .

. . . I believe that with the possible exceptions of the two extended passages for the Girl, I can handle all the text problems myself by using the material already in the play. And if you have no objections I can write the words there too. But should you feel inclined to fill in the Girls "Autobiography" which I wrote about in my last letter, I would feel better about it.

The acting edition gives no running time for the play. Do you know how long it usually takes? As yet I haven't enough music to have an idea about length of the sung version—I should say about 40 minutes but that is little better than a guess.

Sincerely,

(signed: Jack Beeson)

October 19, 1953

Dear Mr. Saroyan,

. . . Last Monday I "finished" the opera, and just in time, too, for my wife is to produce *her* baby this week. I can finish copying the score and the orchestration quickly and easily, no matter what hullabaloo there may be around here in the next few weeks, but *composing* music under such conditions might be more troublesome.

I have been pestering O'Leary for some time now, and as a result had an extended phone conversation with him this morning. He wanted to write you again concerning the business arrangements but I took the liberty of telling him that it was my impression from your letters that he and I were to work out the details and submit our results to you for your approval. This we shall do. I hope that these matters can be polished off quickly. By their having dragged on so long they seem to take on too great importance.

Before I can show the piece around I must finish copying out a piano-vocal score. But already an opera workshop performance in the spring is a possibility. I should like for the Ford people of CBS Omnibus to see it. Have you any objection to this or perhaps suggestions as to *when* it should be shown or would you rather see the score first yourself? Naturally you would get one of the first scores anyhow. In connection with your Omnibus plays are you likely to be in New York sometime soon? If so, then I could "sing" and play the opera for you and we could talk everything out. There is a strong possibility that I may be granted a commission for a longer opera. We could talk over the possibility of collaborating.

Ralph Proodian asks me to send you his greetings, should you remember him.

Sincerely,

Proodian, of Armenian parents, as was Saroyan, was a Columbia College undergraduate who would have a small spoken walk-on role in the premiere and on the Columbia Records recording of *Hello Out There*, hereinafter often to be known as HOT, one of my favorite acronyms.

24848 Malibu Road Malibu California October 24 1953

Mr. Jack Beeson
3 Claremont Avenue
New York 27

Dear Mr. Beeson:

Two babies in two weeks is pretty good going, at that: congratulations to both of you. Good luck with O'Leary. For a number of reasons, involved and uninteresting, I would rather reserve for later on the idea of offering *Hello Out There* to Omnibus: the opera, that is. In the meantime, I am awfully eager to hear it, in any version at all, if only to give me an idea what it is like, and how I might, while there may be still time, improve my part—if it is in order to do so. Could you do it or have it done on a tape recording that I could listen to five or six times on my Revere: or on an LP record, whichever is simplest, easiest, quickest? So far there does not appear to be any indication that I shall be in New York this year at all, and possibly not even next year, certainly not early in the year: that is why I suggest the tape or other recording in the meantime. I hope all goes well, otherwise, that you are granted the commission for a longer opera, and other good things. In the meantime, please let me hear from you as soon as possible. Al the best:

(signed: Bill Saroyan)

Nov. 3, 1953

Dear Mr. Saroyan,

I have been trying since *last* Tuesday to write to you about the latest developments in the case of *Hello Out There* but the new birth has been complicating things, especially since it didn't occur until last Friday. Nature is much too inefficient to fit well into New York living, which somehow requires a much more predictable schedule. The doctors with their crystal balls are very good about giving one a precise date eight months in advance, but as the date approaches they become as full of buts and maybes as the witch doctors they have replaced.

At any rate your letter arrived on Tuesday morning and O'Leary phoned at noon to give me the results of his deliberations that morning with Harold Matson and the head of Samuel French. They had been digesting the information I had given O'Leary the week before concerning usual publication practices and royalty payment arrangements in the non-operetta world. It seems that French *does* handle some operettas, mostly of the high-school senior-play variety, as well as some commercial musical comedies. They have never gone in for the "more serious" variety and so wouldn't be interested in publishing *Hello Out There* in the operatic version. . . .

. . . The upshot of the conversation was that the two agents decided to disclaim any interest in the matter and to throw the arrangements back between us.

I shouldn't be surprised if you were just a little irritated at this, especially since you have several times said that you don't want to be involved in business details. I am, too, since I have had to go to some trouble to get French to inform themselves at all about what is apparently a new field to them and to get them to come to some decision on the matter. But my irritation is tempered by not now having to fool with agents at all. Most of us composers have none and prefer talking to other composers or to authors on the basis of common interests rather than to their agents whose interest is in most cases only financial. I suppose that this reflects the fact that composers are mostly making peanuts and so are not much sought after by agents. Since this particular work, however, might easily make a modest sum of money, perhaps your irritation can be tempered with the knowledge that your share of the money won't have to be shared with anyone else. . . .

. . . It is easier for me to approach music publishers if I have already made arrangements with the author, although they have no real interest in how the amounts to be paid to the creators of the piece are to be split up among the persons involved. Whenever a publication contract is drawn up, the *whole* arrangement will be formalized and the publisher would then be your collecting agent, sending checks, handling publicity, etc. I see no reason, unless you do, for having a lawyer draw up a contract between us. However, if you do, I'll have it done. I should think that our arrangements might be made in a letter. My thoughts on the matter I outlined to you in my first letter to you, of last June 3rd. I think they are fair to both parties, but I am open to suggestions. . . .

[I then copied out the relevant paragraph, omitted here, in case he no longer had the letter to refer to.]

My apologies for having gone on at such length and for any inconvenience that you may be put to by the default of Messrs. Matson and O'Leary. Let us get the matter over with quickly so that I can stop writing business letters and go back to copying out the fair copy of the vocal score. Although that's no fun either.

Sincerely,

(signed: Jack Beeson)

December 22, 1953

Dear Mr. Saroyan,

Yesterday I took several copies of the piano-vocal score to the bindery and when they are ready, on Thursday, I shall send you a copy. These are the first days since last July that I have not been occupied with the opera. As a matter of fact there is still the full orchestra score to be copied out from the pencil score, but though this is a big job, it is purely mechanical.

The opera workshop here is enthusiastic about the new piece and wants to include it on a double bill late in May for 4 or 5 performances. The Ditson Fund, which in the past has often commissioned new chamber operas for this series of first performances, would make the production possible. (The other half of the bill may be another one-acter with a text by Thurber.) We already have a pair of good singers for *our* two main parts, both from "downtown." Since I'll coach them in the music myself, I'll have a chance to do any polishing that may be needed before the piece gets out into the cold world. The stage director, by the way, will be Felix Brentano.

I am seeing some music publishers beginning next week. If I can hook one soon then he *might* take over the 6-700 dollar job of copying out the individual orchestra parts.

I hope that you will be able to find someone to go through the music with you: in places my changes in your text may seem arbitrary unless one considers both elements at once. How simple it would be if I could go through it with you myself! When the singers have learned their parts—at the moment they are out of town for the holidays and have anyway only read their music through once—I'll send you a tape as promised. But I hope that I shall have heard from you before that time.

In the meantime, all best wishes for the holidays.

Sincerely,

(signed: Jack Beeson)

[As it turned out, the curtain-raiser on the double bill was to be *The Malady of Love, A Spoof in One Act*, by Lehman Engel. The libretto was by Lewis Allen, the pseudonym of Meeropol, who was to adopt the children of the Rosenbergs after their parents' executions in 1953.]

24848 Malibu Road
Malibu California
December 31 1953

Mr. Jack Beeson
3 Claremont Avenue
New York City 27

Dear Mr. Beeson:

Happy New Year—it's not too late. I eagerly await the arrival of the stuff you have mentioned in your letters, for which thanks. Alas, I am not scheduled to get to New York—in years, it seems.

Now, our business arrangement, as such: you outlined the whole thing in your early Nov. letter: you don't understand deals and neither do I: how can we go wrong? I suppose the routine thing is to have an agreement drawn up though and signed by both of us. I leave that to you. If you want legal help, my friend Pincus Berner of the firm of Ernst, Cane & Berner, 25 West 43rd Street, New York will be glad to put the agreement terms into simple clear language.

As for developments, I hope they keep coming up, and that good things materialize for the little opera: I am of course eager to know what you have done, and how you have done it.

So please shoot the stuff to me—everything; the more the better, so I can have a clear idea as to what's what.

The best to you and yours:

(signed: William Saroyan)

With the May premiere of *HOT* apparently assured, I lost no time in sending Saroyan's friend and attorney, Pincus Berner, copies of all letters from me, Saroyan, and the two agents that included discussion of rights, royalties, and other matters to be set forth in a Saroyan-Beeson contract. Shortly thereafter we met in his office. It was naïve of me to imagine that the friend-attorney would resemble a Saroyan character: talkative, friendly, poetic, and with sympathy for the little guy. Instead, right off, he demanded that all royalties be split 50-50. I pointed out that Bill's play—I used the nickname that I had not quite yet used in our correspondence—would continue its vibrant spoken life in English and its 22 foreign language translations and that I had devised a libretto based on it, which I had then set to music; Bill, though I had invited him to make changes, cuts, and additions for the libretto, had left all that to me. Simple fairness and all operatic precedent suggested that the librettist-composer's labor be recognized. He was adamant and also puzzled by that new word, libretto.

He stated that my rights would terminate unless I had signed a contract for the publication of the opera within two years. I replied that we both knew that a composer who sought exclusivity in a property—as I was not—would have to relinquish rights unless a production came about in a stated period, but that a publication deadline for an opera was unheard of. Because there were then three publishers interested in *HOT*, I was not unduly alarmed. (One by one all three backed out. By the time the vocal score was published—in 1960, two years after its commercial recording—there had to be foolishly unnecessary pleas for time extensions.)

Berner required that copyright be secured and held jointly in the names of Beeson and Saroyan. He was startled to learn that few, if any, publishers would accept an opera unless the copyright were assigned to the publisher. Though "author's rights" generally are held by the composer, Berner decreed that both Bill and I must agree in writing to anything affecting *HOT*, including performances. Happily, immediately after its premiere there was a flurry of inquiries from small companies about the piece and a series of performances.

Dutifully I wrote Bill about each, asking for his written assent. Fed up with answering my letters, he finally wrote that from then on anything I found OK was OK by him, and that was that—with a couple of exceptions in the future when his signature was necessary for the publication and the recording.

At the close of our meeting, Berner asked me how I wanted the credits to read. Having been defeated at every turn, I then won a small skirmish: "Music by Jack Beeson. Libretto adapted from the play by William Saroyan." The second "by" was nicely ambiguous; he read it his way; I could read it my way, uncredited though the libretto remained.

He promised to draw up a contract in the form of a letter from Saroyan to me, "taking into consideration my suggestions," to be signed by both. I waited patiently for its arrival, then impatiently. Perhaps he tired of my series of phone calls and letters, for he turned the matter over to his colleague, Paul Gitlin, who also remained unresponsive up to and after the first performances in late May.

I interrupt this dismal account of what many may find irrelevant to the writing of operas to include my letter to Bill describing our opera's premiere. In fact, my troubles with agents and attorneys highly protective of their client—and ignorant of the ways of the opera world—are reminiscent of Verdi's numerous extra-musical battles with the censors of his day, and Debussy's with Maeterlinck, from whose play he derived his libretto for his opera *Pelléas et Mélisande*. Maeterlinck resorted to the law and the Society of Authors and threatened Debussy with a caning and a duel.

Columbia University
in the City of New York
[NEW YORK 27, N. Y.]
DEPARTMENT OF MUSIC

June 3, 1954

Dear Bill,

This is an anniversary! A year ago today I went downtown to see O'Leary at Samuel French about the rights to your play. The first performances of the new opera are over—they ran from last Thursday through Sunday—and by now except for the music magazines most of the reviews are in. If they interest you I'll send you copies. Perhaps you will have seen the article in *Time* by the time you receive this letter. Since this was my first appearance in that august journal, I didn't care very much really what was said. But it is pleasant that he is encouraging. The same thing could be said about the reviews in the five daily papers. The music critics in recent years have not been easily pleased by new operas and so by those standards *Hello Out There* is a rousing hit. I was particularly gratified that the libretto came in for special praise. Composers are always being ripped for choosing bum books. And if they have chosen a good play as the basis for their libretto they are usually accused of having ruined the play in the process.

Enough of this.

There was rather general agreement that the production was good. Paul Morrison, who did the sets for *The Confidential Clerk* did a very beautiful setting, and the direction by our regular opera man here, Felix Brentano, was perfectly fine if one didn't mind the strictly realistic, literal, approach.

I would like to go on with all the details, but on top of my being nearly knocked out by the experience of living through the 1st performance (and final rehearsals) of the first work of mine to reach the stage, sub-tenants are driving us out of our apartment to the country a week earlier than we had expected.

Thank you so much for the letter of good wishes. . . .

. . . Lehman sends his greetings. . . .

. . . There are 3 publishers interested and the Louisville opera commission seems to be in the bag—an hour or so opera. . . .

[signed: Jack]

I had surely been correct that Paul Gitlin had intentionally avoided meeting with me until the premiere had taken place. It was not until July that he summoned me to sign the single-page agreement, dated July 8, 1954. All the provisions that Berner had insisted be included were present, including the mutually exclusive ones. When I may have shown some sign of being about to make an objection he said, coolly, "If you don't sign it as it is, we'll sue you for having brought about a production of a Saroyan-based opera without the right to do so." I signed.

I then waited for the final copy, signed by Saroyan. Four months later a letter from Gitlin arrived with two copies to be signed of the retyped agreement (retaining the July 8 date), and "incorporating the additional changes." The only substantive change was that, ". . . in any opera program, advertisement, publication . . . there shall be the words 'text and lyrics by William Saroyan;'" Shocked by the duplicity and the power-play—and assuming that Bill had not initiated the new paragraph—I had no option but to sign again and return them to Gitlin for Bill's signature. The credits for the opera have always remained, nevertheless, as Berner and I had earlier devised, accurate, ambiguous, and disregarding the letter of the binding agreement, which was fraudulent in assigning credit for non-existent lyrics.

A reader might reasonably ask, "Why didn't Beeson just hire a lawyer and let him handle all these matters?" Well, Beeson *did* have an attorney, Philip Wittenberg, well known as a theatre and intellectual property (copyright) specialist and as "the handsomest man at the bar." His advice to me, early on, was, "Jack, act the part of a supplicant, not an opponent, and never that of a potential litigant." Needless to say, I kept him informed of actions taken and inaction endured. Once, when I reported the latest indignity, he said, "Jack, this is the sort of thing that happens when a young and little known composer chooses to collaborate with an older and world-famous playwright, one who is well-intentioned but protected by those who are interested only in his rights and in making money for their boss. The only thing you can do is to age, develop your own clout, and be able to hire your own intellectual goons."

In my anniversary letter to Saroyan I mentioned the *Time* magazine review. The critic mistakenly wrote that "Both [operas] were written with an eye to TV." The article had been read by Norman Manning of KTTV studios in Hollywood, who wrote me soon after on Huntington Hartford Enterprises letterhead. He said that whether or not the *Time* TV comment were true, I should be informed that nobody but they had the right to kinescope (that is, make a filmed copy) of a live television presentation of the play or any work derived from the play. Though Paul Gitlin had once mentioned this fact in passing, he should have included this reserved right in the JB/WS Agreement, but neglected to do so.

A little snooping around then and later proved interesting. Hartford, very rich and with a strong but highly circumscribed taste in the arts, became smitten with Marjorie Steele, a 19-year-old would-be movie actress and married her in 1949. With the idea of providing her with a film role to be shot in his KTTV studios, he approached Saroyan for the film rights to *Hello Out There*. Bill happened to be broke and sold them to Hartford. The film was quickly made in 1949, disliked by Hartford, and never released.

Though I had long thought that *HOT* would be effective on television and both the NBC Opera and the CBS Omnibus had made inquiries, a letter from St. Louis shortly after *HOT's* premiere led to renewed efforts. Harold Blumenfeld, a composer-conductor I'd known slightly at Eastman, led the Washington University Opera Theatre and wrote that his forces would stage *Hello Out There*. He had acquired a Ford Foundation grant to televise a series of shows about aspects of opera that would conclude with *Hello*. The series would first be shown on the local NET (later known as PBS) station and then be shown on the rest of the network. The director of the local station, on his own, phoned Hartford, who was agreeable to the project, but referred Vincent Park to his lawyer, who was difficult to find, then unresponsive and finally refused the request. By that time the Ford Foundation had backed out.

However, excellent staged performances did take place in May '55, just a year after the premiere, which I attended and wrote Bill about at length and lyrically. Local funding was secured to revive the opera in the fall and to televise it live. This time I was asked to try to secure kinescoping permission for other NET network showings. I went to the top and wrote Hartford himself in New York at 1 Beekman Place, applauding his efforts in aiding the arts and asking his permission for this worthwhile, not-for-profit project. There was no response. The dedicated St. Louis people did follow through with their revival, telecast live, and then staged it again four times in the next five years. In most of the performances the conductor was Dorothy Ziegler, the trombonist-pianist who had talked me into writing the *Music for Two Earnest Instruments* at Eastman.

The second televised production caused little trouble with Huntington Hartford Enterprises, probably because they thought it "big time" and worth bothering about. A chance meeting in New York with Stefani Hunzinger, in charge of theater and television at S. Fischer Verlag in Berlin led to her becoming interested in my opera and arranging for its televising throughout Germany in 1960. The production originated in Munich and was conducted by Werner Egk. Notable in the cast were the young Hermann Prey as the Gambler and the famous Tristan, Fritz Uhl, in the small role of the Husband. Titled *Hallo, da Draussen*, the translation was by the bilingual Thomas Baldner.

Later television versions in 1976 and '77 originated in Antwerp, Belgian, in Flemish and Dutch. My troublesome 42-year relationship with Hartford was brought to an end in 1997 by my publisher when PBS was contemplating a production of the opera and Hartford's lawyer wrote that ". . . any exclusive rights he may have had . . . are waived with respect to telecasts of the opera." (Marjorie Steele had married someone else in 1961.)

Though there was, indeed, a lot of *HOT* activity shortly after its premiere, while it was still in manuscript, its publication by Mills Music in 1960 made the piece more widely and readily available. Over the years, it has been the most often performed of my ten operas. I know of about 50 productions here and abroad. That there have been others the following story suggests.

Once, while correcting errors in an extra set of scores and parts, I noticed under the vocal line a second set of words in a language I did not recognize. Nora quickly identified it as Serbo-Croatian. Instrumentalists sometimes record their performances on the final page of their part. At the end of the horn part were the signatures of two hornists and two dates, 5 V '74 and 20 V '74, the second adding Split, identifying Yugoslavian performances I'd known nothing about.

The *HOT* publisher referred to, Mills Music, I joined in 1959. I was pleased to have an exclusive contract that gave all my then unpublished music, and all that I would write, a home. It was not long, though, before my hopes were dashed. Mills was gobbled up by ever larger entities, ever less interested in their non-commercially inclined composers: Belwin-Mills, a gas magnate, Gulf and Western, Filmatrax, and Columbia Pictures. Five thick files contain the forty years of correspondence concerned with the retrieval of my works that Mills had published or had clung to, leading finally to a threatened lawsuit against Mills for breach of contract. Those forty years of frustration are foreshadowed and foreshortened by the following telephone conversation; it led me into becoming an accessory to theft, if not grand larceny.

The vocal score of *HOT* had gone out of print, been reprinted, and as I discovered in trying to buy a copy, again was said to be out of print. I called the Mills warehouse on Long Island and was referred to a pleasant woman who was said to be in charge of the inventory. She confirmed that there were no more copies for sale. I explained that a clause in my Mills contract provided that if a publication went out of print and it stayed out a year, I could request the return of the copyright. I would not request reprinting because I would be leaving Mills for Boosey and Hawkes. "Then you're dissatisfied here?" "Yes," I answered. "So long as Arthur Cohn was here, I was very happy. Now that he's left, I'm leaving." She changed her tone of voice and confided, "It's a terrible company now that he's gone; I work here only when I'm pregnant." I wished her good luck with the pregnancy and asked if by any chance there were a few *Hello* scores stashed away in the rental department. She doubted it, but went to look. She returned saying that there were many packages there where they didn't belong, perhaps 120 or more copies. She added that I was in luck because the next day the whole of the Mills inventory would be trucked to cheaper housing in Hialeah, Florida. "Why don't I just ship all the *Hello* scores to you?" "But if you're found out, you'll be fired!" "Once this place is emptied out, I'll have no job. Anyhow, I'm giving birth soon. Since the score is officially out of print, there are officially *no* more scores. Be my guest!" A day or two later the *HOT* pile arrived; I kept it out of sight until I was signed on at Boosey and then presented the publisher with the 132 scores as a present. They accepted the valuable gift with pleasure and the story about how I'd come by it with a mixture of horror and amusement.

It is not often that a commercial recording of an opera comes about before its publication, but such was the case with *Hello*, which Columbia Masterworks recorded in 1958, two years before it was in print. The sequence is explained by the fact that Jack Mills, insecure about any music not jazz or pop, postponed signing me on to his company until the recording was released and he'd had a chance to read its reviews—then changed the contract date from the original '58 to '59. He was so angry to discover that he did not have the opera's film and kinescope rights that he forced me to do all the dickering with the Hartford interests.

In part, the recording came about because of the enthusiasm of my friend from Eastman, David Oppenheim, who was now the Masterworks "A and R man"—in charge of artists and repertory. Before anything could happen, contracts had to be signed by Bill and me. I was in Rome; according to one tabloid, Bill was in Yugoslavia making a movie; according to another he was there evading IRS for overdue taxes. One of these sources next placed him in a certain hotel in Paris. A composer-friend at the Rome Academy traveling to Paris acted as my emissary, traced him to his hotel, spent a memorable afternoon with him at a café, and returned with the signed contract.

The recorded cast was perfection itself. Leyna Gabriele and Marvin Worden, both of whom had created their roles in the premiere, were the Girl and the Husband. When Douglas Moore and I were invited to a screening of the NBC Opera *Magic Flute* and the Papageno appeared, I knew I had found the perfect Gambler, John Reardon. He was pleased to be cast and I was delighted to be coaching him in the role, which he quickly learned with the perfect and unforced projection of every word. Frederic Waldman conducted the top-flight ensemble of 13 players. At the first of the two recording sessions I asked the engineer several times, please to boost the too-dim orchestra. He replied—as did the engineers of my four subsequent opera recordings—"Who the hell buys an opera recording to hear the accompaniment? We sell records on the voices!" I asked Dave to attend the second session to supervise the balances. He did so, not touching the controls himself, for he was non-union.

It was Dave's idea that Saroyan be asked to contribute an article to be printed on the LP jacket. Bill was sent a test-pressing to listen to, but did not respond until I was asked to beg him for it. When it arrived, the Masterworks editor, Charles Burr, whom I'd known as a Columbia student, thought I would be shocked by what Saroyan had written and wanted it scrapped. I thought it a wonderfully Saroyanesque improvisation on the theme of playwright vs. opera and, in its special way, highly complimentary of the composer.[1]

I give Saroyan the last word on *Hello* by reprinting his jacket-liner piece. My many words about the opera have had all too much to do with matters irrelevant to the piece itself, with agents, lawyers, and publishers. In later operas, often three or four times the 35-minute length of *Hello*, my efforts could be directed mainly to writing the pieces themselves, with few, if any, tiresomely necessary extra-curricular complications.

---

[1] The original Columbia Masterworks recording has been reissued several times by other companies. It is to be included with *Dr. Heidegger's Fountain of Youth* on a "double-bill CD" by Albany Records.

254

[Jacket Liner]

Well, opera. The very word is against us, not that it's foreign, or special, but out of date, except for remembering, and replaced by half a dozen words or combinations of them that mean less inaccurately what we mean or think we mean: musical, musical comedy, musical drama, a play with music and songs, a play with songs and dances—this could go on forever, but if we tried to bunch them all together under the heading of opera nobody would understand us, and there would be no accuracy at all. The Americans are not an opera people. *Porgy and Bess* itself is spurious, if grandly so, although we might say the same of every Italian, French, German, and Russian opera as well. What has changed, or what is the difference? The yeast of the people has changed, out of which art in its various forms is expected to come, or be squeezed.—The foregoing was written as I listened to Part I of Side I, and on its own terms, the music is quite wonderful—lyric, pure, simple. Both the male and female voices are excellent, in song as in speech and in speech-song.

Even American opera can win us, of course. While we listen to a good one we are certainly with it, but after it is over we don't know. Is that us? Is the orchestra the keeper of our time? Isn't it rather the machine? The enormous machine that is the world itself, and then the millions of variations of that one big machine, all of them buzzing, chugging, clicking, clacking, keeping up any number of small steady annoying predictable rhythms and one or two less steady or predictable and therefore less annoying ones. But what if this is so? An orchestra must *still* put it all into some form of meaning, and again we're stumped because again it's opera, it's lyric, it flows, it has tone, texture, and the glue of art. —Part II of Side I continues magnificently, nullifying my cracks about opera, American, past, present, and so on. The stuff is good, it is really good to hear. Jack Beeson has achieved something extraordinary, perhaps a masterwork. But even while I am won completely by his achievement, I have got to carp some more. We can't change the world back to opera, so you have got to change opera over to the world. Somehow. Or you can't call it opera, that's all. Coming to the end of Part II of Side I I'd say that this is somehow opera, still opera, irresistible, and yet not for me. Not quite it.

As Part I of Side II begins perhaps I had better say something about the play. It was written as a *tour de force*, because I had read about a fellow somewhere in the South who was in a tough spot, only because he was in an area, an area of preposterous ignorance, dishonesty, and righteous criminality. He didn't have a chance. It actually happened, not in opera, not in a play, but in the real world in the South of the U.S. And he wasn't a Negro, he was white—or trash. It was in The New Republic. They hung him. Legally.

At the opening of a revival of *Anna Christie* in San Francisco, the director, John Houseman, asked if I had a one-act play to go with Shaw's *The Devil's Disciple*. I said I didn't but would write one. That night I wrote *Hello Out There*. At the Lobero Theatre in Santa Barbara where it had its world premiere about a month after I had written it, it introduced Jennifer Jones and it raised hell with Shaw's play, which came next on the program. The critics thought *Hello Out There* was a great play, and Shaw's only a little lark, or a game. Well, the truth is that insofar as the impulse to write the play was concerned, *Hello Out There* is actually a lark, but only for the writer, however angry he may have been about the wonderful, lying, crooked people who believed themselves to be righteous in their murder of a hoodlum of a gambler-poet. The writing of the play was no more than an exercise, an assignment, the keeping of a causal promise to an acquaintance who might very well have forgotten five minutes after speaking to me that we had talked about a one-act play. And yet the play is world famous. It has been done in Zulu, I believe. And that's the end of Part I of Side II.

Here's the last Part. I can only say that I have found Beeson's music, and the singing and acting, flawless so far—more than flawless, sombre, dramatic and true: really grand, loud, clear, intelligent, artful, right—and dead wrong. I myself have had to confess that among my plays I count this as the only one in which I took the easy way. Put a punk in jail, falsely accused of rape, and in danger of death at the hands of the outraged and righteous who are actually only the criminal mob, and already the dramatist has so much going for him that there is almost no real work for him to do. It is the only play of mine in which violence is central, the core of the whole thing, and while violence is all over the place, and all the time, it is too easy to use as material for art, and I am opposed to such usage. But the writer of a play isn't the boss—the readers and the beholders of the play take over, and the play is theirs, not his. He can have his ignored plays all to himself, without any opposition from readers and beholders—that is, people. But if *they* take over, then it doesn't matter what he thinks. I continue to believe I am right and I would defend to the life my right to believe everybody else is wrong, however pleasantly. —Jack Beeson has writ himself, and myself, and the rest of us, one real beaut of an American opera, out of Matador, Texas, by way of Fresno, California, and wherever Beeson hails from. This is the second time I have listened to it, and damned if I don't like it.

WILLIAM SAROYAN

During my preceding single-minded, seven-year pursuit of *Hello Out There* from its birth in 1953 through its early performances, televising, recording, and publication, it may have been thought that I was living altogether in the never-never land of opera, surrounded only by its strange citizenry of musicians and theatre people. Not at all. By the end of that period, by 1960, our children were 10 and 7 being bused to school, Christopher to Collegiate, Miranda to The Brearley. Nora was a newly-minted PhD and I was settled into my assistant professorship. When we had become family of four we had moved from Claremont Avenue—without losing our friendly Gang members—around the corner to the so-called Gold Coast, to a commodious apartment in a university-owned building, 445 Riverside Drive, where we were to remain for a quarter of a century.

While enjoying the pleasures of playing the father and the husband at home and the professor at Columbia, I had long been working part-time in never-never land on my third opera, *The Sweet Bye and Bye*. Hardly were the 1954 *HOT* premiere performances concluded when my librettist Kenward Elmslie, and I were planning its scenario. I was indebted to Douglas Moore for both its subject matter and its librettist. Drinks with the Moores usually included discussions of possible opera subjects. One that Douglas was partial to, but afraid to tackle, was the famous evangelist, Aimee Semple McPherson. He had once attended one of her mammoth Foursquare Gospel soul-saving meetings in New York and been struck by her singing and preaching voice and her highly theatrical style. He and the whole world had followed the scandal that surrounded her in the middle twenties. I suspected that a story could be concocted around a character based on Billy Sunday, Aimee, and the others on whom Sinclair Lewis had based his character, Elmer Gantry, in his novel of 1927 about evangelism.

I, not having collaborated with a librettist before, suspected that I should not make up a story from almost scratch and then clothe it in my own words. Douglas came to my rescue. He told me of Kenward Elmslie, a protégé of John Latouche and living in John's apartment. It was said that Ken had arrived with scrapbooks of Latouche programs and clippings thicker even than John's. A few years out of Harvard, en had been writing poetry and lyrics for musicals and was looking for a composer-collaborator. At the time Douglas and Touche (as he was sometimes called) were working together on *The Ballad of Baby Doe*. As Ken and I began work on *The Sweet Bye and Bye*, we two pairs passed ideas and rhymes back and forth occasionally; Douglas and I played our latest passages for one another, one of us sometimes finding a careless word-setting or an unwisely judged high note in the other's sketch.

Ken shared a keen and inventive theatre sense with Touche and had a highly personal way with words, rhymed and unrhymed. He was agreeable to his composer's insistence that neither music, drama, nor the verbal surface of the opera, but that musico-dramatic shapes in little and in large should form the piece. He may have found me, accustomed as I was to shaping librettos from plays, a demanding collaborator. Shy and reticent as he was, I was slow in discovering that he was a grandson of Joseph Pulitzer and, in spite of appearance and manner, really quite wealthy; he was determined to make sure that his writing was recognized for its worth, as it was in a long and comprehensive composer-librettist agreement drawn up when we began working together.

Our early and frequent meetings took place in a small barn I was converting into a comfortable and quiet studio. During the summer before, spent in the garage apartment of the Darbys' Anchor Ridge, Nora and I had explored Shelter Island, a few miles to the east and reached only by ferry. We had quickly found a very inexpensive conventional farmhouse—with the barn in back—and bought it. With our summers free and soon to have two children too small for trips to Switzerland, it seemed sensible to have a country place near the city—and pleasant for it to be so near the Moores' Salt Meadow in Cutchogue. Douglas had been appalled that we would take on a house and barn in need of so much repair, but I was delighted to be able to re-shingle and to practice the carpentry that I'd learned in the years of our Michigan log cabin. Because Latouch was often at Salt Meadow conferring with Douglas, and Ken was often there with Touche or with us on Shelter Island, our foursome flourished in summer as well as in the city months.

Once Ken and I had concocted our story-line and its characters, named it and them, and set them in the midst of their loyal and easily duped followers, Ken began writing, happy with this off-beat subject. Later in the summer I began composing. Generally his new words arrived as I needed them. When I ran out of words, I wrote my own, subject to his later approval. Quite often I needed more than he provided, or fewer, or re-writes. He complied without complaint. The libretto and its musical setting in sketch were completed in about a year and a half; it took me another eight months to fashion its vocal score and to orchestrate it; in all, there were three summers and the time snatched in between.

Once we had the libretto completed, I revisited my attorney, Philip Wittenberg. He was also known as a specialist in libel and slander. Ken and I wanted to make certain that we would not be troubled by the Angelus Temple, still, even after Aimee's death in 1944, a powerful force in Los Angeles. When I saw, on his desk, four volumes of Winston Churchill, which he was reading for possible libelous and slanderous passages, it occurred to me that Ken, not I, should be running the risk of a hefty legal expense. Philip, as much a friend as my attorney, put me at ease on that score and promised to read the libretto in a week.

When I returned, he was complimentary about the libretto and said he looked forward to hearing the opera performed. He agreed that of course the setting could not be California and that our choice of Atlantic City was properly dowdy. He wondered whether Salt Lake—and its Mormons!—wouldn't be preferable. Not wishing to argue with him, I discomfited him by remarking that nobody would believe that a drowning could take place easily, or be faked, in the highly salted Salt Lake. He advised us to direct that a disclaimer be included in any program of the opera and we provided the following:

> "The Flock of the Lifeshine Ark is a fictional creation and any resemblance to other religious groups is coincidental. The Ark requires of its leader—who must be a woman—that she have no

earthly ties: she must be an orphan of unknown parentage and she must take the oath of chastity."

Ken and I, from the outset, had planned an evening-filling opera with a serious theme that would be carried out by often comic means. Our heroine, Sister Rose Ora Easter, owed more to the Bellini-Romani Norma than to any latter-day evangelist, though our Flock were far from being Druids. We were taking stands against the misuse of a congregation's faith for private gain and in favor of the homely idea that living is to be savored while one is alive and not in some sweet bye and bye.

There was hardly time for the orchestra parts to be extracted before the opera was in rehearsal for its first performances by the Juilliard Opera Theater on November 20, 21, 22, 23, 1957, aided by a handsome grant from the Alice M. Ditson Fund. This cooperation between Columbia-Ditson and the nearby Juilliard School came about not only because our opera was far too large to fit into Brander Matthews Theatre, but also because opera at Columbia was coming to a close. The Opera Workshop had recently been discontinued; only a few months later, Milton Smith would be retired, his Columbia Theatre Associates disbanded, and Brander Matthews razed.

Only two and a half years had passed since *HOT* had been produced in a theatre ideally suited to a chamber opera. The full-size *Sweet Bye and Bye* was a good fit for the Juilliard Opera Theater. which had fine rehearsal facilities, a large staff, and excellent instrumentalists and singers for the smaller roles and the chorus, all eager to perform.

I was delighted to be asked to take part in the casting and the coaching of the three principals, all young professionals from downtown as guest artists: Shirlee Emmons, spinto soprano, with a strong Columbia connection, as Sister Rose Ora Easter; Ruth Kobart, mezzo, as the terrifying Mother Rainey; and the lyric tenor, William McGrath. My stage director for *HOT* had been Felix Brentano, one of the several German-born and thoroughly well-trained stage directors who had been on the staff of the Opera Workshop since its beginning. I was therefore pleased to have as my Juilliard stage director Frederic Cohen, whom I'd long known as the head of the American section of ISCM. Fritz, as he preferred to be called, was but one of the four German-born and German-trained experts in charge of the premiere of *SBB*, pronounced Ess Bay Bay. When I used this acronym on the four for the first time, they were puzzled. I explained that it was a bi-lingual pun referring both to the opera and to the Swiss railroads, the *Schweizerische Bundes Bahnen*. In charge of the production, stage direction, conducting, and costume design, they had been accustomed since youth to productions of new operas, but they were concerned that some of the highly peculiar American goings-on in *SBB* they might not understand or be able to project. They had no trouble with my occasional twenties jazz. (Virgil was to be complimentary about it.) As young men they would have heard Hindemith's and Křrenek's versions of it. It was the revivalists' songs and actions they found mystifying. I explained that these were watered-down versions of what I'd heard and seen as a teenager in Muncie, Indiana. I had frequently biked out to the edge of town to watch from just outside the tent-meetings of the Holy Rollers, who sang hymns, weaved about, and sometimes fell and rolled about in fits. My explanation was found to be exotic, but unhelpful. It was decided to leave these troublesome matters—and the beauty contest and the danced faked-kidnapping dumb-show in the second act—to the choreographer, Myra Kinch, a Californian.

The chorus of thirty made up in quality what it lacked in numbers; the mezzo Tatiana Troyanos and the tenor Enrico di Giuseppe went on from the chorus to splendid careers. There was also a direct link to Brander Matthews, for our stage manager had studied under and assisted Milton Smith; he was soon to share his name with Jan de Gaetani.

Given the excellence of the chorus, the principals, and the orchestra, all under Frederic Waldman's direction, and the commitment of those who staged it within David Hays's imaginatively wacky sets, *The Sweet Bye and Bye* was warmly received by its four audiences and all but one of its music critics. I was told—very much in private, and against the rules—by the chairman of the Pulitzer Music Prize jury—that I had been a very high runner-up in the competition for the 1958 Prize, awarded that year to the Sam Barber "score of Venessa," oddly seemingly slighting its librettist, Gian Carlo Menotti. Bill Bergsma wrote at length of the *SBB* in the *Musical Quarterly*, quoting a passage from the score. Characteristically thoughtful and knowledgeable, he described the difficulties presented by the first performance of any new American opera.

> ". . . The problem (I trust it is solvable) is to marry living theater with living music. The demands have always been contradictory, music being an implacable master. But any American audience will apply contemporary theatrical standards to any event that takes place in a theater. Think what this means. The entire production (seen complete for the first time at dress rehearsal) is unconsciously compared to a show that opens after six weeks of rewriting on the road. The text must be unobjectionable, and heard from each seat with the clarity of electronic reproduction. The orchestration must permit this and yet sound ample. The prosody must always be natural, yet suited for soaring melody. The music must be appreciable immediately, and yet improve with repeated hearings. . . ."

Bill, as did all the others, lauded the choral music, much of it "appreciable immediately." Had there been a twelve-tone-friendly critic, it would have been damned out of hand. As usual, each critic had his own doubt about this or that. When comments made after one hearing coincided with what Ken and I had come to believe after all the rehearsals and four hearings, we made a few revisions, including a large cut in one of the soprano's introspective arias.

We had awaited a blast from someone about "our anti-religious bias," or some-such, but there was none. The only scandal—one spread mainly by gossip in the opera world—resulted from the review by Jay Harrison in the *Herald Tribune*.

It may have been noticed that until now I have only alluded to reviews of my music. Clearly, press response to a premiere and subsequent productions of an opera forms a part of its history. But I am not writing a history of my operas, only an account of their gestations, births, and occasional events in their later lives. The reprinting of only positive reviews. or—worse—the extraction of favorable sentences and passages are neither history nor playing fair, but only tasteless and false self-advertisement. Out of pure contrariness I could—but won't—reprint the whole of the Jay Harrison review as the worst that I or anybody else could receive. Except for the choral music, everything was reviled: libretto, orchestral music, vocal writing, text setting, even the singing. I could have passed it off as just one person's opinion, printed unfortunately, except that by his writing that ". . . one cannot fathom how it came to be mounted in the first place . . ." Harrison impugned the Ditson Fund/Columbia and the Juilliard School and its Opera Theater. Very upset that Ken and I had been responsible for the good intentions of so many being insulted in the press, I spoke to Paul Lang, chief music critic of the *Herald Tribune*, on which Harrison was one of his juniors. The worldly Paul said that he had been present at one of the performances, but could not review it because, as we all knew, he had for obvious reasons promised himself and us when he took the *Trib* job never to review a Columbia composer's work. He went on to say that Harrison had expected to become the chief critic of the paper in 1954 and had never forgiven "that Columbia musicologist" for having been appointed in his stead. Hadn't I noticed that Jay went out of his way to belittle concerts held on campus and Columbia composers' works played there or elsewhere? Paul thought Jay had acted disgracefully and hoped I was not too offended. I said, truthfully, that I was worried about the others who had been maligned. "So far as I'm concerned, as they used to say on Broadway, 'I don't care what they say about me, so long as they spell my name right.'"

As though a rejoinder to the Harrison review—as many thought it to be— Howard Taubman, the *N. Y. Times* chief critic followed up his generally very favorable review of the opera with a Sunday article, *In One's Blood: New Beeson Opera Shows Advantages to US Composers of Native Themes*. He expanded on this theme from his daily review and described some musical scenes in detail.

*   *   *   *   *   *

Irrelevant to the continuing story of *The Sweet Bye and Bye*, but with some of the same performers recapitulating all the themes of the Jay Harrison review with a much stronger and more lasting effect, was a pair of Sunday articles four years later in the *Herald Tribune*. But first, as introduction to this replay: From 1952 on through the fifties, the Columbia Music Department became the American center for the development of electronic music, at first known as tape-music. With Otto Luening and Vladimir Ussachevsky as its originators and exponents in the US, both American and foreign composers were attracted to their guidance and their ever-expanding electronic-music laboratory. In response to this interest, The Rockefeller Foundation made a large grant to set up and to operate the Columbia-Princeton Electronic Music Center at Columbia under the direction of Luening and Ussachevsky, together with Roger Sessions and Milton Babbitt from Princeton. Many of the compositions created there were first presented on a pair of concerts in McMillin Theatre. They were introduced by the Columbia Provost, Jacques Barzun, who spoke knowledgeably and enthusiastically about this new musical medium.

True to the letter of his vow, Paul Lang did not attend, for his colleagues Luening and Ussachevsky and other Columbia composers were represented on the concerts. He sent a *Trib* staff critic to report back to him what had taken place. Untrue to the spirit of his vow, he then published two successive Sunday articles decrying at length and in detail the new electronic medium, conceding only—and slightingly to his colleagues—that it might prove useful to the "truly creative." As if in imitation of Jay Harrison's criticism of the *SBB's* sponsors, he then upbraided the Rockefeller Foundation for funding the project and the two universities for planning to give credit for the study of a "harmless pastime."

A week later there was a rejoinder in the *Trib* from Barzun, a letter in which Jacques elaborated on the words he had earlier spoken. He added, "It is because audiences and critics approach the new in the self-indulgent mood of a political crowd at a rally, hostile or infatuated, that the history of artistic change is such a sorry spectacle of fighting in the dark."

As may be imagined, Otto and Vladimir were furious with what they considered calculated treachery by their colleague. They would no longer speak to Lang in the corridors or acknowledge his existence in faculty meetings. I risked a short talk with Paul, saying that he could think what he chose about electronic music, but that he ought not to have broken his own very sensible rule about not writing about his colleagues—and the Music Department—in the paper. As usual, when in the wrong and cornered, he was contrite, even grateful, seemingly taking pleasure in being chastised. I spoke to my other two elders, saying that I did not want to be in a department in which there was such obvious animosity, that they should forget Paul's articles as most everybody else soon would, and that they should try to act as collegially as before. I was not so naïve as to think I could heal the deep rifts, but I was successful in applying bandages that made things tolerable. Nevertheless, the bandages tended to slip, or slip off later when there were compositional-musicological altercations during the setting up of the composition DMA in the School of the Arts and in the Wuorinen affair. Hurt and resentment remained until the retirement of all three, and thereafter.

*   *   *   *   *   *

In the late spring of 1944, at the very end of my five years at Eastman, my brother and I had met in Muncie to witness the burial of our father and to settle what very little remained of his possessions. Tom was mustered out of the Air Force a year later and then earned a masters in geology at the University of Colorado. He then settled down in Midland, Texas to prospect for oil. He found some and also a wife, the very sensible daughter of a local banker. Tom was one of my only two remaining links with Muncie; I was to see him again only a couple of times when he and Esther visited us in New York briefly. Otherwise, occasional phone calls and annual Christmas cards sufficed to maintain a cordial, if distant, not very fraternal relationship.

The other Muncie tie was, of course, Mother, Nora and I occasionally drove down to Shamokin to see her and her husband, Will Haupt; after we moved to the large apartment, she often came to visit us and to enjoy her grandchildren.

My only other connections with my hometown were occasional letters from my first piano teacher and a couple of my former schoolteachers. They would enclose clippings from the Muncie *Star* and/or the *Evening Press* about my exploits—the Rome prize, the *HOT* recording, and New York performances. I suspected that my distant cousin, Carl Cranmer, highly placed in the Associated Press, was secretly favoring me by arranging that these minor NYC items were included on the wire services.

Some such local news items I suppose was read by Robert Hargreaves, who wrote me soon after the Juilliard premier as Head of the Music Department of Ball State Teachers College, State of Indiana, Muncie. He enclosed brochures of the '56 and '57, the first and second, Crossroads of America, Ball State Summer Arts Festivals. It was astonishing that there could be an Arts Festival in Muncie, of all places, and that the centerpiece of the first of them had been a chorus and orchestra piece—with dance!—by Lukas Foss, who had conducted it. I knew Lukas, who was about my age; he was—and still is—unsure about whether he was born in Berlin in 1921 or 1922. Also enclosed were Muncie *Star* photos of the new Ball State Music building and its assembly hall-theatre, recently completed. After reading all these improbabilities and re-reading the Robert Hargreaves letter more cogently, I thought that the packet must have been mailed from Oz, not Muncie. Our bedroom on Washington Street had been encircled by a wide wallpaper frieze of scenes from the Oz books. They had been as seductive to me as my teenage visions of the South Seas. Hargreaves wrote that, subject to seeing the score of *The Sweet Bye and Bye* and finding that Ball State had the means to produce it, it would be the centerpiece of the Third Arts Festival in early July 1958. If I wished to conduct it, I was welcome to do so.

There followed extensive correspondence concerning the revisions being made in the scores and parts, casting, and planning for the opera's production. I told Bob that though I could conduct my opera, I would not; that the one who prepared the piece—he—should conduct it. There was a lyric tenor at Ball State who could handle Billy Wilcox, I was told. Could I find guest artists for the two demanding women's roles? Shirlee Emmons was delighted to repeat the Sister Rose role she had created. Kobart was otherwise engaged, but Douglas Moore suggested the mezzo-contralto Beatrice Krebs, who had recently sung Mama McCourt in the Central City premiere of *Baby Doe*. I had the pleasure of coaching her in the role of Mother Rainey.

I had the bright idea of inviting my mother to accompany Shirlee and me out to Muncie, where she could stay with and see her numerous friends. The three of us flew out to Dayton, Ohio, as close as we could get to Muncie by commercial flight. While we were being driven through the familiar flat landscape by Bob Hargreaves, I learned that the stage director had suffered a mental breakdown and was hospitalized. Would I mind taking over the stage direction for the several days of final staging and dress rehearsals? I agreed to try, not admitting that though I'd never been afraid to make suggestions to the directors of my operas, I'd never tried to do it myself.

Though the Arts Festival publicity stated that the Merce Cunningham Dance Company would present an evening performance, I'd thought it as improbable as everything else that was taking place. During the break of one of the piano-dress rehearsals I wandered out into the almost empty house and found Merce himself and his music director-pianist, John Cage. They had been highly amused to see a composer playing stage director, pushing the chorus around to improve sight-lines and the soprano's contact with the conductor, and exhorting the bathing beauties to gyrate more curvaceously.

I was never clear at the time about whether *SBB* was the first opera to have been produced in Muncie, or only its first modern opera. In any case, the locals made a great fuss about the occasion. Just in time to hit the Sunday papers, Mayor Tuhey, in an oratorical outburst that would have been more appropriate for the mayor of Bonn honoring its native son, Beethoven, thanked me for "adding luster to the city of Muncie," urged the whole population to attend the opera, and proclaimed "Wednesday, July 2, 1958 to be Jack Beeson Day."

The events described above could not even have been imagined in the Middletown I grew up in. When I left, in 1939, Muncie had changed little from the Depression-trodden *Middletown in Transition* the Lynds had described two years earlier. The newly-built music building and its theatre and the Ball State Festival were in themselves signs of a better, even thriving, time and city. A striking example of the new wealth occurred at a fancy reception for Mother, Shirlee, and me on Jack Beeson Day. Hosted in Westwood by the son of former, favored, patients of my father, our host discovered that we were to be driven back to Dayton to catch our New York-bound plane. He offered to fly the three of us to Dayton. "But wait a minute. I'll be right back. I have to find out whether I'll take my mother's or father's plane."

There had been some concern that here on the edge of the Bible Belt there might be animosity directed at the opera because of its subject matter. There was none in the press. Only the Muncie *Star* mentioned the matter: "There was delicate irony but so subtly conceived it could hardly be offensive to anyone." If there still were any Holy Rollers in town, they weren't heard from.

There was similar concern when the opera was given for five performances by the Kansas City Lyric Theater in 1973, for Kansas City was home to several pentecostal sects. By that time Aimee's Foursquare Gospel was being led by her son and numbered 672 congregations in North America, several of them in Missouri and Kansas, but there was no outcry. In the seven reviews of the opera there was but one oblique reference to religion: "The opera goer is left to draw his own conclusions about the sect. . . . The opera as a whole expresses no satiric innuendos."

The Kansa City production was handsome, with sets and costumes by the young Robert Israel. The director was H. Wesley Balk, who approached the staging, as he wrote, ". . . as one who was saved as a youth on numerous occasions." That the cast, chorus, and orchestra, conducted by Russel Patterson, were all excellent is easily provable. Immediately after the final performance

Desto Records recorded it and released it on LP; that issue was later released on CD by Citadel Records.

*   *   *   *   *   *

"Back Home in Indiana," as the old song had it—if only for a short week—when I awakened on July 1, 1958, I must have been planning what still could be done, staging-wise, during the afternoon rehearsal before the dress rehearsal that evening. I would have forgotten that July 1st was the first day of my first sabbatical year, that it was also the first day of my Guggenheim year, and that we would be spending it in Rome and the Ticino.

Now recently tenured, I had taught as a professor for six years and, as if by Biblical injunction, there was now a year of rest, free of classes and students, free to compose. My application to the Guggenheim Foundation had been made months before. Applicants were required to submit a Plan of Work, though composers could get by with only "to compose." I stated that I intended to work on an opera, but I was cagey about its subject. For four years Richard Plant and I had been discussing and planning an opera to be based on Lizzie Borden and I hoped fervently that there would be for this composing year at least part of a libretto, but there was only our six-page synopsis. (The long gestation of the opera *Lizzie Borden*, from its conception in discussions between Plant and me in 1954 to its premiere by the New York City Opera in 1965—eleven years later—is to be recounted in piquant detail in the article *The Autobiography of Lizzie Borden*, pp. 299-324.)

News that I had been awarded a Guggenheim arrived in early spring and led me to write to Laurence Roberts, still Director of the Rome Academy, to ask if I could have studio space there from September 1 into the following summer. The answer was that Nora and I would be welcomed by him and Isabel and the Academy, that "my" Villino studio near the Villa Aurelia would be free for my use, and that arrangements were already under way for the four of us to be housed "off-campus" in the apartment house next door operated by Lebanese Maronite Christians.

Back home on Shelter Island and in real time, there were chores to be done in the house, on the barn, and for the children: the long unused privy I was turning into a playhouse and pulling up by their roots the luxuriant poison ivy surrounding it. *In* the barn I completed what I'd begun earlier as a change from the words, action, and the theatre to the visual-musical: *Sketches in Black and White*, five solo piano pieces called Landscape, Portrait, Abstraction, Still Life, and Seascape. The title referred both to the black and white piano keys and to sketches in pen and ink—and, allusively, to the Debussy two-piano work. They were performed soon after, and appropriately, in The Museum of San Martino in Naples and then twice in Rome while we were there. Just before the four of us took off for Rome I finished dipping back into *The Sweet bye and Bye* to arrange for large orchestra three segments of the opera called *Hymns and Dances*, titled Memorial Service; Comic Strip; and Hymn, Interlude, and Dance. The suite not only places the would-be-sacred cheek by jowl to the jocular-sinful; at one point all the instrumentalists but the brass sing one of the rousing Lifeshine Ark marching tunes.

Our apartment sublet for the year, packed, and the children—not quite eight and five—only vaguely aware of what was going on, we left for Europe.

*   *   *   *   *   *

The Maronite priest who was the landlord of our furnished apartment was both friendly and hospitable. On arrival we were invited for coffee in his spacious quarters filled with Near Eastern intricately inlaid tables resembling the ubiquitous Roman Cosmati work; he introduced us to the tenant of his garden apartment, an English architectural historian engaged in doing drawings of all the Roman medieval churches.

Already arranged, a school bus took Christopher daily far across Rome to the American Overseas School. Nearby, in the "Garibaldi Park" abutting the walled grounds of the Academy's Villa Aurelia, was a nursery school in which Miranda spent the year, except for a period when it closed because of a polio scare. Relieving Nora of some household chores, we splurged on a maid who did the complicated shopping and cooked. We enjoyed her Roman specialties, especially her spaghetti con vongole (with mussels). Christopher soon dubbed her "Oily Emma," a nickname that stuck.

The Rome we had known a decade earlier had not changed, except for the traffic. Those who had zipped around on Vespas had now graduated to small cars, dentless, washed, and polished. As the Romans say, the most important thing to keep up is "una bella facciata" (a handsome façade).

Laurence and Isabel Roberts were as hospitable as before to various foreign and Roman scholars, writers, artists, and musicians, and to us. Margarita Rospigliosi, not mentioned earlier, continued as our special friend. Known as La Principessa, she was indeed a princess, a member of the "Black Nobility," with a 17th century Pope in her heritage. Invaluable to the Academy, there was not a closed palace, library, or church that would not be opened for a Fellow at her request. As Nora and I had discovered, many of the descendents of the old Roman aristocratic families were employed—as was she; only a favored few could afford the high life and notices in the Italian tabloids; some of them had married wealthy Americans. Sightseeing with Margerita as a guide was always memorable. Once, on a feast day, we ambled through a church down the hill in Trastevere where a number of her ancestors were interred. We went from one elaborate tomb to the next as she kept up an amusing, running commentary about the foibles and sins of this or that long-dead relative. She accompanied us on a short trip north to see villas and their gardens. As we were admiring the Villa Lante's justly famous formal garden and its fountains, she directed me to look at the Villa itself. She pointed out the window of the bedroom she had slept in as a girl when summering with her Lante della Rovere relatives. In her office or free of it, Margerita was always available for a drink and conversation at the nearby bar, Giovanni's. On one such occasion she admitted that she had had to be dried out, during our absence, when she finally arrived at 19 Camparis a day.

Our friend and once fellow-Fellow, Alexei Haieff, was the composer in residence for the year and ensconced in one of the apartments attached to the Villa

Aurelia, where Sam Barber had been earlier, only a few steps from my idyllic garden studio. As had Sam, Alexei often knocked on my studio door for a musical conversation or an aperitif before lunch. (By this time I'd learned to avoid the latter.) The Fellow in Composition for the year '58-'59 was Salvatore Martirano whom I saw only occasionally. We seldom spoke of music; he could be unpredictably confrontational and pick fights on occasion—with others, not me.

Librettoless, and occasionally receiving brief notes from Richard Plant that implied that I would remain so until our return a year later, I set about writing my first—and last!—symphony. My note in the published score suggests my ambivalence at the time about what I was composing and not composing.

> ". . . The first movement accepts the premise that 'the first movement form' is basically a dramatic confrontation, but substitutes contrapuntal entanglements and various orchestral sonorities for the more usual antagonists. The slow movement [called Aria da Capo] is an aria-duo with a varied da capo section. And the finale, after two Wagnerian reminiscences, remembers Rossini, with drums and cymbals, instrumental virtuosity and general high jinks [marked Allegro Buffo]."

I was happily in the middle of the third movement when the school Christmas holidays intervened. We had already joined the crowds, all in a festive mood, touring the decorated churches and visiting the Piazza Navona, where the *piffari* were to be heard, the pipers from the mountains who come down at Christmas each year to pipe away for the benefit of the buyers of seasonal knick-knacks.

We took the train to Lugano, were picked up by Emmy and driven to Casa Serena. It had lost much of its serenity, for Henry ha died of a second stroke in March 1957, after having only partially recovered from the first stroke suffered two years earlier. Emmy was pleased to be called *Nonna* (with a well-pronounced double-n) by her grandchildren, who had already picked up some Italian in school. She was planning to sell the villa eventually and to move to Zürich, which she had always preferred to Leipzig, Baltimore, and the Ticino.

All together, we traipsed around the local villages, and rode the pokey little train into Lugano, where the others shopped and enjoyed the sweet *cassate* at Saipa's on the arcaded Via Nassa. In short, we made a family quintet-holiday of a couple of weeks, then returned to school and nursery school in Rome.

And back to finishing the buffo finale of my symphony, polishing and editing the whole by January. Oddly, its first professional performance was to be by the Polish National Radio Symphony Orchestra, conducted by an American, William Strickland. That performance was recorded and released by CRI Records, later on CD by Bay City Records. Otto Luening, who somehow knew things nobody else did, always insisted that Bill Strickland's excellent performances and recordings of American music in out-of-the-way places all over the globe were his cover. When I asked him what he meant by "his cover," he added, "Why are his conducting fees so very low? Bill's in the pay of the CIA as a secret agent." There were other "cultural covers" during the Cold War that only slowly became uncovered. When I checked out Otto's story with Douglas Moore, he was unusually evasive.

When we returned to New York the next fall, my briefcase was over-full, with two large orchestral scores and seven smaller miscellaneous works, one of them a collection of three separate pieces, another of seven. When we had left New York, in the briefcase there had been only writing materials and one pre-*Jonah* work that I had long wanted to reconsider and perhaps revise or re-write, I was still impressed by the eight Yeats *Crazy Jane* poems I had selected and by my good intentions in setting them for contralto and piano. Doubtless my wish to retrieve them was related to Bartók's having taken them seriously fifteen years earlier. My Latouche register informs me that one of them was "somewhat revised," two of them "thoroughly revised," and one "rewritten." The other four were consigned to the closet-limbo. Years later, before publication, those remaining were again sanded and polished in honor—so to speak—of their semicentennial.

The pleasure I took in re-working the Yeats songs—in places adjusting the original contralto tessitura to the more sensible mezzo territory—quite naturally had led me to the Academy Library for other poetry to set. The two poems that most intrigued me were, as usual, ones with unconventional subject matter and diction. The differences between the two, *Against Idleness and Mischief and In Praise of Labor* by Issak Watts, from *Divine Songs*, 1720; and *Fire, Fire, Quench Desire* by George Peele, 1599, are so great that their musical conceptions and workings out might seem those of two different composers.

My Watts setting is subtitled, "a practice session for soprano and piano" and is exactly that: the coloratura practices diction while purveying the words, alternating with coloratura passages with two high C's on "ah." The vocal line is liberally provided with seldom-seen musical diacritical indications: where a final t is to be exploded, u and > for unexpected unaccented and accented notes, and, in the second line of text, where the ee-sound in the diphthong of "shining" is to be placed;

> "How doth the little busy bee
> Improve each shining hour?"

Appropriately, this practice session is dedicated to Madeleine Marshall, the Juilliard School English diction teacher and writer on the subject.

While the singer goes on her own way, the pianist doggedly plays scale passages and arpeggios in two hands a tenth apart, occasionally, in the right hand, scales in thirds and in my as-yet unpatented augmented fourths. The effect of the freely tonal whole is not unlike that of a composer leading down a path to its end two rambunctious dogs on two leashes—not unlike the exhortation of Isaak Watts:

> ". . . In Works of Labour or of skill
> I would be busy too:
> For Satan finds some Mischief still
> For Idle hands to do . . ."

The highly sensuous George Peele *Fire, Fire, Quench Desire* led me into one of my few explorations of twelve-tone territory, with its underbrush of discontinuous pulses and rhythmic brambles. Musically, the song, with its extended range and an incidental trill, can present problems to some singers.

I have written about seventy solo songs. Except when several form a cycle they are unlikely to be mentioned. The preceding description of two of that number and most of the following paragraphs are relevant to the subject of my way of writing in the medium, from early on through today.

In the nineties, Angela Brown, a lyric soprano with an unusually expressive voice and fine musicianship and diction, came across some of my songs. (She is not to be confused with hr namesake who has risen to prominence since.) Though she had performed in opera here and abroad, she became partial both to the more intimate recital stage and, apparently, to my songs, ever more of which she included in her programs. At a benefit recital in Saranac, New York for the restoration of the cabin in which Bartók spent his last summer, she sang twenty of them. As a respite from so much music by one composer, I spoke in some detail of my musical experiences with Bartók, then more than a half-century in my past. (The cottage at 93 Riverside Drive in Saranac Lake is now completely restored, aided by a substantial gift from Bartók's son Peter, and can now be visited.)

Angela continued adding my songs to her repertory until she had enough to fill a CD. I was invited to hear and comment on those most recently studied, but she and her excellent coach-accompanist, Dixie Ross Neill, had prepared them so well that there was little to fuss about. Angela and her husband, Kellum Smith, whom I'd long known well, arranged for the release by Albany Records of the CD, with the title of *Fire, Fire, Quench Desire*. I provided a "Composer's Note" which I reprint because it provides some comment about my choices of texts and their settings.

> This selection of twenty-six songs (and two arias from operas) comprises about a third of my works for solo voice and piano and most of those written for soprano.* The poetry dates from the end of the sixteenth century to the late twentieth century and encompasses a wide variety of styles and subject-matter. In order

to reflect this variety, the music ranges widely in style, from the simplicities of the Blake settings to the 12-tone serialism of *Fire, Fire, Quench Desire*. Hughes's black-magic *Death by Owl-Eyes* invokes a traversal of musical idioms from early Renaissance open fifths to some of the habits of the 1960s. The song is dedicated to Otto Luening, another 20th century time-traveller.

As might be expected of a composer and librettist of operas, some of these songs—and many of those for other voices—suggest a dramatic context and the presence of another character listening. For the most part, the words are set exactly as written by the poet, but occasionally I exercise what may be called "musical license." Sung words in recital or in the theatre pass swiftly and cannot be pondered as can words on the page: it can be helpful to hearer and performer if the composer repeats a word or phrase for clarity or for emphasis.

It is often forgotten that a musical setting is, so to speak, an *arrangement* of a poem: it is the composer's interpretation of the words, made audible by means of his or her choice of pitch, tessitura, accentuation, and phrasing in the vocal line, and choice of style, mood, and implied action (if any) in the accompaniment. The line, "To be or not to be, that is the question:" has been delivered in many ways over the centuries. Once set to music, the composer's reading of the line is fixed in all performances, for singers and pianists cannot stray far from the written notes.

*Boosey and Hawkes has published four volumes of *SONGS AND ARIAS*, one for each of the common voice-types.

Back from the future—from 2000, when the CD of songs was released—and in Rome, I was engaged in making inked fair copies of the two songs just written. In March I left my studio for a week to travel by myself to Zürich and Frankfurt am Main to conclude a year of intermittent discussions and correspondence that I had hoped might lead to a Swiss or German production of *The Sweet Bye and Bye*. Rudolf Thomas, my former conducting teacher, had become an advisor and an admirer of my three operas. He was convinced that the *SBB* could succeed in Germany because it would be thought as exotic as Near Eastern and Asian subjects earlier in the century. He went out of his way to introduce me to a friend, Dr. Hans Hartleb, in charge of stage direction at the Frankfurt Opera. Fritz Cohen, who had directed *SBB* at the Juilliard, held the same opinion about a German possibility and led me to Georg Solti, the music director in Frankfurt. Solti informed me that their repertory was fixed for the next two years and included "at most only two or three new works in each season." Nonetheless, he suggested that I send my score to Felix Prohaska at the Frankfurt Opera.

When vocal scores were sent to Zürich—where Ticinese friends, formerly members of its opera's staff paved my way—and to Frankfurt, they were accompanied by a German translation of its detailed scenario and a title, *Jenseits, Diesseits*, by Ruth Yorck. Ruth, born Ruth Levy in Berlin, was also known as Ruth Landshoff (having earlier taken on her mother's maiden name), and occasionally as the Gräfin Yorck. Just before Hitler's rise to power, she had married David, Graf Yorck von Wartenburg; they moved to Paris, then London, divorced, and then, separately, ended up in the US. Ruth's past, talents, and appetites were as various as her names. It was said that she, as a beautiful young woman, had been the first woman to appear nude in a film, a German silent on the subject of Dracula. In my two viewings of *Nosferatu* I've not seen her. Edited out? A myth?

She was a close friend and sometime traveling companion of Ken Elmslie and lived for a time in a small apartment on Cornelia Street (with a small Paul Klee oil on the refrigerator door) across the way from Ken's two-story remodeled former stable. She often gave large parties—elsewhere—at which many of us were first introduced to couscous, which we were required to eat from large bowls with our fingers. It was at such a party that she introduced me to her Berlin cousin Stefani Hunzinger, who then brought about the German Television production of *Hello*; at that or some other gathering Ruth introduced Edward Albee to Stefani, who was responsible for Albee's first success, a German production of *The Zoo Story*.

Ruth was of course partial to Ken's writing and was the third of my German-born friends to believe that *The Sweet Bye and Bye* would quickly find a German production. All three were mistaken and for reasons that neither they nor

I could have predicted. My informant at the Zürich Opera was impressed that its composer was married to a Zürcherin whose mother was an Escher, but he reported that the music staff had been puzzled by the curious mixture of the serious and the comic, by its confrontations of the religious and the raucously secular. That dichotomy, he added, would dictate the casting of the former by opera singers and the latter from their operetta roster—something they could not do, on principle. I refrained, I'm sure, from remarking that Mozart's *Die Zauberflöte* presented much the same problem, everywhere simply solved. In conformity with the orderly reason for rejecting the opera, I had no such problem retrieving my scores and materials as I had had at the disorderly La Scala.

When I arrived in Frankfurt-am-Main I was treated to a fine lunch by my acquaintance Hans Hartleb. He and his music staff had obviously examined my score and Ruth's synopsis in German. They too had been struck by our treatment of the sacred and the profane, but not been put off by it. He confirmed Solti's comment that they were limited to two new works a year, and added that they had to be very careful in choosing them because of the music critics. Subject matter and its treatment aside, the German music critics expected the music to be "cutting-edge," preferably twelve-tone. My music, however appropriate to, or necessitated by, its subject matter would not be accepted by them and therefore could not be considered for production.

Disappointed and somewhat disconcerted by a Rhineland version of the Zürich strict categorization of styles, I was grateful for his candor. I found the Swiss-German and German attitudes toward new operas somehow—well— foreign and unItalian.

Our long and illuminating conversation came to an end when he had to leave for a lighting and technical rehearsal to which he invited me. I have often preferred rehearsals—even tech rehearsals—to performances and accompanied him into the empty theatre. Act II of Parsifal was being lit. Toward the end of the session, Hartleb asked if I would mind standing in for their tenor, so that the spotlight could be focused and the spear-hurling cable be tested. I was agreeable but pointed out that I was much shorter than any imaginable Parsifal. "We've already thought of that and have a foot-high block of wood for you to stand on. You don't have to try to catch the spear. Don't try!" While he determined where I was to stand, the spot was chalked and the block placed. I made my way to the stage and took my place, feeling very much the pure fool. The spear whizzed by my head time after time on the black-painted taut steel cable as the timing and speed were adjusted. As I was dismissed with thanks, Hartleb suggested that I attend *Das Mädchen aus dem Goldenen West* that evening as his guest; they had found a sensational 25-year old American as their Minnie.

I discovered in the program that her name was Marilyn Horne, so far almost unknown in the U.S. She was, indeed, a sensational singer and a believable Californian saloon-keeper. After the performance I rushed backstage, expecting a crowd of fans, but I was the only one. She was pleased to have an American visitor, hearty, and admitted that Minnie was a handful. Most of her varied roles at the time were in the heavy soprano territory. She was amused to hear about my impromptu matinee as Parsifal, which I joked I would add to my resumé. As we were discussing the many American singers at large in Europe at the time, I mentioned my friend Stich-Randall; Nora and I had just heard her as Fiordiligi in Rome. In her dressing room thereafter she had bragged that of all the American singers abroad, she was the only one who could perform Bach's *Jauchzet Gott* correctly. Horne, having sung it often, harrumphed.

Some years later, when she was the reigning mizzo, her admirers marveled at her easy high notes and coloratura; few knew what she had been up to in her early European career. At that later time at some reception, I saw her seated alone on a couch. I joined her, and reminded her of her Frankfurt performance as Minnie, *als Gast*. She was startled that I had been present and that we had met. She did seem to remember a strange story of a composer—who was it?—who had sung a Parsifal there.

After these frustrating experiences with big works in the big world, it was relaxing to be back in my quiet Roman studio writing something small and homely for Christopher and me to play together, four hands. He had begun piano lessons during the year before we left for Rome with the recently widowed Mae Kurka. Mae's husband, Robert Kurka, just my age, had been a graduate composition student at Columbia. Of Czech parentage, he had then based his first opera, *The Good Soldier Schweik*, on the well-known Czech novel of the same name and barely completed it before dying months before its first successful performance by the New York City Opera in 1958, which the three of us attended. His opera has had innumerable productions since, mostly in Central Europe.

Christopher, having heard music since birth, made rapid progress under Mae's excellent teaching. I was happy to share my piano with him and tried my best to make no supervisory comments. He was to continue lessons into high school, by which time he was studying privately with William Beller, our Music Department staff piano teacher. Bill had to put up with the fact that the only music Chris wanted to play was by Bach, whose Goldberg Variations he played almost pre-professionally. Extra-curricularly, his pleasure was anything by Scott Joplin. He chose to attend the University of Rochester for much the same reason his mother had: in order to be able to take private lessons at the Eastman School. Quite by chance, he was assigned to Dennis Andal, who had been a piano major in my class a generation earlier.

While writing the seven pieces for Christopher and the next generation of beginning pianists, I was aware that I was doing in a very small way what my teacher, Bartók, had done extensively in the preceding generation. As a professor of piano for almost thirty years in the Budapest Academy of Music he had every reason for doing so. His best known teaching pieces are the six volumes of *Mikrokosmos*. Composed over several years, they are designed to introduce the young to various 20th century compositional procedures and are graded in difficulty from the first two volumes—dedicated to his son Peter—to the recital pieces in the last volume. *Mikrokosmos* was among the first of his works to be published in 1937 by Boosey and Hawkes. When I became a B&H composer almost a generation later, I heard that the Bartók volumes at first hardly sold at all; selected teachers were given full sets on condition that one of the volumes be kept always on the piano. By 1960 I saw waist-high piles of them in the stock room ready for mailing, to replenish music store stocks.

My title for the seven pieces, *Round and Round*, is the title of the first piece, which is a round, a double canon at the octave; the last piece is *Round and Round Again*, almost identical, except that the upper part (for the student) is exchanged with the lower part (for the teacher). All but one of the other pieces are canons of an only seemingly complicated sort, easy to play and designed to introduce young pianists to the pleasures of counterpoint and canon.

Back at Eastman in 1942, the other composers in Soderlund's advanced counterpoint class may have been inoculated for life against writing canons, having been assigned to write them for Soderlund in specified historical styles. That vaccination did not take on me, for immediately—on my own—I set a passage from St. Luke as a four-part choral round, *I Bring You Glad Tidings*. A few years later I revised the music and changed the title to the punning *A Round for Christmas*. Published, it is still in print. Since then I have written almost sixty pieces in canon, of one kind or another. Following a centuries-old tradition, most of them are for chorus or vocal ensembles, insuring that the individual parts, SATB or whatever, are all of equal importance and interest.

Having had fun writing short pieces for four hands, I continued with several more for four-part chorus, one of which I describe in some detail. Though a scant minute and a half long, it is probably my most often performed piece. The Gregg Smith Singers have performed if for years—"hundreds of times," Gregg says—on tours throughout the US and Asia. The text, anonymous doggerel, is titled *Give the Poor Singer a Penny*.

> I'll sing you a song,
> Though not very long,
> Yet I think it as pretty as any.
> Put your hand in your purse,
> You'll never be worse:
> Give the poor singer a penny.

Altos and tenors sing the stanza through once, in octaves, to the crooked, seemingly wandering, fast tune that forms the basis of the piece. Then the sopranos sing it, joined by each of the other three parts, altos, tenors, and basses in turn, at the same short interval of time. By the time the sopranos begin the tune again, all four parts are busy. The above description could be that of numerous canons of the past. But in this canon *each* entrance of a part is a perfect fifth higher (or its octave equivalent) as are *all* entrances of the tune throughout, leading the piece around the twelve keys of the "circle of fifths" to its beginning and the original key—if it had one. Then the circle is gone around again, and *could* go "round and round" forever unless stopped; I found a way of gradually winding down the energy to a full stop. The visual impression of the printed page is that there is great busyness and outbreaks of accidentals. The *heard* impression is that of an aural kaleidoscope in which familiar phrases, now in the light (high registers), now in the dark (low registers) are heard in constantly changing combinations.

Before and while suffering from canonitis, I made a point of examining the exudations of earlier victims of the disease, from Henry Purcell, whose catches (rounds written for his Catch Club) have texts so dirty that they are now rarely published, to Weberns 12-tone choral canons. I am pleased to say that I found none written in the manner of my piece for penny-begging singers and am proud of my minute and a half of originality.

Because Oily Emma was not always available for babysitting, our attendance at the theatre, opera, and concerts was more limited than during our earlier two years in Rome. Nevertheless, we always heard the concerts of the RAI Orchestra (Radio Italiana). The Academy station wagon drove us composers and interested others to the outlying RAI studios and concert hall. The Academy's Director had recently made an arrangement with the RAI management that premieres of orchestral works by Academy composers would occasionally be programmed for the broadcast concerts. Laurence Roberts, who remained as hospitable and friendly as in the past years, assured me that if I would write a single-movement piece, he would see to it that the RAI would perform it in due course.

I searched for a title for the piece that described what I would write and that would translate easily into Italian. *Variations (Variazioni)* implied more predictability than I wanted; *Transformations (Trasformazioni)* was chosen. A ten-minute work for large orchestra, it was first played by the RAI Orchestra in Torino, in our absence. It was composed and orchestrated in my Cathouse in the garden of Casa Serena during July and August, the score edited on an Italian liner we boarded in Genoa for New York in early September.

We had left Rome at the close of the school year for our last summer's stay with Nora's mother. The five of us continued, as if without interruption, the local sightseeing on foot and by Volkswagen we had enjoyed at Christmas time, now adding swims in and bout trips up and down the Lake of Lugano.

Nora was engaged in sorting her father's extensive library, selecting those parts to be donated to the Zürich, Yale, and Hopkins Medical Libraries. All uniformly and beautifully bound, his own writings amounted to 27 books in 64 editions (many of them translations) and 445 papers, combined in volumes, each containing those of several years. They were but the written remains of a life that included teaching on two continents and impromptu talks and lectures mostly on social, public health, and medical issues on four continents. Each year, on January 1, Henry entered into his private journals a plan of work: what he hoped to study, write, and accomplish during the coming year. In late December, he took some pleasure in what had been accomplished, regretted and looked for reasons for what had not. For a person who professed no religion, Henry was so imbued with the Calvinistic work-ethic that if anyone deserved sainthood in that faith, he did.

In addition to the published books and papers were the numerous folio volumes of journals, handwritten in German and English—for a few troubled years in French. A selection from them was made and translated by Nora and published by McGill University Press in 1966,* after which the Journals were donated to Yale.

Because Henry read 13 languages, a half dozen of which he spoke fluently, some idea of the size and variety of his research library that had to be sorted for distribution can be imagined. Some of his belles lettres volumes in English, French, and German we shipped to New York, together with two oak roll-front cabinets that have served me since for some of my music manuscripts.

Revising and editing the score of *Transformations* on board ship for the eight days from Genoa to New York proved to be a useful time-passer between the swims in the pool and movies with the children—and gazing at the horizon. In the bar, off-hours, there was always an empty table and I was bothered only by an occasional curious barfly. Shortly after our arrival a copy of the score was sent back over the seas to my two half-blind copyists in Rome to have it handsomely copied and the instrumental parts extracted—as they had recently done with my symphony.

By the time the books and cabinets from Casa Serena arrived by slow freighter, three of us were settled back in school and Nora was immersed in her research for her PhD dissertation, carrying on, so to speak, in the tradition of her father. The subject she had chosen was one highly untypical for the Slavic Department, but finally found acceptable: Meyerhold, an early twentieth-century Soviet theatre director and producer, little known in the West in 1959.

During the fifties, now drawing to a close, I was occasionally invited to contribute reviews of new-music scores and recordings to various periodicals, such as *Choir Guide, Notes,* and *The Musical Quarterly.* I noticed that those among my acquaintances who were composers were often in trouble with their friends, about whose music they wrote too honestly and too frankly. Virgil Thomson, Ned Rorem, and John Cage had fallings-out with one another and with others. For this and other reasons, I had begun to doubt that I cared to run such

---

* *Henry E. Sigerist: Autobiographical Writings.*

risks when Paul Lang, editor of the *Quarterly*, sent me yet another score and asked me to write about it. The composer was a Catholic priest somewhere who had composed a respectable, highly conventional choral anthem. I called Paul to suggest that perhaps a mistake had been made because the *Quarterly* never reviewed such run-of-the-mill music. He insisted that there was no mistake and I should do what I'd agreed to do: write about it. I did, but the review was not printed. I wrote no other reviews ever, for anybody, about the music of living composers.

I did not regret my decision no longer to write music reviews, for I had my own music to attend to. But writing prose—occasionally, later, poetry and lyrics—has always seemed to me in most ways not unlike composing music, possibly because as a teenager I had begun writing librettos, with words intended to be sung to music inflected by words. The planning of the length and shape of the whole, the chapters resembling separate movements, phrases—verbal or musical—down to the words and syllables equating pitches: all required choices and decisions differing only in their being read or being heard performed. As a musician writing, not composing, I have noticed that my choices of phrases and words are more often determined by their sounds than are the phrases and words chosen by writers who disregard the unheard sounds they are composing.

With no such notions in mind, I was flattered to be asked to submit an article on a musical subject of my choosing to the newly established Columbia University *Forum*, a quarterly journal of fact and opinion. Its young editor, Erik Wensberg, enterprising and energetic, proved to be also a helpful editorial guide in polishing my first published essay. Writing about music for the uninitiated is often thought to be difficult or impossible. It is possible to find the knack for doing so, I discovered, by teaching Music Humanities to a few hundred Columbia College students over ten years or so. When I saw my *Music, Magic, and Money* in print, I found that I was in good company: Robert Brustein and Seymour Lipset, both more or less of my age, the older Polykarp Kusch, and the elderly T. S. Eliot, among others. In 1968 my essay was republished by *Atheneum*, as the blurb said, as one of "the best articles published in *Forum* during its first ten years."

*   *   *   *   *   *

𝕸𝖆𝖌𝖎𝖈, *music* & MONEY

by JACK BEESON

(as it appeared in *Columbia University Forum*)

Every year more and more magicians disappear. Not so long ago the navigator was magician to the shore-bound, apparently relying on some occult connection with the spirits of the sea and sky, though actually drawing on his knowledge of simple arithmetic, tables, and the known movements of the spheres. Today, with radar, and with the Hydrographic Office's having already worked out most of the problems and tabulated the answers in nine volumes, the magic is almost gone. Navigation can be learned in evening classes, and everybody with even a middle-size boat goes to class. Similarly, the practice of medicine—especially diagnosis—was once very much a matter of sorcery to the layman. But now that *The New York Times* is only a day behind the learned journals in reporting the latest medical advance, and now that we can all participate in the conquest of disease by contributing a dollar to the Muscular Dystrophy or Heart Fund, medicine—even diagnosis—is losing its mystery.

To anyone who still wants to be thought a magician by everybody else, I recommend musical composition. The general public simply refuses to believe that composers create music by any other than occult means. It is of no use to assure an inquisitive music-lover that a composer prefers to compose regularly every day (most write music in the morning, between breakfast and lunch), that he doesn't despise bourgeois comforts, that he doesn't understand what the word inspiration means (at least as the layman uses it), that he makes music the way anybody else makes anything else: by making it.

The facts are against him. When he leaves his study for lunch (he has probably been composing in the living room or in the bedroom), there is some music newly created, seemingly out of nothing, and it can affect a listener in some curious—magical—fashion which defies precise verbalization. It is thought suspicious that his study is invariably neat, with sharp pencils, razor blades, rulers, erasers, and much

286

unused paper. And if composers look like everybody else and mostly talk not composition, but money, rights, commissions, and jobs among themselves, what Inquisition was ever fooled by the looks of a necromancer or by the fact that alchemists among themselves spoke innocently of the fluctuating prices of base metals?

The only magic in music for the composer is the strange power it has to compel him to compose. against all the dictates of reason and cautions of common sense. For, although writing music in the United States may be a way of life for a composer seriously interested in the expressive powers of music, the composer does not very often make a living from composition alone.

This is not to say that money cannot be made in writing music. A person may have only modest musical gifts, little or no training (he may read music only haltingly and not be able to write any of it down), but with luck, perseverance, and the collaboration of a good lyricist, he may make money—sometimes lots of money—writing popular music. But as the tunesmith of a juke box hit he resembles more closely one member of a team designing a commodity than he does a composer. For the process by which his tune is selected, treated by a highly specialized arranger, recorded by a favorite band and a sexy vocalist, plugged over the air or in juke boxes, and listened to and forgotten by millions of persons—all this has more to do with toothpaste and detergents than it has to do with

musical composition, which is communication in tone between two human beings.

The American layman tends to define these musical extremes by the terms *popular* music—music that is very much liked by practically everybody for a short time—and *classical* music—music of the sort that goes on in concert halls and is heard over FM and other comercially unsuccessful radio stations much of the time, and over networks and big-time stations at strange hours. (It is easy to avoid classical music on television because there isn't much.) The third category is *semi-classical* music and consists of popular music which has survived its period of popularity and that classical music which has become almost universally familiar.

As everybody knows, a lot of what sounds like popular music never fulfills its definition and becomes popular. And, as not so many know, classical music is really much more popular than is supposed. As for semi-classical music (that is, semi-popular music), over a period of years it pays better (that is, it is more popular) than popular music. Real jazz is actually much more nearly related, in the attitudes of its creators, performers, and listeners, to classical than to popular music, though its adherents are much less numerous. They are today the smallest minority group among musicians and affect the longest hair.

Statistics reinforce the fact that there is money in music. One speaks, in this country, of the music *industry*. Last year almost half a billion dollars were spent on record players alone. Of the $360 millions spent on records, at least one quarter went for recordings of classical music. And as has most often been the case recently, more money was spent last year on classical music than on spectator sports.

However impressive the bare facts on the widespread use of "classical" music in this country, it is clear that there is a certain rough injustice in democracy as it affects the arts. The kinds of music favored by minorities numbering even in the millions are economically at a disadvantage when pitted against the kinds of music favored by the majority. There is enough money in popular music to make its composers interesting to capitalists, labor groups, lawyers, and legislators. The spokesmen for the national conscience may occa-sionally pay lip service to the "classical" composer, but he is not financially interesting enough to have friends in court or Congress and therefore receives as small a piece of the economic pie as decency permits.

And so it is that the composer of what the masses call classical music rarely lives exclusively from the money he receives from composing.

There are only a few composers who manage (sometimes with two different names) to support their composition of "classical" music by writing "popular" music; for the person is rare who can and does compose serious music and who has also the knack and stomach for the most popular variety. He must move in two quite different social and musical worlds and he must, to say the least, have a flexible esthetic and a thick skin. There are, however, numerous composers whose main energies go into concert—or un-economical—music, but who have no conscientious scruples against writing once in a while (or as often as they can) a score for a movie, a television show, or a Broadway musical comedy or play.

The theatrical forms have always offered the most money for music. In fact, since the mass media will sometimes permit, on especially prestigious occasions, the breadth and depth of expression associated with concert music, a number of highly trained composers with serious musical intentions live out their entire creative lives on the more sophisticated levels of the theater, movies, and television. Many of our most respected composers of cham-ber music, songs, orchestral music, and operas, however, will have nothing to do with those media which must be coerced or shamed into using the good offices of serious composers. They are likely to be scornful of those who write consistently or even occasionally for Hollywood or Broadway. This scorn takes the form of upbraiding the erring composer for having made concessions to the public, though a disinterested person might point out that there is no one public, only different publics.

Those who elect to see a film made by the kind of producer who would choose a score by a high-class composer are not those who flock to a film made especially for adolescents, one of the chief attractions of which will be music designed for adolescents. Furthermore, many of the "concessions" are simply musical practices made necessary by the dramatic media and are no more improper or immoral than the suiting of a composer's symphonic thoughts to the performers and instruments of a symphony orchestra and the customs of the concert hall.

But, not to pursue further matters of musical morals, how *does* the composer make money from creating "classical" music, serious music, concert music, art music, or call-it-what-you-will music? Leaving out of account such windfalls as Hollywood film scores, which are offered only occasionally to composers not regularly employed in a movie studio, let us trace the economic life of a symphony.

It is more than likely that a composer spends between six and twelve months at work composing and scoring a thirty-minute symphonic work. He writes his symphony in the first place because he wants to, or because he feels he should, or because, if he is experienced and well known—and let us assume he is—because some orchestra or foundation has commissioned him to do so for some such sum as a thousand dollars. He may or may not be required to furnish the orchestral parts. If so, he may copy them out himself, or, to save his own time, he may have them done by a professional copyist, who will charge close to a thousand dollars. He can

have the parts copied abroad for a quarter or half that sum, but he may run into trouble later with American union musicians Orchestral parts are almost never engraved nowadays. As a rule, full scores are first circulated among conductors in blueprinted copies of the composer's manuscript. In such circumstances it is not surprising that there is hardly a professional composer alive who does not write music legibly. No one can afford the shorthand scrawl common in earlier days when copyists were plentiful and ill-paid. If, however, the contemporary composer does not write legibly enough, or if he is hard pressed for time, wealthy, or supported in this by a publisher, he will have the score—as well as the parts—copied out by a professional copyist at rates which *begin* at several dollars per page.

When the work is finally performed, the composer will charge a royalty and rental for the use of the score and parts. He is likely to bargain sturdily for the first-performance fee. Nevertheless, he is unlikely to be paid much more than the usual amount paid by a major orchestra for a thirty-minute symphony: about $100. For subsequent performances by the same orchestra he receives, usually, $50. If there are later performances by orchestras not in the top ten (second performances are much rarer than premieres, by the way), the composer will receive half the sums paid by major orchestras. If the symphony is accepted by a publisher, who acts as the publicity and rental agent, the composer splits all fees 50-50, whether the publisher actually publishes or not. In the unlikely event that the publisher does print the work, the composer receives 10 per cent of the list price of the score. If he is extremely fortunate, he may have his symphony recorded. In such a case the royalties will not be great—both he and the publisher receive 4 cents on each record sold; but a recording makes possible radio performances, and each performance will be logged and paid for by one of the performing rights societies—probably ASCAP (American Society of Composers, Authors, and Publishers) or BMI (Broadcast Music, Incorporated) —provided that the composer is a member of one. In case he is not, or is not a member of the group to which his publisher belongs, only the publisher receives payment. The money a composer makes through his performing rights society is substantial, but the complicated and unpublicized payment practices of the societies are not easily broken down to determine how much money a symphony is worth per radio or television performance.

Even if the symphony has been commissioned in the first place, wins the Pulitzer Prize of $500 after the first performance, and is then widely performed, recorded, and played often over the air, the composer is not likely to earn enough money to keep himself and his family for the length of time he invested in the composition of the piece. And of course all these blessings are never visited upon one symphony. The result is that writing symphonies is a losing proposition, economically speaking.

Because opera performances take place in theaters, where larger amounts of money change hands—royalties are larger and extended runs are possible—there is a greater chance that the opera composer will be reimbursed for his time and out-of-pocket expenses. He may even make money. But the majority of composers of successful two-hour-long operas will only lose four times the amount they would have lost on a thirty-minute symphony. It is not surprising that literary men who are accustomed to live by their writing cannot often, if ever, afford the time to write a libretto.

Composing chamber music is, from the economic point of view, hopeless. It is infrequently performed in public, is not often subject to performance royalty or rental of parts, and in the rare instances in which it is recorded, the records are not bought by the public or played over the air. For some reason the record-buying and radio-listening public prefers huge orchestral sounds and operatic cataclysms in their living rooms over chamber music, which is almost always faithfully reproduced electronically and perfectly suited to the size of living rooms.

Concert songs and music for one or two instruments, two other kinds of respectable music-making, are in an even worse fiscal state. They are performed sometimes, but though fifty performances of a piano sonata by a virtuoso on tour may add greatly to a composer's reputation, he is not likely to receive more than 10 percent royalty from the one copy of the music bought by the pianist: 30 cents. (If the work is not published, it is quite likely that the virtuoso was *given* a copy of the manuscript, reproduced by a blueprint process at a cost to the composer of $5). If the pianist happens to appear in an ASCAP-licensed hall, a pittance performance royalty will be paid to the composer, provided he is a member of ASCAP.

In this country the principle is not yet established that the composer should receive a royalty for each performance of his music before a paying audience. The performing rights societies have been making only slow progress in convincing American concert managers and the ladies on civic music associations that if the janitor, the piano tuner, and the ticket salesmen are paid, the composer should really be cut in too.

Breathes there a man with so little economic determinism in his soul that he does not wonder if perhaps even the more enlightened elements of society no longer require some kinds of traditional music-making? The once clear, though often strained, relationship between the composer and his princely or ecclesiastical patron has changed in the last 150 years to a very complex relationship between the composer and the distant, unknown listener, who becomes a patron whenever he buys a record of the composer's music or buys the products advertised on the radio programs which present his music "live" or recorded. The old-fashioned means of communication by way of live concerts and publication still exist (both involving "patronage" by way of royalties and tickets), but it is significant that publication is every year of less importance. Music publishers live these days from their percentage of recording, radio, and television payments, not from sales.

The once clear and close relationship between the man who needed music for a specific purpose and the composer who wrote it for him has become very muddled, not only by the legacy of the nineteenth-century notion that the true artist creates solely out of his need for self-expression rather than to fulfill someone else's need for his music, but also by the hosts of persons who make the composer's music available to listeners by way of the modern means of musical communication. These middlemen too often interpose their own tastes and business interests between composer and listener. In this situation, aggravated by the fact that the American audience for music is growing and learning and changing in mysterious ways, it would not be surprising if composers frequently spent their energies in directions that are as empty of listeners as of financial reward. And at the same time, composers may overlook kinds of musical communication that arise out of new musical needs in a rapidly changing society.

This is not to suggest that composers should write down to a public. As recently as ten years ago new music was still resisted by the large musical public because it did not sound like the fifty works which made up the universal orchestral repertory. The language of musical modernism irritated a public not yet accustomed, as it is now, to some of these same sounds on movie sound tracks. And in these ten years vast amounts of old and new music formerly seldom heard have been recorded and have become available to anyone with an FM radio and a middle-class pocketbook. In the face of this new public sophistication, the fifty works are gradually being retired, resistance to contemporary music is diminishing, and the composer should re-examine his relation to an audience that is changing faster than he is.

Perhaps the day will come when a very large segment of our population will have been educated in their college Introduction to Music course and by their records and radios and local performance groups to a healthy receptivity to modern music. Perhaps by that time the present copyright law, which does disservice to composers, will have been changed. And perhaps the composer will be in a powerful enough position financially to overcome the present sharp practices of all those groups which today make more money than they should from his efforts.

But while he awaits the millennium, the composer must eat. Since he cannot, or will not, or at any rate usually does not live by composing music, he must do something else. Usually it is something musical. He may conduct, or play an instrument, or both. He may work in some corporation concerned with the business of music. He may pay his way by writing criticism, thereby influencing friends and making enemies among his composer colleagues and thereby garnering good or at least polite reviews of his own music from his critic colleagues. He may live for some years on a series of prizes, fellowships, and foundation grants. Or he may teach. By far the largest number of old and young composers, well-known and un-known, are today teaching in colleges, universities, and conser-vatories. There is much argument among composers as to whether this is a good idea. The teaching com-poser is not in the position of the scientist whose research project occupies most of his time. When teaching duties are consuming, the teaching composer becomes a "summer composer," developing a bad conscience and a rusty technique during the winter. But many composers can and do combine prolific writing with teaching. Against the composing-college teaching combination it is sometimes charged that the composer becomes a verbalizer who comes to believe the oversimplified half-truths he passes out to the nonspecializing student, and that he is not called upon to operate at full capacity as a professional musician when working with music majors only half committed to music as a profession.

It depends. With so many composers of such different persuasions now at work on college and university faculties and with the levels of music-making and performance in some institutions approaching the levels of conservatory music, it is dangerous to generalize. One may, in fact, object that the conservatory point of view, with its interest focused on the creative and recreative musician, may also be dangerous for the composer who will spend his life writing music for an audience made up for the most part of nonmusicians.

Surely it should be the business of a composer to compose, and surely the most healthy situation for everyone concerned is one in which the composer can live by his creation. Whether the American composer will be able to do so in the future depends on the extent to which he can communicate musically and economically with a large public. His position will be assured if the American educational ideal should ever be fulfilled: the elevation of all intelligent persons to the condition of what was once an intellectual elite. But the composer will be even worse off if the mass media succeed finally in reaching everybody and then, for financial reasons, succeed in coarsening the response of the individual to the extent that he cannot understand because he does not any longer want to understand or react to a personal musical statement addressed to an individual listener.

The composer of today, whenever he teaches Introduction to Music courses on campuses or on television or radio, is doing more than making money to buy time in which he can compose. He is participating in a social and educational experiment which, if successful, will bring new and larger audiences to his music and to all music in the future.

*   *   *   *   *   *

Chapter 9

Good Deeds and the Ditson Fund

(1960 --)

Lizzie Borden

(1954-65)

Because I had been promoted to tenure as an associate professor shortly before taking a leave for the Guggenheim year in Rome, there was more than a year during which I could bask in the knowledge that I was assured continuance in a friendly department I enjoyed within a university I respected until age 65 or 68. Both Nora and I so relished the excitement of the city that I didn't think twice about turning down composition professorships in Cornell and such far-flung places as Oklahoma and Honolulu. My music courses were in three divisions of Columbia, the Columbia College Faculty, the Faculty of Philosophy (one of the graduate facilities), and the General Studies Faculty. The deans of each faculty were annually on the prowl for newly tenured bodies that might prove to be of long-term use on committees. The College Dean found me and I served for years with the greatest interest on the Admissions Committee; when the School of the Arts was organized in the mid-sixties I exchanged my G.S. seat for a more demanding and musical seat on the Arts faculty and its governing committees until retirement.

Both Douglas Moore and Otto Luening for decades had helped to bring about and to keep alive numerous organizations that served the composer community. It was the two of them, I suppose, who decided that I was now mature and dependable enough to be invited to join various boards and juries—often in the company of one or both of them—that promoted new music by American composers.

In 1960 Robert Ward and I were elected members of the Advisory Committee of the Alice M. Ditson Fund, which determines how the income of that Columbia University endowment is to be spent. Because Douglas was to retire in 1962, he would have to relinquish his position as the Fund's Secretary, in charge of the day-to-day management of the Fund. I was asked to become the Acting Secretary in the interim.

I was not altogether inexperienced in taking over this responsibility, for already in the fifties Douglas had asked me to carry out three interesting projects funded by Ditson.

1) I was made a committee of one to weed out scores and tapes of composers who applied for aid for one or the other purpose; the final decision resting with the Committee's composers and the Committee itself. Already, a dozen years earlier I'd been asked to read through and report on a great pile of one-act opera vocal scores in connection with a competition sponsored jointly by the Fund and the Metropolitan Opera. The jury selected as the winner *The Warrior* by Bernard Rogers; its libretto retold the Samson and Delilah story hyperrealistically. Because the Met idiotically paired the premiere with *Hänsel and Gretel*, few in the audience enjoyed both. The critics flayed the Rogers music and the Met and Ditson for selecting it. Bernard was so upset for himself and his sponsors that he fell into a clinical depression. My pleasure in the whole affair was in the opera itself and in the numerous rehearsals I attended, observing a wonderful Met cast and the conductor Max Rudolf.

2) Concerned that little attention was being paid to composers of song, the Committee made me the producer of an album of *Songs by American Composers*. Inasmuch as the only competent jury to decide its contents would have to be three experienced composers in the genre, I had the bright idea of avoiding

embarrassment at our meetings by assuring each juror that he would be represented on one of the four LP sides. The first thousand of the albums were mailed out as gifts, from the Columbia president's office to carefully selected voice teachers. My payment came in the form of coming to know well and to attend the recording sessions of the four singers I had chosen, one from each voice type, Eleanor Steber, Mildred Miller, John McCollum, and Donald Gramm. The album was later issued on CD.

3) This third assignment I was responsible for initiating and carried out until 2007.

In 1952 Virgil Thomson took me to lunch to ask me to intercede on behalf of Arrow Press with the Ditson Fund and Columbia University Press (hereafter CUP) with his plan to place Arrow under the umbrella of CUP, with aid from Ditson. Some years before, he, Copland, Marc Blitzstein, and Lehman Engel, not being able to find publishers for their music, had set up Arrow as a publishing cooperative. Now they wanted to unburden themselves of Arrow and wanted me to superintend the CUP takeover and its continuance there. In a typical Virgilian inducement, he said, "Jack, if you're in charge, you can publish your own music and that of your friends and turn down the music of the enemies." As it turned out, the Arrow catalog went elsewhere, but it seemed to me—aside from the indecent proposal—something valuable could be made of the failed project. I sent a detailed proposal to the Advisory Committee for the publication of American music by CUP, its costs to be met by the Fund. Douglas reported that his colleagues were enthusiastic about the possibility, particularly because Mrs. Ditson's Will called for the publication of music. The Ditson Fund would fund the project once it was set up and ready to publish if I were prepared to carry it out. Charles Proffitt—whom I always called Mr. Non-Profit—was pleased with the idea of being President of the only American university press with a music publishing imprint, and one fully funded; the cautious assistant director, Henry Wiggins, dithered for a couple of years at such a radical venture. Finally, after more years of talk, contracts discussed and signed, and the Ditson money promised, the publication of new music by American composers commenced by CUP two decades after lunch with Virgil. The project faltered after my retirement in 1988, but there is hope of its revival.

Having passed the test of serving a year as Acting Secretary of the Fund, I was then elected Secretary and served until I retired in 1988. I soon learned that making grants to the most worthy applicants is far less simple than putting money on the plate while the Doxology is sung: "Praise God from Whom All Blessings Flow." Our blessings implied much correspondence, coming to understand budgets and the Office of the Controller, through which our checks flowed. I was aided by the Secretary's secretary, for most of my twenty-eight years by the knowledgeable, patient, and indestructible Betsy Mahaffey.

On rare occasions it was necessary to defend the Fund against rapacious members of the administration, always seeking money in odd places, from the unknowledgeable and the weak. One well remembered example will suffice. I was invited to lunch at Faculty House by the then Vice-President for Finance, a short, wiry economist who made a point of being seen on campus coatless, even in the coldest weather. He began his pitch by saying that the Ditson Fund file was red-flagged, indicating that we had an unspent balance over a couple of years; we seemed unable to spend our income. I replied that we were building up an amount to be spent on a coming major project. Nevertheless, he said, surely it would be better for us to underwrite graduate fellowships in music than to underwrite performances and recordings enjoyed by only a few specialists. I quoted from Mrs. Ditson's Will, parts of which I'd long since memorized: ". . . The said income shall not be applied directly for educational purposes." He replied, illogically, that their prohibition would not apply to unspent balances and that he would transfer the sum to some more useful purpose. I brought our luncheon to an end by warning that if he did so, I would report his action to the two on our Advisory Committee with law degrees and to the New York State Attorney General, in charge of such matters, adding that—as he surely knew—gifts to a university are made with the assurance that provisions of Wills are strictly carried out. There was no more plundering attempted from that source.

The mission of the Ditson Fund is to aid emerging American composers, chiefly by means of grants to record companies and performing groups specializing in new music—giving shots in the arm to keep them alive and active, as Otto Luening quipped. Because there were—and still are—few sources of funds for that purpose, Ditson's reputation was and still is far greater than its resources. Early on, I devised a friendly reply to the question, "How much money do you have?" "Less than some people think; more than some people think." Sometimes, because fund-raisers believed that electing me to their board would enhance their chances of gaining support from the Fund, I was over the years elected to serve in this or that organization. When I accepted I would point out that becoming privy to their problems would lead me to read more easily between the lines of their often too rosily written grant applications. Frequently I settled for leading my name to their advisory boards; their members were almost never asked advise, and those who offered it, un-asked, were usually resented.

I have known composers who have been paid, *quid pro quo*, in performances of their music by serving on the boards of performing organizations. In my stiff-necked—even priggish—way, when invited to join the boards of three small opera companies, I agreed to do so on condition that they promise not to perform any of my operas. In each case, with surprise, the invitation was withdrawn.

I have occasionally asked myself why I so often have agreed to do what I did not have to do in the university and in the new-music world. I have settled for the fact that I have no idea what I did, if anything, to deserve the Citizenship Award of the Muncie Exchange Club when I was in the seventh grade. Perhaps it is true that the child is father to the man.

That there was so much non-compositional activity after our return from Rome in September, 1959, was partly due to these new duties and partly to the fact that I was involved in helping to shape the scenario of my fourth opera, *Lizzie*

Borden, while waiting to receive some of its libretto to set to music. I did take some time out to compose something more parochial. Columbia College commissioned me to write a short work for the Columbia Band and Glee Club for the opening of its new student activities building and theatre, Ferris Booth Hall. Called *Commemoration*, most of its audience would have thought that the composer was fancifully playing around with the College alma mater, *Stand, Columbia*, not realizing that he was writing variations on a string quartet movement written by Joseph Haydn. In a somewhat similar example of institutional forgetfulness, the name of Ferris Booth has long ago disappeared in favor of the name of the donor who provided for the enlargement of the building, now known as Lerner Hall.

Quite some time after the premiere of *Lizzie Borden* in 1965 I thought it wise to write down the long and complicated story of how the opera had come into being—if only for myself—while the details were still vivid and I had my journal notes, letters, and postcards still on hand. When the editor of the *Opera Quarterly* invited me to submit an article on some operatic topic, I revised what I'd written and asked my two *Lizzie* collaborators to read it and make comments. Each wrote saying that I had included too much about the other; since I couldn't satisfy both except by cutting material about both, I left it essentially unchanged. I thought that a decade after its first and several subsequent productions, their mutual dislike would have disappeared. I naively thought that two gay writers living in the West Village within a few hundred yards of one another, each with one Jewish parent and a stepmother, would have more in common than frustration and jealousy: ill health had prevented the one from completing the libretto, circumstances had prevented the other from collaborating on the scenario and writing the first act of the libretto.

In the following reprint of the article, most of the material concerning *The Sweet Bye and Bye* has been deleted.

The Autobiography of *Lizzie Borden*
(1954 – 1965)

New York City
30 May 1954

A little man about my size—but with blue eyes and a vaguely Central European accent—came backstage after the last performance of *Hello Out There* last night. We talked for a while in the alleyway outside the stage door. He was complimentary about the lyric passages, startled me by remarking that obviously I must have the same water fixation Debussy suffered from—for throughout *Hello* I seemed never to set San Francisco without evoking the sea, usually with foghorn sounds. He's right, though mot more than half were conscious. It turns out that he's Richard Plant, the person Oliver Daniel phoned me about, the one who has been brooding for years over a libretto based on the Lizzie Borden murders. So far he hasn't found a composer, and it's not hard to see why, with such a subject. Anyhow, we agreed to get together next week to talk about it.

Early June 1954

Richard's place is in the East Forties, dripping with books, mostly 19th and 20th C. German Lit., which he teaches. It seems he lived next door to the Frankfurt Opera as a boy—his father was a doctor to the company; and he seems to have spent a lot of time in opera houses since, for he knows the repertory backwards and forwards, including the names of librettists. He's a mystery story buff and wrote several in Switzerland, as well as radio plays and a retelling of the Borden story. I'm to look up his Doubleday novel. He says the Calvinism he love/hated in Basel, where he did his Ph.D. (on one of the more neurotic playwrights) after leaving Germany, is the same Calvinism that accounts for those Yankee accomplishments in which, he insists, we take so little pleasure. He sees the Borden family in its Fall River setting as a distillation of the main currents of New England history. Mr. Borden is the latter-day version of the hanging judge of Salem; Lizzie is the passionate, repressed, upper-class unemployable Victorian spinster. Richard admits that many may consider the story a threadbare subject but, as he says, it's constantly being reused because the story is archetypal (Elektra with the parents switched—"and don't forget that everybody hates a wicked step-mother") and because it has a peculiar fascination for Americans. He says the fact that it's been several plays, a ballet, and nobody knows how many novels and articles proves the story has dramatic power; it has exactly the kind of outsize people and emotions that are the stuff of opera. In that he's right, of course. By the end of the evening I was almost ready to say yes to the idea.

300

The next morning

I really can't imagine how one could do another *Elektra*, even a New England one. Nobody could beat Strauss at his own game, and who'd want to play with his rules anyway? As we agreed last night, the whole story is about *why* she did it—there's no story at all if one doesn't assume she did do it—and the opera would therefore be a psychologically oriented opera of characterization. If the music, words and the dramatic shape work together to convince the audience that Lizzie not only can but also *must* murder her parents, the piece could work; but if there is any substantial miscalculation, the audience won't go up the stairs with Lizzie to murder her—their—parents. And if they won't go up the stairs, there won't be any point at all in their having come to the theatre.

It's been obvious to me for a long time that an audience at an opera premiere, including the critics, is a *theatre* audience; most everybody is so busy taking in the plot, the characters, the surface of things, that not much of the music is heard, even if it's actually animating and shaping the whole. If a new opera can survive this kind of premiere, it may be performed often enough for the music finally to be listened to. Eventually the opera audiences take over; by that time nobody is interested in anything but the singers and maybe the musical "numbers," least of all in the plot and the characters. I don't know which treatment is worse. In any case, a Lizzie opera would be an awful risk. Most operas have something to get through life on, tho' some organ may be found to be weak or missing on opening night; a Lizzie opera would either be born or die in the general bloodletting.

Luckily I didn't have to be so ambivalent over the phone with Richard. It seems he's full of other projects now and couldn't work on a libretto until the summer, probably not even then. He says that in spite of finding me "a little far out musically" he thinks I might be right for the subject "even though you lack the requisite neuroses." I let that pass and made him promise he wouldn't look around for any other composer so long as I am interested. After all, it might work out someday!

With the first performances of *Hello Out There* out of the way and *Lizzie* in cold storage, tagged with my name on her, the search began for another subject . . .

Having written libretti as a teenager and twice adapted plays for operas, I was tempted to write my own libretto. But I thought then, and still do, that it is very risky for a composer to undertake from scratch his own play-and-poetry writing. The large-scale shaping of a libretto is essentially *musico*-dramatic shaping, to be sure, furthermore, musical necessity often determines the verbal middle ground and foreground, as well as the presence or absence of rhyme and the choice of vowels and consonants. The composer has enough to do in planning these matters, writing and scoring his music, and adjusting his ideas to the dramatic and verbal discoveries of his librettist, without trying to acquire the specialized craft and experience of the playwright/poet. Besides, one of the attractions of opera is precisely this varied play of tension between word and tone, as is manifest in the correspondence between Strauss and von Hofmannsthal, and in *Capriccio,* for that matter.

The search for a librettist for what was to become *The Sweet Bye and Bye* never really got underway. Through Douglas Moore, who was in the throes of collaborating with John Latouche on *The Ballad of Baby Doe,* I met John's apprentice/collaborator, Kenward Elmslie . . .

Lizzie slunk in the shadows, intruding into dinner conversations. I tried the idea of a Lizzie opera on everyone. Reactions were mixed and tended to extremes: "Terrible idea—people singing about their frustrations is a contradiction." "It's a natural, why hasn't it been done before?" I noticed, however, that even those composers who were most enthusiastic showed no signs of stealing the subject. My sly plan of nudging Richard into writing *his* libretto while I was composing *SB&B* came to nothing more than amusing phone calls. He was busy at other things. He also implied that having lived for so long with the idea and the Strauss/von Hofmannsthal letters, he was not to be deprived of a real-life, down-to-every-last-word-and-note collaboration with a composer . . .

In the spring [of 1958], I learned that a Guggenheim Fellowship would give me the coming year free to compose. It was obvious to me that I should have at least part of a libretto in hand by September, when my family and I were to leave for a year at the American Academy of Rome; large-scale works are not best written during summers and time snatched between classes in the winter. . . . I badgered Richard into discussing a Lizzie libretto seriously.

It was immediately clear that he had read all the extensive Lizzie Borden literature, as well as the trial testimony, newspaper accounts, and even a book on the Fall River Steamship Line. Furthermore, he had long since decided at what points in the "true" story we should depart from the "facts" and by how much. The ages of the two sisters would have to be changed in order to conform to psychological necessity—in this case the precedent of Elektra and Chrysothemis. And the name of Lizzie's sister, Emma, would have to be changed. We agreed that the overall style would be New England *verismo,* as little like its German predecessor as possible. Nevertheless, the veristic fact that the Bordens had mutton broth, bananas, cookies, and johnny-cakes for breakfast on that hot day of the murder was unusable for our purposes, though it might be the touchstone for some other, more surrealistic Lizzie opera.

Several meetings in New York and a weekend on Shelter Island resulted in a six-page outline that put Richard's years of thoughts and notes into a dramatic shape that could be handled musically. Though much of the detail was unclear, the main outlines of the work as it was to be finished six years later were already present. A first scene in the living room of the Borden house, beginning with children singing a Sunday school hymn and ending with "Andrew's Credo," with father and daughter arguing about a dress in between; a second scene in the daughters' room, beginning and ending with arias for the younger daughter, Amanda (alias Emma, finally to be called Margret); and a scene with Lizzie in between. The third scene of the first act was later to become the second act; to the original plan were added, years later, the quintets, and the Genet-like sadomasochistic scene enjoyed by Andrew and Lizzie, but the bulk of the second act, in broad outline, existed in this early tentative Outline I.

The synopsis of our second act (now the third) reflected problems in arranging the elopement of Margret and the Captain, deciding whether Lizzie should murder her parents singly or together, and effecting a transition between the murders and the epilogue, which was originally longer than it is today. Richard and I had agreed in our first talks—already four years before!—that we were averse to long trial scenes in opera; we chose not to put Lizzie in court. But there remained the problem of showing her in the act of murder and then free of the law, though imprisoned by her memories and burned-out passions. To make the transition clear to those ignorant of the historical Lizzie (including European audiences who might never have heard of one of America's national heroines), we planned to indicate the trial proceedings and the passage of time by using slide projections of newspaper articles, newsboys shouting headlines, three town gossips, and finally a gentleman reading (in a speaking voice) an editorial from Joseph Pulitzer's *World*. (The *World* wrote that the jury had done well in acquitting Lizzie, for to imagine that a woman of good family, devoted to the church, could carry out such a deed would call into question the whole basis of society.) Out purpose was not only to convey significant information, but also to effect a transition to the moody, quiet, and time-obsessed epilogue. A final scene was essential to our purpose; we were not writing an opera about murders, but about why a woman (largely of our making) would kill. It was important to know what would happen to such a person, in such a time and place, after killing. We thought it important, also, to highlight the one wholesome result of her act by permitting our Margret/Chrysothemis, who had fulfilled herself in these years, to return for a few words with her sister.

We were aware of the risk involved in leading an audience for two hours up to murder and then continuing, but such a "falling action" was essential to our whole intention. The musical and dramatic means of handling the murders, the transition, and the epilogue were not found until after another four years of worry and trial and error. The paraphernalia of slides, newsboys, gossips, and the editorial were eventually eliminated; they seemed out of keeping with the theatrical style planned for the opera as a whole—domestic intimate, involved with psychological motivation, not with exteriorized decoration.

By the end of summer, another weekend in the country and an occasional letter had added more detail to plot and character, but there was still not one word of the libretto itself.

East 48th Street
27 October 1958

Dear Jack,

A hurried note. I wish you a wonderful time in Rome. . . . I hoped you would let me know your new address but you are no Strauss who wrote faithfully. (You may add, correctly, that I ain't no Hofmannsthal either. . . .)

Very herzliche regards as ever,
Richard

East 48th street
Christmas 1958

Dear Jack,

I am adding all the time to our project. It is always close. I am reading things for it, rewriting lyrics, thinking of scene improvement, getting the hang of Calvinism. Want to get many Cotton Matherisms in, so as to make Andrew prototype of a Calvinist money-happy, but truly believing man. Insufferable, but no villain. Am studying Newman's opera books—informative, witty—and took course in voice. Learned about vowed singing, voiced consonants, and so on. So, either in Europe, or after your return, we go to work. . . .

Richard

Columbus, Ohio
21 January 1959

Dear Jack,

I waited so long to answer your note . . . because I had hoped to be able to come forward with at least snippets and scene I.

Hélas, things have nor worked out that way. I need to do a bit of research on Sunday school, church songs, etc., and some more thinking about how to get the children off, get a singable dialogue, and move things quickly into the first encounter. I have tried but nothing came of it, and so you get this hurried note from Columbus . . . Well, you may as well know, they are having a new play on Broadway, *Legend of Lizzie.* Not by any particularly famous man—he has done TV and some playwriting. But, of course, someone else may make an announcement that he is going to use the play . . . There is nothing we can do. We were there before, but people will say that we got influenced . . . I have not seen the play, but shall do so later.

As ever,
Richard

East 48th Street
16 March 1959

Dear Jack,

    This is going to be a contrite note. To be frank, I have not only a bad conscience but am in poor shape . . .

    First, duty, Good sport that I am, I rushed to the box office the day of *Legend's* premiere. This was Friday, my ticket for Sunday. But it never made Sunday! I got my filthy $$$ back, but never saw as much as a set. Too bad. You saw the review. No one will accuse us of plagiarizing now.

    Two new ideas . . .

Yours, defective librettist,
Richard

East 48th Street
23 May 1959

Dear Jack:

    . . . And now I cannot swing the trip to Europe, hélas. I shall stay here, take a short trip South, and work on Puritanism, Old New England, and Lizzie. I have been overwhelmed with work and worries . . . BUT I am looking forward to fall and your return. As a matter of fact, Lizzie is never far from me. I have sketched a few more items, and hope, in June, to start in earnest. I admit: I need your stimulation, our arguments and struggles. Things emerge then in terms if opera. I am trying to see the characters as musical characters: Old Borden is thrift, acquisitiveness, and tyranny. Strictly the old mold, the overbearing Father, the hoarder, humorless but not without grandeur. And the thing that we must suggest is that he still has sex with fat Abbie, the poor member of the family, and that Lizzie knows and feels it. Margret is all lyrical soprano, and FEAR. Her big aria I have nearly done . . . she knows when He and She are home, even though she has not heard them . . .

Yours,
Richard

    Upon my return from Rome in September, we did set to work in earnest. We began by talking through the changes that should be made in Tentative Outline I. While Richard pondered, and then typed these changes into Tentative Outline II, I leafed through shelves of hymnbooks. To set the time and place of the opera we had decided to use an actual Sunday school hymn text in the opening children's chorus. But the right text was difficult to find. It had to be free of copyright, characteristically a children's hymn, and shaped in such a manner that my musical setting would also fit the traditional doggerel with which we wished to *end* the opera:

        Lizzie Borden took an axe
        And gave her mother forty whacks.

When she saw what she had done
She gave her father forty-one.

The right text, when it was found, leapt from the page, for it not only fulfilled my requirement that the first lines given to characters in opera should limn them verbally and musically, but also expressed the "work for the night is coming" aspect of the Calvinist ethic:

Toiling early in the morning,
Catching moments through the day,
Nothing small or lowly scorning,
While we work, and watch, and pray.

The new and more detailed outline completed and the opening text discovered, we continued meeting almost weekly to determine the layout of musical numbers, transitions, and the particulars of the stage action. By the middle of October Richard had the first scene in first draft.

West 11th Street
13 October 1959

Dear Jack,

There can be cuts. I have suggestions for more, mainly in (1) Andrew, preceding and introducing his Credo, and (b) in the Credo itself. I also realize that my rhythms change. This, too, can be adjusted to fit your rhythmical ideas.

I have more stage suggestions and musico-dramatic ideas, which I noted down and shall tell you when we meet. The scene is undoubtedly too long. We may have to cut the Cavatina to Old Harbor, in addition to the Introduction and Credo. Curtain in American Gothic, frozen, unspoken, and full of hidden emotions. It must be a tableau. Call me soon.

Regards,
Richard

More meetings followed, concerned with refining the verbal detail of the first scene and the dramatic detail of the next two scenes. The better part of an evening was spent in finding an appropriate name for the Captain. It had to be Anglo-Saxon Protestant, in order that Mr. Borden should distrust and dislike him for other reasons that his background and breeding. In addition, because the Captain was to symbolize all that the girls longed for—not only a man, but the attraction of faraway places as well—it could be no ordinary name. The Bible, genealogies, and the telephone directory finally led us to Jason Macfarlane, two names that subliminally, subaurally, accomplished our purpose.

Frederiksted
Virgin Islands
2 February 1960

Dear Jack,

Andrew would have disliked it: sun, sand, and bronzed bodies, fish, crabs, and no work. But Lizzie might have been liberated in every respect and there was a Captain Eggleston (USN) for Margret. I always cast. Will see you in February, first week.

As always,
Hugo von Hofmannsthal

West 11th Street
March 1960

Dear Jack,

Here it is up to the Credo, which we shall discuss next. I hope to see you next week—if I am still alive. I have finally thrown out versions and versions of I,1. I still have three left, and I have discovered one thing: they are getting shorter and shorter each time . . . so I hope to be able to start soon on I, 2. I am a little afraid of it, just like Margret . . . and of course, I postpone and postpone and one cannot keep Jason Beeson waiting forever . . .

Regards,
Richard

When the first scene was finally "right" for both of us, I was anxious to begin composing the music. . But with the spring Richard's depressions deepened, and he was finally hospitalized uptown.

During the six years we had lived with the Borden family of Fall River, shaping facts to fit fantasies, Richard's European reticence occasionally permitted fleeting references to the *Plaut* family of Frankfurt am Main. The Catholic mother had died in 1932; Richard fled to Basel in 1933. No entreaties could induce the Jewish father to leave the still-flourishing medical practice and the *Heimatland*—but perhaps one could have been more forceful? By 1938 it was too late to emigrate, and in desperation Plaut took his own life and that of Richard's stepmother, with means easily available to a physician.

With or without the "requisite neuroses" to compose a Borden opera, I could see plainly the parallels between Richard's two families: the strong, obdurate fathers, the stepmothers, imagined patricide and matricide, and the guilt of survivors. Was his work on the libretto a writing out and transferal of suffering, or was it actually contributing to his illness?

Neither the duration nor the outcome of his illness could be predicted. I could not bring myself to begin the music, not knowing if he would ever be able to continue; nor, as it was becoming clear how intimately Lizzie's story was entwined with his own, could I bring myself to suggest inviting another librettist to continue. When somewhat recovered, Richard sensed the difficulty and wrote:

New York
15 June 1960

Dear Jack,

It was nice seeing you . . . and talking things over.

In the event that I will not be able to work on our opera concerning Lizzie Borden in the fall—say by October—you must feel free either to hire another librettist, or write the text yourself, or provide me with a collaborator. In any case, you are free to do with the material whatever you wish, and this includes the material we have so far finished.

This is fair, I think, and will set your mind at ease. I am quite sure that when the first flurry of the term is over, I will be not only able but eager to get back to our cooperation, but this release will provide you with the necessary security . . .

Yours sincerely,
Richard Plant

Within a week I had retyped the "final" agreed-upon version of the txt, changing a word here and there, stealing a word here and there from one of the rejected versions; within another week I had begun the music, many of the ideas having been germinating for a year. As usual, working into the musico-dramatic world, "musical" considerations dictated "dramatic" changes, or the other way round. A case in point: We had agreed that the end of the first scene would be mimed; but Abbie's entrance required some added vocal flourish. The composer was not hard put for words, for "da-da-da-da" sufficed. (Similarly, when completing the second scene a year later, I added the offstage voice of Abbie as an extension of the long-held final note of Margret's "Fear Aria." This dramatic effect "makes" the first-act curtain, but was in origin a musical, an operatic, idea.)

While I was composing on Shelter Island, Richard was nearby in East Hampton casting off the remnants of illness, regaining his memory and sense of humor. We picked up the threads of our story and its tangled characters, on the East Hampton beach, on Shelter Island, and in the fall by telephone and letter in New York. The third draft of the second scene was under way, together with four successive drafts of what was to become the second act, each draft fleshing out the scenario in great detail.

Columbus, Ohio
20 August 1960

Dear Jack,

. . . the window duct, a few suggestions. I do not have the second scene here in Ohio. But it could be rewritten:

Alone in the window
Before the garden
I see (watch) the flowers
Fading away.

Then simply leave off the wall item, and we can give it to Lizzie later. If this is important, write me and I'll try to redo the lyric, perhaps add a line for Margret for the wall item left out . . .

. . . Now, the most difficult because I am not convinced quite. The repetition of "long" in Andrew's Credo does not bother me. Repetitions in opera are useful. But here are alternatives:

I worked hard, I worked long
The years were barren and lean.

Bad: more syllables, not as Puritan-plain. Good: barreN aNd leaN, plus loNg. We get N sounds to tie us together . . .

One more word to duet in window. Margret feels the prison as much as Lizzie does. One must NOT assume that she does not suffer. She is simply too timid, and not a fighter, being truly Evangeline's daughter, to make troubles. Lizzie is the born rebel, troublemaker, and instigator. She has forever things going, is in permanent turmoil, enjoys—if she can enjoy anything in the basic mode of suppressed rage in which she lives—fighting back. So that Margret could notice the wall Father made. It should NOT appear that Lizzie suggests to her sister that *la vie* in Fall River Gothic is nice and pleasant. It is just that Margret is truly feminine and yielding. But inside she suffers and loathes. I realize that this makes her love for Jason more of an opportunity to escape—but this is typically Victorian, too, gives an element of puzzlement in the last scene when she decides to go West and cut all ties to the East (that is, her murderous sister) . . .

I am enclosing the first version, so-called Chick Version of Abbie's Bird-Song. We simply cannot escape tradition: I remembered, while working on it, that there is Nedda, damn her. But Opera, after all, has tradition, *toujours* . . .

Yours, Illlica-Giacosa
Ricardo

Columbus, Ohio
Post-Labor Day 1960

Dear Hänsli,

No. 1: I can hardly read your handwritten notes. So it may happen that I cannot answer your questions, comments , requests.

No. 2: It is often difficult for me to change something that we have set. You, too, *mon cher ami,* have changed your mind. First, the bit with Mrs. Perkins, Hale, & Co. was left out—against my wish—then put back in again, to my joy . . .

This leads to I, 2, the window scene. I am *quite* satisfied the way it is now. It has a certain poetic flow that, I think, none of your changes will improve. I stewed over it quite a lot. I want you to be happy, as happy as Strauss ever was with Hofmannsthal—and then changed the Composer in *Ariadne* behind H.'s back into soprano—so that he could indulge in his pastime of having 3 sopranos together!

. . . Andrew's Credo: I still say, leave as is, the two "long"s do not matter. Further: barren for Andrew *does* work—because he made little money, the years were barren. Lonely, I admit, is out of character . . .

. . . Where is the kitchen? Right of dining room, in back? I must visualize it . . .

. . . Could we put in that Abbie nursed Evangeline—to death? You know I plan to have a few phrases to the effect that Lizzie wanted to work, office, nurse, but was refused, denied, not allowed . . .

. . . Now a few things about Lizzie Mad Scene. I have been thinking a lot about it. I would like her to Remember Mama, "She never left me," etc. But: what about her having dreamed that Andrew is not her real father? This is known as "foundling fantasy." Many children in conflict with parents have it. It would fit Lizzie. Think about it . . .

. . . Too bad I cannot have more dreams—another, if foundling one meets with your disfavor, is the one about burning. Burning the ledgers, the books, the bills, the furniture, seeing the house in wrack and ruin . . .

. . . Don't worry about too many fantasies—we have one, after all, before the mirror, sheer sex and Cinderella. But as mentioned, Lizzie lives in a good deal of fantasy, like many prisoners. . . .

Yours, old
Riccardo . . . Piave

Shelter Island
Friday the ninth
[September 1960]

Dear Richard,

. . . The situation reminds me of the late summer 1954. I had finished the first scene of *SB&B (not* the *Schweizer Bundesbahnen)* and was panting to go on, but the opening aria text didn't suit me. So I writ my own. Probably Ken never forgave me, but he put up a bold front and after causing me no end of trouble by changing a line or two—worsening them, I thought, naturally—came to love it. Go to, thou, and do likewise.

Here for your condemnation or commendation is the [beginning of the window scene, I,2], already set. I hope you can accept it as yours.

MARGRET
In the garden
the flowers wither and die.

In the garden
the towers of the house
and the high wall
cast shadows at all hours,
and nothing grows in the darkness.

In the garden
the stunted flowers
lean toward the light.
Their petals
  withering
    pale from the long night
    yearn for the bright air,
    the sun's caresses,
for nothing lives in the darkness.

Is it spring?
Is it fall?
The shadows lengthen,
deepen, darken.

In the garden,
  the flowers by the sunless wall
  find no light, no hope,
  no change of season.

Is it spring?
Is it summer

LIZZIE
  Is it fall?
  Is it winter?

MARGRET & LIZZIE
  The seasons turn,
  the years grow older.
  We wait in the shadows.

MARGRET
  Time passes us by.

LIZZIE
  Time passes us by.

I have no general objection to the repetition of words and phrases. My objection to Andrew's two "long"s is that they mean two different things too close together. The solution can wait.

. . . I visualize the kitchen to the right of the dining room—from the spectator's point of view. You too, I imagine. You say you have to know where everything is before you can write words; I can't write the music unless I see in my mind's eye where each person might be at every moment in a scene. I don't say they *will be* in those positions, but it's a kind of private stage direction, nevertheless. Most people don't realize that adding music to a libretto is, in at least one respect, staging it—for the composer is responsible for the *timing* of all the dialogue and much of the action.

Dining room should have more windows than living room. Then the four characters can be thrown into good light (during the tableau) and, furthermore, when the sliding doors are first opened there will be an effective spilling of light into the living room.

All the ideas on your page are good ones; it is all a matter of fitting them in—and into places where they make units. Not too much dial tone, please! ["Dial tone" was his word for those words and phrases that are essential for dramatic reasons, but that are embarrassing to the composer.] The more dreams and wishes and such, the better. They make the 'realism" more operatic.

Yrs,
Jack

New York
31 October 1960

Dear Giacomo,

Finally Version III. I hope we don't have to do more than Version IV [which was worked out in a series of December meetings]. I have concentrated as much as possible. . . . Leave out or leave in as necessity dictates. I want you to have enough to chew on, but on the other hand I wanted a lean story line. Saw three operas since I saw you last—understood each time not more than 1/19 of text, even in a German *Rosenkavalier!* Distressing! But it means that we do not have to quarrel about every single word. . . . See you Thursday, November 3.

Regards,
Rix

In the dead of winter Richard again fell ill and returned to the hospital, where our meetings continued in February and March. He was having recurrent nightmares: summoning Lizzie from the dead to force her once again to kill her parents was also summoning his parents. He was convinced that these dream spirits would be exorcised only when the opera should be finished, finally, and his surrogate, Lizzie, driven by motives in part on his own invention, should murder her father and stepmother before him and an audience. And, in fact, they were to be exorcised at the first performance of the opera, not to reappear thereafter.

312

The opera, too, was in one of her several crises, brought on as usual by frustration. I had just played and sung both scenes of act I for Julius Rudel, general director of the New York City Opera. He had found the completed part "interesting", and though he thought my description of the next two acts "full of problems," he requested a synopsis of them and the audition of scenes as they were completed. But Richard, now in traction in the Hospital for Joint Diseases, was in no position to type a synopsis, much less think through, alone or with me, the numerous unsolved problems of the third act. Nor did he find amusing my comment that I'd always thought of *that* hospital as one for venereal diseases. With his permission I set about finishing the synopsis myself; without his permission, but with the intent of shortening the epilogue, I substituted for Margret a letter from her to the Reverend. He was annoyed and quoted Hofmannsthal at me.

Easter 1961
Visited R. at his apartment. He's back teaching, but tentatively. He says he has neither the physical nor the emotional energy to continue *Lizzie,* unless I can wait. And he doesn't suggest I wait, for he's characteristically very pessimistic about the future. I told him I'm willing to discount the *Mitteleuropäischer Pessimismus,* but with another free summer coming up I have to get on with the composing and the second act of the libretto's not yet right. Fortunately it was he who first alluded to his letter of a year ago. He said that perhaps he should not force himself against body and spirit and asked if I'd considered inviting Kenward Elmslie to help. I said, "Of course," but I hadn't wanted to mention it until we'd arrived at an impasse. He added that as the specialist in neuroses and mystery stories on our team he believed he'd put the best part of himself in the creation of the characters and the emotional growth of the story line, that I should invite Ken—with whom, after all, I'd already written an opera—to add his special talents as poet and musical-theatre man to our drafts of the second act and the scenario of the third. I left with mingled elation and regret.

4 April 1961
Ken said I could deliver my mystery immediately if I'd meet him at a party at Morris Golde's—as it turned out, only a couple blocks from Richard's. There was such a crowd I couldn't make myself heard, and it was impossible to sit, for there was no knee room. We fled to Ken's apartment down the street. I told him how things had started almost seven years ago, sketched our labors to the present, the NYCO interest, etc. Asked if he'd continue from the beginning of II, following our latest version of it and the third-act scenario, free to change things dramatically so long as he could convince me he had better ideas. He's intrigued, took the completed music, sketches, and scenario. He'll phone.

A few days later

Ken called and we talked at least an hour. He says that at first he was disinclined to get involved; he's already tried two murder-mystery plays that were troublesome and abortive, one on the Snyder-Gray case and one about three teenagers who killed an Ann Arbor nurse. But he says that R's idea of a "Bird-Song" has won him over; he's begun filling it in—"like a magpie" he'll be able to use some of the leftovers from R's nest—and now he's hooked. He's falling in love with Abbie, he says. Coincidence, *he* has a stepmother, too, his mother—a Joseph Pulitzer daughter—having died when he was quite young.) He thinks Lizzie herself is something of a drip and that it will take some doing to fix her up and to think of things for her to sing. He'd like permission, when the libretto is finished, to go back over the first act and make whatever changes in the text might be necessary to keep everything in one style. I agreed, so long as there will be only "in line" changes that will not require more than minimal changes in the already-written music.

I think he really does understand the kind of piece we've been writing: as he says, there's very little plot in the usual sense—but certain threads, such as the dress, hold things together. He knows from our *SB&B* days that I'm the first to want the best possible verbal surface and the first to do everything I can musically to get words across in the theatre. But he sees a strong point of the scenario is that the action should be clear even if none of the words project. (He relished my story about Puccini's choosing for libretto subjects those plays—Belasco's, for instance—that he'd seen and "understood" and been moved by, even without knowing English.) He's impressed with the crucial importance of the murder scene, doesn't think we have it right—neither do I—but doesn't yet know how to improve it. He's quite taken with the idea of the Turkish corner and plans to play it up. It's not only in character for Abbie and therefore becomes her part of the living room—she's superficially pleasant but actually very bitchy, and the T. corner is full of cushions *and* blades and sharp points—even more important is that it puts the murder weapon in full view of the audience from the first curtain-up. There'll be no sudden "*Ich habe ihm das Beil nicht geben können*" line. It was one thing for Elektra to scrabble in the dirt and stones of Mycenae, but something else for a 19th C. old maid to go get the ax out of the cellar and chop up her parents in Massachusetts. If we've led our audience up to that point in the right direction, they'll be tense and a wrong move onstage—such as a trip to the cellar—might lead someone to relieve his tension in a giggle, as happens all the time in horror movies. Of course, if the audience isn't ready to go up the stairs with Lizzie, it won't make any difference what mistakes we've made.

15 June 1961

Ever since Ken sent me his last draft of "Abbie's Bird-Song," I've known what the musical setting will be, but I hadn't sat down to write it out until today. Singers will love it (if they have a high C-sharp) and some composers will think I'm out of my mind in writing "such stuff." The trouble is that most "serious" composers have gained their good reputations among other composers via their instrumental compositions. Most of them have little knowledge of the voice and even less affection for it, not to mention their lack of knowledge about English word setting—their lack of affection for *that* is shown by the number of German texts they set. And really nobody ever stops to think that it is only in the opera house that an audience is subjected to two or three hours of one composer's music, and that this circumstance requires a broader musical palette than that proper for a symphony or a chamber work. This circumstance implies, too, the fact that musical-theatre pieces are inconceivable except in terms of their having audiences, and relatively large ones, including many of the musically unwashed. But a string quartet can have an existence if only four people in the world experience it.

We three agree that we're writing a family portrait in words and music. With characters as diverse as those in *Lizzie*—or whatever we'll title it—there must be as much musical as verbal and dramatic differentiation in the characterizations. Let those who may call it "eclectic" be damned to endless rehearings of works composed from too-limited palettes!

Shelter Island
15 July 1961 [my fortieth birthday]
Ken's here for the birthday weekend—the Moores come for dinner tonite—and has been out in the barn working ever since he arrived. He came with a new draft for the entrance of Jason and the Reverend. It doesn't have the slow tableau-quintet I *must* have to balance the long set number of "Abbie's Bird-Song," but it does have the terribly good idea of a parlor game. I suspect he's picked it up from all those murderous Moore-family parlor games we've played together. Now that we have an active quintet-game, it's all the more certain that we need the static quintet first. He's coming around to the idea, for we've decided to make a special thing of the piece. I need expandable vowels for the lovers and short vowels together with sharp consonants for the gossipers if I'm to make the double canon for the two pairs make sense; and I've ordered dactyls for Lizzie, to make her musical line stand out from the others. He's taking up my dare and working all kinds of cross-references into the text —garden, green, vines, weeds, and such— that occur in different parts at the same time, but mean different things.

During that summer of 1961 the composer and his librettist were racing neck and neck, the librettist hardly ever ahead by more than a page. Kenward remained patient and sweet tempered as I rejected early versions or cooed over final versions—"final" versions in which I would later cut, transpose, or rewrite lines or words while setting them to music. But such changes were made only with his permission, usually cheerfully given. After I had played and sung a completed version for him, we would occasionally return to an earlier version of the words, occasionally seek some new solution. The first quintet was completed musically, though in part without text; it proved difficult to find the short vowels and spit-out consonants for one of the fast-moving musical phrases of the Reverend until "what with the burdock and the briars and the blackberry brambles" was hit upon [by his composer].

If in libretto discussions with Richard I had most often been on the side of the least conventional "operatic" solution, with Kenward I argued constantly for a plain, strong dramatic shape. When this line was made clear, I was happy to go along with his delight in making layers of verbal and psychological detail and role reversals. I, too, took pleasure in evolving a complicated manner of weaving patterns of recurrent thematic, textural, and stylistic references, but these, too, had to take their places in the plainer, stronger overall shape. We had long since settled for ourselves which of the two overall shapes was the more important: neither. An opera is a prize won in a dead heat by composer and librettist, each urging the other on, the librettist unfortunately to be forgotten.

We were taking chances. Even with the strength inherent in the building up to a well-known murder, perhaps our family portrait, painted with such psychological detail in music, action, and words, could not be projected by even the most gifted singing actors in a large theater. They might find the completely unaccompanied recitatives impossible to keep in tune. (These were used primarily for musical and dramatic punctuation, not simply to project words.) Kenward was doubtful of and more than a little embarrassed by the overt "theatricality" of some of our ideas, particularly the moment in which Mr. Borden tries to sell his elder, rather than his younger, daughter to the Captain; I insisted that high temperature in the music could justify, even require, this action—an action that would indeed seem overly Belascoish in the spoken theater. There was no discussion necessary concerning his expansion of the Lizzie/Father confrontation, briefly sketched in the synopsis, into a ritual of some significance. It was a valuable gift to the composer.

By the end of the summer the libretto was completed as far as Lizzie's mad scene at the end of act 2, and the music was coming along nicely. But the verbal treatment of her madness was difficult, Kenward discovered. One attempt after another arrived, accompanied by little undated notes, each version on paper of a different color.

48 West 10th Street

Dear Jack,

Here is the aria, minus the Dark Hunger section. I'll keep at it until I come up with something satisfyingly scary.

yrs,
KGE

Dear Jack,

During office euphoria—perhaps she could destroy some of Andrew's files and ledgers. Should we get together in a week or ten days?

yrs,
KGE

Dear Jack,

Her *real* answers to What do you want to harvest? seem the way to end the aria—the supplication "protect me" part wild and hysterical as can be, & the final harvest part eerie and scary and crazed. And hell bound.

yrs, (Let me know)
(What you think)
KGE

While the mad scene found its final shape, I continued composing my way through the second act. And while I worked my way through that act, we talked our way through the third. We were annoyed at there being a third act at all, for we were partial to the one-intermission evening. Furthermore, though we held to the theory that acts should diminish in length as theater time changes its pace over an evening, it seemed clear that our three acts would follow the opposite pattern. In an excess of frustration and originality, Kenward drafted a third act in one short scene, telescoping some of the elements of the Plant/Beeson scenario I had typed a year earlier and eliminating the rest.

The Borden family was not to be killed off so quickly and easily. The psychological diseases with which we had infected them had to run their courses, and these diseases had drama-making and music-making time scales of their own. As is often the case in planning the final sections of any imaginative work, the closer we approached the end, the fewer were the choices left, almost everything having been determined by earlier choices.

And so we returned to the original scenario, working out together a more detailed synopsis of act 3, scene I. A first draft of the scene up to Lizzie's love scene with herself arrived typed on green paper.

Dear Jack,

Here is the beginning of III—a little too garrulous, perhaps, but I think the mood is right. THEN comes a duet (Lizzie sings about what she'll sew on from now on, Margret sings about marriage fears) which leads to Jason's entrance. Margret admits him, Lizzie flees to room. How about next week? For further clearings in the woods? . . .

yrs,
KGE

A second draft followed on blue paper, and a third and final version on white paper. A work week on Shelter Island—it was already summer again—with

Kenward under self-imposed barn arrest, resulted in the words for Lizzie's love scene aria (actually a kind of masturbatory scene) as well as a synopsis of the following Abbie/Lizzie bitch scene, as it was later to be called, worked out in the greatest detail down to the layer of the words themselves. The bitch scene would be crucial, for in it all aspects of these two complex women would be exposed nakedly to themselves and to the audience. As Richard had planned from the beginning, the opera was to consist of a series of ever more important battles between Lizzie and her parents. She meets her first defeat by simple withdrawal; deeper humiliation leads her to retreat into fantasy. In the bitch scene Abbie's dirtying of Lizzie's fantasies results in Lizzie's destruction of her own mirror image; this self-destruction is also, and for the first time, a physical act and one that draws blood—her own, as she smashes the mirror with her arms. By the end of the bitch scene we intended to have built all the motivation and tension necessary to bring about the murders. In the next scene we would need only to play the trump card of Lizzie's mad seduction of the Captain and her final degradation by Abbie. (Lizzie's realization, at last, that her success in furthering Margret's elopement with her unacknowledged lover will leave her alone in a barren triangle with the elder Bordens would be the joker in the deck). In portraying Mr. and Mrs. Borden there was always the difficulty of staying on a line between making them interesting enough to spend the evening with but disagreeable enough to deserve being chopped up. Mr. Borden remained, perhaps dangerously, close to the line. But Mrs. Borden lurched violently, deliciously, from one side to the other. It was a pleasure to seek out the musical parallels to these extremes of sweet and sour.

A few days after Ken left the island, I finished the music of act 2. When he left for the Yucatán and Central America a few days later, I did not worry because, for once, the libretto was more than a page or two ahead of the music.

Mérida, the Yucatán
6 August 1962

Dear Jack,

Another beefy chunk. Abbie seems beautifully endless to me, a slow grinding of malice. Three more selections, which I'll chip away at, in the next respite—

(A) Abbie's "I should have known you weren't and couldn't be anyone's bride." Sex taunts.

(B) Lizzie's neurotic harping (Evangeline + Andrew wrecked by Abbie).

(C) Abbie's threat. Will tell Andrew all, wants Lizzie out of the house, along with Margret. Before it's dark.

MIRROR break

Shouldn't go on too much longer. Tighter and tighter, and tenser and tenser.

The journey so far, all four days of it, has been a complicated and surprising pleasure, full of hazards, heat, incessant movement, and gaiety. I am at present in Mérida, at a declining pension, once a hacienda, once a "good" hotel, now quite empty, $1-a-nite, & with a semipublic swimming pool. Huge white pillars, big tiled patio, and a jungle garden to roam in. Jason is quite right to refer this area to New England, and Margret is quite sensible to carry on about hose green islands so.

yrs,
KGE

P.S. I'll send the final—whew! —scene installment when it's jelled and been sat on a few days. . . .

Ogunguit, Maine
1 September 1962

Dear Jack,

Cher amis—Full of New England fog, this nice spot only confirms my conviction that thrift and Puritanism lead to suppression, greed, and bad food. . . .

Regards,
H. von Hofmannsthal

Another academic year rolled around, that of 1962-1963. The music was going well, if slowly, composed in time sandwiched between classes and administrative duties at Columbia. At intervals we met to hone the action and words of the bitch scene to an ever-sharper edge. As a relief from the raging we provided a short song for Abbie, but the urgency of the scene made it seem superfluous; as the spirals narrowed toward the center there was no time for pleasnatires.[2]

The details of the next scene, act 3, scene 2—and the last but for the epilogue—had been worked out up to the murders. We had invented a package of love letters that unified and justified all the actions from Lizzie's "Kill Time" song at the beginning through the seduction scene. Tearing up the letters at the close would convey the idea of her loss of Jason and her readiness to act; throwing the shreds against the weapons in the Turkish corner would attract her attention to the axe. The murder of Abbie followed almost as a matter of course; we would have no trouble making Andrew's murder seem even more necessary thereafter.

But at the time I had no notion of how to handle a musical climax divided between two murders, and I would have nothing to do with a dramatic solution that was not also a musical solution. I invited Richard's counsel, as I had on several occasions since the end of our active collaboration in the spring of 1961. He was still arguing that Lizzie should kill both parents in one time and place. Such an action would make for musical simplicity, but I agreed with Ken that it was not credible. Nagging uncertainty dragged on far into the summer.

Hightowers
Shelter Island Heights
28 July 1963

Dear Ken,

I've sometimes wondered what you must have thought when your card, two installments, invitation to stay overnight if I came into town, apology for not being able to visit us next weekend—all coming more or less at once—didn't get any rise out of me. I hope you didn't take it amiss. The piano arrived and I went to work is part of the answer. Part of the rest of the answer is that III, 2—with its murders—is crucial to the whole—obviously—and neither you, nor Richard, nor I has ever come up with something that seemed—as a right thing must—suddenly right. Since I couldn't quite accept your solution but had nothing better to suggest, I just moped, carpentered, and went on composing III, 1.

For the rest of the reason, well, last Monday I went to the hospital with what *I* had diagnosed as appendicitis. I was told that it was *not*, given quantities of expensive antibiotics, and sent home. . . . [Six weeks later it was discovered that not only had there been appendicitis, but also that the appendix had burst.]

It has given me time to think—with fever and without—and I submit my ravings to you. (You are *not* to consider them ravings.)

First: I'll accept *Lizzie* as a title if we can think of nothing better. [The title finally chosen, *Lizzie Borden*, was Rudel's idea.]

As to the epilogue draft: I like the form—the sequence of events—just fine. The movement of the whole is direct, it's terse, and there are immanent numbers, as there ought to be in this little scene. I'm sorry to say that I like the song very much and that it won't do at all at this point. It is pleasant rather than parched, comfy rather than dead, resigned rather than wholly without flavor, color, or life. Sorry. Surely some lines are recoverable:

> midnight & noon . . .
> wait for the snowfall . . .
> seal out the rain . . .

and maybe the last two lines. There should be no action suggested, at any rate at the beginning.

I have no objection to the winter garden image, tho' it's likely to lose most of its point sung from the big room. . . .I still like the idea of getting across the impression that these are the dead coals of a once too-hot fire, that she now neither sleeps nor wakes, and when she sleeps cannot dream. But I certainly don't press them, only wish for something we both find right.

Length of song just fine. It might be longer but must not be shorter.

Entrance of Reverend fine.

If we are to do away with Margret's return, as we are both delighted to do, you *must* give me more words behind which I can let the music do what we both decided it must do: bring into the last scene a pool of warmth that lets the switching of Lizzie and Margret (life and death once, now the reverse) come through. There need not be more than 6-8 lines more than there are. Perhaps Lizzie comes once almost to life, but Rev. says . . . not to write, or won't come back, or something that stifles the glimmer. . . .

Now to the scene *before*, III, 2: We've been through a few versions of the opening. I like it except for the very beginning, which is not striking enough in its imagery. Besides, it confuses or might confuse, with its talk of winter—a word that should be heard for the first time in the epilogue opening, to set time. It is ghastly hot, late afternoon, killing weather, supposedly. The last four lines are terrific. . . . Couldn't we begin with them? . . . On page two I'm still averse to the lines about Abbie that seem, under the circumstances, merely petty—and not the kind of pettiness (like mutton soup too often for breakfast) that adds up. Then all good . . . (with maybe just a few wee word-queries—"particulars," for instance) through Abbie's nasty, almost spoken eight lines.

Congratulations on the whole well-turned two pages between Andrew and Lizzie. I think it is well done in itself, but I can't bring myself to believe in the action. . . . As I said in one of our meetings, my objection to having the two murders separated in time has to do with what seems to me the difficulty of leading an audience for two hours carefully and slowly and sometimes deviously to believe in the climactic action of a moment, and then dividing that moment in two. I'd be willing to concede the argument to the wordsman if I weren't, as the composer, responsible not only for the sounds but also for the dramatic timing. It was your very good, simple—even obvious—suggestion that led to the solution of the space between III, 2 & 3: that the interlude should be the "murder music," You were altogether right. This means that I can't compose any kind of similar music to accompany an earlier murder. . . .I know your objection, strongly and long held, to having Lizzie do them in one after the other—against historical fact, even—and in one room. . . . As it stands in your version they are both awake when they are done in—singly. That's open to logical objection too, especially since Abbie has been asleep (we've always said so—that she was asleep during the packing scene—but there isn't a line anywhere saying so in the first part of III, 2, and there should be, to add tension to the packing and to justify the muttering). She might just as well be imagined as having drifted off after "cold collation" and during the first murder music, if there's to be a 1st and 2nd m. m. (One more line in her "cold collation" speech would establish this very easily.)

*   *   *   *   *   *

Well, all that thought over and written down, I've taken a breather to reread several times what I've written here and the *whole* libretto with your II, 2, ensconced within it. I am neither so obstinate nor so blind to the merits of your draft solution as not to use it as the key to unlock my musical problem. I see now how, maybe, I can avoid the musical-excitement duplication of two murders. (I should add that this letter has been going on for two days—it is now Monday, 4:30.)

You remember that for over a year I've known I'm going to start the opera with a 3 or 4 minute prelude, beginning with a great smash that gradually subsides into the quiet children's Sunday school hymn. . . . The 2d act begins with exactly the same orchestral introduction, subsiding into "Abbie's Bird-Song." (After these two surprises, there'll be *no* intro. at all to the 3d act.) In the past weeks it has occurred to me that I might let the "murder music' be the crescendo that leads to the climax, the great smash with which I & II began. By playing the prelude a third time, in an expanded form leading to the quiet epilogue, the three acts are tied together. It will look—sound—like this (the sketch isn't time-scaled):

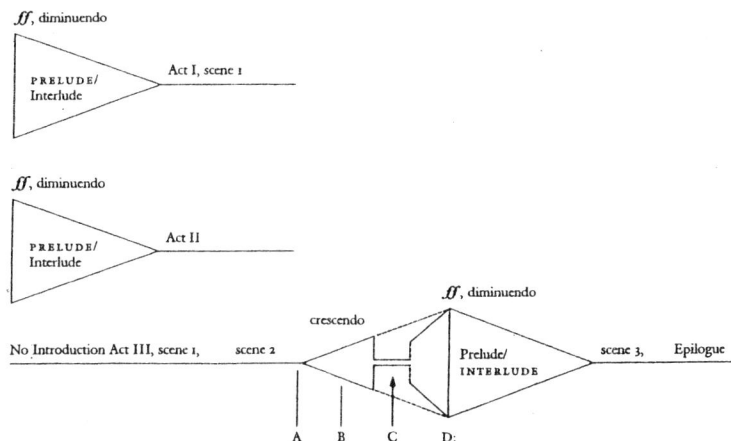

A: Abbie's nasty speech, "cold collation."
B: Lizzie throws letters, gets scimitar, goes upstairs, disappears into bedroom, Abbie's screams merge in the orchestral crescendo.
C. The short Andrew/Lizzie seduction scene on the stairs—on the green sheets you mailed—ending with the continuation of the interrupted crescendo accompanying Lizzie's following her father up the stairs and into the bedroom. . .
D: Blackout and/or curtain; beginning of an extended version of the prelude/ interlude.

A few details: How does Andrew know the mirror is broken in the girls' room if he comes in through the main door and the hall, not by way of the open gate, the girls' room, to living room? . . .

Has Lizzie left the scimitar—the "axe," that is—in Abbie's room after doing her in? I assume so. Or is it hidden under the shawl?

I don't like Andrew to call out "Abbie" brokenly. Pity isn't onstage at this point.

. . . The short page six (having to do with C in the sketch, that is) I have my doubts about. This time it is the blood father she must kill, not the wicked stepmother. She has been ambivalent all along about him, has shown only dislike or worse for Abbie. I don't call for lots of words—fewer, even—but there should be some final degradation. As she walks enticingly down the stairs during her speech (cut a couple of lines for brevity) he sees Abbie's dress worn by Lizzie at this point, cuts into her sweetness with a harsh line, pulls at it, tearing it. I should like her to fall on the stairs, or on the floor if she makes her way all the way down. In this fashion we have some repetition of the "Genet scene," but this time as he (wordless) dashes up the stairs; Lizzie hardly waits, follows, kills: It's all mimed, and fast.

*　　*　　*　　*　　*　　*

I won't tire you with the alternative I was working out and going to suggest. . . . Let's hope it won't be needed. I feel all the better for this workout, for *I* was becoming quite neurotic about the end. Perhaps my fever will go down. At least it's been lower today.

I need new first lines for the opening of scene 2. They should have a lot of rhythmic variety, lots of consonants, as in the marvelous "flies" section, and a mixture of long and short vowels.

Jack

With this ancient problem solved (and an appendiceal abscess removed in early September) the music was swiftly written up to and including the murders. Ten bars into the following interlude—which is to say, also ten bars into the twin preludes—I stopped. It has been two years since the audition of the first scene at the New York City Opera. In the interim, though prodded, Julius Rudel had said neither yes nor no to a Ford Foundation commission "to complete the opera" and to an option on the first performance. I decided not to write the interlude/prelude and the last scene until there should be a decision of these matters and turned to the task of reducing the *Particell* to a playable—or almost playable—piano-vocal score, thus making it possible for Rudel to examine the work. By June he was still equivocal and the epilogue was singing itself in my head, but I did not write it down and turned to the huge, but pleasurable, task of orchestration instead.

In August Rudel gave an answer: yes. Immediately I set about composing the interlude, arranging it in such a manner that it would glide into the differing beginnings of acts 1 and 2, and its expanded version would lead into the epilogue. A search for a fresh sonority to open the epilogue, to place it in winter and "some years later," led to a series of bell and clock sounds, timed in arithmetic progression. And this musical idea led naturally to the association of Lizzie's time obsession throughout the opera with her checking bookkeeping totals at the outset of the epilogue. To carry out this new idea, Kenward several times rewrote the opening lines, the final version arriving on Thanksgiving. By 21 January the music was complete, and we had worked at length over words, phrases, and lines in act 1 to bring unity to the verbal style of the libretto as a whole. Emancipation from the 650 pages of orchestral score came on Lincoln's Birthday 1965. Five and a half years of work were finished.

The premiere of *Lizzie Borden* was scheduled for the all-contemporary spring season of 1965, nearly eleven years after Richard Plant and I had first spoken of an operatic Lizzie. Julius Rudel's decision to produce the work was followed by asking whom I had in mind to sing it. I confessed that because I had undertaken the work without more than a hope for performance, I had not dared conceive the roles of specific singers. Months after composing Abbie's final phrases and death screams I looked across the room at a New Year's party and saw Abbie, big as life, in the person of an old friend, Ellen Faull. She was cast forthwith. A mezzo-soprano was needed for the title role; more importantly, a phenomenal actress was required. I nominated several mezzos; Rudel nominated a phenomenal actress, Brenda Lewis, who, though a soprano, had sung such roles as Carmen and Marc Blitzstein's Regina, a role not unlike Lizzie. I auditioned Miss Lewis and she auditioned Miss Borden. They got along famously with one another.

The singing actor Herbert Beattie was cast in the difficult role of Mr. Borden, and the three more conventional roles of Margret, Jason, and the Reverend were cast from the company's roster: Anne Elgar, Richard Fredricks, and Richard Krause.

Casting a stage director proved frustrating. Given the special nature of our opera, we favored a director who would be particularly responsive to its dramatic values, but by this time most were already committed for the season. Gian Carlo Menotti was asked first but could not say yes. At almost weekly intervals I played and sang an act or two for Alan Schneider, Robert Lewis, and Carmen Capalbo. Richard, Kenward, and I thought that some of our hopes for the piece might be justified when each director in turn agreed to stage it if his schedule for plays, films, and whatnots could be rearranged. But the schedules of Schneider and Capalbo could not be changed. Bobby Lewis, who had been excited by my "performance" and who had left with a briefcase of Borden books, decided, after a sleepless night, that he was not sure he could project a piece of such subtlety with singing actors in so large a theater.

This reaction was unsettling, for there *were* many dramatic and musical subtleties in the work. We had from the first believed that the opera might for this reason be effective on the television screen. (In early 1967 NET Opera, with the original cast and conductor, Anton Coppola, and the staging of Nikos Psacharopoulos adapted for the camera by Kirk Browning, showed that the many subtle layers of the opera were indeed effective on the screen, at whatever loss in overall shapeliness.) Fortunately, however, the first performances in the City Center and the revivals in the New York State Theater indicated that the stronger, plainer main lines of the piece do project in large theaters, at whatever loss of musical, verbal, and psychological detail.

Because as the composer I wished to try out and change, if necessary, some chancy passages of vocal writing and word setting and because as a one-time vocal coach and conductor, I enjoyed working with singers, I offered my services to the New York City Opera as unpaid coach. By the opening night I had clocked 130 hours on the piano bench.

Both Nikos Psacharopoulos, the stage director, and I were nervous about the length of Lizzie's mad scene and in our nervousness made cuts. Subsequent performances restored these passages, with the curious result that the scene seemed shorter and more sturdily shaped, not longer. We were also concerned about the length of the bitch scene, and the two singers were convinced they could never learn the difficult music at its climax. They did. But mostly we were anxious about whether the opera would project as a whole. As I thought from the beginning, it would either work well or not at all; there could be no middle ground for an opera on such a subject. As is well known, no one involved in the theater can possibly stand far enough away to look and listen to a work as it is being written and rehearsed; until an audience entered the house, we could not know if they would go up the stairs with Lizzie.

24 March 1965

This afternoon was the dress rehearsal; tomorrow's the premiere. We had every intention of stopping for musical and dramatic repairs—and there were reasons enough to have stopped half a dozen times. But we were astonished to discover hundreds of people in the house. The cast (and Coppola and Nikos) apparently decided to give them a performance, not a dress rehearsal. There was "interested" applause after the first act (I must clean out some brass in the first scene) and real laughs at the beginning of the second act (where we expected them), growing excitement up to Lizzie's mad scene, and great applause thereafter. There were plenty of March coughers in the house—coughing is one of the best indications of inattention in the theatre—but they remained marvelously quiet throughout. Nikos & I were more than a little sweaty as the Big Moment approached—I don't know where Ken & Richard were—but up the stairs they went—no giggles and many of the audience sitting on the edge of their seats (I looked around, coolly, hoping they might be)—up the stairs they went with Lizzie to chop up her parents in Massachusetts. I guess we can quit worrying about tomorrow's premiere. I haven't felt so sane since just before I went to live with the Bordens in '54.

Notes
1. *Lizzie Borden* libretto (© 1967) and vocal score (© 1967) (New York: Boosey & Hawkes, 1967). The original cast recording (1966) of *Lizzie Borden* is on Desto Records DST-6455/6/7, the CD on CRI/New World.
2. Though this arietta appears in the Boosey & Hawkes score, it is rarely performed and is not heard on the Desto recording.

*   *   *   *   *   *   *

In the foregoing *Autobiography of Lizzie Borden* there was a long letter from me to Kenward Elmslie recounting—and graphing—my solution to the problem of how we might handle the double murder, a solution found while I was contending with appendicitis. I did not tell Ken that I thought that the key to the problem might have been found at the moment of the bursting of the appendix, for such a dramatic coincidence seemed too improbable to mention.

It is even more unlikely that anyone would have noticed—not to speak of remembering—that my letter was dated 28 July 1963 and written from the address Hightowers, Shelter Island Heights.

The new address was the result of our having exchanged our farmhouse and barn near Shelter Island Center for a very large Victorian house just outside Shelter Island Heights, on the crest of the highest hill of the island. Built by an affluent New York attorney in the nineties, in the nomenclature of that time it would have been a villa, with "two, three or more servants in residence." Hightowers for some years had served as a summer bed and breakfast hotel run by an ageing widow and her alcoholic son. The three-story house, with 100 feet of wrap-around porch, had its romantic aspects. Almost attached was a very small walled-in tea garden. Built on to the back of the house was the servants quarters wing, its door in a tunnel through which the private road led down a hundred feet through an allée of trees to the garage, which had a second-floor apartment. For a few months, until he was hospitalized, Ace, the alcoholic son, refused to move out of the apartment and would zip up the allée in his jalopy and through the tunnel unexpectedly and dangerously. During our first summer occasional fancy cars appeared, with middle-age men and their paramours who asked for their favorite rooms. We were tempted, but unlicensed, and refused rental politely. After our first moving-in summer, we rented out both the wing and the garage apartments to mostly interesting tenants. In later years we installed heat in the wing and could weekend on the island in winter.

Taking on such a large and complicated establishment was perhaps more than a little crazy, but there were inducements: it was sold at a ridiculously low price and completely furnished. A set of 14 matching 1920 Bar Harbor wicker chairs, tables, and settees dated from the original Otis family or the wealthy second owners; a Chinese black vase was later identified by Chou Wen-Chung as K'ang Hsi (1661-1722). Once the piano was maneuvered up the narrow steps to the third floor, my aerie of a studio was perfect, giving its name to the house, Hightowers. A built-in, drawered, workspace could accommodate the largest scores; its three windows looked out on Peconic Bay; the north and south windows shared a view of salt water. The water itself was only a comfortable walk downhill to the village and a sheltered harbor where we were soon to moor our sleek black 19-foot sloop, a Nova Scotian Bluenose we christened *Mnemosyne*. After a quarter century of life as a landlubber, I had not lost my love or knack for sailing. Christopher quickly acquired both from me. It was not long before he was racing and winning, later crewing on two Bermuda races, then serving as first mate on a 35-foot sloop on a round trip from Shelter Island to Penzance, England, and, finally, beginning professional life as an expert on the upkeep of large sailing yachts.

Not least of the attractions of our new summer were our neighbors, John and Helen Lamont, whose capacious, book-filled, house and gardens covered the rest of the top of our undulating hilltop. Helen Otis Lamont had been conceived and spent her girlhood summers in Hightowers, long before it had acquired its B and B name. She was now retired as the editor of the Women's Home Companion during its literate years. She had become a prime mover in the local historical society and had long pursued Shakespearean studies, having published her edition of the *Sonnets*. She was planning to stage at least two of the Shakespeare comedies on Shelter Island and was to do so. John had been a book editor, was the grandson of the brother of Thomas Lamont and cousin of the leftist philosopher at Columbia.

*   *   *   *   *   *

But, to return to proper chronology, at the time I was figuring out how to go about murdering Lizzie's parents, we had just moved into Hightowers and I into my studio. There I remained with the Bordens when not with the other Beesons or the Lamonts, or not repairing things—there were seven toilets to superintend—or cutting hilly grass, or clipping high hedges. The same varied company and activity continued during the next two summers, '64 and '65.

In the seasons between them, when on our other island, Manhattan, one sometimes wished for less varied company and activity; but teaching and meetings were interesting and instructive in themselves. Some of the music of the half-dozen composers in the graduate seminars was new to me; the subject matter of Humanities and lecture courses was new to the students. Attending meetings on- and off-campus taught me that any meeting of three or more persons is in some sense a political meeting: one learned how to make one's words count, if he ventured any. Verdi's admonition to his librettists, only "la parola scenica" (the dramatic word), is as persuasive off-stage as on-stage.

Unfortunately, the Music Department was no longer as convivial as it had been before Douglas Moore had retired three years earlier, in the spring of 1962. Anyone—teaching staff, graduate students, secretaries—anyone with a home-bought or store-bought lunch had been welcome to join in the general talk in the one large room from noon on; Douglas didn't so much lead the discussion as animate it. Always charming, a vastly-grown cherub with wit, he was known to the secretaries as "Peaches." He was comfortable in seeming not to be running the department alone, as he was, indeed. He had been appointed chairman "at the pleasure of the Trustees" in 1940. As his generation of chairmen retired, each department's tenured members wee required to form an Executive Committee and to elect a Chairman for a term of three years, renewable once. Ruth Ihrig and I arranged the members' teaching schedules so that nobody had an excuse to be absent on Tuesdays from noon until two for the Executive Committee meetings.

As the election approached, Douglas, Otto, and Paul Lang spoke to me privately to say that they would be pleased to nominate me for Chairman, "though I was a little young." I responded to each with thanks, that Bill Mitchell coveted the position and thought himself to be the heir apparent, that I didn't want to be

Chairman if it would upset him, and that I was anyhow far too busy composing to take on anything else.

While I was involved in all these extracompositional matters, our opera progressed as detailed in *The Autobiography of Lizzie Borden* at an ever more rapid pace. When the music was completed, a playable piano vocal-score had to be devised, then what turned out to be 633 pages of orchestral score. Quite some weeks before the premiere, our neighbor, David Truman, came to my rescue. When we had moved on to Riverside Drive, he was a friendly professor of government living in the adjoining apartment to ours, two apartments to a floor, sharing a service-elevator door and a garbage pail. By this time he had become Dean of Columbia College and was shortly to become Vice-President just in time to take part in the Time of Troubles. He was aware that I had an important production scheduled and that I wanted to participate fully in its rehearsals. Perhaps when we met at the garbage pail or on our way to Columbia I was looking more harassed or peaked—or both—than usual. Quite on his own, he arranged that I be given a month-long leave with pay through the rehearsal period of *Lizzie*. I was therefore free to coach the principal singers and to play all the staging rehearsals, aided by David Effron.

By the time the Borden family had been brought back to life by the New York City Opera on 55th Street I could tell the other Beesons that we would be in Rome for the next year. Two or three years earlier I had received an open invitation from Frank Brown, the new director of the Rome Academy, to attend as Resident Composer. He had finally been able to arrange that the year could coincide with my coming sabbatical. We would be housed in the larger apartment of the two attached to the Villa Aurelia, in the smaller of which Sam Barber had been during our first Roman stay, and Alexei Haieff during our second. I was to keep an eye and an ear on the two composer-fellows, be available to them if they asked for counsel on whatever, and to superintend the Academy chamber recitals and the continuing relationship with RAI—not quite a sinecure, but surely not onerous.

The only person disappointed by our going abroad was Mother. Now widowed, she had sold their Shamokin home and taken an apartment in East Stroudsburg, halfway between her siblings and their families and us in New York City. She came to visit us occasionally in the City and on the island. During the coming '65 summer we arranged that she be at Hightowers to bid us farewell when Nora's mother would be there from Zürich, where she now had an apartment after having sold Casa Serena. If I have correctly guessed the year of an undated photo of the two grandmothers, Christopher, and Miranda, it was during that summer when all four were first and last together.

On September 3 we boarded the Raffaello for a week's crossing of the Atlantic to Gibraltar and then to Naples, where the Academy stationwagon picked us up and then dropped us off at our apartment in the park-like grounds of the Villa Aurelia.

Practically the next day the Overseas School bus drew up to the Academy's gate to pick up Christopher, soon to be 15, and Miranda, soon to be 12. Now that they were old enough to appreciate what Rome and its environs had to offer, our weekends were spent mostly inside the city and in the hilltowns outside sightseeing. On one memorable occasion I took the two of them for several days to Naples, all over the city, hiking on Capri, and around the rim of the smoking Vesuvius crater.

By the time the three of us went off to Naples, Nora was engaged in editorial work on the huge *History of World Art* undertaken by the Rome office of McGraw-Hill. She saw the 5 volumes almost to their completion when we returned to New York, then moved on to the Encyclopedia Britannica and to the Metropolitan Museum. Her continuing affection for museums and interest in buildings of the past and the present and her fluency in German, French, Italian, Russian, and Polish made possible a long career as an editor of art and architecture books for the Met, Harry Abrama, Inc., the Morgan Library, the Architectural History Foundation, and sundry others.

As for me, I was still uncharacteristically librettoless, as I had remained since the completion of *Lizzie*, but I was still pursuing two subjects that greatly interested me.

The first of these was the Tennessee Williams *Camino Real*, which I had enjoyed on Broadway in 1953—the same year I was writing *Hello Out There*. At that time, my friend and recent composition student, John Kander, confided that he had attended six performance of it and memorized the important part of Kilroy. In a Walter Mitty imagining, he was ready to leap to the stage and complete the performances if anything should happen to the actor Eli Wallach. John and I agreed with the one or two drama critics who wrote that *Camino* was more of a libretto than a play, an opinion that I learned had dismayed Williams.

Now, years later, I happened to discuss my commitment to the play and my present need to obtain the right to use it with Bobby Dolan, a well-known film composer teaching film music at Columbia and later to write an opera himself. He offered to put in some "good, loud words" for me with his close friend Audrey Wood, who had been Williams's agent almost from the beginning of his career. She promptly invited me to a long, lavish, lunch, during which she agreed that of all his long plays, *Camino* was the most suitable for operatic treatment. I believed her promise to try to pin down her indecisive, changeable charge and we exchanged letters for months until she wrote me in Rome, two days after Christmas," . . . Williams still feels very strongly that he doesn't want this made into an opera. I grant you that this can change any time, but this is his present feeling." I was as doggedly decisive as Williams was changeable; just as I had once been in pursuit of John Collier's *Evening Primrose*, I returned to Audrey Wood five years later for another try at *Camino*.

The other project I had in mind also dated back to the HOT years, *My Heart's in the Highlands*, by Saroyan. The play was his third and largest treatment of what had started life as a short story, then been turned into a one-act play, and finally expanded to the modest full-evening that set the theatre world talking and arguing when the Group Theatre first performed it in New York in

1939. I made a point of studying all the versions to make sure that my early affection for this poetic and touching tale of displaced persons was still intact and then wrote Saroyan in July from Hightowers asking him for permission to adapt *Highlands* as an opera. I made a point of reminding him that I had kept him informed of my changes to his *Hello* while constantly inviting his suggestions, without flat-out saying that I hoped he would let me fashion my libretto for *Highlands* also completely on my own.

For once he was at home in Fresno and answered immediately and chummily: he had already three versions of *Highlands* and at this point he didn't want it to go into a fourth. Instead, he wanted me to make an opera of his *The Human Comedy* or of one of his other novels or plays that were being mailed to Shelter Island by his publisher. I was extremely disappointed with his response, but he had not said, "No, you can't!" My native Midwestern optimism led me to think I could make him change his mind.

Meanwhile, I continued to while away my composing time by writing some miscellaneous pieces, a couple of which I had been asked to write.

The President of Boosey and Hawkes, citing the large number of US bands, talked me into making an arrangement for band of the orchestral suite, *Hymns and Dances*, that I had fashioned from the opera *The Sweet Bye and Bye* during my librettoless Roman year seven years earlier. I did what he asked, though having written only one earlier band piece I needed some study and coaching in the medium and all too many weeks of copying out the large score. When the new President of B & H received his copy, he cited the very small number of US bands that could and would play anything but marches; he accepted the piece and promised to have the parts extracted. My time and trouble are now only a poor investment I made years ago: the piece—actually three movements—is still unperformable, there being no instrumental parts available.

The Juilliard School asked for some teaching pieces for its Repertory Project, to be carried out in cooperation with the US Office of Education. I complied with *Homer's Woe*, twelve rounds for treble voices mostly on anonymous riddles, simple to complicated, written and copied out in a high good humor in ten days.

Unasked for but cheerfully accepted by its dedicatee, Nora Beate, was *Sonata Canonica* for two alto recorders. Nora had added to her violin playing recorder lessons with those in the circle around Joel Newman and Pro Musica Antiqua, who played it first.

And, a couple of nicely titled cappella pieces for grown-ups, *Greener Pastures* and *Boys and Girls Together*—also rounds, and very likely the result of this renewed attack of canonitis.

It is not my intention with the phrase "whiling away my time" to disparage what I was writing or what most composers do most of their lives: write instrumental works of varying lengths for one performer, or a few, or an orchestra, and occasionally a choral or vocal work. Any sensible person would do so, rather than be bothered with the jumble of those—some of them non-musicians—involved in the writing and production of an evening-long opera. As the astute Copland used to say, "One can write with a greater hope of success four long symphonies with far less trouble and time than it takes to write an opera."

If my smaller works are but briefly described or even unmentioned, it is not because I disavow them or believe that the bulk of an opera in itself assures its importance and quality; it is surely possible to believe that the single operas of Schumann and Wolf are outweighed in importance and quality by any of their song cycles, even by some single songs. It is, rather, that this account of my early addiction to opera and my subsequent wrestling with its pleasures and perils is my main subject. Of course an opera exists only in its performance, but because of its verbal and dramatic content it can be at least limned in words, as purely instrumental music cannot be.

As I have often said, writing an opera is rather like playing an oversize slot machine. One invests large amounts of time, energy, even money; if the opera is performed, the machine makes a large noise heard by many and widely read about in the press; some or all of the investment may even be recouped. If a composer plays the machine half a dozen times, or a dozen, he becomes known as an "opera composer," no matter what else or how much else he has written. The smaller pieces—if there are any—tend to be disregarded. Of my 134 works (244 by another count) 10 are operas.

For several speculative reasons, none persuasive—except that success breeds success— a composer such as Floyd, Moore, or Ward, has only one of his 10 or 12 often produced, another not very close runner-up, and the others rarely or never produced after their premieres.

Given these realities, it was comforting to hear in the spring that another *Lizzie* production might take place only months after its premiere—on television.

Almost the only operas to be seen on television these days are televised performances from Lincoln Center or elsewhere. Once upon a time, beginning in 1950, CBS produced some repertory works and NBC, not content with its own symphony under Toscanini, organized NBC Television Opera, with Peter Herman Adler as conductor and Kirk Browning as director. For years, beginning with Kurt Weill's folk opera *Down in the Valley* and the commissioned Menotti *Amahl and the Night Visitors*, NBC Opera introduced recent European works—always in English translation—and commissioned new American operas. They were performed by singers who looked their parts and seemed to be reinventing *drama per musica*. During these years both Adler and Browning were friendly with Douglas Moore and me, inviting us to screenings and inquiring about what we were writing.

When NBC Opera came to an end, the Ford Foundation underwrote a successor with the same leadership and ideals: National Education Television Opera, NET Opera for short. NET later changed its name to PBS. Adler, as a Czech, had known Janáček in Brno; the first try-out production was his *From the House of the Dead*, in English, the American Premiere. For their second production they sought an American opera, preferably with a recently rehearsed intact cast, and chose *Lizzie Borden*. Preliminary arrangements for rehearsal and filming were being made while we were still in Hightowers and then finalized by mail to Rome. The NYCO cast and Anton Coppola, the conductor, were all re-engaged. I was invited to re-coach the cast, play all the staging rehearsals and to be assistant conductor at the filming. In return, I was paid a fee (my first ever for work I'd have done again for nothing) and all my travel and living expenses from the middle of December in New York for almost two weeks of rehearsals and in Boston for filming through the 30th at the studios of WGBH.

Assuming that the singers had not by then lost their voices—the TV microphones would ease their stress—December 31 provided a perfect day to make a commercial recording. Horace Grenell of DESTO RECORDS was agreeable if I would raise the necessary funds, which I did, finally, just in time.

I flew to New York twelve days before Christmas for yet another long visit with the Bordens; when the holidays came for the others, they went to Zürich to be with Emmy and the other Swiss relatives. Never having been in a New York hotel before—or since—I chose the Algonquin because of what I'd read of the high-powered conversation that had once taken place there at its round table. When I checked in I was disappointed that the bar was so small and there was a round table that seated only two, obviously only a symbol. My single room was hardly large enough for one.

Kirk Browning began the first staging rehearsal modestly and sensibly by saying that he thought that the NYCO production had been superbly directed by Nikos Psacharopoulos and that he had no intention of altering the characterizations or restaging scenes between two or more of the six characters. He would merely adapt everything for the cameras and to fit the quite different sets being built by WGBH in Boston. He remarked that even long shots on TV—not to speak of close-ups—are revealing of gestures and facial expressions invisible to everybody in a theatre except maybe to front-row sitters and that most large gestures and strenuous singing would be ruled out. The cast was to make the most of subtleties that the stage prohibited. With me at the piano and the singers mostly marking, the full days passed quickly and fruitfully.

When we moved to Boston the singers and I encountered a set-up largely invented by Peter Adler and Kirk during their NBC Opera years. They would have nothing to do with the system often used in televising opera: singers and orchestra pre-recorded together; the cast, on camera, then acted their parts to the playback while lip-synching the words. Not only was the lip-synching often flawed; the muscle-play associated with singing was absent.

Instead, during rehearsals and in the filming two studios were used, linked with mikes, speakers, and TV monitors. In a nearby soundproof studio were the conductor and the orchestra; in the film studio were the sets and the singers who could see the conductor's beat over several TV monitors and hear the orchestra dimly—to avoid feedback. The conductor heard their voices over headphones and saw them over his monitor. Only one passage was lip-synched, in Lizzie's mad scene when she was running distractedly through the house with her face averted. On this and other occasions when the singers could not see the monitors, I hid off-camera behind the rented antique furniture or behind open doors, relaying the beat from a monitor to them.

Counterpointed against the elaborate rehearsals of *Lizzie* was the foreplay that was to lead to the conception and birth of another opera. Peter Adler had modestly and sensibly given way as conductor to Anton Coppola, who had conducted the premiere. As the Artistic Director of NET Opera Adler attended all the rehearsals and was staying at the Treadway Inn with the rest of us. He, Kirk Browning, and I were at dinner there when he seemingly casually asked if I had any intention of writing a fifth opera. No doubt I answered, "Yes, and more thereafter, if Fate cooperates." Did I have a libretto subject in mind? I mentioned the two, with *Highlands* the more probably available. Kirk was immediately enthusiastic, for he loved the play, which he had recently directed on television's Play of the Week, with Walter Matthau as the poet-father. Intermittent conversation followed in which Kirk and I discussed the cuts and changes that would be needed in the play if it were to be turned into a libretto. Kirk and Peter must have spoken together in my absence, for Peter suddenly announced to me that if I could obtain the libretto-setting rights to Saroyan's play—in writing—NET would commission me to write an opera based on it for production whenever I had completed it. Disbelieving him, for I now was sure that Bill would change his mind, I asked if he were serious about the commission and whether and how much the commission amounted to in money. When he answered "None, just the production shown nationwide on the ever-enlarging network," I added, "You know, copying out the parts will be expensive." "Yes, I know, But that's how it is, and I'm sorry. How much would you settle for?" Being realistic, but also realizing that a commission implies, though often does not include, a payment, I said, "One dollar." He gave me a bill from his wallet and we shook hands on the big deal.

I had been insistent on the matter because by that time I'd learned how un-Saroyanesque Bill could be when the subject was money. If the opera came about and he learned from the attendant publicity of a commission to me, he'd want his 50%. I would then pay him 50¢.

I tried phoning Bill at every rehearsal break and, 10 days later, wrote him a brief note saying that all I had to do was to write our opera to have it performed nationwide on NET. I thought such hyperbole would change his mind about the rights and then went back to watching, listening to, and occasionally relaying Coppola's beat to the singers from my hiding places.

On schedule, *Lizzie* was "in the can" late on December 30th. The next day, scheduled for recording for Desto Records, began unpromisingly. While the orchestra sat or loitered about for four hours waiting for the suddenly broken-down recording equipment to be replaced—being paid handsomely and running us over budget—the singers had time to become nervous. Brenda Lewis, Lizzie, claimed that she couldn't speak, let alone sing. She insisted that I ask for advice from a laryngologist. I called my old friend Doriot Anthony Dwyer, who gave me the number of a friendly specialist. He told me to tell the singer that if she couldn't sing, she shouldn't. For Brenda I translated that unhelpful advice into something more useful to us and added some encouraging words of my own. I knew that she was rarely ill and never cancelled a performance and suspected that she distrusted her recorded voice alone to convey the dramatic force that had made her famous. By the time we were ready to record, she was in fine voice and ready to sing the first line of the opera. Ann Elgar, the Margret, insisted that I look closely at her sore throat. I did so and pronounced it to be "just beautifully red and ready to be used."

After more than two weeks of rehearsing and filming and in spite of the lost four hours, by New Year's Eve the recording, too, was "in the can," many of the scenes having needed but one take. This original NYCO cast recording has remained available ever since, most recently on the CD of CRI/New World Records.

*   *   *   *   *   *

Chapter 10

My Heart's in the Highlands
(1966-1970)

Riots and the Bust on Campus
(1968)

Back in New York from Boston, I stayed with the Trumans and Celia Hecht and visited friends in the Department, where I spent some hours with Elias Dann, our band director, who suggested I make some changes in my new band arrangement of *Hymns and Dances*. I then did my family a favor. My brother and I had been brought up with English bulldogs and I thought our children deserved no less. The one thing they missed in Rome was Rorschach, who had been left with friends in Providence, R.I. He had acquired his Swiss name from the evocative splotches on his belly. In a complicated maneuver I drove to Providence and then he and I flew together to Rome, terrifying baggage handlers all along the way. The gardeners at the Villa Aurelia had never seen such a slobbering animal and remained wary of him until they learned that his looks belied his friendliness.

While I waited impatiently for Saroyan to answer my "good news letter" to him, little by little I polished off the last of the miscellaneous pieces and incorporated the changes recommended by Elias Dann in the already inked fair copy of my band *Hymns and Dances*.

Following is a letter from Saroyan regarding *Highlands*.

2729 West Griffith Way Fresno California 93705 January 26 1966

Mr. Jack Beeson
Accademia Americanana
Via Angelo Masina 5
Rome Italy

Dear Jack: Thank for your January 7th letter . . .

. . . I'm here until further notice, although soon enough I shall be obliged to return to New York and then to Paris. When you kept phoning, I was in Europe: Lebanon, Syria, Jordan, Greece, Israel, and Paris—skipped Rome. A lot of action seems to be taking place for you, and that is something every man should be pleased about. I'm eager to hear the opera, and the symphony, and anything else you have that you want to send.

My Heart's in the Highlands—well, let's pick it up again. Business terms—well, refer to the Hello Out There form and follow it, I guess. I am no longer with Gitlin or any other lawyer, except Aram Kevorkian, at Coudert Frères, 52 Avenue Champs Elysées, Paris 8e: and I have no literary or other agent. If Audrey Wood is your agent, she is among the best of them—and a delightful lady. I know her from a few more or less accidental meetings in the elevators or the lobby at the Royalton in New York which is where I generally stop—about fifteen bucks a day, $10 less than the Gotham or the St. Regis, for instance, and big rooms. —Will I be hearing from you soon? All the best, always:

(signed: Bill Saroyan)

I lost no time in trying to pull together the various ideas I'd long had about the plays and testing them against my re-readings of them. I then spent two days writing a very long letter that summarized the general problems that exist in turning a Saroyan play into a libretto and a few of the particular problems posed by *Highlands*. I include an edited and much abbreviated version of my letter.

[Rome]
February 8, '66

Dear Bill,

Your letter came three or four days ago and I've been a new man ever since. . . .

. . . It didn't arrive very promptly, for there has been an on-again, off-again postal slowdown here; since there's no government at the moment, it isn't very clear who they're striking against.

Ever since it came, with the implication that I can do the piece, I've been reading the short version (my copy here is the one in the Bentley collection) and the long version (my copy here is the Faber & Faber ed.) every eight hours or so. I think I told you that I don't like to get too emotionally involved with a subject unless I "can go all the way;" I think I also said that there are a lot of problems to be solved before I can start thinking up the tunes and un-tunes, whatever they are. (This one should be tuney.) I'm a long way from having solutions to the problems, but at least I'm finding out what the problems are. Unfortunately, I'm not the fast worker you are—it's not in the nature of composing that one can be, anyhow—but if I plan things out carefully to begin with, I don't usually get mired later. Furthermore if the whole dramatic-musical shape is clear and strong to me from the first I don't get into the thing & then have to give up. Perhaps you feel the same way about writing plays as I do about writing operas: it's knowing what the thing is all about before it is written that makes it possible to write it down.

Well-meaning people are always asking me the stupid question, "Which comes first in writing an opera, the words or the music?" O course the words always do—except for maybe a phrase or part of a song here or there—but in all the good operas I know, the words were shaped to the musical and/or musico-dramatic needs in the first place. The last two operas I did were close-close-close collaborations with the librettist. In fact it was Hell, but I got what I wanted, and so did, finally, the librettist—since he, as much as I, was mostly interested in the final thing. In a sense, working with a pre-existent play is easier. First of all, selecting the play in the first place means one has found something that has some of the right makings of an opera and in the case of your two, *HOT* and *Highlands*. most of the main makings. The problem, though, is then so to shape it, that the opera sounds and looks and feels as though its libretto had been designed for music in the first place. That's where I am at the moment, which is just where I was in the summer of 1953, when I was worrying *Hello Out There* into a libretto. Same pleasure, same pain, same problems. In a way this one is easier—there are more people and there are many and varied scenes. Bringing off *Hello* was something of a gamble, what with those two people going on for almost half an hour without stopping. If you remember, the way the other one was worked out was that I wrote asking permission, you said ok, then I started out with a couple of editions to re-shape and cut, writing you occasionally to let you know what I was up to. Somewhere along the line I talked to Berner and a page was worked out;

the contents of the page, somewhat altered, became the gist of the publication contract later. . . .

. . . Once, much later, I played a lousy recording of the rather lousy first performance for you (it had been the first performance of any opera of mine) and you said you were sorry you hadn't taken the chance to help more directly in the words. (I don't know whether you were referring to my cutting and transpositions, or to the new words and occasional lines I made up for it.) Remember?

Now, on the whole, I was pleased with the early "working arrangement," except that when I needed more words, as I constantly did, I was sometimes hard-put to combine what had been alternating speeches into longer units and I was always a little embarrassed about adding my own to yours, on the few occasions when I did. *Highlands* presents this same problem to the composer: how to give the music a chance, not to take over, but to work with the words, the people, and the stage, as well as on its own. The short lines, alternating between two people are almost always good in the spoken theatre, they work only for a little while with singing actors. In *HOT*, as I've said, I sometimes cut alternate lines, making longer speeches. I can do this too in *Highlands*. But there are places that just need to go on longer, where a kind of aria or arietta, a little song, would be in order.

Oddly enough, one needs more words sometimes—but one needs to cut too. It takes longer to sing words than to speak them (even when I set them, for I set them rather fast, on the whole). So it is that if all the words of a play are set, it runs over half again as long, usually. If one allows for the places where the words have to be expanded beyond their prosy necessity (in the way that poetry often expands them, in Shakespeare for instance) then one is down to the minimum of text, a minimum that consists of all the pregnant words, phrases, and sentences that make the characters, mood, and story vital, and all those many more that in themselves & with the music make the whole thing worthwhile. One can, with music, get along with fewer words of explanation, oddly enough. The first trumpet note of MacGregor's return, even in the play, makes his coming—no grape stealing—everything, clear. Real operatic moment, sir! . . .

. . . Obviously, if we can collaborate more closely on this piece than we did before, I'd be delighted. On the other hand, I'm happy to go ahead on my own as I did the other time, shaping it to what I think are the musical-dramatic necessities, if you can trust me. . . .

Aside from the verbal changes within the scenes, of the sort I've already talked about, I'd leave the number and order of the scenes in what was the short play pretty much alone. However I couldn't do much of anything with scene 3 musically. We could go directly into the next scene. . . .

With music involved, as in an opera, the plainer the dramatic line and the broader the emotional sweep, usually the better. Such cutting and such an ending would be in line with what seems more and more what I'm trying to head for: in main outline, the short version of the play, but ending with the final scene of the long play and using as much of the preceding parts of the long play as are necessary to motivate the use of the last scene.

I have to watch the length of Johnny's part like a hawk. He can't have anything that's not essential, everything has to be thrown into relief, for a boy's singing voice has nowhere near the staying power of his speaking voice. If it's used right it can be very effective and touching, as in *Amahl* and in Britten's *Turn of the Screw*.

In the two plays MacGregor's age varies. The younger old man may be better, for he sings! I'm not committed, though . . .

Father should be a tenor, so that he seems to be singing in the same register as the boy—sound alike, look alike, but a short generation apart. MacGregor's a bass, or bass-baritone.

If there's to be a bunch of neighbors, obviously they'll have to sing. The isolated lines that exist are ok in part as far as they go, but something more is needed, of some kind or other. (By the way there's at least one line from the short version that I want to put in the opera, the one about bird seed and maple syrup. It hooks right on to the popcorn and cheese. This is the kind of expansion I meant, way back on an earlier page.)

++ ++ ++ ++

I don't know whether all this excites you, interests you, bores you, makes you angry or just annoys you. I'm only trying to find out how to go about writing a little musical theatre piece, opera or call it what you will, that, though it will be different from the play necessarily, will carry the spirit of the play, even deepen it. As I said earlier, I'll be happy to do all the worrying myself and not bother you with much or any of it, but it would be nice to have someone to talk—write—to, and even nicer to have your ideas and words. In any case, you can see that I'm serious about it and raring to go. . . .

++ ++ ++ ++

Yours,

(signed: Jack)

Raring to go as I was, I was nevertheless gratified to find two of my operas jostling one another: some unfinished *Lizzie* business forced a postponement in beginning another. There had been some vague talk about a half-hour NET show called Creative Person. It suddenly became definite that I was to be featured as such a person, the program to precede the 2-hour *Lizzie Borden* as a kind of publicity "turn on." The filming days were not many, but widely spaced so that I would be back in New York for almost two weeks, from late February through early March—with time to see the *Lizzie* videotape, help edit the recording of it, and to spend two days with the other MACS on the Guggenheim Foundation jury—my expenses for the whole stay met by NET.

The director of the show was Marc van Cleefe and it was amusing to act the part of a creative person as he defined one. I was told to walk purposefully on upper Broadway and to be lost in thought while sauntering on the Columbia campus. The office staff was impressed by having a camera crew about and provided an empty office where I sat at the piano chewing a pencil, posed over a blank sheet of music staff-paper. All this was accompanied by the usual "voice-over" with biographical details alternating with interviews on camera.

Back again in Rome, having missed Nora's birthday celebration—as I had missed the festive Roman Christmas holidays during my first trip—it was clear that if Rorschach had not been quite the man of the house, he had been the center of affectionate attention. During my second trip to New York I learned from Adler and Browning that now that Bill had agreed to let me use his play, NET would commission and produce the opera when it was completed. Enthusiastically, I lost no time in beginning it, writing out the long-planned first words and music on March 18, 1966. I had finally pinned down a memory from my early Muncie school days. I seemed to recall that we had sung "My heart's in the highlands, My heart is not here" to a tune I remembered all the way through, but to words I'd mostly forgotten. In a search through the Academy Library music collection I found the song in *Twice 55*, the music to the Robert Burns poem by J. M. Courtney. My search there and in other Roman libraries led me to other settings of the words, none of which I liked. The first line of the poem, which serves as the title of both the play and the opera, is quoted or alluded to often by one of the main characters, Jasper MacGregor. A Scot who was once an actor, he had fled from the Old People's Home and been taken in by the Armenian family who are the main characters in the play and the opera, the 12-year old, his father, and grandmother. I planned to thread the tune—with some Beesonish inflections—throughout the opera, occasionally with the words. Uneasy about Bill's reaction to what I wanted to do, I wrote him a letter which included the tunes I had found and over the phone sang to him my chosen Courtney melody. In my letter I elaborated:

. . . Not just any setting will do for me, for I have to have one that makes it possible for me to integrate it into the parts before and after it, in fact into the whole score, so that it sounds natural when it comes in, and so that my music around it sounds natural, too. It is one of the major problems I'll have.
    I started the music yesterday, to see how it feels. . . .

He responded promptly:

2729 West Griffith Way Fresno California 93705 Monday March 28 1966

Dear Jack: I am rushing this pell-mell-like so that in case I get swamped you won't have to try to guess which song it is: it is the first one in your letter. W. B. Courtney is the name of the composer. The singing of the song was required in California when I went to school at Longfellow Junior High in Fresno almost 50 years ago. It is the best of the versions by various composers, to the words by Robert Burns. I know nothing about Courtney or the others. I think you will find that it is the most suitable of any you may come upon. Let me repeat then, it is the first tune: a young music student played all of them for me just yesterday, because I don't read music I'm sorry to say. What else can I say to you at this moment, when you have just started work, excepting good luck (which helps more than any of us may be willing to say, I think). Please remember that the key to the whole thing is a warm crazy toughness in which profound earnestness is real simultaneously with comedy and delight in all things, including even sorrow. I am really rushed, but please do a great job and please leave the play as it is and let me know if you need help of any kind that I might give. Again, good luck:
                                  (signed: Bill Saroyan)

So we had both known our "title tune" since junior high school days! By the time his letter arrived, I'd already alluded to the tune in a phrase whistled by a newspaper boy and then written it all out to be played offstage by a cornet supposedly by the old actor, just before his first entrance. I was uncomfortable in using the tune because I could find nothing in Rome about its composer. If his music was in copyright, he or his heirs could later cause all kinds of rights and royalty problems. As I progressed in shaping the libretto and its music, for months I was all too often accompanied by an incubus named J. M. Courtney. Many, many months later, in the course of a long letter to Bill I recounted how I had been burdened, from early on, by that ghost and how it had finally been exorcised.

January 1, '67

Dear Bill,

This is a good day to look backwards and forwards and, besides, I owe you a "progress report." . . .

. . . Getting back into the University and into New York has been more trouble than I'd thought, after 18 months out of it. The result is that I haven't got as much farther as I'd hoped into the second act. But the Christmas vacation—a vacation to do "real" work—has let me finish one of the scenes that had worried me since the beginning. I cut it some, but it's there. It's one thing to have a scene with two boys talking—quite something else to find the right things for them to sing conversation to! Fortunately there's a lot of whistling.

Quite apart from having my time cut in on, just to make a living, one of the things that held me up early in the fall was a ghost that kept hanging around the studio. The first act is so full of J. M. Courtney's tune that I could hardly go on without knowing who he was, when he'd died, and whether his publisher, heirs, or ghost would be around to make things unpleasant when it was discovered that I'd been playing around with his tune. So I spent more than a solid week tracing the damn tune and its composer. I won't trouble you with the whole story, though you could do a fine short story on the subject, but last spring I had the Music Library here on the job, the reference librarian in the big CU Library, and the head of the New York Pub. Lib. Music Div. and one of his minions on it—all flunked miserably. Finally, I sat me down in the dusty and unused old choral-music stacks of Teachers College to look for the oldest publication of the tune I could find—preferably one before the US Copyright Act went into effect. The earliest printing (I went through several hundred song books, by actual count) has the date 1898-1899, in a series of school tunes edited by Eleanor Smith. By the time I'd found it I had by pure chance come upon a footnote concerning the tune, in a later printing, and had discovered that J. M. Courtney was only a pseudonym for Eleanor Smith! I suppose it doesn't make the tune any less good. She was a somebody—friend of Jane Addams and the founder of the Hull House Music School, died in 1942 at the age of 84. Apparently she didn't want it to appear that she was leading her own series with her own tunes and so divvied them up under at least these two names. Copyrights and credits have been checked thoroughly by me and by my publisher and there are no problems about the use of the tune, either here or abroad. As soon as I discovered that we wouldn't be infringing on anyone, I went back to composing, unblocked.

There's another problem, too, maybe. Do you know whether the words and music of "Ghendsoreen dzareen dahgeh . . ." are really a folk tune? An Armenian friend of mine . . . has dug up a copy of the song, copyrighted in 1930 by the Armenian Music Society, words by A. Isahakian and music by H. Mehrab. My friend has talked to the widow of Mehrab, who claims her husband wrote it. I'd rather skip that whole subject, by finding a tune and words that are for sure free. In fact I've found material in the Komitas collection that works in better with the surrounding material. I'm giving her (Grandmother, that is) another folk song to sing while she's sweeping off the porch. After the boys' singing conversation I have to have a "number" to keep the music from losing its shape completely. . . .

Happy New Year!
Jack

(The Armenian-American friend referred to was Anahid Iskian, who had met Nora when she was studying Russian in one of the classes at Hunter College taught by Nora. Not only the two folk songs, but also all of Grandmother's role is sung in Armenian; I needed help in setting those of her words not already set in the folk songs.)

*   *   *   *   *   *

Bothered as I had been from the beginning with the ghost of Courtney, I was to suspect very much later that some other occult power seemed to have chosen the date I began writing the opera, March 18 (1966), and then decreed the timing of my progress through the opera to its end and the date of its premiere.

I had often read in the play, but taken no special notice, that in the third scene "eighteen neighbors gather in front of the house" and that at the beginning of the next scene "Eighteen days have passed." When the music sketch was completed and I was reviewing it, I took notice of my beginning date, March 18, and then wondered why Bill had been so unnecessarily specific in choosing his number twice; unfortunately, I had never thought to ask him. Intrigued, I examined the dates in my manuscript of the completion of the scenes and found what, surely, my subconscious could not have accomplished. At the end of the sketch of the opera—its music, that is—I had written "Hightowers, Shelter Island, September 18, 1967." Again an eighteen and a quick computation disclosed a period of exactly eighteen months. I had begun the piano score immediately and then continued with the orchestration. While composing the sketch I had concluded that I would need about 17 instruments, but because there were to be 18 voices in the chorus of neighbors, I decided—if it was I and not the occult power in charge—on eighteen. I have often rushed or dallied in order to be able to inscribe some approaching holiday at the end of a manuscript. At the end of the *Highlands* orchestral score is written, "Easter, 1969." Another quick computation disclosed that the piano and orchestral scores had been written in exactly eighteen months and eighteen days. The first New York showing of the NET production of *Highlands* was March 18, 1970, the fourth anniversary of its beginning!

Aside from my consciously changing the size of the small instrumental ensemble from 17 to 18 players, all explanations for the numerous eighteens are improbable: an occult power, a remarkably calendrical subconscious, or pure coincidences.

Though, as I wrote Bill later, the Courtney ghost was finally exorcized, I am today still puzzled by the problem of the eighteens—a Sherlockian phrase. The entries in my 1966 date book for the dates before its first occurrence, though uncharacteristic of a Roman week, suggest that I began writing the opera when I did simply because I was ready to do so.

I see that on the 10th I wrote Mother, worked on the *HH* libretto and met with Whittenberg (one of the music fellows I was to look after if need be; unfortunately, he had been drinking so heavily for so long that the Academy Director and I had him hospitalized). On the 11th: wrote Otto; worked on the libretto and then spent the day with Whittenberg in the hospital; Nora and I heard *Die Winterreise* at Santa Cecilia. On the 12th: taxes all day. On the 13th:

sightseeing. On the 14th and 15: taxes only. 16th: exhibition of Marino Marini and more *HH* libretto. 17th: still seeking Scotch songs (i.e., settings of the Robert Burns poem); bought music staff-paper (for *HH* composition sketch); N. and J. to opera, Pizzetti, *Fedra*. And on the 18th: wrote Mother, Morton Baum and two others, and—in red crayon—"began *Highlands*." Leafing on through the pages, I'm delighted to find that the occult power—if there was one—was inattentive or otherwise engaged on April 18th, for on the *19th* in red ink appears "finished 1st scene of *HH*."

My work on *Highlands*, as well as on the preceding miscellaneous pieces, was mostly done at the fine large Steinway in our living room and a worktable there while the children were in school and Nora at McGraw-Hill. I also had free access to use the concert grand in the intimate recital hall that was the top floor of the Villa Aurelia next door, from which, looking east, one had the finest of all views of Rome.

In the recital hall a few concerts took place each year for invited guests and other interested Romans. Touring American performers were heard, as were Italian musicians playing works by Academy composers. it was my duty as Resident to schedule the events, help find the performers, and, in part, choose the music to be heard—all things I'd been doing at Columbia for years.

It was more a pleasure than a duty to make sure that RAI orchestral performances of Academy composers would continue, acting as a friendly liaison between Academy and RAI. We would have attended all the RAI concerts anyhow and it was hardly onerous to make a point of greeting the conductor, Ferrucio Scaglia, in the green room thereafter. I enjoyed visiting Renata Bertelli, practicing my Italian and drinking expressi with her. She was known as *la eminenza grigia* (the gray eminence) and was in charge of music programming at RAI. She and I had in common friendship with Teresa Stich-Randall, whom she hired as often as possible to sing on the network.

Aside from these American Academy music resident duties, such as they were, my time was my own to shape the libretto of the opera and to compose it—

and to attend the theatre and the opera with Nora and to visit churches, museums, and monuments with our teenagers.

We all interrupted what we were doing to fly to Athens for the Easter holidays, leaving Rorschach with a friend. As guests of the American School we were lent one of the two white marble houses flanking its main building. On one of the holiday evenings we had a splendid view of a long procession of celebrants carrying torches along the side of the hill nearby. In a hired car we visited Mycenae and Epidaurus, the ancient medical center about which Henry Sigerist had written extensively in his *History of Medicine*; after this visit to the south we spent two days at Delphi, where I was awed by one of the earliest musical "manuscripts," a Hymn to Apollo inscribed in stone. When the eleven days were over, it was impossible to tell which of us had been most impressed, each in his or her own way at ages 44, 43, 16, and 13, by what had been seen and experienced.

It was the very slobbery Rorschach who was most pleased with our return from Greece, although I was eager to get back to composing and Miranda to her dance classes at the Overseas School. These introductory classes were to lead to her being accepted by the Martha Graham School—alluded to earlier in this memoir—and then for a while to becoming a dance major at Sarah Lawrence College.

And so we continued as before, with that mixture of daily duties without stress and the unexpected—an almost always closed church with its door open for its saint's name-day, finding shards at the ancient port of Ostia (which we still have), a trip to the Academy's dig at Cosa—a mixture uniquely Roman. Then followed the farewells to the gardeners and new and old friends. Among the latter was Alexei Haieff, who was still in Rome, living in a large apartment in a downtown palace with Lady Bridport—also known in Italy as the Duchessa Bronte—whom he was later to marry. When the celebratory luncheons and dinners were over, we were driven to Naples where we boarded the Michelangelo, sister ship of the Raffaello, on which we had arrived. I occupied myself with reading proofs of *Lizzie* and *Transformations*, as I would have to do much of the summer. Christopher and Miranda were put in charge of walking Rorschach. Bulldogs are known for their unsteady gait and it was amusing to see him coping with the often-slanting upper deck.

We had not been in Hightowers long when I found myself in rehearsal. Our neighbor, Helen Lamont, was producing and directing the third of her Shakespearean comedies, *Midsummer Night's Dream*. In 1962 she had presented *As You Like It*, in which Miranda had appeared as a fairy. Two years later the play was *Twelfth Night*, in which Christopher was a handsome page and I was assigned the role of Sebastion. Now he was to be a page and I was cast as Lysander. If it seems odd that a man of 43 and 45 would be cast at those ages as a young lover, it is because, so to speak, I have had *two* long-lived chronic diseases, diabetes and the inability to look my age. Of course, like Dorian Gray, I may be cured of my second disease at any time now.

Just as I had once studied voice because I was working with singers and wanted to know what they had to cope with, so I wished to experience memorizing a part and learning to take direction. What Helen lacked in stage directing experience, she made up for in her knowledge of the text and how to project it. The Shelter Island High School gymnasium included a decent stage and ranks of lights; our casts included several with acting experience and one, Warren Teixeira, a painter, textile designer, flutist and a sometime professional actor. My only problem in *Dream* had been that my Hermia was in real life married to a large, muscular, buff man who resented little me throughout rehearsals, performance, and thereafter, for acting out a romance with his wife. Nevertheless, I enjoyed all the rehearsals, the performances and benefitted from the experience.

At one of the performances, there were at least two notables in the audience: Julius Rudel, General Director of the New York City Opera, and Harold Schonberg, chief music critic of the *New York Times*. The two were so astonished to see me in costume and makeup that they could barely mumble something about my having been a convincing young lover.

Harold was already a Shelter Islander when we arrived. In those days the Island was relatively unpopulated, so the social circle that would include a composer and a major critic of the *Times* was small enough to insure our meeting often. For a while he seemed to me distant and uncommunicative. He then explained, apologetically, that he made a point of never becoming acquainted with performers and composers so that he could remain objective should he have to review their performances or compositions and could be seen and known to be unprejudiced. (Very likely another major critic's name entered our first real conversation: Virgil Thomson believed that a critic's prejudices should be made clear, even flaunted, so that his reviews could be correctly interpreted.) In our subsequent conversations it became obvious that we disagreed on a number of musical subjects: he firmly believed that all operas should be performed in their original languages; I thought that many, if not most, should be translated, or at least sung only by those expert in the foreign languages. We disagreed on the merits of most contemporary composers. He disliked the singing of Callas, as I treasured the *whole* of her performances; he was shocked that I considered Sutherland to be a glorious living flute with that instrument's agility, accuracy, and almost its range, and with no more than a flute's dramatic projection and ability to pronounce any language. We agreed to avoid these and other subjects and then became fast friends.

Once, leaving the lobby at the end of a City Center intermission, I was goosed by someone behind me. It was Harold, unsmiling and silent, being friendly in secret.

At another time, having drinks on our porch before dinner I broke our compact and mentioned a forbidden topic. A few days before he had been off-hand and highly critical in his review of a Britten opera. I asked if he had more to say about it than he had written. He replied that on the whole he disapproved of music by homosexual composers. I was too shocked to pursue that subject. Instead, only half-joking, I asked him whether there wasn't something to be said in favor of the 19th century Parisian practice of performers and composers paying critics for writing favorable reviews. He was too shocked to reply.

When I asked Virgil the same question, he answered quickly, probably having asked himself the same question often. "Yes, but only if its public knowledge how much money has changed hands."

Though Harold had once been a Golden Gloves boxer and had broken one—or both?—legs as a paratrooper during WWII, he rarely exercised. One day, after my swim, I way lying on the beach drying and reading when he ambled along with his Labrador retriever for his daily dozen—throwing a large stick out into the water for his dog to retrieve. Impishly, I asked him if he'd mind if I raced his dog for the stick, thinking he would get a kick out of putting a composer in competition with his Labrador. We raced out several time, the dog taking the stick back to his master a few times, I doing so at least as often. Harold, grinning broadly, enjoyed the match.

On the *Times* for many years, Harold Schonberg often reviewed the music of Arnold Schönberg, about which he almost never had anything good to say. In fact, he disparaged all serial music by any composer and managed to hold responsible for its faults his umlauted namesake. I finally had the opportunity of politely alluding to this forbidden subject. During the final illness of his first wife, Nora and I tried to be of some comfort to Harold. He then married a recently widowed friend and neighbor of ours. Together with a conventional letter of congratulations to the newly married pair, I sent a larger stiff card inscribed in my best calligraphy. On the first line was Harold C. Schonberg, centered; under it were his initials, H.C.S. and their musical equivalent on staff lines, B♮ C E♭; thereunder the words "trichord in retrograde:" S. C. H. and their musical notation, E♭ C B♮. In the last and lowest line "H C S = S C H = SCHonberg, showing that the retrograde of his initials is the same as the first three letters of his last name. Though the argument and the terminology derive from Arnold Schönberg, poor Arnold was not so serially named as Harold had been. He was apparently amused by my discovery, thanked me profusely for the card, framed it, and displayed it on the wall of his living room.

More important than my disclosure of the trichordal relationship of Harold to Arnold was the result of a casual remark Harold made when we met by chance one afternoon at the post office. He had just been in the office of Walter Shumann, editor and publisher of the weekly *Shelter Island Reporter*. Walter had told him that he had at home a large shoebox of musical manuscripts and letters passed down through the generations to him from his great grandparents, Robert and Clara Wieck Shumann. Harold asked me if I would examine the trove and report to him what I'd found, which might serve him as a subject matter of a Sunday article.

I lost no time in going to visit Walter, whom I knew well from social events at which he usually sat at the piano playing pop songs not very well, and *Traümerei* soulfully. In the shoebox was the manuscript of *Fugue in A♭ minor* for organ by Brahms and other music I could not identify offhand, and a stack of letters to "Lieber Johannes." I convinced Walter that it was unsafe to have these manuscripts in an island frame house and to permit me to borrow them and make copies. I deposited one complete set in the Columbia Music Library and have kept another set. In my research I discovered to my wry amusement that "the whereabouts of the Brahms *Fugue* manuscript is unknown;" that the letters were more varied than I'd thought—not all from Clara to "Lieber Johannes" —that there were Schumann and Weber manuscripts and a page in Schubert's hand. When I returned the collection to Walter I told him that I had phoned an acquaintance in charge of the huge musical manuscript collection at the Morgan Library who would be pleased to meet him and to view the originals with the possibility of purchasing them, especially the Brahms *Fugue*. Walter did not bother to do so, died, and bequeathed them to his two surviving daughters, so their whereabouts are no longer unknown.

The library copy of this small treasure became the subject matter for a semester of a graduate musicology seminar offered by Ed Lippman, in which every page was thoroughly examined and identified.

*   *   *   *   *   *

These varied vignettes from the long—and from Harold's point of view, secret—acquaintance of a composer and a music critic took place over many years, both before and after our midsummer production of *Dream*. Playing at being Lysander for a few weeks interrupted the writing of *Highlands*, but it was another enjoyable way of experiencing make-believe. In fact, cutting, transposing, and occasionally rewriting Saroyan's lines of dialogue or writing my own, followed by setting and accompanying them, progressed pleasantly and fruitfully, if more irregularly once classes began and other commitments uptown and downtown had to be tended to.

The problem of setting to music words intended to be spoken, whether those of a play being adapted as a libretto for an opera, or those of a poem for a solo song or a chorus, is in some sense the problem of working with and overcoming verbal gravity. It is not often noticed that the average adult male's speaking voice lies in the space between B and D in the bass clef. Female voices speak in the same range an octave higher. Minute inflections within those limited ranges, together with varied timbres and accentuations suffice for self-expression and to identify individuals by others. Of course, for emphasis and in the voices of trained actors, forays into higher pitches often occur.

The trained singing voice spends most of its time in the octave and a half or two octaves above the usual speaking voice. The disparity between he two ranges can be problematic if a composer makes use of spoken words in a predominantly sung work and seeks smooth transitions from one to the other. The solution is simple: let the sung line end in or near the spoken spoken range and then let the sung line begin again in that range. A composer of whatever style can find numerous examples of the problem and its solution in Marc Blitzstein's *Regina*. In an opera, if conversation of a mundane sort is not relegated to speech, it should be set in the lower part of the voice, as it has been in Italian opera for four centuries; to force such text up into the "expressive" part of the voice—against gravity, metaphorically speaking—leads to that kind of boring artificiality that curses too many 20th century operas.

From the *Highlands* play I cut pages of everyday chatter and palaver, retaining a few spoken lines, setting the rest. What remained of the mundane was enlivened by the great variety of characters and voice types: Johnny, boy-soprano, and the newspaper boy, whistler and boy-alto; Johnny's father, Ben Alexander, dramatic tenor, with a clarion high B; the old actor, bass-baritone; and Mr. Kosak, the grocer, a bass with a low D. The only women's voices were the Armenian grandmother, a contralto, and Esther, girl-soprano—and of course, those in the chorus. And a dog, listed as "Barker."

Notwithstanding the fact that words seek the lower part of the voice (as exemplified by most pop singers) well-trained voices have always endeavored to sing words clearly as though speaking them. Some learn to do so throughout at least their middle range. For physical and physiological reasons most vowels except for ä and ē must be modified at or above "the break," as it is called; consonants on these high notes tend to be dropped or slighted.

Consequently, there are but few words that can be projected clearly in the high register; in the stratosphere of the coloratura voices there are usually only ahs. The tenor high B mentioned above is sung on "fire," preceded by the same word sung on A♭ and F to trick the listener into understanding the word on high B. Though the vowel in that word is a diphthong, the ä is available and the ē is brilliant in the tenor voice; the throat remains open and the final r takes care of itself.

In twice fashioning librettos from Saroyan plays I was twice confronted by the few passages and monologues that could be expanded vocally and musically into ensembles and arias—songs was the word I used with Bill, though they were rarely songs. The *King Lear* mad scene on the heath recited by MacGregor as the climax of the play—ill-remembered by him, who infuses it with bits of *Hamlet*—

was a blessed exception, which I seized upon, as would have Verdi, who planned but did not write a *Lear*. The one Armenian folk song in the play became two in the opera. Hard up for an ensemble, I fashioned an odd trio, the tenor reading an August 2, 1914 anti-war editorial from the N. Y. *Tribune* while Johnny and his grandmother carry on in a mix of English and Armenian.

In my long letter to Bill written when I was beginning work on the opera I explained that there would be sections, strategically placed dramatically and musically, where more words would be needed, where the main characters should become expansive in song. When I was nearing such a place and knew that another would follow, I wrote Bill to suggest a prose-poem by him that would provide the words for both. The first occurs when Johnny brings the mail to his father, a rejection letter from *The Atlantic Monthly* that includes the prose-poem he had submitted. He erupts angrily: "Who the hell is *The Atlantic Monthly*? Go ahead, kill everybody! . . ."

It is important to note that both *Highlands* and *The Time of Your Life* were first performed in 1939, when World War II began and that—not by accident—*Highlands* takes place in Fresno in 1914, the year in which World War I began. The prose-poem I refer to is printed before the text of *The Time of Your Life* and in the programs of its productions. Bill refers to it, not as a preamble, but as his Credo, as it is mine too. It is best if I describe my plan for finding needed texts in the words of that time, in a letter written to Bill on March 27, 1967.

> 445 Riverside Drive
> New York, N.Y. 10027
> March 27, 1967

. . . One of these spots is coming up shortly, after the rejection slip from the *Atlantic Monthly* arrives; Johnny's Father reads thru the poems swiftly, then launches into the furious section, "Go ahead, kill everybody." . . . There may be barely enough words here for a fine furious vocal piece, but the furious part should be only the second part of a solo scene, aria-song, the first part of which could very well be made up of his reading part of the rejected manuscript, not to himself silently, but to himself out loud with us listening in. (The part is obviously long enough in the spoken play, but with music the dramatic time scale is always different.) My first thought months ago, when I was listening and thinking ahead, was to write you to ask whether you have a lyric (rejected or unrejected) that would work suitably. But I've since had what I think is a brilliant solution. It's an idea out of left field and maybe you'll think it too crazy, but I have to know what you'll let me do before I can go on. I'd like to form the first part out of setting the first half of the preamble to *The Time of Your Life*, "In the time of your life, live—so that . . ." I'd use about half of the long paragraph, which I've been shaken by for about twenty years. (So it's no new infatuation.)

Another place that has to be expanded to make more room for singing is [the scene in the grocery when Johnny's father gives Mr. Kosak his manuscript in lieu of cash]. It's just fine as far as it goes, but I need twice that many words, at least. Part of my "brilliant" idea is to have Mr. Kosak sing the <u>rest</u> of the preamble, beginning toward the end of what the Father had sung, and going on to the end. In this way the whole passage from *The Time of Your Life* will be used, forming, in a sense, one "song," sung by both. I think it would make dramatic sense under the circumstances and I <u>know</u> it will make musical sense, and be a fresh thing.

Of course it makes it seem as though the *Atlantic Monthly* has rejected a wonderful page of prose-poetry, but that's the only objection I see, if it is one . . .

Could you let me know your reaction to the idea as soon as you have one? . . .

If you do like my idea, as I hope you do, I just need your permission to quote the passage. From what you wrote me some time ago about rights, I assume there's no publisher from whom I need to ask permission.

As you'll have noticed, the passages fit in as though written to fit. They not only add more weight musically to the two scenes, they also solve my not having enough words as is, and they let me set words I've always wanted to set anyhow.

I trust you're fine. I just read somewhere that you're writing a short story a day, so I guess you must be in fine fettle.

Yrs,

(signed: Jack)

- - - - - -

1821 15th Avenue San Francisco 94122 Wednesday March 29 1967
Dear Jack:

I leave in a few hours for a drive-around California but the above will be the address where I can always be reached, as anything of importance is forwarded to wherever I may be: my first impulse was to argue that the words in My Heart's in the Highlands should be all we ought to believe are needed, and stuff from one work should not be transferred to another. But let me go along with you, and let's see how it turns out. Also, you might think about the possibility of having the Credo from The Time of Your Life turn out to be some kind of very desirable and useful and popular song for special occasions, and temper the music accordingly. And of course that would mean very likely a separate publication of the work as a song, I suspect. And you and I understand that whatever happens, I am always free to use the words involved in whole or in part as I choose, including in another opera, for instance, or as a song, or a recitative [sic] or whatever. Incidentally, how is it going, and when do you see it being finished? And when will I hear some or all of it? (Incidentally, I worked with a Russian composer teaching at the U. of Chicago five or six years ago (for two or three years) by correspondence on the play called The Cave Dwellers, but I haven't heard from him for three or four years. I forget his name, at the moment, but perhaps you know him.) In any case, good luck and all best:

(signed: Bill)

(Thanks for the discs—I'm enjoying them very much.)

According to my former composition student, Phillip Ramey, the forgotten Russian composer was Alexander Tcherepnin (1899-1977), who taught in the Windy City not at the University of Chicago, but at De Paul University. Ramey, a Tcherepnin student in the early 1960s, remembered that Tcherepnin had an opera commission from the Koussevitzky Foundation and had mentioned that he'd corresponded with Saroyan concerning a libretto, but ultimately found Saroyan too difficult as a potential collaborator.

* * * * * *

The writing of letters concerned with borrowing a part of one Saroyan play for use in the libretto based on another dates from when I was a little more than a year into the writing of *Highlands*. As indicated earlier, 18 months were to be spent altogether in shaping the libretto and setting it to music; another 18 months and 18 days would be required before there were inked copies of piano-vocal and orchestral scores. During these three years changes took place in the Music Department and in the other arts offerings, and in the University as a whole, of lasting effect. Cast by chance and circumstance in walk-on, supporting, and leading roles, in addition to the usual teaching and counseling duties. I had seemingly endless meetings, conversations, and solitary thoughts about this and that—including how best to convince x, y, and z, of the wisdom of carrying out a, b, or c. Surely there were times on campus when I thought of the Burns lines:

> My heart's in the highlands,
> My heart is not here.

*   *   *   *   *   *

By the late fifties, when Brander Matthews Theatre and Earl Hall were razed for the building of the Law School, the few remnants of activities in Theatre, Painting, and Sculpture became the Program in the Arts administered by an Executive Committee, which included a music representative, at first Douglas Moore, then Otto Luening, then me. The Committee was led by the brilliant Jacques Barzun, Provost of Columbia. Our larger task was to revivify Dramatic Arts (to include Theatre, Film Radio, and Television), Painting and Sculpture (to include Drawing, Printmaking, and Photography) and to combine them with Creative Writing and Music, the whole to form a School of the Arts to be housed in a new Arts Center. There had been serious talk of such a new building for at least a decade. Our Committee was to draw up the requirements of facilities and space for them. Because the Arts Center was to include at least two theatres, I joined USITT (The United States Institute for Theatre Technology) and benefitted from new theatre friends, their seminars and reports.

The building site was originally that usurped by Law, then the whole block from 115th to 116th from Amsterdam all the way east to the privately owned buildings. The cost was to be borne by a Trustee, William Paley, the enlightened President of CBS whose headquarters was being designed by Eero Saarinen.

There were those on campus who considered the arts to be what had been accomplished by masters of the past, that which could be seen in the museums and heard in the concert halls and the opera houses; time, effort, and money should not be spent instructing would-be creators and performers of today. According to rumor there was a group of trustees that thought the University should convert the Paley twelve million to the really new, to science facilities.

Paley, angered by what he was hearing, withdrew his promised gift and built the museum of Broadcasting and Television with the money.

Although there have been no more than mumbles about an Arts Center in the forty years since, the School of the Arts came into existence in 1965 and has flourished. We of the Program of the Arts who had engineered its transformation into the School became the School's first Executive Committee. Homeless, we had our first meetings on 110th Street in the leased quarters of an abandoned hospital. I felt rather at home there, for our two children had been born in Woman's Hospital.

While we were defining the nature of the new School of the Arts, the Department Chairman received notice from Princeton that it would soon offer the PhD in composition, the first in the Ivy League to do so. Our. MA in composition had served as our terminal degree in the subject since the late twenties. Given the joint management of the Columbia-Princeton Electronic Music Center and the tendency of many in the music world, including the press, inaccurately to speak of composers at Columbia and at Princeton as all of one kind, Luening, Ussachevsky, and I decided that we should follow Princeton in offering a doctorate in composition. Of the three of us, only Ussachevsky had earned a PhD from Eastman; I had intentionally dropped out of that program; Otto had completed the seventh grade and was to be awarded an honorary high school diploma in the early 1970s. We realized, though, that young composers now wishing to teach in universities were disadvantaged without a doctorate.

We spoke with our friendly Provost, Jacques Barzun, who confirmed our belief that a PhD in a "creative" discipline could not be awarded at Columbia. All of the graduate degrees earned in the Department were granted by the Graduate Faculty of Philosophy; the other humanities departments in the Faculty would look askance at our requirement of a large musical composition as the dissertation—even if accompanied by an essay—fearing that such a precedent might lead to demands that novels or epic poems become acceptable as dissertations. Jacques believed, though, that my hunch was correct; the new

School of the Arts, empowered to grant the specialized M.F.A. (Master of Fine Arts), could also grant the D.M.A. (Doctor of Musical Arts) often offered in conservatories in specialized areas. He promised to pursue the matter with the N.Y. State Department of Education. He was successful in Albany, with the graduate committees and with the Trustees at Columbia. Meanwhile I was successful with my colleagues in Arts, but on one condition: all their divisions led to the MFA; our DMA should be preceded by an MFA in composition. I agreed to pursue the matter, but since the Department already had a flourishing MA, I saw no point in setting up a competitor. I dragged my feet in semblance of pursuit until the DMA was in place and everybody else forgot about the condition.

There remained some problems to be solved. The Arts Music Division, housed in the same building with the Department and staffed by the composers who would now teach their composition seminars in both the Division and the Department, would deprive the latter of what had been its unique status and might lead to administrative difficulties and rivalries. To be sure, the Department would profit from the arrangement; DMA candidates with MA degrees from elsewhere would elect many Departmental graduate courses, as would those of our own masters who continued. In fact, from the point of view of students then, and today, with little interest in administrative matters and power politics, there was but one overall curriculum, course numbers prefixed by one or the other identification, taught under the same roof (except for the Electronic Music Center uptown), by the same grown-ups.

Nevertheless, the status quo had been upset by what was interpreted by some historians as a power-play by the composers. In carrying out this joint enterprise there were at first many meetings of the Department Executive Committee to discuss composers' teaching assignments in one or the other Faculty and the courses to be offered to one, or the other, or both student bodies; too often there were ruffled feathers and veiled unpleasantries.

In the spring of 1968 there was to be an election for Departmental Chairman, Mitchell's limit of two three-year terms to come to an end June 30.

There were hints that I would be nominated as his successor, though I certainly was not eager to take on the added responsibility. Paul Lang spoke to Jacques Barzun and to me of his fear that Ussachevsky and the two assistant professors, Wuorinen and Sollberger, would soon form a troika in the Music Division of Arts and secede from our joint enterprise. Paul threatened to withdraw his support for the DMA and its program unless Luening or I were to lead the Division and I the Department. I refused to do both—though I was later on occasion to do so. If peace and unity between the Department and the Division were to be maintained, I had no choice but to accept the flattering unanimous vote to become Chairman. Jacques arranged for Otto to take over the Division for a while, even though he was to retire at 68 in '68, to be followed long-term by Chou Wen-Chung.

Though I thought Paul's fear was paranoid, he had to be paid attention to, for the 66 graduate students in musicology numbered almost double the total number of students registered in the other three graduate disciplines, composition, theory, and ethnomusicology. Exactly twenty years later the total of MA and DMA composers had grown to the earlier record, 66, and the historians had dwindled to 39. It is not simple to account for the varying drawing powers of subjects in a department or division, but the influx of composers—from 15 to 66 in two decades—was from early on marked by many students from abroad, attracted by the very varied group of composers on the faculty: Otto Luening, German-American; Vladimir Ussachevsky, Russian; Chou Wen-Chung, Chinese; Mario Davidovsky, Argentine; and I, from Middletown USA, who attracted Jim Stepleton, son of my junior high school music teacher.

These parochial matters were as nothing compared to the so-called Crisis at Columbia experienced by the University as a whole, its administration, faculty, and students during the spring of '68. In the spring season of earlier years there had been pantie raids carried out by the men of the College near the Barnard College dorms across the street. Much shouting under the windows led to scuffles over who were to keep the panties thrown out of the windows by the girls. But such high-jinks had disappeared by the 3rd or 4th year of the Vietnam War, the military draft, and widespread protests on and off-campus. Curiously, most campus unrest, including violence, occurred in the spring, as it had on the Berkeley campus a year earlier. I have no wish to review those intense controversies or to describe in detail a campus often in anarchy for five weeks. All these and other matters are described and documented in *Up Against the Ivy Wall* by editors of the Columbia *Spectator*. Rather, by describing some of what I experienced, the whole of the craziness can be imagined.

On Tuesday, April 23, 1968, the College Dean phoned to ask me if I would attend the rally of SDS (Students for a Democratic Society) at the sundial, an enormous granite ball, now gone, in the middle of the campus. A mob of some 400 were there with their leader Mark Rudd (pronounced Mar Crud by some). They were surrounded by counter-demonstrators, the curious, and, I suppose, other observers like me. After several angry speeches, Rudd urged his followers on to Low Library, our Pantheon-like administration building, too heavily guarded to be invaded, then across Amsterdam Avenue to Morningside Park and its new gym site, one of the precipitating causes of the unrest. On our way, a young woman in a miniscule skirt just in front of me began screaming slogans and I told her—did I shout?—to pipe down. Shortly after, squeezed up against a construction fence, I was approached by a policeman with a clipboard who wrote down my name and address and told me that I'd be hauled in on an assault charge. She must have changed her mind, for I was not arrested. A couple of days later, after she and others had occupied the President's office, the *Times* ran a photo of her in the window—still in the same skirt. She was a Barnard undergraduate, said to be the daughter of the Chief of Protocol in the White House.

In short order, some five buildings were occupied by 800 protestors. Those teachers and professors who were not on strike taught the few willing students on the lawn or in their apartments. Mostly white protestors occupied Hamilton Hall, the main Columbia College building, and took Dean Henry Coleman hostage. Shortly thereafter, the whites were ejected by Black activists from nearby Harlem and all over NYC—with guns, it was rumored. I found myself one of the half dozen members of Dean Coleman's committee parleying with the Black leaders holding out in a room across the hall. As I remember, we didn't settle very much, if anything; mostly each group kept to itself. At some point I left to go to the men's room in the basement but was quickly stopped by a huge man standing guard over us. He announced that I couldn't go by myself, so, like an ill-assorted father and son, we trotted off to the men's room and adjoining urinals, both of us more amused than talkative.

From the third day of the crisis on, an Ad Hoc Committee of concerned professors met in almost constant session receiving bulletins from the front and wringing their hands. It was decided that volunteers should form a constant cordon of bodies on the yard-wide base of the sides of Low under the windows of the president' office, in order to help those of the 75 who wished to climb out and to prevent others from climbing in. A professor of chemistry was appointed to be in charge of the recruitment and deployment of the troops.

It was my friendly neighbor, David Truman, who suggested to the Ad Hoc Committee that I share the command of the motley professorial cordon; he had been a popular College Dean and now, as Vice President, he was the only member of the administration to inspire any confidence in the contending groups. He confided to me one morning over coffee that he had two or three times dissuaded President Kirk from unwise actions by threatening to resign. I rather enjoyed the irony of standing guard half-time at all hours—once or twice until 2 am—as a once-upon-a-time would-be conscientious objector. But we were, after all, trying to be peace-makers, although at times we were anxious that we might be overcome by a large group of SDS invaders. A few days after our duty began, my colleague failed to appear and I learned that he had collapsed from nervous exhaustion and been taken to the hospital.

I cannot even today enter the President's office without remembering the several times when I lifted out and down the large bags of SDS garbage from the upper window to the ground—and was then thanked profusely for my trouble.

Some time later when things had become more tense, I was called while on duty by Truman. Did I realize that those standing about, seemingly idly, were plain-clothes-policemen? Should we be in danger of being rushed by a large troop of SDS, I should alert them, who were empowered to call in the hundreds of NY police who were at the ready. I told him that I certainly would not be the one to call in the police, something that had been threatened and feared from the beginning. If he would put an extension phone on the first floor window ledge and there were a threat, I would phone him to say so. Then he could do what *he* wished to do.

Near the end of April, with great relief and without much guilt I left, more or less AWOL. I flew to Indianapolis to hear its Symphony rehearse and give the first American performance of my *Transformations*. On May 1, the Hoosier papers were full of news about "The Bust at Columbia," which had taken place a day earlier, to the effect that the police had been called in to clear the buildings of Commies and Blacks. When I returned the next day, the *Times* was more temperate and factual: there were 712 arrested, 148 injured.

As a reaction to the police action, thousands of students went on strike and classes were cancelled. For a couple of weeks the neighborhood was only slightly more quiet: local activists seized Columbia-owned apartment buildings; Hamilton Hall was re-occupied and fires broke out in two other buildings, with 138 arrested, half of them suspended.

One day a number of us went downstairs from the Department to a packed McMillin Theatre to an SDS meeting because we had heard—but hardly believed—that Harvey Sollberger and Charles Wuorinen were to perform there the Pierre Boulez *Sonatine* for flute and piano. When the unruly audience quieted, the performers were introduced and it was announced that we were to hear an example of music of the future, when the new democratic society would have prevailed. The briefly attentive audience soon lost patience with the piece, the quiet sections of which were obliterated with hisses and catcalls and the outbursts of which were greeted with whoops and hollers.

I attended the makeshift Commencement held for safety in the Cathedral of St. John the Divine at which the historian Richard Hofstadter spoke eloquently, in lieu of President Kirk. At the counter-commencement held in the open on campus a crowd of a thousand listened to Dwight Macdonald and Harold Taylor and the psychoanalyst Erich Fromm, who quoted Nietsche: "There are times when anyone who does not lose his mind has no mind to lose."

*   *   *   *   *   *

And so, finally, in this highly unacademic fashion the academic year came to its end. On June 5 a far less ambiguous graduation ceremony took place at the Collegiate School, founded in 1687, the oldest school in New York. With Christopher newly graduated from high school, the four of us and Rorschach left for Shelter Island and Hightowers, where, in my third floor aerie, I could return to my *Highlands*.

Back near the beginning of that academic year, on September 18, the pencil sketch of all the words and music of *Highlands* was complete after 18 months of writing and rewriting. I informed Peter Adler and Kirk Browning that their opera could be performed in two or three acts and that it would play about an hour and forty minutes.

Hardly had I begun arranging the sketch of *Highlands* into a playable, neatly inked, vocal score—as usual making revisions as I went along—when I was asked yet again to be the rehearsal pianist for *Lizzie Borden*, for its revival by the NYCO to take place this time at Lincoln Center. In the bowels of the State Theatre I coached two new cast members and re-coached the old ones, all of us using the recently beautifully published vocal score. In almost a month, including the re-staging rehearsals, I put in 63 exciting, if unpaid, hours on the piano bench, including the piano-dress-rehearsal, stashed away in the pit with the new conductor, Franco Patanè.

After my immersion in the *Lizzie* piano score—and the excitements of the performances—I returned as often as I could to the making of the new one. I marveled at the differences between my fourth and fifth scores, *Lizzie* and

Highlands: the elaborate textures and seas of chromatics brought on by the tortured Bordens and the thinner and plainer textures, the more sunny, tuney, and tonal nature of the latter, to be scored for only 18 instruments, not 50 or 60, after all.

Given the already recounted difficulties of the year in the Department, between it and the emerging Arts Music Division, and later the all-University troubles, it was fortunate that the task at hand was easily interruptible—and unfortunate that it progressed so slowly. But Commencement promised a steady daily stream of pages.

As, act by act, the score came into being, copies were sent to Adler and Browning inviting their questions and suggestions; though the performance date was far from fixed, they could now consider who could be cast in the several highly idiosyncratic roles.

In August I simplified achieving the over-all goal of having a piano-vocal score and an orchestral score without the notational conflicts that often exist in such pairs, by writing out both more or less at the same time. My large built-in work space in Hightowers gave me both the idea and space for the experiment. Because the orchestral parts were to be copied out in Rome by my two one-eyed Carnevalis and there would be much to-ing and fro-ing by airmail for proofing and correcting, it was in any case best to begin the orchestral score early.

For the rest of the summer, work on the two scores proceeded pleasurably and fruitfully in tandem, broken only by sailing and yard work shared by father and son. Then, with Christopher off to the University of Rochester for his freshman year and me on my campus as a first-year chairman, the *Highlands* pace slowed considerably. Because chairmen of the humanities departments taught only two classes a term, not the usual three, it was possible to arrange my other appointments more conveniently than before. Unfortunately, though, I was elected to the first University Senate and then stuck with its Rules Committee, which was assigned the almost impossible task of codifying the rules of behavior for everybody on campus. After months of discussion they were finally in place, to be broken, on and off, for the duration of the Vietnam War. Then, by fiat from Low Library, all departments were for the first time to set up their own rules of organization, subject to their acceptance by the administration, which finally accepted ours.

Notwithstanding these and other uptown and downtown commitments during 1968-69, the two scores were completed almost at the same time on Easter Sunday. As remarked earlier, I sometimes make an effort to complete a large work on a holiday, as I did on this occasion. But that the scores had been 18 months and 18 days in the making I discovered only after Easter had been chosen—if, indeed I chose it, and "some occult power, a remarkably calendrical subconscious, or some benign coincidence" was not responsible.

Whatever the answer to the "problem of the eighteens" may be, the manuscript pages were very real and numerous. The inked piano-vocal score ran to 216 pages. (When Boosey and Hawkes published it there were 285 pages and the volume was granted a Paul Revere Award for typographical excellence.) The orchestral score in two volumes numbered 538 pages. The beautifully copied extracted orchestral parts had been arriving in batches for months and continued to do so into August. The total price in lire, 486,660, looked as unreal as the sequence of eighteens, but at 620 lire to the dollar the 572 handsome pages had cost less than 800 dollars.

When all these many parts pages had been checked and re-checked, there remained only the duplication of them and the scores and then the composer-librettist's work would be completed. Life in the city during the new year of 1969-70 was to be the mixture as before, diluted with weekends on Shelter Island, sailing Mnemosyne to Greenport and laying her up for the winter.

Downtown near the Columbus Circle in what had been the Henry Hudson Hotel were the offices of NET Opera, to which I delivered the great pile of *Highlands* material and to which I was soon summoned by Peter Adler and Kirk Browning. The good news was that the opera would go into rehearsal in New York for three weeks in November and then be filmed in a week or so at WGBH in Boston thereafter—much the same schedule that had been followed with *Lizzie* four years earlier. The disappointing news was that on television hour and half-hour units are inviolable; *Lizzie* had fitted perfectly into two hours; my estimated time for *Highlands* was an hour and forty minutes; there would have to be cuts to fit the playing time into ninety minutes. I acquiesced—at the last minute writing and scoring, and copying out parts for accompaniment to the credits.

I was asked to return to record my playing and singing of the opera so that they could check its timing, tempi, and its style. Because I had heard Douglas Moore and others give such bizarre and often amusing performances, I agreed, provided they'd not play the tape to entertain their friends. After I'd gotten the notes back into my fingers—if not into my voice—I returned for my "performance." When I came to a passage of spoken dialogue I turned to ask if I should speak all the lines. "Yes, of course." When I had recorded the whole opera I was thanked excessively and as I left to find a drinking fountain they were muttering together. When I returned Peter said that Julius Rudel claimed he had seen me act; could that be true? "Yes," I answered, "some Shakespeare." Kirk complimented me on my line-readings and said I wouldn't do in the brief spoken role of the Real Estate Agent, but if I agreed, I could be cast as the Young Man who had spoken lines in two scenes; AGMA, the singers' union, would permit a non-member one service. I accepted before he had a chance to change his mind.

With that minor part just cast, I asked whether they had succeeded in signing on two of my obvious suggestions: the Armenian-American, Lili Chookasian, the usual Erda at the Met, and Spiro Malas, everybody's favorite Osmin, he with the lowD, as the grocer Mr. Kosak. Both had been cast. As the eccentric poet and father there would be Alan Crofoot; the huge, overweight Canadian tenor would be at least as appropriate as he was as Salome's stepfather, Herod. And as Johnny, the son, there would be Gerard Harrington III, a 13 year old soloist and member of the Met Children's Chorus.

Because for once I would not be playing staging rehearsals and only occasionally coaching principals, it was not necessary to attend all the three weeks of daily 6-hour rehearsals and I could juggle uptown and downtown commitments. At the first I attended I met the principals and those playing secondary roles, all of whom lived up to or surpassed the NET Opera's high reputation for excellent singing and diction and embodying their roles to the life.

Early on, I met Rhoda Levine, a former dancer who was assisting Kirk in choreographing movement and who was introduced to me as my wife. She hastened to explain that she'd had to accept the assignment as the Young Wife, but because she planned a career as a stage director she didn't want such a small walk-on-carrying-a-baby role on her resume and would use a pseudonym, Dhora Nevile, for Rhoda Levine. She was surprised that the opera's composer had been offered the part of the Young Husband and astonished that I'd accepted it. I must use a pseudonym as the actor, she said. Thinking fast, I pointed out that if I used an anagram, as she planned to do, Kacj Noseeb would sound Turkish and wouldn't do at all in a partly Armenian opera. Besides, I added, there would be about 170 stations telecasting an opera with new music and most television critics would be hard up for something to write about. Having a composer in the cast would give them a "handle," as they call it. I turned out to be correct: nobody even mentioned my acting ability—or lack of it—or my suitability in the small spoken role, but the rare example of a composer in his own opera was always mentioned, given headline notice, or even a picture in costume. One learned critic opined that such a thing had not taken place since the 17th century, when Lully had danced in one of his own works.

Rhoda introduced me to the cover (understudy) for the part of Johnny, of similar age and build to Gerard. He was sitting alone in a corner of the rehearsal room writing music, seemingly deaf to what was being played and sung in the hall. When I asked what it was, he answered that he, too, was writing an opera! He kept at it throughout the rehearsal period, for Gerard remained in good health, incapable of forgetting a line or making a musical mistake. I happened never to have a chance to hear Timmy Lloyd sing; he came by his operatic interest naturally, for his father was a leading tenor in the New York City Opera and in charge of the Lake George Summer Opera Company. Timmy enjoyed a performance of his three-act opera *The Witch Boy* somewhere downtown when he was only 24 years old and died the same year. One can't know what was lost.

Eldon Elder was engaged to design the sets and costumes. (One of his designs is on the cover of the published score.) We had met when as a young designer he had worked on a Columbia opera production at Brander Matthews. He invited me to his studio to renew our acquaintance, to see the set designs and the water-color sketch of my costume as a cowboy hippie. He told me to let my hair grow and that it would take but little make-up to make me believable, which I took as a compliment. (I would be 48 when on camera.) I was to have a cowboy hat, boots and bracelets. And I was to make an appointment with the costumer Barbara Matera to be measured for the jacket and pants and to be outfitted with the rest of it.

Her workshop was in the middle of the theatre district, but she was elegant and greeted me with a ripe British accent. She and an associate were sorting through a pile of dark suiting swatches; she interrupted to summon someone to take my measurements. A young man entered, took me over to the window where there was light and began asking questions.

YM: This your first time here?

JB: Yes.

YM: Your hat size?

JB: 6 7/8.

YM: Shirt?

JB: Neck, 14 ½ inches.

YM: Shoe size?

JB: 6 1/2, I think. I'm not sure.

YM: Width?

JB: I don't remember. Narrow?

YM: Glove size?

JB: I've no idea. I don't wear them in this show, anyhow.

YM: We need all this info for when you come the next time.

JB: I won't be back, I'm sure.

YM: Oh? Sorry!

[With that, he took out his tape measure and spent an unnecessarily long time measuring my waist and the inseam of my trousers. Finally he released me and as I was leaving I stopped by Matera and her associate, still trying to choose the right swatch from the pile.]

JB: You realize that the old man wearing the suit was once an actor and that it was probably of good cloth and fashionable cut. He's now in an old people's home, has worn it for decades, and now it's shiny and frayed—maybe torn?

Barbara Matera: Are you sure? How do *you* know?

JB: He's in my opera; I wrote the music.

BM: Oh, dear. I'm sorry! It's so seldom we take the measurements of composers!

*   *   *   *   *   *

During the rehearsal period, which passed without incident, I wrote a *pro forma* letter to the provost asking for a week's leave for the December filming in Boston. The reason was so unacademic and I had come to know Jacques Barzun so well that I hazarded "Dear JB" as the salutation and "Cordially, JB" in closing. An informal message of "OK JB" was the response.

At the WGBH studios, when I was not being rehearsed, I could listen to and watch the others and the two pianist-assistant conductors, Martin Smith and John DeMain, transferring cues to the singers from the TV monitors while hiding from the cameras, as I had done during the *Lizzie* filming. There was the same Adler-Browning system of the "sets and singers studio" and the "orchestra studio" linked in both directions by speakers and monitors. I could watch and listen to the orchestra, or sit in one of the few banked seats of the control room and observe a busy Kirk keeping track of what the cameras were seeing—or ought to be seeing—and literally calling the shots to the engineers nearby.

This filming process was so riveting that I phoned Nora to come and share it with me. She arrived on a day when we were rehearsing in costume. I was in the control room with my hat and make-up still on when she arrived and sat down beside me. Almost half an hour later she realized that the cowboy hippie next to her was her husband.

There were two physiological events. The excellent, if high-strung, lyric baritone, Robert Shiesley, in the small but important role of the Young Man from the Old People's Home, is to knock on the door and be terrified, shouted at by the angry old actor whom he's come to take back with him; the pretense is that MacGregor is needed there to play King Lear. Shiesley was so terrified by the prospect of being on camera that he ran out and vomited. He returned, just on cue, so pale and upset that his scene was perfectly done in one take.

The size and shape of our tenor were such that he suffered from severe back pain for which he usually took muscle relaxants. When on a singing engagement he dared not to do so for fear of relaxing his throat muscles. In rehearsal he sang the "Fire B♮" perfectly; in the filming of the scene his voice cracked on the note. Had he broken his rule and taken a pill? A day or so later, at the end of our filming, he repeated the phrase two or three times and the perfect high note was spliced in equally perfectly. Since then I've not written a high B for any tenor of any size!

One of the great problems of televised opera had always been the poor sound of the voices and the orchestra caused by the deficiencies in the outgoing signal and the receiving television sets and their speakers. With the expenditure of a great deal of ingenuity, time, and money, NET Opera succeeded in improving the sound quality of televised opera for the first time in its production of *Highlands*.

In the control booth at all times was Richard Mohr, on loan from RCA Records, supervising the recording on 16-track tape, of which seven sound tracks were Dolbyized, others used for editing and synchronizing with the video. The recorded stereo sound was equivalent to that of an RCA recording; it could be enjoyed by those listeners by turning down the volume on their television sets and tuning their radios to the local FM "good music station" if there was one; the telecast and broadcast were exactly synchronized, insuring both first-class video and audio.

Already at the beginning of the rehearsals I was told by David Griffiths, the associate producer of the opera, that NET would film a half-hour teaser to be shown on the network some days before the opera's telecast. Would I please find out from Saroyan if he would come to New York to be filmed with me and Peter Adler; there would be a $250 honorarium and all his expenses paid. For once, Bill was in Fresno and answered my letter with all its news of our opera and the request from David. Bill was not coming to New York to see the rerival of *The Time of Your Life*, but would I send him "articles, letters, or even ads" about the production. As to the projected half-hour teaser, "I never take up free transportation and lodging offers. It's free here, too, that is."

Because the editing of the new and extremely complicated inter-related video and audio tapes would require weeks of work, there was sufficient time for Griffiths and Adler to trace Bill's always changing whereabouts and to entreat him by phone and exceedingly long letters to cooperate in making the show. When he was found he remained obdurate, I was hauled in to try again and did so, also at length.

He wrote to Griffiths in early February agreeing to come later in the month to be shown the opera and thereafter to participate in the talk-show. His letter was a splendid example of incendiary writing by a seemingly abused and underpaid author " . . . but there it is, show business again, phone calls, urgency, schedules, and all the rest of the shenanigans of the Busy Spenders of the Public Money, or the Private, even—and then we got it by the standard traditional secretarial telephonic persistent nagging. —Well, now what opera is that? That's the real opera that doesn't tend to lend itself to lyric tenor arias . . ."

Put off by reading his letter to David, I didn't look forward to meeting Bill for the very first time, after years of friendly correspondence and phone calls. But we watched together the screening of the still not completely edited videotape and he could not have been kinder or more complimentary. The filming of our three-way conversation—illustrated with short clips of the opera spliced in later—showed us all in high good humor. He and I were then invited to lunch by Peter, Kirk, and David Griffiths. David had earlier taken me aside to say that the standard NET honorarium for talk-show guests was $250. "Because Saroyan had refused to come for less than expenses and $500, would I . . ." He was too embarrassed to finish the sentence. Over after-lunch coffee David handed Bill and me our checks. Without comment I wrote on mine "Make payable to William Saroyan" and gave it to Bill, who took it without a word, smile or expression of thanks.

Nevertheless, while he was in town, Nora and I invited him and Sarah Moore to dinner with us and Miranda. Though we three could be talkative on occasion, Bill monopolized the conversation all evening with one story after another, each so shapely that it could have been written, published, memorized, and then spoken. One, about a fly, went on for some twenty minutes, always engrossing and amusing.

Saroyan liked to direct his own plays, though he was rarely given a chance to do so. He would have produced them too, as I suspected when he called me one morning and asked me to accompany him for the afternoon, traipsing around the theatre district. We must have visited a dozen theatres to find one he thought best suited for a production of his *The Cave Dwellers*, a kind of predecessor of *Follies*. He asked me to stay on and have dinner with him in a favored Armenian restaurant. When he asked our waiter for the check, it had already been paid by an attractive middle-aged woman across the room—whom he seemed, or pretended, not to know.

Years later we met for the last time unexpectedly, in a restroom, before a members meeting at the American Academy of Arts and Letters and then remained together for the meeting, drinks, and dinner. That he seemed subdued was not surprising, for he was suffering from prostrate cancer that he had refused to have treated. His pronounced deafness caused trouble, for whatever was said during the meeting or to him later, he asked me—in an unnaturally booming voice—to repeat.

Only occasionally during our long acquaintance did he seem as Saroyanesque as I would have expected during my teenage and early-twenties years when I was enraptured by his short stories and early plays. At other times his personality seemed mis-shaped, as though in a series of funhouse mirrors. How else to explain his announcement to the press late in life that he had cancer of the heart, disinherited his two children, and left his copyrights to the William Saroyan Foundation to promote his writings after his death?

When editing of video and audio and the complicated scheduling of paired performances by television and broadcasting stations were finally completed, some pairs premiered *Highlands* on March 17, 1970. The New York pair premiered it on the next day, the last of the eighteens and the fourth anniversary of the first one, when my pencil wrote the first notes of the opera. The teaser talk-show had already been shown and with the new system of simulcasting in place many stations repeated the opera. As time passed and simulcasting became common, this process took less time and effort.

Because of the wide advance press coverage and the mostly positive critical reception of the opera, its cast, and the improved sound quality—there are 116 clippings of all sizes in my scrapbooks—it is not surprising that there was interest in a first staged production. Julius Rudel was musical director of the Caramoor Music Festival and had long since seen the score, asked me to play and sing parts of it for him, and hoped to produce it in the summer after its telecast. The death of Lucie Bigelow Rosen, however and patroness of the Festival made it impossible. However, Julius attended an early screening of *Highlands*, was enthusiastic and said he would do it at the New York City Opera. He was surprised—as was I—when I responded that my chamber opera, with its slender plot and a part for a child much longer than Amahl's—and two other children—

would be lost in the too-large State Theatre. We argued about it and, for better or worse, I turned down the highly tempting and well intentioned offer.

Peter Mennin, my Eastman classmate, was now president of the Juilliard School and promised to produce it the following season, but died during the summer and his successor had other repertory plans.

There was also the hope that it would be performed at the Lake George Summer Opera with its director David Lloyd singing the poet-father and his son playing his son. The hoped-for Ford Foundation funding was not forthcoming and the production could not be postponed a year because Timmy's voice was about to change.

This short list of non-productions is included because these five examples suggest a few of the odds against which an opera composer and his producers contend: unexpected deaths, insufficient funding, an unsuitable theatre, and puberty. In the case of *Highlands* the composer and his producers were of one mind and equally beset: more often the composer, for a host of other reasons, cannot find a producer for his work. Indeed, after the flurry of activity in the wake of the premiere's hullabaloo, years passed before the Center for Contemporary Opera produced *Highlands* in its staged premiere, as the first theatre production in the newly rebuilt Miller Theatre on the Columbia campus.

*　　　*　　　*　　　*　　　*　　　*

Chapter 11

Tempers and Tantrums in the Department

Captain Jinks of the Horse Marines
(1968-1975)

After four years in the highlands I descend briefly to the lowlands and to the Morningside Heights Campus of Columbia University. To be sure, I had never left Hightowers on Shelter Island or Riverside Drive in Morningside Heights to spend time among the displaced Armenians and the elderly Highlander except by traveling to them as often as possible by means of pencil and pen. The first two years of this four-year span had been filled with uptown and downtown commitments, the former accompanied ever more often by noisy, mostly anti-Vietnam War demonstrations that climaxed in "The Bust" in late spring, 1968. Taking over as chairman of the Department on July 1 could not have occurred at a worse time, for in the wake of that violence and during the continuing war everybody became quarrelsome; a disagreement that once would have led to a discussion now provoked an argument and flushed faces.

Such contentiousness continued throughout the last two years of the *Highlands* four and then into 1970-71, the last of my three-year tenure as chairman. It certainly played a part in the Wuorinen affair that erupted in the spring of that year and involved many issues: personal, interpersonal, departmental, and University. These were so entangled with varied opinions about the new-music scene of the time that not only composers and composer-teachers, but also music critics of the daily press and national magazines entered the fracas at its height. Today it is remembered and misremembered by few, but the subject-matter, the plotlines, and the characters of the drama are not outdated.

Charles Wuorinen was born in 1938 into Columbia, for his Finnish-American father was both a professor in and long-term chairman of the History Department. In 1953 Willard Rhodes talked me into accepting Charlie as a private beginning composition student, the first of only three I've agreed to teach outside the university. He came to our first meeting with a thick ring-binder of choral settings of the psalms. After some months I sent him off to Ussachevsky for counterpoint lessons.

He enrolled in Columbia College as a music major, as a professor's son tuition-free. Because he entered with advanced standing and was very clear about his goals, as his advisor I approved his very special curricular wishes, remembering the somewhat similar circumstances in which latitude had been shown me by the principal of Central High in Muncie. In doing so, I was reproved by Bill Mitchell, our theory man. I responded that because of Charlie's obvious talents and accomplishments he merited the exceptions. At one point, when Ussachevsky and I sensed that Charlie's musical activities were causing tensions at home, we invited the somewhat square father-professor to lunch to assure him that to become a musician—even a composer—was perfectly honorable and, given his extra-curricular studies, an occasional B+ or even a B- was not dishonorable.

Parenthetically, I mention the coincidence that John Corigliano, also born in 1938, was a music-major classmate of Wuorinen. His father, too, was a man of consequence, the long-time concertmaster of the New York Philharmonic. They were as different from one another in those days as they have been as mature composers, alike only in their strongly held opinions and attacks on opposed points of view.

By the time Charles had earned his BA and MA and dipped into the DMA, he had for two years been a member of my composition seminars. He, as did most of the graduate students, began teaching with a section of Music Humanities. Though the instructors were free to present the music of the past and present in their own ways, they were to follow chronologically the styles and composers as scheduled in the parallel listening sessions. Charlie managed the late eighteenth century without a note of Mozart's music or without mentioning his name. When a number of the more alert students complained to Bill Mitchell of their dissatisfaction with their instructor's explanation—if, indeed, he had offered one—Bill questioned Charlie. His answer was touching, if unconvincing to Bill: when he compared the amount and quality of music that Mozart had written at his age, he found it impossible to speak of the man and his music to his class.

A similar solipsistic attitude was clear at CRI Board meetings (Composers Recordings Inc.), where he spoke little or at length. On one occasion he objected to the presence of three jurors on the Editorial Committee, who determined what works would be issued by the company; there should be, instead, a committee of one, to insure quality and a CRI identity; he volunteered to serve in that capacity. Instead of listening to the discussion that followed, he left abruptly. A short time later he dropped into my office to say that he had decided that he was not really a "committee person." He asked if I agreed. I did.

In '62-'63 he organized the Group for Contemporary Music, on the impressive concerts of which he often appeared as a pianist and conductor and for which he in the main chose the repertory. The Group received annual grants for years from the Ditson Fund, even after Charlie left the university; he, too, benefited from it on occasion, as he did also from grants to CRI to release recordings of his music. During the passing years, his fertile composition of highly personal, even idiosyncratic, works, often difficult to perform and for some to understand, aroused widespread interest, climaxing in the Pulitzer Prize for Music in 1970.

When the time came for the Executive Committee, the tenured professors, to survey the status of assistant professors, who could serve six years in that rank before being promoted to tenure or leaving, there were four in the fields of composition and theory nearing their limit, including Wuorinen, with two years remaining. With the rapidly increasing number of graduate composition students, at least one other tenured composer was sorely needed, as I tirelessly repeated to the dean, but new tenured professorships were not being made at the time for financial reasons; fund raising was suffering in the wake of the '68 events.

Early in the spring three composers nearing their "up-or-out" dates, without speaking to any of their elders but Ussachevsky, devised a plan for reorganizing the teaching of music at Columbia and sent it to President McGill, with carbons to three deans, and to Ussachevsky, Chou, and me. Their plan envisaged moving all undergraduate and graduate composition and theory teaching to the School of the Arts, leaving everything else in the Department, including, of course the twenty-some sections of Music Humanities and its General Studies equivalent, which provided the basis for graduate fellowships. Their goal was clear, but there were no means toward their end. The cause of the tenure problem was financial and the Arts School had far less access to funds than did the Department and few professorships of its own. The asserted dichotomy between composition and musicology—assigning theory arbitrarily to the former—was decades old, not special to Columbia (where they'd recently been getting along) and not to be overcome by segregation. Four days later a petition to the same effect but differently worded and signed by 32 students was sent to McGill.

In the wake of these letters my tenured colleagues were in favor of considering Wuorinen's future in the Department a year earlier than necessary. As Chairman I tried to remain even-handed in the animated and peevish discussions that ensued. When driven finally to reveal my thoughts on the matter, I said, evenly, "I'm not sure we would be prepared to take on as a colleague until his age of 65 or 68 a thirty-three year old Berlioz or Beethoven." A motion that I inform

Wuorinen that he would not be promoted to tenure two years hence was passed. Because the Chairman voted only to break ties, my vote was not needed.

During this trying period Charlie and I spoke in private several times. One exchange sticks in the memory. I asked why he would want tenure and long-term presence in a department that was so full of, as he had called them, "ass-holes." He responded that he had not asked for tenure.

News that a department had voted to terminate after two more years the services of a recent Pulitzer Prize winner reached President McGill, who asked to vet my letter to Wuorinen; I was soon thereafter asked by him to vet his answers to those who wrote objecting to the administration's and department's action.

Charlie's response to my letter was to resign.

Thereafter, in a lengthy phone conversation with me he disclosed that he was writing a substantial letter to the *Times* decrying Columbia's and the Ivy League's lack of support of the arts and their creators, particularly composers. Toward the end of our talk I invited him to take over in the following year, as a part-timer, a graduate seminar in composition. Enclosed with his formal acceptance of my offer was a personal letter expressing his gratitude for my ". . . honor, sincerity, and sympathy . . . and support." His words enabled me to define much of what was spoken and written about the Wuorinen affair over the following months as the flexing of egos and the advertising and selling of personalized points of view about the place of the arts in universities and this or that style of new music.

Wuorinen's essay printed by the *Times* provoked an extensive reply from Paul Lang (who had played no direct part in the tenure vote, having retired a year earlier) and a large number of varied outspoken letters to the *Times.* The last in the series was a rather angry response to the Lang essay by Wuorinen. Not only did the local *Spectator* have its say; the music critics of *New York* and the *New Yorker* expressed their differing opinions, as did those who wrote me letters, all of which had to be answered.

*   *   *   *   *   *

If only to suggest that it is not only composers who can lead to melodramatics in a Department, I relate the tale of Denis Stevens, the eminent musicologist. A compressed account of that long, drawn-out story would be resented by the ghost of Denis, who died recently. An account as long as that of Wuorinen is unwarranted, for no large issues were involved that were of interest to the musical public outside the ivy walls. Mainly it is the sad story of a presumably untreated paranoid schizophrenic. I was alerted to his illness by his fellow Oxonian Alan Tyson, both a highly specialized musicologist and a psychiatrist in charge of the psychiatric supervision of Oxford students. Alan was a visiting professor in our department and warned me that those suffering from the disease can become violent if their paranoia becomes focused on one person as "the enemy." Because Denis strongly objected to composer-chairmen he wrote a letter, copies mailed out wholesale, expressing his intense resentment of my presence. Thereafter I visited him in his apartment to try to gain his confidence with a friendly conversation, which I discovered he was surreptitiously recording. Because of these and other unusual acts, Tyson's warning, and the fact that I passed Denis's nearby apartment twice daily, in a letter to Dean Frankel that enclosed a copy of another poison-pen letter, widely distributed, I included the following paragraph:

> The main purpose of this letter, however, is to inform you of the following: Should Professor Stevens's delusions concerning me become so focused as to result in personal injury to me, I shall—if I am alive—consider the University as accessory before the fact, and —if I am not alive—have assumed that my heirs will share this opinion.

In the wake of the Wuorinen affair and the continuing misbehavior of Stevens there was no one willing to become chairman at the end of my term, which my colleagues assumed would have been the first of the usual two, and which I told them had been my last. This impasse was overcome by compromise:

I agreed to serve another year if *appointed* by Dean Frankel, giving my colleagues time to find a successor.

*　　*　　*　　*　　*　　*

At one of the regular meetings of departmental chairmen, chaired by the President, we were told that HEW (the Department of Health, Education, and Welfare) had decreed that we would be responsible for reporting to a designated University official the gender and ethnicity of each member of our teaching staff. It was rumored that only Columbia and MIT had so far been directed to do so; non-compliance would result in the withdrawal of federal funds. The chairmen could determine the ethnicity either by visual inspection or by questioning individuals, assigning each by name as Black, Asian, American Indian, Hispanic Surnamed, or White or Other. Most of us thought the government's purpose in promoting diversity admirable, but HEW's program absurd and demeaning; we all thought the categorization crazy.

So we did as we were told. It was said that the Chairman of Sociology chose the option of asking his faculty members their ethnicity and reported that they were 60% Black—to the consternation of the administration. Seething, I made by "visual inspection" from my desk.

Because I remembered that my father, when drunk, would say sometimes to Mother, "The trouble with you is that you're part Indian" and—from earlier— that the enlargement of a photo of my youthful maternal grandparents over their bed in Benton, Pennsylvania showed a woman with distinctive Indian features, I began to wonder about my own ethnicity. When I next drove to Stroudsburg to see Mother I asked her about her ancestry for the first time. She said that a ninety year old uncle had always told her that her grandmother had been an Indian. She showed me a tintype of her paternal grandparents from the 1860s that settled the matter for me. Unsettled was whether Francis (sic) Delphine Sutliffe was a full-blooded member of the Susquehannock Tribe, long since dispersed. If so, then I was one-eighth Susquehannock and on the form I wrote American Indian. It is to be remembered that in the early seventies, all kinds of minorities, including gays and lesbians—not to speak of women and Blacks—were parading their otherness. It was not long before I was phoned about my entry, which was considered a bad joke, and asked, "You are what percent Indian?" I replied that we had not been asked to fill in that information and so far as I knew nobody had been asked for it since Germans in the thirties and forties. She repeated angrily, "What percentage?" "I'm not certain, but I'll tell you if and when you have found out what percentage of white blood each of our few Black faculty members have." She hung up on me.

*   *   *   *   *   *

Our first chairman, Edward MacDowell, convinced President Low that there should be a music conservatory at Columbia or that he be permitted to affiliate his department with one, but neither came about then or later. My main uncalled-for task during my unexpected fourth year as chairman was to try to bring about an affiliation with the nearby Manhattan School of Music. I was well acquainted with its practice rooms, rehearsal facilities, and vocal and instrumental faculty, most of which we lacked; I also knew that in order to offer the New York State required academic courses, the School hired as teachers PhD candidates from our campus across the street. I wondered if our use of its facilities and teachers in exchange for Columbia instruction in non-musical subjects could be worked out. I spoke to President McGill—during the recent imbroglio we had become Bill and Jack—of my scheme and he seemed abnormally enthusiastic; he confessed that he had recently tried to *buy* the Manhattan School and its buildable vacant lot, been turned down, and had not even told me or anybody else but his trustees! He gave me carte blanche to pursue my idea, which I confessed had been MacDowell's.

Our School of General Studies provided adults over the age of 21 with a full range of courses that could be taken separately or toward a degree. The G.S. Dean was interested in any plan that would increase his enrollment and assured me that if I could manage such a joint program, he could accept Manhattan students younger than 21. The President and Dean at Manhattan were also approving of a program that would assure their access to course taught by more experienced faculty than PhD candidates.

Following up on these promising conversations implied numerous conferences with interested parties in both institutions. I never passed the G.S. Dean on our campus without his saying, "Jack how's it going?" By the end of the year both boards of trustees had given their agreement in principle and there remained only the tiresome financial and exchange-of-academic-credit arrangements to be worked out.

Howard Shanet was elected as my successor and once he had settled into his chair, I asked how the Columbia-Manhattan arrangements were proceeding. He answered that he was not pursuing the matter because he was afraid he would lose too many members of the University Orchestra. Probably trying to inhibit my irritation and disappointment, I said something like "We musicians all know that young performers when high school seniors—and their parents—are confronted by the choice of continuing their studies in a conservatory or in a college. If, in our joint program there would be those who discover that they have made wrong choices, they can transfer to the other institution, and we shall have done what we're here for—aided them."

My efforts were not all in vain, for Barnard College made a limited arrangement with its near neighbor. In 1989 Columbia College and the Juilliard School collaborated in a comprehensive program in which students enrolled in either could earn a BA, a Bachelor of Music, or both. It was just such a common-sense solution as would have pleased MacDowell, and I wrote letters to all those who brought it about saying so.

Our new chairman, Shanet, was the only tenured performer in the department and as a conductor-chairman soon became the other resident devil in Denis Stevens's imagination. It was he who had the unenviable but necessary task to bringing about the resignation of the tenured Denis just before his threatened dismissal for cause in 1976.

With these pages, mostly concerned with two very different errant colleagues, I conclude what I have to relate about music at Columbia. During the last 21 years of the half century I taught there—and since—nothing comparable has taken place. There are professors with a yen for administration who consider a chairmanship a first step to a deanship and then a presidency. Both my three-year stint and its extension were undertaken without complaint, but somewhat under duress. They confirmed my belief that I preferred the selfishness of practicing my private vice, composing, to serving the local public welfare as a chairman or dean. Twice I scotched talk to my becoming Dean of Columbia College, three times the deanship of the School of the Arts. Nor did I follow up offers to consider becoming the director of the Eastman School of Music or the Rome Academy, or the Vice-president of Indiana University, all of which would have required leaving New York City, which neither Nora nor I would do.

*   *   *   *   *   *

During the last two years of my 4-year stint as Chairman too many unscheduled small and large crises had arisen to permit undertaking another opera project, though I was always on the lookout for the subject of one. Instead, I managed to write ten smaller works, nine of them to bizarre and/or amusing texts. During a recurrence of canonitis there was a set of nine rounds for men's voices called *Everyman's Handyman* (including "To Cure a Kicking Cow" and "How to Revive a Chilled Pig") and a similar set of nine for women's voices called *The Model Housekeeper* that included such useful recipes as "Strawberries as a Dentifrice" and "Plumpening cream for Hollow Cheeks." All were dedicated to various members of the Douglas Moore household. Of the other two single choral pieces and three songs, the scary/funny *To a Sinister Potato* has attracted the most attention, recorded in Europe by an American Black bass, and even semi-staged in New York.

Zelda Goodman, a mezzo soprano from my Eastman days, commissioned and with a first-rate string quartet first performed *A Creole Mystery*, written to fit her expressive talent. I had long since run across a very short story by Lafcadio

Hearn and now adapted it to serve a ten-minute quasi-dramatic scene. The medium was so attractive that I followed up with three longish settings of Peter Viereck poems, the last of which serves as the work's title, *The Day's No Rounder than Its Angles Are*; the faster second song, "The Dance of the Haemophiliacs" usually provokes murmurs from its audience.

The last of these miscellanea was commissioned by the Shelter Island Grove and Camp Meeting, which was celebrating the centenary of its founding in 1872, the era in which such Methodist Chautauquas flourished. The chorale-prelude I wrote for the Shelter Island group was designed to be useful in their services and at first titled, *Prelude and Doxology*. After a series of contrapuntal variations in ever-shorter note values on the hymn, *Praise God from Whom All Blessings Flow*, the piece ends in G major, the usual key of the hymn, which can then be sung while the offering is made and collected. When the piece was written and a fair copy made, I opened my Latouche book to enter the new work's title, date, and other relevancies in the registry to discover that it was number one hundred. With a grin, In changed the title to the hymn's nickname, *Old Hundredth*, and demoted *Prelude and Doxology* to its subtitle.

*   *   *   *   *   *

My interregnum of four years between operas spent as chairman coincided exactly with Christopher's years at the University of Rochester earning his BA. He applied to the Historical Preservation Program of the Columbia Graduate School of Architecture, but lacked the required prerequisite courses and was not admitted. He refused to permit me to intercede with its admissions committee. He was now studying navigation toward applying for a Coast Guard License "to operate and navigate passenger carrying vessels," which he received the following December.

Miranda had chosen nearby Sarah Lawrence College after graduating from the Brearley School and was flourishing as a theatre and dance major. It was an easy drive there and back, as Nora and I did on the evening we attended her first public performance. She followed up on her special interest by attending the summer dance program at Connecticut College in New London. One of the events of the summer was to be the cruise by Christopher and me across Long Island Sound to bring her back to Shelter Island. We had exchanged our sleek *Mnemosyne* for a fiberglass 22-foot sloop equipped with galley, head, and two bunks, and stayed overnight in the New London harbor before taking Miranda on as our passenger.

Nora had been presented with an elegantly boxed, leather-bound presentation copy of the *Guide to the Metropolitan Museum of Art*, which had just been published and for which she had served as author and general editor. Although the Met had existed for a century, there had never before been a comprehensive catalog. With many curators, some of them as difficult and as jealous as opera singers of one another, no one had succeeded in creating such a volume. Her ability to speak the languages of foreign-born curators had made her task easier. Now she was planning to remain in our neighborhood while working on the Columbia Encyclopedia.

And, as for me, seven years had unaccountably passed since our last Roman year and another sabbatical had been earned, 15 months free to work my way well into a sixth opera. I had been rereading *Camino Real* by Tennessee Williams and still found it enchanting and more libretto-like than play-like. For the last couple of years his friendly agent, Audrey Wood, had kept me informed: Tennessee could not be teased or coerced into approving "our" project, hers and mine. My letter to Williams remained unanswered. By chance I made the acquaintance of an admirer of my operas, Andrew Lyndon II, an intimate friend of Williams. He promised to pursue the project with "Tenn" by way of "pillow talk."

Now that the matter had become urgent to me, I discovered that Williams had exchanged Audrey Wood for a young man. As someone in the know said to me, "I prefer the real grade A. Wood to that sapling!" It was tiresome starting all over with the new agent and having to write at length telling him of my years of waiting, enclosing a resumé. He was, in fact, acquainted with *Lizzie* and pleased to attend the screening of *Highlands* I arranged for him, but he arrived very late and then, after the screening, was in a hurry for his next appointment on First Avenue and 49th. I pretended to be headed for that neighborhood in order to have an uninterrupted chat with him in the taxi. His description of "Tenn's" travels around the world and around in his own head resembled Audrey's. He seemed to be in favor of what I wanted to do and promised to try to set up a meeting of the three of us. He phoned later in June to tell me that in a meeting of the two of them, Tenn and he had agreed that of all his plays *Camino* was the one most suitable for operatic setting, nevertheless the answer was No. There were other composers he knew who wanted *Streetcar* and *Glass Menagerie*, but he didn't trust them. He could not accede to me while turning the others down; consequently, only his one-act plays would be available as opera material. If I would wait until the fall, perhaps he could get "Tenn" to relent. I was non-committal to him, but fed up with waiting.

*   *   *   *   *   *

It may be remembered that I was invited to initiate a series of lectures in 2001 to mark the centenary of Verdi's death. My extemporaneous words were recorded, transcribed, and edited, and dealt mainly with two subjects, both related to Verdi and his music. The first was my first opera, *Jonah*, entered in the La Scala international competition for a new opera in 1951, held to mark the semi-centennial of Verdi's death; the retrieval of my signalized score from La Scala led to an amusing adventure recounted earlier.

The other subject was a discussion of my sixth opera, *Captain Jinks of the Horse Marines*, appropriate to the occasion because both its libretto and its music are derived in part from Verdi's *La Traviata*. Because there was a concentration on these parallels, I shall twice interrupt the following publication of the second part of the lecture with two short essays on other aspects of *Jinks*, both originally written to accompany the original-cast recording of the opera.

Extract from *Contemporary Opera Composers on Verdi*

Pierpont Morgan Library, March 30, 2001

. . . I discussed my libretto predicament with John Kander. Since our time together in the Opera Workshop and his year as a graduate composition student of mine he had remained my friend—and had become the successful composer of the Broadway team, Kander and Ebb. He suggested that I should collaborate with Sheldon Harnick, whom I'd long since met casually. I asked why and he answered, "When two people collaborate on a theatre piece, an opera or a musical, they should complement one another. Fred and I are very different; I'm the sentimentalist of the pair. Sheldon is also a sentimentalist and you are . . . well . . . you're not." John, who is familiar with the whole operatic repertory, then mentioned the similar pairing of Strauss and von Hofmannsthal. It did occur to me at the time that my composer-friends might think it odd that I would be hobnobbing with a Broadway star, and that Sheldon's friends might wonder what he was doing with the MacDowell Professor Music, that "uptown composer." My friends would not have known that Sheldon for a while was a professional violinist, played chamber music, or how much I valued his FIORELLO, FIDDLER ON THE ROOF, and SHE LOVES ME. I was—and remain—in favor of librettists who know all about the theatre, as I imagine you are, too, as audience members. Kander told me that the long-time collaboration of Bock & Harnick had come to an end: I would not be intruding.

We were summering in those years on Shelter Island and Sheldon was but a few miles and a ferryboat ride away in East Hampton. After a simple phone call we sat by his pool and began our collaboration. He said that he was not good at making up stories and plots and preferred, therefore, to adapt existing material such as plays. He would, as a first libretto, want to work with a comedy, one with lots of songs or arias. Having already guessed all this, I went over to my car and brought back a copy of CAPTAIN JINKS OF THE HORSE MARINES, by Clyde Fitch, the Broadway hit of 1901, in which Ethel Barrymore had made her debut and then played for all too many decades. Oddly enough, he had read it two weeks earlier, searching for the subject of a musical, cast it aside as unsuitable, but thought it perfect for what we wanted to do together.

HOW DO YOU WRITE A LIBRETTO?
by Sheldon Harnick

My introduction to opera was bewildering. As a 17-year-old violin student in Chicago, I was beginning to expand my musical horizons and decided I was ready to tackle opera. The San Carlo Opera Company was giving *The Barber of Seville*, and, ignorant as I was of operatic literature, even I knew the aria that went "Figaro, Figaro, Figaro!" Since it was to be sung in Italian, I obtained a copy of the libretto, read it through and trotted off to my first opera.

Somehow, by the end of the first act I was sure I had seen the entire opera: I had accounted for every dramatic event in the libretto—and there was still one act to go! I stayed and watched Act II with the miserable feeling of being hopelessly at sea. This experience, regrettably, left me with the conviction that opera was something mysterious and incomprehensible.

Some 25 years later I reluctantly went to see another opera. Julia Migenes, who created the role of Hodel in the Broadway production of *Fiddler on the Roof*, was performing the title role in Menotti's *The Saint of Bleecker Street*. From a mixture of friendship, good will and curiosity, my wife and I went to see how Julia did. I expected to understand little of what I saw. Surprise! It was a stunning evening of musical theater! I had an exciting new image of what opera could be. Soon after that I became a regular operagoer, and soon after *that* I accepted an offer from a composer friend to collaborate on an opera.

Once again I found myself hopelessly at sea. I found that my previous experience writing lyrics hadn't prepared me to write a libretto. The first few pages I handed my composer friend seemed to baffle him completely. He murmured that my approach was "wrong" but was unable to give me a hint as to what approach might have been "right." Stalemate. My friend suggested that perhaps we should drop the project. I wholeheartedly agreed.

Thus, when Jack Beeson called early in the summer of 1972 and asked if I would write an opera with him, I was able to tell him three things: 1) I liked opera; 2) I had seen (and been impressed by) his opera *Lizzie Borden,* and 3) I had tried to write an opera and found I didn't know how. Jack promptly assured me that he would furnish guidance on the construction of the libretto. I hesitantly asked if he had a specific project in mind. He did: Clyde Fitch's turn-of-the-century play, "Captain Jinks of the Horse Marines." I was familiar with the play and knew Jack was not asking me to join him in a venture as formidable as, say *Wozzeck.* "Jinks," as I recalled, was a sunny, free-wheeling, romantic comedy about an opera singer. I felt that (with Jack's help) it might be possible to create an opera from this material that was both amusing and poignant. On my side, I told Jack that the operas I had come to prefer were those liberally sprinkled with arias. I enjoyed hearing beautiful voices singing stirring music.

The first steps were simple enough. One role was eliminated and one major role added. Then we made a scene breakdown, deciding which scenes and locales were valuable and which new ones would have to be invented. We took a close look at all the characters to determine whose roles should be expanded and whose shrunk. We decided which motivations were cogent (for our purposes) and which had to be explored anew. With regard to our leading lady, we made an essential alteration. The heroine . . . as drawn by Clyde Fitch, is a relentlessly coquettish, 18-year-old, an "adorable child," not a woman of any emotional depth. Since we were aiming for a work of some depth and substance we decided that Aurelia would have to be older, more serious, a woman of great emotional range.

Then my problem started. How do you write a libretto? This time I had tried to prepare myself by reading biographies of opera composers and volumes of correspondence between composers and librettists. One thing had become clear; in the majority of cases it was the composer who took the lead; his was the dominant influence in the shaping of the libretto. How many times had I read of Verdi or Puccini or Strauss badgering their librettists with demands for changes, cuts and rewrites? And, I thought, it stands to reason. Without minimizing the importance of a good text, it is apparent that the quality of the music is what ultimately determines the life of an opera. I knew, therefore, that it was my obligation to accommodate my composer in every way I could.

So I sat down to write scene one with a copy of the play in may hand and a feeling of inadequacy in my heart. I brought my first efforts to Jack wondering whether once again my approach would prove indefinably "wrong"; Jack read the pages carefully and, to my intense relief, said, "Not bad for a first draft." Then he explained in some detail what he could use and what he couldn't and why; and why expository passages had to be as succinct as possible; and why (in the stretches between arias) I should try to evolve a style of writing that was neither dialogue nor lyrics but somewhere in between the two, with elements of both, and why—but that's another article. This time I found I could do my job because my composer was articulate about what he needed to do his.

Finally, after three years of discussions and questions (not to mention changes, cuts and rewrites), I find that we have actually written an opera—and one that is both amusing and poignant and liberally sprinkled with arias. And, as I told my wife, I know now how to write a libretto—at least for Jack Beeson.

It is to be kept in mind that the play that is the basis of our opera—the title often to be shortened to *Jinks* hereafter—frequently alludes to *Traviata*; in our opera we have broadened and deepened those allusions to Verdi's opera. *That* opera was also based on a play, that was based on a novel by the same author,, based on his own experiences! *La Traviata* was a failure at its first performance in 1853, largely because the "naughty" subject matter was played in modern dress; once the costumes were changed to an earlier period, the subject matter became acceptable, if still controversial. Our opera is laid in the 1870s, as is the play on which it is based. Our heroine, with six arias, is Aurelia Trentoni, born Johnson in Trenton, New Jersey. Her name-change has no doubt aided her in becoming an important singer in Europe, famous for her Violetta in Verdi's *Traviata*. When the curtain rises on the first act she is arriving in New York on the steamer *The Flying Dutchman* (my idea, obviously). She is met by five reporters eager to get the low-down on her supposed affairs with princes and khedives. As usual, they are confusing her stage role, Violetta, in which she is soon to make her American debut, with her off-stage behavior. A little later, two vice-presidents of the Ladies Anti-French Literature League implore her to make her debut in an oratorio, rather than in *La Traviata*. Her manager, Colonel Mapleson, argues with the reporters. In Clyde Fitch's play Mapleson is only mentioned; Harnick turned him into a major character. Though not at all a colonel, he played a large role in 19th century New York operatic life as the head of the Fourteenth Street Theatre, which at one point almost bankrupted the Met, which, in turn, *did* bankrupt him. Then three well-off young mean appear: Jonathan Jinks meets and is enchanted by Aurelia. He bets one of his friends $1000 that he will make love to her and the third man holds the written note. How the bet turns out, and how the rehearsals and the performance of *Traviata* in the Fourteenth Street Theatre turn out, form the substance of this "romantic comedy in music," as the subtitle of *Jinks* defines the piece.

But, have no fear, I do not plan to follow the slim but complicated plotline, even to mention all the many characters. Rather, I'd like to examine what the two operas, separated in time by more than a century, have in common. I have long believed that different characters and changing dramatic situations in an opera demand different, appropriate vocal and instrumental music. Such an idea Monteverdi put into practice 400 years ago. Those who hold that belief and act on it will also believe that the varied libretti they choose to set, tragedy (domestic or dynastic), comedy (romantic or farcical), or whatever, will require different parts of their musical vocabularies, so to speak. Verdi wrote with such a belief: *Trovatore* and *Traviata* were premiered in the same year. Their musical *grammar*—separate sections of arias, recitatives, ensembles, and orchestra preludes are similar, but Verdi chooses from his musical vocabulary two very different kinds of melody, harmony, rhythm, and instrumental colors. *Jinks* has in common with *Traviata* much of its grammar: it is a "numbers opera," with its many sections amusingly listed on the Contents page. Its musical language is designed to provide a context for the Verdi quotations without undue jarring and to be appropriate for a somewhat stylized romantic comedy.

- - -

...AND WHAT, IF NOT WHO, IS *CAPTAIN JINKS OF THE HORSE MARINES*?

by Jack Beeson

Probably everybody realizes that a lot of time and effort and tempers are lost in finding the right title for a theater piece, one that describes briefly—or at length—what, or whom, the piece is about, one that suggests the style of the piece and tickles the curiosity of the ticket buyers. But the collaborators on an opera (or any musical-theater piece) will invest at least as much thought on the subtitle. What the writers are up to is put down under the title in smaller type on the program and the title page of the printed score, to be left off the posters and flyers and to be put out of mind. A glance at the title page of a dozen "operas" and a dozen "musical comedies" has a jarring effect on one's easy generalizations.

So, what is *Captain Jinks of the Horse Marines?* Is it an opera? Yes, it is, but more specifically it is "A Romantic Comedy in Music."

It is belligerently *romantic* in manner and matter. What, if anything, it has to do with upper-case Romanticism is for others to discover. In its matter it remains faithful to the main plot of Clyde Fitch's hit, placed in time in the early 1870s. In Act I boy meets girl; in Act II he loses her; by the end of Act III they are engaged to be married. A simple enough scheme, to be sure, used often enough (especially in the 19th and early 20th centuries) to prove that it is threadbare or that it has the stuff of life in it, according to taste. But if the plot is simple in essence, one can concentrate on other things. Romantic? It has to do with a romance, and even more romantic is the fact that it is an operatic version of a romance, than which nothing can be more other-worldly, thereby bringing us full circle on a slippery pun to Webster on romance, a definition that works equally well for opera: "A falsehood, especially one showing ingenious or imaginative fancy."

But enough of the adjective *romantic*. Whether it is *comedy* or not remains to be heard. Some of what was comedy in 1901—and might still be in the spoken play; topical allusion and making fun of half a dozen immigrant accents, for instance—we have cut. They make no effect when the matrix is music. Sheldon has kept some of Fitch's funny lines and retained the gist of others; more often he has sought the comic in *relationships* among more fully rounded characters. It is a truism that two of the sources of comedy are exaggeration and, related, the incongruous. There are other sources of comedy, of course, but some are less useful for lyric theater and some disastrous. It is also a truism that the nature of music in the theater is (among other things) to heighten the expressivity of word and gesture. I have relied chiefly on the combining of these two principles in undertaking a comedy in music—oddly enough the most difficult challenge to a composer.

" . . . Comedy *in* Music"—the *in* is intentional and important. Not only does music heighten verbal, gestural and scenic expressivity; as Sheldon implies the shape of the whole and the forward thrust of an act also come from the music, though the dramatic skeleton and verbal surface will have been designed to those ends. Our modest preposition *in* is but a way of aspiring to the original and continuing ideal of opera, *dramma per musica*, drama by, or through, music.

We know the characters of an opera from their words, but we believe them because of what they sing. The music will appear to reflect them, as in an enlarging mirror; rather, as though the music were a magic mirror, it will appear to create them. It follows, therefore, that the music (and the words) for the lovers must be different from the music (and the words) for the entrepreneur Colonel Mapleson; the confidante Mrs. Greenborough; the kindly Italian uncle, Belliarti, and the five Reporters, who are distinguished from top tenor (the august *Times*) down to the bass (the cretin on the tabloid *Clipper*). In part for musical variety and in part for the implied irony, Law and Order—in the persons of the Policeman and the Customs Official—are represented musically by serial procedures based on a 12-tone row. There are numerous other subaural activities. For example, when Mrs. Jinks arrives to break up the liaison . . . the meeting-music of the lovers is played backwards. Contrapuntal goings-on, in fact, abound, as do conscious attempts to find and to insist upon symmetries, important for both musical and comic structures. Act I begins and ends with band music; Act II opens and closes with stagehands busy on the stage-within-a-stage. Between Acts II and III one is to imagine Aurelia making her American debut in *La Traviata* . . . . And our curtain goes down a short act later with the plot untangled, two couples entangled, and the ensemble singing a paean to the power of music, as much for itself as for the audience.

In short, Fitch's play is about an opera singer, but our opera is an opera about an opera, *La Traviata*, in particular, others in passing, and a love letter to Italian opera and the English language. Half-truths are more often true than not; whole-truths rarely so, and one should keep them to himself. Accordingly, I may say that *Jinks* is for singers and opera buffs. Any composer and librettist who provide their leading lady with six arias display a certain liking for singers (some would say a latent sadism), not to speak of arias for the others and ensembles all the way up to a *tredicino*. As is usually the case, if the composer is aiming towards the throat—"the vocal cords set in motion by the heart strings"—the orchestra must play a subordinate role. But a romantic comedy invites restraint, and who would wish to cover the flavor and freshness of Sheldon's text with a rich orchestral sauce?

I address the buffs at their most inclusive: For the high-note specialists there is an F *in alt* for Aurelia, three high Cs for The Times and a two-and-one-half-octave compass in Mapleson's aria; to the specialist in quotation I recommend the dog-walking scene. (The more learned may wish to examine a trichord in retrograde related to The Times.) But the quotations in *Jinks* are not included (with some exceptions) just to be ferreted out, nor are they there out of modishness; the tensions between *Traviata* and *Jinks* are very much related to the intended pathos and humor of the latter, to the "Romantic Comedy" of our subtitle.

In this country there are those who do not approach the operatic repertoire historically, but attend performances as chance wills. For their sakes Sheldon and I have tried to make *Jinks*, at least on the surface level, perfectly comprehensible without a prior knowledge of middle Verdi. And while we welcome the newcomers to opera in the hope that we have at least succeeded in sending them sometime, somewhere, to a *La Traviata*, may we all welcome the Fiddler down from the roof and into the opera house, where everything is as it never was and never, ever, shall be.

- - -

In the Fitch play the second act operas with a ballet rehearsal of the Act I party scene of *Traviata* taking place, incongruously, in a large hotel room. Sheldon and I took that idea and ran with it. In our version it is the afternoon before the evening's *Traviata* performance. The curtain opens on the Fourteenth Street Theatre's stage, bare of scenery except for the pieces of Act I that are being put in place by several noisy stagehands. In addition to the painted drops and pieces of scenery there is a rehearsal piano to the audience left, downstage. Mrs. Gee, Aurelia's accompanist and friend, is at the piano practicing the piano reduction of the dance music played by the stage band in *Traviata I.* What she plays is pure Verdi, except that she occasionally practices the difficult trills, repeats passages, or interrupts to shush the stagehands. Occasionally she sings (in Italian, naturally) phrases given to Violetta and Alfredo by Verdi during the dance scene. Casting Mrs. Gee is not easy, for besides playing piano well, as a contralto she sings an important role.

Shortly after she begins playing, Col. Mapleson enters in a foul mood. As an impresario he must put up with sopranos who are jealous of one another, undependable, pretend to be sick, and, worst: fall in love, marry, and give up singing. He has obviously noticed the developing romance between Aurelia and Jinks. Mapleson's aria is a tour de force for the bass voice, ranging from the low E♭ to the B♭ two and a half octaves higher in the falsetto that he uses to imitate various complaining sopranos. For the first 20 of the 25 pages he is accompanied by Mrs. Gee's playing of Verdi. But the orchestra is also accompanying, discreetly. The instruments pick up, vary, and develop phrases from the Verdi piano-playing and from the newly invented Beeson vocal line set to the words of Sheldon Harnick. Bear in mind that, as I said earlier, I am a composer who believes that both the over-all subject matter of an opera and its differing characters and dramatic events should be strongly characterized by varied, appropriate music. It follows that such a composer will strive to find the appropriate vocal line, instrumental color, and harmonic inflections for the phrases, even the individual words, of the text. But to do so is not easy when there is a tuneful, harmonically simple *cantus firmus* almost always in unclouded A♭ major. Chromatic inflections in the vocal lines could be used to color important words. When words are difficult or impossible to fit into the inexorable Verdi, I could ask Sheldon for an extension here, or a small cut there, or make my own adjustments in timing. For relief from A♭ major I could direct Mrs. Gee to shuffle through her pages while the Colonel and the orchestra digressed. Twice she's directed to leave the piano and to quiet the stagehands; while she's absent, the digression goes on longer and farther. And when she returns the second time, she's forgotten the key signature and plays a few bars up a half-step, in the orchestra's key.

In short, it is possible to combine only slightly tinkered-with Verdi with one's own vocal and instrumental music, a librettist's words, stage action, and noisy stagehands, but it is not easy. To make it *sound* easy, natural, and funny was my aim. This long aria/scene is the most difficult I've ever attempted, and one of the most pleasurable to write.

As already mentioned, both *Traviata* and *Jinks* are Number Operas. Accordingly, in the latter there's now a Love Scene, an Aria for Jinks, a Duet (in which he and Aurelia agree to become engaged), and then an Aria for Aurelia's musician-uncle, Belliarti, in which he wishes the couple happiness in their life together. Then Mrs. Gee enters with 3 or 4 couples of ballet dances and sits down at the piano. Belliarti picks up the violin that has been sitting on the piano since the curtain rose and the dress rehearsal of the *Traviata* Act I begins. It was common in the 1870s for these instruments to accompany dance rehearsals, the violin playing the fast, high notes, and the piano the ¾ pum, pum, pum, in this case.

With the dancers onstage, the duo plays the transcription of the original without pauses or repeats. The orchestra enjoys itself with take-offs from the solo violin's pyrotechnics and with my longer, flowing counterpointed lines. Coming through the clutter of Verdi and Beeson—violin, piano, and orchestra—are the vocal lines sung by Belliarti, Jinks and Aurelia, the Stage Manager, and Aurelia's maid, Mary. The treatment of these lines and the action is similar to Verdi's treatment of the lines sung by Violetta, Alfredo, and Flora against the chorus and orchestra in *Traviata I*. When Belliarti is called away on an emergency, Mrs. Gee takes over the right-hand notes she'd been practicing earlier.

Later, when I played our scene through for Sheldon (called simply Rehearsal in the score) I remarked that I thought it a bit short. I've remembered the gist of his reply because it contains a general truth: "Yes, it is, a bit, as it should be. If a number is just a bit short, the frustrated anticipation of the audience will push it happily into the next scene or number."

As the dancers leave, the stagehands strike the *Traviata I* set pieces and bring in the *Traviata II* garden backdrop and a pergola for painting touch-ups. The scene-change was Sheldon's and my invention, to offer a visual parallel to those I'll be describing. It's now clear that the "emergency" was the unexpected arrival from Virginia of Jinks's mother. Those familiar with *Traviata* will remember the touching scene between Violetta and the elder Germont known to opera professionals as The Germont Père Scene. In that scene Alfredo's father visits Violetta at a villa outside Paris where she is living, unmarried, with Alfredo. Germont implores her to leave Alfredo, whose sister cannot marry if her brother is living in sin.

Clyde Fitch cleverly wrote a Germont *Mère* Scene, as we came to call it. In the Mère Scene of the play and our opera Mrs. Jinks implores Aurelia to give up her plan to marry her son, who will lose his chance at a diplomatic post if he is married to an opera singer—to an actress! Sheldon and I capitalized on the resultant Pirandelloesque parallel: Aurelia realizes that she is in life living the scene she will be acting out that evening. She once quotes an apposite line of Piave in Verdi's setting, in Italian. Because the dramatic conflict between Germont père/Mrs. Jinks and Violetta/Aurelia is all one and the Piave/Fitch/Harnick words express the same sometimes tense interchanges between the two pairs of characters, it is not surprising that the Verdi and Beeson settings show some similarity, though each in his own musical language.

There is one passage in *Jinks* of 35 measures that is pure Verdi, except that a sung passage is played by an instrument. Because Sheldon and I have always agreed that what is important in the theatre should be clearly set forth on the stage, not just written about in the unread program, we had a problem: how to show that our Act III takes place shortly after the end of the evening's performance. Solution (at least for those familiar with *La Traviata*): simply use as our prelude to the act (humorously called Death and Transition) the final bars of *La Traviata*, supposedly as they are taking place in real-time. On the final loud chords, the curtain falls on the performance in The Fourteenth Street Theatre and our curtain rises on preparations for the post-performance party at the Brevoort House, a few blocks away.

There are other allusions and quotations from *Traviata* in *Jinks*. One of the more extensive will be obvious to *Traviata* buffs in Act III when Aurelia puts on a dying Violetta coughing fit to prevent a policeman from arresting Jinks.

In the first act, Aurelia, in order to be alone with Jinks, asks his three opera-buff friends to take her pet dogs for a walk. When she mentions that one of them is named Leonora, they are surprised. "Leonora?" they exclaim together in counterpoint what the footnote duly credits:

Florestan, FIDELIO, Act II
Alvaro, LA FORZA DEL DESTINO, Act III
di Luna, IL TROVATORE, Act I

There must be some among you who have been wondering: how can a living composer so shamelessly and parasitically use the music of a composer now dead for a hundred years? Why doesn't he write his own music? Doesn't he fear having it compared to Verdi's? I could point out to the questioners that I've not been so choosy: in Aurelia's opening aria she remembers her singer-mother's voice by singing her—and my—favorite phrase from "Casta Diva" from Bellini's *Norma*; and she remembers the voice lessons with her Uncle Belliarti by singing at length, only on "a", coloratura exercises by the long since forgotten Francesco Lamperti. The title of the play and the opera is the same as that of a popular 19th century music-hall song that became a favorite in New York. Who ever heard of *its* writers, Leybourne and Marriott? We couldn't very well use their title and not use their words and music.

If I were to be tried in court for having betrayed a composer's duty always to be original, I could plead that of the almost two hours of music in *Jinks* not more than 15 minutes are derived from others' music, most of that counterpointed against my own. Or I could plead that writing an opera about another opera and its heroine is an idea original in itself and invites, forces, one to make use of the parallels between the two.

Ten years after the premiere, the handsome vocal score of the opera was published and reviewed at length in *Notes* by the composer-critic Marshall Bialosky. He proceeds in his own way to provide a précis of what I've been talking about: my nonchalance in quoting Verdi and other "art" composers, my daring to use the popular Captain Jinks song, and whatever else from the past that suited my present purpose. In short, he claimed that *Jinks* was a very early example of musical post-modernism. I'm no great believer in these stylistic isms, but it was nice to read that I was in on the beginnings of a new ism, today much in vogue.

There's one more not quite routine matter that could have become very newsworthy. In writing the part of Aurelia I had in mind a soprano who copes with Acts I and III of *Traviata* equally well. In the sixties, one of the few who could was Beverly Sills. The Director of the New York City Opera at that time was Julius Rudel; we had become friends a decade before at the time of the performances, filming, and recording of *Lizzie Borden*. Rudel asked me . . . to audition *Jinks* for him . . . He seemed to be so unnaturally interested that I asked why. Well, Beverly planned to stop singing at age 50 and wanted a new opera for her last performances. Julius had talked her into singing Aurelia in *Jinks*!

Why she didn't, and why *Jinks* ended up in Kansas City and on RCA is, to me at least, a fascinating back-stage diva story. But I'm in such a talkative mode that I'm afraid I might become indiscreet and shall stop right now!

*   *   *   *   *   *

Whether for the reason that John Kander gave when he suggested that Sheldon Harnick and I should collaborate, or for it and other reasons, we worked together as close friends on three operas for twenty years with only an occasional difference easily resolved and never an argument. There were no agents or lawyers to contend with. As already mentioned we were but a short drive and a pleasant ferry-ride apart during summers; in town, we were both West Siders, he in an apartment on Central Park West with an elevator shared by Beverly Sills.

On rare occasions we drove out to the East End together during summers, our *Jinks* discussions spiced with Sheldon's reports on the progress of *Rex*. I was sharing Sheldon's gifts with Richard Rodgers! Sheldon was not enamored with the subject of their musical, Henry VIII, but he could not turn down the invitation to work with Mr. Rodgers, as he deferentially spoke of him, especially as *Rex* was thought to be his last work. (One more was to follow.) Sheldon regretted, he said to me, that he had not been keeping a log of their collaboration; had he done so, we would have *his* account of his and Rodgers's self-doubts.

Sheldon took even greater care than usual in writing his first lyric for *Rex* before sending it off to his composer. Rodgers was famous for setting the lyrics of Hart and Hammerstein almost instantaneously. As day after day passed without a response from Rodgers, he despaired, certain that he had failed the great man.

Sheldon knew his reputation for being free with the usual shapes of lyrics—something that I encouraged in the *Jinks* aria texts. He wondered: should he have stuck more closely to the usual AABA shape? When the Rodgers office finally phoned to invite him down for a conference, he left fearing the worst.

Rodgers, long ill and hardly able to speak after an operation for throat cancer, greeted Sheldon hastily. Then, nervously, as he passed on his way to the piano, he croaked something like "Let me play this shit for you." Rodgers for some time had come to doubt his ability still to compose. Sheldon was to learn later from Dorothy Rodgers that her husband had tried over and over during several days to set the lyric; during the other days he tried to find the courage to play the song for the lyricist he valued so highly.

When I had the Fitch/Harnick amusing words for the boisterous opening of Act I, I began setting them in sketch on August 18; I did not notice the 18 at the time, nor did I pay attention to the possible significance of March 18, 1973 at the end of the sketch of Act I, seven months later, the seventh anniversary of the first notes of *Highlands* and the third anniversary of its television premiere. It seems unlikely that I was being controlled by some Gaelic gremlin, interested only in Scottish subjects. The newly recurring eighteens were perhaps only coincidences or my overactive calendrical subconscious.

Less mysterious but equally interesting was the origin of the staff paper I began to use on the 18th. A few weeks earlier I received a letter addressed simply to The MacDowell Professor of Music, Columbia University, NY, NY. written by Mrs. Robert Evans of Tacoma, Washington. She wrote that she had been a close friend of a recently deceased Miss Richardson, who for forty years had been the secretary of Marian MacDowell, the very long-lived widow of the composer. Mrs. Evans had come into the possession of MacDowelliana that she wanted to donate to Columbia via its MacDowell Professor. She and her husband were setting out cross-country in their motor home. When and where could we meet? I suggested Claudio's, a fine restaurant in Greenport, just down the hill from Hightowers and near the ferry dock just across the bay.

Mr. and Mrs. Evans proved to be an uncomplicated, well-meaning couple carrying two large cardboard boxes, which, after lunch, we opened. Inside was a foot-high silver presentation cup with the engraved names of his last (1904) Columbia students (now usually on display in the Columbiana Collection), a double page manuscript of an early song (which I've kept, framed, in my studio pending its eventual deposit in the Columbia Rare Books and Manuscript Library), some miscellanea, and some unused music manuscript paper. When we had finished our small-talk and I had expressed my thanks for the University and promised a more formal letter, we parted.

Back in Hightowers, we all examined the gift more carefully. The thick fascicle of music paper was held together with ancient broken twine, which I retied. In doing so I was startled to discover why it had been kept all these years. MacDowell was something of an artist and an expert caricaturist; he insisted on designing the covers of his publications by Breitkopf and Härtel. There, on the last page were color splotches, trial colors presumably, and several versions of "Eight Songs, opus 47, by Edward A. MacDowell." My Grove's Dictionary informed me that the songs were published in 1893, so the paper had been purchased in that year or before. I felt little guilt in inscribing the essence of the above on the first page and then filling all the empty pages with the whole of the sketch of Act I of *Jinks*. The few other blank unbound pages in the trove I used for the sketches of the final number of *Jinks*, "Paean to Music." The Beeson manuscript, "illustrated by MacDowell," will end up also at Columbia.

Sheldon's libretto and its musical setting were finished in mid-August 1974. When we were jinxed—as we joked—in puzzling out our deviations from the play or I was waiting for more words, I worked on the inked vocal score and orchestrated section by section, so that both were completed on my birthday, July 15, 1975. Just three years had passed since we began. Small parts of the orchestra score serve as a travel journal, for during a month-long winter trip to Zürich, through Germany and the Netherlands, and two summer stays in London and out-of-the-way English counties, I dutifully entered the places and dates when pages were scored.

Quite some months before by fifty-fourth birthday I applied to the National Endowment for the Arts for a grant "to complete the opera," which meant to me the completion of the vocal and orchestra scores. The application was successful and covered the expenses of parts extraction and blueprinting. Because I was required to file a report on my work, thereafter to be designated "Commissioned by the NEA"—implying that all the labor had been underwritten—I estimated all the hours that had been spent in writing the piece and divided the total into $5,000, which resulted in a number considerably smaller than the federally imposed minimum wage. I trusted that my irony would be found amusing in Washington.

Perhaps in part because Rudel had been disappointed in my refusal to have *Highlands* performed in his too-large theatre, he was interested in *Jinks* from the time we began work on it. I confessed to him that our Aurelia would require that rare kind of voice that could perform the first and third act of *Traviata* equally well and that therefore the voice of Beverly Sills was my model. He asked me to keep him informed of our progress and when the first act vocal score was completed, he invited me to audition it; while I played and sang, he sight-read the coloratura passages on the upper end of the keyboard. Later, during the audition of Act II, he stopped me. He confessed that he and Beverly had been discussing what work she should perform in her farewell season at the NYCO and that he'd more or less talked her into doing *Jinks*, though she hadn't yet actually studied the score.

Not long after I heard from a friend of her hairdresser that she wouldn't sing a comic opera as her farewell. Too bad, for she was an excellent comedienne!

The hairdresser's gossip was confirmed by Julius himself, who summoned me one Friday to come immediately. He then added what I'd not known: that Beverly had been urging him for years to revive *Lizzie Borden* for her.

JB: "Oh, she wants to do Ellen Faull's part?" (Faull had so far always sung Abbie, the evil stepmother, written for a spinto soprano with coloratura.)

JR: "No, Lizzie herself!"

JB: "But that's for a mezzo!" He shushed me and shut his office door, saying "She's in the outer office . . ."

He added that Beverly considered the Lizzie role a great dramatic challenge and believed the Mad Scene to be one of the finest mad scenes in the repertoire. When he told her that he'd not be responsible for tearing her throat out, she's answered, "It's *my* throat!" Now she refused to do the comic *Jinks* and insisted that he schedule *Lizzie* for her final performances. He had again refused, for the same reason, and she had replied, "But I won't be singing again!"

They had compromised, he said. Jack would be asked to write an opera for her, with mad scenes. Julius offered me a large commission, many performances and pointed to the coffee table on which was the libretto they had chosen for me. Before examining it I told him that I could not supply an evening-filling work in just two years, what with teaching and completing the orchestration of *Jinks* for the Kansas City Lyric, which had accepted it on the rebound from NYCO.

JR: "Well, just take two years off from Columbia and postpone the *Jinks* premiere—after all, it's just Kansas City!:

JB: "But I can't leave Columbia for two years; and KC has to do *Jinks* in September '75 because RCA will record it immediately thereafter, for release on July 4, '76. It's to be RCA's bow to the Bicentennial. Tom Shepard tells me their PR will emphasize its all-American aspect: its composer, part-Indian from Middletown, USA; its librettist from Chicago; based on a 1901 hit that made a star of Ethel Barrymore; and a Midwestern opera company."

Miffed, Julius said I couldn't say no until I'd read the libretto. Over the weekend Nora and I read the material. I was already familiar with the story because for years Douglas Moore and I had spent cocktail hours swapping possible opera subjects and Carlotta and Maximilian had come up occasionally, without arousing our interest. The treatment at hand was by a competent librettist, who had written an NET Opera libretto. It boasted *three* mad scenes: in Washington, where Lincoln was busy with the Civil War, in Vienna, and in the Vatican. I couldn't imagine it as appropriate for our Bicentennial, dealing as it did with keeping a Hapsburg on the throne of Mexico. Nora added that only a Viennese would find it appropriate.

I returned the script on Monday, telling only the bare truth; that I couldn't write the opera in the time allotted. But Gian Carlo Menotti could and did, providing Beverly not only with mad scenes, but also a madwoman, *La Loca.*

During the following holidays at a party at our neighbors on Shelter Island, Harold Schonberg introduced me to Beverly's personal representative, Edgar Vincent. "Oh," he said, "you're the composer who refused to write an opera for Beverly." "No," I said, "I'm the composer who wrote an opera for Beverly that she refused to sing." We took our drinks into an empty room where we could compare our versions of this top-secret backstage gossip.

Indeed, *Jinks* was to be produced by the Kansas City Lyric Theatre in late September, barely two months after its completion. Russell Patterson, who had founded and led the company and conducted most of its performances, had enjoyed the experience of reviving and recording *The Sweet Bye and Bye* just two years earlier and was gloating over—as he put it—having "won out over the NYCO." I knew that the Ford Foundation was underwriting the costs of recording new American works up to a maximum of $15,000; he and I talked Ford into doubling that maximum in support of the RCA recording of an opera two hours in length.

Fortunately, as described earlier, the opera had been scored scene by scene from early on and the instrumental parts could be extracted soon thereafter. Aldo Carnevali, my one-eyed Roman copyist, had died recently; his one-eyed wife had come to New York, married a Russian piano teacher, and was living in the ornate Ansonia Apartments just five stops south on the subway. Her remaining vision was unimpaired and there were no problems in transatlantic packages and dollar-lire exchanges.

The pace of checking parts and score quickened over the summer, enlivened with occasional coaching sessions with the New York-based principals: Bob Jones, my favorite tenor as Jinks and his wife, Carol Wilcox, (formerly of the Met) as Aurelia; Eugene Green, paragon of dialectical characterization, Col. Mapleson; Carolyn James, Mrs. Gee; and Walter Hook, Charlie.

Several of the above and Russell and his chief coach from Kansas City, assembled in Hightowers for several days of intensive music rehearsals. Hightowers was as it had been in its most palmy days as a bed and breakfast, with every room and bed occupied, singers serving as waiters and cooks. The only time off was one trip to a secluded beach where the women and I swam and the burly men waded only up to their knees, all of them having recently seen the movie *Jaws*. The climax of the rehearsals was a partial run-through next door for an audience of Helen and John Lamont, with Russell conducting and me at their fine Steinway.

There is some truth to the comment often made by Douglas Moore, "I'm fully alive only when I'm attending the rehearsals and premiere of one of my operas." I was more than fully alive for a good three weeks for I not only attended rehearsals, but also occasionally coached singers and wielded a baton. I had arrived with the last batch of orchestra parts in my suitcase. Nora and Sheldon arrived for the dress rehearsals; Christopher and Miranda, John Kander (a native of Kansas City and a member of the Lyric's Board), and Douglas's younger daughter, Sarah, arrived for the premiere. There was time to introduce the other Beesons to Jack Edleman, our stage director and choreographer—a decent singer who could sing all the parts in the opera—and Patton Campbell, who had designed the sets and costumes. Pat had been involved with the first production of *Baby Doe*, was on the staff of the New York City Opera and had cannily designed our sets so that they would fit the stage of the State theatre. (I was to alert Rudel that he would be able to rent sets and costumes, rather than build them, and that we had an excellent cast from whom he could take his pick in case he could revive *Jinks*.) After Pat had met Christopher he took me aside and confided that he had never before met a young man who so exactly embodied his idea of Billy Budd. I was to remember his words with a pang eleven months later. I'm afraid that just before the curtain rose I may have been overheard when I whispered to Miranda that "that pubescent critic representing *Opera News*" was sitting just in front of us. The performance went splendidly; after applause, bows, and flowers, there were hugs and kisses backstage, a brief night's sleep, and we all returned to New York, Miranda and I a week late for classes.

I returned for the last performance and the three long recording sessions. RCA had sent its top producer, Jay Sachs, and his staff by air and a truck filled with equipment. The cast, chorus, orchestra, and conductor, buoyed by five sold-out performances, were intent upon doing their best, and did. There was but one unexpected and amusing interruption.

It may be remembered that in our version of *Jinks* the second act opens on the Fourteenth Street Theatre's stage, bare of scenery except for the pieces of *Traviata*, Act I, being put in place by several noisy stagehands. During the performances there had been no problem: the two percussionists left the pit and went backstage, picked up a small and regular hammer and a sledge-hammer and played the rhythms notated in their orchestral parts. A stagehand was cued to begin sawing off a 2x4 piece of lumber and continued until he finished, as instructed. But at the recording session of Act II, Patterson had barely begun when the Musician's Union representative called a halt. He objected that percussionists could not hammer on wood as though they were carpenters. I countered with the observation that there were no recordings of *Das Rheingold* without union percussionists pounding on anvils like blacksmiths. "OK," he said, "but what about that guy with the saw. He's a member of the Stagehand's Union, not the Musician's Union. He can't be recorded, especially on RCA." I made some ridiculous statement about the sawing-sound being important to the over-all artistic message, but he didn't buy it: "Just cut it!" Then I remembered that I'd been permitted to act in my own opera on NET because non-AGMA members were permitted one "service." Taking a chance, I asserted that as a non-member of the Musician's Union I was permitted one "service" and that I'd be the sawyer. I got away with it, bringing the long argument to a close—it had been much enjoyed by the orchestra, paid on the high recording scale—and becoming the only composer-sawyer on a recording.[1]

During the eight-month wait for the recording's release on July 4, 1976—with 80 radio-plays scheduled for that Bicentennial date—there was consideration by Rudel of producing *Jinks* at the NYCO. He was still interested in the piece itself, though the bloom of its premiere was off, but with Stills still on the premises there could be embarrassments. . . . For over a year I had been in correspondence with Bonynge and Joan Sutherland, who had requested the opera's vocal score, but she was committed for two years and she would, of course, expect to create the role of Aurelia, not to recreate it, so . . .

Capitalizing on the hullabaloo of our Bicentennial, RCA advertised its main contribution to that event widely. The press and magazine critics followed, for the most part praising the opera and its performance even more enthusiastically than they had its staged premiere. But, as time passed and there were no offers to revive it, I was at first puzzled, then disappointed, and then finally resigned to the obvious reason: though comic operas of the past are in the standard repertory and *Il Barbiere di Siviglia* ubiquitous, with the exception of Kirke Mechem's *Tartuffe*, there are no evening-length contemporary American comic operas that are revived. For most of the general managers who choose the repertories of their companies on the basis of the real and imagined tastes of their audiences, Fitch's, Harnick's and my barbed wit is no match for my operas with handguns and axe whacks.

*   *   *   *   *   *

---

[1] As of, July 2008, Albany Records plans to reissue the original RCA recording on CD.

Chapter 12

Two Jinxed Subjects
Awards and Passings
Dr. Heidegger's Fountain of Youth
(1976-1978)

Writing at length about the composing of *Jinks* has resembled in little its creation over the three years from '72 to my birthday in the middle of '75. Both tasks are comforting evasions of life as it is lived, for characters in an opera—or in a play or a musical—rarely age in their allotted two hours, though they often die; when the curtain rises again on the first act, they are rejuvenated or revived. But we all live offstage lives in which aging and death, sooner or later, are real.

Mother, once a nurse and during our years in Rochester employed in a hospital, could recognize her own failing heart and inability any longer to visit us in New York, where her grandchildren seldom were. Miranda was still in college; Christopher, after a European tour with his girl friend, visiting his Swiss relatives, was now intermittently captaining millionaires' yachts, "stinkpots" as he and I called them. With the first in a series of slight strokes Mother left her apartment for a nearby lakeside retirement home. My brother Tom, for the first time in years, came from Texas to Stroudsburg for a few days where he and I amicably divided her few furnishings between us, all of them dating back to the Muncie house or before. The 5 x 7 oriental rug under my Baldwin today is the same one that was under my Gulbransen piano when I began piano lessons at age 7. Still, almost daily, I practice scales and exercises to keep my fingers in shape and play Bach's *The Art of the Fugue* in four clefs to keep my mind in tune.

Sheldon and I were in the middle of *Jinks* when Adriana Zahn, soon to become the president of The National Arts Club, began discussing with me a commission to write a one-act chamber opera on an American subject to be presented in their generous gallery space as part of their 80th anniversary celebration; though the subject of the opera was up to me, Adriana suggested Samuel Tilden, who in the 1870s had converted two houses in Gramercy Square into his sumptuous mansion, now the Arts Club. Tilden, Governor of New York and Democratic candidate for President, who lost by one electoral vote in the election of 1876—the most disputed election in history before 2000—seemed to me too outsize a subject for a chamber opera! His larger than life-size bronze statue on Riverside Drive and 112th Street was familiar; it is now just outside our windows. There is an irony in the Tilden quotation graven in its pedestal, "I trust the people," for as the enemy of the Tweed Ring he had good reason to have steel shutters built into the street-side windows of his mansion.

For the two remaining *Jinks* years there could be only discussions with Adriana—sometimes in Italian—and two members of her music committee, Ruth and Thomas Martin well-known translators of opera, he on the staff of the NYCO as coach and conductor.

When *Jinks* was finished and performed and, for the rest of 1975-76 we were awaiting the release of its recording, I pursued another irony that might provide a subject for our chamber opera. I read somewhere that when the second Mrs. Aaron Burr sued her husband for divorce on the grounds of adultery, her attorney was Alexander Hamilton Jr. Sheldon and I thought we might be able by means of flashbacks and introspections during the single-set scene in court to limn our flamboyant characters: Burr, successful attorney, former Vice-president; found not guilty of treason, and the killer of Hamilton; his wife, whom he had married when he was 77, once a prostitute and madam in Providence and former mistress and wife of Stephen Jumel, one of the richest men in the US who had died mysteriously; Hamilton Jr., out for vengeance against the defendant; and a nondescript judge.

Essential to us would be the trial transcript. I learned at the Hall of Records that in New York State divorce proceedings are not disclosed, that I should visit the County Clerk. I had come to know him slightly over decades of jury duty. He was sympathetic to my story because he had just been given elegant display cases for the rotunda and wanted to be able to exhibit the Burr papers. They could become public only if someone successfully sued the State for their disclosure. Would I do so? I envisaged an expensive, long drawn-out trial, but he said he could simplify matters. He accompanied me to a clerk-cashier, for whom I filled out a form and wrote a modest check. Through back stairs he led me to a judge in chambers, one he thought would be prejudiced in our favor. I made my pleas as he took notes and left for uptown.

Weeks later I was peacefully—and, I hope, usefully—seeing my graduate student composers in private sessions when the office staff and I were overcome by calls from the news services, the *Times*, and magazines: Judge Stecher had ruled in my favor and now everybody wanted the lowdown on the Burr divorce, which I didn't yet have.

A quick trip to the Hall of Records, where a copy of the trial transcript awaited me, and a quick glance—the whole of it would turn out to be a long, dull, read—sufficed to rule out the subject: Hamilton Jr., to be sure a friendly neighbor of "Madame" Jumel, had *not* been her attorney. None of the trial testimony would be usable in a libretto.

That would have been the end of the matter except for the emergence of another example of the importance of names. As admitted earlier, I am in agreement with Tristram Shandy's father that they can be determinant. Surely my middle name, Hamilton, accounted for the somewhat surly tone of the first letter I received from the President of the Burr Society, written before he learned that Sheldon and I had given up on the Burr subject.

In early April, when Judge Stecher's decision had the effect of bringing about our divorce from Burr and Co., Sheldon began the search for another subject while I busied myself coaching a mostly new cast for the NYCO revival of *Lizzie Borden* in the spring season that included a revival also of Douglas's *Ballad of Baby Doe*.

While daily juggling appointments at Columbia and rehearsals at Lincoln Center, one evening in March, the National Arts Club awarded me their Gold Medal in Music. Honored as I was to be added to its list of laureates, I was even more touched that President McGill accepted the Club's invitation to speak of me at the presentation ceremony. A condition of the Award was that I agree to sit for a portrait in charcoal by Everett Kinstler. His studio was in the Club's tall attached building stacked with artists at work. Placed in the strong north light, I soon became uncomfortable under his long examination of my face. "You have very high cheekbones. Are you a fourth or an eighth American Indian?" "Yes, one eighth, I think." Nobody else has said such a thing to me. Portraitists see: the rest of us just look.

Two weeks after the gold medal evening, Nora and I attended The American Academy and Institute of Arts and Letters dinner welcoming their new members. We were familiar with their impressive buildings on West 155th Street because we had attended their annual late-spring Ceremonial in 1968 when I had received their Marc Blitzstein Award for Musical Theater. According to the *Times*, Gore Vidal had also been elected. I looked forward to meeting him, for I had recently read two of his historical novels on our two failed libretto subjects, *1876*, concerning Samuel Tilden, and *Burr*. Gossip among the writers that evening was that he had rejected membership in a telegram because ". . . I'm already a member of the Diners Club." Twenty years later, when John Updike, the editor of the Academy's *A Century of Arts and Letters*,[*] talked me into writing its 1968-77 chapter, I discovered that Vidal had sent no such smart-aleck telegram.

---

[*] Columbia University Press, 1998.

Also elected that year was Alice Neel, the well-known and eccentric painter of portraits, often so acutely observed as to be invasive. During drinks before dinner I spied a former student, Richard Neel. He introduced me to his mother, with whom I had a long chat. At one point an acquaintance of mine, glass in hand, ambled slowly from behind Alice, clockwise around back of me, and then disappeared from her sight. She had been eyeing him intently as he made his circuit. "Do you know him?" "Yes. Do you?" "No, but let me tell you about him." And she did, accurately. It was my second experience with those who can see beneath the skin. After that performance, she began stroking my blue velvet jacket and remarked that much time had passed since she had used that expensive pigment. After caressing my hair inquisitively she asked if I would sit for a portrait. I agreed to do so during the next year, for what turned out to be seven sittings. Years later, after her death, Richard and his brother donated the valuable large oil to Columbia, where it hangs above the busts of Varèse and Bartók in the Wiener Music and Arts Library.

Squeezed into all these gratifying events were several visits to see Mother, near Stroudsburg, 80 miles away on the new highway 80. Her heart was giving out; she herself drew the blood samples for the lab and her doctor to determine the constantly varying dosage of blood thinners. I was shocked when she confessed that she prayed every night that she would die before morning. On the drive back to attend the last of the *Lizzie* performances—to which I was late and had to talk my way into—I wondered if there could be some Calvinistic accountant somewhere who was arranging that I pay dearly for my springtime of good fortune.

There was one more item he would have to add to the debt column of the ledger: Kellum Smith, my colleague on the Ditson Committee and Secretary of the Rockefeller Foundation, asked if we would care to be residents at the Foundation's Villa Serbelloni on Lake Como, near our old stamping ground in the Ticino. Yes, we would, and it was arranged that we could stay for five weeks, from late May through most of June.

Before leaving there was time for many meetings with Sheldon. He had found a Hawthorne short story, *Dr. Heidegger's Experiment*, we thought an excellent basis for our chamber opera. We changed the title to *Dr. Heidegger's Fountain of Youth*; altered somewhat the characters and their relationships, five to be singers, the maid to be an actress. We exchanged Hawthorne's use of magic by enhancing the doctor's ability to suggest and convince. During our absence Sheldon would work on the libretto, using the story's meager dialogue when he could and adding lyrics where appropriate. I would not be able to begin the music until early October.

Miranda, Christopher, and Laurie, his friend and partner in their business of yacht maintenance, drove us to Kennedy Airport. At Mal Pensa, the airport north of Milano, we were met by a chauffeured limousine and driven to Como—which we had often visited during our Ticino summers—and then on a narrow road above Lake Como to the Villa Serbelloni, spread out on the crest of a hill facing the southeast arm of the lake. Our elegant room with balcony shared the same magnificent view.

As the days passed we seemed to be visiting an even more luxurious Rome Academy: the same Italian ambiance, the long tables set for lunch and dinner and conversation, but with residents of a certain age or older from many countries and professions. The gardens, the beach and the ruined monastery, and the paths through 53 acres on the high promontory invited first visits and then daily revisits, as did the solitary watchtower, Santa Caterina, my music studio.

That small stone building, already listed in a 1492 inventory, is situated a couple of hundred yards from the Villa on the edge of a cliff just above the village of Bellagio. The bells in the church tower are tuned to a partial D major scale; their frequent tolling was contended with differently by the few composer-residents in the early Rockefeller years. At the excellent rented upright piano or at the desk they could disregard D major or succumb to it. In my song cycle, *From A Watchtower,* mostly composed there, the first two songs compromised with necessity and began with the exploitation of D and A and other fifths, ranging widely thereafter. The five poems of the cycle, *Mutability* by Wordsworth, two scherzo-like ballades by W. H. Auden, with the whole-tone quiet Hopkins *Heaven-Haven* between them, and ending with the de la Mare *The Listeners*, I chose with some care and trouble in the Villa library. They are unified by their allusions to towers and battlements as places of refuge, sieges, and sorties and as symbols of mutability.

While I was sequestered in my tower, Nora, on vacation, was free to do as she wished, to make friends among the other residents—an English couple we later visited in their home on the South Downs—and see relatives in Zürich. On one occasion, her cousin Pips Nussio and her husband Otmar Nussio (the several-times mentioned composer-conductor of the Swiss-Italian radio orchestra in Lugano) were our guest for lunch at the Villa and then drove us to Lugano, where we over-nighted and revisited old haunts. And there were boat trips up and down the lake together, with stop-overs at villas and villages and long walks to crumbling old fortifications on the less-traveled paths.

I became fascinated with the sometimes elaborate expressions of thanks in the guest book written by departing guests. Aided by a typescript of the history of the Serbelloni site and no doubt influenced by my tendency to do things the hard way, I tried my hand at suggesting the past and the present of the Villa in *terza rima*, the Italian verse-form not often attempted today in English. Though it and the song cycle were not completed until August and published still later, I include *Ruminations of a Dowager-Villa* here in context.

RUMINATIONS OF A DOWAGER-VILLA
Villa Serbelloni: 1976

Cradled in granite, yet verdant with vine and olive,
the villa nods in her garden, a dowager, ancient
facade lifted, painted afresh (her novel

and recent rejuvenation fools no-one who's trenchant
enough to discern the old lineaments hidden by surgery)
nods, dreams, blinks and awakens: French and

Italians, Germans and Swiss, emerge, err, re-
form at the portal—is that their baggage or arms? —
taken in charge, led in, by the butler in livery.

The dowager villa, long since accustomed to alarums
and excursions both real and theatrical, extends hospitality
coolly, eyes half-shuttered, immune to all charms

not the equal of those she'd succumbed to long ago. Virility
pleases, but he—over there—that leonine Luchino
(what's he to that early and richer and cod-pieced Visconti,

who forced the portal and toppled the towers) a *contino*
dal cinema, faking for films and the opera his dreams
of the grand and aberrant. And *she*—over there—does she know

as she simpers and primps at the mirror near the columns, the streams
of duchessas who've passed down that corridor or through the *cortile*
shivering the silver of mirrors without turning? It seems

to be those with no beauty who look—no breeding, no *stile*!
How would she know of Francesco Sfondrati who erected
those columns—only five of them left—*un uomo gentile*;

of the Countess d'Agoult, in the evenings often neglected
by Liszt (down below in Bellagio composing some works
for piano), dancing up here, calm and collected,

enceinte, little knowing her daughter'd repeat her own quirks
by leaving her husband for Wagner—while still a von Bülow—
and mother two Siegfrieds and anti-Semitic Young Turks.

And speaking of Germans: there was Adenauer *there*, across Como;
that loose-gaited Kennedy—a Berliner? no, an American;
and that Ghibbeline Maximilian who forced the rich Sforza from Milano

to marry in fourteen ninety-three, to give him a son.
She didn't. Too bad, for though ugly, at least she had style;
when he stayed here years later, as Emperor, he dressed like a baron.

Those Germans are right when they accuse us Italians of guile:
since Caesar brought Greeks to put in the vineyards and Pliny
the Younger built there on the terrace—we've been here a while—

this point has been sought out and fought over, bought out and held (inef-
fectually for long) by pirates, and soldiers, and prelates.
Stanga, Sfondrati, Serbelloni, and Frati Capuccini,

they survived by their guile and their papal connections, no zealots
but one, the Inquisitor Cardinal, safe in his tower,
directing the burning of witches and priests and their helots.
      *   *   *   *   *   *
Now, with the guests all assembled for drinks, the shower
of the fountain diluting the babel, the flowers well watered
and nodding, and all in the topiary drowsy, the dowager

villa, enveloped in shadows, on three sides surrounded
by lakes, on four by the mountains, tries her best to forget
that last duke, who left as his heir that ninny who traded

this Eden for money. Hotel! This elegance to let
for two generations to those who could pay for a week
in the villa and gardens their betters had bred for and bled

for. No wonder the ghost in the bell-tower appeared, to seek
out the brides and to tell them the story of how he'd been shoved
off the cliffs by his fiancée's friends and relations, wreak-

ing their vengeance on him and all knights and the peasant he'd loved.
There was more than a moral to his story, for surely he wished
for much more than an audience, more than the brides to be moved

by his tale: he wanted them gone. Finally vanquished—
by financial depression—the guests left; the hotel was sold.
Only at night does one hear armor clanking; the ghost's form has vanished.

Those tall ones with long drinks who slouch but who never seem old,
they're the new Romans, with talent for roads and good plumbing.
Americans, emigrants all, returned to the fold

in their two-hundredth year. (Amusing: Columbus discov'ring
the New World the year that the Stangas were digging foundations.)
No matter if new money's looking for roots; creating

and nursing a lineage or vintage takes striving, patience,
and time. The Italian nobility, titles denied them,
permit their own villas to languish while chasing sensations

and sending their lire abroad. But let's not deride them;
let's hail their successors: Ella the millionaire heiress
of Walker, distiller (she married two blue-bloods, survived them)

who offered the Pope—he said, "No!"—all the grounds and villa's
possessions, then turned to those greatest refiners of life
and of oil, the Rockefellers, who acquired, not a title, but status.

    *   *   *   *   *   *

A seventeenth-century stage-set, the garden perspective
is quickly foreshortened: triangular mountains, cut out
as the wings of the setting, dissolve in the mists of a restive

south wind bringing rain and the lights are put out
as the sun's rays are splintered, then cut off, by peaks in the west.
But the scene-transformation is played to the glasses left out

on the tables and the wisps of polite conversation and contest
still hovering in mid-air and mixing with mist and the fountain's
spindrift; the audience-parquet is now empty. Each guest

by the dining-room door now peers at the salver, his countenance
fixed on the place-cards. Savants and professors, and wives
in long dresses, and artists and writers unused to such elegance,

pretend no objection as footmen—who've spent all their lives
civilizing barbarians—attend to precedence and chairs.
Barbarians? No, nouveau riche of a new kind, in the hives

of whose minds is the honey collected by muses, computers,
assistants, and students; in return for the honey, they manage
on money doled out by executive hirers and granters.

Though paid by the pipers, this new intellectual peerage
will dance to no tune but its own. In time they'll take over
the world, then this villa and gardens, and then—the old adage—

they'll settle down here, collect pictures and wines of good vintage,
talk with the gentry of box-hedge and rock-slides and clover,
and learn to distinguish more nicely between those from the Villa and village.

At the end of our residency I entered a brief thank-you in the guest book
and promised that something more elaborate would follow. We were driven in
style to Milano, where we remained for two days before taking off for New York.

There we were picked up by our three young chauffeurs and the next day I made the round trip to see Mother briefly. She was sorry to be causing me so much trouble and angry that her prayers had not been answered, that she had not died during our absence abroad. Her opinions were reminiscent of her better days; in other respects she was failing. The next day I spent visiting Christopher on his *Jed*, the houseboat he had purchased second-hand and docked in the Hudson at the Boat Basin at 79th Street. Once in a while he ran the engine to keep the battery charged; this time we struggled against the ebb tide upriver to the George Washington Bridge and speeded back, much to my delight. It was comforting to know that his boat business was thriving and that he could live so exotically, able to invite John Kander down from his townhouse not far away on 70th Street to the waterfront for drinks on board.

July was "a mixture of incongruous elements," as Webster writes of mélange. To celebrate the Bicentennial Fourth we listened on our excellent Hightowers speaker set-up to an advance copy of the long-awaited RCA *Jinks*; an oil tanker spill in the harbor had deposited sticky sludge on our sloop, which over days was finally removed; hedges that had become shapeless in our absence were trimmed; the 102 lines of the *Ruminations* were tinkered with, completed and neatly typed and the last of the songs in the cycle finally finished by my birthday on the 15th. The next two days were spent in part on planes discussing with Sheldon the *Heidegger* libretto on our way to and from Kansas City. There the Lyric Theatre was throwing a "Benefit Autograph Party and Cocktail Buffet Celebrating the Premiere Release of the RCA Recording of the Pulitzer Prize Nomination of *Captain Jinks* . . ." Ah, the fund raising ingenuity of an opera company's board of directors!

My annual birthday party at the Moore's Salt Meadow was a few days late. As usual in those years, the painter Isabel Bishop was a guest, this time presenting me with an inscribed etching. Also present were Christopher and the Moore daughters' cousin, Darby Moore. That handsome couple were then living briefly together in Anchor Ridge, her family's summer home nearby, in the garage apartment of which I'd composed most of *Hello Out There* in 1953 when Christopher was two years old. His liaison with Darby was the closest the Moore and Beeson families ever came to a matrimonial connection.

On the last day of July, while I was at work copying in ink the first of the songs in the cycle, *Mutability*, I was interrupted by a phone call from Mother's doctor. She had died that morning after her last stroke, suffered during the night. Though the timing was not quite what she had wanted, her prayer had been answered. She was 79 and had been mother and dependable friend to me for 55 years. I was, nevertheless, to remain dry-eyed throughout what followed: Tom flew to New York immediately; he, Nora and I drove to East Stroudsburg where a simple Methodist funeral service was held and then on to Benton for the burial in the family plot in the cemetery on top of a hill just outside the village. I recalled that I'd last been there as a boy, sunning myself on the larger flat tombstones; most of her close relatives taking part in the service—and mine, for that matter—I had not seen for many years. Tom and I remained until the next day to settle Mother's affairs with her attorney, then drove to New York to pick up Nora, drive Tom to La Guardia to catch his plane, Nora and I continuing in heavy rain and a rough ferry passage to Shelter Island.

Perhaps as a delayed reaction to Mother's death only five days earlier, I seized the few hours of good weather to work on and sail the *Grayling* with Christopher, once with Patton Campbell, the *Jinks* designer, as passenger. We were then all at Salt Meadow on Saturday evening to celebrate Sarah's—and, in memory, Douglas's—birthday. Miranda and Laurie, living together in the West Village, left for town. On Sunday it was predicted that hurricane Belle was headed north and that its eye might pass near or over New York City. Christopher was concerned about his houseboat and decided to check its tire-bumpers and its lines to the dock—and then ride out the storm, if it came, on *Jed*.

He left early on Monday, in his Volkswagen, the ninth of August—my brother's birthday—thanking me for the offer of our heavier station wagon. With a similar purpose I drove down to the harbor, rowed in the dinghy out to the

Grayling, stowed the sails in the cuddy cabin, and secured the lines and the tiller. As I was casting the anchor close to the mooring I saw Nora waving on the end of the dock. "Christopher is in the Greenport Hospital. I'm going ahead. Come quickly." I did so, with a reason for evading the line of cars at the ferry.

At the hospital we learned what had happened. At 10:15 on the North Road, our usual two-lane route along the Sound, a farmer's wife had heard a crash where the potato fields give way to woods. She released the young man from the seatbelt and called the ambulance. A year earlier a nurse had lost her life in the same place when her front wheels hit a large rut hidden by standing water and she crashed into a tree. The same thing had happened to Christopher. After all that sailing on blue water, to be wrecked on land by a puddle! He was still unconscious when we saw him, very pale, his curly blond hair invisible under a huge bandage. Nora and I, both tuned into things medical, tried to understand the implications of what we were told by the doctors: he was unlikely to survive; if he did, there was such extensive brain damage that he would be severely impaired for life. We went out to the waiting room, shaken, hardly aware that Sarah, Mary and Darby Moore had appeared. Neither of us could imagine a severely impaired Christopher and directed that no extreme measures be taken to prolong his life. He died at 2:15 p.m. without regaining consciousness. He was not yet 26 and I was obsessed with what Jack Eddleman had said about his resemblance to Billy Budd.

Each of us had to cope with the loss in his or her own way. I could not remember ever having cried, not to speak of weeping. I was told that there were drugs that could aid during the mourning period, but that they could not prevent its return in another form, perhaps depression. I took none, but it was difficult to contend with an unexpected *Times* obituary, headlined "Christopher Beeson, composer's son," and with a telephone call from the mortuary suggesting that I bring some clean and more formal clothing for the cremation. I replied that there were to be *no* clothes, please.

Nora and I drove thereafter to Southold to pick up the ashes in their urn and then on to Reel Point, a deserted beach on Shelter Island across the channel from the North Fork. There I waded out into the deeper water, dropped my shorts and, nude, emptied the ashes and threw the urn into the outgoing tide.

* * * * * *

Only once, early in the more than thirty years that have passed since hurricane Belle caused the accident that has affected so many of us since, have I been able to drive the North Road that had in earlier years been driven without any special meaning or connotation. On that occasion I saw that the deep rut in the narrow road had been repaired. Nearby was the sturdy maple, still defaced by the paint marks of the crushed car. Next to the tree trunk I strewed a bouquet of wild flowers.

* * * * * *

During the month before classes began yet again I sailed with some of the numerous guests who arrived with their well-meant but mostly unhelpful condolences, completed the fair copy of *From a Watchtower*, and began to plan the musical shaping of *Dr. Heidegger's Fountain of Youth*. As Otto Luening said at the time, "We who compose music or make things have an outlet for our feelings that others, unfortunately, do not." It was understandable that our choice of the *Dr. H.* subject, made months earlier, with its emphasis on the differences between youth and age suddenly took on added layers of meaning for me. I have long been certain that some of the musical passages would have been less expressive had the words and action not brought to my conscious or unconscious mind memories of my young son's death.

In brief, our story concerns an aged doctor who invites four ageing friends for an evening of experimentation. They form a quartet: soprano, mezzo, tenor, and lyric baritone; there is much ensemble writing in the opera, often with the doctor, a bass-baritone. The doctor shows his friends a large flask of liquid he claims is from the fountain of youth in Brazil. He places an ancient withered rose in a vase of the elixir; by his sleight of hand it blossoms handsomely. As the guests sip the wine-like liquid, sip again, then drink, then drink again, they seem to sense their youth returning and with it their earlier passions, jealousies, and entanglements. These lead to a fight between the two men. During their struggle they knock the flask and vase of the elixir to the floor, the rose seemingly again withered. The guests revert to their older selves and leave to find the source of the fountain of youth. Heidegger at the close sings:

> . . . If your years so little have taught you,
> so little have brought you,
> if the vast and varied richness of life
> can no longer fill your glasses,
> why then in truth, I pray you find it.
> [He turns upstage and toasts his departing guests.]
> I pray you may find your Fountain of Youth.
> [Then turns front . . . holds up his glass again . . .]
> I pray you may all find your Fountain of Youth.
> [and toasts the audience.]

This simple but evocative tale was to be animated by the music, the instrumental and vocal styles of which were intended to limn the varying moods and actions to an extent uncommon even for me. The spooky beginning, including the dusting by the maid of the hanging skeleton and the rearrangement and rattling of its arm-bones by the doctor, is accompanied by the exposition and development of a twelve-tone row not unrelated to the *Mutability* fifths and a derived crooked theme that pervades the entrance of the halting guests. Later, when the Widow begins to dance with the Colonel—both now rejuvenated, they remember a song and she sings it, a slow waltz, AABA, in sumptuous D♭ major. Variations and then perversions of it develop into the fight music. The reversion of the quartet to their ageing selves brings back some of the opening serial music that leads to a final cadence in C major as Heidegger toasts the audience.

These synoptic sketches of the story line and its musical setting can hardly suggest the sheer labor that brings about even a chamber opera lasting three quarters of an hour. Not to speak of the writing of the libretto and the revisions of its words and phrases as it is set, there are literally thousands of notes and indications of dynamics and tempi written first in sketch, multiplied in the orchestral score and then arranged for two hands and inked in the piano score; the composer will have copied out his librettist's words three times! One need not mention the decisions that bring about the notes and how they are to be played, whether pondered briefly or at length—sometimes sketched—or, suiting them to the words, characters, and situations by simply writing them down as experience dictates.

My delayed start on the composition of *Dr. Heidegger's Fountain of Youth* was but one of the dislocations brought about by the deaths, ten days apart, of my mother and son. At the simple memorial service at the Shelter Island Heights Chapel in the Grove, when parts of Christopher's transatlantic log were read I almost fainted, for the first time ever. Two of my three courses were composition seminars with a half dozen each of students in their early or mid-twenties, all looking forward to their lives; once or twice I found myself—then stopped myself—following Christopher look-alikes on the campus.

It had been a simple matter for Tom and me to arrange with Mother's attorney the settlement of her modest estate. It was upsetting to inherit my son's *Jed*, still docked at the 79th Street Boat Basin. In his houseboat, as sailors say, "there's a place for everything and everything's in its place." In my many trips by car downstream and then upstream I displaced everything for elsewhere and finally found a buyer for the boat.

Otto was correct, as usual, in pointing out that composers have defenses against adversity. I realized that if I could find the music that aided our characters to forget their age and relive their youth, I could relegate the still vibrant immediacy of the recent past into my memory, to be recalled only when I wished. In early October I began the composition of the opera.

*   *   *   *   *   *

Before continuing with an account of the writing of the opera I offer three amusing stories, at least two of them distantly related to the events of August 9.

Our Hightowers summer tenants in the former servants quarters for several years were Dr. Ernst Bartsich and his Berber wife, Asisa. Ernst, a surgeon in the Columbia Medical School, had been of great help to us during and after

Christopher's death. Ordinarily the Beesons and the Bartsichs never met in the city, but all of a sudden Asisa phoned to invite us to a reception at the United Nations, where she was one of the few women from her country on staff.

We were barely started on the exotic hors d'oeuvres and drinks—there was alcohol available at this mostly Moslem event—when I spied across the room a crowd of rather formally dressed autograph hounds surrounding a tall Black who looked familiar. "Yes, that's Muhammad Ali. He's a Black Muslim and often comes to our parties," Asisa explained. I joined the fans and when at last Ali towered above me and extended his hand, I naturally grasped it even more strongly than usual. (I had long since noticed that the arthritic elderly avoided me at a second meeting.) I didn't expect him to wince noticeably and to ask, "Where'd ja get that handshake?" "Oh, I'm a piano player," I answered. He thought it a bad joke and I returned to my friends. Shortly thereafter one of his managers approached and asked if I were the one who'd hurt Ali. Didn't I know that boxers over time break many fingers and hand-bones that remain painful? I admitted that I didn't and would he please tell Muhammad Ali that I was very sorry I'd hurt him.

*   *   *   *   *   *

Quite some time later, on December 5 to be precise, I attended a cocktail party of a different sort. In what year I had first attended the Claire Reis annual party for composers I don't remember, unfortunately, for at that time I was told by one of my seniors that the initial invitation signified that one had made it as a composer on the New York scene. On this latest occasion I greeted my hostess and a number of my composer friends; then, as I went out to the large empty foyer to freshen my drink, the outer door opened and a disheveled man in need of a shave quickly entered, poured himself a large Scotch, turned, and said, "Hi, Jack . . ." By that time I realized it was Lenny Bernstein. Gossip had it that he had recently left Felicia and was living in a hotel with a man. Certainly he looked uncared for and frazzled. ". . . Let's go somewhere and talk." As I backed away uncertainly a step or two I found myself penned into the nearby corner by his

428

outstretched arms, one hand holding his drink, the other his cigarette. He began our talk by saying how shocked he'd been by seeing the obituary in the late summer, and asking if he wasn't right in thinking that Christopher had known his son Alexander at the Collegiate School. I said that I thought they had at least known of one another, Alex having been some four years younger than Chris. He, and then we, expanded on the subject of fathers and sons, youth and age, and he was fascinated to learn that Sheldon Harnick and I were working on an opera about that subject. The conversation continued for at least the length of two or three cigarettes, each lit from the butt of the last, and concluded with his remarking, approvingly, that he'd always considered me Jewish. I replied that, unfortunately, I wasn't; the best I could claim was being one-eighth Indian.

LB: I know a lot of Jews who aren't Jewish, but only a few Gentiles who are.

JB: Then what does it take to be Jewish?

LB: Oh, you have to be attractive, intelligent, and creative.

During our literally tête à tête conversation I could see many coming out to the bar, some of whom spied the pair of us in the corner and seemed to pause, as though trying to overhear what we were talking about. When Lennie and I joined the crowd in the other rooms a couple of my close friends asked me outright and looked doubtful when I told them the truth. Another of the curious passers-by waited five months to ask.

*   *   *   *   *   *

It was on a Friday the thirteenth of May that I went to Philadelphia to present the 1977 Ditson Conductors Award to Eugene Ormandy during the intermission of a matinee concert of the orchestra. It was my annual pleasure to draft the citation for the president, and then to represent him at the conferral by reading it, handing its fancy copy and a check to the conductor who had been chosen by the Advisory Committee for having programmed a large body of music by American composers over a long period of time. On that May concert was included the Fourth Symphony of David Diamond, whose music was often performed by Ormandy. On our way to pay our respects to the conductor after the concert, David asked me if I knew that Ormandy had been born in Budapest with the German name of Eugen Blau. I didn't, but, however named, he turned out to be jovially informal. After asking whether it was really true that I'd studied with his friend Bartók and if I knew any funny Hungarian stories—I told the only one I knew—we discussed briefly Bartók's aversion to teaching composition. He invited me to send him one of my orchestral scores, and he continued at length about Hungarians.

After enough of this, we took our leave and I invited David to join me at dinner as the second guest of Alice Ditson at the nearby excellent Bookbinder's restaurant. During drinks and the fish course he kept up a constant stream of salacious stories about himself and his friends, the Eastman School and his quitting it the day before he was to be dismissed from it, his flight from New York City to Florence the day before he might have been arrested, and others surely to be found in his *Memoires* if it is ever published. Now, having died a year ago, he can no longer endlessly tinker with it. (I've done what little I could to urge on its publisher.)

By coffee time he got around to asking me what Lenny and I had been talking about so earnestly at Claire Reis's party back in December. I gave him the same truthful answer I'd given the others.

DD: And did he invite you home with him?

JB: No. Why would he?

DD: Would you have gone with him if he'd asked?

JB: No, certainly not. I was already late for dinner. Why would he have asked?

DD: Well, for the obvious reason. We all thought you were gay when you first came to New York.

JB: Who were "we all?"

DD: Well, I did, and Lenny, and Ned, I guess. You know the crowd.

JB: Yes, I did, and do. What does a person have to be, to be thought gay?

DD: Well, he has to be attractive, intelligent, and creative.

Now insecure in the knowledge that anyone with these three qualities could be thought to be both Jewish and gay, I apprehensively took the train back home to New York.

*   *   *   *   *   *

These three amusing and mildly thought-provoking stories, however long in the telling, describe events spaced over the first months of composing my seventh opera, what Otto called "the restorative treatment of Dr. Heidegger." With the story line, characters, and the first draft of part of the libretto in hand, I had begun the music in early October. Only about 18 months later—a short time for me and this time fortunately not exactly 18 months later—the music was completed and its piano-vocal and orchestral scores readied for the eyes and ears of others.

Both the modest space of the Arts Club and the intimacy of our opera dictated a small instrumental ensemble. I chose eleven players, omitting the too-insistent oboe: flute, two clarinets, a busy percussionist, harp, piano, and five strings (with provisions for added strings); doublings on piccolo and alto flute, bass clarinet, celesta and harmonium would add to the available colors. To be sure, in such a score there are fewer notes and other indications to be written, but even greater attention must be paid to keeping the colors varied and clean; for example, an instrument should not be used in the same register accompanimentally just before it is to come to the fore. I seized every opportunity to use the unaccompanied vocal ensemble, for in three quarters of an hour an ear tires of the over-use of an instrument, of the same combinations of them, of too-similar textures and registers, of the ensemble itself.

As with *Jinks*, I scored some of the opera as I proceeded with the sketch, the first pages written in London where we three spent the Christmas holidays in a somewhat unsuccessful attempt to erase their associations. I completed its modest

177 pages a year later on Twelfth Night, 1978, and after revising and correcting them for my remarkable monocular copyist, went on with the vocal score. All parts were ready for the rehearsals and performances in November '78, barely two years after the music was begun. I note with some satisfaction that the three performances included one on the eighteenth—17, 18, 19.

Shoehorning even a small chamber opera into the gallery space of the National Arts Club, accommodating an audience of 150-200, required much ingenuity. Patton Campbell, who had designed the sets and costumes for *Jinks*, and Jack Eddleman, its stage director, were again on hand. I remarked to them that in a sense we were re-inventing the past, presenting a new opera in a private space, just as the new *Orfeos* of Peri and Caccini had first been heard in Florentine *palazzi* in 1600 and 1602.

Rambling through the Club's upper floors I discovered a wide and tall backless bookcase that was brought down to fill the entrance of a narrow offshoot of the gallery and performance space; with scrim tacked to its back and the conductor and the eleven instrumentalists behind—invisible but audible with a sound reflector, we had a practicable piece of our set and—as Peri had at his premiere in the Pitti Palace—"the instruments behind the scene." In a contemporary fillip, the conductor, Thomas Martin, and his beat were visible to the singers on a TV monitor suspended from the ceiling over the heads of the audience. As a critic wrote, "It was a happy choice to stage the work in a corner of one of the National Arts Club's large rooms, allowing the audience to enter the ambience . . . as they entered the house itself—one was simply another of Dr. Heidegger's guests."

Our Aurelia Trentoni from *Jinks* was to be the Widow Lockhart, with the most lyric music of the opera, the waltz-aria. Because of our conductor's NYCO connections, we were able to cast the other four roles with singing actors able to make the most of their closeness to the audience. When my colleagues learned that Miranda had been appearing off-Broadway as an actress, they suggested she be cast as Heidegger's maid. I agreed enthusiastically, for Sheldon and I had already adjusted the opening scene to make a family connection in the text.

The maid enters the darkened stage carrying a tray of glasses to a table; then the business of dusting the skeleton—the stage directions are all elaborately written in the score. She dusts the large volume lying on the table and haltingly reads its title, the syllables provided with rhythmic notation: "On Nymphs, Sylphs, Pygmies and Salamanders." She is interrupted by the sounds of bones rattling, lets out a little shriek, flees, bumps into Heidegger and shrieks again; curtsies and exits. Heidegger turns to the book, scans a page, and reads, as notated rhythmically:

"What a spirit wishes to have, he has,

and all his wishing, desiring, is thus;

but man is the most earth-bound of all creatures.

He obtains nothing by wishing, desiring.

What he must have and wants he must make by himself."

The title of the tome and the quoted words are those of Paracelsus, the 16th century Swiss physician alchemist, translated by Henry Sigerist, Miranda's grandfather.

Dr. Heidegger then turns approvingly to the bust of Paracelsus and sings, *parlando*, "How true, Paracelsus." All of this opening action was made up by us from vague hints in the Hawthorne story, one of them that the good doctor had a bust of Hippocrates in his study. It was amusing to traipse up and down 8th Avenue with Patton Campbell and to find and to rent various props for the production and a bust that might pass for Paracelsus.

In addition to helping put our stage and rudimentary set together and renting props, I was again coaching singers, particularly the numerous quartets that are unique to this opera and the most difficult music in its score. Also special to *Heidegger* and tricky to manage are the quartet's two transformations. Jack Eddleman's inventive suggestions for facial expressions and carriage, the entrances and exits with canes and limps and their elimination during the youthful phase, hair and costume adjustments—not to speak of the words and the changing instrumental and sung music—all helped to make Hawthorne's inexplicable believable. That such was the case was proved by the reactions of the producer and others from the CBS "Camera Three" staff who attended the dress rehearsal and performances. They were quite free in telling music critics that the opera would be presented on their series during the next season. Doubtless it would have been had not CBS suddenly dropped "Camera Three" after 26 years. With its end, and the demise of NBC Opera and NET Opera, came the end of opera produced for television in the US. We are left with only the occasional televising of a staged production nowadays.

Though the televised production did not take place, *Heidegger* became the fifth of my operas to be recorded, this time by CRI (Composers Recordings Inc.).[1] As had been usual, the recording sessions were scheduled after the final performance, to take advantage of the readied—and rested—cast and orchestra. The CRI album was particularly well done sonically, with a handsome cover and the libretto conveniently bound within. The published vocal score, with the same striking artwork on the cover, followed within a year from Boosey and Hawkes, as did other productions in New York and elsewhere shortly thereafter.

*   *   *   *   *   *

---

[1] Available from CRI/New World and on a "double bill CD" that includes *Hello Out There*, issued by Albany Records.

Chapter 13

Miscellanea and *Cyrano*
(1979-1990)

To clarify chronology from the preceding welter of varied events and detail: though Sheldon and I had worked out our revision of the Hawthorne story and he had written the first part of its libretto by the one unforgettable date of the period, August 9, 1976, such were the effects of hurricane Belle and its aftermath that I could not plan its complicated musical beginning and its first notes until early October. In the interim I finished the inked fair copy of the cycle *From a Watchtower*, dedicating its first song, *Mutability* "in memory of my son Christopher." Thereafter, until those first notes and the rest of the notes of *Heidegger* were brought to life in their first performance two years and a month later, November 17, 1978, whenever I could I spent my time with the good doctor in his study rejuvenating four lives and then returning them to their earned deserts. In real time, though, life made demands not to be trifled with.

Our apartment was now larger than we needed. After a thorough search of the Columbia neighborhood, a smaller one, recently renovated in an attractive cooperative building, was finally found. Separated from Riverside Drive traffic by a small park, all windows face the river and look out not only on the bronze statue of Samuel Tilden, already mentioned, but also on the elaborate sculptural figures dedicated to Lajos Kossuth, the Hungarian revolutionary hero.

Shelter Island had been wonderful during long summers with two growing children. Now, with only one, grown and absent, it was too distant and Hightowers too large for a couple of weekends, Nora now a senior editor at Abrams during the week. A much longer and wider search for a smaller weekend retreat nearer the city resulted in a house that fitted perfectly our tastes and needs, one with huge windows looking out on a fresh water pond and—rare from a noted modern architect—many doors, essential for a composer-pianist husband and his violinist wife. We were to discover only after we had committed to purchasing it, that a private beach on Cold Spring Harbor was but a few hundred yards away. Two acres of woods and numerous millionaires surrounded the house, barely into Suffolk County and only a little over an hour by train or car to the city.

The change of address on Riverside Drive from 445 to 404 was accomplished early in the *Heidegger* two-year period. The removal from Shelter Island to Lloyd Neck took place later, in the summer of 1980, and led to the final dispersal of our small fleet: the houseboat, the sloop *Grayling*, and the dinghy. The only tangible remainder of the three stands in a kitchen corner of the apartment: a sturdy boat hook now on land duty and reduced to helping to open and close the upper parts of tall windows.

There is another reminder of my sailing years in the apartment's studio-living room. As part of the 1905 design of the entrance to our building and its elaborate canopy is the semicircular window in our second floor apartment. Similarly shaped windows even of this size—12 feet in diameter—are often found in downtown New York and always present the problem of providing curtains or drapes for shade, the solution disfigured with a square or rectangle of cloth. My as yet unpatented solution is simple. Center and shape onto the inside of the wooden curve and fasten with screws two pieces of sailtrack meeting at the top. Take the measurements or a model of the two needed quarter circles to a sailmaker, who, after overcoming his astonishment at the shape of your pair of "sails," will hem the sailcoth—or fabric of your choice—insert grommets and tie to them the slides that fit your sailtrack. If you are fussy about design unity, stop in at a nearby sailing equipment shop and purchase two small cleats and sufficient line for your "halyards." The two lower corners that meet in the center should be belayed to a fixed screw eye. Go home or to the office, rig and set your sails!

At the end of these two years our small family was enlarged with a son-in-law when Miranda and Laurie were married, thereby aiding him in obtaining US citizenship. We had all known one another since he joined Christopher in their yacht-tending enterprise. He had proved to be a good sailor and Hightowers handyman. Laurie, Laurence Reid, born in Liverpool and a littler younger than the Beatles—who were also Liverpudlians—had been educated in Windsor and in London. He told stories good enough to be true. While hitch-hiking in Yugoslavia the only language he and the driver had in common was Latin. He had been close with his paternal grandfather; the two of them pored over the records of births and deaths in Somerset House in London, trying to trace the Reids back to their supposed source, one of the illegitimate sons of Lord Wellington and to a fortune made and misplaced somewhere along the line.

Nora and I acquired the habit every summer—after the sale of Hightowers—of visiting London and its theatres—always staying in the Hotel Russell in Bloomsbury and then touring some new part of the countryside. On one such trip, with a wish to be helpful and having examined several Wellington biographies, I visited Apsley House, the Duke's residence near Buckingham Palace. There I found yet other biographies, but not what I was seeking. I asked the librarian if she could provide me with a volume that mentioned the names of the Duke's illegitimate sons, all of whom he was said to have provided with important army commissions. She was at first huffy; when she became angry I left to hear others ranting on Hyde Park Corner.

*   *   *   *   *   *

As usual, when between operas I turned to writing shorter works, almost always those with words, more often than not of an odd and/or humorous sort not appealing to most other composers. The 1979 examples were two songs: *Cat!*, a Keats setting for mezzo and *Cowboy Song* for baritone; *Hinx, Minx*, a nursery rhyme round for a cappella chorus, and *Knots*, also for that medium, with four solo voices in addition. The odd words of the seven pieces in *Knots* were chosen from a small volume of the same name by the unconventional London psychiatrist R. D. Laing; no doubt my choice was determined by the fact that the simple but tangled ideas and their knotty expression cried out for a similarly contrapuntal setting, which they duly received. While writing them, I discovered that Laurie and Laing, as frequenters of London's Washington Pub, had known one another well enough to have had a falling out.

It took a month of Hightowers time to weave together seven times the competing, closely interrelated strands of words and music in such a way as also to make a satisfactory over-all shape lasting only a quarter of an hour. But I've rarely so enjoyed an attack of canonitis. The registry of my works in the Latouche volume includes the date of the completion of the inked fair copy of *Knots* as August 9, 1979. I must have dallied or rushed to make that self-imposed, all too literally punning, deadline. Over thirty years later I am still strangely ill at ease on that date. It must have been such a state on that third anniversary that led me, compulsively, to add to the date the time: 11:59 a.m.

*   *   *   *   *   *

The opera that was to be written after the miscellaneous events and smaller pieces just described was to be my eighth and by far the largest and longest of the ten I have written. In some post-*Heidegger* conversation with Sheldon I pointed out that, with one exception, I had always alternated writing more or less standard-size operas lasting two hours or so with chamber operas, one of which—exceptionally—lasted over an hour and a half. I hoped that I could continue this pattern by our finding a subject that required the full operatic panoply, including chorus. He reminded me that he was not good at starting a story from scratch, that he was not—in Broadway parlance—a book writer, but a lyricist. Consequently, we both began reconsidering once-set-aside subjects and seeking new possibilities, mostly plays.

Toward the end of 1979, as a kind of Christmas present, he suggested *Cyrano de Bergerac*, a play we had both seen and long admired. (At one of the intimate evenings at the Villa Aurelia the guest of honor had been the best-known Cyrano of the period, José Ferrer. I seized the opportunity to discuss with him the play, his role, and the film of it, for which he had received an Academy Award in 1950.) Nevertheless, I had my doubts about the subject, as several other composers of the past had not. I said to Sheldon, "I'm afraid that when the curtain goes up, it will look like *I Puritani*." He responded, "That's just the trouble with modern operas; they never look like operas." Our comments were very much in character. All my operas had been on American subjects; even Jonah and his family were Brooklynese, though supposedly from Gath-Hepher. However little I knew about being a gambler in a Texas jail, an Armenian in Fresno, or a Borden in Fall River, I could imagine some affinity with them; I knew I had no connection with 17th century France. Nevertheless, I agreed and would try. The essence of the characters transcended their place and time; Lizzie, after all; was a reborn Electra.

The duality of the real-life Cyrano (1619-55), famous as a swordsman-duelist and as a poet-fabulist, was the theme on which Rostand wrote his fantastic variations in his immediately successful play in 1897. Only a year later there were three English translations and it was played in New York. Most of the other main characters, their motivations, and the highly original serio-comic story they enact, are of Rostand's invention—tweaked somewhat by Sheldon and me. Cyrano and Roxane, cousins, are brought up together in the country. Later, when they remember that place and time I use some of the folk melodies from Bergerac and—at John Kander's suggestion—allude to them in the tragic final scene in which both finally admit to their lifelong love for one another. There are quite a few other examples of pre-existing music in the score—including bugle-calls—most credited.

Throughout the tale Cyrano's too-large nose serves as both the excuse and the cover for his ability to express everything but his passion for Roxane. We eliminated Rostand's need for backstage instrumentalists by substituting—and often using—a young and handsome bugler. When Sheldon and I were asked by the stage director of the premiere performances to write our reasons for choosing our subject and our treatment and changes of it, I wrote to him at great length, including the following:

"Buglers are usually teenagers. Without wishing to play up some implied closeted homosexual tendencies on the part of Cyrano—whose motives, to be sure, are various and complicated . . . There may be merit in having a touch of that which some in the audience would like to find in it. Nuff said, and not too much to be made of it, I think."

Sheldon was also asked to write, as the translator-librettist:

". . . More specifically, Jack told me he was eager to try his hand at an opera which called for large choral forces . . . *Cyrano* struck me as ideal: the THEATERGOERS in Act I constituted a natural mixed chorus; the SOLDIERS gave us a men's chorus; and the NUNS in Act III provided a women's chorus. Moreover, the story is dramatic, the characters are 'operatic' (in that they are larger than life), and passion is the motor which drives the actions of the four principals: CYRANO, ROXANE, CHRISTIAN and DeGUICHE.

Rostand chose to write the original play in alexandrines. I suspect that he chose this verse form not only as a challenge to his creative abilities but also to give the play both a 17th century flavor and a kinship with the work of those 17th century playwrights, such as Corneille, who traditionally wrote in alexandrines.
I deliberately chose *not* to write in alexandrines because I felt that to do so would impose a severe constraint on Jack's ability to compose music in a wide variety of rhythms. Since this was to be an opera after all, the music had to be paramount, so it was vital to give the composer as much flexibility as possible with regard to metric structures.

Consequently, I chose to use alexandrines in only two places:
1. the scene in which we meet the 'Intellectuals': BARTHÉNOIDE, URIMÉDONTE, et. al. Since they are commenting on the quality of a 17th century play, it seemed appropriate [and not without humor] to have them do so in 17th century dramatic verse;
2. the lines we hear recited by MONTFLEURY from Balthazar Baro's play [in Act I].

There was another choice I had to make: how and when to use rhyme. I chose to write in a style I have adopted before, a style in which the lines, generally unrhymed, have a strong sense of rhythm while at the same time having the easy flow of natural conversation. However, I like to surprise the listener by using rhyme in unpredictable places (generally speaking). I believe this adds a freshness and musicality to the lines and also contributes to the feeling that the ear is hearing more rhymed lines than it actually hears. At times, of course, I felt that a more formal use of rhyme was called for, such as in LIGNIERE'S song about the COUNT de GUICHE; CYRANO's comments to VALVERT about the size of his own nose; the improvised 'ballade' CYRANO sings as he duels VALVERT, etc.

One last note regarding my feelings about the play, *Cyrano*, which echo Jack's. Although I love the play for its poetry, its poignance, its passion, its drama and its theatricality, I have always felt that it is simply too long, too wordy. To adapt it for the operatic stage it was incumbent upon me to trim some of the excessive verbiage, beautiful as it is in the original, if only to make room for a few extended arias. This was a task I welcomed.

In adapting the libretto, I have tried to remain faithful to Rostand's conception of his characters. However, Jack and I discussed the character of ROXANE and agreed that, as written, she seems somewhat shallow. When she discusses her love for CHRISTIAN, she tends to sound foolish. She doesn't seem entirely worthy of CYRANO's passion, beautiful though she may be. We felt that the audience should see a ROXANE who is intelligent, articulate, poetic in her own way, a fitting heroine for CYRANO to adore.

Thus, in her Act II aria we tried to show, by following her reasoning, what an eloquent, high-minded young woman she is; and at the same time, we tried to show that all of her reasoning is an elaborate rationalization, a transparent exercise in self-deception, whereby she disguises from herself the fact that she is simply infatuated with CHRISTIAN'S physical beauty. We have also introduced a note of irony: in order to accomplish this self-deception, ROXANE has persuaded herself that she is an excellent judge of character and that she can, therefore, find in CHRISTIAN'S face all those poetic qualities which she already attributes to CYRANO. Thus, unconsciously, she acknowledges the deep love she has for CYRANO, a love she will only discover, consciously, at the end of the opera.

No doubt it was Sheldon's interest in the French repertory that led him to the Rostand play; he had already translated *Carmen* and Ravel's *L'Enfant des Sortilèges*. The choral director of the Houston Opera *Carmen* objected to

Sheldon's translation of "Des oranges pour grignotter!"—"Oranges, good to nibble on"—in the fourth act and had it changed. Because there are orange-sellers near the beginning of *Cyrano*, Act I, hawking their produce in the theatre before the play within a play begins, I used his rejected, delicious, words and stole the Bizet musical setting, changing it slightly to fit the context. So far as I know nobody has ever noticed the theft.

Some years earlier, when Sheldon and I were working on *Jinks* and he was completing the lyrics for the Richard Rodgers *Rex*, he mentioned ruefully that he regretted not having kept a record of his collaboration with Mr. Rodgers. That comment led me to keep a log on our very long and closely collaborative work on *Cyrano*. It begins in April 1980, notes that I began the music on Columbus Day, 1980, and ends on the Columbus Day weekend, 1989, when I finally completed its music and its scores.

My log, or *Cyrano* Journal consists of carbons of letters written to Sheldon and letters from him to me, my notes on what we discussed by phone, and my longhand scrawls, written daily or at intervals, of ideas to be pondered and to be discussed. There are also a few letters to and from Christopher Keene concerning its production at the New York City Opera, and a few irrelevant matters mainly related to other of my works. After the turn of the century, my friend Susan Hawkshaw borrowed and ordered the material, deciphering and typing my handwritten notes. In her version the whole of the Journal consists of 224 pages.

I first met Susan when she was a PhD candidate in musicology and published an article concerning the Brahms manuscript I found on Shelter Island. She became Susan Hawkshaw when she married another Columbia musicologist. When both were later at Yale and she was associated with the Music Oral History project there we met again, often, for she taped 18 hours of her questions and my answers, which presumably sparked her interest in my operas and their composer, about which and whom she has several times written. Her labor on the Journal was undertaken in the hope that, shorn or not of the more extraneous material, it might serve as a uniquely detailed monograph about the collaboration of a composer and his librettist in writing a single opera. It would be an honor to have such a volume shelved somewhere near the wonderful exchange of letters between Strauss and von Hofmannsthal, concerned mainly with their collaboration on twelve works from 1900 and 1929, six of them operas.

Not long after our 1979 Christmas-time decision to write a *Cyrano* together—and to title it that, simply—and no doubt influenced by my predilection for American subject matter, I was struck suddenly by a soundless but vivid transposition of our opera to New Orleans, beginning at the outbreak of the Civil War and ending there some years later, the battle scene taking place elsewhere. That this daytime vision was laid in the one French part of our country was natural enough, but may have been influenced by my having just received the annual Christmas letter from my favored cousin who lived near Lake Ponchartrain and by my reading at the time Otto Luening's recently published *Odyssey of an American Composer*. His autobiography describes in detail his sojourn among the Louisiana Cajuns when writing his opera *Evangeline*, which I had coached in 1948.

Curious as to whether my vision was merely a daydream or a subconsciously conceived précis of an opera laid in New Orleans in the early 1860s with parallels of places, events, and characters to those in Rostand's play, I began reading extensively in obscure volumes and journals in the Columbia Library. I was astonished to discover that there were almost no discrepancies. Rostand's five acts would become our first act and the two scenes of our second act and the two scenes of our third. His first act takes place in an improvised theatre; New Orleans was home to several theatres—opera had been performed there often since 1791—or ours, too, could take place in an improvised space for the play-fragment within an opera. His Acts II and III, our II (1 and 2), a patisserie-rotisserie and then the front of Roxane's house with a balcony and climbable foliage, present no problems. His Act IV would be the first scene of our III: the Siege of Arras the 1863 "Battle Above the Clouds," as the battle of Lookout Mountain or Chattanooga came to be known, or just "A Battle." And his

Act V, our last scene, could be paralleled by the well-known Ursuline Convent, the first on our continent.

Anybody would think that the duel between Cyrano and Valvert would be an impossibility in 1860. Not at all. Until the Civil War's end, all young men of good families were taught to fight with pistol and sword. Duels were common and St. Anthony's Garden near the rear of the Cathedral was the usual place to fight them.

The Gascon Cadets of the play, including Cyrano and the other lead, the tenor Christian, would become the well-known Orleans Cadets, enlisted April 11, 1861. All the names of the characters in the play could be retained in the Frenchified New Orleans version except for that of the Comte de Guiche, who would become General Beauregard, born in the St. Bernard Parish in Louisiana and whose character resembled closely the de Guiche of the play.

These and other discoveries I duly reported to Sheldon, who was fascinated by the parallels and amused by my diligence in finding them. He was interested in my idea of a simple transposition of the time and place of the play to New Orleans in about 1861, but he was immersed in his translation of *Carmen* for the Houston Opera and our discussion of that possibility would have to be postponed until he was free to translate and revise the play into our libretto.

I had accomplished what I had set out to do, proved that there was something useful in my seeming daydream. Unfortunately, I had become so enamored of the new time and place that I sought for unneeded details and failed to rein in my tendency to poach on the playwright's and librettist's territory. The only point in my discovering the dates when Beauregard resigned as commander of West Point, became a Confederate brigadier general, gave the order to fire on Fort Sumter, and returned to New Orleans, was to make sure that he could be there for Mardi Gras. I was possessed with the notion that our first act should take place at that time and read widely—to no practical purpose—about the history and the masked goings-on on that special holiday.

Similarly, no one can read about pre-Emancipation New Orleans without being fascinated by the many self-contradictory meanings of Creole and the flexible exactitude of the vocabulary for identifying the fractional amounts of black and white blood in the population. For example, quadroons, officially one-fourth black, could be 1/64 black, or even less. As was said at the time, "Those who need to know will know."

I found a quotation from a travel book by Sir Charles Lyell that recounted the story of a white man who wished to marry a quadroon. Because mixed marriages were unlawful, using a penknife he squeezed a drop of her blood into his arm and thus became a black man. They lived happily ever after. It is possible that Edna Ferber read this story too and borrowed it for her *Show Boat*. Nevertheless, my librettist-self was enamored of the idea of turning Roxane into a quadroon. She and Christian would then go through the blood exchange before the brief marriage ceremony that is in the play—and would be in the opera— thereafter unconsummated in both because he is summarily called to battle. Had I not been on sabbatical, I would not have had the time for such misadventures.

The background material for these two too-imaginative flights, the Mardi Gras timing and Roxane as quadroon, together with the substantiation of all the parallels I had discovered fill a spring-binder of bibliographic notes and Xeroxes of my reading. At the end of almost five months of pre-compositional thinking about our opera and collecting twelve different English translations of the play, I sent to Sheldon a 5-page précis of my thoughts and suggestions, including the two outré ones. That summary became the first entry in the *Cyrano* Journal, April 18, 1980.

The summary was written to coincide with Sheldon's completion of the *Carmen* translation. When he had considered the implications of its complexities he invited me over to East Hampton for our first long and comprehensive *Cyrano* discussion. He was still intrigued by the idea of what we called the simple transposition. He was agreeable to the Mardi Gras-timing change, though he believed it unnecessarily troublesome. His real doubts about Roxane as a quadroon and the changes in plot and characterizations that would have to be made he had prepared as a long list of questions that he read one by one. I had not thought my ideas through, as had he, and I could not improvise answers. He was adamant that the crux of the matter, the exchange of a drop of blood, could not be used. We'd be accused of stealing from *Show Boat*. I had known that, but blocked it, and now agreed.

After lengthy discussion of these and other matters, we agreed to return to France and the 17th century, with those revisions we had already agreed to make, most of them already alluded to herein. For some reason, probably fatigue on my part, I did not argue for, or even mention, our earlier agreement that a simple transposition of time and place was a lively possibility. I put the idea in my forgetery—Otto Luening's term—for some years, until long after we'd finished the opera, and then I retrieved it.

*   *   *   *   *   *

As it happened, there was not enough of the libretto of Act I completed for me to plan the shaping of its many segments into a trajectory and then to begin composing until Columbus Day, 1980. It was a fitting day to begin a musical voyage that was to last nine years. That so much time was required is partially explained by the extreme variety of characters and dramatic events and my wish to search for and find the right expression and temperature for each. And, obviously, an opera for large forces that has a playing time of two hours and forty minutes—exclusive of two intermissions—takes a while to conceive and to write down. That part of the writing of the opera which can be verbalized, together with all of Sheldon's and my labors on the action and the characters, are in the *Cyrano Journal*. The resultant music is to be found in the two scores, the vocal score of 401 pages and the orchestral score of 763 pages.

During the later of the nine years I could devote more time to composing. I retired a little early, in 1988 at age 66; for the preceding three years I chose to teach only during the spring term. The part-time teaching served to prevent any withdrawal symptoms that might have arisen from suddenly breaking my teaching habit. Sensibly, but unnecessarily, upon retirement I relinquished my leadership of the Ditson Fund and its publication of new music by the Columbia University Press to two colleagues. I retained my commitments to them, nevertheless, as well as to other juries, boards, or committees that aided American composers, The American Academy of Arts and Letters, the Guggenheim Foundation, AAR, ASCAP, CRI, and other acronymically named, as well as my then still secret connection with the Pulitzer Prize in Music. If I had had any guilt about teaching less, such service on behalf of somewhat older composers would have allayed it. After retirement, I initiated and taught, off and on, the seminar for composers on voices and the setting of English for them until my half-century at Columbia came to an end.

*   *   *   *   *   *

Some two years into *Cyrano* I gave a copy of the first act piano score to my friend Richard Woitach, a coach and conductor at the Met, who thought that Jimmy Levine should be informed that such an opera was under way. I drafted a letter to Maestro Levine saying that I did not wish to get in the way of my friends Jacob Druckman and John Corigliano, both of whom had commissions from the Met, but that if either should withdraw, he might wish to consider the work of Sheldon Harnick and myself, the first act of which I'd given to Woitach. On the day I planned to type and mail it, the *Times* announced that Beverly Sills, the Director of the New York City Opera, had appointed Christopher Keene as Musical Director of the NYCO. I had known and admired Keene since the time he had been scheduled to conduct a *Lizzie* revival; he didn't, as it turned out. When I phoned to congratulate him on his new post and mentioned our work in progress and my draft-letter to Levine, he asked me not to mail it until we could lunch together. At the Ginger Man he told me that *Lizzie* would be revived in 1984 and asked to see what I had of *Cyrano*. After he had examined the score, he arranged another lunch and announced that he would premiere the piece in '86. Stunned, I admitted that I couldn't have the orchestration ready by then. Not to be outdone, he replied that the pair of years between the *Lizzie* revival and the *Cyrano* could be postponed until I would be ready; no problem! He added that he thought *Cyrano* "an audience piece," but that because he was only second in command to the unpredictable Beverly, I'd be wise to alert the Met to its existence. I polished my letter to Levine, mailed it, and received no response. No matter, for across the Plaza it seemed that when the opera was completed, it would be produced in the State Theatre. During a meeting of Sills, Keene, Sheldon, and me, we went so far as to discuss casting the title role. In code she said to Chris, ". . . that difficult one, the star, would make himself available whenever to do such a role." I guessed who she was talking about, for whom the tessitura would lie too high. I recommended a director to them. When in London Nora and I had been at the box office of the Donmar Warehouse when I spied Jonathan Miller, simply went up to him, introduced myself, and said that Sheldon Harnick and I had a *Cyrano* opera awaiting a premiere. Would he be interested in directing it? His answer was just as brief. "Sure." Later in New York we met again by chance and discussed the matter at some length. Beverly and Chris were impressed.

Shortly thereafter I received a letter from Keene, quoting Beverly, for whom he wrote "no-letters"—she wrote her own "yes-letters." It included ". . . the Rostand subject . . . in its 19th century Romanticism departs from the forward-looking direction we would like the new works we present to make." As it turned out, for fiscal reasons the *Lizzie* revival couldn't be afforded. The rumor that Beverly had changed her mind became irrelevant because Keene, our loyal partisan, resigned as Music Director just before '87.

Not long after he returned as General Director two years later, he asked to see the almost-completed orchestral score. He was planning a '93-'94 retrospective to include *Lizzie* and, I dared hope, a *Cyrano* two years later—but labor and money troubles intervened.

Thee was another intervention, totally unexpected. In the Rhineland city of Hagen the *Intendant* (director) of the opera and his Music Director, married to an American choreographer, decided to produce an American opera. They acquired a pile of scores and then eliminated them, one by one, except for *Lizzie*, with which they intended to open their '92-'93 season. By mail I came to know and to be of some use to the company's dramaturg and public relations director, Astrid Rech-Rechy, married to a Kentuckian and practically bilingual, who accomplished a fine translation into German. During the week that Nora and I spent in Hagen attending rehearsals and the premiere of *Lizzie*, Astrid sat beside me at interviews with the press. She enjoyed my opening sentence at each: *"Ich habe im Kopf nur ein kleines Wörterbuch."* "In my head I have only a small dictionary" and fed me words when I needed them—as in the *Cyrano* garden scene trio.

It must have been she who mentioned to the *Intendant* that I had an as yet unperformed *Cyrano* only informally committed to the New York City Opera. Astonishingly, on the morning of the final dress rehearsal Peter Pietzsch called me to his office and asked if Hagen could give the *Welturaufführung* of *Cyrano* to open their next season. In saying yes, I'm afraid that I added that they ought to discover how *Lizzie* would be received and that they really ought to look at the score of the new work. He was not to be put off: the play had always been foolproof, my translator-librettist was famous for *Anatevka* (the German title of *Fiddler on the Roof*), and he'd heard enough rehearsals to trust me! *Lizzie* turned out to be a success, with twelve performances and then a tour of the Rhineland.

After the years of equivocation in New York, it now appeared that *Cyrano, A Romantic Comedy in Music*, would be premiered in Hagen, joining the impressive roster of English and American operas first performed in Germany. The list so far includes, among others, one or more by Dame Ethel Smyth, and Frederick Delius; among the Americans Roger Sessions, Gunther Schuller, Louise Talma, and Elliott Carter.

Astrid sent me batches of her translation as it progressed; I checked it insofar as I could and occasionally changed the vocal line to fit. As I refamiliarized myself with the libretto, working through it word for word in two languages, one day I suddenly retrieved the phrase "simple transposition" from my forgetery. I began to notice, for the first time, that here and there words and phrases would have to be altered, even in a simple changing of the place and time to New Orleans in 1860-61. I resolved one day again to take up the matter with Sheldon.

As it turned out, the time required to translate the lengthy libretto and to schedule the large chorus rehearsals led to a postponement of the premiere as the season-opener from '93 to '94. That September I was in Hagen for three weeks of rehearsals, for the first time at the birth of one of my operas not as an insider sitting on a piano bench coaching singers or waving a baton at them, but as an overly voluble consultant trying to restrain himself.

In 1999 Opera America asked me for an article for their *Encore* that would describe some of my experiences during the productions of my operas. I reprint the last part of *Way Back, Later On, and Now*, which is briefly concerned with my two operas produced in Hagen.

Whatever the reception of the premiere, subsequent productions always differ from the first, and their receptions may differ as well. Even the move to another theater may change the character of a piece. When *Lizzie Borden* was premiered by New York City Opera in its old house on 55th Street, nobody mentioned difficulty with understanding the words. Such a reaction usually implies that the words are singable and set idiomatically, the singers have good diction, and that there are healthy acoustics. When the production was revived eighteen months later in the State Theater [with the same cast and conductor], there were complaints about diction and I was accused of over-scoring. In fact, I had *eliminated* some brass from the first act. Fortunately, the acoustics of the State Theater have been much improved since the 1960s.

In that revival I was on the piano bench, coaching and playing rehearsals. I remember vividly the piano-dress rehearsal—I could see nothing from the pit, but at one point Julius Rudel leaned over the railing and beamed approvingly. I thought to myself: "No wonder he's pleased. He has his composer where he can't interfere with how things are going on stage, and he's playing his own damnedly difficult piano score—and not being paid!"

To be sure, such an intimate relationship between a composer and a production of his opera is uncommon, but it is ideal for the composer if the company is tolerant. It cannot be maintained if productions become far flung or take place overseas. Even if the composer arrives a week or so before the opening, sets and costumes have long been built, and the director's concept has been integrated into the staging. Singers' diction, if improvable at all, can be sharpened in the early private coaching sessions, but not in the final days of rehearsal— beyond exploding a consonant or purifying a vowel here and there. It is possible to ask for adjustments in tempi and balances—even to open small cuts—but the composer and the work gradually, inexorably, and finally posthumously, become the property of others.

Turning an American opera over to the highly skilled and stylized German theater has special rewards and surprises: I remember trying to explain (in German) to the director of *Lizzie Borden* that the female Bordens were members of the Women's Christian Temperance Union and those gleaming glasses of red wine would have to go from the luncheon table. And I remember being incensed that in the world premiere of *Cyrano* (in German) all spoken passages were to be spoken and acted in slow motion, in imitation of the UFA films from the twenties. My well-known director from Berlin reasoned that he could entertain such a *Konzept* because, in most of those passages, the orchestra was silent; never mind that I had indicated the tempo of the spoken text in my own finicky way. Most of my intent was finally realized when the cast insisted on being coached on the slow motion by a mime, for whom there was no budget.

Because German and Austrian (and Swiss!) opera houses still, as a matter of course, perform many new and recent works, they welcome the presence and aid of living composers, even Americans. In our own country, companies so seldom perform new operas that directors, designers, and general managers have little practice in coping with living composers and librettists. Imagine their predecessors in the Italian opera houses of 1899 in the presence of Mascagni, Leoncavallo, Giordano, the youngish Puccini, and the aged Verdi!

But a composer who has lost minor skirmishes can be useful even at a dress rehearsal, with a quiet word to the love-stricken tenor that he really ought to remove his wedding ring onstage, or the suggestion to the countertenor dressed as an elegant lady that perhaps he should consider shaving his forearms.

It was fascinating during those three rehearsal weeks in Hagen to learn something of the inner workings of a highly respected middle-sized German opera house. Astrid, the General Director, and the Music Director were all nervously worried about their new financial straits, hardly discernible to a visiting American. Their season's seating capacity was 85-90% assured by subscriptions that were passed down from one generation to the next; city, state, and federal subsidies were made to some fifty opera houses in Germany. These grants to Hagen had just been cut by two million marks. The three of them were curious about the financing of opera in the US and asked me about it. I explained that our subscriptions were smaller and much less prized; that we received little, hardly any, funding from government sources; that much advertising was necessary for the important box office sales; and—most important—that our tax code was designed to encourage what was called generosity, large gifts from corporations and wealthy individuals, all duly acknowledged in numerous pages in each program.

The four of us agreed that the Americans were as unlikely to grant more government funding as the Germans were to change their tax code, and that there was little transferable from one system to the other. My three friends were just beginning to make two small steps to deal with what they thought a crisis. The Hagen Theater had just put on sale small replicas of their elegant art nouveau building immersed in water inside plastic domes—covered with "snow" when shaken—and issues of non-voting stock certificates at 100 marks each. I bought one of the former and two of the latter.

Nora and Miranda and Sheldon and Margie Harnick arrived for two dress rehearsals and the opening night. The lyricist of *Anatefka* was able to bring about what I'd been unable to: more light on the stage. When I mentioned to him that there were 400 light cues, he quipped that "too many of them are dark cues!" He convinced the lighting designer to make some changes by pointing out that "audiences never can hear the words of an opera if the light is too dim." He was as surprised as I had been at an early staging rehearsal to see Cyrano weep, not once, but three times. I had been told that stage directors from Berlin and the east tended to look for places in libretti in which their male heroes could break down. Sheldon was the first of us to discover that the handsome program booklet contained the whole of the libretto in German, most of which he could not understand.

At the premiere there were ten Swiss relatives from four countries and Robert Tannenbaum. Robert had been a student in my Opera Survey course. He was one of those who dropped into my office for chats, for he was intent upon becoming an opera stage director. I was pleased to offer him advice as to how he could serve as apprentice and assistant to an established director. He succeeded so well that he became the director of the Giessen Opera, not far from Hagen, to which he'd come with a small entourage. We chatted at length during an intermission during which I told him of my recently revived idea of transposing *Cyrano* to New Orleans at the outbreak of the Civil War should it be performed in the US, a conversation that was later to bear unripe fruit.

The three of us returned to New York shortly after the opening night. Ten performances were scheduled and two were added. Astrid sent me copies of articles and reviews of the opera. Because she had enjoyed my story of how Sam Barber had once told me that he did not read his reviews, but only measured them, I measured ours and sent her the result: 11 yards: 10.25 meters. New operas in Germany created more of a stir in Germany than they do hereabouts, apparently.

I dropped a note about the Hagen production to Christopher Keene, now the general director of the New York City Opera. He responded immediately and assured me that "A European production is no obstacle to the work coming here—our problem has been too many projects and too few opportunities." With several important and difficult European works scheduled, "our" opera had to wait and then, this time, Keene's illness and death intervened.

Another hopeful story began some time later and had a more ambiguous ending. Tannenbaum phoned to say that he had left Giessen and had just been appointed to lead the New Orleans Opera. He had not forgotten our intermission conversation in Hagen and my wish to translate the place and time of the work should there be an American production. Though he remembered well the size of the production—it was the largest so far undertaken by the Hagen Theater—he was planning to make a project of producing *Cyrano* with his company. Would I grant him the right to present the first US performances? I said that with the death of Keene it was unlikely that City Opera would produce it and that, anyhow, New Orleans was the ideal place for the first production; I was certain that Boosey & Hawkes would agree. In short, "Yes, of course!" That was the last I heard of the project or from him. I learned later that after only some three months he left New Orleans and returned to Germany.

*   *   *   *   *   *

As I implied earlier, my retirement from Columbia, June 30, 1988, preceded by a little more than a year the completion of the *Cyrano* scores and the final revisions of its music and words. For several years before my retirement the provost and his deputy attempted to talk me into presenting one of the three annual University Lectures. I finally agreed to do so during my final term, but not in the traditional place, the prestigious Rotunda, the acoustics of which would prevent my including a soprano, baritone, and piano in my presentation. I insisted that the ongoing transformation of McMillin Theatre into the Miller Theatre be hurried so that the certificate of occupancy could be granted before my lecture and the term's approaching end.

The first part of *Composers and Librettists: Marriages of Convenience* bade farewell to the old theatre, hailed the new, and was relevant only to that audience seated in the space of both. It is included here as a part of my discontinuous account of my half century at Columbia, but was omitted from the main body of the lecture that was published soon thereafter in *The Opera Quarterly*. What I had to say therein about Mozart and da Ponte as collaborators was colored, surely, by what I as a composer had experienced in collaborating with Kenward Elmslie (twice), Richard Plant (once), Sheldon Harnick (thrice), and myself (five times, if I include the two operas to be written thereafter).

COMPOSERS AND LIBRETTISTS: MARRIAGES OF CONVENIENCE

The tearing down of theatres, and their building and rebuilding, can be the very stuff of theatre. In William Saroyan's *Cave Dwellers* homeless actors live out their lives and roles on the stage of an abandoned theatre about to be dynamited. In the recent musicals *Follies* and *The Rink*, the destruction of old buildings leads to memories of old performances and to new resolve; destruction structures the drama.

We are here this evening in the little that's left of McMillin Academic Theatre: it's a rather well-appointed cave. In fact, we are in a reconstruction; we are not yet in the Kathryn Bache Miller Theatre, for the Miller Theatre is not yet quite completed; the proscenium has yet to receive its dark, non-reflective color. The new theatre will not be dedicated until October. We are, properly speaking, nowhere, and from *there*, perhaps, we should devote a moment to remembering

McMillin, which many of you—perhaps most of you—have visited often and have long since given up trying to spell correctly.

At the time McMillin was built, in 1924, the Little Theatre movement was burgeoning in colleges throughout the U.S. There was agitation also at Columbia for theatre performance. As one means of thwarting this imprudent, even indecent, activity, McMillin was designed without fly-space, wing-space, or a pit—and the stage, such as it was, was placed on the side that would ensure the worst sight-lines and acoustics for a theatrical or orchestral event. Accordingly, plays and operas were rarely performed here, though Martha Graham's company—with an orchestra—first performed Samuel Barber's *Serpent Heart* in this space (*Medea*, as it is now known), on a program with a first New York performance of Aaron Copland's *Appalachian Spring*; Alwin Nikolais's first foray uptown from the Henry Street Settlement was to McMillin. It was for decades the home of the Columbia University Orchestra and host to innumerable recitals and chamber music concerts. In the forties and fifties, here in McMillin, the NBC, CBS, and Juilliard Orchestras premiered works by Piston, Sessions, Louise Talma, Riegger, and Hindemith, among many others. The first (or second) all-Ives concert in the world was here; *The Unanswered Question* and *Central Park in the Dark* were heard here for the first time. In these same years the *Herald Tribune* regularly, and with reason, proclaimed McMillin to be the worst concert hall in the city.

The architects of 1924 had their way so well that their design of the building has made it impossible to place the stage, fly-space, and wing-space *there*, but in many other aspects their puritanical intentions have been subverted. There is some irony in the circumstance that McMillin Academic Theatre was designed primarily for lectures and we celebrate its destruction this evening with a lecture, though it may be perhaps insufficiently academic and will be concluded with singing actors.

There *is* something suitably academic, however, in my mentioning that McMillin and Miller will have in common the spelling of Theatre with an RE. This is in accordance with Jacques Barzun's dictum of the mid-sixties that, at Columbia, the proper spelling of theatre was to be the *proper* spelling of theatre.

In the same vein, I should confess that it was my mistake, and mine alone, that your invitation implied that I would speak this evening only of musi*cal* theatre. My subject, rather, has to do with musi*c* theatre, that is, with music and drama together in the theatre—with opera primarily, and also with its more popular relative, musical theatre. I shall not pause to define and discuss that embattled word opera, largely because the examples I'll cite are indubitably operas by anybody's definition. If we were discussing the contemporary scene, we'd find that the word opera has now entered Humpty Dumpty's vocabulary; that is, it means whatever one chooses it to mean. Because it's generally thought to be a classy sort of word, it's even used by those seeking artistic respectability, climbing, I think, the wrong ladder.

Webster says that marriages of convenience are those "contracted rather for the advantages arising out of them than because of mutual affection." Fanciful or not, the term describes most of the relationships entered into by composers and librettists for the purpose of writing for the music theater. Clearly, not all the reasons that bring the two together for a short or long period—or for life—are mentioned in the dictionary. Husband-and-wife collaborations—not to speak of other pairs brought together by "mutual affection"—*do* exist. I might observe, though, that couples couple for other reasons than collaborating on music theater pieces and it is rare that a pair includes both an accomplished composer and an accomplished librettist.

I should add that operas and musical theater pieces have also come into existence *asexually*, so to speak, with words and music conceived by one person, thus "allowing beneficial combinations of characteristics to continue unchanged," as the *Columbia Encyclopedia* explains in quite another context. In the early decades after opera's beginnings around 1600, some of those known primarily as librettists occasionally wrote their own music. Examples in our own day include Sheldon Harnick and Stephen Sondheim. During the last century and a half there have been examples of composers serving as their own librettists: Wagner, Busoni, Richard Strauss (in one instance), Schoenberg, Menotti, Floyd, and Sondheim, if he doesn't belong in the first category.

But all too often, composers have thought that the advantages of conceiving words and music together can compensate for what everyone else recognizes as their clumsy dramaturgy and lame writing. However, if a composer bases his libretto on an already-written play, his chances for success may be improved, for some small part of his librettist's task has been accomplished. Debussy and Berg, in successfully adapting plays by Maeterlinck and Wedekind, respectively, may be said even to have transferred them back to the theater from the library. If the composer conceives his work alone because he will not, cannot collaborate with a librettist, he should not write for the theater at all, for he will not be able to tolerate *enforced* collaboration with theater directors, conductors, stage directors, designers, singers, and theater audiences—which are not concert audiences . . .

. . . Why have I chosen often to collaborate? Why have most works of music theater for four hundred years been written in collaboration? I think the answer is implicit in my earlier comments: composers are rarely also poet-playwrights; poet-playwrights are rarely also composers. The individuals who form these couples are, furthermore, specialists. Not every composer is willing to accommodate his musical ideas to the demands of words with music, and of those who are, only some are willing to adapt also to the time scale and other requirements of the theater. It is uncommon for a poet to have a sense of the stage and to be able to speak in the voices of stage characters in addition to his own; it is also uncommon for a playwright to write words that permit, that *demand*, singing, and to accommodate his sense of dramatic timing to the musico-dramatic timing of the composer.

Given the tensions inherent in any kind of marriage, the combining of text and drama and of music, and the well-known tensions that have sometimes existed within pairs of collaborators, it is understandable that historians and critics have taken the side of one against the other. Ironically, these opponents have borrowed their battle cries from the title given by one of the most elegant late eighteenth-century librettists, Giambattista Casti, to an opera composed by Salieri, *Prima la musica e poi le parole (First the Music and Then the Words)* —or from its inversion "Prima le parole e poi la musica" (first the words and then the music). As if to repay Casti's generosity, some composers of a radical disposition have insisted on the primacy of text and drama in their polemical writings, if not in their compositions.

Mozart, who was no radical, put his first thing first—if I may oversimplify. Writing to his father, he said, "I should say that in an opera the poetry must be altogether the obedient daughter of the music." But then he begins to qualify, "An opera is sure of success when the plot is well worked out, the words written solely for the music and not shoved in here and there to suit some miserable rhyme. . . . Verses are indeed the most indispensable element for music—but rhymes—*solely for the sake of rhyming*—the most detrimental" (my italics). And he ends, "The best thing of all is when a good composer, who understands the stage and is talented enough to make sound suggestions, meets an able poet, that true phoenix; in that case no fears need be entertained as to the applause even of the ignorant."[1]

I think that the arguments concerning the preeminence of librettist or composer are overly facile and reflect, if not just the prejudices of an individual, the dominant musical and theatrical conventions of a given time and place. Let us consider the matter chronologically.

There is no doubt that the poet dominated in the first years of opera, the poets of the quasi-dramatic pastorals, which could be set to music throughout because of new developments in music around 1600. By the middle of that century the first major opera composer, Monteverdi (and then his pupil Cavalli), commanded a musical style of great flexibility and intensity. At hand was the first major librettist, Giovanni Francesco Busenello, who was both poet and dramatist, and whose six libretti were models of their kind. If, for a brief period, a happy balance between text and music was achieved, the virtuoso singer was soon to seem more important than either.

Few male or female singers could compete successfully against the power, flexibility, and beauty of the castrato voice. The castrati dominated the serious opera, the court opera—the *opera seria*—throughout the eighteenth century. The singers' needs were attended to by the librettist shaping the drama to provide the proper number of arias for each of the usual six characters. He served the composer with elegantly turned, highly compressed lyrics, often with as few as six or eight lines. These few lines the composer repeated and fractured at length, decompressing the text, so to speak, into large musical structures over long time spans.

The singers' chief competitor for the attention of the audience was the machinist, the stage designer. The librettist furnished excuses for conflagrations, inundations, and the appearances of gods and goddesses from above, demons and denizens of the deep from below. One intends no disrespect to Handel, Hasse, and the other prominent opera composers of the eighteenth century in claiming that it was the librettist who dominated, who determined the subject matter and the form of the *opera seria* in that century. Even the reforms attributed to the composer Gluck were in fact shaped by his librettist Raniero de Calzabigi.

The great master of providing these vocal and scenic necessities within a formal, poetic structure that also provided the composer considerable scope was the librettist Pietro Metastasio. Aside from his other writings, during a half-century period he wrote thirty-some libretti that were set to music more than a thousand times, often rewritten by other librettists to conform to local requirements. Doubtless part of his success was due to the fact that he was a trained musician, an excellent harpsichordist and something of a composer.

By the end of the late 1700s, however, social, theatrical, and musical changes were bringing about the end of the Metastasian opera, of the *opera seria*. From then until recently it was just those libretti, once held in such high esteem, that were thought to make impossible the revival of works in that style, even when the scores were by Handel—the outmoded libretti, *and* the lack of castrato singers. But there are no more castrati singing opera today than there were in most of the nineteenth century, and nineteenth-century producers could have compensated for their absence by making the same vocal compromises that *we* make. No, the death and rebirth of Handel operas—and the death and rebirth of other music theater styles—have more to do with the cyclical changing of theatrical conventions than with changes in musical style and musical performance practice. That the *opera seria* and other supposedly defunct music theater styles can now be exhumed and enjoyed is largely because theatrical conventions today are loose enough to make acceptable the revival of almost any once-lively, then outmoded, set of conventions. *We* accept formality, informality, even formlessness. The baroque practice of composing men's and women's parts without reference to gender, or lack of it, does not seem outlandish to a late twentieth-century public familiar with *Tootsie* and *La cage aux folles*.

Such considerations are relevant also to the lives, deaths, and rebirths of Mozart's operas. The casual operagoer may imagine that those of Mozart's operas most often performed today were always widely performed. They were not. Or it may be thought that the less frequently heard works were always to be found if one traveled around a bit; in fact, a number of them were to be found only in libraries. *Don Giovanni* was once absent from the Metropolitan Opera's repertory for nearly a quarter of a century; the Met was in its thirty-ninth year, in 1922, when it first performed *Così fan tutte*, and that was apparently the first American performance. In Italy, Mozart's operas have *never* been performed much.

Mozart's thirty-five years do not quite encompass the second half of the eighteenth century, but his operas include examples of all the genres of that century. At the age of fourteen and in his last year (and occasionally in the years between these extremes), he followed the custom of the time; he accepted Metastasian libretti with equanimity and castrato singers with delight. At other times he was less compliant, imposing his sense of theater—his own sense of musical characterization and pacing—on his librettists. One of the most interesting records of composer-librettist collaboration is the correspondence between Mozart, in Munich composing *Idomeneo*, and his father, in Salzburg relaying his son's demands to the irritated librettist, the Salzburg chaplain Abbate Varesco.

I quote from the letters of Mozart a few of the comments and demands that were to be put more politely by the go-between:

The second duet is to be omitted altogether—and indeed with more profit than loss to the opera. For, when you read through the scene, you will see that it obviously becomes limp and cold by the addition of an aria or a duet, and very gênant for the other actors who must stand by doing nothing.[2]

Tell me, don't you think that the speech of the subterranean voice is too long? . . . Picture to yourself the theatre, and remember that the voice must be terrifying—must penetrate—that the audience must believe that it really exists. Well, how can this effect be produced if the speech is too long, for in this case the listeners will become more and more convinced that it means nothing. If the speech of the Ghost in *Hamlet* were not so long, it would be far more effective.[3]

The scene between father and son in Act I and the first scene in Act II between Idomeneo and Arbace are both too long. They would certainly bore the audience, particularly as in the first scene both the actors are bad, and in the second, one of them is; besides, they only contain a narrative of what the spectators have already seen with their own eyes. These scenes are being printed as they stand. But I should like the Abbate to indicate how they may be shortened—and as drastically as possible—for otherwise I shall have to shorten them myself. These two scenes cannot remain as they are—I mean, when set to music.[4]

The speech of the oracle is still far too long and I have therefore shortened it; but Varesco need not know anything of this, because it will all be printed just as he wrote it. . . . There is a good deal that might still be altered; and I assure him that he would not have come off so well with any other composer.[5]

In the stern replies of Leopold to his son, much of the anguish of Varesco is reflected. But, after all, *he* was more interested in having his libretto published than in how the audience made its way through an opera by some twenty-four-year-old composer. One has to understand that since the beginnings of opera, printed libretti had usually been available at first and subsequent performances; the music, with the text as set, was often not published at all. *Idomeneo* was published five years after Mozart's death. This sequence of publication of text and non-publication of music was indicated in the credits. In my studio hangs a copy of the program of the first performance of *Die Zauberflöte*, Mozart's last opera. Translated, it says, "For the first time: *Die Zauberflöte*, a large opera in two acts, by Emanuel Schikaneder"! Then follows the cast. Down at the bottom of the page, somewhat lost in a mass of small type, it states, "The music is by Mr. Wolfgang Amadé Mozart, who is to conduct." Then there is an ad for the libretto and its price.

When Mozart had the opportunity to choose his librettist and could assert his musico-dramatic needs in close collaboration, he was prefiguring a relationship that has since become usual. To be sure, in the early nineteenth century, Italian composers still frequently accepted assigned subjects and librettists, and composed swiftly, quoting from themselves and others in the older manner. Beethoven, in contrast, searched widely for a subject, found one, wrote *Fidelio* with care, rewrote it twice, and was then unable for the rest of his life to find a second subject suited to his musical, dramatic, and psychological needs. At the end of that century, Debussy—another one-opera composer—went through the same before-and-after searches.

Certainly the opera composers' growing expenditures of time, energy, and money—and their growing insistence on projecting *their* views of the world, of life and love and death—made the finding of acceptable subjects and compliant librettists ever more difficult. The subjects rejected by Verdi and Puccini—not to speak of more recent composers—are as revealing of those composers' lives and personalities as are the subjects they finally chose and browbeat their librettists into fashioning for them. The copious correspondence of Verdi and of Puccini with their librettists indicated that composers had become the dominant collaborators in their marriages of necessity and *in*convenience. On the other hand, the vast exchange of letters between Richard Strauss and Hugo von Hofmannsthal over a twenty-three-year period is a valuable lesson in how two very different personalities can collaborate on friendly and equal terms in creating music theater that is a reflection more clearly of the pair than of either one individually.

These days, particularly in this country, an opera house audience tends to disregard the libretto—except in the case of new works—and to forget the librettist's name. This is not surprising, for libretti in languages not understood by audiences can hardly make much of an impression. The audience is let in on the secret of what is happening onstage if supertitles are used, but the librettist's care with words is not apparent in the cut version being screened.

In the popular musical theater the lyricist's words are heard: they are in English and miked, after all, and his name is not forgotten. His name is paired with that of the composer, though most often in second place: Rodgers and Hart, Rodgers and Hammerstein, Kander and Ebb—and with credits reversed, Gilbert and Sullivan, and Lerner and Loewe. But a lyricist is not usually the whole of a librettist. In the musical theater there are the composer, the lyricist, *and* the book writer: "Who wrote the story and all that talk?" "I dunno, look in the program." "Never heard of him."

It is a sign of both the reemergence of the librettist and of the cross-fertilization that is occurring between opera and musical theater that we now hear of the dialogue of a musical, or the dialogue and the lyrics of a musical referred to as the libretto. In another quarter, the libretto is beginning to be considered a respectable literary genre and even an acceptable dissertation topic. Some of this recent interest dates from the publication, eighteen years ago, of Patrick Smith's nicely titled book, *The Tenth Muse*, a history of the opera libretto. This kind of attention is welcome, for histories of opera are usually written by music historians who are quite naturally prejudiced in favor of composers. Historians of theater, on the contrary—when they write about opera at all—favor the librettist.

At the end of the twentieth century it is really not worthwhile for a composer-librettist pair to squabble about whose task is more important. As at the end of the seventeenth century our joint efforts, whether for the opera house or Broadway, are often thought less important than the stars and the spectacular stagings that sell the tickets. As it has always been in the music theater, he who pays the piper and his poet calls the tune.

Let us turn now to a particular librettist, his collaboration with Mozart, and to an example of their work together. It is timely to speak of Lorenzo da Ponte, for 1988 in the 150th anniversary of his death; it is fitting to speak of him here at Columbia University, for he was Columbia's first professor of Italian. Da Ponte would certainly have applauded the university's transformation of the old McMillin Academic Theatre into the new Miller Theatre. He would think it a minor effort though, for *he*, at the age of eighty-five, raised the funds, helped design, supervised the builders, and then co-managed the first theater in New York City intended only for opera performance.

Da Ponte was born of Jewish parents in a ghetto eighty miles north of Venice in 1749, seven years before Mozart was born, and named Emanuele Conegliano. His mother died when he was five and he turned bookish. He was later to write in his memoirs that, as a child, his favorite author had been Metastasio, "the Poet Laureate of Austria whose verses aroused in my soul the very emotions of music itself."[6] When the boy was fourteen, his father decided to marry a Catholic woman and so it became necessary for him and his children to convert to Catholicism. At his baptism Emanuele Conegliano took the name of the officiating bishop, Lorenzo da Ponte. With Lorenzo da Ponte, Sr., so to speak, as his mentor, he entered a seminary, became an excellent Latinist, learned Greek and Hebrew, and began to read widely and to write poetry in Latin and Italian. He was soon promoted from student to professor and then vice rector. He also had the energy to carry on three love affairs at the same time.

At the age of twenty-four he was ordained, celebrated his first Mass, and was posted to Venice as priest in San Luca. There he spent a good deal of time in coffeehouses and theaters and made the acquaintance of Carlo Gozzi (*The Love for Three Oranges* and *Turandot* are based on his work) and the librettists Caterino Mazzolà (who was later to collaborate with Mozart) and Carlo Goldoni. He became a friend of Casanova. He also arranged entertainments for the brothel in which he was living with a married woman. None of this was extraordinary in the Venice of that time, but some of his poems were found to be seditious and *this* led to his dismissal as professor of rhetoric and to an investigation of "Radicalism in the Schools" of the Veneto. At last he was denounced—only in part for having twice gotten a married woman pregnant—brought to trial, and banished. He had already left town.

He was then thirty, and for three years he caroused his way through the operatic centers of central Europe, unencumbered with priestly duties. He was to remain a priest for another sixty years, though he kept that matter rather quiet until he took confession and received absolution on his deathbed. During those three years he translated and reworked the libretti of others, doing hackwork, experiencing, in Patrick Smith's phrase, "a paradise of the journeyman and the graveyard of the talented."[7] But in 1782, with the help of his Venetian librettist friends, the kindly Salieri, and Metastasio himself, da Ponte settled in Vienna. Metastasio, for many years the Caesarean Poet to the Hapsburg Emperor Joseph II, died soon after. Da Ponte had long aspired to that position and was to achieve it in all but name, as Poet to the Court Theater.

Mozart's landlord, a friend of da Ponte, introduced the two to one another, probably shortly after da Ponte arrived on the scene. The year in which da Ponte gained his title, 1783, was the year in which Mozart received a court commission for an opera in Italian. He would have preferred to compose a German opera, and, as he wrote his father on 7 May:

> I have looked through at least a hundred libretti and more, but I have hardly found a single one with which I am satisfied; that is to say, so many alterations would have to be made here and there, that even if a poet would undertake to make them, it would be easier for him to write a completely new text—which indeed it is always best to do. Our poet here is now a certain Abbate da Ponte. He has an enormous amount to do in revising pieces for the theatre and he has to write *per obbligo* an entirely new libretto for Salieri, which will take him two months. He has promised after that to write a new libretto for me.[8]

Though the libretto for Salieri was written on schedule, the opera was not performed for more than a year. It was a terrible fiasco. Da Ponte blamed Salieri, who said he would rather cut off a finger than collaborate with him again—and did not for four years.

After the two months mentioned in his earlier letter, Mozart wrote his father, "An Italian poet here has now brought me a libretto which I shall perhaps adopt, if he agrees to trim and adjust it in accordance with my wishes."[9] Because he did not name the Italian this time—and for other reasons—there is a continuing argument about whether it was da Ponte who collaborated with Mozart on *Lo sposo deluso (The Deluded Husband)*. It is pointed out that the libretto was not up to his later Mozart standard, but then neither was the preceding Salieri libretto, actually the first da Ponte had written on his own. Perhaps he would not agree to rewrite in accordance with Mozart's wishes. In any case, the matter is of no great importance, for Mozart composed four numbers and quit.

The pair went on to write some occasional pieces together and then three operas: *Le nozze di Figaro* (1786), *Don Giovanni* (1787), and *Così fan tutte* (1790).

Between the time of *Lo sposo deluso* and *Figaro*, Mozart had been deeply impressed by at least two new operas by others, and da Ponte had become a more experienced writer. It was Mozart's brilliant idea to adapt the Beaumarchais play *Le marriage de Figaro*, which the emperor had just banned in his empire. Mozart was in some ways a much more practical man than he is popularly thought to have been. It was da Ponte who gained the emperor's permission to base an expurgated libretto on the banned play, with the characters altered and warmed by the music, *not* Mozart, as the film *Amadeus* has it. That excellent film, in my opinion, shows a caricature of Mozart; but it is to be remembered that any caricature enlarges upon very real peculiarities. In fact, this pair of collaborators, in spite of their differences in background and training, had much in common. All three of their completed works deal obsessively, and often comically, with the relationships of the sexes. The first two, *Figaro* and *Don Giovanni*, have political and demonic elements carried over from their borrowed material. When the pair was more freely inventing, as they were in *Così*, they were more single-mindedly amatory.

Such was their preoccupation—not theirs exclusively in the eighteenth century—that Beethoven and Wagner among many others in the nineteenth century were contemptuous of da Ponte's libretti, except for the political and demonic content, and were totally at a loss to understand how the composer could have sullied his music with such frivolous obscenities. John Ruskin put their case best: "To follow and fit with perfect sound the words of *Zauberflöte* and of *Don Giovanni*—basest and most monstrous of conceivable human words and subjects of thought—for the 'amusement' of his race! No such spectacle of unconscious (and in that unconsciousness all the more fearful) moral degradation of the highest faculty to the lowest purpose can be found in history."[10] That is but an exaggerated statement of the case brought by those who would save instrumental composers—the "pure" composers—from polluting their music with text and theater.

Figaro and *Don Giovanni* were thought to be bad enough as subjects, but *Così fan tutte—All Women Act That Way* is one of several possible translations— was thought to be the worst of the three. It was seldom performed in the nineteenth century and then only when heavily revised. Actually, Mozart and da Ponte were not altogether freely inventing. Couple- and wife-swapping had—and have—long been a staple of comedy. Five years before *Così*, da Ponte's hated Rival, Casti, had provided Salieri with a *buffo* libretto on just such a subject. The two heroines of *Così fan tutte* are two sisters from Ferrara living in Naples. There *were* two sisters from Ferrara, both renowned singers, living in Vienna at the time, known as the Ferraresi. The part of Fiordiligi in *Così* was written for yet another Ferrarese, a married woman who was da Ponte's mistress. If it is difficult in the twentieth century to figure out which of these five sisters were sisters to which, it is partly because da Ponte and Mozart intentionally mixed reality and theater. And Mozart knew all about relationships with and among sisters, in particular the four Weber sisters, two of whom were singers. With one of these, Aloysia, he fell in love, but he married Constanze instead. At that time he was writing a leading role for a character named Constanze, sung during the first run of the opera by Aloysia.

If I have stressed matters that may seem inconsequential and irrelevant to some, I have done so because they explain in part why this pair could so easily agree on the choice of subjects and then work so agreeably together. Da Ponte's most elegant poetry and best-crafted scenes were for Mozart; at least half of Mozart's finest stage music was to da Ponte's libretti.

In the next year and a half Mozart wrote two more operas, with two other librettists. Perhaps he would have collaborated again with da Ponte, but in 1791 Mozart died, not quite thirty-six years old. In that same year da Ponte was dismissed upon the accession of the new emperor, to whom he wrote a letter in verse filled with democratic ardor and his usual paranoia. And in that year Columbia College was thirty-seven years old.

Da Ponte's journey to Columbia was circuitous and lengthy. I shall describe it only briefly. Again almost penniless, he set out in search of a new position, in the company of la Ferrarese, who was soon reclaimed by her husband. Da Ponte, unable to return to Venice, went on to Trieste where he met a very young Englishwoman with reputedly rich Jewish parents. They decided to marry, but there were problems. He was still a priest and she had converted to the Church of England. Gossip had it that there was a Jewish wedding, that there had been no wedding at all. Nevertheless, they were ever afterward known as Mr. and Mrs. da Ponte (or Diponti), Anglicans, as were their five children. When he was called the Abbate da Ponte, the title meant only that he had *studied* for the priesthood, not that he had taken priestly vows.

He sought advice from Casanova, to whom he introduced his wife as his mistress, just to keep up appearances. Casanova made three suggestions: (1) that they settle in London, avoiding Paris, (2) that Lorenzo stay away from the Italian coffee houses in London, and (3) that he not sign his name to anything. They lived in London for twelve years. He was poet to the Italian opera at the King's Theatre, where he wrote, translated, adapted, and printed libretti, while running a shop for fine and rare books on the side. But he was not following *all* of Casanova's advice. He was dismissed, and when threatened with arrest for debt, he took ship for the United States in a packet named Columbia. He was never to write for the theater again.

For a while da Ponte wasted his time running grocery stores in downtown New York City and in Elizabethtown, New Jersey. Then a chance encounter in Riley's Bookshop on lower Broadway with a recent graduate of Columbia College, Clement Clark Moore, led him to take up teaching again. His charm, erudition, and devotion to Latin, Italian, and French literature soon attracted a number of private students, some of them also students in the College. The fact that Clement's father was bishop of the Anglican Church and president of the College was a help, of course, and with such connections da Ponte became something of a social lion.

But, unfortunately, the distillery business that Mr. Diponti was running on the side went sour. He fled with his family to his in-laws, who had settled in Sunbury, Pennsylvania, of all places. This sojourn was to last seven years. Mostly things went very well for him. He was the second largest taxpayer and built the first three-story brick building in Northumberland County. To the store in Sunbury he added another—and another distillery—in Philadelphia, with a cartage service in between. But the former Poet to the Hapsburg emperor and the King's Theatre in the Haymarket began to find life on the Susquehanna River somewhat limiting. He changed his base of operations to Philadelphia and there he failed again.

He moved back to New York City at the suggestion of Clement Moore, who had by then written and published "'Twas the Night Before Christmas." Da Ponte's new bookstore, specializing in Italian literature, and the rooming house he ran at 343 Greenwich Street, specializing in fascinating tales of his European past—and good Italian cooking—were popular with the young and were the first centers of Italian studies in the United States.

By this time Clement Moore had become a trustee of Columbia College, and some of da Ponte's earlier students were professors there. Presumably with their connivance, he applied for a teaching position and was appointed professor of Italian in 1825, at the age of seventy-six. In those days instruction in modern languages was not considered academically respectable and so he was unsalaried. Italian—and for that matter, German and French—had to be paid for in addition to the regular tuition. It is not surprising that there were no students after a year or two. He did make some money from the College by selling books to its library. But the College did not accept his scheme for attracting students by giving them textbooks; nor did the trustees accept his letter of resignation. He remained a professor until he died just short of ninety years old. He may have been the first Jewish-born professor in the College; he may have been the first Catholic priest to have been a professor. He was surely the first to have been one or the other—or both—*and* to have been thought an Anglican.[11]

The other memorable event in that same year was the visit to New York by Manuel Garcia's troupe with a repertory of Rossini operas. At da Ponte's suggestion, the company presented the first Italian performance in the United States of *Don Giovanni*. Four members of the cast were also members of the Garcia family, including the seventeen-year-old Zerlina, later to be known as Maria Malibran. It is easy to imagine the impression that performance made on his students and the flood of memories that welled up in the aging librettist. In fact, da Ponte was much given to reminiscing about the good old days in the company of Mozart and the emperor. Some of these memories were recorded and published by his friend and physician, Dr. John Francis. At least *his* report can be trusted, for he was founder of the New York Historical Society. I quote Dr. Francis: "Mozart determined to cast the opera exclusively as serious, and had well advanced in the work. Da Ponte assured me that he remonstrated, and urged the expediency on the great composer of the introduction of the *vis comica*, in order to insure a greater success, and prepared the role with 'Batti, batt,' 'Là ci daren,' etc."

Anyone who treasures *Don Giovanni* does so, in part, because of its wondrous mix of the serious and the comic, of *opera seria* and *opera buffa*. Da Ponte's recollection, as reported by Dr. Francis, jibes with the following quotation from da Ponte's memoirs, written earlier:

> *Maestri* Martini, Mozart, and Salieri . . . came all three at the same time to ask me for books. I loved and esteemed all three of them. . . . I wondered whether it might not be possible to satisfy them all, and write three operas at one spurt. Salieri was not asking me for an original theme . . . [but] a free adaptation. Mozart and Martini were leaving everything to me.
>
> For Mozart I chose the *Don Giovanni*, a subject that pleased him mightily; and for Martini the *Arbore di Diana*. For him I wanted an attractive theme, adaptable to those sweet melodies of his, which one feels deep in the spirit, but which few know how to imitate.
>
> The three subjects fixed on, I went to the Emperor, laid my idea before him, and explained that my intention was to write the three operas contemporaneously.
>
> "You will not succeed," he replied.
>
> "Perhaps not," said I, "but I am going to try. I shall write evenings for Mozart, imagining I am reading the *Inferno*; mornings I shall work for Martini and pretend I am studying Petrarch; my afternoons will be for Salieri. He is my Tasso!"
>
> He found my parallels very apt.
>
> I returned home and went to work. I sat down at my table and did not leave it for twelve hours continuous—a bottle of Tokay to my right, a box of Seville to my left, in the middle an inkwell. A beautiful girl of

sixteen—I should have preferred to love her only as a daughter, but alas . . .! —was living in the house with her mother . . . and came to my room at the sound of the bell. To tell the truth the bell rang rather frequently, especially at moments when I felt my inspiration waning. . . . In a word, this girl was my Calliope for those three operas, as she was afterwards for all the verse I wrote during the next six years. . . . The first day, between the Tokay, the snuff, the coffee, the bell, and my young muse, I wrote the two first scenes of *Don Giovanni*, two more for the *Arbore di Diana*, and more than half of the first act of *Tarar.* . . . I presented those scenes to the three composers the next morning. They could scarcely be brought to believe that what they were reading with their own eyes was possible. In sixty-three days the first two operas were entirely finished and about two thirds of the last.[13]

Pungent and brief as they are, these passages from the memoirs, and the later reminiscences that I first quoted, tell us as much or more about da Ponte and Mozart's collaboration *Don Giovanni* than do any sources from 1787, when it was written and to which year we now return.

The two were living in Vienna and not far from one another; correspondence was unnecessary. There were no chatty, newsy letters from Wolfgang to his father, who had recently died. Whether the subject of Don Juan was really da Ponte's idea or the suggestion of the Prague Opera's director, who commissioned it, is not certain—we have only da Ponte's word for it. In any case, it was convenient for a writer of three libretti at one time to rework a well-known story and to have at hand the original Spanish play, and Goldoni's and Molière's versions, not to speak of a recently performed one-act version by a rival librettist, Giovanni Bertati. From that libretto da Ponte took what he wanted, exercising his great gift for rewriting, improving the verse, adding to and fleshing out the characters, and inventing incidents to fill out a full-length evening. Mozart dipped into the same score and took a small dollop of music from its composer, Giuseppe Gazzaniga. Mozart and da Ponte had been working together on *Figaro* barely a year earlier and had the opportunity to develop a smooth working relationship. If there were disputes, we know nothing about them. In this connection, it is interesting to note that Mozart, who was said by da Ponte to want to "cast the opera exclusively as serious," designated *Don Giovanni* an *opera buffa* when he entered it into his list of works; da Ponte, who maintained that he wanted to pursue the *vis comica*, called the opera a *dramma giocoso*, a facetious or jocular drama. Clearly, in working together they exchanged positions of that important question, however ambiguously.

If we know next to nothing about their work together on *Don Giovanni* in Vienna, we do know a little more about the events leading up to the premiere in Prague. The manuscripts that exist tell us what music had not yet been composed when Mozart left Vienna to spend what turned out to be a month in Prague. There, in keeping with the custom of the period, he wrote the music for the singers whose voices he was not already acquainted with: arias, two duets, a chorus, the second-act finale, and the overture. Presumably he had brought texts of the planned-for sections with him. But some of the new music was written because singers felt shortchanged. Did he write back to Vienna for more words from his librettist? We don't know. We do know that Casanova was in Prague at the time, that there is a sketch in his handwriting for the second-act Leporello aria, and that he heard the first performance. For the eight days before the premiere, da Ponte was in town to direct the singers' acting, but he had to return to Vienna to take care of one of his other two composers and missed the premiere. The opening night was an enormous success. What a quartet: Mozart, da Ponte, Casanova, and Don Giovanni!

Mozart and da Ponte, possibly with the help of Casanova, rewrote *Don Giovanni* considerably for its first performance in Vienna six months later. Nobody liked it much at first. If the opera these days seems long and the libretto in some places pretty much of a mess, it is because we are hearing almost everything from both versions jumbled together. Few dare to eliminate anything written by such a pair.

About thirty minutes of theater time after Don Giovanni's presumably unsuccessful rape of Donna Anna, the Don is again on the prowl. He and his manservant, Leporello, find themselves in a crowd that is celebrating a country wedding. The Don soon meets the couple about to be married. Because he considers the girl sufficiently attractive, he commands Leporello to remove the protesting bridegroom and invites the merrymakers to his castle for an impromptu party.

In keeping with the conventions of the period, what follows between the Don and Zerlina begins in *recitativo secco*. The Don starts by insulting Zerlina's bridegroom, then offers himself as lover and husband, while Zerlina's initial shock dissolves into guarded interest. A conventional treatment of this dramatic situation in 1787 would have continued the recitative through Zerlina's acquiescence; next there would have been a duet, orchestrally accompanied, formally organized, in which the pair would have sung together of their present and future felicity.

Instead, in this recitative, da Ponte warms the prose with an occasional rhyme. (During that period—and since, for that matter—prose was used in recitatives, verse for the solos and ensembles.) The occasional rhymes coalesce in the last lines into a small rhymed quatrain. The final vowel sounds are echoed in the formally rhymed first stanza of the *duettino* that ensues. In this way the librettist has avoided the more usual formal close to the recitative and formal beginning of the duet.

I would guess that the initiative in the making of this transition was da Ponte's. Mozart follows his lead beautifully. He sets the final lines of the recitative more suavely than those of its beginning, and the register and pitches are those used in the first phrase of the *duettino*. *He*, also, seems intent upon linking the close of the recitative to the beginning of the number.

Their joint purpose is, of course, to carry out the later part of the seduction and Zerlina's acquiescence with more expressive means than *recitativo secco* can provide, with orchestral accompaniment, two voices in full song, the predator pursuing and the prey finally succumbing. Mozart includes very few stage directions in his manuscript, but many are implied. For example, over Zerlina's last "Andiam" (Let's go) he writes a fermata that brings an end to this little dramatic scene. That fermata is placed, structurally speaking over a half-cadence that propels the listener into the second part of the *duettino*, which is in the same key, but has a different meter, implying a quickening of pace even if one is not imposed. The two then sing the same words at the same time on mellifluously parallel tenths, because they are blissfully in agreement on everything else. The short orchestral postlude is just long enough to start them offstage toward the castle, as Donna Elvira rushes in to save the girl from a fate worse than death.

Throughout *Don Giovanni* one finds elisions of the sort described above. It is notable, too, that Mozart writes few extended instrumental introductions and postludes to arias and ensembles. He seems always to want to get on with the drama, to keep things moving. It has been suggested that he suffered from hyperthyroidism; the symptoms are apparent in his eyes and in his operas. If he did, we benefit from his disease.

"*Là ci darem la mano*"—for obviously that is the *duettino* I have been discussing—was encored three times at the Prague premiere, or so legend has it. Its music, extracted from its dramatic context, has been subjected to countless arrangements, and its delectable first tune has served for sets of variations for two centuries.

This is not the place to make an exhaustive musical analysis of "*Là ci darem la mano.*" Let me say only that the music behaves itself as would any similar instrumental work of the period, whether examined in terms of the common practice of the late eighteenth century or by more recent systems of analysis. To be sure, it is rather more stuffed with events than would be a four-minute piece for flute, bassoon, and orchestra. Musical theorists, on the whole, prefer not to tangle with music that is associated with words and theater, for these free radicals, highly reactive and unstable, can disturb systems of analysis that are designed to deal primarily with purely musical elements. On the other hand, verbal and theatrical elements can often add *why* it happens to the theorist's description of *what* happens.

For example, the Don begins—actually he is continuing his plea—with a four-bar phrase in 2/4 meter. Woodwinds enter to mark its end and to cover his breathing. He then repeats it, varying it slightly, as he *must*, for the second pair of lines in the quatrain is different from the first pair (see ex. 1).

Descriptively speaking, the first phrase begins on the downbeat. *Why?* After all, more melodic phrases in Western music begin with an upbeat, an anacrusis, than on the accented beat. This one begins on the accent because da

470

Ponte's first line begins with a dactyl, as do almost all the Don's lines in the first section of the duet, and the others have to be set to music accordingly. It is not that Mozart could have played no part in this. If da Ponte had first

Example 1

"Là ci darem la mano"

submitted the line *"Mi dia la mano bella,"* Mozart might have said, "Look, I want the Don to be more forthright, more insistent. Fix it so he starts out that way and stays that way!" It is much more likely that da Ponte, through instinct and experience, got it right the first time. The two collaborators were directing their separate means toward the same end. The last note of each of the Don's phrases is also squarely on the beat, lending musical and dramatic symmetry.

I do not imply that these niceties exist because of conscious decisions on the part of da Ponte or Mozart. Writers and composers who write as swiftly as did those two and who develop highly personal styles respond instantaneously and idiosyncratically to the flow of what to others may be subjects for cogitation. (The sum of Mozart's reactions defines his style. The more varied and less predictable, and therefore less coherent, reactions of smaller talents are known as their bad habits, borrowings, and pilferings.) It is to be assumed that Mozart and da Ponte working together may have conferred and compromised, but it is not unknown for congenial, long-acquainted collaborators to work together as quickly as either working alone.

Zerlina then varies the Don's pair of phrases, extending the second by two measures (see ex. 2).

Example 2

Her variation of his melodic line is more fluid and fluent than the squarish, blunt original and avoids the partial stop in the middle of his first phrase. More to the point, her phrases begin with upbeats, as they must, given the iambic beginnings of da Ponte's lines for her. Furthermore, at her first cadence the force of the downbeat is dissipated by distributing falling pitches over the moment. I hate to say it, but Mozart is writing for her a kind of feminine cadence. Given the scansion of the text he did not *have* to do this, any more than he had to give the Don his masculine cadences.

I suppose one need not labor the fact that we are dealing here with the man as pursuer and the woman as the pursued, in accordance with the subject of Don Juan and, one assumes, Mozart and da Ponte's views on the matter. My terminology for the cadences is old-fashioned, but appropriate in this case, I think. A pair of collaborators on the musical version of *Fatal Attraction* would have to pay close attention to their cadences and anacruses.

For the next exchange between the two, the dynamics for the orchestra are raised from soft to moderately loud. There is a new short phrase for the Don, with its affirmative downbeat; Zerlina also has a new short phrase. For the first time she mentions her bridegroom, Masetto, and the thought sends Mozart and her into an indecisive wavering between A-sharp and A-natural. Her anacrusis and feminine ending, though, are still intact (see ex. 3).

Example 3

The Don then repeats his phrase exactly, but with different words. She varies and extends her phrase, more undecided than before and vacillating longer between A-sharp and A-natural. What could have been a trap for a less gifted pair than da Ponte and Mozart is turned to an advantage: Zerlina's only trochee is "Presto"; the first syllable *must* be accented, but she is not allowed such masculine ways. So the *"Pre-"* of *"Presto"* is placed on the weak part of the measure—where her anacrusis is always to be found—and tied over through the following downbeat, forming a syncopation. The resultant off-beat accent can be used by the singing actress (see ex. 4).

The Don is now well aware that he is having his way and returns to his winning tune, singing the first half of the initial phrase, thereby effecting a conventional musical repetition. That *she* is being won over is shown by *her* singing the second half of his original phrase, but in her way, with the upbeat and the cadential fall, both provided for by da Ponte. They repeat the exchange, more or less. She and Mozart tremble a bit together on *trema* and the Don, now thoroughly aroused, breaks in on her last note with *"partiam, ben mio, da qui"* (my dear, let's get out of here). She doesn't wait for him to finish his line either, but breaks in.

Example 4

In the play it is the director who controls the pacing of spoken dialogue. In an opera the composer carries out this directorial function, fixing the speed at which the musically set lines are to be delivered, judging the length of pauses between lines or their overlapping in moments of excitement. In the first section of this duet the gradual quickening of the dialogue and the concomitant shortening of the phrases given to each character in large part predetermine the stage direction.

Now that the voices have briefly touched one another, they are brought together for four measures. We hear his and her earlier phrases again, but they are arranged to fit together in such a way that each retains its own identify. The orchestra plays loudly for him, softly for her. Her voice is left over singing *"Presto non son più forte"* three times. But her amorous predicament has worsened and is reflected—or created, if you will—by her wavering between D-sharp and D-natural, B-sharp and B-natural, and G-sharp and G-natural. He sings *"Andiam"* twice more; she melts on her *"Andiam"* —the one with the fermata— and then, as I said earlier, they sing together the same words at the same time because they are no longer in disagreement.

Do not think that there is anything very special about this little duet—except for its perfection, of course. What da Ponte and Mozart did here is what they did consistently in their work together. And what they did is what every other pair of collaborators—each in its own way—has always aspired to do.

Notes

1. Mozart to his father, 13 October 1781, *The Letters of Mozart and His Family*, ed. and trans. Emily Anderson, 3d ed. (New York: W.W. Norton and Company, 1985), p. 773.

2. Mozart to his father, 13 November 1780, in ibid., p. 662

3. Mozart to his father, 29 November 1780, in ibid., p. 674.

4. Mozart to his father, 19 December 1780, in ibid., p. 693.

5. Mozart to his father, 18 January 1781, in ibid., p. 708.

6. *Memoirs of Lorenzo Da Ponte*, trans. Elisabeth Abbott (New York: Dover Publications, 1967), p. 33.

7. Patrick J. Smith, *The Tenth Muse: A Historical Study of the Opera Libretto* (New York: Alfred A. Knopf, 1970), p. 169.

8. Mozart to his father, 7 May 1783, in *Letters of Mozart*, pp. 847-48.

9. Mozart to his father, 5 July 1783, in ibid., p. 855.

10. John Ruskin, "Time and Tide," *The Works of Ruskin* (New York: Bryan, Taylor and Company, 1894), 14:139.

11. Gerskom Seixas, the first American-born rabbi, was a trustee of Columbia College from 1787 to 1815.

12. John W. Francis, *Old New York* (New York: Charles Roe, 1859), p. 266.

13.*Memoirs of Lorenzo Da Ponte*, pp. 174-76.

(Soprano Jenny Hayden, baritone Allen Roberts, and their accompanist Jorge Martín—who has composed several operas since—performed the excerpts printed in the text and then performed the whole of the duet after I had finished speaking.)

* * * * * *

Chapter 14

More Miscellanea
Sorry, Wrong Number
Practice in the Art of Elocution
(1990-1999)

Not long after the two Harnicks and the three Beesons returned from the Hagen *Cyrano*, Sheldon, remembering that I liked to alternate writing long and short operas, asked if I would collaborate with him on a one-act comedy, preferably based on a French farce. We had enjoyed working together for eighteen years and surely not only for the reason that John Kander had brought us together. I was pleased to be asked, quickly agreed, and began reading one-act comedies in English translation from Moliere to Labiche and beyond, as he did the same, but in French. Many months passed before either of us found something interesting to recommend to the other. Meanwhile, he was busy with other projects and I was immersing myself in Black Magic.

Forty years earlier I had conceived the idea of writing a Black Mass, but Bernard Rogers, though intrigued, talked me out of it and I settled for *Three Settings from the Gaelic* for chorus and orchestra, one of which was an exorcism. Now, in addition to reading French farces, I fascinated myself by searching out and arranging texts for the five movements of *Magicke Pieces*, for mixed chorus, bass-baritone, three winds, and tubular chimes. I chose and wove together ancient charms and spells into a movement so-named; Robert Herrick's *The Hag* and *The*

Hagg became my *Hag Ride*; a *Conjuration* began the series appropriately. There is a brief quotation from the terrifying excommunication, *Malediction*, early in this volume when I was acknowledging my various debts to Laurence Sterne, who translated the original Latin into English.

At the beginning of the first rehearsal of *Magicke Pieces* by the Gregg Smith Singers, Gregg asked me to speak about what might be thought the outrageous words I had chosen to set to music. After I had done so, one of the tenors asked whether I "believed the words" and then added that one of his friends who had dabbled in black magic had committed suicide. I replied somewhat evasively that several of the texts had been written by clerics, one of them a bishop, and that I suspected that not every composer who had set the Catholic Mass necessarily believed every word in the Credo or Dies irae. Though the first performance of *Magicke Pieces* served it well, a few of the numerous difficulties were sufficiently audible to force the cancellation of the scheduled recording session. Theodore Presser Co accepted them for publication in spite of their texts and musical difficulties, or perhaps because of them.

During the long hiatus of almost five years between the finishing of one opera and the beginning of another, thee was time for another choral work of some size, *Epitaphs*, in four sections, a cappella, touching and humorous by turns and Protestant by implication. It was as time-consuming to find usable epitaphs and to organize them—sometimes to combine them—into unified pieces as it had been to find and deal with their devilish counterparts. What composer would not be enticed to set the following punning lines?

Death has decomposed them
And on that great day of resurrection
Christ will recompose them.
(John Adams died 1811, age 79, Newbury, Mass.)

Emboldened by "decomposed" and "recompose" I set this epitaph to one of the subjects in Bach's *Art of the Fugue*. The other two epitaphs in the first of the four pieces are:

Such as thou art, sometyme was I;
Such as I am, so shalt thou bee.
   (Edward, the Black Prince, 1376, Canterbury Cathedral, translated
   from the French.)

As I was, so be ye,
And as I am,
So shall ye be.
   (St. Dunstan's Church, Stepney, UK, on Robert Knight.)

The measured tread of these two led me to use fragments from another work of the past, the slow movement of Beethoven's *Seventh Symphony*. Accordingly, the piece is titled *Composers*, music by Bach, Beeson, and Beethoven (listed alphabetically).

There are sixteen epitaphs set in the four pieces, one as long as eight lines. One of the shortest and most amusing was written, presumably in anticipation of his death, by the deceased, John Gay, whose *Beggar's Opera* became the basis of Brecht and Weill's *Threepenny Opera*:

Life is a jest, and all things show it;
I thought so once, and now I know it.
   (Died 1732, age 47, Westminster Abbey.)

The ever-faithful Gregg Smith also premiered *Epitaphs* and then recorded them. This time I helped Theodore Presser design the cover of the publication. Most of the printed matter on the cover appears to be engraving on a tombstone. I suggested that *Music by Jack Beeson, 1921*—be included also on the tombstone, but the idea was rejected as too ghoulish.

As the only instrumental piece of that period and the last that I have so far written—some would say the only real piece, undefiled with words—a small suite for two Baroque (or modern) flutes, *Fantasy, Ditty* and *Fughettas*. Commissioned by that virtuoso on the pre-Boehm flute, John Solum, for him and his colleague Richard Wyton to premiere; they have played it often since and recorded it for CRI. Before accepting the commission, I phoned Doriot Dwyer for some tips about the Baroque flute. After giving me some she added, "Anything playable on the Baroque flute is more easily playable by the thousands of flutists with modern instruments, including me."

*   *   *   *   *   *

Sheldon's and my search for a usable one-act comedy came to an end when we could not find a libretto-subject about which we were both enthusiastic—a necessity for collaboration. I found *Le Soprano*, coauthored by Eugène Scribe, that paragon of 19th century French grand opera librettists. A farce having to do with a soprano passing herself off as a castrato, I thought it had intrinsic musical possibilities and worked out some revisions for a libretto, but Sheldon was not interested. I didn't want to have anything to do with the one he found. While rummaging around in other French farces I came across the script of the radio play, *Sorry, Wrong Number* that had frightened Sheldon, me, and everybody else who heard it in the forties with Agnes Moorehead as the heroine. Would he collaborate with me in turning it into a one-act opera? "No," he said. "It's too *Grand Guignol* for me and I don't like the murder at the end. You've collaborated with yourself before. You do the whole thing." So I did, with enthusiasm.

Because the two plays and the short story on which Sheldon and I had based our operas were safely in the public domain, we could revise them as we pleased, and did. The publication of *Sorry, Wrong Number* carried the copyright date of 1948, and a stern warning that professional producers and those seeking other rights should address their inquiries to the William Morris Agency. The young people who spoke to me at the Agency thought that Lucille Fletcher, the author of *Sorry, Wrong Number*, other plays, and novels, might once have been represented by William Morris, but knew nothing of her present agent or her whereabouts. I was surprised, for her play had been translated into 15 languages, including Zulu. While watching the film *Sorry, Wrong Number*, made in 1948 and starring Barbara Stanwyck, I was surprised to see that it was Lucille Fletcher who had written the script that seriously diluted the menace of her radio play of only 22 minutes of playing time. The last of a dozen phone calls to agencies in

Hollywood and New York led me back to William Morris and to the ageing Owen Laster who had represented Fletcher for the forty years since the beginning of her career. Laster understood immediately what I wanted to do, was supportive, and gave me Lucille Fletcher Wallop's address on Maryland's Eastern Shore and her phone number. She, too, was friendly and helpful, both a good talker and a good listener, in her early eighties, ill, and lonely, I thought. She mentioned that Jerry Moross had once written an opera on *Sorry* and that she had heard it "somewhere in the West Village in 1957, accompanied by two pianos. Anything that you and Owen Laster work out will be ok with me." I learned that Wallop was the name of her deceased second husband, who had written the novel that became the basis for *Damn Yankees*. Earlier she had been married to Bernard Herrmann, Hitchcock's favored composer. When I told her that many changes would have to be made in her play she made no objections and hoped I would phone her often about how I was getting along with the words and the music.

Owen Laster was equally agreeable and eventually sent me a copy of the contract he had drawn up for Jerry Moross; he suggested that *I* write the letter of agreement between Mrs. Wallop and me and then send three copies to him for forwarding to her for her signature.

With the three principals informally in agreement in early February 1995, one might think that signatures would soon be on a formal contract. A phone call by me to him could be answered in as little time as two weeks; a letter or a draft could be reacted to by him—or by his apologetic assistant—in a month or two. On the first of June I mailed three drafts of the Letter of Agreement; on July 27 arrived by hand on William Morris Agency letterhead, re-typed, were the three copies of the final document. I signed them and returned them immediately for the signatures of Lucille, as I had come to know her. My copy of the Letter of Agreement, now in effect, was delivered by hand—presumably for security, surely not to save time—on September 5, still bearing the date of June 1.

Because I had known for six months that I was likely to acquire the needed rights, I had not hesitated to study the play thoroughly, to write drafts of the libretto, and to plan at the same time the shaping and some of the details of the music.

It happened that the contract permitting me to write my ninth opera arrived as I was reading proof of the piano score soon to be published of *Dr. Heidegger's Fountain of Youth*, my seventh. On those red-letter days of August 27-28, I was attending rehearsals for a pair of concert performances of *Hello Out There*, #2, and Paul Kellogg phoned to confirm that the New York City Opera would revive *Lizzie Borden*, #4, during the next season and to discuss casting. This sudden jostling of so many operas against one another—a unique experience in my life— led me to write down the long-planned first pages of my new one in August '95.

Fourteen months later the music was composed and orchestrated and I wrote the last notes of the piano-vocal score. My estimated performance time was about 35 minutes, which turned out in performance to be accurate. The nine characters, several with doublings, can be cast with only five singers. In keeping with the work's chamber opera qualities, the instrumentation is for only 17 players.

The simple stage setting for the murder mystery that is *Sorry, Wrong Number* is so important that my suggested design for it is sketched on the page that lists the characters and the instrumentation. More or less centered downstage is a small side table on which is a lamp—the only light source onstage—a rotary dial telephone, a glass of water and a pill bottle. Enclosing the space is either an arc of scrim or two scrims on the diagonal that serve as the sidewalls. There is a door on the audience right and a window upstage through which one can see the lights of distant buildings. Behind the scrims, near the proscenium on both sides, is a telephone booth, behind the scrim, on the left, upstage of one another, are two telephone switchboards (the time is the forties); opposite them and behind the scrim, on the right, are the desk of the precinct police station and the desk of a Western Union office. When a telephone call is made by or to a person behind a distancing scrim, the lighting makes him or her visible. Also onstage are at least suggestions of expensive furnishings in the second floor living room of a private home on North Sutton Place near the river on Manhattan's East Side.

The sounds that begin the opera are as unconventional and integrated into the special nature of the piece as is the stage arrangement. The conductor enters unobtrusively and cues the oboist to play the A to which the others begin tuning. As the tuning continues, later to dim and to disappear, the conductor begins, "Quasi Lento, quarter equals 52: the tempo of rotary phone dialing" and an offstage clock or church bell chimes 10 o'clock in quarter notes. At two-beat intervals one solo string after another enters on an A in a higher or lower octave until all available A's are sounding pianissimo. By this time the stage is dimly lighted, supposedly by the table lamp, Mrs. Stevenson, of middle age and in a striking kimono, is in her wheelchair downstage from the table dialing UN7-5432 [Murray Hill 4-0098] in the prevailing tempo. (Brackets indicate the original play text.)

This number and all others are of my invention. The two initial letters and the other five numbers are the analogues of pitches sung and/or played by an instrument and are sometimes used in the orchestra to unify a small scene. Her dialing is accompanied by A F# G E D C# B♭, woodblock quintuplets filling in the sound of dialing between pitches. The line is busy, the sound simulated in the orchestra.

She slams down the receiver. Frustrated, she takes a pill with water, tries the number again. It is still busy. She calls the operator; as the bell rings at the first switchboard, its operator answers, "Operator." Mrs. Stevenson explains that the line has been busy for forty-five minutes, though her husband is supposed to be working late in his office. She adds that she is ill, is alone because the maid is out, and asks the Operator to try the number, please.

The Operator tries, crossing the lines so that Mrs. Stevenson remains connected while the phone in one booth rings, called by the phone in the other booth. Light comes up on Capo (Italian for Boss) and Giorgio. [First Man and Second Man.] She overhears their conversation but they cannot hear her exasperated questions to them. The two hit men discuss a murder they are to commit at 11:15, when any screams of the victim would be covered by the racket made by the train crossing the Queensboro Bridge. All of Capo's instructions to Giorgio seem to her to describe her neighborhood, home, and her one light in the upstairs front room. When jewelry is mentioned—to make the crime seem to be a simple robbery—shocked, she hangs up and calls the Operator again, the first of her many calls for help. These first minutes of the opera, described in some detail, introduce the main character, three of the several others, and the use of the telephone as the medium for conveying the increasing tension and mystery leading to the murder that takes place half an hour later.

Mrs. Gugliemo Stevenson [Mrs. Elbert Smythe Stevenson] I renamed in order to clarify an ambiguity in the play. Her husband's Italian first name suggested a possible Italian Connection that may have led him to hire two Mafiosi to commit murder. I also thought it would be amusing to have an operator cope with the spelling and pronunciation of Guglielmo—and did so. On two occasions when Mrs. Stevenson is at ease, she speaks of her husband affectionately by his nickname, Googly.

In addition to changing numbers and names, I cut many passages, rewrote many others, and invented far more than I cut, in order to provide vocal solos of some length and variety. Two of these, not on the phone, are quietly introspective and sung by Mrs. Stevenson. While writing new lines I sought to maintain regular rhythms and used much assonance, alliteration, and false rhyming. Strict rhyming would be out of place in an opera to be subtitled A Conversational Chamber Opera in One Act.

The first of her introspections takes place well into the opera. Because it is late in the evening, Western Union calls to read a telegram to her. "Darling terribly sorry, line always busy . . . leaving for Boston in an hour. Urgent business. Back tomorrow at three. Stay happy. Love, Googly." In the play she reacts in anger and frenzied panic, with few words. In the opera, touched by the kindly tone of "Thank you, Ma'am. Good Night", after an outburst of disappointment and disbelief, she reflects, in a quasi-aria:

> . . . After all these years beside me, why now?
> Is there someone else he loves, someone he sees,
> and speaks and sleeps with?
> I'd be the first to understand,
> and the last to blame him.
> (She glances yet again at her stopped watch.)
> Our lives are like the hands of my poor watch,
> his, moving swiftly,
> mine more slowly, by the hour.
> And so they meet, and fall apart,
> But when they twist together
> then they slow, then break, then stop . . .

Shortly thereafter, too rattled to call her husband's number, she asks the Operator to try it. While she does so, Mrs. Stevenson sings softly to herself. "*Sola . . . sola, perduta, abbandonata.*" (Alone, lost, abandoned.) "There's no answer Madam. What are you saying?"

"No matter, no matter. My husband loves Italian opera. It's often apropos."

In addition to this quotation from Puccini's *Manon Lescaut*, there is another, the greater part of the tuniest marching song for chorus and orchestra from my *The Sweet Bye and Bye*. When Mrs. Stevenson calls the precinct station for the first time, a policeman and his assistant are listening to it in their radio. The phone rings six times before it is answered. "Police Department, Duffy speaking."

The following is set to vocal lines for my ninth opera and accompanied by part of the broadcast of my #3:

Mrs. S.	I'm calling to report a murder.
Duffy	What's that? I can't hear you.
Mrs. S.	Well, turn off that gospel music.
Duffy	It's *not* gospel! What murder? What murder?

He turns down the volume while she explains that it's not yet taken place but it will at 11:15 and tells him everything she'd overheard not long before. He interrupts to ask and write down her name and address; he's interested in her story but unconvinced of its truth. He speaks with a brogue and has the gift of gab, remarking that his mother, "God bless her, lives in Dublin in a house in Sutton Place near a bridge across the Liffey." (My long conversation with the Dublin operator and her informants assured me that my invention could be true.) His friendly manner leads Mrs. S. to speak of her absent husband who rarely left her side in the twelve years she's been housebound; he, in turn, waxes lyrical on the subject of New York's rivers, bridges, and murders elsewhere, trying to be helpful. In short, their effusions are a relief halfway through the opera from the tensions earlier and later.

And, much later, terribly apprehensive because her watch does not work and she knows that the murder is set for 11:15, she calls her by now friendly Operator to ask the correct time. It is 11:13. She, but not the Operator, hears a click on her phone and is certain that someone on the downstairs extension is listening in and sooner or later will come up the stairs. Three times she demands that the police be called immediately.

During these final few minutes of high tension and murder I wished to avoid the usual clichéd orchestral crescendo on ever more dissonant agglomerations. As my alternative, each of the restless lines that accompany the telephone interchange comes to a close on a pitch that is sustained softly until the end. New lines that enter are treated similarly, the sustained pitches each a perfect fifth above or below the other forming by the end a stack containing eleven of the twelve in the chromatic scale. This quietly held string sonority—with three interjections by four raucous woodwinds—is oddly undefinable and seldom heard; I used it twice to similar effect near the end of *Lizzie Borden*; it is similar only in its structure to the consonant stack of octaves that begins *Sorry, Wrong Number*.

On the last of her three cries to the Operator, "The police!" she sustains the last syllable *ff* at length while, as she thrashes about, the phone cord catches the lamp, throwing it to the floor and the stage into darkness. Her high A♭ is taken over in the octave above by the highest G♯ of the E♭ clarinet, piercingly long held. The clarinet then descends and doubles the beginning of the Operator's "I'm ringing the Police Department!" Overlapping this line, the door opens and there is a shadowy figure with a flashlight who rushes in. As the (recorded) sound of the train on the bridge increases in volume it mixes "with the moans, whimpers, or screams of Mrs. Stevenson" (as the stage direction has it).

The rest of the action is accompanied only by the quiet, colorless tapestry of the strings. Giorgio efficiently stabs Mrs. Stevenson to death. The light has dimmed on the Operator and now comes up on the precinct station desk on which Duffy is sleepily resting his head. He finally answers the phone, when it has rung five times. "Police Department, Duffy speaking." Giorgio takes the sparkling diamond ring from her hanging, lifeless hand. "Police Department, Duffy speaking." Giorgio picks the phone up off the floor and answers, "Sorry, wrong number," then replaces the phone, turns off his flashlight and disappears. The musical cadence follows: the two last fifths to be sounded, the highest and the lowest.

After the first performance of the opera, John Kander hurried to greet me and to ask, "How did you get the idea of using the high E♭ clarinet?" I was surprised and delighted to be asked, for his question helped to confirm my impression that those four measures of thirteen notes played by that instrument in that register formed the most effective passage that I had ever composed.

*　　*　　*　　*　　*　　*

Though Sheldon and I were still eager to continue working together, we had by now long tried but failed to find a subject for an opera that interested both of us and each went on his own way. Mine, for the moment, was a triple collaboration related to the celebration of the centennial of the American Academy of Arts and Letters: a large print consisting of a reproduction of the manuscript of my setting of part of Allen Ginsberg's *Pull My Daisy* superimposed over Paul Resika's design of a vase overflowing with giant daisies. A subterfuge made possible the presence of all three signatures on the hundred expensive copies of the print, Allen having died while the project was under way. The miniature song, unadorned, then appeared in two of the Boosey and Hawkes volumes of my songs.

That one-page song was followed, after much thought and planning, by the 111 score-pages of *Interludes and Arias from Cyrano*, four of the baritone arias and two purely orchestral sections woven together in an 18 minute synthesis of the opera. My model was the similar *Three Pieces* for soprano and orchestra that Berg fashioned from his *Wozzeck*. While writing the opera from 1917 to 1921 neither he nor his publisher could find a theatre willing to produce such a difficult work, though only ninety minutes in length. It was the conductor Hermann Scherchen who urged Berg to extract the 16 minutes of vocal and orchestral sections, the successful performances of which led, finally, to the premiere of *Wozzeck* in 1925. Though *Cyrano* had already been premiered, in German, I thought my *Interludes and Arias* might lead to the opera's production in English. Because it was important both to portray Cyrano as a developing character and to shape the parts of the suite into a satisfying whole, some revising, rewriting, composing and orchestrating were necessary. In addition, new words and phrases were needed to clarify the new sequence of solo sections now out of their contexts. In our last collaborative meetings, Sheldon examined my by now already set-to-music words and phrases and, as usual, either found them acceptable as his own or bettered them on the spot.

*   *   *   *   *   *

While still checking the *Interludes and Arias* orchestral parts for errors— for many had to be extracted from the newly reordered orchestral score—I found serendipitously the excuse for, if not quite the subject of another opera. On the ninth of August, uneasy as I have been always on that date, I was idly browsing through Miranda's collection of theatre and dance books in her room in our Lloyd

Neck house and discovered a battered tome she had found at a yard sale. Quite a few of the 452 pages were missing from *The Standard American Speaker and Entertainer* (Beautifully Illustrated by Celebrated Artists), but its author's name was present and amusing, Frances Putnam Hoyle-Pogle, B.E., as was her flaunting of a bachelor's degree in education.

Mrs. Hoyle-Pogle's book was free of copyright, fortunately, published in 1901. Serious in intent and hilarious in effect almost a century later, its purpose was to instruct public speakers, actors, and singers in deportment, bodily movement, and vocal projection; it also provided many lengthy and sometimes imaginative exercises to develop and perfect them. Throughout were full-page photographs of actors and singers in "attitudes" of grief, horror, lust, contentment, amusement, and whatever. Also included was a collection of songs written for the volume by George Vickers, A.M.—*he* had earned a Master of Arts degree! The songs were to be used as vocal-expression exercises, which sometimes sported a high-flown vocabulary:

> . . . Whether reciting or singing the selection, the performer must use the Oratund Voice, to be distinguished from the natural voice by being stronger, deeper, and more resonant. Of the three divisions of the Oratund Voice, the Effusive, the Expulsive, and the Explosive, the first named . . . most appropriate . . . as it is in rendering all grand, sublime, reverential styles, in everything that expresses awe, despair, wonder, reverence, and horror . . .

Throughout her book Hoye-Pogle pays lavish credit to her teacher, François Delsarte, often quoting from his treatises. Delsarte (1811-1971), French teacher of voice and acting, originated the Delsarte System that defined the ways in which the voice can, and should, be coordinated with the parts of the body. Toward the end of his life several American Singers and actors attended the courses in "applied aesthetics" in Paris; others, including Hoyle-Pogle, imported his ideas and then taught them in modified form. The specialty publisher of her large volume ran pages of advertisements by studios—not all of them in New

York City—aimed at public speakers, actors, and singers and each promising them the road to success.

I suppose that my only connections with this bizarre period of codified behavior were some of the attitudes struck by actors in silent films and some of the illustrations in my early edition of *The Victor Book of the Opera* purchased when I began listening to the Met broadcasts in 1933. Some of the remnants of those olden days are still to be seen on the opera stages.

That I thought some of the attempts of early film and opera stars at high tragedy resulted in low comedy and that Hoyle-Pogle's serious intent in 1901 seemed so hilarious in 1997 suggested a kind of dramatic conflict, though of an unusual kind. In any case, Hoyle-Pogle's basic subject matter was words and music and their dramatic projection singly or together, something that had animated my composing for decades. It might, in itself, form the basis for a music theatre piece if I could invent a context for it made comic by the use of the choicest passages and exercises from her book.

Eight months after discovering Hoyle-Pogle's book, to the day, I delivered a copy of the completed score of *Practice in the Art of Elocution*, an operina for soprano and piano, to Boosey and Hawkes. I didn't mind that the publisher claimed that it now had ten of my operas, but I had coined the Italian word *operina* (a little opera) to describe accurately and honestly what I had written, perhaps to be counted as number 9 1/2. With nothing required onstage but a piano and a music stand, a soprano and a male accompanist—*both* of whom can perform dialog as well as act—and lasting about half an hour, it can be part of a double or triple bill of chamber operas or it can serve as the costumed quasi-dramatic half of a voice recital. I have heard it performed in both contexts.

In whatever company, *Practice* is an unconventional music-theatre piece in subject matter, form and content; for the most part its music is unashamedly anachronistic, what I was writing in the late 1990's. Though I was not inhibited in such a piece as this from doing anything I wished, I could not be as silly musically as I could in choosing what to quote from Hoyle-Pogle, what texts to use for the four songs, and in inventing the dialog and action.

Our unnamed Soprano comes onstage, paying no attention to the audience. She carries a music stand and a large book that purports to be *The Standard Speaker and Entertainer* but is actually the score of *Practice in the Art of Elocution* disguised, perhaps filled out with blank paper. She arranges the volume on the stand, leafs through a few pages, as though for the first time, then reads aloud a bit about the Delsarte System, that "gesture is the language of nature," and that "Practice makes Perfect."

"The following exercises are designed to encourage the Harmonic Poise of Arms and Hands: Assume the Military Position: Head erect; shoulders well up . . . Abdomen back in place."

"Exercise I.
1. Place your left foot forward and put your weight on it.
2. Drop your handkerchief to the floor on your right side."

Suddenly aware that a handkerchief is needed, the Singer turns to her accompanist—who is not yet present. Annoyed, she is about to exit audience-left to find him, when he enters, carrying what appears to be his copy of the Hoyle-Pogle (his copy of the operina), a sheaf of newspaper clippings, and a scrapbook. She addresses him as "E.B."—my posthumous tribute to Emanual Balaban, an Eastman faculty opera coach and conductor who left Rochester for New York at about the time I did. She helps herself to his large white breast pocket handkerchief; he's also dressed à la 1900. She asks him if he'd mind if she did a couple of these new exercises. E.B. replies, "No, not at all. I have to organize all these press clippings for your scrapbook." He adjusts his round piano stool and goes about his work. She continues Exercise I, reading the complicated instructions and carrying them out . . . until "In this way the left leg does all the work, and none of the vulgar parts of the body are brought into prominence." The instructions say that she should repeat the movements ten times. "Oh no! (or

Surely not! Or perhaps *once* more.)" This kind of flexibility is built into the spoken lines as is stated in the Performance Notes in the score:

> The performers are encouraged to elaborate on the written words, particularly while the singer is performing her exercises: miming distress, incomprehension of the instructions, fatigue, or whatever. Other words, phrases—even dialog—may be added with discretion from time to time.

The singer reads the instructions for another exercise.

> "Imagine feathers to be floating around you, and press them down so carefully that they will not stick to your fingers. . . . In this movement, when the hand goes down, the fingers should go back and when the hand goes up, the fingers should trail."

As she begins to try trailing her fingers and then the imaginary feathers begin to fall, float, and be pressed, and as E.B. becomes intrigued by her curious motions, we hear the first tentative notes of the operina. Very likely E.B. is often also a dance-rehearsal pianist, accustomed to improvising. He begins to play music appropriate to her slithery motions. He has either memorized the music in my score or pretends not to be reading it. Beginning with isolated very soft high notes, it becomes a filigree as she reads the instructions and returns errant feathers. The filigree fills out into cascades of notes as the feathers pour down and she presses them together; then, as she discards them delicately in a pile between her feet, the music disappears and E.B. returns to his press clippings.

The Soprano selects one more exercise, one intended for Focusing the Tone. I overcome my temptation to include here the five directions given for preparing the waist, lungs, and lips to explode the word Boat. When she does so, she startles E.B. who listens to her read #6: "Imagine yourself on a storm-tossed rowboat." He responds with low, loud thumps on the keyboard while his right hand damps the strings. "You see a rescuing sail and with your hands at your mouth sing out 'Ship ahoy!' five times . . . for your life depends on it. E.B.

provides a crescendo as she reads and then appropriate chords to accompany her five stentorian "Ship ahoys!" He applauds her effort politely.

She then reads the words written by me to lead into my choice of the text for the first musical number of the operina: "Now expand and extend this brief nautical image by reciting or singing the musical setting of Rupert Brooke's sonnet *A Channel Passage*." These lead to Hoyle-Pogel's instruction that such a piece must be sung in the Oratund Voice and to her explanation of its various subdivisions quoted earlier in part.

Singer: Do you have your copy of it?

E.B.: I think so . . . Yes . . . Here it is.

Because the two musicians are meeting in order to read through the music supposedly included in their new copies of the Hoyle-Pogle volume, both must pretend to be sight-reading the five musical numbers that follow. To assist in this deception, the Performance Notes include:

> …In the musical sections . . . if mistakes are designed to occur, passages may be repeated *ad libitum*, with or without spoken comment between the performers; it is suggested that such interruptions take place near the beginning of a number (or of a section) with a repetition "from the top" in order that the overall effect of the number not be lost.

Four of the five song texts were very difficult to find. I wanted the poems to date from the early 1900s or shortly before and they had to share the zaniness of their context. In the case of the first of the four, *A Channel Passage* was a perfect fit, for it followed naturally the Ship Ahoy exercise. One of the earliest of Rupert Brooke's poems, it became known to his critics as one of his "unpleasant poems" for good reason. A passenger recounts her stormy crossing of the channel, trying to quell her seasickness with fervent rememberings of her beloved, finishing with

> "It's hard I tell you
> To choose twixt love and nausea,
> heart and belly."

I provided no dialog immediately thereafter, not being certain whether their reactions would be of amused surprise, disbelief, or repugnance, and leaving it to them to improvise comment or to shrug off the experience with grimaces.

The Singer returns to the Hoyle-Pogle text and to one of my hobbyhorses, "Distinctness and Diction. After pronouncing *slowly* and distinctly, then *quickly* and distinctly" a few complicated and varied polysyllable words, she goes on to "Difficult Sentences," all in the form of little-known tongue-twisters. Two of them are,

"Say, Susan, should such a shapely sash such shabby stitches show?" and:

"One sheet-slitter, he slit sheets;
Two sheet-slitters, they slit sheets."

The last one I included was an old friend of mine. I had set it as a choral round in Rome almost 40 years earlier and had seen it through two publications.

"Swan swam over the sea,
Swim, swan, swim!
Swan swam back again,
Well swam swan!"

Inventing my own Hoyle-Pogle prose, I sent the performers to my made-up page number where they will find the words set as a round. After some palaver they begin to "sight-read" it. She sings the first two lines by herself, then the last two lines, as E.B.'s left hand begins the tune a fifth higher. As he continues, she begins the tune again, up another fifth, forcing her to perform the whole of the transposing tune a step higher. She is surprised and disconcerted. The process continues as the "third voice" enters a fifth higher in E.B.'s right hand. When she begins the tune for the third time, she must sing it all again yet a step higher. The tune is so written that she now becomes uncomfortable with its tessitura and turns to the pianist who is preoccupied sight-reading and "improvising" a free decorative counterpoint. When she reaches the High B she is in vocal trouble—or fakes it—and quits. She is angry at the round's composer, who is supposed to keep a round in one key. E.B. explains that it is a spiral canon, bur she doesn't understand and, exasperated, says "Even Tetrazzini couldn't keep going up twelve steps! I won't have anything more to do with it!"

Still irritated, she returns to Hoyle-Pogle and a tongue-twister read angrily, rapidly, and forcefully.

> "Amidst the mists and coldest frosts,
> With stoutest wrists and loudest boasts,
> He thrusts his fists against the posts
> And still insists he sees the ghosts."

Her verbal tantrum leads to a mixture of Hoyle-Pogle and Beeson prose and then to my own, which introduces *Hiawatha* and "our great, gray poet Henry Wadsworth Longfellow, who was very partial to word and phrase repetition. There is just such a passage of it . . . on page 76." They turn to the *Longfellow Variations* as she says "Maybe the music is by somebody good, like Cadman or MacDowell and has some Indian melodies in it." It doesn't, but aside from my feeble attempt at writing *Redwing* in my teens, it's my only music with Indians involved; the words, by some anonymous Longfellow parodist, are wonderfully absurd. When the two of them have read it through, they approve of my partially pentatonic music and decide to keep the song in mind for their tour out west, for Sioux City and Cheyenne.

She turns in the volume to a paragraph on Humor and Music in which we learn that "Physiologists tell us that the lachrymal glands and the risible muscles are the nearest neighbors on the human countenance. . . . Flights of notes always produce mirth." This paragraph is the last read from the Hoyle-Pogle. The remaining dialog is of my invention, however Hoyle-Pogleish.

The Soprano then leafs through the other songs in the volume and finds "something very modern with words by that charming Hoosier post James Whitcomb Riley. *While Cigarettes to Ashes Turn.* Can you find it?" "Let's see . . . well . . . yes, let's try it."

The Riley poem, of some length, begins quasi-operatically with a young woman's parents violently objecting to her boyfriend because he smokes cigarettes. The music relaxes into a tango-like accompaniment as she calms herself in her room at sunset. Through her window and his across the way she sees him light a cigarette; she lights up, too, then

> ". . . gleam for gleam and glow for glow,
> Each pulse of light a word we know,
> We talk of love that still will burn
> While cigarettes to ashes turn."

During the brief conversation thereafter, the Singer remarks that her mother would have a fit if she found out she had anything to do with tangos and smoking. E.B. adds that he lives in the house of his grandmother, who doesn't like his practicing "this dissonant modern stuff . . . and these new dance rhythms—rags, or blues, or tangos."

The Singer suggests that they might program it "when there aren't so many old fogies around. Let's try one more song and then have some coffee and a cigarette."

The last song, which ends the operina, is a setting of another Riley lyric to be sung with a Hoosier twang, *The Lugubrious Whing-Whang*. It is a humdinger, fast and various, and anything but lugubrious, having to do with a pair of bird-like creatures whose constant refrain is some variant of "Tickle me, Love, in Me Lonesome Ribs." The peroration is

> "Tickle me, Dear, tickle me here,
> Tickle me here, and here, and here
> in my no longer Lonesome Ribs."

She is directed to leave her last note on a giggle or laugh. The performance of their rehearsal now at an end, they "acknowledge the presence of the audience for the first time, bow, smile, and leave the stage in the usual manner."

By the time I had completed *Practice* it had become clear that its four main musical numbers had enough in common to form a song cycle. Given their contents—seasickness, making fun of Longfellow and his Indians, cigarette smoking, and tickling—*Four Forbidden Songs* seemed a highly proper title. Its separate score was delivered to Boosey and Hawkes together with that of its parent, the operina.

Only a few weeks later the *Four Forbidden Songs* were performed twice by Lauren Skuce and Joel Sachs on the Summer Garden 1998 series at the Museum of Modern art. It was a pleasure to hear the music so well played and sung, and every word expressively and clearly projected; it was heartening to discover in this partial preview of the operina that the audiences seemed amused and interested by the unconventional words that had been so troublesome to find and to adapt and such fun to set to music.

Some months later the songs appeared in their original setting when *Practice in the Art of Elocution*[1] was premiered in Merkin Hall on May 12, 1999 as the chamber-opera half of a song recital. The performers were again excellent musicians, and accomplished actors to boot, Lynne Vardaman and Marc Peloquin, both specialists in new music. A stage director and costumer aided in bringing about a convincingly staged make-believe rehearsal. My pre-performance worries about whether anybody would find my first attempt at comic opera libretto writing as amusing as I did turned out to have been needless. The song-recital audience, already treated to song cycles by Schoenberg and Messiaen, may have been thrown off guard by Lynne's re-entrance newly old-garbed and carrying her own music stand, and by her reading out loud Hoyle-Pogle prose, but they soon accepted the intended absurdity as hilarious, sometimes drowning out lines with laughter. No doubt Miranda, sitting next to me, having read the script and able to anticipate the jokes, was unintentionally cueing the audience with her infectious giggles and laughs.

---

[1] *Sorry, Wrong Number* and *Practice in the Art of Elocution* were released on a "double-bill" CD by Albany Records in 2008.

By coincidence, two weeks later, *Sorry Wrong Number* was first performed on May 25 and 26 by the Center for Contemporary Opera at the Danny Kaye Playhouse. That excellent singer-actress Patricia Dell was memorable in the demanding role of the wheelchair-bound Mrs. Stevenson. *Sorry* was on a double bill with the very different *Angel Levine* by Elie Siegmeister, which included several black singers in its cast. No doubt the budget demanded that two of them double in the small roles of Capo and Giorgio in *Sorry*. Unfortunately, my carefully structured plan for a mafia connection at the beginning and end of the opera and the naming of three characters was obliterated by this cross-casting, not because the two did their parts in any way but well, but because they couldn't be expected to impersonate Italians.

Because the press was unaware that *Sorry* had been completed some two years earlier, its comments about my fecundity, based on two premieres two weeks apart, were completely undeserved. Both productions no doubt benefited by the half-dozen performances of *Lizzie* that had taken place at the New York City Opera only a few weeks earlier, the sixth of them televised by Live from Lincoln Center.

*　　*　　*　　*　　*　　*

Chapter 15

Coda

(1999 -   )

My teenage ambition to write operas had now been fulfilled in some measure with the satisfactory round number of ten of them written; the last two had been brought to life in the spring and *Lizzie*, now 34 years old, seemed to be doing well in her maturity. With my heart and diabetes under control, 72 years had passed since the Chicago diabetes specialist, Woodyatt, had said to my father, "Dr. Beeson, I'm sorry to say that your son has only about six months to live." Nevertheless, my 78th birthday was looming ever nearer and with no small-scale or large-scale opera subject at hand I was hesitant to search and find one and then to undertake the long-term commitment that would inevitably follow.

Instead, seven smaller, but substantial compositions, all text settings for one medium or another came into being before I set aside writing notes for singers and instruments for the writing of words for this volume.

The first three of the seven pieces were commissioned by those who were first to perform them, two for a voice and chamber ensemble, the other for two voices and ensemble. Not only do these three very different pieces have traits in common; they share some of these with the chamber opera and the operina that immediately preceded them. They are inherently dramatic and narrative rather than lyric and their words are partly mine; when not written or rewritten by me, they are rearranged to fit my over-all musical and quasi-dramatic plan. One might wonder whether, in my wide searches for texts to set I sought out maimed and incomplete poems so that I might then repair and finish them. Surely, as I have remarked before, those that I have chosen, often humorous or bizarre—or both— are unlike those most composers choose to set.

During drinks after the second MOMA Summergarden performance of the *Four Forbidden Songs*, Joel Sachs invited me to write a work for solo voice and his New Juilliard Ensemble. That the first of these last compositions was likely to be *The Daring Young Man on the Flying Trapeze* for countertenor and chamber ensemble (or piano) seemed likely when I leafed through my "Texts for Setting" file and found the typescript I'd once made of the poem. Nora and I, on our annual visit to the Glimmerglass Opera, had recently been struck by the remarkable voice, musicality, and diction of the countertenor David Daniels and as I reread the doggerel I giggled at the sudden idea of a countertenor's losing his girl to an athlete and at the rare invitation presented by the flying trapeze for writing coloratura passages. At the next opportunity to hear Daniels I visited him at length after the performance and asked him if he'd be interested in the piece, which I described in some detail and which would be scored for about eight instruments that would certainly be present at any chamber concert of eighteenth century music. I had thought of several reasons he might have for resisting a piece on such a subject, but he thought it "a swell idea" and added that he'd thought of commissioning a new piece by somebody because, "I can't go on doing music only from the 17th and 18th centuries forever."

Buoyed by his enthusiasm, I began learning everything I could about a type of voice unfamiliar to me—his in particular. Because the music and the lyrics of the once popular song would have to be used in some fashion, I needed to know if they were now in the public domain; I discovered, finally, that they were and that the credited lyricist was in reality George Saunders. Using the music lent a more than usual tonal cast to my music, but the tune was altered and developed as it reappeared. Credits are all-inclusive: Verse by George Leybourne, 1842-84 and Jack Beeson; Music by Jack Beeson and Alfred Lee (1839?-1906).

Before beginning the music and then while composing it, I made a number of changes in the lyrics and, to add more action to the thin story—and more coloratura—three more stanzas of my own, a quarter of the whole. When the sketch was complete in pencil I sent David a copy of it and a clearer typescript of the text. He responded that the vocal line fit him like a glove and that he liked my new words particularly. He looked forward to seeing the final fair copy and to performing it a few times with piano before doing it with the instruments, if I didn't mind.

I didn't, in the least. What I *did* mind was that in spite of David's insisting that he liked the piece and looked forward to performing it—and his repeating the same to third parties, whom I could believe—and in spite of speaking to him after New York performances, telephone calls, letters, and finally asking the aid of his personal representative, Matthew Horner, after four years, *The Daring Young Man* remained earthbound, unperformed.

During my final chat with Matthew Horner I learned that Thomas Adès has composed a Shelley setting for David that he'd liked and promised to sing; after waiting only one year, Adès found another countertenor. When I asked Horner what he would advise me to do if I were his client, he answered, "Go find another one!"

Much earlier, when I delivered the piano-vocal and instrumental scores to Joel Sachs, I learned that Daniels could not have sung the premiere at the Juilliard in any case, for *all* performers had to be Juilliard students. As there were no countertenors in the school at that time, I had the pleasure and the duty of writing another voice and ensemble piece to fulfill the commission.

*   *   *   *   *   *

I had long since mentioned to Joel an abandoned project dating back more than a third of a century, which he urged me to reconsider. During our last Roman year I had spent some time with my old friend Teresa Stich-Randall and tried to interest her in performing an as yet uncomposed quarter-of-an-hour piece for soprano and chamber ensemble based on songs and other passages from *Hamlet* and to be called *Ophelia Sings*. Her refusal was simple and direct: "Jack, I'd love to, but I don't sing any modern music." Librettoless in Rome at that time, I tried to put together a synthesis of the Ophelia role, but when extracted from their context, the sections seemed scrappy and directionless. I had tried in later years, but always failed, and thought that now I would make one last effort.

Armed with four editions of the play, with six weeks of pondering I fashioned a short one-character libretto for what amounted to a musical monodrama. My few minor word changes (pronouns mostly) might escape the scrutiny of a scholar, as might my borrowing of one line from Hamlet's part and another from a Gentlemen's role. Given the difficulties of handling a long text ranging widely from madness to distinguishing true love from false, from ditty to threnody, from calling for her coach (its arrival signaled by the cornet) to her drawn-out good-nights, composing the music demanded all my attention for three months and all the tricks and traits in my vocabulary. To avoid the implications of the silly-maiden-soprano and to have the clearer diction of the lower voice, my Ophelia was written for mezzo soprano, her highly attentive accompaniment to be played by a dozen instruments. In an instrumental quodlibet of ditty fragments I seized the opportunity to quote the *Highlands* tune and just before the double cadenza of voice and cornet found the place to quote my trademark "Tristan chord," this time boldly untransposed.

The Juilliard students, including the mezzo Leah Summers, rehearsed and performed their piece beautifully in September 2000. I tended to think that Joel Sachs's letter of thanks for my having written the work for him and his forces exaggerated his affection for *Ophelia Sings, A Mad Scene with Ditties*, but he chose to revive it with Sasha Cooke as the singer on a special concert celebrating the fiftieth anniversary of the Juilliard School.

*   *   *   *   *   *

The last of these three concerted pieces was commissioned by the Contemporary Chamber Players of the State University at Stony Brook, and first played by them there and in New York City. It resembles *Ophelia Sings* in length—thirteen minutes—and in its instrumentation for twelve players. Two singers, a tenor and a soprano, share the four movements. Completed and premiered in 2001, it had its origin in a duet for soprano and tenor with piano accompaniment composed exactly a half century earlier called *Piazza Piece*.

In 1951 a young married couple asked me for a duet that they could sing on joint recitals. But before they got around to performing P.P. as they called it, they separated and divorced. As the years passed, whenever another couple asked for copies I usually revised the piece, in the late eighties even adding suggestions for semi-staging it. However I altered it in detail, I remained intrigued by the musical form I had found for paralleling exactly the shape of John Crowe Ransom's sonnet. The tenor, representing a man of middle years, observes and describes a young woman he desires, while singing the octet (the first eight lines); the soprano, awaiting her lover, sees the man hidden behind the vines and threatens to scream, while singing the sestet (the last six lines). The two vocal lines are so written that they can be—and are—sung together, the accompaniment altered to fit the pair of voices.

For that half-century I had also been an admirer of Ransom's very long poem, *The Equilibrists*, which had always seemed to me resistant to musical setting. Now it occurred to me that if *Piazza Piece*, scored, were to be the first of four sections, a setting of *The Equilibrists*, the poem suitably cut and edited, could be the last section and provide the title for the set; the pair at odds in the first resembled the couple in the last after two lifetimes of equivocation. The problem was to find two poems that would account for the passage of time. No other Ransom poem would serve, but I found two quatrains of the four in *Because I liked you better* by A. E. Houseman, supposedly spoken by a man, that would serve perfectly for a tenor solo. Because I could find no poem by anyone that could serve for the following soprano solo, I was forced to write my own fourteen lines and then a couplet leading into the Ransom *Equilibrists* sung by both. I was uneasy about following Houseman and preceding Ransom, but I used the rhyme scheme of the former, the pentameter of the latter, and verbal linkages to both to form transitions into and out of my effort. I was confident that the sauce of my music, spread over the whole, however varied its ingredients, would tend to give unity to three writers' words. A more comprehensive account of the verbal, musical, and physical travails of this subtitled *An Elegiac Cycle* is in the Latouche registry.

*   *   *   *   *   *

Of the last four of the seven post-operas compositions three had demanding verbal complications. For several decades on the wall just behind my piano bench was hung a very large framed decorated reprinting of "Reasons briefly set downe by th' author, to perswade everyone to learne to sing." There are eight down-to-earth reasons given in straightforward rather flat prose written by that wonderful composer William Byrd (1542-1629) and first published in 1588. I had long been tempted to try turning Byrd's words, some with humorous and rather touching implications, into something more settable. Cutting some and adding some of my own, I left almost nothing untinkered with. In a week I had four versions and while setting the fifth to music for chorus, made the most of Byrd's reasons for singing—as a cure for stuttering, improvement of diction and oratory, "strengthening all parts of the brest and opening the pipes," and "the better to honour and serve God there-with." All kinds of vocal acrobatics and expressivities were invited, justified, and included. Byrd ended his *Reasons* with the Latin phrase, "Omnes spiritus laudet Dominum" with which I concluded my *In Praise of Singing.*[1] Given the nature of this seven-minute piece it was performed and recorded by the Gregg Smith Singers and published by Boosey more quickly than usual.

*   *   *   *   *   *

The other a cappella choral piece came about as the result of an "o.j. high," my invented term for a sudden increase in a diabetic's blood sugar level.

---

[1] *In Praise of Singing* serves also as the title of an Albany Records CD of Beeson choral works from 1951 to 2002, sung by the Gregg Smith Singers under the direction of Gregg Smith. The seven works include *Summer Rounds and Canons* of 2002.

On June 19, 2002, immediately after my usual swim of 150 yards, in six segments, at my usual beach on Cold Spring Harbor Bay, I had my prescribed 3 o'clock snack of an ounce of cheese, four saltines, and a cup of orange juice from my thermos. This snack, and the rest of the daily diet regimen had been strictly adhered to since I went on insulin in 1980. The combination of the considerable expenditure of energy and the intake of the quickly assimilated orange juice led, as it often did, to the pleasant "high," modest, normal, and healthful compared to the illegal and dangerous drug-induced "high." It led me, as experienced on a lovely early-summer afternoon, to repeat obsessively as much as I could remember of the words and tune of *Summer is acomin' in*. I went on to make up other words to the head of the tune: "summer is arunnin' around . . . summer is agoin' away . . ." I wondered: would it be possible to add other stanzas of words and variants of the music to the original? to make something new of the old?

Back in the city, while worrying these questions I spoke to my friend Ernest Sanders, who had published his transcription of the original Rota (round) dating from 1240-50 and his literal transcription of its Middle English text. I was surprised that I hadn't long since become intimately acquainted with this earliest six-part double canon, given my frequent episodes of canonitis. The four upper voices sing the well-known melody as a four-part round; at the same time the two lower voices repeat "Sing cuckoo" endlessly in their own two-part round.

Using Ernie's translation as a pony, I made my own highly rhythmic and rhymed version of the words. As "librettist" I kept ahead of the composer, revising my new words and phrases often while composing. I tried to maintain the verbal style I'd set as translator: words derived from Middle English were preferred, a good deal of assonance (always welcome in a sung text), and occasional rhyme. The new stanzas were indebted to my beach improvisation. My fanciful translation led to some "modern" syncopations in the 13th century tune and to ever more melodic variations in what followed: "Summer is arunnin around . . ." and a section on summer thistles, spiders, bugs, bites, poisons, and the enjoyment of flowers and caroling warblers. Everything is in canon (with two repeatable rounds) except for a crow-cawing section that parodies the F-D "cuckoo" of the original and provides the dying-away transition to the "agoin away" conclusion. Some variety is provided by using only six solo voices at the outset, then the chorus. A coded sign of the overall unity in the constant variation is the initial F in the soprano part. In its own time it would have been known as the Ionian Final, later as the tonic of F major. In the course of the six minutes of *Summer Rounds and Canons* (see footnote 1) the initial F is transmuted into E♯ as the final soprano note, the third degree of the key of C♯ major, its function changed, but sounding the same, of course.

*   *   *   *   *   *

The last two compositions of the seven—I hesitate to say my last two works, though as of this date they almost are—are song cycles: A *Rupert Brooke Cycle* and *Three Viereck Songs*.

The first of these shared with all the other recent pieces textual problems to be solved before and during musical composition. My early affection for Brooke's poetry had been remembered when searching for poems written shortly after 1900 and led to the setting of *A Channel Crossing* as the first large number in *Practice in the Art of Elocution* and its inclusion in *Four Forbidden Songs*. Now, only a couple of years later, on the hunt for poetry for a set of songs for bass-baritone and piano, I re-read all the work of Brooke and his 1919 biography, *Memoir*, written by a friend only a year after the poet's far too early death.

As might be expected, I was partial to those few of his poems that came to be known as his "unpleasant poems," of which *A Channel Passage* was one. The vocal line of it I transposed down a tenth and rewrote the accompaniment to serve as the centerpiece of the new set of five. Another "unpleasant poem," *Wagner*, I re-titled A *Wagner Lover*, afraid that an inattentive musical audience might think the gross sensualist in the poem was a portrait of the composer himself. For fun I sent a copy of the just completed song to John Kander, a perfect Wagnerite, who responded with a note that it described him accurately and that he'd identified all the many entangled quotes from the *Ring* and *Tristan* that formed most of the accompaniment. Given the 19th century music quoted in the context of my music written in 2002, *A Wagner Lover* became the first song in the set.

On my search for other unpleasantries I found the torsos of two in Brooke letters reprinted in the little-known biography. Just before WWI he traveled across the US, coast to coast, on his way to the South Seas. In a letter to a Miss Nesbitt he described some of our folkways and sketched part of two amusing quatrains about chowder. I repeated some of his lines, added two of my own, and my punning title, *Spooning with Chowder*. Another letter, to his close friend Violet Asquith (daughter of the Prime Minister), was written from the Fiji Islands. He assures her that nobody has been eaten there recently and then tosses off a sonnet in which the victim—himself—watches himself being cooked and eaten piece by piece. He discusses his sonnet in some detail and includes rejected variants. I used the sonnet and its variants and some words of my own in a poem of twenty lines. As a small concession to USA 2002 I changed "a Black Man" to "a native" and the obsolete "incoctible" to "inedible" as the final word. I set our words to music with the same delicious pleasure he seemed to take in writing to Violet and, I hope, to some of the same mock-heroic effect. Naturally, nothing could follow such a song, which closes the cycle. It is preceded in this cycle of five, for variety, by a quiet and lyrical setting of the conventional and thoroughly pleasant *Waikiki*.

*   *   *   *   *   *

The other song cycle, the last of these post-opera works, was written for bass voice and piano and consists of three longer-than usual settings of poems by Peter Viereck—my friend, very recently deceased at 89—and the last of more than a dozen Viereck-Beeson songs and choral pieces. The choice of the lyrics was made before the choice of the bass voice, the color of which seemed the most appropriate for the subject matter and the mood; the three form a unity, having to do with a wife, a daughter, and a brother, in this case Peter's, killed in WWII at Anzio. Titles and a few words were revised somewhat for musical setting in close collaboration with the poet himself.

As usual, I forego detailed comment about composing the music. Words can describe the finding of texts and the worrying of them thereafter; words, in whatever language, are too bluntly specific to translate easily or accurately the seemingly secret ways music comes into existence or its sound and import. When sung words are part of the music, some of these secrets are revealed to the ear and others by the eyes of those who can read its code, its notation.

*   *   *   *   *   *

But enough of this and all other vexed matters. Today, my 87th birthday, is my self-imposed deadline and some secrets will have to await revelation.

July 15, 2008
Jack Beeson

*   *   *   *   *   *

Appendix A
Repertory and Direction of the Columbia Opera Workshop

1943-44	Musical Director: Stage Director:	Nicholas Goldschmidt Herbert Graf
1944-46	Musical Director Stage Director	Willard Rhodes Herbert Graf
1946-48	Musical Director Stage Director	Willard Rhodes John Wolmut
1948-54	Musical Director Stage Director	William Rhodes Felix Brentano
1954-57	Musical Director Stage Director	Rudolph Thomas Felix Brentano

Summer Opera Workshops were under music direction of both Otto Luening and Willard Rhodes. The stage directors were Ernst Lert and Elemer Nagy.

Operas and plays with live music in Brander Mathews Hall from 1941 to 1958, produced, for the most part, by the Columbia Theatre Associates (CTA) in collaboration with the Music Department and its Opera Workshop. Certain operatic productions were undertaken at other venues, sometimes in collaboration with the Columbia Theatre Associates. All works performed are operas except for those indicated with a (†), which are mostly plays with newly-composed incidental music.

Season	Date of Performance	Work(s) Performed	Collaborators	Production Information
1941	February	*The Devil Take Her*	Alan Collard (librettist) John Gordon (librettist) Arthur Benjamin (composer)	Produced in collabora- tion with the Opera Department of the Juilliard School of Music
		Blennerhasset	Norman Corwin (librettist) Philip Roll (librettist) Vittorio Giannini	World Premiere. Produced in collaboration with the Opera Department of the Juilliard School

Season	Date of Performance	Work(s) Performed	Collaborators	Production Information
	May	*Paul Bunyan*	W.H. Auden (librettist) Benjamin Britten (composer) Hugh Ross (conductor) Milton Smith (stage director)	World Premiere. Produced by the CTA and the Columbia Music Department with the chorus of the Schola Cantorum. (?) Six performances.
1941-1942	Fall	*The Burglar's Opera*	Edward Eager (librettist) Alfred Drake (Librettist) John Mundy (composer)	World Premiere. Produced by the CTA.
	February	*The Music Master*	Edward Eager (translator) G.B. Pergolesi (composer) Richard Falk (conductor) Milton Smith (stage director)	Probably the first performance in English. Produced by the CTA and the Columbia Chamber Opera Players. Six performances.
	March	*Iphigenia in Tauris* †	Witter Bynner (translator) Claude Lapham (composer)	Produced by the CTA. Incidental choral settings for Euripides' play.
1942-1943	December	*The Village Barber*	Joseph Weidermann (librettist) Edward Eager (translator) Johann Schenk (composer)` Nicholas Goldschmidt (conductor) Milton Smith (stage director)	Very likely the first American performances. Produced by the CTA and the Columbia Music Department. Five performances.

Season	Date of Performance	Work(s) Performed	Collaborators	Production Information
	May	*A Tree on the Plains*	Paul Horgan (librettist) Ernst Bacon (composer) Nicholas Goldschmidt (conductor) Milton Smith (stage director)	Commissioned by the League of Composers First New York performances. Produced by the CTA and the Columbia Music Department. Five performances.
1943-1944	December	*The Two Misers*	Edward Eager (translator) André-Ernest-Modest Grétry (composer) Nicholas Goldschmidt (conductor) Milton Smith (Stage director)	Probably the first New York performances. Produced by the CTA and the Columbia Music Department. Five performances.
	May	*Pieces of Eight*	Edward Eager (librettist) Bernard Wagenaar (composer) Otto Luening (conductor) Milton Smith (stage director)	World Premiere. First opera commissioned by the Alice M. Ditson Fund. Produced by the CTA and Columbia Music Department. aided by the Ditson Fund. Five performances.
1944-1945	December	*The Jealous Husband*	Edward Eager (translator) G.B. Pergolesi (composer) Otto Luening (conductor) Milton Smith (stage director)	World Premiere in English and probably the first performances of the opera in the U.S. Produced by the CTA and the Columbia Music Department.[1] Five performances.

---

[1] From the fall of 1944 onwards, the Music Department was represented primarily by its sponsorship of the Opera Workshop.

512

Season	Date of Performance	Work(s) Performed	Collaborators	Production Information
	May	*The Scarecrow*	Dorothy Lockwood (librettist)	World Premiere.
			Normand Lockwood (composer)	Based on a play by Percy MacKaye.
			Otto Luening (conductor)	Commissioned by Ditson Fund.
			Willard Rhodes (conductor)	Produced by the CTA and the
			Jack Beeson (asst. conductor)	Columbia Music Department, aided
			Milton Smith (stage director)	by the Ditson Fund. Five performances.
1945-1946	December	*The Imaginary Invalid* †	Jack Beeson (composer)	Produced by the CTA. Incidental music for Molière's play.
	February	*The Barber of Seville*	Phyllis Mead (translator)	Based on Beaumarchais' play. Only previous
			Giovanni Paisiello (composer)	American production had been in French
			Otto Luening (conductor)	(New Orleans, 1810). Produced by the CTA and the Columbia
			Jack Beeson (asst. conductor)	Music Department. Five performances.
			Milton Smith (stage director)	
	May[1]	*The Medium*	Gian Carlo Menotti (librettist, composer, and stage director)	World Premiere. Commissioned by the Ditson Fund. Produced by the CTA and the Columbia Music
			Otto Luening (conductor)	Department, aided by the Ditson Fund. Five
			Jack Beeson (asst. conductor)	performances.
			Robert Horan (stage assistant)	

---

[1] Also in May were several performances of Stravinsky's *L'Histoire du Soldat*, produced jointly by the American Section of the International Society for Contemporary Music and the CTA, conducted by Dimitri Mitropoulos, and directed by Frederick Cohen.

Season	Date of Performance	Work(s) Performed	Collaborators	Production Information
	May 17-28		Willard Rhodes (conductor) Jack Beeson (asst. conductor) Jacob Avshalomov (musical assistant) John Wolmut (stage director) Elena Allegro (stage assistant)	The Workshop in a program of scenes and acts from the repertory.
	August 14		Willard Rhodes (conductor) Elemer Nagy (stage director)	The Summer School Opera Workshop in a program of scenes and acts from the repertory, including the whole of Menotti's *The Old Maid and the Thief.*
1946-1947	n.d.			A competition for a new one-act opera was sponsored by the Ditson Fund, in collaboration with the Metropolitan Opera. The winning work, *The Warrior* by Bernard Rogers, was performed by the Met in January 1947.
	December 17-19		Willard Rhodes (conductor) Jack Beeson (asst. conductor) John Wolmut (stage director) Elena Allegro (stage assistant)	The Workshop performed scenes from operas with texts taken from the works of Shakespeare.

514

Season	Date of Performance	Work(s) Performed	Collaborators	Production Information
	February (double bill)	*Stratonice*	Winthrop Palmer (translator) Etienne Méhul (composer)	Believed to be first American performance of both of these one-act operas. Produced by the
		The Man with the Terrible Temper (L'Irato)	Phyllis Mead (translator) Etienne Méhul (composer) Willard Rhodes (conductor) Jack Beeson (asst. conductor) Jacob Avshalomov (musical assistant) Albert Rivett (musical assistant) John Wolmut (stage director)	CTA and the Opera Workshop of the of the Columbia Music Department. Eight performances.
	May	*The Mother of Us All*	Gertrude Stein (librettist) Virgil Thomson (composer) Otto Luening (conductor) Jack Beeson (asst. conductor) John Taras (stage director)	World Premiere. Commissioned by the Ditson Fund. Produced by the CTA and the Columbia Music Department, aided by the Ditson. Fund. Nine performances.
	August 11 and 14		Otto Luening (conductor) Jack Beeson (asst. conductor) Ernst Lert (stage director)	Demonstration by the Summer Workshop of opera scenes, mostly Mozart ensembles.
1947-1948	January 26-28		Willard Rhodes (conductor) Jack Beeson (asst. conductor) John Wolmut (stage director) Lee MacBurney (stage assistant)	The Workshop in scenes from the repertory.

Season	Date of Performance	Work(s) Performed	Collaborators	Production Information
	May	*Evangeline*	Otto Luening (librettist, composer, and conductor) Jack Beeson (asst. conductor) Nona Schurman ((stage director)	World Premiere. Aided by the Ditson Fund. Produced CTA and the Columbia Music Department. Eight performances.
	August 6			Demonstration by the Summer Workshop.
	August 13		Willard Rhodes (conductor) Albert Rivett (musical asst.) Ernst Lert (stage director) Ruth Ives (stage assistant) Lee MacBurney (stage assistant)	The Workshop in scenes from the repertory.
1948-1949[2]	December	*The Belle of New York*	Hugh Morton (librettist) Gustave Kerker (composer) Albert Rivett (musical asst.) Milton Smith (stage director) Louis Grifford (stage assistant)	Operetta produced by the CTA and the Opera Workshop of the Columbia Music Department.

---

[2] Operas by Henry Cowell, Paul Nordoff, and, later, Hugo Weisgall *(Six Characters in Search of Author)* were commissioned by the Ditson Fund but not produced at Columbia.

516

Season	Date of Performance	Work(s) Performed	Collaborators	Production Information
	January	*Sir John in Love*	Ralph Vaughan Williams (composer) Willard Rhodes (conductor) Albert Rivett (musical asst.) Felix Brentano (stage director)	Based on Shakespeare's *The Merry Wives of Windsor.* First complete performance in the U.S. (for 2 pianos). Produced by the Opera Workshop with various members members of the School of Dramatic Arts
	February	*The Little Clay Cart*†	Jacob Avshalomov (composer)	Produced by the CTA. Incidental music for the play by King Shudraka.
	May	*A Drumlin Legend*	Helena Carus (librettist) Ernst Bacon (composer) Otto Luening (conductor) Albert Rivett (musical assistant) Anley Loran (musical assistant Milton Smith (stage director) Oreste Sergievsky (choreographer)	World Premiere. Commissioned by the Ditson Fund. Produced by the CTA and the Columbia Music Department. Four performances.
	May	*The Emperor Wants a Son*†	Albert Rivett (composer)	Produced by the CTA. A play with incidental music.
	August 6 and 11		Otto Luening (conductor) Albert Rivett (musical asst.) Everett Lee (musical assistant) Ernest Lert (stage director) Ruth Ives (stage assistant) Lee MacBurney (stage assistant)	The Summer Workshop in scenes from the repertory.

Season	Date of Performance	Work(s) Performed	Collaborators	Production Information
1949-1950	December	*The Way of the World*†	Albert Rivett (composer)	Produced by the CTA. Incidental music for the play by William Congreve.
	January	*The Barrier*	Langston Hughes (librettist) Jan Meyerowitz (composer) Willard Rhodes (conductor) Albert Rivett (musical asst.) Felix Brentano (stage director)	World Premiere. Produced by the CTA and the Opera Workshop of the Columbia Music Department. Ten performances.
1950-1951	December	*The Old Maid and the Thief*	Gian Carlo Menotti (librettist and composer)	A double bill of Menotti operas performed by a Workshop group at Cedar Crest College, PA
		The Telephone	Gian Carlo Menotti (librettist and composer) Albert Rivett (conductor) Ruth Ives (stage director)	Produced by the Opera Workshop.
	March-April	*Giants in the Earth*	Arnold Sundgaard (librettist) Douglas Moore (composer) Willard Rhodes (conductor) Albert Rivett (musical asst.) Felix Brentano (stage director)	World Premiere. After novel by Ole Edvart Rølvaag. Awarded the Pulitzer Prize in Music for 1951. Aided by the Ditson Fund. Produced by the CTA and the Columbia Music Department. Ten performances.

518

Season	Date of Performance	Work(s) Performed	Collaborators	Production Information
	April 2			The Workshop in scenes from Verdi operas (at Casa Italiana).
	May	*Come Down Daniel†*	Albert Rivett (composer)	Produced by the CTA. A play with incidental music.
	May	*The Old Maid and the Thief*	Gian Carlo Menotti (librettist and composer)	A double bill of Menotti operas performed by a Workshop group in White Plains, NY. Produced by the Opera Workshop. Two performances.
		The Telephone	Gian Carlo Menotti (librettist and composer) Albert Rivett (conductor) Ruth Ives (stage director)	
1951-1952	May	*Acres of Sky*	Zoe Lund Schiller (librettist) Arthur Kreutz (composer) Otto Luening (conductor) Jack Beeson (asst. conductor) John Kander (musical assistant) Edward Reveaux (stage director) Letitia Evans (choreographer)	First New York performance. Aided by the Ditson Fund. Produced by CTA and the Music Department. Five performances.

Season	Date of Performance	Work(s) Performed	Collaborators	Production Information
1952-1953	May	*Sweeney Agonistes*	T.S. Eliot (librettist) Richard Winslow (composer) Willard Rhodes (conductor) John Kander (asst. conductor) Felix Brentano (stage director)	First performance in New York; presented, with a small orchestra on a program that included scenes from repertory.
	March	*Poor Eddy*†	Elizabeth Dooley (librettist) Albert Rivett (composer and conductor) Albert Smith (stage director) Doris Humphrey (stage director and choreographer) Charles Weidman (principal performer)	A dance drama based on the life of Edgar Allen Poe, with songs. Produced by the CTA. Aided by the Ditson Fund. Five performances.
1953-1954	April	*The Beggar's Opera*	John Gay (librettist) J.C. Pepusch (composer) Willard Rhodes (conductor) John Kander (asst. conductor) Felix Brentano (stage director)	Produced by CTA and the Opera Workshop. Five performances.

520

Season	Date of Performance	Work(s) Performed	Collaborators	Production Information
	May (double bill)	*Malady of Love*	Lewis Allen (librettist) Lehman Engel (composer)	World Premiere.
		Hello Out There	William Saroyan (librettist) Jack Beeson (composer) Willard Rhodes (conductor) John Kander (asst. conductor) Felix Brentano (stage director)	World Premiere. Both operas produced by the Opera Workshop in cooperation with the School of Dramatic Arts. Aided by a grant from the Ditson Fund. Five performances.
1955-1956	March 1		Rudolph Thomas (conductor) John Crosby (musical asst.) Felix Brentano (stage director)	The Workshop in scenes from the repertory. In McMillin Theatre.
	May	*Pantaloon*	Bernard Stambler (librettist) Robert Ward (composer) Rudolph Thomas (conductor) John Crosby (asst. conductor) Felix Brentano (stage director) Thomas DeGaetani (stage assistant)	World Premiere. Based on a melodrama by Leonid Andreyev. Performed at the Juilliard School of Music in a collaborative production. Produced by the CTA and the Opera Workshop of the Columbia Music Department. Aided by Ditson Fund and the Juilliard School. Three performances.

Season	Date of Performance	Work(s) Performed	Collaborators	Production Information
1956-1957[3]	November	*The Dream*†	Louis Huber (conductor) John Reich (stage director) Oreste Sergievsky (stage assistant) Louise Grifford (stage assistant)	A production combining the major part of Shakespeare's *Midsummer Night's Dream* and the music to Purcell's *Fairy Queen*. Produced by the Opera Workshop of the Columbia Music Department. Five performances.
	May	*Panfilo and Lauretta*	Chester Kallman (librettist) Carlos Chavez (composer) Howard Shanet (conductor) Kurt Saffir (musical assistant) Walter Baker (musical assistant) Bill Butler (stage director)	World Premiere. Produced by the CTA and the Columbia Music Department. Aided by the Ditson Fund. Ten performances.
	May 24	*Love is a Game*	Marivaux (librettist) Milton Feist (translator) Pierre Petit (composer) Rudolph Thomas (conductor) John Crosby (asst. conductor) Felix Brentano (stage director)	First American performance of the one-act opera based on Marivaux's play. Followed by scenes from the repertory, all accompanied by piano.

---

[3] The Opera Workshop was discontinued after the season 1956-1957. A grant from the Ditson fund made possible a production of *The Sweet Bye and Bye* by Kenward Elmslie (librettist) and Jack Beeson (composer) on November 21, 22, and 23, 1957, at the Juilliard Opera Theater.

522

Season	Date of Performance	Work(s) Performed	Collaborators	Production Information
1957-1958[4]	March (double bill)	*The Boor*	John Olon (librettist) Dominick Argento (composer)	New York premiere.
		Gallantry	Arnold Sundgaard (librettist) Douglas Moore (composer) Emerson Buckley (conductor) Kurt Saffir (musical asst.) J. O. Scrymgeour (stage director) Day Tuttle (stage director)	Work Premiere. Produced by the CTA and the Columbia Music Department. Aided by the Ditson Fund and the Recording Industries Trust Fund. Five performances.

---

[4] On April 10-11, 1949, Columbia University, in cooperation with the University of Illinois, presented *The Bewitched* by Harry Partch, "a dance-satire" with choreography by Joyce Trisler. The work was produced by Tom DeGaetani in the Juilliard Concert Hall and was aided by the Ditson Fund.

Appendix B

Musical Works by Jack Beeson[*]

Operas

Captain Jinks of the Horse Marines (1975)   ca. 120´
A romantic comedy in music in three acts
Libretto by Sheldon Harnick,
based on the play by Clyde Fitch
Commissioned by the National Endowment for the Arts
First Performance: 20 September 1975 Kansas City,
Missouri Kansas City Lyric Theater, Russell Patterson,
Conductor Jack Eddleman, director and choreographer,
Patton Campbell, designer

Cyrano (1990)   ca. 160´
Heroic comedy in music
Libretto by Sheldon Harnick,
based on the play by Edmond Rostand
FP: by the Theater Hagen in German translation,
September 10, 1994

Doctor Heidegger's Fountain of Youth (1978)   ca. 40´
Chamber opera in one act
Libretto by Sheldon Harnick,
based on the short story by Nathaniel Hawthorne
Commissioned by the National Arts Club
FP: 17 November 1978, New York, National Arts Club,
Thomas Martin, conductor, Jack Eddleman, director,
Patton Campbell, designer

Hello Out There (1953)   ca. 40´
Chamber opera in one act
Libretto adapted from the play by William Saroyan
FP: 17 May 1954, New York,
Columbia University Opera Workshop
Willard Rhodes, conductor, Felix Bretano, director
Paul Morrison, designer

---

[*] All works for which no publisher is listed are published or controlled by Boosey & Hawkes.

Jonah (1948-50)   ca. 115′
Opera in two or three acts to be played, danced and sung
Libretto by the composer, adapted from the play by Paul Goodman

Lizzie Borden (1965)   ca. 120′
A Family Portrait in three acts
Libretto by Kenward Elmslie,
based on a scenario by Richard Plant
Commissioned by the Ford Foundation
FP: 25 March 1965, New York, New York City Opera
Anton Coppola, conductor, Nikos Psacharopoulos, director
Peter Wexler, designer, Patton Campbell, costumes

My Heart's in the Highlands (1969)   ca. 105′
Chamber opera in two or three acts
Libretto by the composer, adapted from the play by William Saroyan
Commissioned by the National Educational Television Opera Theater
FP (telecast): 17 March 1970, New York, NET Opera Theater
Peter Herman Adler, conductor, Kirk Browning, director
Eldon Elder, designer

Practice in the Art of Elocution   ca. 35′
Operina for soprano and piano (1998)
Libretto by the composer
FP: 12 May 1999, Merkin Hall,
New York City by Lynne Vardaman and Marc Peloquin,
staged by Stephen Quint

Sorry, Wrong Number (1996)   ca. 35′
Chamber opera in one act
Libretto by the composer, based on the play by Lucille Fletcher
FP: 25 May 1999 in the Kaye Playhouse, New York City,
by the Center for Contemporary Opera, Richard Marshall, producer
and conductor, Charles Maryan stage director

The Sweet Bye and Bye (1956; rev. 1958)   ca. 110′
Opera in two acts (five scenes)
Libretto by Kenward Elmslie
FP: 21 November 1957, New York, Juilliard Opera Theater
Frederic Waldman, conductor, Frederic Cohen, director
David Hays, designer
FP (revised version): 2 July 1958, Muncie, Indiana,
Ball State Teachers College

Orchestral Works

Fanfare (1963)   2´
for brass, winds and percussion
Commissioned by the Kirkwood Symphony
FP: 23 October 1963, St. Louis, Kirkwood Symphony
Dorothy Ziegler, conductor

Hymns and Dances (from *The Sweet Bye and Bye*) (1958)   15´
for large orchestra
Memorial Service; Comic-Strip; Hymn, Interlude, Dance
FP: 27 February 1965, New York, Columbia University, Orchestra
Howard Shanet, conductor

Interludes and Arias from Cyrano (1997)   18´
for baritone and orchestra

Symphony No. 1 in A (1959)   20'
for orchestra
FP: 27 February 1965, New York, Columbia University Orchestra
Howard Shanet, conductor
First professional performance (and CRI Recording):
7 December 1966,
by the Polish National Radio Orchestra,
William Strickland, conductor

Two Concert Arias (1952/53)
for soprano and orchestra, or piano
FP: 7 January 1954, Radio Svizzera Italiana
Annalies Gamper, soprano, Theodore Bloomfield, conductor
The Elephant (1953) Text: D. H. Laurence   4'
The Hippopotamus (1952) Text: T. S. Eliot   5'

Transformations (1959)   10'
for large orchestra
FP: 2 July 1966, RAI Orchestra
Torino, Ferruclo Scaglia conductor

Two Pieces (1967)
for film, radio or television
The Hoosier Balks, The Hawkesley Blues
1(=picc).1.0.0—2.2.2.0—perc(1):*timp/susp.cym/tgl—pft*

526

Solo and Chamber Works

Fantasy, Ditty, and Fughettias (1992)   8'
for two Baroque (or modern) flutes
Commissioned and first performed by John Solum
and Richard Wyton 25 May 1992, Music Mountain
C.F. Peters

Fifth Piano Sonata (1946; rev. 1951)   14'
FP: 24 November 1951, New York, Composers' Forum
John Kirkpatrick
Theodore Presser

Fourth Piano Sonata (1945; rev. 1951)   9'
FP: New York, WNYC Music Festival, Rafael de Silva
Theodore Presser

Interlude (1945; rev. 1951)   3½'
for violin and piano
FP: 24 November 1951, New York, Composers' Forum
Zvi Zeitlin, violin, Robert Starer, piano

Old Hundredth: Prelude and Doxology (1972)   3½'
for organ
Written in honor of the Shelter Island Grove and Camp
Meeting Association centenary
FP: 4 July 1976, Shelter Island, New York, Phyllis Clark

Round and Round (1959)
Easy duets for piano, four hands
Oxford University Press

Sketches in Black and White (1958)   10'
for piano
FP: 22 April 1959, Naples, Museo di San Martino, Joseph Rollino

Sonata Canonica (1966)   5½'
for two alto recorders
FP: 3 September 1966, Provincetown, Massachusetts
Joel Newman and Elloyd Hanson
Galaxy Music Corp.

Sonata (1953)   15'
for viola and piano
Theodore Presser

Song (1945)   2'
for flute and piano
FP: 18 February 1947, New York, WNYC Music Festival
Allen Jensen, flute, Robert Gunman, piano
Shawnee Press

Two Diversions for Piano (1953)   6¾'
revisions of 2nd and 3rd movements of the third sonata ('44)
Scribner Music Library, Vol. 4

Works for Solo Voices,
accompanied by piano or instrumental ensemble

Abbie's Bird Song (1965; rev. 1967)   3'
for high voice and piano
Revision of an aria from *Lizzie Borden*
Text: Kenward Elmslie
Available separately or in *Nine Songs and Arias for Soprano*

A Creole Mystery (1970)   9-10'
for mezzo-soprano or baritone and string quartet
Text: Lafcadio Hearn, adapted by the composer
FP: 17 July 1971, Music Mountain, Connecticut
Zelda Manacher, mezzo-soprano, Berkshire Quartet

Against Idleness and Mischief and In Praise of Labor (1959)   3'
a practice session for high voice and piano
Text: Isaac Watts
Available separately or in *Nine Songs and Arias for Soprano*

Aria in praise of Sopranos (1975)   3'
(from *Captain Jinks of the Horse Marines*)
for tenor and piano
Text: Sheldon Harnick
In *Songs and Arias for Tenor*

528

A Rupert Brooke Cycle (2002)   12-13'
for bass-baritone and piano
    A Wagner Lover   2:40-
    Spooning with Chowder 1:20-
    A Channel Passage   2:30
    Waikiki   2:20
    Scherzo Cannibalistique 3:10-

A Tale Told by Mary's Lamb (1991)   4'
for tenor and piano
Text: Peter Viereck
In *Songs and Arias for Tenor and Piano*

Big Crash Out West (1951)   2'
for baritone and piano
Text: Peter Viereck
Galaxy Music Corp.
In *Nine Songs and Arias for Baritone*

Cat! (1979)   3'
for soprano and piano
Text: John Keats
In *Nine Songs and Arias for Soprano*

Cowboy Song (1979)   4'
for baritone and piano
Text: Charles Causley
Galaxy Music Corp.
In *Nine Songs and Arias for Baritone*

Death by Owl-Eyes (1971)   2½'
for high voice and piano
Text: Richard Hughes
Available separately or in *Nine Songs and Arias for Soprano*

Eldorado (1951)   2'
for high voice and piano
Text: Edgar Allan Poe
FP: 24 November 1951, New York, Composers' Forum
Hazel Gravell, soprano, Robert Starer, piano
Galaxy Music Corp.

Fire, Fire, Quench Desire (1959) 2½'
for high voice and piano
Text: George Peele
In *Nine Songs and Arias for Soprano*

Five Songs (1946; rev. 1950) 8'
for soprano and piano
Text: Francis Quarles
FP: 4 November 1951, Town Hall, New York
Hazel Gravell, soprano, Arpad Sandor, piano
Peer International Corp.

Four Crazy Jane Songs (rev. 1992) 8'
for mezzo and piano
(see Lullaby and Three Love Songs)
Text: William Butler Yeats
In *Songs and Arias for Mezzo-Soprano*

From a Watchtower (1976) 16'
five songs for high or middle voice and piano
Texts: William Wordsworth, W. H. Auden,
Gerald Manley Hopkins, and Walter de la Mare
FP: 21 December 1982, Merkin Hall, New York
Marie Traficante, soprano, William Vendice, piano

The Gambler's Song (1953) 3'
for baritone and piano
Revision of an aria from *Hello Out There*
Text: William Saroyan, adapted by the composer
In *Nine Songs and Arias for Baritone*

Hide and Seek (an Easter ballad) (1991) 3'
for tenor and piano
Text: Peter Viereck
In *Songs and Arias for Tenor*

Indiana Homecoming (1956) 2½'
for baritone and piano
Text: Abraham Lincoln
FP: 29 April 1957, Town Hall, New York
Everett Anderson, bass, Arpad Sandor, piano
Available separately or in *Nine Songs and Arias for Baritone*

In the Public Gardens (1991)   3'
for tenor and piano
Text: John Betjeman
In *Songs and Arias for Tenor*

Killing Time (1965)   2'15"
for mezzo and piano
aria from the opera *Lizzie Borden*
Libretto by Kenward Elmslie
In *Songs and Arias for Mezzo-Soprano*

Leda (1957)   20"
for reciting voice and piano
Text: Aldous Huxley
FP: 30 October 1957, Town Hall, New York
Inga Lind, voice, Maxim Schur, piano

Love Song, Arietta, and Aria (rev. 1992)   7½'
from the opera *The Sweet Bye and Bye* (1958)
for tenor and piano
Text: Kenward Elmslie
In *Sings and Arias for Tenor and Piano*

Lullaby (1944; rev. 1959)   3'
for alto and piano
Text: William Butler Yeats
See *Four Crazy Jane Songs* in the Mezzo volume

Margret's Garden Aria (1965; rev. 1967)   3½'
for high voice and piano
revision of an aria from *Lizzie Borden*
Text: the composer
Available separately or in *Nine Songs and Arias for Soprano*

Mary Magdalen's Song (1991)   4'
for mezzo-soprano and piano
Text: Peter Viereck
In *Songs and Arias for Mezzo-Soprano*

Mother Rainey's Aria: The Wages of Sin and Her Reprise:
To the Seducer   4' and 1'
from the opera *The Sweet Bye and Bye* (1958; rev. 1992)
for mezzo and piano
Text: Kenward Elmslie
In *Songs and Arias for Mezzo-Soprano and Piano*

Nine Songs and Arias for Baritone
see under individual titles for details
      "Big Crash Out West"
      "Calvinistic Evensong" (see *Two Songs*)
      "Cowboy Song"
      "The Gambler's Song" (from *Hello Out There*)
      "Indiana Homecoming"
      "Prescription for Living" (from *Doctor Heidegger's*
         Fountain of Youth)
      "Senex" (See *Two Songs)*
      "To a Sinister Potato"
      "Wedding Song" (from *Captain Jinks of the Horse Marines*)
(B&H, pub. 1990)

Nine Songs and Arias for Soprano
See under individual titles for details
      "Abbie's Bird Song" (from *Lizzie Borden*)
      "Against Idleness and Mischief and In Praise of Labor"
      "Cat!"
      "Death by Owl-Eyes"
      "Fire, Fire, Quench Desire"
      "Margret's Garden Aria" (from *Lizzie Borden*)
      "To Violetta Valery" (from *Captain Jinks of the Horse Marines*)
      "The Widow's Waltz" (from *Doctor Heidegger's Fountain of Youth*)
      "The You Should of Done it Blues"
(B&H, pub. 1990)

Ophelia Sings, a Mad Scene with Ditties (2000)   12'
for mezzo and chamber ensemble
Test adapted from Shakespeare
Commissioned and premiered by the Juilliard School
September 23, 2000
Fl(alt picc), Ob(alt E.H.), Cl(alt bass cl), bassoon, horn, cornet in B^b,
harp, string quintet

Piazza Piece (1951: rev. 1988)   4½'
duet for soprano and tenor with piano
Text: John Crowe Ransom
FP: On tour 1988 (revised version)
Mary Burgess, soprano, Gary Glaze, tenor,
Diane Richardson, piano

Prescription for Living (1978: rev. 1990)   4¼'
for bass-baritone and piano
An aria from *Doctor Heidegger's Fountain of Youth*
Text; Sheldon Harnick
In *Nine Songs and Arias for Baritone*

Pull My Daisy (1997)   1'
for soprano or tenor and piano
Text: Allen Ginsberg
In both *Songs and Arias for Tenor* and
Songs and Arias for Mezzo-Soprano

Six Lyrics (1952; rev. 1959)   12'
for high voice and piano
Texts: Thomas Lovell Beddoes (2), Herman Melville,
Percy Bysshe Shelley, Jasper Mayne, Sir Walter Raleigh
FP: 9 April 1959, Villa Aurelia, Rome
Magda Laszlo, soprano, Jack Beeson, piano

Songs and Arias for Mezzo-Soprano and Piano
Four Crazy Jane Songs
    Lullaby   2:50
    Crazy Jane Reproved   2:30
    Crazy Jane on God   1:20
    Her Anxiety   1:40
Mother Rainey's Aria:
    The Wages of Sin, and   4:00
    her Reprise: To the Seducer   1:00
    (from *The Sweet Bye and Bye*)
Killing Time (from *Lizzie Borden)*   2:15
The Spinster's Anguish   2:00
    (from *Dr. Heidegger's Fountain*
    of Youth)
Mary Magdelene's Song   3:50
Two Millay Sonnets
    I Shall Forget You Presently   2:30
    What Lips My Lips Have Kissed   3:00

Pull My Daisy	1:00

(B&H, pub. 1999)

Songs and Arias for Tenor and Piano

Three Blake Songs	
I Laid Me Down Upon a Bank	1:30
Never Seek to Tell Thy Love	1:40
I Asked a Thief	1:10
Love Song, Arietta, and Aria	
(from *The Sweet Bye and Bye*)	
Love Song	2:45
Arietta	2:30
Aria	2:15
Two Cavatinas	2:00
(from *The Sweet Bye and Bye*)	
Aria In Praise of Sopranos	2:30
(from *Captain Jinks of the Horse*	
Marines)	
A Tale Told by Mary's Lamb	3:30
Hide and Seek (an Easter Ballad)	3:00
In the Public Gardens	3:00
Pull My Daisy	1:00

(B&H, pub. 1993)

The Daring Young Man on the Flying
Trapese (1999)   9:00
for countertenor and chamber ensemble
Verse by George Leybourne and Jack Beeson
Music by Jack Beeson and Alfred Lee
Commissioned by the Juilliard School
Fl, Ob, bassoon, horn, (perc ad lib.) string quintet
(augmented ad lib.)

The Day's No Rounder Than its Angles Are   12'
three songs for mezzo and string quartet.
Texts by Peter Viereck (1971).

The Equilibrists (2001)   12:30
for soprano, tenor, and chamber ensemble
Text by John Crowe Ransom, A. E. Houseman
and Jack Beeson.
Commissioned by the Contemporary Chamber
Players of Stony Brook New York State University
and premiered by them, April 4, 2001.
Fl(alt fl in G), Ob (alt EH), C1 in B^b (alt bass cl), bassoon,
horn, harp, string quintet (bass with C)

The Spinster's Anguish (1978)   2:00
for mezzo and piano
An aria from *Dr. Heidegger's Fountain of Youth*
In *Songs and Arias for Mezzo-Soprano*

Three Love Songs (1944; rev. 1959 and 1992)   5'
for alto and piano
Text: William Butler Yeats
See: Four Crazy Jane Songs in the Mezzo volume

Three Songs (1945; rev. 1951, and 1992)   4:20'
for soprano and piano
Text: William Blake
FP: 24 November 1951, New York, Composers' Forum
Hazell Gravell, soprano, Jack Beeson, piano
See: Three Blake Songs in the Tenor volume

Three Viereck Songs (2003)   13½'
   A Too-Late Love Song   4½'
   If Blossoms Could Blossom   4½'
   A Farewell: Vale from Carthage   4½'
Poems by Peter Viereck; for bass voice and piano, first
performed: Kevin Maynor and Eric Olsen, pianist, at
Smith College, October 30, 2004

To a Sinister Potato (1970)   3½'
for baritone and piano
Text: Peter Viereck
Available separately or in *Nine Songs and Arias for Baritone*

Violetta Valery (1975)   2'
for soprano and piano
An aria from *Captain Jinks of the Horse Marines*
Text: Sheldon Harrick
In *Nine Songs and Arias for Soprano*

Two Cavatinas (1958; rev. 1992)   2'
from *The Sweet Bye and Bye*
libretto by Kenward Elmslie
In *Songs and Arias for Tenor and Piano*

Two Concert Arias (1951/53)
for soprano and piano
"The Elephant" (1953)   3½'
Test: D. H. Lawrence
"The Hippopotamus" (1951)   4½'
Text: T. S. Eliot
For complete listing see *Orchestral works*

Two Millay Sonnets (1992)   5½'
for mezzo and piano
Text: Edna St. Vincent Millay
In *Songs and Arias for Mezzo-Soprano*

Two Songs (1952)   5½'
for baritone and piano
Text: John Betjeman
"Calvinistic Evensong"
"Senex"
Available separately or in *Nine Songs and Arias for Baritone*

Wedding Song (1975)   2'
for baritone and piano
An aria from *Captain Jinks of the Horse Marines*
Text: Sheldon Harnick
In *Nine Songs and Arias for Baritone*

The Widow's Waltz (1978; rev. 1983)   2½'
for high voice and piano
Revision of an aria from *Doctor Heidegger's Fountain of Youth*
Text: Sheldon Harnick
In *Nine Songs and Arias for Soprano*

The You Should of Done It Blues (1971)   2½'
for soprano and piano
Text: Peter Viereck
Available separately or in *Nine Songs and Arias for Soprano*

Choral Works

The Bear Hunt (1957)   6'
for TBB chorus and piano
Text: Abraham Lincoln
FP: 21 April 1961, New York, Columbia University Glee Club
Bailey Harvey, conductor

Boys and Girls Together (1965)   2¼'
Rounds for mixed voices a cappella
Text: Anonymous

Commemmoration (1960)
see *Works for concert band*

Epitaphs (1993)   14:50
for mixed voices a cappella
   Composers (Bach, Beeson, Beethoven)   2:15
   Heavenly Harps and Organists   4:30
   Humoresque and Hymn (Grave Matters)   4:30
   So Let My Living Be; So Be My Dying   3:35
Theodore Presser

Evening Prayer (1959)
see *Rhymes and Rounds*, under title *Night Spell*

Everyman's Handyman (1970
9 rounds and canons for men's voices a cappella
Text: Elizabeth W. Smith, adapted by the composer

Four Gallows Songs (2007)   9-10
for mixed voices a cappella
Text: Christian Morgenstern (Eng. trans.)

Give the Poor Singer a Penny (1959)   1½'
Round for mixed voices a cappella
from *Nursery Rhyme Rounds*
Text: Traditional nursery rhyme

Greener Pastures (1965)　　　　　　　　　　　2½'
Round for mixed voices a cappella
Text: Anonymous

Hickup, Snicup (1959)　　　　　　　　　　　1½'
for mixed voices a cappella
from *Nursery Rhyme Rounds*
Text: Traditional nursery rhyme
See *Rhymes and Rounds*

Hinx, Minx (1980)　　　　　　　　　　　1¾'
Nursery rhyme for SATB chorus a cappella
See *Rhymes and Rounds*

Homer's Woe (1966)
12 rounds for treble singers a cappella
Text: Anonymous nursery rhymes
B&H, Canyon Press (#1-8)

In Praise of the Bloomers (1969)　　　　　　　　　　　1½'
for men's voices a cappella
Text: Anonymous, from *Mrs. Partington's Carpetbag of Fun*
FP: 17 October 1969, New York, Columbia University Glee Club

In Praise of Singing (2001)　　　　　　　　　　　6¾'
for mixed voices a cappella
the words by William Byrd
revised and versified by Jack Beeson

Knots: Jack and Jill for Grownups (1979)　　　　　　　　　　　12'
for SATB chorus a cappella
Text: R. D. Laing
FP: 9 March 1980, Shelter Island, N.Y.
Gregg Smith Singers, Gregg Smith, conductor
Theodore Presser

Magicke Pieces (1991)　　　　　　　　　　　22'
for SATB chorus, bass-baritone, three winds and three bells
Text: Reginald Scot, Bishop Emulf of Rochester,
Robert Herrick, and Anon.
FP: 18 January 1992, New York, Gregg Smith Singers
Gregg Smith, conductor
Theodore Presser
Oboe, English horn, bassoon, and 3 tubular bells.

Matthew, Mark, Luke and John (1959)　　　　　　　　　　2'
for mixed voices a cappella
Text: Nursery rhyme
See *Rhymes and Rounds*

The Model Housekeeper (1970)
9 rounds and canons for women's voices a cappella
Text; Elizabeth W. Smith, adapted by the composer

Nursery Rhyme Rounds (1959)
for mixed voices a cappella
Text: Traditional nursery rhymes
see under individual titles:　Hickup, Snicup
　　　　　　　　　　　　　　Swan Song
　　　　　　　　　　　　　　Give the Poor Singer a Penny

Rhymes and Rounds (1984)
for mixed voices a cappella
Contents:　　　　　　　Hickup, Snicup (1959)
　　　　　　　　　　　Hinx, Minx (1980)
　　　　　　　　　　　Night Spell (1959; previous titles: Evening Prayer;
　　　　　　　　　　　　　Matthew, Mark, Luke and John)
　　　　　　　　　　　Swan Song (1959)
Galaxy Music Corp.

A Round for Christmas (1942; rev. 1951)　　　　　　　1½'
for SATB chorus a cappella
Text: from The Gospel according to Saint John
FP: 8 December 1951, New York, Columbia University Chorus
Jacob Avshalomov, conductor

Summer Rounds and Cartons (2002)　　　　　　　　　6'
for SATB chorus a cappella and several solo voices
The editing of *Sumer is Icumin In* and the translation
of its Middle English verse and the rest of the words are
by Jack Beeson.

Swan Song ((1959)　　　　　　　　　　　　　　　1½'
for mixed voices a cappella
Text: Traditional nursery rhyme
see *Rhymes and Rounds*

Three Psalms (1951)   8'
for mixed chorus a cappella
Psalm 107 (TTBB), 121 (SSA), 140 (SATB)
Text: The Bay Psalm Book
FP: 4 April 1976, New York, ISCM,
New England Conservatory Chorus

Three Settings from The Bay Psalm Book (1951)   8'
for SATB chorus a cappella with optional piano accompaniment
Psalm 131, 47, 23
FP: 25 April 1953, Boston, Chorus Pro Musica
Oxford University Press

The Tides of Miranda (1954)   3'
madrigal for five voices
Text: Sarah Moore
Oxford University Press

To a Lady Who Asked for a Cypher (1969)   3'
for SATB chorus a cappella
Text: Anonymous, from *Mrs. Patington's Carpetbag of Fun*

Works for concert band

Commemoration (1960)   5-6'
for band and optional unison chorus
Text: Columbia College Alma Mater
Commissioned by Columbia College
FP: 5 April 1960, New York,
Columbia University Band and Glee Club
Elias Dunn, conductor
picc.2.2E♭cl.3.E♭acl.bcl.2—2asax.tsax.barsax—4.2.3crt.3.euph.basstuba—
timp.perc(3)—piano(four hands)—db

Hymns and Dances
(from *The Sweet Bye and Bye*) (arr. 1966)   5.6'
picc.2.2E♭cl.3E♭acl.bcl.2—2asax.tsax.barsax—4.2.3crt.3.euph.bass
tuba—timp.perc(3)—piano(four hands)—db

Index